The One For Her

A bundle collecting parts 1 - 9 of the previous titled Mr White series by J A Fielding.

A BWWM Billionaire Marriage And Pregnancy Romance.

The longest complete BWWM romance story ever! A complete story with no cliff hangers.

This is a bundle collecting parts 1 - 9 of the previously titled Mr White series by J A Fielding (see titles of each book below).

About:

Natasha Black is a strong African American woman who has always been career focused and level headed.

Nothing has ever been able to knock her off her game... Until now.

Enter billionaire Mitchell 'McDreamy', an eligible bachelor and hunk of a boss at her new dream job.

Pretty soon the two find they have much in common, and start dating despite their working relationship.

But with Mitchell wanting marriage and possibly even a family one day, will Natasha be ready to give her new man what he desires?

Find out in this complete story bring Natasha and Mitchell through meeting, complications, falling in love, marriage, starting a family and more...

A must read for all fans of BWWM romance stories!

Suitable for over 18s only due to smoking hot sex scenes a plenty.

Collects all stories in the 9 part series:

1. 'Is Mr White Mr Right?',

2. 'Mr White Proposes',

3. 'Wedding Planning With Mr White',

4. 'My Honeymoon With Mr White',

5. 'Making Babies With Mr White',

6. 'Giving Birth To Mr White's Baby',

7. 'My Future With Mr White',

8. 'Igniting The Passion With Mr White', and

9. 'Healing Mr White'.

Get Free Romance eBooks!

Hi there. As a special thank you for buying this book, for a limited time I want to send you some great ebooks completely **free of charge** directly to your email! You can get it by going to this page:

www.saucyromancebooks.com/physical

You can see a the cover of these books on the next page:

ONE LONE COWBOY, ONE WOMAN ON A MISSION...

THE LONE ★ COWBOY

EMILY J.

ROCHELLE

...IRE MET HIS MATCH?

UCH
...ASS

...LDING

IF IT'S MEANT TO BE...

Him

KIMBERLY GREENFORD

PLAYERS GONNA PLAY?

SHE'S THE ONE HE WANTS
BUT CAN SHE TRUST HIM?

ONE VAMPIRE. ONE COP. ONE LOVE.

VAMPIRES OF CLEARVIEW

J A FIELDING

These ebooks are so exclusive you can't even buy them. When you download them I'll also send you updates when new books like this are available.

Again, that link is:

www.saucyromancebooks.com/physical

ISBN-13: 978-1515199304

ISBN-10: 1515199304

Contents

Book 1.

Is Mr White Mr Right?

Chapter 1

Natasha Black checked her phone again. She could not believe that Jay was late, again. He was always late. Even when she gave him an hour's head start, he would still be late. She took a deep breath as she dialed his number. "Where the fuck are you Jay?" she asked.

"I'm sorry baby, I'll be there in ten." He said. Natasha sighed again as a waiter approached her table. "*Why am I even here?*" she wondered. She knew she had made a mistake as soon as she accepted a dinner invitation from her ex Jay.

"Ready to order now?" he asked with a smile. Natasha looked at him with a smile.

"Oh yeah," she answered. "Get me a nice glass of red wine, your choice," she said as she looked at the menu. "Oh wow, the chef's special is the chicken and chorizo jambalaya?" she asked in excitement.

"Yes, ma'am," the waiter said.

"Alright, change up,' she said as she handed him back the menu. "A nice cold glass of chardonnay and some of that jambalaya," she added with a smile. The waiter bowed respectfully and walked off. "*Maybe it's time I officially ended things with Jay,*" she thought.

The two had been together for a little over two years before she finally called it quits. The last year of the relationship had been characterized by fights and trust issues. That was just too much for Natasha to handle but she still had a weakness for him and he knew it.

"Maybe that was why he knew that I would agree to meet him

today," she thought angrily. "*Dumb ass.*" A few months back, she had decided to jump back on the dating horse but it was not as easy as she thought it would be. Everyone she tried dating was simply put, a train wreck. They were either too high or out to get laid. These were not people she wanted to be in a relationship with.

Today would have been the third month since she spoke to Jay and she was unsure what they would talk about. I mean it had been three months. From the corner of her eye she noticed Jay coming in as the waiter walked towards her with a bottle of Chardonnay.

"Hey baby," he said smoothly. Natasha looked at him as the waiter poured her a glass.

"Don't hey baby me, fool," she said angrily in a hushed whisper. "I have been here for almost half an hour... what were you doing anyway?" she asked as he took a seat. By this time, the waiter was already heading back to their table with Natasha's jambalaya.

"You ordered already?" he asked as she elegantly draped the napkin on her thighs.

"I was here for thirty minutes Jay," she said leaning forward so he could hear the urgency in her voice without her shouting. "*Thirty,*" she said again hoping he got the point.

"Anything for you sir?" the waiter asked as he handed him the menu. Jay skimmed through the contents and sighed.

"*Typical,*" Natasha thought. "*You couldn't decide what color of underwear you wanted if your life depended on it.*"

"I'll have what she's having," he said finally. "And maybe some red… no… white…what is she having?" he asked.

"Chardonnay, sir," the waiter answered. Natasha looked at him as she took a bite of her jambalaya.

"Yes that will do," Jay said giving back the menu. "Or…" "…for the love of God Jay have the damn Chardonnay!" Natasha cut him short as the waiter walked off. He mouthed a 'thank you' to her as he walked.

"So, how you been ma," he asked in a soft sexy voice. Natasha rolled her eyes. She was not going to fall into this trap. Not again. Jay almost always managed to get back in her good graces by his words.

"Don't do that," she said as she sipped her wine. "You know you are not in my good books right now," she snapped.

"I know and I am sorry," he said with a smile. He looked at her hoping that she would smile back but she wouldn't barge. "Come on, Tasha. Give us a smile," he pleaded.

"What for?" she asked taking another bite, acting as if what he had just said didn't matter at all. "We both know it won't go very far in changing you," she added. Jay took a deep breath.

"So we're already dealing with the elephant in the room, huh," he said as the waiter walked back with his order. "Thank you," he said quickly as the waiter left.

"Unlike you, I do not procrastinate," she answered curtly. She was not about to give this to him on a silver platter.

"Let's just enjoy the dinner first then talk," he said as he began eating.

"Oh please, Jay," Natasha said. "I am enjoying my dinner just fine. And we both know that you are always too busy for me."

"Come on, that's not true," he said. Natasha looked up and gave him a scornful laugh.

"Really." Tasha leaned back in her chair. "When was the last time you made time from your busy schedule to spend time with me?" she asked. Jay looked down at his plate. She had him cornered between a rock and a hard place. "I know Jay, three weeks ago and that was after I pressured you," she said finally.

"Yeah about that." "…you better make up your mind whether you want to be with me or not," she cut him short.

"Whoa, baby hold up," Jay said holding up his hands. "Are you serious?"

"Tell me Jay, do I look serious enough to you?" she asked looking straight at him. Jay reached for her hand and looked at her.

"Why would you want to do that to me?" he asked in a soft voice. She looked back at him, this time unable to keep up the tough act. "You know I've got nothing but love for you," he said looking into her eyes. She pulled her hand away and went on eating. Jay knew that this was just a ploy for her to avoid eye contact.

"Then you better get your shit together Jay," she said, her voice almost quavering.

"I will, I promise," he said reaching for her hand again. "Come on, why don't we finish up and head back to my place..." "...Nah ah, Jay," she said suddenly yanking her hand from his again. "You ain't getting freaky till you prove that you do got your shit together," she added sitting back. She looked at him and smiled. His look said it all. He was defeated. She was loving this. It was about time he realized that he couldn't just disappear on her when he wanted then make reappearance just because he was horny. That was **not** going to happen again.

*****

"Ready to go?" he asked after about another hour and a half. She pushed the plate away and took a final sip. Jay took that as a yes and signaled the waiter for the check.

"Did I tell you how hot you looked today?" Jay asked her as they headed toward the parking lot. "You know what Jay, you've already forgot that little but important fact," she said with a smile as they approached his car.

"Well allow me to apologize," he said pushing her against the car. He smiled down at her as he brought his face down for a kiss. She felt a wave of energy go through her as their lips met. It had been almost a month since they last had any form of intimacy. She raised her arms and wrapped them around his neck as he slipped an arm around her waist.

As they kissed she could feel her nipples harden against the flimsy material of her silk blouse. She felt his hand ran up the small of her back then all the way down to her ass. She whimpered when she felt him squeeze her ass. He then trailed his lips to her neck where he let his tongue follow the contours of her slender neck.

"Is this your idea of an apology," she asked in a low voice as he went on nibbling at her neck.

"Oh yeah," he said quickly as he fumbled with the car door. He gently pushed her inside and followed quickly just in case she changed her mind.

"We cannot do this, Jay," she said as he brought his face down on hers.

"Shhh, no talking," Jay said as he engaged her lips again, his hands softly making her run wild. She was whimpering and moaning against his lips as he gently made her lie on the back seat. He went back to kissing her neck while one of his hands found its way under her skirt. She twitched when she felt his hands make contact with her pussy.

"Jay please…" She started slowly as he playfully stroked her cunt. *"Don't let him back so easily Tasha,"* she scolded herself as his other hand kneaded her breast. He was almost pulling her panties off when the shrill ring of her cell phone ruined the moment.

"Hi daddy," she said panting.

"Hey Tasha," her father Eric said. "What's going on? Have you been running?" he asked concerned.

"Shit!" she thought. "No, just thought I'd hit the gym," she said looking at Jay. "But I just ran into Jay, he'll be dropping me home," she added giving Jay a 'you-better-do-it-or-else' look.

"See you soon then," Eric said before hanging up. Jay gave her a smile and moved closer to her.

"Where were we?" he asked as he brought himself forward to kiss her again. She pushed him off as she adjusted the buttons on her blouse.

"You were taking me home," she said as she jumped to the front seat. Jay looked at her in disbelief.

"Really?" he asked, shocked.

"Yes, really," she said giving him the same sharp look as she had earlier. Jay knew he was already fighting a battle he could not win. He jumped to the driver's seat and put the key in the ignition. "You still have my gym bag in here right?" she asked as she fixed her hair. "I would hate for daddy to know that I've been lying," she added fastening her seat belt. Jay took a deep breath.

"It's in the trunk," he said as he started driving away. Natasha smiled to herself. It was about time Jay realized that she wasn't a toy. She would hold off till he begged.

*****

On Thursday morning, Natasha looked at her reflection in the mirror and then at the humongous pile of clothes on her bed then sighed. She had no idea of what to wear and this was not one of the days you throw an outfit together. Today would be her third and final interview with Nolan Schmidt Communication Solutions, a media company she had long dreamed of working at. It the only media company she knew that was all rounded. Television, radio, public relations and advertising. NSCS was one of the most reputable media companies in the country, and she was always afraid she would never make the cut.

"Tasha, breakfast!"she heard her nan call from downstairs.

"Be there in a minute!" she yelled back as she pulled out three outfits from the huge pile on her bed. *"Red is too damn loud,"* she thought as she narrowed it down to a black dress. *"You never go wrong with the little black dress,"* she thought as she walked to the closet for a pair of red and black soled platform heels. *"This is really good,"*she thought as she smoothed the bottom of the dress down after pulling it over her head.

The dress was the perfect contrast to her light African American skin tone. The pencil design of the skirt made her hips and well rounded ass seem exceptionally beautiful. The v-neck was definitely showing off her nicely sized tits. She took a red and black polka dotted scarf and gracefully laid it on her shoulders. It would match her shoes and shut nan up about her revealing dress. She always had something to say about her clothes.

"My girl be killing them today," her dad, Eric said as she walked into the kitchen. Natasha smiled as she put her handbag on the table.

"Thank you daddy and good morning," she cooed as she walked to the table. Eric smiled at her as he rose to join her at the table. "Hi nan," Natasha said as she took a seat.

"Hey baby, I made you pancakes," her nan Estelle said with a smile. She smiled back as she dug in. She was certainly nervous but her stomach had none of those nerves.

"So, third time's the charm, huh?" Eric asked with a smile. It was obvious that he was proud of his daughter.

"Yeah, so I've heard," Tasha said between mouthfuls.

"You are going to be great honey," Estelle said touching her hand.

"Fingers crossed," Natasha said as she looked at her phone. "Oh my God, is that the time?" she asked no one in particular as she gulped down her juice. She grabbed her bag and headed out. "Hey dad," she called from the door. "I'm taking your car," she said as she grabbed his keys.

"Whoa, let's not get ahead of ourselves," Eric said as he stood up.

"Daddy, look at me," Natasha said as she twirled around. "Do you really picture all of this, in *that*?" she asked pointing at her car, a mini cooper. "I hardly look serious in that car," she added.

"The girl does have a point," Estelle said matter-of-factly as she took a sip of coffee. Natasha shot her a dirty look. Eric sighed. "Fine," Eric said as he succumbed to his fate. He never seemed to win anytime he was against these two.

"Yes!" Natasha shrieked as she headed out.

"A thank you would have been nice,' Eric said to Estelle who replied by taking a nice long sip.

"I heard that," Natasha called out as she got in the car.

*****

Though NCCS was just a few minutes away, the drive there seemed to take forever. But when she finally pulled into the NSCS driveway, she found herself a bit more relaxed. She was feeling fairly confident as she got out of the car, even though her feet wobbled lightly under her. She was not sure what happened but the next thing she knew, she was glancing up at a friendly looking face. She suddenly realized that the friendly face was a stranger who had her cradled on his lap.

"Welcome back," he said with a smile.

"What… What happened?" she asked sitting up. "Who are you?" she asked as she smoothed her skirt down.

"Mitchell Schmidt," the man said. "You passed out. Drink this, it will give you some energy," he added handing her some grape soda.

"I passed out?!" Natasha said in a panic. *"Great. Now I have definitely lost it."*

"Relax," Mitchell said as he made her sip some soda. "Nothing is ever that serious," he added.

"Yes it is," Natasha said as she struggled to get to her feet. "I am supposed to be interviewing for this position today…" "…I'm sure they'll understand," Mitchell cut her short. She smiled weakly.

"Hope you are right," she said as she struggled to stand up. Mitchell helped her up and stood next to her for a while.

"I better walk you to the lobby," he said. Natasha looked at him and nodded. She hated feeling so weak. Mitchell put his arm around his waist as they walked together towards the reception.

"If ever there was a time I felt insecure, it's now," she thought as they walked through NSCS' lobby. The other interviewees, or whatever they were, were already there. All seated giving her a 'you are so done' look.

"You okay?" Mitchell asked looking at her. She could see concern in his eyes but she was not sure what it was for. "Hey, you better clear that grape soda," he said gesturing at the can in her hands.

"This is embarrassing." Natasha said under her breath.

"Oh please. I pass out in front of strangers all the time," Mitchell said looking at her. She laughed as she tucked a strand of her hair behind her ear.

"Thanks, really," she said as Mitchell looked at his watch.

"Oh crap," he started. "I'm really sorry but I will have to leave you now," he said with that same killer smile.

"I can't thank you enough," Natasha said clutching the can in her hands. She could feel her palms getting a bit sweaty. *"Damn it, girl, stay down,"* she thought as she tried calming herself down.

"Don't mention it, just stay strong," Mitchell said as he walked off. He turned his head and gave her a little wink.

"Fuck that's sexy."

As he walked away, she couldn't keep her eyes off his ass. He did have a sexy one, so she couldn't be blamed. His dark wavy hair bounced with every step he took. He kind of reminded him of Grey's Anatomy's Derek Shepherd. Maybe he was her very own Dr. Shepherd. Her very own McDreamy.

"Natasha Black," the receptionist called snapping her out of her daydreaming state.

"Yeah, that's me," she said quickly.

"They are ready for you," the woman said.

"This is it," she thought as she took a deep breath. She took her clutch bag in her hands and slowly but surely made her

way to the board room. She knew exactly where to go but she had no idea what to expect.

"Miss Black, nice to see you again," Patrick, the head interviewer said as she walked in.

"Thank you for having me," she said as she took a seat in front of the four man panel.

"Well, today Mr. Schmidt will be joining us," Patrick said. Natasha took another deep breath.

"You are playing with the big guns now."

"Meet Mitchell Schmidt, the CEO," Patrick said as McDreamy walked in. Natasha flushed. She could suddenly feel a sea of emotions overwhelm her. Her cheeks were flushed, her nipples felt a bit hard and her pussy, well, her pussy was almost completely drenched.

"Fuck."

"Nice to meet you Mr. Schmidt," she said surprised that her voice did not shake at all.

"Nice to know your name," Mitchell said with a smile as he sat down. "Shall we begin?" he said as he got his questions ready. Natasha wanted to scream or something. This would be a hard interview, the hardest one yet.

Chapter 2

"What the fuck was that?" Natasha wondered as she walked back to the parking lot. A few hours ago she was sure that she would ace the interview. Now though she did not have as much faith in herself. She got into the driver's seat and threw her head back with a sigh. She ran her fingers through her thick hair as she recalled the last couple of hours.

"This is so damn messed up." She thought as she took the phone out of her purse. "Celia would know exactly what to do," she said to herself as she scrolled for her best friend's number. She finally found it and swiped the screen to call. Her fingers were trembling as the phone rang on the other end. A soft knock on her window sent her into panic mode. The phone dropped to the floor as her hand landed on the car horn, resulting in a resounding honk in a otherwise calm environment.

"Fuck!"

Tasha turned her head to see a smiling Mitchell standing outside the car. She nervously placed a finger on the power window and smiled as the window slowly rolled down.

"Do I need to get you some ice for that?" Mitchell asked gesturing to the bruise that was now forming on her wrist. She looked at her hand and let out a nervous laugh.

"I'll be fine, Mr. Schmidt," she said politely. She felt her heart skip as he smiled at her again. *"Darn, Tasha. What is with you today?"* she wondered. Could it be that her dry spell was playing into her personality making her the biggest klutz she knew?

"Call me Mitch. Mr. Schmidt is my dad," Mitchell said looking at her. She smiled at the statement. For some reason, even the most cliché remarks made this man unbelievably desirable.

"OK, Mitch," she said feeling a bit more relaxed.

"You seemed really nervous in there," he said leaning against the car. "I really thought you to be a bit more confident," he added.

"I passed out and the CEO of the company I was interviewing for gave me first aid," she said looking at him. "Tell me that wouldn't make you a bit nervous," she said again. She involuntarily tucked a hair strand behind her hair. She always did that when she blushed.

"True that," Mitchell said. "You still did well enough." Natasha felt her cheeks flush.

"I guess we'll see in a few weeks," she said laughing nervously again.

"There is a coffee shop around the corner that makes a killer latte," he said passively. It seemed obvious to Natasha that this man had not had so many negative answers in his life. She smiled up at him.

"Mitchell Schmidt, are you asking me out?" she asked surprised at her new found boldness.

"Matter of fact I am," he answered. "Now get out of the car. You're making me look creepy to onlookers," he added looking around. Natasha laughed as she reached for her purse. Once she was out of the car, she found herself looking at her rear view mirror for self approval. For some reason this would have to be the first guy she had met in over two years who wasn't a complete douche. She almost wanted to kick herself as she stood in front of Mitchell who was obviously making his own mental judgment.

"You know between the passing out and me carrying you, it might have slipped my mind to tell you how good you look," he said effortlessly. She smiled at him and adjusted her skirt waistline.

"Thank you, Mitch," she said finally getting the courage to look him in the eye.

"You know, not many women are able to pull off the glamorous but official look all at once," he said. It was obvious that he was hard at work trying to charm her pants off and she did not want to let him know that it was working.

Natasha nodded her approval as they began walking away from the parking lot. The walk, though short, was quite uncomfortable as far as Natasha was concerned. Her loins were still heating up, and the fact that this man made her blush almost every other second wasn't helping. She kept her head low as she followed him out of the company premises and onto the street.

She looked around as vehicles sped by like police cars in hot pursuit of some criminal. She suddenly felt an overwhelming wave as he slid his arm around her waist. She looked up at him and almost jumped in her skin. *"Oh my God, he is going to make a move right here,"* she thought as she looked into his intense eyes.

"Let's get you on this other side," he said softly moving her to his left side, away from the oncoming traffic. "I would hate for anything to happen to the future of NSCS," he said with a smile. Natasha felt her heart skip a beat. Was this one of the people who expected you to sleep with them for a promotion or a position in the company?

"No Tasha, stop that," she scolded herself. She pushed the perverted thought to the back of her mind. Sometimes people were nice for the sake of being nice, right? She shrugged in

an attempt not to think about it anymore.

"Thanks," she managed to say as they approached a coffee shop.

"Would you believe it if I told you that this place has been around for more than ten years?" he asked as they walked through its doors. Natasha looked around. The place looked absolutely fabulous. It was kind of like Starbucks, only better.

"A couple of years back, the lady who owns the place wanted to close down because she couldn't afford the costs. It wasn't as busy back then," Mitchell explained as they walked in. "NSCS offered to partner with her fifty-fifty and voila," he added with a smile.

"*Shit, he can be so full of himself,*" Natasha thought looking at him. That would have to be the first negative quality he had.

"Good investment?" she asked looking at him.

"Never regretted it, especially since it doubles up as a bar after ten," he said with a wide grin on his face.

"Hey Mitch!" A young man called from behind the counter. "The usual?" he asked. Mitch waved at him and nodded. "Make it two." Mitch looked at Natasha waiting to see if there was any objection, but found none.

"You are a popular guy," Natasha said to him with a smile.

"Just around here," he said as a waitress brought them two lattes. He lifted his cup and smiled. "To the start of something nice?" he asked looking at her. She took her cup and lifted it before flashing him a smile.

"Here here!" she said before taking a sip. He was right. The latte was like an orgasm of milk, coffee and caramel inside her mouth.

"Good right?" Mitchell asked with a smile.

"Awesome, actually," she replied after finally swallowing. She looked into his eyes and felt a shiver down her spine. She did not know what it was about him that made her feel a bit... weak?

"So, Natasha Black," he started as he took another sip. "What else don't I know about you? I mean apart from what you said in the interview." He softly fixated on her eyes.

"Nothing much," she said breaking the long gaze. "I lead a pretty boring life," she said leaning back in her chair.

"Really? You're going to make me work for it?" he asked. Natasha felt cornered.

"Really. There is nothing to tell... Except for no one calls me 'Natasha'." she said shrugging.

"There we go," he said with a smile. "What do people call you then?"

"Tasha," she quickly responded.

"Tasha," he echoed. She could almost swear his eyes twinkled when he said it. "I like it," he said finally.

"What about you?" she asked. "Do you take all your interviewees on a date the first time you meet them?" she asked. It was her turn to put him on the spot.

He smiled.

"No, just the ones who pass out in my parking lot," he said with a smirk. She giggled as she felt her cheeks grow hotter.

"Well played," she said circling the rim of her cup with her finger.

"Well, I try," he joked leaning forward. "So, Tasha, are you seeing anyone?" Mitch was again looking straight into her eyes. She felt a chill go down her spine as she struggled to maintain eye contact.

"No," she said. "You?"

She surprised herself at the question she had just thrown back at him. "Not that I...."

"...Don't sweat it," he said before taking a deep breath. "Well, let's say... 'it's complicated'," he finally answered. Natasha felt a wave of rage go through her. This was just what she needed. Another guy with a whole butt load of drama.

"Oh," she said as she lifted the cup to her lips to take another sip.

"Does that make you uncomfortable?" he asked. Natasha was sure that he had seen her facial expression change. She was never good at hiding what she felt.

"It's not like we're doing anything wrong, right?" she said with a smile.

"Right. Just two adults enjoying a latte," he answered with a smile.

"Walk away, Tasha," she thought as she glanced at her watch. *"This won't end well."*

"This was nice," she said placing the cup on the table. Mitchell looked at her and shook his head.

"Was?" he asked. "Are we done already?" Natasha smiled at him.

"This will have to do," she said as she stood up. "We have to save some talk for next time," she added.

"Can I call you?" he asked standing up. She looked at him. This time her gaze was more targeted at his lips than eyes.

"You got my number," she said with a smile before walking away. As she slowly but surely walked out, she could still feel his eyes on her. She wondered whether it was so obvious that she liked him. *"You can't like him, Tasha,"* she thought as she walked towards the NSCS parking lot. *"He just might be your boss. And things with him are 'complicated'."*

This sucked. McDreamy, or Mitchell, was the greatest guy she had met in a while. Yet he just had to be the boss of her dream company. *"This is fucked up,"* she concluded as she got into her car.

She quickly picked up her phone and speed dialed Jay. It was either her long dry spell was making her find Mitchell, though ill mannered, outrageously attractive. OR... well, she would find out soon enough.

Jay had used her one too many times before. It was time to return the favor.

"This is a surprise," Jay said when he picked up the phone.

"Yeah I know," she said as she started the ignition. "No small talk. I need you to be at your place in twenty," she said before hanging up. She loved the fact that she left him hanging. She would soon know whether Mitchell Schmidt was really her McDreamy or it was really her pussy that needed some well deserved action.

*****

"What's the big emergency?" Jay asked when he opened the door. She looked at him and pushed him out of the way as she made her way to the bedroom. "Tasha? What's going on?" he asked as she pulled her blouse over her head. Tasha turned around and undid her skirt's zipper and let it fall to the ground.

"What do you think?" she asked as she stepped out of her heels. "I'm horny," she said as she walked to the bedroom without looming back. She knew he would come after her. He always did so long as sex was on the table.

She walked to the bedroom door, placing her hand on the door knob and turning it around. By that time, Jay was already undoing his shirt buttons while trying to quickly walk towards her. "Leave it," she said as she pushed the door open. She swayed her hips slowly as she walked towards the bed.

She could hear Jay's labored breaths at the door, but she was careful not to turn too quickly. She wanted him to enjoy the view before she gave it all to him.

She slowly turned, revealing her full breasts that looked like they were about to break free from the lacy restraint that was her bra. She smiled at Jay as he walked towards her. His buttons were barely undone.

Natasha put her hands on his waist. She undid his belt buckle, pulling it sharply. She smiled as she ran her hand over his crotch, feeling that he already had a raging hard on. She leaned forward and kissed him lightly on the lips as she undid his pants and then his buttons. His hands were already making their way to the small of her back and finally down to grope her ass.

She yanked the shirt off his shoulders before pushing him on the bed. He lifted his head to look at her.

Natasha smiled when she saw how cute he looked with his pants around his ankles. Pathetic, but cute. She licked her lips seductively as she undid the clasp of her bra.

"Beautiful," Jay mumbled under his breath as her breasts finally bounced free.

Tasha slid her panties down her womanly thighs, before finally stepping out of the last of her restrictive underwear. She climbed on top of him, kicking off her shoes as she done so. They made a resounding thud on the wooden floor.

Jay brought his hand up to cup her face, before bringing her face down for a kiss. She felt herself shiver as his lips slowly worked hers. Before long, their tongues were gently intertwining together.

She sighed as her one of her breast rested softly in his palm. He pulled away from her, bent down, and took one of her nipples inside her mouth. She moaned softly as his other hand softly kneaded her opposite breast.

He had clearly not forgotten what to do when it came to pleasing her body. She stretched her hand to the bedside table where she knew he always kept the rubbers and took one out. He was still busy giving her breasts great oral pleasure while she slipped the rubber on his rigid black cock.

She pressed herself against his head as he sucked her harder, making her moan loudly. She felt herself melt onto his waiting cock and knew it was time.

She pulled herself away from him and held him by the wrists. Natasha could tell he was surprised when she secured her position, pinning his arms over his head. She looked down on his face as she lowered herself on his hard cock.

"Oh... Tash...oh fuck," he mumbled as her wet cunt engulfed his cock. She smiled as she looked at his face, his cheeks wincing with pleasure as she worked herself on his rigid pole. She lifted herself slowly; up, down. Jay couldn't help but moan her name.

The pace became increasingly steady with every jolt, a sign that her pussy was getting used to his size.

Tasha slowly moved herself on and off his cock, pushing his

pelvis down as she did. Deciding to switch things up, she then began working short strokes on him, only letting herself fuck his highly sensitized cock head. His moans grew louder as she cock teased him; she was liking every minute of this!

Jay tried to lift his pelvis up to bury himself inside her hot, wet pussy... But Tasha was having none of it! She used her knees to grip him tightly around his waist and keep him in position.

"Down boy," she said as she brought her face down to kiss him. He moaned softly as she again made their tongues dance a hot moist dance.

The slow strokes were obviously driving Jay insane. She pulled away just in time to see him closing his eyes, slowly resigning to his fate. "That's it," she said before allowing her pussy to take in the whole of him.

He groaned loudly as he sunk himself inside her hot depths. Her speed increased as her strokes got longer and more intense. His pelvis was now freely rising to meet her own long thrusts.

Jay opened his eyes to see breasts bouncing freely in front of his face. Again, he took a nipple inside his mouth and began sucking.

Tahsa began to work her pussy, faster, harder on his hard shaft. Slurpy, sloshy sounds filled the room as his cock moved in and out of her vagina. Juices from her pussy began flowing freely, slowly but surely drenching the covers as time went on. He let go of her right nipple, only to take in her left one and suck it with the same intensity.

When he finally let go, her beautiful full tits stood alert and highly aroused. He freed his hands and made her head lie on his shoulder. He placed his hands around her waist and took over the dominant role, driving his cock deeper inside her.

Using his strong grip on her waist, Jay pulled himself inside her wetness which was suddenly getting tighter. He always wanted to see her when she had her climax. This time however, he could not let himself pull out of her.

The way her tight pussy closed over his penis when she was about to give in to her pleasure made him achieve his own orgasm. Jay groaned, Natasha screamed out loud; They could both feel a warm fluid coating the insides of their inner thighs.

"Damn," was all Jay could verbalize as he slowed down his thrusting; Tasha shivering in his arms. Beads of sweat were all over her back and breasts.

She pulled away from him as she felt his limp cock slip out. She looked down and smiled. "Does this mean what I think it does?" he asked inbetween short breaths. She looked at him and scoffed before letting herself drop on the bed.

"It doesn't mean anything Jay," she said as she reached for tissues to clean herself up.

"But why..."

"...please Jay, don't ruin my mood for round two," she cut him short as she brought her face to his to kiss him again. He wrapped his arms around her as he responded to her kiss. She felt an inward victory as she felt his arms on her back. She was over him. She was completely over Jay.

But wait, then this meant that her attraction to Mitchell Schmidt was genuine. It wasn't the dry spell. *"I am officially screwed,"* she thought as Jay came on top of her.

Chapter 3

Natasha walked through the living room with a big bowl of chips as her best friend followed closely. She had been dancing around the details of the interview, namely the parts including Jay and Mitchell. She had no idea how to break the news because she knew Rita would judge. She had always been judgmental, and was not known to ever mince her words.

Natasha had no idea how she was going to begin or how she would end. That's if Rita even allowed her to finish her story that is...

"Girl, you are killing me," Rita said rolling her eyes. Natasha sighed as she sat down. She put the bowl of chips on the couch as Rita also took a seat. She crossed her legs and looked Natasha right in the eye. Natasha felt her cheeks flush. She hated being so light skinned.

"You have to promise not to overreact," Natasha said taking Rita's hands in hers.

"What?" Rita pressed. "Are you selling our country's secrets to the soviets?" she asked in cynicism.

Natasha smiled. "Very funny," she said leaning close. "Okay, me and Jay," she started after taking a long breath. "did the nasty." she added giggling like a teenage girl in love.

"Oh hell no!!" Rita said yanking her hand from Natasha's grip. "You fucked Jay? What the hell is wrong with you?!" she asked in surprise. Unfortunately, Rita was being a bit more dramatic than Natasha had hoped she would.

"Could you say that a little louder, I don't think my dad heard you," Natasha said in a hushed whisper. She looked over her shoulder at Eric who was busy at the kitchen table working on his laptop.

"Seriously girl, " Rita started again, her voice thankfully lower this time round. "I thought you said you were done with Jay." she said crossing her legs on the couch. Natasha shrugged.

"Well, I was horny," Natasha snapped back. "A three month dry spell tends to do that to you, you know," she added in a whisper.

"There are so many other people, why Jay?" Rita asked. "If all you wanted was a fuck then you should have gone to Craigslist," she added. Natasha rolled her eyes again.

"I also wanted to be sure that my sexual drive was not a basis for my attraction to Mitchell," she said ignoring Rita's earlier comment.

"Tasha Black, what are you not telling me?" Rita asked looking intensely at Natasha. "Who is Mitchell?" she asked, suddenly more interested in what Natasha had to say than anything else.

"Well, I met a guy," Natasha said blushing. "The hottest guy I have ever known, Rita. Thick dark hair, muscular body, toned skin," she added. By now, she had a dreamy look in her eyes.

"Who is this guy, Derek Shepherd?" Rita asked as she made herself more comfortable on the couch. Natasha looked at her in surprise.

"I thought so too, " she squealed. "We are so alike right now," she added throwing an arm around Rita's shoulders. Rita looked at her in disgust.

"You sound like a white girl," she said in a sarcastic voice before they both laughed.

"Is that Rita Johnson," Estelle's voice filled the room as she came through the front door.

"Hey Mrs. Black," Rita said smiling. She got up and walked to the door. "Here, let me help you with that," she said as she took the grocery bags from Estelle's hands.

"Bless you child," Estelle said with a sigh. "How is everyone back at home?" They both walked over to the kitchen table. Eric stood up, reached for a glass and began pouring her some cool lemonade.

"Fine, Mrs. Black, just fine," Rita replied. Natasha walked over to the newly formed group and began helping with the groceries.

"I hope you are staying for dinner," Estelle said as she took a seat next to Eric. "I am making my famous fried chicken," she added, taking a sip of the lemonade.

"Mmm, I got to make sure I don't miss that," Eric said shutting his laptop. He pulled his chair back, grabbed his car keys and began walking towards the door.

"Where are you going?" Estelle asked as he opened the door.

"Work," he said. "I want to get that chicken hot and fresh and the mere thought is a distraction," he added closing the door behind him.

"And that's the boy I raised," Estelle said feigning sadness. "You have such high hopes as they grow up only to have them crushed," she added.

"When all they think of is food, what do you expect?" Natasha asked, feigning the same sadness as her nan. Rita laughed as she looked at the two.

"The drama never really dies down in this house, does it?" she asked shifting gazes from Natasha to Estelle. Natasha shook her head.

"Do you expect anything less?" Natasha asked flipping her hair dramatically.

"Speaking of drama," Estelle started turning her attention to Natasha. "I met Jay's mother at the farmer's market." Rita and Natasha exchanged glances. "She said she will be stopping over later today," Estelle added holding her glass. Rita looked at her best friend. She could have sworn that she literally saw color drain from Natasha's face.

"It looks like that later is now," Rita said as they all looked at the old Sedan pulling up in the driveway. Natasha felt herself panic. She had nowhere to run. There was only one way out of this mess and that was through the front door. The same door Jay's mother, Sherea, intended to walk through in the next few seconds!

She looked at her nan and sighed. Estelle reached out and gave her now cold hand a little squeeze. Natasha had always been open with with her nan. She knew when she and Jay began dating, when they started having issues, and eventually when they broke up. She even knew the reason why their relationship hit the rocks. Actually, the whole town knew why. The only person who never understood Jay was Sherea. To her, she had raised the perfect son. The responsible son rather than the lying, irresponsible bastard he truly was.

"Hellur," they heard the all too familiar tone of Sherea's voice at the doorway. They all looked more like zombies, standing rooted to the ground rather than the welcoming house guests they should have been.

"Hey, Sherea," Estelle said with her usual charm. Natasha had always wondered how her nan managed to remain charming even when she was obviously agitated.

"Well, don't just stand there," Sherea said to Natasha. "Come and give your future mother-in-law a hug," she chimed. Natasha looked at Rita who was trying hard not burst out laughing. Estelle gave a nudge, causing Tasha to involuntarily walk towards their house guest.

"You are still losing weight," Sherea said as she embraced Natasha. "Maybe after the wedding we can get some meat on these bones," she said laughing.

"After the wedding?" Rita asked looking directly at Sherea.

"Oh yeah," Sherea said walking towards the kitchen table. "We know how ya'll girls like looking nice and skinny in them Vera Lang wedding dresses," she added as she pulled out a chair.

"You mean Vera *Wang*," Rita corrected.

"Whatever, Lang, Wang they all Chinese anyway," Sherea said throwing her arms up. Estelle smiled. Sherea was never one to accept when she was in the wrong.

Ever!

Even if she drove the wrong direction in a one way street, she'd still manage to get out of the situation without a ticket thanks to her argumentative nature.

"Well, nice to see you," Natasha said as she walked back to the kitchen. "But, we were just leaving." She took Rita's hand.

"Where to?" Sherea asked as she helped herself to some lemonade. *'She didn't even ask if the glass is clean'*, Natasha thought as she looked at Sherea in disgust. "You do know that it's not everyday you get to sit down with your future in-laws in a friendly setting," she said lightly.

'Oh this has got to stop. Jay owes me big time,' she thought again as she cursed Jay for not telling Sherea about the break up. Natasha wanted to scream! Or even better, drop dead right where she stood!! Instead, she sighed and tried to relax. A conversation with Sherea was going to require every last nerve of her sanity.

"I guess not," she said as she walked towards Sherea and took a seat.

"So tell me," Sherea started as she took Natasha's hands in hers. "When are you planning to make an honest man out of my Jay?" she asked looking into Natasha's eyes.

"Don't torment the girl, Sherea," Estelle said in Natasha's defense.

"I am not tormenting anyone," Sherea said as her voice got a bit higher. "The one being tormented here is me," she added. Rita scoffed making Estelle give her a sharp look.

"How so?" Rita asked. "You are not the one in a relationship with Jay," she added in a low tone. Estelle looked at her again. Thankfully, Sherea had missed that last part.

"Well, I ain't growing any younger and I need grandchildren," Sherea said winking at Natasha. Rita saw her friend's eyes grow big.

"Sherea..." Natasha started before Estelle came to her rescue.

"Let the children be, Sherea," Estelle said. "why don't we sit out on the porch and catch up?" she asked in an attempt to help her clearly drowning granddaughter. Natasha gave her a thankful look as she stood from the table.

"I guess we could talk about this later," Sherea said picking her glass up.

"I guess," Natasha said in a small voice.

"We'll just be outside, " Estelle said as she opened the door.

"Maybe I should get you and Jay over for dinner and talk about when I get to be a grandmother." Sherea said walking towards the door to Estelle.

"Okay that's it," Rita said standing up. Natasha jerked around and looked at her.

"Rita, what are you doing?" she asked, her heart pounding hard and fast.

"She needs to know," Rita said looking at Natasha and then back to a confused Sherea.

"Need to know what?" Sherea asked looking around. "Estelle, what is this?" she asked.

"Nothing," Estelle said grabbing her arm. "Don't pay her no mind," she added.

"Please nana Black let me tell her," Rita said.

"No, it's not your place," Estelle said sharply.

"We both know Tasha's cowardice will never allow her to say it," she said matter of factly.

"Rita!" Natasha said still looking at Rita.

"What the hell is going on?" Sherea asked. She was already getting agitated. It was obvious that there was something going on and she wanted to know what it was. She **needed** to know.

"You perfect little son Jay," Rita started as she put up finger quotes.

"Rita Johnson you better shut up before I shut you up," Estelle said sternly. Rita looked at her and shook her head.

"What is that thing you say nana Black? Speak the truth and the truth shall set you free?" Rita asked looking at Estelle who was now dumbfounded. Natasha knew that her nan always quoted the Bible, and now that Rita had done the same, she knew Estelle had nothing more to say.

"Rita please," Natasha pleaded.

"What about my boy?" Sherea asked ignoring the two Black women. It was obvious that Rita had something to say about her son and she was not going to leave until she had all the gory details.

"Well, Jay and Tasha..." "RITA!" Natasha yelled interrupting her sentence.

"Someone's got to do it girl and that person is me!" Rita yelled back at Natasha before turning back to Sherea. "Sherea, Jay and Tasha are done," she said finally. Sherea looked at the two of them and then at Estelle.

"You're kidding, right?" Sherea asked looking at Rita.

"Why would I kid about something like that?" she asked looking right back at her.

What did you do Rita? Now I'm never going to hear the end of this.

"Is this... Is this true?" Sherea asked Natasha, whose eyes were now fixated on the floor.

"Yes, ma'am," Natasha replied I a low voice. "We broke up four months ago," she added lifting her head to look at Sherea.

"Sherea, I'm sorry," Estelle said walking back to the kitchen. She placed her hand on her friend's arm to console her.

"It's okay," Sherea said. "Things don't always work out," she added sadly as she sat back down. Natasha felt heavy in her heart. This was exactly what she never wanted to happen. Sherea was an annoying woman. but she did have her good side, her sensitive side. She walked towards Sherea and gave her a hug.

"I'm really sorry Sherea," she said in a low voice. "If I could do anything differently you know I would," she added.

"I know," Sherea said managing a smile. "I wonder where Jay will get another one like you," she added, patting Natasha's hair.

"He'll probably move to some place and fuck another white

bitch," Rita said under her breath. This time everyone heard her.

"RITA!" Natasha and Estelle said in unison. Rita looked up in surprise. Natasha could see the 'oh fuck' written all over her face.

"What did you just say?" Sherea said suddenly getting angry. "I ought to wash your mouth out with soap."

"Sherea! Chill out," Natasha said trying to hold her back. Sherea's large form effortlessly pushed Natasha to the floor.

"Tasha!" Rita shouted as she ran to her aid. Estelle quickly intercepted Sherea's hand which was hell bent on slapping Rita.

"Let her be," Estelle said looking at Sherea. From where she lay, Natasha could tell that her nan meant business. The two older women were now in a tight staring contest, with Sherea waiting to see who would break first. "You better get out of my house if you can't respect it enough," Estelle said still looking at Sherea.

"Did you hear what she said about my son?" Sherea asked, her voice shaking.

"You know she is right, Sherea," Estelle said, her voice a little softer now. "Everyone knows what he is like. You cannot tell me you're the only one who didn't know the son you raised," she added looking at Sherea.

"I'm sorry, Sherea but someone had to tell you," Rita said helping Natasha to her feet.

"If what you all say is true," Sherea said in a low voice.

"It is true Sherea," Natasha said looking at her sadly. "All of it," she added.

"... Then you had all better prepare yourselves to face him," Sherea finally said as she picked up her bag and headed for the door.

"Wait, what?" asked a confused looking Rita. "What do you mean? Why would we have to face him?"

Sherea was already at the door.

"Because he is moving back here," Sherea said. "Next week, Jay is moving back." She said again before walking out. The Black house was dead silent. You could have heard a pin drop from miles away.

"Did she just say Jay was moving back to the neighborhood?" Rita said breaking the serene environment. "That boy causes enough damage from wherever he is," she added as she sat down.

"It's okay," Natasha said. "He's my past and I've moved on," she added. Rita rolled her eyes.

"Yeah right," Rita said rolling her eyes. "You can't keep your panties on for one second when you're around him," she added before realizing what she had just done. She quickly slapped her palm over her mouth and looked apologetically at Natasha who was now staring daggers at her.

"Gee, thanks Rita," Natasha said cynically.

"Natasha Renee Black, I raised you better than that," Estelle said sternly looking at her granddaughter. Natasha was thankful when her phone rang breaking the growing tension in the room.

"Hello," she said, avoiding eye contact with her nan.

"Hi this is Angie Roth calling from Nolan Schmidt Communications Solutions." Natasha felt a chill go through her.

"You ok?" Rita whispered.

"Who's that?" Estelle asked, eager to know who was calling. Natasha put a finger on her lips before setting the phone on loud speaker.

"Yes," she said in anticipation.

"Well, I am pleased to inform you that you passed the interview," Angie said in a neutral tone.

Natasha jumped up and down in excitement as the other two came and gave her a group hug.

"Thank you so much" Natasha said, trying not to sound as excited as she felt. "I don't know what to say," she added, out of breath.

"You have to come in tomorrow to sign the contract and then you can officially begin working with us," Angie said.

"Sure, I'll be there first thing tomorrow morning," Natasha replied happily.

"We look forward to seeing you." Angie promptly hanging up.

"Thank you so much," Natasha said as she heard the click from her end of the line.

"Congratulations!" Rita said giving Natasha a hug. "This is the job you've been waiting for girl!"

Estelle stepped over to her granddaughter to once again make the hug a group one.

'Is this really happening?' Tasha wondered in disbelief.

"Now, what was this Rita mentioned about you and Jay? And the lack of panties?" Estelle asked, swiftly switching the subject and holding her granddaughter at arms length.

"You know what nan, me and Rita are headed to the salon for a mani-pedi," Natasha responded grabbing Rita's arm.

"We are not done yet," Estelle called out as the two quickly walked out the door giggling.

"See what you and your big mouth did," Natasha exclaimed as she fumbled with her car keys.

"I'm really sorry," Rita said as she got in the passenger seat. "Make it up to you? Manicure's on me," she added, quickly looking to appease her friend. Natasha looked at her.

"Throw in a facial," she said as she started the ignition. Rita frowned.

"What? Nan's probably going to bite my head off later today, I may as well look good while it's going down!"

Rita thought for a second. "Guess that's the least I could do," she finally let out admitting defeat. "No need to be pissed off while exfoliating though."

The pair looked at each other before both bursting out in

laughter.

Chapter 4

It was a Thursday morning. As Natasha stood under the warm running water of the shower, she wondered what her first day at Nolan Schmidt Communications Solutions would be like. She took a deep breath as she felt the water trickle down her spine to her crack. She turned around and leaned on the wall, allowing the water to fall on her full breasts.

She ran her hands through her wet hair and then down her torso, palms slightly brushing her hardened nipples. She gasped lightly as the thought of seeing Mitchell Schmidt again crossed her mind. The thought actually aroused her a little.

She put her hands on the knob and turned the water off before grabbing her towel. As she wrapped herself in the fluffy towel, she pictured the look Mitchell would have when she walked through the doors of his office. Mitchell had tried to get a hold of her socially over the past few weeks, but each time Natasha wouldn't budge. For Natasha, it was merely to protect herself. After all, the man had admitted to being in a 'complicated' relationship.

However complicated the relationship was, she was not interested. All she carted about was that she got into her dream job. Besides, she was going to have to work her ass off if she was ever going to take her place in the Forbes 'Top 30 Under 30' list. She smiled when the thought crossed her mind. Her best friend Rita had put the thought in her head and she had come to appreciate the prestigious feeling that this title would bring.

"What to wear," she thought as she looked at her three choices. There was a black sleeveless dress, a blue skirt coupled with a black button down blouse, or a navy blue pencil dress. On the floor was the one thing the three outfits revolved

around: A new pair of blue peep toe heels.

She had a quick ponder, threw her towel on the bed, then walked to the dresser for some lotion. *"The blue is glamorous and says I mean business,"* she thought as she rubbed the sweet smelling oil on her already smooth brown skin. *"Blue it is,"* she thought as she slipped on a pair of black panties. She matched this with a black bra before finally pulling the dress over her shoulders. She then walked to the full length mirror and looked at her reflection. *"Well hello there sexy mama,"* Tasha thought as she smoothed down the bottom of her dress.

"Damn," she thought when she looked at her watch. It was already 7.30am. She had another half hour before she officially became late on her first day of work. Not cool.

Tasha quickly blow dried her hair and pulled it back in a low bun. She then quickly applied her make up, careful not to overdo it. Natasha had always had well accentuated features, all she ever needed was some mascara and lip gloss. Today though, she thought she could do with some eye shadow.

She looked at her reflection again before walking back to the bed and finally putting on the shoes. *"Utter perfection,"* she thought as she looked at her feet. The peep toe feature was perfectly showing off her well manicured toes. She glanced at her wrist watch again. 7.44am. Perfect.

Slowly she walked down the stairs to the kitchen where her dada Eric and nan Estelle were. Her nan had made waffles specially for her first day at work.

"There she is," Estelle said as Natasha made her way to the kitchen table. "The new head of corporate advertising at Nolan Schmidt Communications Solutions." She had put on her best commentary voice.

"You know it," Natasha said as she kissed her nan's cheek. "And thanks for the waffles," she added as she took a plate.

"You look beautiful princess," Eric said as he stood to kiss his daughter's cheek. "You will knock them dead in that dress," he added before sitting back down.

"I am the head of corporate advertising," Natasha said as she helped herself to some waffles. "I need to look the part."

She took a big bite.

"These are really good, nan..."

The end of her sentence got mixed with chomping sounds as she took another bite.

"Hey, don't talk with your mouth full," Estelle said pointing at Natasha using a spatula.

"Don't worry, she does that to me too," Eric said as he gathered his stuff. Natasha smiled at him as she rushed to finish her breakfast. She had exactly three minutes to be on the road.

"I better go too," announced Tasha as she stood up.

"But you haven't even had juice," Estelle protested. Natasha walked over and gave her a quick hug.

"I will have it before I have dinner," she said as she grabbed her bag. "But now, I have really got to go," she added as she kissed her farther goodbye.

She stopped on the way to the door and turned around. "Daddy, do you think..."

"...don't even say it," Eric said grabbing his car keys off the table. He had loaned her his Ford Lincoln on her last interview with NSCS. Estelle smiled. Natasha knew her nan had seen that answer coming long before she even asked the question.

"It was worth a try," she said as she walked out to her own mini cooper.

Eric had always told Natasha that her mini cooper was classier than most. Her first two salaries had taken care of completely pimping her mini coop into one of those 'pimp my ride' vehicles you saw on TV, just without the crazy colors. However, Natasha still thought she looked more classy in a Lincoln than a mini.

*****

As she drove down the street, she felt herself being more relaxed as the cool breeze brushed her soft cheeks. Her heart rate was getting faster and faster as she got nearer to the NSCS offices. By the time she drove through the company parking lot, she almost felt like she was hyperventilating. *"Relax, Tasha,"* she told herself as she walked towards the office building. *"You already got the job,"* she thought as she approached the reception. A wide eyed brunette smiled at her.

"You must be Angie," Natasha said smiling. "I sure am!" Angie replied enthusiastically. "And you're Natasha Black right?"

Natasha nodded.

"Well, before you get settled in, Mr. Schmidt would like to see you in his office," Angie said as she pointed her to Mitchell's office.

Natasha felt goose bumps on her skin as she walked down

the lobby to Mitchell's office. "Oh no, why would he possibly want to see me?" she wondered. She took a deep breath when she got to his door and knocked softly.

"Natasha Black, the most difficult woman to find this side of California," Mitchell said as Natasha slowly walked in. She smiled at him while still standing at the doorway. "Well, don't just stand there, come on in," he said standing up. She could feel his eyes looking up and down her well defined curves.

"Nice to see you, Mr. Schmidt," Natasha said as she took a seat.

"Can I offer you anything?" he asked walking to his mini-bar. "I have cognac, champagne….," he looked at her disapproving expression and smiled. 'Doesn't he know it's a Thursday morning' though Tasha.

"Okay, juice?" he asked.

"Sure," Natasha said crossing her legs. She knew he had noticed that involuntary gesture. She cursed herself for dressing up, she should have worn a pants suit instead. Maybe something that didn't show too much skin.

"To a new beginning," Mitchell said after handing her a glass of orange juice. "I am looking forward to a very healthy professional relationship with my new head of corporate advertising." Natasha could hear the stress in his voice when he said 'professional'. She smiled.

"Me too," she said as their glasses touched with a quiet clink.

"So, why didn't you return any of my calls?" he asked. He had a smile on his face. A sly but sexy smile.

"What happened to the professionalism?" she asked taking a sip of her juice.

"It's still there," he said, his gentle gaze not leaving her for a second.

Natasha hated this. She had successfully avoided this conversation for three weeks but it had now caught up with her. She leaned forward and put her glass down.

"I want to keep things strictly business between us, Mr. Schmidt," she said her voice suddenly becoming a bit more serious than she had expected it to be.

"Mr. Schmidt? I thought we agreed on Mitchell," he said leaning back in his chair.

"Alright, *'Mitchell'*."

Mitchell smiled, stood up and walked to the door. She felt her heart skip a beat. *What the hell was he about to do?*

"Donna," he called from the door. "Hold my calls for an hour or so. I need to go over contract details with the new HCA," he said before shutting and bolting the door.

Natasha felt her heart rate rising again. Her body numbed put when she noticed that Mitchell's office had only one window and it overlooked the Californian sky scrapers. She panicked and stood up, quickly walked to the door and eyeballed Mitchell.

"I need to get settled in," she said, swinging her bag over her shoulder. Mitch smiled down at her. Funnily enough, Tasha felt like she would melt right there. The mixed feelings she felt were confusing.

"Nice shoes," he said completely disregarding her request. She felt butterflies in her stomach as he moved closer to her. "They make you look..." He got even closer.

Their noses were now inches away from each other. She could actually feel his orange mint breath brushing over her skin. "... sexy." he finally finished before sliding the bag off her shoulder. She was now breathing hard and fast.

Natasha tried hard not to show it but it was a bit too obvious. Mitchell Schmidt turned her on. She wanted to move but she couldn't. Even when she felt his hand on her waist she still couldn't move. She was now sure of one thing: Mitchell Schmidt, her real life McDreamy, was her very own Kryptonite.

"Mitchell..." "...don't talk," he whispered as he put his other hand on her waist. Her eyes were fixated on the floor. She was sure if she looked up she would advance on him faster then he was making moves on her.

"You are denying what is already a done deal," he whispered as he began backing her up. She moved back one step and then another. Then another till she felt her calves against the office couch. "You know you want me as much as I want you," he said as he brought his lips to her neck. His warm breath was driving her crazy.

She raised her arms to push him off, but instead found herself wrapping her arms around his shoulder.

"No, Tasha. This is your boss," she thought as she ran her fingers through his thick hair.

She felt him slowly plant a soft kiss on her neck. The soft kiss quickly turned intense as he began trailing kisses along her slender neck. She felt him pull her even closer and she could smell his well groomed skin under her nose. Her heart was beating faster as he kissed her neck, and then her chin. He worked his lips up to her own soft lips and brushed them softly. *"Oh my God,"* she thought as she felt his arm slip around her small waist. She put an arm on his chest and tried pushing him off.

"If you manage to push me away, I will let you go and never bother you again," he said softly. Natasha could still feel his arm around her waist but she could not move. She knew she wanted to push him off... Or did she? She closed her eyes and sighed. She wanted him. She knew she did.

"Mitch...." "......do it and I walk," he interrupted again, slowly kissing her. She looked into his dark eyes and realized that she still had one hand on his head. "I thought so," he said as he bent down to kiss her. She gasped for breath as she once again felt his soft lips slowly massage hers.

She suddenly decided to give in to her body's desire and wrapped her arms around him, kissing hard and with urgency. Her heart was pounding harder and harder as she felt his hands slowly caress her. She was sure she wanted to pull back, but all she found herself doing was holding him close, her hardened nipples pressing against her dress.

He let his hand go low to where her waist was and slowly started lifting the dress, peeling it away from her smooth skin. This was going to far. It had to stop.

She pulled away and looked at his warm eyes. Something in them dazzled her. Something in them got her blood rushing.

She surprised herself as she took a seat on the couch and looked at him invitingly. She lifted her head and undid the bun her hair was in before shaking it loose. Mitchell smiled and slowly began to loosen his tie. She knew she was making him get hotter by the second and for some reason, she was loving it.

He took a seat next to her and brought his face to hers, but never allowed himself to go low. She looked up at him and smiled. Mitchell wanted to see if she could take control.

Natasha slowly grabbed his tie and pulled him down, her lips slowly meeting his. She felt his hand slowly go up her dress and caress her thighs, making her pussy hot and moist. Her eyes were closed when she felt him undo the zipper behind her back.

She heard him breathe a low smooth wow when her breasts became exposed to him.

"Ah…." She gasped when his warm hand cupped a full breast. She opened her eyes to see him marveling at her tits.

"You are the most beautiful woman I ever saw," he said in almost a whisper. Natasha put her hands on his face and tilted him upwards.

"Really?" she asked cynically.

"Oh yeah," he said as he effortlessly undid her bra clasp. She felt a shiver run down her spine as he pulled the bra away. She could almost see his cock twitch as he looked at her breasts. Her gasps quickly turned into moans when he took one of her nipples in his mouth and began twirling his tongue around it. She felt a warm flow of liquid blot her panties as he sucked her hard, his other hand now carefully brushing her other nipple.

She held onto his bobbing head as he moved up and down

her heaving chest, almost as if her life depended on it. Natasha could feel Mitchell's hand slip away from her breast down to her navel. She quickly opened her eyes to see him kissing her stomach while lifting her dress.

"Oh my God, is he going down there... NOW????" she wondered as his lips trailed the inside of her thighs. Her pussy was now fully wet, almost staining the couch. "Mitch... what...," his hand soon blocked her words as he made her suck on his index finger. He suddenly placed both hands on her waist and pulled her down on the couch before spreading her legs wide. She felt vulnerable as she lay there, legs spread eagle like in front of a fully dressed man. She watched him closely as he lifted her manicured foot and admired her heels.

"Great woman, great taste," he said in a low voice as he smiled at her. She smiled back as he threw the shoe on the floor. He surprised her when he lifted her foot, kissing her well manicured toes. The kisses soon turned into slow sucking.

"Fuck, this dude is fucking kinky," she thought as she surrendered herself to the pleasure.

He worked his kisses up her leg, then finally to her warm, wet center. *"Oh fucking shit,"* she thought as she felt those warm lips on her dark throbbing vagina.

The sight of his white lips on her dark brown ones was a thing of pure beauty.

He was slowly sucking and almost tugging at the hair which covered the top of her feminine area, triggering shivers and chills a plenty. She was sure his face was now a hot, wet mess, but he never stopped. It was like he didn't want to. He lapped at her cunt as his fingers toyed at her opening. She gasped, trying hard not to cry out as he worked his oral prowess on her wet, ripe pussy.

Seemly wanting to give her a shock, Mich suddenly plunged his tongue deep inside his new play mate, activating a serious orgasm that ripped through her walls. Natasha slapped a hand over her mouth as she screamed out, her orgasm matching some of the best ones she had with Jay.

This was Mitch's cue to pull away from her pussy and get himself standing again. Smiling, he took Tasha's hand away from her mouth and kissed her gently.

"I want to hear you scream," he whispered amidst kisses.

"No... I can't... the office..." "...yes you can, baby," he said kissing her again. "Insulated walls."

Natasha nodded as he slowly and softly kneaded her breasts. "I want to hear it," he said again before going back down on her. She felt him fumble with his fingers for a while before shoving two of them inside her wetness.

She arched her back as he quickly worked his fingers in and out of her. He was watching her get multiple orgasms, and he loved every minute of it.

Her vocal chords were strained, but as a final orgasm approached, she couldn't help but squeal and scream, her body slowly drifting down the couch. She knew he was having a hard time maintaining his finger fuck as she came, but her body's actions were now involuntary.

She opened her eyes to see him looking at her. His cock was already out of his pants looking angry, rigid and ready to plough her. Mitch withdrew his fingers making Tash shiver; the last bits of sexuality draining out of her cunt.

He brought his face down and kissed her lips, then her breasts, before collapsing on her. She could feel his cock pressing against her body and all she wanted to do was have his beautiful hardness buried inside.

"Mitchell, you..." "...next time, I won't stop there," he said kissing her forehead. He didn't want to hear what she had to say. She didn't want this moment to end. But it was the first day of work and it was 9.30 in the freaking morning. She had to pull herself together, and fast!

Chapter 5

Rita looked at a bright faced Natasha and smiled. She wasn't sure whether she was happy or altogether proud.

She had just got Natasha to spill her guts about her little office encounter with Mitchell at the office. It had been already five weeks since she started working at Nolan Schmidt Communications solutions and she had been glowing ever since the first day. But perhaps what made her most proud of Natasha was the fact that finally, her best friend was over Jay.

"At least I don't have to hear anything else about that jack ass," Rita thought as Natasha handed her a bottle of water.

"I have got to ask," Rita said as she fumbled with the bottle. "Could McDreamy be the reason you haven't missed a single day of work, **even** when Aunt Irma visited?"

Rita smiled as Natasha shrugged, taking a long sip from her own bottle.

"Come on, don't even go there," Natasha said as she led Rita to her room.

"We both know I'm right, Tasha," Rita said in a decisive voice.

"Mitchell has actually been in Brazil for the last couple of weeks," Natasha said, making her way to the bed. "Some company promotion thing," she added before fluffing up some pillows and taking a seat.

"So, you've been the good girl ever since you joined NSCS because you want him to give you his full blown daddy dick?" Rita asked, a naughty smile playing on her face. Natasha threw a cushion at her.

"Rita!" Natasha said giggling. Rita put her hands up in defense as the cushion came flying towards her face. "You are disgusting," Natasha said. She could already feel her cheeks flushing again.

She could not deny that she had indeed gone to bed many a night wondering what it would be like to have Mitchell deep inside her. The way he had eaten her out in his office made her want more of him. It was almost as if her mind was enslaved to him.

To his hands. To his lips. To his tongue. And even though she was yet to have it, to his cock.

She had wanted to know what his cock was like since they met that day at the parking lot. There was an aura of sexuality around her boss and she could feel it.

That said, Tasha wasn't sure what his reasons for wanting to be with her were. Maybe he liked the idea of having an African American woman. Maybe he just had to confirm the rumor that black women were great in bed. Or was it for street cred? Whatever it was she didn't care, she just wanted to be with him. To fuck him, to feel his warm skin against hers as they both got into a wonderful world of climax.

"Hello, earth to Tasha!?" Rita asked, waving her arms in front of her bestie who suddenly blinked and took another sip from her bottle. "Still here?"

"Where else would I be?" Natasha responded, answering a question with another question. Rita ran her fingers through her thick braids.

"I don't know, McDreamy's bed?" she said laughing.

"He has a name, you know," Natasha said looking at Rita. "It's Mitchell!" She put on her most serious joke face.

Rita smiled before bursting out into a laugh.

"You're the one who said he was your very own McDreamy," she said amidst laughter. "Shonda Rhimes should have your head on a pike for stealing her best selling product," she added.

"Don't even... You know the only reason I watch Grey's Anatomy is Derek Shepherd," Natasha said feigning seriousness again. Rita laughed before putting her bottle on the floor.

"Well, enough said." Rita suddenly became more serious. Natasha looked at her closely. She looked like she was about to drop the atomic bomb on Hiroshima all over again. "There's something I want to talk to you about," Rita finally said. "*I knew it!*" Natasha thought as she held her hair up.

"What is it? What's going on?"

She hated when Rita got serious. Seeing as she never really got serious at all, this had to be major.

"Well, I couldn't say this earlier because I wasn't sure," Rita started. Natasha felt her heart rate go up a little. She needed time to process something, this was nothing small...

"Come on, out with it," Natasha pressed. Rita took a deep breath and held her friend's hand.

"Jay's finally moving back," Rita finally said. Natasha felt like her world had just come to a stand still. "*Did she just say...*"

"Did you just say that Jay is moving *here*? Back to the neighborhood?" Natasha asked almost in a panic. "I thought he wasn't going to any more..."

Rita squeezed her hand.

"This guy is like a bad smell. You can't get away from him," Tasha thought.

"How do you know this? I mean, who have you been talking to?" she asked feeling the anger within her building up.

"Miranda was bragging about it all over the nail salon last weekend..." "...Miranda? What the fuck?!" Natasha interrupted as the anger finally blew over.

Miranda Johnson had been her sworn enemy since middle school. Their relationship became even more stained when she went on a rumor mongering spree in an attempt to break Jay and Natasha up. For some reason, Natasha always thought that Miranda would grow out of her childish phase, but it seemed that even in her twenties, she was still living back in high school.

Natasha took a deep breath. "So, do you know when exactly he's coming back?" she asked feeling a lot more calm than she had been a few minutes ago. Rita shook her head.

"Maybe Miranda knows," Rita said with a smile. Natasha smiled back.

"You know I really don't care," Natasha said lying down on the bed. "Jay is my past and that's where he belongs. History," she said crossing her legs. Rita looked down at her and smiled. Natasha could tell that she was proud of how far she'd come.

"That's exactly what I wanted to hear from you," Rita said as she followed suit and lay on the bed. "I mean, you guys were a baby short of being the next hit on VH1," she added cynically. Natasha grabbed another cushion and hit her knees.

"What? You know I'm right," Rita said trying to yank the cushion out of Natasha's hands.

Just then, the loud shrill of Natasha's cell pierced the room.

"Saved by the bell, " Natasha said as she rose to pick up her phone. When she looked at the screen she froze. Her heart was suddenly beating faster and her palms seemed sweaty all of a sudden.

"What? Who is it?" Rita asked crawling on the bed to where Natasha was. "Is it Jay?" she asked, looking at Natasha's frozen phone bound gaze. Natasha shook her head and managed a half smile.

"McDreamy," she whispered before finally picking up the phone. "Hello?" she said trying not to sound as nervous as she felt.

"There's the mellow voice I have gone so long without," Mitchell said from his end of the phone. Natasha was grateful he wasn't there to see her blush.

"How you doing?"Mitchell asked. She could tell he had a smile on his face even without seeing him.

"Good," Natasha replied not wanting to sound too excited. "How about you? How's Rio?"

"Good good. Not as comfortable as home though," he answered. "Eating alone is a bit of a bummer." he added.

"I thought it was a seminar... Why don't you make a few friends while you're there?" Tasha asked. She looked over at Rita who had a wide smile on his face. Natasha knew that she could not hide the fact that she was attracted to Mitchell much longer. The placid voice she had while talking to him was a sure tell-tell sign.

"I don't like these rich snobs," Mitchell said causing Natasha to give him a sarcastic laugh.

"Rich snobs? Have you met yourself? Your family name is on 300 acres of land and that's just corporate property," Natasha said.

"I don't want to talk business right now," Mitchell said dismissively. "Let's talk food," he added.

"I've never had Brazilian," Natasha said quickly.

"And I'll make sure you try it one day. But today, I'm in the mood for some good old Mandarin pork," he said.

"Well then, order in or just take yourself out," Natasha said shrugging. Was this all he had to say to her? Not even a flirty 'I miss you'?

"Fine, but only if you come with me," Mitchell said. Natasha rolled her eyes.

"Do you have a super fast jet? Because that's the only way I'll get there in time for dinner," she joked, half laughing.

Mitchell didn't laugh back.

"As a matter of fact, I do..."

Natasha's eyes widened. Mitchell didn't sound like he was joking at all."*He has a super jet... No, he has a personal jet?* She wondered cursing her average lifestyle.

"So what, you're just going to send your jet for me or something?" Natasha asked nervously laughing.

"Well, first I need to know whether you want to have dinner with me tonight," he said casually. Natasha looked at Rita and smiled. "*He wants me to have dinner with me,*" she mouthed to Rita.

"Urm, sure, I guess..." Natasha finally replied.

"Great. I'll pick you up at seven," Mitchell quickly responded. Natasha could hear the relief in his voice as he said so.

"Alrighty, see you then" she said as she hang up. Rita looked at Natasha in disbelief.

"Girl, you are rolling high, aren't you?" Rita asked as she looked at an obviously over excited Natasha.

"Oh shut up and help me decide what to wear," Natasha replied as she led Rita to her closet.

*****

Natasha was unsure of her outfit. She hated this situation. Usually she was never undecided about her clothes; everything she had always seemed to be a good fit anywhere she went.

After Rita left for work that afternoon, she had left four dresses on the bed. For the last twenty minutes though, Tasha had done nothing but stare at the choices in front of her... Until now.

"Too slutty," she thought as she put away a hot pink mini-dress. She looked at the other three and sighed. One was a short black sleeveless dress that made her boobs put Pamela Anderson to shame. Another was a red strapless gown.

"You are not going to the Grammys Tasha," she thought as she put the red gown away.

Now, it was either the black dress or a purple halter dress. The black dress would obviously draw attention to a specific part of her body, but that wasn't what she wanted. She put the black dress away before putting on the light purple option. She carefully fastened it behind her neck, careful not to mess up her straightened hair. She had chosen to wear her hair down in a side sweep. She thought it was elegant and classy. Not too much, just enough to make Mitchell drool.

She giggled at the thought of seeing Mitchell again. It had been a long time since Tasha last traveled and she didn't want to make a fool of herself when the two met again.

She picked up and inserted a pair of black dangling earrings which matched her peep toe heels. It also matched her black Marie Claire clutch.

Slowly, Tasha walked to the full length mirror and checked herself out. She loved what she saw. The dress was modestly short, reaching just above her knee, showing off her smooth, long legs. *'Everything's perfect'*, she thought as she made her way downstairs.

"Oh honey," her nan Estelle said as Tasha made her way to the living room. "You look so beautiful!"

"Agreed," her dad added, "more so than you did on your prom."

Natasha smiled.

"Thanks guys," she said before taking a seat.

"So, this Mitchell. He's your boss I hear?" Eric asked putting the TV on mute.

"Oh man, here comes the lecture."

"Yes, daddy," she said crossing her legs. "Mitchell Schmidt is my boss at NSCS."

"It's just, I don't like this whole idea," Eric said shaking his head. "Dating your boss?"

"Don't use that as an excuse daddy, you never like any guy I meet," Natasha said with a laugh.

"That's true, Eric" Estelle added, grinning knowingly at her son.

"Don't blame me, Tasha's my baby," Eric mentioned in his defense. "I just don't want you to get hurt again." He took his daughter's hand.

"Oh come on Eric," Estelle said. "It's not like the girl is running off to marry this Michelle guy..." "...Mitchell!" Natasha corrected her with a smile.

"Fine, this 'Mitchell' guy, any time soon." Estelle continued. "And besides, I think he's so much better than that Jay character," she added. Natasha turned to look at her.

"Nan, you never liked Jay?" Natasha asked in surprise. She had always thought her nan liked him.

"Oh no, honey," Estelle said. "I was sure you could do better... Well look at the time."

Natasha wasn't sure if she was saying that to change the topic or because she was generally shocked at the time.

"Eric, you have to drive me to Chantal's for bible study. You know I hate being late," Estelle added, grabbing her purse. Natasha smiled. "*It was genuine,*" she thought as she looked at them heading towards the door.

"Bye honey," they called in unison as the door closed behind them.

"Later guys," she called back before relaxing in her seat.

Natasha took a long deep breath before finally switching the TV back on. She stared at the box without taking in what was going on. All she was thinking about was Mitchell. How he planned to jet her off to Rio on such short notice. She would've been just as happy him taking her to a restaurant around the corner, or for a sit in the park. All she wanted was to see him.

She felt herself getting hotter at the thought of seeing him again. She longed to run her slender fingers through his luxurious hair as he held her close, close enough to smell his manly scent. Her panties were already feeling a little moist as these thoughts went through her head... She was lost in the moment.

Natasha leaned into the couch, bringing her hand to the back of her neck and carefully undoing the knot that held the dress in place. The fabric of the dress fell like petals on her lap.

She began slowly rubbing her nipples against the lace that was her bra. The other hand reached up to her other breast, before slowly but deeply kneading her mounds. She managed soft moans as pleasure shot through her body. She thought of how great Mitchell's warm, wet mouth had felt on her clit, and felt a hot surge of warmth shot through her body.

One hand slowly went down her navel and finally hit her leg. Before long, the same hand was traveling up her thick thigh to her now hot pussy. She closed her eyes as she let her index finger make contact with her sensitive bud. She touched herself again and again until her clit became as wet as her pussy was.

With a gasp, she slipped a finger inside her vagina and then took it out.

She reintroduced her pussy to her finger again, this time coupling her index finger with her middle finger. She let a shriek escape her throat as she began to slowly finger fuck herself.

Her juices were now making it easier to move her fingers in and out of her pussy. She wished she was holding on to Mitchell's head... or hand... or even his nice hard cock.

The pace at which she thrust her fingers in and out increased until it reached a point where she couldn't take much more. She threw her head back as the pressure inside her built up. She unintentionally slid on the couch, pushing her hips forward and making her palm put pressure on her clit. She felt herself give in to an unknown force as she finally lay down on the seat, exhausted, happy, and satisfied. Just then, the doorbell rang calling her out of her dazed state.

She quickly sat up as reality once again hit her. She was a self sexed mess.

"Just a minute!" she yelled as she rushed to the bathroom. She roughly rubbed her hands under the 'cold turning warm' water, scrubbed in some soap, then rinsed it off as the hot water had just started to show. She then wet some tissues to clean the wetness that was trickling down her thigh.

Tasha re-fastened the dress behind her neck before running fingers through her hair. She looked at her reflection and smiled. *"You are still perfect,"* she told herself as she rushed back to the living room.

She squared her shoulders and walked to the front door. She couldn't help but smile when she lay eyes on a clean shaved Mitchell. *"Fuck, Tasha! Get it together!"* she thought as she stood dumbfounded on the doorstep.

"Don't I get a hug?" Mitchell asked with a smile as he held his arms out. Natasha smiled and allowed herself to be locked in his brief but warm embrace. *"He's really here!"* she thought excitedly as he pulled away. Just then, Mitchell lifted her chin with his finger and brought his lips down to meet her own. Natasha felt herself melt as she responded to his warm expert kiss.

"I never know whether to give a girl a kiss at the start or end of a date," he said when he pulled away. "I don't get the whole awkward situation, but that's over right?" he added with a smile. Tasha pulled the door shut behind her and smiled back.

"Real smooth Schmidt," she finally managed to say. Mitchell smiled and took her hand.

"Shall we?" he asked. Suddenly Natasha gasped as she caught glimpse of the sleek black limo in front of her house.

"A limo?" she asked in almost a whisper.

"I figured since I was already back, the jet would have to wait," he said as he led her to the vehicle. "Besides, limos have no turbulence," he added with a wink.

"True, but limo rides can also be bumpy," she said as they approached the long car. Mitchell again smiled.

"You're not wrong there. Nice dress by the way. Though I'm not sure you'll be able to keep it on with the bumpy ride ahead," he said as the limo began driving off. Natasha felt herself blush, not knowing if pun was intended. Either way, all she cared was that she was in a limo with Mitchell Schmidt, her very own McDreamy.

Chapter 6

As she rode home after the date, Natasha felt more relaxed than she had going into it. One thing she had to admit, was that even though he could be cocky, Mitchell had been right. Kissing her at the beginning of the date made her feel a lot more relaxed. She never had to worry that he was leaning in for some action every time he reached for the salt.

Looking out the window, she could see buildings speeding by as they cruised down the streets. She was eager to get home and sleep off the buzz that was already working its way to her head.

"Hope you're not too tired," Mitchell said softly. She looked at him and smiled.

"I wouldn't say I am," she replied before looking out again. She suddenly realized that the driver was taking them downtown instead of driving her back home. "Mitchell, I live way back that way," she said pointing in the opposite direction of where they were heading. He looked at her and smiled. Right then, she knew he had something up his sleeve. Whether or not she wanted to know what it was, he didn't really care.

"I thought you said you weren't that tired," he said reaching for her hand. Natasha looked at him and twisted her head.

"Where are you taking me?" she asked looking into his eyes for an answer.

"Don't you trust me?"

"Depends," she said. She loved the fact that alcohol made her so chatty. She would have probably not talked this much under normal circumstances. "Do you have any feel good drinks in here?" she asked. Mitchell reached for a bottle of champagne from the limo's mini bar.

"More than you can handle" he answered as he stretched out to get a glass. Natasha grabbed the bottle from his hands and waved her index finger in his face.

"No glasses," she said pulling the cork out with ease. Mitchell watched as she began to drink straight from the bottle and laughed.

"Classy!" he joked. "But I have to admit, I am loving this new you!"

Natasha didn't respond. She was still focused on consuming more then her fair share of alcohol.

"Where have you been all my life?" he asked when she finally put the bottle down. Tasha smiled as she felt his hand on her cheek. She was feeling a bit buzzed, but she knew exactly what she was doing. She also know what she wanted... Or **who** she wanted for that matter. She put an arm around his neck and kissed him deeply.

Mitchell pulled away. "Was that you or the champagne?" he asked.

Natasha let off a half tipsy smile and put the bottle back in the bar.

"This is all me, Mitchell." she said as she kissed him again. "All... me." she echoed as she secured both arms around him. She felt his hand slowly running up and down her leg as their tongues softly made contact. But, the limo came to a halt just as things were heating up. Natasha sighed against Mitchell's hot lips as she felt his hands tracing the curve of her back.

"Damn," he said with a laugh.

"Damn is so right," she said as she smoothed her dress and puffed her hair up. "Where are we?" she asked as the driver opened her door.

She suddenly gasped when she saw the whole of Los Angeles at her feet. She marveled at the array of lights and well mowed lawns beneath her feet. "Oh my God," she whispered as she made her way out of the car. "The Griffith Observatory?" she asked in surprise. She looked at Mitchell who stood smiling as if he had just done the most normal thing in the world.

He nodded as he made his way around the car to where she was. He took her hand and stood behind her. She felt her emotions take the better of her as a tear slowly rolled down her cheek. "I can't believe that I'm really here," she said in a low voice. She suddenly turned to look at him. "Wait, it's Monday right?" she asked him. Mitchell nodded.

"Yeah it is, why?"

"The observatory is usually closed on Mondays," she said. "Oh my God, Mitchell, are we here illegally?!" she asked looking around for any sign of security guards coming their way.

"I am sure they would have noticed a black stretch limo on their cameras," he said holding her waist. She looked up at him and felt her cheeks flush a little despite the cool evening air.

"You did *this*?" she asked realizing what was going on. He brushed off the tear using his finger.

"In your application, you mentioned that one of the things you would like to do was visit the Griffith Observatory alone," he said. "Well, you're not really alone right now, but I guess I wanted to share your dream moment with you." he added, planting a kiss on her forehead.

Natasha felt her stomach turn. She couldn't believe he had put so much thought into their date, this wasn't something Jay had ever done! Mitch had gone the extra mile to make private arrangements just for her, and her panties were again suddenly feeling very wet.

She wanted to give herself to this man now more than anything.

"No one has ever made me feel so special," she said looking up at him. He smiled and spun her around.

"Then enjoy this," he said making her face Los Angeles. He then took his jacket and draped it over her shoulders to shield her from the cold air. As they stood there watching Los Angeles in the glory of the evening light, the driver was busy clicking away on a camera he had obviously carried at Mitchell's request. When she realized what was going on, she shyly resorted to posing; something she would normally not do. Though the moment was wearing it off, the champagne certainly helped.

After taking enough pictures, the two went back inside the limo. They were in one of her favorite places in the world, but Tasha just wanted to be in Mitchell's arms again.

She hated that she was already feeling this strongly for him after such a short space of time. She wasn't sure if what was happening was a good or bad thing, but she did know this: She wanted to live in the here, the now! That moment was right here with Mitchell in the limo, and it was the highlight of her day...

No, actually her week.

"Tell me one thing," Natasha started as she looked at Mitchell. "Why me?"

Mitchell took a long deep breath. *"Maybe he's been asked this before,"* Natasha thought as she looked at him.

"You're not fussy," he said without blinking. Natasha looked at him questionably.

"Fussy." she said. "I don't know what that means..." she finally said shrugging. Mitchell laughed before running his fingers through his thick waves.

"My surname is my biggest cross," he started as he took a grape from a dish in the mini bar. "Every woman I've been with was with me for the alimony checks and flashy lifestyle," he added as he popped the grape in his mouth.

"That really happens?" Natasha asked. "I thought it was just something people did to popularize films."

"Oh it happens," Mitchell responded. "Remember when I told you that I had a complicated love life?" Natasha nodded. "Well, I was going through the final phase of my divorce. The woman I was married to, well, let's just say that her drama should have its own reality show." Natasha couldn't help but laugh. Mitchell could be funny when he wanted to be.

"So, I'm not fussy?" she asked with a smile. Mitchell shook his head, running his hand up and down her arm.

"You are maybe my best decision yet," he said. "I really want to see where this goes," he added looking into her eyes.

Natasha looked at him, wondering if this was the moment she had been waiting for. She slowly let his jacket slip off her shoulders and onto the limo floor. She was a bit nervous about making the first move, but thanks to the wine at dinner and the champagne she had earlier taken, she felt more confident than ever.

She shifted her weight a little so she could get closer to him. Before she could get fully in position, Mitchell leaned forward and claimed her lips in a long, sensual kiss that almost left her breathless. She slowly put her small hands on his broad chest and began working his buttons with her trembling fingers. Feeling her nervousness, Mitchell held her closer, a move which made his cock twitch.

Tasha felt him work his tongue inside her mouth, her hands focused on getting the last button of his shirt open.

Success.

Underneath were carefully crafted abs, a sight for any woman's sore eyes. Slowly, she ran her fingertips along the length of his torso before leaning to kiss him at the waist.

As Natasha's hot mouth pleasured his body, Mitchell's breath soon turned to short sighs and gasps of pleasure. She ran her tongue down his torso before trailing short, soft kisses on him. He felt small pimples forming on his skin as he closed his eyes in pleasure.

Natasha worked her way back up and took one of his pecks in her mouth. She let her tongue swirl around his tip, making his cock twitch again. She then withdrew from him and smiled.

Mitchell opened his eyes and caught her undoing the knot at the back of her dress. He gasped as the smooth purple fabric gave way to her two glorious breasts, now only covered by the black strapless bra she wore. The bra was carefully crafted so that her cleavage was well showed off. He breathed a long, low wow as his hand slowly moved up her thigh.

Using that as her cue, Tasha looked down and began working his pants. She was careful not to go too quick, wanting this moment to last as long as possible.

As she undid his zipper, Tasha felt her throat tighten. Her eyes were now witnessing the biggest bulge she had ever seen. OMG, how was she going to handle that?!

She pushed the thought to the back of her mind and continued to pull his pants off. He helped her with his boxer shorts, releasing a long, thick cock from the constraints.

Natasha knew she was staring but couldn't help it. Not only was this the first time she'd ever seen a white man's cock before, but she was now able to prove the stereotype of white men having small penises very, VERY wrong.

She felt her heart beat faster and faster, so fast in fact that she didn't realize Mitch pulling her dress down all the way.

Natasha finally came to her senses when she felt the tightness of her bra relax; he had undone the clasp of her bra. She trembled as he ran his palms on her hardened nipples.

Mitch pushed her on the seat, knelt in between her knees, and leaned forward to pull her panties off. *"Of course, you have to level the playing field,"* she thought. But instead of pulling her black panties off, Mitchell began kissing her navel, one hand still slowly rubbing her breast.

"Oh shit he's good. He's so... so... what the fuck..."

Natasha's thoughts were suddenly interrupted as he slowly pulled her panties down with his teeth.

She had never felt so turned on.

There was a hunk of a while man, between her legs, with a pair of knickers in his mouth. THIS WAS THE DREAM!

Mitch threw her knickers on the floor and let his body slowly descend on hers. They both marveled at the feeling of their two naked bodies touching.

As he went on to nibble her neck, Natasha closed her eyes and ran her hands up and down her new lover's back. Her wetness was now rubbing against his large member, making her breath faster and harder.

Withdrawing his mouth from hers, he slowly worked his tongue down to one of those breasts he so much adored. He took a nipple in the mouth, sucking long and hard enough to make her tremble under his weight. He let the nipple out of his mouth, only to take the other one in.

She moaned and squirmed as she felt herself inside his hot mouth. His hard tongue twirled around her nipple wildly, almost as if he was revenging for her earlier action of similar nature. His involuntary rubbing was gradually pushing her over the edge as he continued sucking on her. She suddenly raised her legs and wrapped them around his waist, again shivering wildly under him. She knew there was no way she could hide the fact that she had just had her orgasm from him.

He finally pulled away from her, releasing her nipple in the process. He wriggled out of her grip as she weakly collapsed on the seat. "Now, you're ready for me," he said in a whisper as he took a condom from his pants pocket.

"You knew this would happen," she whispered panting.

"You did too," he said as he eased the condom on his raging shaft. "I saw the condoms in your purse before you went to 'freshen up'" he said as he repositioned himself. *"Oops"* Tasha blushed.

"Ok, I knew..." she whispered as he came down to kiss her again. Natasha was unaware that this kiss was there to prepare her for what came next. She could feel his head on her well lubricated opening. He went on kissing her as he slowly nudged the head in. She appreciated the fact that he was slow and patient with her; she was not a virgin, but she had never had someone as big as him!

"What is he? Like eight, nine inches?" she thought as he slowly pushed himself inside her. As soon as his cock head slipped inside her wet pussy, she knew she was in trouble. She moaned against his lips as he worked the rest of his length inside her. *"Ten! Definitely a ten or eleven..."* she thought as he slowly withdrew his mammoth cock. He then pushed himself back in.

A few thrusts later, Mitch pulled away from her mouth to better analyze the situation, still slowly worked his cock in and out of her. He could see Tasha's face giving off both pain and pleasure as her cunt struggled to get used to his shaft.

Soon enough, the wetness inside her allowed him to slowly move in and out of her with ease. However, she was still whimpering. He pulled himself out of her and saw her face twitch as he did. He looked down at her pussy. It was no longer small and tight lipped, but wide open, gaped, and waiting for him to sink himself inside her.

Natasha opened her eyes to see him re-entering her, this time pushing himself to her hilt.

She gasped loudly as he sunk himself inside her smooth, inviting hole. Her fingers held on to the car seat as he picked up his pace. She had officially graduated from pain to desirable pleasure, and she was loving every minute of it.

Her tits bounced up and down as he worked himself in and out of her. Beads of sweat were forming on his forehead as he worked himself into a piston like frenzy. The car soon became filled with the sound of Natasha's loud gasps and moans. Her body fluids began to work their way to the surface, dripping down her thighs as they did. Mitchell's pace and closed eyes made Natasha know he was near the point of no return.

Before this thought had even left her head, Mitch suddenly lay down and flipped his lover over with ease. He was now lying on his back, Natasha on top and in the driving seat. *"I'm not sure I can do this,"* she thought as she struggled to move herself on his hard length.

As if he could read her mind, Mitchell put his hands under her ass cheeks and helped her work her way up and down. Soon enough, Natasha was being drop fucked onto Mitchell's long dick. She was surprised that by this time, he could bury himself inside her all the way.

She slowly began twisting her waist as she fucked him, causing Mitchell to let out a loud groan and put his hands on her breasts as she did so. It was quite evident that she was doing a good job, judging by the way he moaned and how his once gentle grip tightened. Or maybe the grip tightening was his way of trying to hold on to the wild woman on top of him...

Natasha tried to fuck Mitchell without exploding for as long as she could. Eventually though, she couldn't hold it any more.

Still sliding up and down, she felt herself burst against his shaft, orgasmic vibrations running throughout her body. She screamed and moaned as he kneaded her breasts, gently but deeply until she stopped shaking.

Just when she thought she was done, she felt Mitchell pushing his cock through her now highly sensitized walls. His spasms had got the best of him, making her scream out loud.

Mitch brought her head down to rest on his shoulder as he continued thrusting upwards. Natasha was confused. Normally, men collapsed after an orgasm. That said, Mitchell was clearly cut from a different cloth. He fucked her longer and harder until she finally felt him spasm again; this time, harder and longer than the first time around.

She shook uncontrollably as she felt the effects of his orgasm in her pussy. It was almost a never-ending pleasure for Mitchell.

He finally stopped thrusting and held her quietly. The only sound in the limo was their heavy breathing and occasional moans.

"You can come clean with me about the enhancers you took," Natasha joked, still resting her head on his shoulder. He laughed and planted a kiss on her forehead.

"I told you I had to get you going before I started," he replied as he ran a hand up and down her back. Natasha suddenly realized that the limo was no longer moving.

"Where are we?" Natasha asked. "We are not moving

anymore." *"Oh shit, the driver probably thinks I'm a whore"* she thought.

"I told the driver to drive us a couple of blocks from your house and take an hour's walk before we took you home," Mitchell said, putting Natasha's mind at ease. Natasha smiled as she cursed the thought of having to wake up alone after such great sex.

Chapter 7

"These came for you Miss Black," Stacy Reynolds, Natasha's assistant said carrying a bouquet of flowers. Natasha looked up to see Stacy placing them next to another four bouquets that had come over the space of two days. *"This is ridiculous,"* she thought, eying the colorful collection.

"Wait Stacy," she said as her assistant started to walk out. "What does the card say?"

Stacy picked up the card and opened it.

"Same as all others," she said after a short pause. "Dinner. Jay" She walked to Natasha's desk and gave her the card. Natasha took a long deep breath.

"Thanks Stacy," she said as she crumpled the small card. "Actually Stacy," she called again as Stacy approached the door. "Take them all with you."

"What would you like me to do with them?" Stacy asked looking confused. Natasha looked up from her computer.

"Trash them, burn them, I don't care," she said with a cheeky smile. "And any other that come in, do the same."

Natasha went back to focusing on her computer.

"Alright Miss Black," Stacy said in a voice Natasha translated as 'whatever you say boss'.

"She probably thinks I've lost it" Natasha thought as she looked at the time. It was almost six, time to go. She grabbed her purse and cleared the desk of all her personal effects. She was just walking out of the office when her phone beeper went

off. She looked with excitement, knowing full well who it'd be.

"Coffee?" the text from Mitchell said. She looked at it and began typing.

"Actually kind of hungry."

Send.

She stood by the door as she waited for a reply.

"*Meet me at the parking lot in five."*

Walking out of the office she smiled, feeling on top of the world.

As Natasha passed Stacy's desk, she noticed the flowers were already gone. She walked over to where her workmate was now sitting.

"Hey Stacy," Natasha said to her with a smile. Stacy looked up and flashed her own pearly whites. Natasha liked Stacy. She was a genuinely nice person, never too eager to kiss her ass. Stacy Reynolds was just what she needed going into a new company.

"Hey Miss Black," Stacy said. "What more can I do for you?"

"Nothing really. I just wanted to thank you for dealing with that floral situation for me."

Stacy shrugged.

"No problem Miss Black, its all part of the job." Natasha smiled as she began walking away. Her phone buzzed again.

"*Where you at?*" it now said.

"*Lobby.*" she replied within a matter of seconds. Tasha picked up the pace, her stilettos clicking along the ground as she did so.

Getting outside, she noticed Mitchell leaning against his black SUV. She then realized that this was the first time she had seen him all day. He had an early morning meeting, and by the time he was back to the office, Natasha was already in a meeting with some potential clients. She was just now laying eyes on her very own Derek Shepherd, a man who looked as sharp as ever in a gray pin stripe suit with complementary soft purple shirt. His wavy hair shone in the evening sun, a heavy contrast from his light toned skin.

"You look good. I mean, really good." she complemented as she approached the vehicle. Mitchell gave her a smile and looked at her. Her body looked exceptionally great in the white wrap around dress and silver platform heels.

"You don't look so bad yourself" he replied as his eyes savored her beauty. He held his hand out and she looked at him confused. *"Is he going to hug me here?"* she wondered as she took his hand in a nervous handshake. Mitchell smiled and pulled her in a close embrace. *"Oh boy, the office gossip machines have something to tweet about,"* she thought. He slowly pulled away and brought his head down to meet her lips.

"Mitch, what are you doing?" she asked looking at him. It was strange enough that he was holding her this close in full daylight, but to kiss her in full view of her co-workers? That was just ridiculous.

"Can't I be happy to see my woman?" he asked looking at her.

Natasha looked at him and smiled.

"You don't mind if everyone here knows about us?" she asked. He smiled again and pulled her close for a long, lingering kiss that almost left her gasping for breath.

"Not at all," he said after letting her go. She felt a shiver go through her. *"This might very well be the real deal,"* she though as she looked at him.

"So where are we going?" she asked still in his arms. He smiled a smile that made her a bit nervous.

"I'm not telling you, it's a surprise," he said as he opened the passenger door for her. *"He's never let me down before"* she thought as she climbed in.

"This had better be good" she teased as the car started up. "I'm not generally into surprises." She said this despite knowing Mitchell's surprises were far from your average.

"I've known you for four months and can guarantee that you'll love it," he replied as he drove them off the company premises.

Tasha relaxed in her seat as they cruised down the streets. She suddenly got uneasy when they began heading out of town, towards the outskirts of LA. *"He best not be some serial killer,"* she thought struggling to regain her composure. *"Four months my ass, he may very well kill me."*

She looked over at Mitchell who was busy humming to the smooth tunes that were now playing. Soon, they drove into what looked like a landing strip.

"Where are we?" she asked as she looked at the landing strip in front of them. There was a small plane on the strip and a man who looked like a butler standing right next to aircraft steps. "Who's that man? Are you going to kill me?" she asked suddenly. She bit her lip when she realized she was thinking out loud.

"What?" Mitchell asked looking at her with a smile. He slowly pulled over and got out of the car. In true gentlemanly fashion, he made his way round to her door to let her out."Come on," he said as he took her hand. They walked together to the plane where the butler greeted Mitchell with a professional smile.

"Everything set Edward?"

Edward the butler nodded.

"Everything is in place, Mr. Schmidt"

With this, Mitchell led Natasha inside. Her eyes widened as she boarded the plane, the private jet clearly having been prepped for just the two of them. There was a table romantically set for two, complete with a bottle of champagne on ice.

"Tonight, we are having dinner in San Diego," he said, smiling and fastening his seat belt. Natasha looked at him and smiled. Mitchell Schmidt was all that and a bag of chips.

She relaxed as they took off, wondering what the next few hours had in store for them.

They finally arrived in yet another private landing strip in San Diego. This time, there was a car waiting to take them to Luca Bellini's, a new Italian bistro in town. The restaurant had been popular from the get go thanks to celebrity chefs and its many high end clients, and Mitch was keen to take his new woman there.

As they walked through the doors of the bistro, Natasha could feel sophistication all around her. They were swiftly greeted at the door, the hostess leading them to a private table with a great view of the ocean. Natasha looked over at Mitchell and sighed. This man was out to spoil her and she was loving every minute of it.

After a great dinner, Mitchell decided to take her for a walk on the coastline. Tasha carried her heels in one hand, Mitchell's hand in the other. They strolled at a easy pace, walking hand in hand while eying the beautiful sun kissed ocean. They had only been walking for a few minutes when Natasha thought she heard someone call her name.

"Tasha" she heard a male voice call out again. This time she stopped to check. *"Who would possibly know me in San Diego?"* she wondered as she turned this way and that. "Hey ma," she heard a voice behind her. She suddenly turned around to see her ex Jay smiling at her. *"Oh fuck!"* she thought.

"Hey Jay," she said passively. "What are you doing here?"

"I came for a seminar. What are *you* doing here?" he asked. "And who is this?" Jay looked at Mitchell.

"This is Mitchell," she said, her hand intentionally on Mitchell's abs. "We were just having dinner." Mitchell responded by slowly putting an arm around her shoulders. She could tell Jay felt jealous seeing her in the arms of another man.

"You doing white men now?" Jay asked clenching his fist. "Why, black men not good enough for you? Or is it because you're a little lighter than us so you think you're better?" he asked.

"Jay my skin tone ain't none of your business. I am just as black as the next person," Natasha said angrily.

"So, is he the reason why you won't take my calls or reply to the flowers I sent?" he asked moving closer to Mitchell. Natasha got in the middle of them and pushed Jay off.

"Jay, grow the fuck up and just go," she said looking at him. Jay was still getting closer to Mitchell... Threateningly close.

"You had better listen to the girl man," Mitchell said as he gently pulled Natasha away.

"Oh yeah?" Jay asked sarcastically. "Why, what are you going to do?" he asked as he shoved Mitchell. Natasha was getting scared. She just wanted to get out of there.

"Man look, walk away," Mitchell said shoving him back. Curious onlookers began to form a crowd. Natasha took Mitchell's hand and began walking away, Mitchell keeping his eyes on Jay the whole time.

"That's right Tahsa, run away with your little bitch" Jay yelled. "Guess you both bitches anyway."

Mitchell stopped in his tracks and ran his fingers through his hair. Natasha would have laughed at his James bond move if she wasn't so scared.

"What did you just say?" Mitchell asked Jay who was already moving towards him. Jay got so close to Mitchell that the only distance between them was the combined length of their noses.

"I said you a little bitch," Jay said, shoving Mitchell again. Natasha could see Mitchell wanted to be the bigger person, but Jay raised his fist and begun to swing for his face. Almost at lightning speed, Mitchell ducked and gave Jay a couple of punches to the stomach. It seemed Jay was winded, but Mitch gave him a swift boot on his now bent over shoulder blade just to be sure. This move brought Jay to the ground, just as a couple of the onlookers stepped in to break up the fight. "It's not worth it" one of them said. Mitch again ran his hand through his hair, looked at the hurt Jay, and put his hand out for Tasha to take.

"Not fucking good" thought Tasha, who took Mitch's hand and decided to get out of there as soon as possible.

Mitch was unusually quiet as they drove back to the airstrip. In fact, they both were. At the strip, Mitchell exchanged a few words with Edward before the plane finally took off. "I'm sorry about that," Natasha said finally. Mitchell looked at her and managed a weak smile. He held her hand and squeezed it a little.

"You were not the one being disrespectful," he said as he looked at his black beauty. He gently pulled her hand, making her unbuckle the seat belt and get closer to him. She stepped closer and sat on his lap.

"Where did you learn how to do that?" she asked as he put an arm around her waist.

"I have a black belt." he replied. "I spent eight years learning martial arts."

Natasha was as surprised as she was turned on.

"Is there anything else I need to know about you that I can

learn in 20 to 30 minutes?" she asked in a sweet voice.

"Plenty" he said kissing her lips. *"Right answer!"* thought Tasha.

Mitch trailed his lips to her neck, and quickly got to work on the knot that was holding her dress together. He was getting good at this.

He pulled away and roughly pushed the dress off her shoulders. He then quickly unclasped her bra without wasting any time, attaching himself to one of her tender breasts. She moaned as she felt the intense pleasure of his mouth engulfing her nipples.

Sex with Mitch last time was good, but this time things were seriously intense!

He soon began working his hand up Tasha's dress. She raised herself a little, allowing him to pull her panties off. As they slid down her legs, she got up and quickly kicked them away from round her ankles. She then sat back down.

Mitch slowly used a finger to caress her now moist cunt as he again started sucking her. When he finally pulled away, her nipples were fully erect and loudly screaming for attention.

He undid his seat belt and sat her down, before completely pulling the dress from her body. She felt a little shy being so bare in front of him, especially as he was fully clothed. Soon though, her thoughts would be else where.

He got on his knees and slowly caressed her smooth, chocolate brown thighs, all the while aiming his head for her center.

She felt herself almost burst as he slowly let his tongue brush her raging clitoris. He did this again and again before finally taking the entire bud in his mouth and sucking hard. Tasha managed to awkwardly edge the top of her head up the seat as he sucked away, ensuring she had a good view of the action.

Suddenly, Mitch pulled away and looked at the results of his work. He smiled. Her clit was now just as hard as her nipples.

He lowered his head again and slowly began kissing her lips. She shivered when she felt him handle her labia the same way he would her mouth. He spread her legs further. He then lifted them, before resting each leg on either of his shoulders.

Tasha closed her eyes tightly when a pleasurable heat wave pierced through her body. Mitch had once again dipped his tongue inside her wet, salty self.

She began squirming as he tongue fucked her hard, his hands resting on her breast and inner thigh. He retracted his tongue from deep inside her before lapping on her wet cunt. She found herself involuntarily wrapping her legs around his neck, not far at all from climax.

Mitchell managed to wriggle away from her grip and stood up. She looked up at him wondering why he wouldn't let her finish.

"We'll do it together," he said as if he could read her mind. She looked on as he stripped down to his birthday suit. He then held her hands and pulled her from the seat.

Natasha stood looking at him, almost at the verge of losing her mind. He kissed her softly as he slightly parted her legs using his knee.

Natasha heard him moan lightly when he let his cock head slightly touch her wet, naked pussy. She closed her eyes and wrapped her arms around him before the couple locked in an intense kiss.

Mitchell lifted her up. Natasha responded by wrapping her legs around his waist. Without breaking the kiss, Mitchell used one hand to guide his cock inside her waiting vagina, using his other hand to support her weight.

Natasha moaned loudly as the familiar discomfort of his large member got reintroduced to her pussy. She was almost crying out when he pushed himself inside her. He pulled away from her lips and held her tightly as he worked himself in and out. By this time, Natasha was trying not to moan too hard as he pushed himself in.

"I'm sorry if I'm hurting you," he whispered as he worked his large member inside her. She kissed his neck as her pussy got used to the humongous length.

"Don't be," she managed to say amid her labored breath. "I love what you do to me." His thrusts were becoming more manageable.

Although her eyes were closed, Tasha could tell he was smiling when she told him this.

He pulled out and pushed back in with as much ease as it would be if they were lying down. They fucked standing up for almost ten minutes before Mitchell lowered her to a seat.

He managed to get her legs well secured as he got on top of her. Then the thrusts started again; long and hard.

Every time he thrust inside her, Tasha would moan and gasp.

Somewhere in-between her moans, she called out his name once or twice.

"You love what I do to you?" he asked looking into her eyes. She nodded as she held on to the seat.

"I want to hear you say it," he said in a smooth sexy voice. *"How is he able to remain so calm and collected considering he is like a bull inside me?"* she wondered as she looked at him.

"I... love... what... you... do... to... me..." she finally said. He smiled and brought his face down to kiss her.

"And do you love *that,*" he asked suddenly thrusting inside her. Natasha arched her back and shut her eyes tightly.

"**Yes**! Oh yes I love that" she replied as he continued thrusting deep inside her.

Mitch brought his face down and kissed her again. This time he kissed her longer and more deeply then the time before.

"I love you Natasha Black," he said as his thrusts slowed down. Natasha opened her eyes to see a gazing Mitchell Schmidt. She knew she had intense feelings for him, but had no idea he was feeling the same. She couldn't help but let off the biggest smile she had conjured up all year.

"Do you love me?" he continued. She nodded and kissed him again.

"I did a long time ago. I wouldn't be here if I didn't," she whispered, holding his face in her hands.

"Fuck Natasha, I'm falling for you bad" Mitchell said as he

resumed his powerful thrusts. She held on for dear life as she felt a orgasm coming on.

"Cum for me baby" Mitch softly requested. Tasha nodded her head and pushed his bum towards her, making his cock poke deeper inside her drenched pussy. She was ready. She gave in to fate.

A huge orgasm ripped through her body, causing a wild quaking of her walls. Seeing what was happening Mitch set off on his own orgasmic path, making him thrust deeper, longer, and harder.

Bliss.

Tasha's screams were getting lower as he slowed down on top of her. That was great.

A few seconds passed before Mitch picked his head out of the slumped state they were both now in. He paused before opening his mouth.

"Is this real?" Mitch whispered close to Tasha's face.

"It is" she whispered back.

He slowly pulled out of her pleasure hole, causing a mixture of their love juices to pour onto the seat and floor. He grabbed one of the napkins and slowly cleaned her sensitive pussy. He then sat up and went on to clean himself off.

Once done, he looked Natasha's way and slapped himself on the thigh, signaling his lover to come and sit on him. She did. Mitchell then went on to cradle her like a mother would a child, showing nothing but love to the person he shared an embrace with.

"So, we've had limo sex and plane sex," she started with a tired but sexy voice. "When are we going to have bed sex?"

Mitch took one arm away from the embrace, looked at his watch and smiled. He pressed the intercom button.

"Edward, what's closer? The Ritz or my house?" he asked.

"The Ritz is fifteen minutes further than your house," Edward's voice came through the intercom.

Book 2.

Mr White Proposes

Chapter 1

Natasha stood in the bathroom as the warm water trickled down her body. She placed her hand on the wall, leaned in and then threw her head back. She smiled involuntarily as she felt the warm water get to her scalp and then again trickling down her back.

"This has to be my best moment of the day," she thought as she ran a hand through her wet hair. *"A bath would be better but this is as good as it gets."* She loved having showers at Mitchell's place. He had the most beautiful up-market townhouse. And it was not just a house, it was the whole damn shebang. Mitchell's house was basically every interior designer's dream when it came to small-time decorating. The three bedroomed house was a cool blend of white, oak brown and black. The master bath came complete with a cream colored Jacuzzi and the best shower she had ever known. When it came to décor, Mitchell definitely knew his stuff.

Natasha looked up when she felt a cool breeze blow in. She smiled when she saw Mitchell standing at the doorway. "Enough room for two?" he asked as he wriggled out of his pajama bottoms. Natasha smiled and looked at him.

"I have already been here for long enough," she said as Mitchell pulled her close. He smiled down at her and kissed her.

"A few more minutes wouldn't hurt," he said kissing her again. At that very minute Natasha knew she was in trouble. She felt Mitchell's hands slowly go down her body and grab her ass.

"Whoa there, mister," she said looking up at him with a smile. "I wouldn't want you to get started on something you have to wait hours to finish."

"Too late," Mitchell said before they both looked down at his hard erection which looked angry enough to drill a hole through concrete.

"I warned you," Natasha said before kissing him lightly on the lips. "But too bad," she added as she stepped out of the bathroom.

"What the...?" Mitchell said looking puzzled as he watched her sexy ass, her wet sexy ass walking away from him. "What about us, Tasha?" he asked, feigning neglect. Natasha grabbed a towel off the towel rack and wrapped it around her body before looking at him.

"Not now," she said as she wrapped another towel around her hair.

"Aaaw, why not?" Mitchell asked in a whiny voice as he walked towards her. Natasha walked to her dresser as she dried herself.

"Because today is the big meeting with Rango's," she said. "And I can't be late," she added as she squeezed some lotion onto her hand.

"Well, I suppose you are right," he said slowly walking up behind her. "But that meeting's at eleven and I only want five minutes," he said as he turned her around. His eyes dropped from her face to her well shaped breasts and hard nipples.

"But...."""...shhh," Mitchell said before kissing her sensually, interrupting whatever she was about to say. He suddenly carried her to bed and slowly lay her down. She looked up and smiled at him as he began planting small kisses on her body.

"I thought you said five minutes," she said as his kisses got closer to her navel.

"Mh hm," he said without looking up, his hands slowly spreading her cool legs. She suddenly gasped when she felt his warm lips going lower, almost getting to her labia. Her tough act was now totally and completely replaced by sheer intense pleasure and longing. She arched her back when she felt his lips on her smooth shaven pussy. Her heart was beating faster as he slowly kissed her lower lips making her wetter than she ever intended to be. She felt pleasure shooting through her body as Mitchell's tongue and her clit made contact.

Thanks to Mitchell French kissing her pussy, all she could think about was how she would lower herself onto that massive shaft she loved so much but for some reason, he did not show any signs of slowing down. She let out a small gasp when she felt him push his tongue into her hot, wet depths. She grabbed onto the bedding as he intensified his tongue fuck.

She felt one of his hands roughly caress her breast as he went on sucking on her wetness. She was not sure whether it was the slurping noises or the way his hand tweaked her nipples that brought her closer to the edge than she intended to be.

"Stop…come up here," she whimpered, yearning for that great feeling of his cock inside her. She felt him retract his tongue before she could finally see his face. He smiled at her and shook his head. He kissed her thigh and then went up to her breasts but he only teased her hard nipples.

She could not take it any longer. She raised her hips but Mitchell also raised his, denying her the pleasure she was so determined to find. She looked up at him in surprise as he turned around and leveled his pelvis with her head before lowering himself back to her wet cunt.

Natasha sighed and gasped as she took Mitchell's hard cock inside her mouth. The position made it possible for him to push himself further down her throat without even realizing what he was doing. She struggled to suck and lick him as she heard him moan out his pleasure on her pussy. Just when her throat was getting used to the length, Mitchell pulled himself out of her and reached for a condom on the bedside table.

She watched as he quickly rolled it onto his shaft before mounting her. Her wetness made it possible for a smooth entry making her gasp as he buried himself deep inside her. She started moaning loudly as Mitchell worked himself in and out of her.

He put a hand under her knee which was dangling on the edge of the bed and pulled it up. She gasped when she felt his cock get a few inches deeper. She was surprised this could even happen. *"I thought I had all of him,"* she thought as Mitchell allowed himself to be lost in his thrusts. It was not long before she felt him gradually pulsating. The feeling made her walls feel like a tsunami. She suddenly arched her back again and let put a loud moan as she felt her body weaken from the orgasm. Her body quavered as he slowed down.

"He was too quiet," she thought. *"He is not done yet, he shouldn't be done yet."* As if Mitchell had just read her mind, he resumed his strong thrusts into her now over sensitized pussy. Thanks to the orgasm that had just ripped through her, Natasha's pussy was like a sea of hot cum. She whimpered as Mitchell started grunting in time with his thrusts. She again held on to the bedding as his thrusts got harder and faster. She was like his little rag doll.

"Oh fuck…Tasha….shit….oh…" she heard him say before he finally slowed down.

"Now that's more like it," she thought as he collapsed on his body. "Five minutes huh?" she said when she got her strength back.

"For the quickie," he said as he slowly lifted his face. "I never said anything about the foreplay," he added with a smile.

"You do realize a quickie is so called because there isn't supposed to be any foreplay, right?" she asked him as she felt his limpness slipping out of her. She sighed as she felt release when the warm cum ran out of her.

"What can I say, when I decide to do something I go all in," he said as a bead of sweat trickled down his forehead.

"Now I've got to shower again," Natasha said pushing him off.

"I'll join you," Mitchell said as he quickly walked after her. Natasha spun around and shot him a dirty look.

"Just because I let you have your morning fun does not mean I'll let it happen again," she said before stepping inside the bathroom.

Mitchell smiled as the sound of the shower being turned on filled the room. He stood up and walked to the bathroom. He had a naughty smirk on his face as he opened the bathroom door.

"No, Mitchell….not this time," she said as the water trickled down her body once again.

"I promise not to feel you up," he said as he walked in.

Natasha gave him a cold hard stare before she finally stepped aside.

"You better not," she said as Mitchell wrapped her arms around her.

"At least not anywhere that might make you hot again," he said. Natasha gently shoved hr bum in his pelvis. "Now that's not helping," he said.

"I know," she said before quickly scrubbing herself down using her loofah. She then quickly walked out and went straight to bed where she had last left her towel. She would never admit this to Mitchell, but she loved it when he trapped her into morning sex. She smiled as she slowly oiled her body. It had been a year and a few months since she and Mitchell decided to be exclusive and even though they had their ups and downs, it was still the most satisfying experience she had ever had.

A few months after working at Nolan Schmidt Communications Solutions, Natasha had decided to move to an apartment a little closer to the workplace and of course for some privacy, something her old neighborhood knew nothing about. She loved the fact that she could be out of the house and not have to answer to anyone.

She walked to the closet after putting on her underwear and pulled out a royal blue pencil dress. *"That ought to command some respect in the board room,"* she thought as she slipped the dress on.

"That's what you are wearing to the Rango pitch?" she heard Mitchell ask. She turned around and smiled at him.

"Why? You don't like it?" she asked. Mitchell shook his head.

"No..It's just a bit too sexy, that's all," he answered as he lotioned up. She smiled and began doing her makeup.

"Well, Rango is the next big thing after Bloomingdale's, Woolworths and Victoria's Secret," she said as she held the blow dryer at arm's length. "This little number got you Calvin Klein and it sure as hell will get you Rango," she added with a smile.

"You make a valid argument," Mitchell said as he began dressing up.

"Besides, the only other clothes I have here are evening wear," she said looking at him. Mitchell walked up to her and placed his hands on her shoulders.

"We can fix that, you know," he said as he slowly massaged her shoulders.

"I am not going shopping, Mitchell," she said, looking at their reflection in the mirror. "I have too many clothes."

"Then bring them over here," Mitchell said.

"Why? I have everything I need right here," she said before standing up. "A week's worth is more than enough, Mitchell." She took a pair of blue suede heels from the closet.

"I am not talking more clothes, Natasha," Mitchell said, looking at Natasha who was busy making the bed. She looked even more beautiful than ever as she tried doing household chores in a couture dress and heels. "The whole thing, move in with me," he added in a small voice. Natasha sat on the bed and looked at him.

"We have talked about this, Mitchell," she said. He could

almost hear the pit in her voice. "I am not ready to move in with you yet. I just moved into my place." She stood up and slowly walked towards him.

"Are you ever going to be ready?" he asked as she wrapped her arms around his neck. She nodded.

"I would not be here if I didn't think so," she said before kissing him softly on the lips.

"What can I do right now? What can I do to change your mind?" he asked, holding her close. She shook her head.

"You are already doing more than enough," she said. Mitchell looked into her eyes and smiled.

"Really? Why is that?" he asked.

"Well, there is the little fact that you are faithful and responsible," she said smiling at him. "I would not have it any other way," she added before kissing him again and turning around. "Zip me up," she said in a small voice. She heard Mitchell take a long deep breath before pulling the zipper upwards. He then brought his face down and kissed her shoulder.

"I just want you to be mine so much," he said holding her. "I'm sorry it feels like I'm rushing you." Natasha smiled and placed her hand on his.

"When I'm ready, you'll know," she said before pulling away from his grip. "Now I'd better get going if I am to get that six figure commission." She smiled, then walked to the dresser and grabbed a pair of earrings and her purse.

"I thought we were doing breakfast together," Mitchell said as she headed towards the door. She turned around and smiled at him.

"You already used up breakfast time with a little something-something," she said before blowing him a kiss.

After she left, Mitchell smiled and sat on the bed. He took his phone and quickly sent Natasha a text. *"See you in a few."*

He had just placed his phone on the bed when he heard it vibrate loudly. *"Sure. We can make up breakfast with lunch."* He smiled and walked to the closet. In one of the jackets he rarely wore, he pulled out a small velvet case and briefly stared at it. *"Dinner's better. Lunch meeting with some associates,"* he typed.

"Sure."

He smiled to himself as he put the case back in the jacket pocket. It wouldn't be long now.

*****

"You were on fire in there," Sealy Moran, CFO of the Rango departmental stores said to Natasha as they walked out of the board room. Natasha smiled at him.

"I had to," she said. "After all, a $30 million contract was on the line," she added with a smile.

"I have heard a lot about you, Natasha Black," Sealy said. "You have quite the track record," he added smiling at her.

"I am happy that my work speaks for itself," she said as they approached her office. "Well, here I am," she said as she came to a halt in front of her office.

"You will not be joining us for breakfast?" he asked. "If there is anything I have learned about NSCS is that they have great personnel and even more excellent buffets," he added with a smile. Natasha laughed.

"I'm afraid not," she said. "The contract signing is the easy part. The real work is what I have to get done," she said shaking his hand.

"Here's my card," Sealy said after a rather long handshake. "Call me if you ever want to leave NSCS," he added. "For a change of scenery or maybe even coffee," he said quickly before walking off.

Natasha smiled and looked over at Stacy's desk. She laughed when she noticed her pretend to work.

"I know you heard it all, Stacy," Natasha said opening the door. Stacy looked up and smiled at her. "Bring me some coffee, would you please?" she said as she walked into her office. She sighed as she finally took a seat kicking off the heels she had on. She leaned against the seat and closed her eyes, feeling a rush of happiness and pride.

She heard a knock and looked up to see Stacy walking in with a Styrofoam cup and brown bag. "Well hello, Flash," Natasha said as Stacy walked towards her desk.

"I sent for it just as you were winding up the Rango meeting," Stacy said walking towards her desk. She placed the cup on her desk and then pushed a file towards her. "These need a signature, pronto," she said as Natasha took a sip of her coffee.

"Oh, that's good," Natasha said closing her eyes again.

"You're welcome," Stacy said to her with a smile. "But signatures," she said again as she stood next to her boss.

"What am I looking at?" Natasha asked as she slowly flipped the pages.

"Consent forms for the new corporate responsibility project," Stacy said. "We're collecting clothing and food for Hurricane Sandy victims," she added. Natasha felt the joy drain from her body as she looked at the photos and letters, mostly from children who resided in New York.

"Devastating," she said as she signed the papers.

"At least you re doing something to help," Stacy said picking up the file. "Anything else you may need before I leave?" she asked. Natasha shook her head.

"I'll let you know," Natasha said, leaning back in her chair as Stacy walked to the door. She smiled when she remembered how weird it had been coming to NSCS at first. Stacy had become more of a close friend than an assistant over the time she had been working there. She did an outstanding job of handling all her affairs, business and personal alike. "Wait," she said as an idea struck her. "The Rango deal went through as I'm sure you know," Natasha started casually.

Stacy nodded and looked at her.

"You did a lot of the research work and I feel you should be rewarded for it," Natasha continued. She saw Stacy's eyes grow wide when she said this.

"It is all part of the job you know," Stacy said trying not to sound proud.

"I know but it would not be fair if I didn't show my appreciation," Natasha said with a smile. "That's why I am going to talk to Vasquez in accounts about a nice bonus this month," she added. Stacy's alabaster skin flushed bright pink when Natasha said this.

"I don't know what to say," Stacy said, dumbfounded.

"Thank you, would be nice," Natasha said as Stacy quickly walked towards her and embraced her. "Or that," she said as Stacy hugged her.

"Thanks Natasha," Stacy said. Natasha smiled as she thought of how best to break the news to Mitchell. This was her eleventh successful pitch and she could not wait to see what the future held in store for her at NSCS.

Chapter 2

"If I knew this is what I was in for I would have worked harder in school," Natasha's best friend Rita said as a woman rubbed her feet. Natasha laughed as she leaned back in her own seat.

"It is nice isn't it?" Natasha said softly. She had decided to treat Rita to a spa date not far from where she worked. Since she started working and got serious with Mitchell, it seemed like they barely got time to hang out. Rita always joked that with Natasha, dick trumped friendship.

"But your art career is doing well, isn't it? Your mom…"

"…My mother would get me a husband if I let her," Rita interrupted. "I would not even dare tell her that my business is struggling," she added rolling her eyes.

"Ok, hold up, Rita," Natasha said sitting up. "What about the Swedish guy who ordered the…how many pieces were they, again?"

"One freaking hundred and thirty," Rita said. "But all he was interested in was 130 feels of this fine black ass," she added before taking a sip of her fruit flavored water.

"What?" Natasha said laughing.

"Oh yeah, he recanted his order as soon as I gave him a good kick in the balls, " she said looking at Natasha. "Literally," she added before leaning back in her seat.

"You did what?" Natasha asked laughing.

"The asshole had it coming," Rita said smiling. "It was all downhill from there. I'm even looking to change career, be a waitress or something," she added taking a deep breath.

"No, don't," Natasha said looking at her. "I have seen your work. You re awesome," she added matter-of-factly.

"You have to say that, you're my best friend," Rita said looking at her.

"No, for real," Natasha said trying to get comfortable. She could see the woman servicing her giving her a dirty look every time she moved. "Do you know how many people have wanted to buy that housewarming gift you got me?" she asked. Rita smiled at her.

"The abstract?" Rita asked surprised. Natasha nodded.

"If you want I can have a talk with Mitchell," Natasha started. "He knows a number of high end collectors and exhibitors," she added looking at Rita suggestively. Rita looked at her for a while before finally shaking her head.

"I am not a parasitic friend," Rita said leaning back in her seat.

"Come on it's nothing like that and you know it," Natasha said as the woman moved to her right foot. "Let a sister hook you up," she said making a sad face at her.

"Okay fine," Rita said finally. They both smiled at the two women who had just concluded their manicure and pedicure session left. "Enough about me, how are you and money bags doing?" she asked looking at Natasha.

Natasha blushed as she reached for her own fruit flavored water. "Good," she said smiling. "He asked me to move in with him," she said looking at Rita.

"Hadn't you already moved in with him?" Rita asked in a sarcastic voice. Natasha laughed as Rita stared daggers at her. "What? You're never home any time I drop by," Rita said smiling. "I would so make your house a personal brothel," she added.

"Really?" Natasha said laughing.

"What, a girl still needs to get her groove on," Rita said laughing.

"Oh, okay. So we have someone special now?" Natasha asked as her interest suddenly grew.

"Well, nothing serious yet," Rita said holding her hands up. "Don't start offering your maid of honor services yet," Rita said laughing just as Natasha's phone vibrated wildly on the table.

I am employing my culinary skills for you my queen. She smiled as she silently read the text.

"Will you share the joke?" Rita asked looking at a smiling Natasha who shook her head.

"Just Mitchell telling me he's making me dinner," Natasha said as she typed on her phone. *Mani pedis with Rita then I'm all yours,* she quickly typed. Rita smiled at her and took the last sip of her water.

"Hope me and Dave get there some day," Rita said sitting up.

"So that's his name," Natasha said placing her phone on the table next to them. "Dave," she said in a mock dreamy voice.

"Stop that," Rita said, gently shoving her. "And anyway, we were talking about your sick reason not to move in with Mitchell. What's up with that?" Rita asked looking at Natasha. There was a serious look in her eyes as she gave her best friend a hard, long stare. One that said, she had better tell the truth. Natasha took a long deep breath before taking her glass again for another sip.

"It's not that I don't want to," Natasha started, trying to look for the right words. "It's just that I don't want to rush things," she said before finally looking up at Rita.

"Who said you were rushing?" Rita asked taking Natasha's hands in hers, careful not to smudge the newly polished nails. "You know what I really hate about you?" she said still looking deeply into Natasha's eyes. "You over think everything. Sometimes it's fun to just follow what your heart tells you to do and this is one guy I feel is right for you Tasha," Rita said.

Natasha's cheeks flushed a little. For some reason, hearing her best friend say those words made her feel more comfortable about Mitchell. She probably just needed someone who had known her all her life to make the call even though the call was hers to make all along.

"You really think so?" Natasha asked smiling.

"Oh yeah and I am a pretty good judge of character," Rita said before leaning back in her seat. "And don't get me wrong, I'm not bragging or anything," she added laughing

"That's subject to confirmation," Natasha said blowing on her nails. "I am yet to meet him," she added.

"Well judging by the way I reacted to you dating Jay and Dane..." "...what was wrong with Dane?" Natasha asked interrupting her just as a spa attendant brought a huge bowl of fruit to where they were. Rita rolled her eyes and helped herself to a grape.

"I never liked the way he looked at women's feet," she said as Natasha looked at her. "For all I care he would have been making wild sweet love to your Manolos while you were away," she added laughing. Natasha laughed and leaned back in her seat.

"Whatever, Rita," Natasha said just as her phone buzzed again. She picked it up and another wide smile played across her face as she looked at the screen.

"That must be McDreamy again," Rita said as Natasha typed away.

"Yeah," Natasha said as she looked at her watch. "And it's about time I left," she added as she took an apple from the basket.

"We're still supposed to do lunch," Rita said frowning.

"If we are going to make it, then we'd better leave now," Natasha said before she slowly brought the tip of her tongue to one of her nails.

"What the hell are you doing?" Rita asked as she stood up. "Are you licking your nails?"

"I'm testing to see if the nails are dry," Natasha said as she took a bite of her apple.

"Of course you are," Rita said in a condescending tone. "If you are that hungry then I'd better drive," she added.

"No, if the polish has a bitter taste then it isn't dry yet but if it's neutral then it's fine," Natasha quickly said in an attempt to defend her methods.

"I won't even ask how you know that," Rita said as they walked to the cashier.

"By the way, we'll need to do a quick detour to my place," Natasha said as she handed her credit card to the lady behind the counter.

"What for?" Rita asked catching her reflection in the mirror behind the cashier.

"Grabbing a few clothes and my lease agreement," Natasha answered as Rita retouched her lip gloss. Rita smiled at her and gave her little wink.

"Now that's more like it," Rita said smiling.

*****

Mitchell looked at his wristwatch and smiled. He was just in time. Everything was where it was supposed to be. The table was romantically set for two, complete with a bottle of Natasha's favorite red wine on ice and a single unlit candle. He never understood the notion of having cold red wine.

"Red wine is usually taken at room temperature," he had explained to her once she told him of her fascination with cold red wine. She only shrugged and smiled at him.

"Well, I am different and I like cold red wine," she'd told him, a warm, sexy smile on her face.

There were red rose petals lined up on the floor leading up to the bedroom and the bathroom where the Jacuzzi lay in wait with petals floating on its surface. There were scented candles all over the house giving the house a wonderful caramelized scent.

He looked around and took a deep breath. He reached for his pocket and pulled out the black velvet case that housed the three stone three carat diamond engagement ring that he had picked out. He hoped that it would be good enough for Natasha. She hated being flashy. He saw this in her personality, the way she carried herself and the way she related with others. Even though in looks she would most likely be said to be a nine or ten, she still tried to live on the down low, not attracting too much attention to herself. He smiled when he thought of her reaction. In a way, he was nervous, unsure of what her answer would be. He had wanted to pop the question for the longest time but the time was never right. There was that time at the sushi restaurant but the man sitting in the table next to them ended up choking, and then there was the time when he took her to the Eiffel Tower but there was a power malfunction. He laughed lightly when he recalled the last trip they took to Niagara Falls. He was just about to go down on one knee and pop the question when the world came tumbling down at his feet.

After two failed proposals, the falls were a sure bet. Everything was set: the beautiful sound of the water gushing against the rocks, perfect scenery and of course, the woman of his dreams right where he wanted her. Just as he descended to ask her, there was a commotion and when they asked around, they found out that a canoe had just capsized in the lake. He remembered being pissed off at the idiot who decided to go canoeing at Niagara Falls. After that, he felt as if the world was telling him to hold his horses. Perhaps he needed to just go slow with Natasha…but he could not. He would not stop until he saw her walking down the aisle to him. She was the most perfect person and he wanted her in his life. There was just something special about her that he couldn't place his finger on. He had been happy with other women before but what he felt with Natasha was more than just happiness. It was security. The feeling that you would only get with that one special person.

Mitchell was still deep in thought when Natasha came in. He turned towards the door and smiled at Natasha who was awestruck at the romantic mood Mitchell had managed to set.

"You did all this?" she asked looking around as she smiled. Mitchell nodded as he slowly walked towards her. His hands went down to her waist as he looked into her brown eyes. He slowly brought his head down to meet her soft lips in a long, deep kiss. His kiss was so deep that he could literally feel her almost collapsing in his arms.

"Wow, I should really get out more," she said in a whisper when he finally pulled off. "If that's the reception I will be getting on a daily basis then I can't wait to go out again," she said as she ran her fingers through his thick hair.

"That and much more," he said taking her purse from her. "So, dinner first," he said as he put her purse on the table next to the door.

"You are seemingly too eager," she said as he led him to the dining room.

"Well, I hate reheating food," he said pulling a seat put for her.

"Okay," she said as he poured her a glass of champagne. "So, what's for dinner?"

"Braised lamb shanks," he replied proudly. She smiled and

rested her elbows on the table.

"When did you have the time?" she asked as he busied himself with serving. He looked at her and smiled as he set a plate on the table in front of her. "Looks delicious," she said as she breathed in the sweet aroma of the food. "Oh my God, you didn't...." she said as he walked towards her with a plate of baked potatoes. She smiled as she looked at him carrying the plate of perfectly done potatoes. Baked potatoes were her favorite, right up there with fried chicken and mashed potatoes.

"Yes I did," he said as he took a seat across from her. "Here's to us," he said raising his glass. She smiled and picked up her own glass.

"Hear, hear," she said as the glasses met in a soft clink. "So, are you going to tell me why you did all this? What's the occasion?" she asked as she took a bite of her lamb shank.

"Can't I just spoil you for funsies?" he asked looking at her. Natasha smiled and took another bite.

"I can't wait to see what you have planned for my birthday," she said helping herself to some potatoes.

"How was your day at the spa?" he asked as he took a sip of his wine.

"We didn't get any massages done," she said in between bites. "Just a manicure and pedicure," she added. Mitchell smiled at her before he finally laughed.

"And that' a big deal?" he asked looking at her.

"Yes," she said her eyes widening. "My back is literally in

knots," she added matter-of-factly.

"Oh I can take care of that later," Mitchell said with a wink. Natasha smiled at him.

"I know you can and I honestly can't wait," she said in a sexy voice.

"Yeah, dessert first," he said as he took another bite. Natasha dramatically slammed her fists on the table and looked at him. "What?" he asked. "You think I was going to make a three course dinner without the final kick?"

As Natasha looked into his eyes at that moment, she could hear Rita's words echoing in her ear. Mitchell was more than perfect. *"Oh shit...Rita's art,"* she thought.

"By the way I need to talk to you about something," she said as she put her fork down.

"Anything," he said suddenly sensing the serious mood that had befallen the room.

"Well, you know Rita does art right?" she started. "Well, the gallery is not doing so well. She is low on sales..."

"...what about that guy Gomer?" he said, cutting her off.

"Yeah, that didn't work out. Turns out her art was not all he was interested in if you know what I mean," she said.

"Bummer," he said as he took a long sip of his wine. "How can I help?" he asked.

"Do you think you could market some of her art to some of your collectors?" she asked looking into his eyes. "It would mean the world to me and to Rita of course," she said giving him a smile.

"Well, the NSCS Foundation is holding an art exhibit next week for charity. She could bring her stuff in and keep 70 percent of the sales, charity and all. That way people would get to know about her work," he said slowly.

"You would do that?" she asked smiling at him.

"Anything for you, you know that," he said smiling back.

"In that case, I have something that I've got to tell you," she said walking up to him. He smiled as she came to where he was and sat on his lap.

"Really?" he asked as she secured an arm around his neck and kissed him. "Something special I hope," he said when he pulled away.

"That it is," she said before kissing him again. She slowly pulled away and looked into his eyes. "Remember that thing you asked a few days ago?" she said.

"If you like jam better than honey?" he asked looking at her confused.

"No, silly," she said laughing. "Whether I'd move in with you," she said.

"Yes," he said looking into her eyes. Natasha looked back at him in silence, just smiling at him. "You are going to do it?" he asked excitedly. She smiled at him and nodded. Mitchell excitedly held her and kissed her again. He was so lost in the moment that he almost forgot the whole purpose of the dinner. He lifted her off him and sat her down on his seat.

"What are you doing?" she asked as she looked at him going down on one knee. He reached into his pocket and pulled out the black velvet case. Natasha felt herself freeze as he opened it and presented it to her. "Mitch…" she started before he put his index finger on her lips to silence her down.

"Natasha Black, you have been in my life for a year now and I just can't think of my life without you. Will you make me the happiest man on earth by being my wife?" he asked smiling up at her. Natasha was unsure of what she was supposed to do. She just stared at him, stuck, frozen in time.

Chapter 3

Natasha looked at the ring and then back at Mitchell as she felt her throat dry up. She was not sure whether to talk or act. This was something she had dreamed about for almost her whole life and she knew that this was good but she was not so sure how good. She just sat there as if she was frozen in time. For her everything was going in slow motion. Mitchell's wavy hair slowly waving as he gently shook her hand. She felt her heart palpitating in her chest, almost threatening to get out of her body. *"What are you doing Tasha, this is it. This is what you've always wanted. This is the man you have so much fallen in love with, the one man who has done right by you,"* she thought as she looked at him.

"Babe...did you hear what I said?" Mitchell asked looking at Natasha's blank eyes.

"Say something!" she scolded herself still looking at him. "Mitch...I, I don't know what to say," she started in a sad voice. Her eyes shifted to the ring in the black velvet case. *"That is beautiful,"* she thought looking at the large rock. *"That must be worth at least 25 grand,"* she thought still looking at the ring.

"You could say yes," he said looking at her. Natasha looked at him as she felt a tear roll down her cheek. Mitchell panicked. This was not going the way he wanted or expected it to go. "What's wrong Natasha...should I not have asked?" he asked her getting confused at her reaction. He lifted her hand and used her index finger to wipe away her one tear.

"It's just that...,"

"...you don't love me enough?" he asked unsure of what was going on at that particular moment. *"That was a pretty damn thing to say,"* he thought. *"But what other reason would she have to say no?"*

"No, it's nothing like that," she said shaking her head. "I love you to the end of the world and back," she said cupping his face in her hands.

"Then what is it? Don't you want me to marry you?" Mitchell asked looking at her. "Because it sounds like you don't want to marry me," he said as he pulled another seat to sit next to her.

"Mitchell, I'm just surprised that's all," she finally said looking at him. "You have to understand that this is something never thought would ever happen to me," she said.

"Why would you think that?" Mitchell asked looking at her.

"Because, in my entire family no one has ever, *ever* gotten married," she answered. "At least not in the last two generations," she added laughing.

Mitchell gave her a confused look as he placed the velvet case on the table. "Okay, you lost me," he said looking at her. Natasha took a long deep breath and looked at him.

"My nan's ma is the last person I know who got married and even that ended badly. Marriage has never been a big thing to me because…well, I don't see the big deal in getting a piece of paper to prove that I love you," she explained. Mitch looked at her still confused.

"So you think just because the marriages in your family didn't work out that ours will be the same? That I'll leave you?" he asked looking into her eyes.

"I didn't say that," she said looking at him. "All I mean is that marriage changes people, most times for the worse."

"Don't you trust me?" he asked looking at her, not believing his ears. "Do you really think I would do…whatever those other guys did," he asked as he felt a cold sweat breaking out on his forehead. Natasha looked at him and sighed for the millionth time.

"It's nothing like that," she said "I just…I don't feel ready," she said in a low voice.

"For what?" he asked angrily. "What could you possibly not be ready for?" he asked again. Natasha looked at him. He was clearly not understanding the reason for her not saying yes to his proposal.

"Baby, I love being with you," she said looking at him. "I am ready to make that lifetime commitment to you. Just not right now."

"Let me get this right," he said leaning back in his seat. "Are you saying that you are not saying no but you do not want to marry me?" Natasha nodded, stood up, and slowly walked over to him.

"No, you are getting it all wrong," she said burying her face in her hands. "I do want to marry you, really I do but I just think it's a bit early," she added. He looked at her and sighed.

"I love you Mitchell Schmidt but let's take this one day at a time, okay?" she asked looking into his eyes.

"So, am I just supposed to sit and wait for you to make up your mind?" he asked. He was having a hard time understanding what exactly she wanted from the relationship. Was she in it for fun? Was he just another guy in the Natasha Black male spree or was she actually serious with him? He looked at her questioningly, his patience gradually reaching its limits. "What exactly are you saying, Natasha?" he asked again.

Natasha took a deep breath and sighed. "I have already made up my mind but I don't think I can say yes right now," she said sounding desperate the more she tried to explain herself to him. "I do want to be with you Mitchell," she said. "I wouldn't be here if I didn't," she added closing her eyes. She felt Mitchell's arms around her.

"How long do I have to wait?" he asked.

"As I said, we can't rush it babe," she said, resting her forehead on his. "Let's just focus on what we have,"

"But…" Mitchell started before Natasha interrupted her with a kiss. "Tasha…" he whispered as he wrapped his arms around her. He slowly kissed her, savoring every moment as he walked her to the couch. "We really need to talk about this," he said in between kisses. She pulled away and took his hands, then slowly placed them on her breasts. He involuntarily felt her perfect mounds as she put her hands on his chest.

"Right now?' she asked as she slowly undid his shirt buttons. Mitchell took a deep breath and closed his eyes as he felt her lips on his neck. Her lips slowly trailed kisses from his chin, up his neck and then slowly to his earlobe. He felt a shiver go through his body when she slowly used her tongue to caress his earlobe. He moaned softly as Natasha slowly sucked on his lobe, his cock increasingly getting harder against her ass, slowly pressing on her soft ass.

Right then he didn't care whether she had just said yes or no. All he knew was that he wanted her, that she had said she still loved him. He pulled away from her and looked at her. He marveled at her perfect body underneath the strapless maxi dress she had on. He stood up and took her hand, leading her to the couch. Natasha noticed the trail of rose petals leading towards the bedroom and felt a tightness in her throat, she had let him down. She suddenly stopped and tugged on Mitchell's hand just as they approached the couch. "What?" he asked looking at her.

"I am sorry," she said as a tear threatened to roll down her cheek.

"I know," Mitchell said looking into her eyes. "But I really don't want to talk about that right now," he said pulling her close. He cradled her in his arms and kissed her passionately, almost too passionately if it were up to Natasha.

"But I do love you, Mitch," she said in between kisses. "More than you would ever imagine," she added as Mitchell sat down on the couch. She straddled him and undid the last two buttons on his shirt. She slowly brought her lips back to his and engaged him in a long kiss as she slipped her hands underneath his shirt.

"Yeah baby," he moaned as he felt her lips take in one of his pecks. She slowly twirled her tongue on his hardened peck as her other hand slowly caressed his neck with her flicking fingertips. She pulled away from one peck and Mitchell breathed a sigh of relief but his reprieve was short lived as she quickly began twirling her tongue over his other peck. "Tash….fuck," he moaned as she trailed her tongue down his navel to his abs. She then stood up and looked at him, as he looked back at her, confused.

The slow music that he had previously started was already in tune with the mood she had set. She swayed her hips slowly as she slipped two fingers underneath the top of her strapless dress. She could almost see him get harder as she pushed the dress off to expose her full breasts in her black strapless bra. He looked at her and smiled as she slowly caressed her full breasts. She continued doing a slow, sexy routine as she wriggled out of the dress.

His eyes traveled up her long legs to her well rounded ass and finally to her pussy. She stepped out of the dress and posed for him. He smiled as he slowly undid his belt buckle. He was about to stand when she placed her foot on his thigh, keeping him down. He gasped when she pulled his belt off the loops of his pants. She went down on her knees and quickly pulled down his pants. She smiled up at him when she saw the bulging hardness in his boxer shorts.

"Someone's happy to see you," Mitchell said in a low voice as she pulled down his boxers. She smiled and positioned herself in between his knees.

"He's about to get a whole lot happier," she said in a low whisper as she took his head into her mouth. Mitchell felt a shiver go through his body as she slowly kissed the head of his knob, slowly sucking on it. He threw his head back when she began to lower her mouth on his length, slowly letting him get deep inside her mouth. He struggled not to hold her head as she continued bobbing her head up and down his long cock. He was actually surprised this was happening. In the one year they had been together, this was the first time he was on the receiving end of oral sex. His heart rate was increasing rapidly as she let her tongue run along the end of his length. She looked up at him as she twirled her tongue on his head, slowly licking the oozing precum.

"Tasha...I can't take it much longer," he whispered as she sucked him long and hard. It was as if what he had just said made her even more excited. Instead of slowing down, her sucking intensified as Mitchell held on to the edges of the couch. His moans were getting louder as she felt him grow rigid inside her mouth. Thankfully, she pulled him from her hot mouth and slowly stroked him. He could feel her writhing at his feet as she struggled to take off her panties. She stood up and unhooked her bra letting her tits bounce free. She knelt between his legs again and held his cock captive between her tits. He moaned loudly as she began rubbing her firm breasts against the sides of his cock. *"What has got into her today?'* he wondered as she watched the expression on his face. *"First the blow job and now a tit job…"* his thoughts were interrupted by the sudden move of Natasha's head, her tongue repeatedly making contact with the head of his hard cock.

"Baby…" Mitchell moaned as Natasha finally stood up. She looked at him and then straddled him again. She slowly wriggled her hips, making his cock rub against her wet pussy. "Tasha…baby that's really good," he said again when he felt himself slip into her wet pussy.

"I know baby," she said as she slowly began to raise herself on and off his cock. Mitchell felt like he wanted to die. He held her hips and began raising his hips, he needed more. He wanted more. But for some reason, she couldn't let him have her that way. Mitchell sighed in desperation. Why would this woman tease him like this? He gasped and moaned as she fucked him slowly, raising her hips on and off him. She placed her hands on his and raised them above his head. "You know that I love you, right, Mitch?" she asked as she fucked him.

"Yeah, baby…I know that…" he said gasping for breath. For some reason, the slow fucking was really driving him over the edge. "I love you too," he added as she slowly picked up her pace.

"Don't ever forget that," she said before she kissed him, a long passionate kiss. Mitchell tried to bring his hands down, but he couldn't. She had pinned his hands hard above his head and was now fucking him hard, relentlessly as if she was under some kind of spell. She moaned loudly as she ground her hips against his, forcing his cock further inside her wetness. She heard his sounds graduate from moans to loud grunts as her firm ass cheeks slammed against his thighs.

"Tasha…!" he moaned out loud as he felt himself coming closer to the edge. "I'm going to cum, baby," he managed to say as she ground her hips harder on him. She lifted her hips pulling her pussy away from his hard cock. He looked up at her in disappointment, panting. "Why would you do that?" he asked smiling up at a heaving Natasha. She smiled back as she climbed down from his thighs.

"Not yet," she said as she turned away from him, her firm buttocks facing him. She slowly brought her hips down to sit on his hard cock. He placed her hands on her hips and closed his eyes, taking in the pleasure of the moment. The mere feeling of his cock buried balls deep in her hot, wet pussy made him shudder. "Give it to me Mitchell Schmidt," she said in a sexy whisper. Mitchell needed no second bidding. He suddenly began raising his hips, sinking further inside her pussy. She began screaming loudly as he bounced her on and off his cock. She felt her pussy make squelching sounds as she fucked him harder, faster….or was he the one doing the fucking? Mitchell did not care. All he knew was that at that moment he was balls deep inside the woman of his dreams, the woman he would one day make his wife, the woman who would bear his children.

"Baby, I love you!" she screamed as she felt his cock spasm inside her, depositing gallons of his cum inside her waiting pussy. The force of his pulsating cock made her own pussy get wetter as she succumbed to her own powerful orgasm ripping through her. She leaned against his shoulder as he slowly pushed himself in and out of her as his cock gradually grew limp. "Babe…" she moaned as she felt his cock slipping out of her drained pussy. She felt hot liquid drain out of her as she collapsed on the seat. He lay next to her in a spooning position and held her close.

She felt him drifting off to sleep as he mumbled his love for her, slowly kissing her at the back of the neck. She took a deep long breath as she settled into his arms. What was she going to do? She felt more confused than a fat kid with cake. She slowly turned so as not to wake Mitchell and faced him. Her hand slowly cupped her face and caressed his perfect facial features.

"You really going to screw this up, Tasha you stupid, stupid girl," she thought as she looked at him. She ran her fingers through his dark hair and planted a kiss on his forehead.

"I love you so much Mitchell," she said in a low voice. She didn't care whether he was awake or not, whether he heard her or not. "If only you knew just how much you meant to me," she said again still looking at him. She did not know what exactly she was expected to do after this. All she wanted was have a long chat with Rita, just get all this off her chest. She planted a kiss on his forehead and was surprised when Mitchell wrapped an arm around her. "You're awake," she said in a whisper. Her thigh moved closer to his crotch. She smiled up at him. "And I think someone is ready for round two," she said giving him a long kiss.

"What has gotten into you today?" he asked as she kissed him down his abs, getting dangerously close to his navel. She looked up at him as her body hovered over him, her hardening nipples brushing against his skin.

"Is me being horny a problem for you, Mitchell Schmidt?" she asked looking at him. "Can't you handle it?" she asked again as she went down on him. Mitchell felt himself suddenly get harder. He pulled her up and flipped her over so that she was under him. He looked down at her and smiled as he aligned his cock with her pussy. Whether she had said yes or no did not matter. She was doing an excellent job of making it up to him and he was loving every minute of it.

Chapter 4

When Natasha's eyelids fluttered open on Thursday morning, she sighed and rolled over to the other side of the bed.

"Why isn't today a holiday or a weekend?" she wondered as she stared out her apartment window. Today would mark the sixth day, almost a week since Mitchell dropped the proposal bombshell on her, and ever since that day, avoiding him was at the top of her to-do list.

The first two days were easy since Mitchell had a closed door meeting with investors but the rest of the week had simply been brutal. When she wasn't ducking under her desk, she was busy leaving the office early just so she would not have to face him. She hated herself for doing this. She actually didn't remember the last time she felt so guilty. The thought of looking into Mitchell's brown eyes, seeing the pain on his face and knowing that she was the one who had caused it was just too much for her.

Her phone suddenly buzzed loudly, the loud ring piercing the silence that had been prominently present in her room. Without even looking at her phone, she knew it was him. She reached over to the bedside table and picked it up before taking a long deep breath.

Where you at? I miss you. Nowadays finding an honest politician is easier than actually getting you.

She smiled as she sat up on the bed.

I miss you too. So much...you have no idea. I just woke up. Where you at?

She hit send and threw the phone on the bed unsure of what to do next. Suddenly, her phone rang loudly. *"Isn't he satisfied with a single text? Clingy bastard,"* she thought as she picked the phone up. She felt a pang of guilt when she saw that it was her dad on her caller ID.

"Hey daddy," she said leaning back.

"She lives!" her father Eric said excitedly. Natasha felt even guiltier at this moment. Lost in her own little, stupid world trying to get away from Mitchell as much as she possibly could, she had forgotten all about the other people in her life who mattered to her. Like her dad and Nan and Rita…

"I am sorry I've been so distant,"she said. "It's just work and a whole lot of other stuff," she added as she twirled one of her curly locks around her finger,

"It's the 'stuff' that makes me worried about you, princess," Eric said. Natasha could almost immediately guess that he had put up finger quotes when he said stuff.

"I am fine daddy. No biggie," she said dismissively.

"Really?" Eric asked. "Is this something you would want to talk to me about?" he asked. Natasha suddenly felt a panic go through her body. Did she really want to tell her dad about Mitchell or was it still too early. What if she could never actually say yes? Would her father be disappointed in her? "Are you still there?" Eric asked when Natasha got a bit too silent.

"I think I would want to talk, daddy," she said in a soft voice. "But just not right away. There's too much on my plate right now," she added quickly. She heard her father sigh on the other end of the phone.

"Okay, but you know that I am always here when you need me right?" he asked. Natasha suddenly felt another wave of guilt. She wanted to cry or for a bus to run over her or better still, for the ground to open up and swallow her.

"I know, daddy," she said.

"And our Sunday father daughter breakfast culture is seriously severed," he said feigning a sob. Natasha laughed.

"This Sunday, we have a date," she said.

"Written in stone?" Eric asked hopefully.

"Yes daddy. Even Moses couldn't break it," Natasha said before laughing heartily. Eric went silent for a while.

"I don't get it," he said finally. Natasha sighed.

"Come on dad," she whined. "Moses, the ten commandments engraved on the stone tablets?" she asked waiting for a word or sound of confirmation.

"Yeah, I know Moses and the ten commandments. What does he have to do with Sunday's breakfast?" Eric asked.

"Daddy! He broke the tablets at some point. Smashed them right on the ground," she said wishing her father was right in front of her so she could punch him or something.

"Ah," Eric finally said. "That's a bit farfetched, don't you think?" he asked. Natasha almost screamed.

"Farfetched, daddy? Really? Engraved in stone?" she asked before finally rolling her eyes. "You make it so hard for me to love you, daddy," she said. Eric laughed.

"But you love me anyway," he said. She could tell that he was smiling when he said that.

"Yes I do, unfortunately," she said. "Got to go now," she said.

"Okay princess, good day," Eric said before hanging up. Natasha smiled. Somehow, talking to her father always lifted up her spirits. Maybe that's why she would always be daddy's girl. She smiled as she climbed off the bed and walked to the bathroom. She got the shower started and then held out her hand, letting the warm water trickle down her forearm to her fingers. She then quickly took off her night shirt and stood under the shower head. She felt goose bumps forming on the surface of her skin as the water trickled down her spine to the crack of her ass. She then turned around and leaned against the wall as the water flowed down her torso, the warm water gradually hardening her nipples.

She took a deep breath as she envisioned what the day had in store for her and then closed her eyes. This would be either a very long day or just a disastrous one. When she finally got out of the bathroom, it was already eight but for some reason she didn't really care. She had no drive to get to work early or actually get to work at all. She quickly made her bed before walking to her closet. She pulled out a pair of black pants and a green sleeveless top.

After quickly getting dressed, she let her hair loose, then sprayed it up before tying it back up again. She thought it looked better that way especially since it wasn't straightened. She then took a pair of silver loop earrings and put them on as she headed towards the door. After slipping on a black pair of heels, she quickly got out and headed to the elevator. As she waited, she involuntarily played with the phone in her hands, wondering who to call or text. Her phone vibrated again just as the elevator door opened in front of her.

So lunch?

She smiled as she looked at the phone on the ride down.

Dinner. I need to check up on my Nan before I get to work. Might take a while.

When she got inside her car, she quickly dialed the office , her heart pounding.

"Nolan Schmidt Communication Solutions. Natasha Black's office, Stacy speaking," she heard Stacy's melodious voice chime. She smiled. She was had never been able to understand how she managed to say all that in under fifteen seconds or at least without biting her tongue or something.

"Hey Stacy. It's Natasha," she said.

"Oh hi boss lady. How can I be of service to you?" Stacy asked.

"Just calling to ask you to take down all my messages. There is something I need to take care of and I don't know how long it might take," Natasha said.

"Sure. So tomorrow?" Stacy asked. Natasha smiled. It had worked.

"Yes, please," she said before hanging up. Her cell vibrated again just before she put it down. She looked at the screen and for the umpteenth time, felt her remorse taking over her body.

Dinner's perfect. Feel like some Tapas tonight though.

She sighed as she quickly typed on her screen.

Tapas it is. Kisses.

The minute she secured her seat belt, she knew she needed to talk to someone. Normally, she would talk to Rita but this time, she needed someone a little more experienced. Someone who knew what the stakes in life were worth because she had lived long enough. She had already thought of going to see her Nan and maybe that wasn't such a bad idea.

*****

Estelle felt especially proud of herself as she took her pound cake out of the oven. She always enjoyed her little culinary adventures when Eric was not in the house. He would always dip his fingers in the mix and eat the ingredients, leaving a frustrated Estelle to prepare a semi-sweet thing…or just something she would want to give to the dog. She carefully put the cake on the counter to cool off and then walked to the refrigerator to get herself a cool drink.

She had just poured herself a nice cold glass of orange juice when she heard the front door slam shut.

"Eric Black, you put your hands on my pound cake and so God help me I will cut them off," Estelle said without turning around.

"Wow, dad has never really grown up, huh?" Natasha said with a smile. Estelle turned around and a smile beamed across her wrinkled face.

"Tasha! What are you doing here…why are you not at work?" Estelle asked as she placed the glass on the counter so she could hug her granddaughter.

"I'm taking a personal day, Nan," Natasha said. Estelle finally let go and held her at arms length.

"You are not eating well, are you?" Estelle said looking at her like a child would inspect a puppy at a pet shop. Natasha cringed.

"What?" she said. "I have…."

"…that McDonald's crap ain't food and you know it," Estelle said as she finally let her go. "Let me get you some proper food," she said walking to the stove as Natasha sat down.

"Oh my God, thank you. I'm starved," she said reaching for Estelle's juice. Estelle turned around and gave her one of those I-knew-it smiles. "Oh come on, Nan. It's just because I didn't have breakfast yet," Natasha said in her defense.

"A mother knows Tasha," Estelle said as she stirred some pancake batter. "A mother always knows," she added in a low voice.

"Okay, Nan. You win," Natasha said with a smile.

"So, what brings you to this side of town on a weekday when you are supposedly taking your quote unquote personal day," Estelle asked as she poured the batter onto a pan.

"Nothing really," Natasha said. "I just needed to see you. It's been a while you know," she added as she took another sip of the orange juice.

"Mh hm," Estelle said as she looked at her.

"Really, Nan," Natasha said trying to convince her. Estelle smiled at her before turning back to her pan.

"If you say so," Estelle said just as the front door slammed shut again. "Better hide that pound cake," she said turning to the counter.

"What on earth are you doing here on a weekday?" Natasha heard Rita's voice coming through the kitchen.

"Me? What are you doing here?" Natasha asked as Rita walked towards the kitchen counter.

"Me and Estelle have a date," Rita said. "We are going shopping for new wallpaper," she added smiling at Estelle.

"Hey Rita," Estelle said smiling back at her.

"Hey Mrs. Black," Rita said before turning her attention back to Natasha. "So, what are you doing here? Everything okay at work?" she asked. Natasha put the glass down and looked at Rita.

"Fine, Rita. How have you been? Me, just cool. Can't complain," Natasha said cynically.

"I'm sorry sweetie. I'm just confused, that's all," Rita said as she leaned towards Natasha for a hug.

"Apparently, she is taking a personal day," Estelle said in the same cynical voice Natasha had used talking to Rita. Natasha looked up at her grandmother who was now pouring more batter onto the pan.

"A personal day?" Rita asked looking at Estelle and then back at Natasha. "What for? You and Mitchell okay?" she asked.

"Yes, a personal day. I am entitled to one every so often," Natasha said dismissively. Estelle and Rita briefly exchanged glances as Natasha silently took the last sip of her juice. She then stood up and walked to the pantry from where she grabbed a bag of chips.

"Okay, she is binging. Something is definitely wrong," Rita said as Estelle walked towards them carrying a plate of pancakes in one hand and syrup in the other.

"Ooh, pancakes," Natasha said as Estelle placed the plate on the counter.

"Definitely something wrong," Estelle said as she grabbed some plates and joined them. "So, what's going on, baby?" she asked as she finally sat down. The two looked on as Natasha squeezed a generous amount syrup onto her pancakes.

"Okay, I don't want you to overreact or anything," she said amid mouthfuls.

"Okay," Estelle and Rita said in unison.

"Last week Mitchell proposed," Natasha said in a low voice. Her grandmother and Rita were unusually quiet. You could literally hear a pin drop.

"Oh, honey!" Rita squealed.

"Congratulations baby," Estelle said as she quickly walked around the counter to embrace Natasha. "It's about time I got me some great grandbabies," she said as she held Natasha close. Natasha's heart skipped a beat as Rita joined in the hug.

"I told you guys I don't want you making it a big deal," Natasha said as she tried to wriggle away from the group hug.

"I'm sorry," Estelle said when they finally pulled away. "We're just so happy for you," she added wiping a tear from the corner of her eye.

"Yeah, we are so happy," Rita said as she and Estelle sat down on either side of Natasha. "So, where is the ring?" she asked looking at Natasha's hands.

"That's the thing I need to talk to you guys about," Natasha said as she put her fork down.

"Did he get you one that you didn't like?" Estelle asked. Natasha shook her head.

"No, it was nothing like that. It was beautiful," she said.

"Then what?" Estelle asked.

"Oh my God, you lost it," Rita said her eyes growing wide.

"No!" Natasha said looking at Rita. "It's just that…"

"…wait, did you just say *was*?" Rita interrupted. "Did you tell him no?"

"Natasha Black, tell me you did not break that sweet boy's heart," Estelle said sharply. Natasha's face fell.

"Not really," Natasha said in a low voice. "I just didn't say yes at that moment," she finally said. Estelle and Rita looked at her.

"Why? Mitchell is by far the best man I know," Rita said looking at her.

"Why would you say no to Mitchell?" Estelle asked. She could almost feel her heart break. She had met Mitchell a few weeks before and to her, he was the epitome of a perfect man. She could not have wished a better man in Natasha's life. "Did he cheat on you? Did he propose out of guilt?" Estelle asked again.

Natasha felt a tear threatening to roll down her cheek. "It's nothing like that," she said as she dubbed the corner of her eye using her index finger. "I just don't think it's a good idea," she said to the surprise of her Nan and best friend.

"Why wouldn't it be a good idea?" Estelle asked.

"Our family does not exactly have a great record as far as marriage is concerned, Nan," Natasha said looking into Estelle's eyes.

"So?" Rita asked jerking her around. "Does that mean that you're like them?" she asked looking at Natasha in disbelief.

"I mean, no offense Nan. You were married and you saw how that turned out,." Natasha said obviously choosing Rita's comment. "And mum and dad…" her voice trailed off as she shifted her glances from Rita to Estelle. "I am scared guys," she said finally as the tear finally rolled down her cheek.

"Baby," Estelle said draping an arm around Natasha's shoulder. "Any man who would think of leaving you is a damn fool and Mitchell is not so stupid," she added with a smile.

"Why do I feel like you gave daddy the same advice when mum left?" Natasha asked sniffing.

"Because I did," Estelle said before they all laughed. "But seriously, I hate white people and you know it. But Mitchell is another brand of white," she added with a smile.

"Yeah. Definitely not the same cloth your mum was cut from," Rita said smiling at her bet friend.

"So then, what should I do?" Natasha asked.

"What do you want to do?" Rita asked. "Because at the end of the day it is all about you," she added looking at Estelle.

"The girl has a point," Estelle said looking down at Natasha.

"I love him. Really, I do," Natasha said looking at her pancakes even though Estelle and Rita knew very well that she could not see them. "And I do want to spend the rest of my life with him. But does that really rely on one piece of paper?" She asked looking at Estelle and then at Rita.

"Mitchell is traditional," Estelle said. "That much I can say and I am sure he wants to make sure he does everything the way his parents would have wanted him to," Estelle said.

"Yeah and if you are so scared about marriage, didn't his grandparents marry like sixty years ago or something?" Rita asked. Natasha smile and nodded.

"Yeah and his parents have been together for 40 years now," she said in a low voice.

"Then you have nothing to worry about," Estelle said as she slowly rubbed Natasha's shoulder. "Now, eat up and come with us to the market. An extra eye wouldn't be so bad," Estelle said with a smile. Natasha smiled and picked up her fork. She still was unsure of what she was to do but getting it out of her chest definitely helped. She felt lighter already.

Chapter 5

Mitchell was not so sure what he was feeling. It was anxiety, anger, something in between or both…maybe. Ever since he proposed to Natasha, he had only seen her three times and two of those times were during work meetings. She had recently resorted to canceling almost every single date they had. He failed to understand why she would not agree to marrying him.

After all, it was not like he was marrying her that very moment. He only needed to know that she would be there when he did and he intended for this to be soon. And anyway, not to sound too proud, there was one thing that he was sure of. Mitchell Schmidt was a catch. He had it all, the full package. Looks, package, the 'other package'. Seriously, what did this woman want? If she loved him, she would have not taken this long… or would she?

He picked up his phone and scrolled down to her name.

Natasha, this is messing me up. How long should I wait before you are ready to talk?

He hit send and sat there staring at the phone. Almost a few minutes later, his phone vibrated.

We will talk when I'm ready.

"Ready?" he thought. *"When will that be?"* he wondered as he typed on his cell frantically.

Could you maybe give me a time span so I know what I should be prepared for?

He looked at the screen and took a long deep breath before finally hitting send. He placed his phone on the couch next to him and took the remote. He flipped through the channels as his thoughts took complete control of his mind. He almost dropped the remote when the phone vibrated loudly against the leather covered couch.

I can't really tell but I do know that I want to be with you. I do love you, that has not changed.

He smiled as he quickly typed in a *'Then why are you avoiding me'* message. It was not long before his phone vibrated gain.

I'm sorry about that. I guess it's just that seeing you disappointed in me is simply killing me slowly.

Mitchell felt a pang of guilt when he read her last message. He was a bit angry with her but he would never be disappointed in her. If that was the way she felt…shit. He could almost shoot himself if he had the guts.

Can I see you tonight? Maybe now, preferably now.

He hit end again and looked at the phone hopefully, waiting for an affirmation text.

Be there in 20.

His heart almost skipped a beat. He felt as if he was courting her all over again. Wait a minute. Courting? *"Who even says that anymore?"* he wondered as he typed a reply.

Can't wait.

True to her word, there was a knock on his front door. He

quickly walked to the door and opened it. He looked at her perfect dainty face and pulled her close for a hug.

"Why didn't you use your key? Did you lose it?" he asked looking into her eyes after pulling away from her. She shook her head.

"I guess I never even…" he cut her short by leaning in for a kiss. The kind of kiss you would only see at the end of cliché love story movies and read about in romantic novels.

"I don't care, I missed you," he said when he pulled away.

"I missed you too," she said a she stepped aside. "Come on in," he said. She slowly walked in and just then he noticed what she was wearing. A long pink mink coat.

"Isn't it a bit too hot for that?" he asked as she walked into the living room. She looked at him over her shoulder and smiled.

"Maybe it is," she said walking to the kitchen. "But then maybe it's all in your head," she added as she headed to the refrigerator. He slowly walked in after her and watched as she took out a box of apple juice. To his surprise, she lifted the juice to her lips and began taking long gulps without taking any pauses.

"Are you okay?" he asked as she finally put the juice down on the counter.

"Excellent," she said as she put the juice back in the refrigerator.

"So I was thinking we would talk…" Mitchell began before she slowly walked away towards his bedroom. "Tasha…Tasha!" he called as he followed her to the bedroom. He found her standing right in front of his queen size bed smiling as if she had just done the most normal thing in the world.

"Are you sure you're okay?" he asked. Natasha shook her head.

"Perfect," she said. "I've been reading these past few days," she said looking into his eyes.

"Okay," he said looking at her confused.

"Have you heard of E.L. James?" she asked. Mitchell shook his head as he looked at her wondering what she was up to. "Fifty Shades of Grey?" she asked. Mitchell suddenly snapped his fingers.

"That book on sex? Everyone's reading it now. I wonder why?" he said rolling his eyes. Natasha smiled.

"It's not about sex. It's about dominance," she said still looking at him.

"About what now?" he asked looking at her still confused. "Tasha, I'm sure that it's a really good book, maybe one that I'll read one day. But right now I really need to talk about us," he said as she slowly opened her coat.

"Dominance, Mitchell. Sexual dominance," she said as she slowly removed her coat. "I want to try it," she added as he gasped, his eyes traveling down her body as the soft mink caressed her body. Whatever had happened to Natasha, his sweet loving girlfriend, he had no idea. The woman in front of him right now was something he would have picked out of the Playboy Mansion given a chance.

*"Did she really drive for two hours in **that**?"* he wondered as

he looked at her body in a sexy maid costume. Actually there was no costume. Just a tiny bodice that made her waist look Dolly Parton small. The tightness of the bodice pushed her breasts upward, giving her the most perfect cleavage. Her thighs were covered in fishnet stockings and on her feet were the longest heels he had ever seen.

He felt himself choke on his own words as she dropped the coat on the floor and slowly made her way towards the bed. His cock was suddenly not the humble member anymore. It was now a raging animal, fighting to be freed. They were obviously not going to have any talking tonight.

"Did you happen to run into traffic police?" he wondered as he stared at her. "Because if you did…" he stopped when she placed her index finger on his lips.

"How do you feel about bondage?" she asked in a sweet voice as she pulled a bag from underneath her bed. His eyes grew wide and his skin pale when she opened the bag. There were spanking paddles, butt plugs, handcuffs, chains…you name it.

"When did you even get all that under there?" he asked surprised. Maybe she had taken the Fifty Shades of Grey literature a bit too seriously.

"That book was…I want it all, Mitchell," she said looking up at him. "I want you to be my master," she added as she began to slowly undo his belt buckle. He quickly pulled his t-shirt over his head and then placed his hands on hers. She looked up into his eyes and almost felt scared. The expression he had was one she had never seen in him before. He looked like a bull ready to charge. His normally brown, warm eyes were staring down at her in an almost sadistic manner.

"Say that again," he said looking into her eyes. She felt a thrill go through her body as the words rolled off her tongue.

"I want you to be my master," she said in a shy voice. She saw a small smile threaten to form at the corner of his mouth as he sat down next to her. He looked at the contents of the bag and smiled.

"Let's start a bit slower," he said taking her hand. "Come, bend over my knee, you naughty girl," he said as she lay on his knee, her bare buttocks exposed to him. She expected him to hold back but the rate at which he was responsive oddly turned her on, a bit too much actually. She felt his hand on her buttocks, slowly rubbing and kneading. She longed for him to spank her hard at that very moment. She yearned for the feeling of pleasurable pain, whatever that was. Her wish was suddenly fulfilled when he lifted his hand only to bring it back down on her ass with so much force that she almost cried out. She whimpered as he slowly rubbed her other cheek as the first remained stinging from the immense slap she had just received. Even though it stung, she was surprised at how much delight it gave her. She felt her other cheek sting as Mitchell spanked her again, this time a bit harder than the first time. She found herself wondering whether the paddles would be this painful or pleasurable. She whimpered again as she felt him spank her again but this time, instead of giving her ample healing time, he just spanked her other cheek without any warning.

Mitchell could feel his cock strain against the pressure of Natasha's stomach. He wanted to get himself inside her so bad but first, he would enjoy this new world she had introduced him to. He had heard of bondage and submission but he had never been one to be more adventurous than most.

This was definitely one area he was yet to delve in. even

though it was his first time being a dominant sexual partner, he found himself questioning why he had never tried this before. The way she squirmed on his lap every time he spanked her was extremely erotic. He looked on in awe as her butt cheeks became incredibly flushed as he spanked her harder and harder till he heard her let out a loud moan. Almost as if she wanted him to stop.

He slowly lifted her off his lap and placed her on the bed before proceeding to take off his pants. He then reached into the bag and got two pairs of handcuffs. He secured her hands to the bed poles and fastened them firmly on either side. Natasha lifted her ass higher as Mitchell stood at the foot of the bed. He then walked round the bed to where the bag was and rummaged through it till he emerged with a big vibrator and one small spanking paddle. He switched the vibrator on and began to slowly run it along her g-string covered slit, making her moan.

Natasha suddenly felt the vibrator removed from her pussy, making her moan her disapproval. She tried looking around to see what was going on but she could not see anything. Out of the blue, she felt Mitchell ripping her fishnet stockings and g-string apart and away from her body. For some reason, her pussy got wetter when he did so.

She whimpered when she felt the vibrator again, this time against her bare flesh. The exposed flesh of her budding clit. For some reason, she held in the sounds of her pleasure. This must have prompted Mitchell to finally use the paddle on her. She gasped when she felt a sting as Mitchell slapped her ass using the paddle. She moaned loudly when Mitchell began pushing the tip of the vibrator inside her wet pussy but never all the way through. He used the paddle on her again as he pushed the vibrator inside her again. The intensity almost made her squeeze her legs shut but she managed to hold back lest she get another whack on her ass.

Mitchell's cock was now harder than he had ever felt it. He could almost swear he could see his pulse just by looking down at his raging manhood. He suddenly heard Natasha's loud gasp making him look up. Without realizing it, he had pushed the vibrator inside her pussy, almost all the way in. He slowly pulled it out and threw it on the bed. He dropped the paddle as well and grabbed her big ass, kneading it and gently slapping it. The way she writhed made him realize that her cheeks were a bit too sensitive from all the spanking. He positioned his cock at her opening and slowly pushed his length in. She gasped and her breath became labored as Mitchell pushed himself into her, inch by inch.

"You like that?"He asked as he began to slowly move himself in and out of her. She nodded before saying a gasping 'yes.' Mitchell slapped her ass hard not caring whether she was in pain or not.

"Yes…what?" he said as he suddenly thrust into her.

"Ah! Yes master," she moaned as he thrust himself inside her. He incredibly managed to maintain a slow and steady pace despite the way the situation aroused him.

"And what about…that?" he asked as he bucked his hips out before jamming them into her again. She screamed as she felt him filling her up.

"Yes, master," she said. "I love that too." Mitchell smiled as he began thrusting into her, hard and fast. He loved the control the present situation gave him. It was almost as if there was nothing else in the world that mattered at this very moment. All he cared for was filling her up. For her to call him master. For him to dominate her to the fullest. His fast pace gave him a false sense of security as soon he began feeling his orgasm approaching fast. He reached over to the bed posts and quickly undid her cuffs.

"Turn around baby," he said in a loving but commanding voice. She quickly turned around and lay on her back, panting. Her skin was slightly damp and some of her hair was stuck to her forehead. She moaned as she watched him quickly undo her bodice, freeing her tits. He then quickly went down and began sucking her hard as he roughed up her other breast.

Natasha moaned and groaned as she tried arching her back in an attempt to redirect his stiff penis back into her wet pussy. She almost felt triumphant when she found the head of his hard cock and arching her back further, she moaned loudly as he slid right into her. Mitchell moaned against her nipple as he felt the familiar heat of her cunt engulf his hard cock. *"Wait. This is all supposed to be me,* he thought. *"BDSM 101. Dominance means I am the boss,"* he thought as he secretly smiled to himself.

"I have to punish you for that," he said when he pulled away from her hard nipple. Natasha felt a wave of panic and excitement go through her as she wondered what he would do this time. "Turn around," he said again. She looked up at him and turned around positioning herself on all fours. She heard him rummage through the bag again and wondered what he would emerge with this time.

"I want you relaxed, Tasha," she heard him say. Mitchell soon ended the suspense when she felt a cold plug being pushed into her tight ass. She felt shivers go through her and whimpered as she felt the plug being pushed all the way to its base. Just when she was getting used to the plug in her ass, she felt pressure in her ass and pussy all at once as Mitchell pushed himself inside her.

The pressure from the plug and the huge length of his cock made the feeling more intense making her moan loudly as he stretched her out. "Just like that baby, just like that," he said in a low voice as he slowly moved in and out of her, careful not to let the plug get out of her ass. His orgasm was now dangerously close. He needed his release. He needed to finish right there and then. He slowly pushed the plug in further before he held on to her ass and began pummeling into her.

Natasha held on to the headboard as Mitchell fucked her hard. The way he punched himself into her reminded her of old soldiers trying to take down a fortress door using a battering ram. By now, she was moaning loudly, not caring who heard her. She could feel herself at the point of no return.

"Master, permit me to cum….I need to cum master, please," she begged in between panting breaths.

"Cum for me, baby," Mitchell said sounding surprisingly calm even though he was about to spill himself into her. Natasha suddenly screamed, forcing his cock out of her pulsating pussy. He looked down just in time to see her pussy squirting out hot liquid onto his thigh. He moaned as he plunged back inside her. The image of her squirting had just made him want to finish off inside her. He threw his head back as he felt hot jets of his own cum draining into her. As his cock began to slowly get limp, he pulled the plug from her ass leaving it gaped before collapsing on the bed. Natasha lay down next to him, breathing heavily.

"So I guess that means we will talk tomorrow," Mitchell said as he closed his eyes. Natasha smiled and slowly raised her head to plant a kiss on his forehead. She felt guilty for using sex as an escape mechanism so that she didn't have to talk about the proposal. She was not sure how long she could keep that going.

"Yeah," she said as she felt herself drifting to a deep sleep.

Chapter 6

Mitchell looked at his wristwatch and then took a sip of his cappuccino. He was supposed to be meeting his best friend Leo Hayes for the first time in eight months. Leo and Mitchell were old friends all the way from their high school days. As they grew up together, they realized that they had more than just the same taste in girls. Their career choices were also strangely similar. They both had a liking for management… crisis management was where they really clicked.

However after graduating from college, Leo had been poached by a pharmaceutical company and after that they rarely got any time to just sit and hang out. Getting some time, any time, even half an hour for a quick beer had literally become wishful thinking. When he wasn't traveling the world trying to fix everything that had gone wrong with a drug launch he was busy sourcing for all the foreign clients he could stomach. When he was free, Mitchell was on some business meeting in Chicago, or Washington….just out of reach. Mitchell smiled as he looked at his watch again. He could not wait to just catch up on all of Leo's foreign conquests.

"Buddy!" he heard an excited voice behind him. He smiled as he stood up and turned around to look at Leo.

"Dude, what the hell are they feeding you in…where were you this time around anyway?" Mitchell asked as the two embraced.

"Depends on when you are asking about," Leo said when they pulled apart. "But this, is all Dubai, dude," he said rubbing his huge tummy. Mitchell smiled as he sat down.

"I took the liberty of ordering some cappuccino for you,"

Mitchell said as he signaled the waitress to come to their table.

"Really? You still do that?" Leo asked. Mitchell looked at him as he took a sip from his own cup.

"Why? What's wrong with that? Did you give up caffeine?" he asked looking at him.

"Hell no...actually never!" Leo said laughing just as the waitress brought his coffee to the table. "So, Schmidt, what's new?" he asked as he slowly played with his cup handle.

"Nothing much. Just the usual suspects," Mitchell said with a smile.

"Nothing much? Dude you are at the top of the Nolan Schmidt financial food chain and you tell me that there's nothing much going on?" Leo said laughing. "Like really man..." he said as his voice trailed off.

"I knew that would come up," Mitchell said with a smile. "I know I said there was no way in hell I would ever work for my family's company," he said looking at Leo. "Things change you know," he added as he ran his fingers through his thick wavy hair.

"They sure do," Leo said smiling. "I mean back when I knew you, you were just some geeky guy with bad hair and glasses...,"

"...hey, feelings," Mitchell said clutching his breast pocket dramatically. Leo smiled.

"You know I'm right, man. Now you are this ...this....sex god gracing the cover of Forbes sexiest men under 40," Leo struggled to say without sounding negative.

"Yeah, there is that," Mitchell said looking down. "There is a perfectly good explanation for that," he said holding his hands up in his defense.

"There has to be. I'm sure Lisa wouldn't have taken it lightly having you in all your naked glory on the cover of a magazine," Leo said. Mitchell frowned.

"You do know we got divorced right?" he asked looking at him. Leo looked back at him surprised.

"I thought that was just one of those many separations the two of you were always going through," Leo said. "Man, this is some fucked up shit," he added before taking a sip of his cappuccino.

"Actually, that's part of the reason I wanted to see you today," Mitchell said.

"Why? You need a good lawyer?" Leo asked.

"Seriously, has it been that long?" Mitchell asked frowning again.

"Well, it's been almost ten months but the last time we hooked we just got hammered," Leo said smiling. "Ah, Vegas," he added, a far away look in his eyes.

"Good times," Mitchell said smiling. "But my divorce was finalized a long time ago and Lisa got the money she wanted. We are done, have been done," he added with a smile.

"So…I'm lost," Leo said as he looked at Mitchell. "What's the big emergency since we already established that I am not here because you missed all of this," he said gesturing at himself.

Mitchell smiled. "So, there is this girl Natasha Black," he started as Leo rested his elbows on the table. "I have been with her for a year and a half now and I think…"

"…no," Leo said interrupting him. "You really want to go down that road again," Leo asked surprised. Mitchell smiled at him and nodded. "Even after Lisa?" he asked, still surprised.

"Yes, even after Lisa," Mitchell said as he smiled broadly. Leo shook his head and took another long sip of his cappuccino.

"This Black Natasha must be really something," Leo said smiling.

"It's **Natasha Black**…as in the surname Black, you bozo," Mitchell said. "She's not a cast in the Black Swan," he added laughing.

"Well, I guess then congratulations are in order, huh?" Leo said as he looked at Mitchell who smiled as he reached into his inside pocket.

"Kind of," Mitchell said as he pulled out his handkerchief. He dubbed his forehead as he took a long deep breath. "I asked her to marry me two weeks ago and…"

"…She said no?" Leo asked cutting him short yet again.

"No, she just didn't say yes," Mitchell said. Leo looked at him, a confused look on his face.

"I am sure that doesn't make any sense even to you," Leo said. "So, that was it? Maybe you did it wrong?" he said.

"No. I did every mushy thing I could think of. I even Googled how to make the perfect proposal," Mitchell said as he signaled the waitress for yet another cup. "Down on one knee, dinner and everything," he added as the waitress brought him another cappuccino.

"Seriously dude, do you like own the joint?" Leo asked as the waitress left. "Normally people have to like place orders and shit," he added in a whisper. Mitchell smiled.

"Actually, yes. I own it but back to the more important matters," Mitchell said in an attempt to change the subject.

"Wait," Leo said. "You never told me what she was like, " he said looking at him. Mitchell smiled as he reached for his phone.

"She is the most perfect woman you could ever imagine. She is the girl high school boys jerk off to and the same girl men leave their loyal wives for," Mitchell said proudly as he scrolled his gallery for Natasha's photos. "There," he said when he finally came to a decent album of the two of them in Rome.

"Fuck…!" Leo said in a low whisper. "Great piece of chocolate right there," he said smiling.

"Hey, watch it," Mitchell aid. "That's my future wife you are talking about right there," he added.

So, what do you think should I do?" Mitchell asked.

"What do you want to do?" Leo asked. "I don't think I am the best person to advise you on this," he added.

"You are actually the best person I would ask right now. You are the lord of the female ring," Mitchell said before they both burst in laughter. "That sounded a bit dirty," he said amid laughs.

"Yes it does," Leo said. "That kind of talk could get you stoned in some countries of the Middle East," he added. Mitchell smiled. "So, why is it so important to get advice from me? Why don't you ask someone with a functional relationship or even marriage?" he asked.

"Because I need to know what my best man thinks," Mitchell said. Leo looked at him in surprise.

"For real?" he asked as Mitchell nodded. "Twice the honor, man," he said as he reached across the table to slightly fist bump Mitchell on the shoulder.

"So, tell me," Mitchell began as he leaned back in his chair. "What do you think about my situation?" he asked.

"Well, have you asked her what's going through her mind?"Leo asked. "Because it would help to know what the hell she's thinking," he added.

"Dude, I'm telling you I've tried it all," Mitchell said. "But every time I try to talk, we just end up in bed and I must say that in the last two weeks I have had the best lays ever!" he added in a loud whisper.

"Really?" Leo asked. "Now you're just making me feel bad, man," he said looking at Mitchell.

"I kid you not," Mitchell said leaning towards him. "Just last week, she made me do bondage stuff. One word, awesome!" he whispered excitedly.

"Wow," Leo breathed out. "And here I was thinking that I was lucky to have twins in Bangkok," he said looking at Mitchell in disbelief.

"Crazy man. I might just call her today to quote unquote, talk if you know what I mean," he said winking at him before he took a sip of his cappuccino. "Wait, you had twins in Bangkok?" he said as he put the cup down. Leo looked at him and smiled broadly.

"Oh yeah," Leo said nodding. "The perfect ménage a trois for sure," he said as he raised his cup at him.

"You pathetic lucky bastard!" Mitchell said. His facial expression suddenly turned and he held up his hands. "But I am in a committed relationship right now," he added.

"So, she never gave you a reason not to marry you?" Leo asked. Mitchell shook his head.

"Something about marriages in her family not working out," Mitchell said.

"There it is. You are overreacting," Leo said. Mitchell looked at him. He almost wanted to punch him right in the face.

"How so?" he asked.

"All the marriages she's seen don't work out so well," Leo said. "I think she's just scared of being hurt," he added. Mitchell looked at him. He had a point. He needed to find Natasha and tell her that. Maybe she needed to hear the words from his mouth.

"I think I need to talk to her," he said. "Who knew, Leo Hayes, world class pimp, could give such sound advice?" he added laughing.

"Hey, the only reason I am a world class pimp is because I get the women," Leo said. "We speak the same language you know," he added.

"Could this language be somewhat vertical?" Mitchell said as he took one final sip from his cup.

"You know it," Leo said smiling. "But seriously that's cold, man," he added feigning sadness. "How's the rock anyway?" he asked looking at him.

"Not so rocky," Mitchell said as he reached into his pockets and pulled out the black velvet case.

"Why not?" Leo asked looking at him in surprise.

"She hates flashy stuff," Mitchell answered. "So, I got the original ring redesigned to a smaller size," he added as he handed Leo the ring.

"No wonder she said no. You got her a small diamond!" Leo said looking at him.

"I just said she hates flashy stuff. And she didn't say no…"

"…you've heard the line that diamonds are a girl's best friend, right?" Leo asked as Mitchell's mouth remained gaped mid sentence. Mitchell nodded and looked at Mitchel unsure of where he was going with this.

"Then get her something cool. This is nice and all but really, you are Mitchell Schmidt," Leo scolded. Mitchell looked at him and slowly nodded.

If you think it will work," Mitchell said.

"If and when she says yes to you, it won't be because of the ring," Leo said looking at Mitchell. "Put that away," he said slamming the case shut and handing it back to a smiling Mitchell. "What the fuck's the matter with you?" he asked looking at him.

"You said when," Mitchell said. "You believe in me," he added dramatically as they stood up.

"As much as a lot has changed, the most annoying aspects about t you are still the same," Leo said as Mitchell dropped a couple of bills on the table. "Why are you even paying? I though you owned the joint," he said as they walked out.

"Didn't your mother teach you about tipping your waitresses?" Mitchell asked as they slowly walked towards his car.

"Do you really want an answer to that question?" Leo asked as Mitchell opened his door.

"Bye Leo," Mitchell said as Leo walked away laughing.

*****

Natasha sat on her bed, looking around at her old room. There was a sense of comfort being back here, the house she grew up in. She walked to her closet and opened it. She smiled when she saw the secret compartment on the floor where she hid her diary. Slowly, she bent down and took her diary out. She smiled as she flipped through the pages before walking back to her bed. She rummaged through her bag and when she finally got a pen, she leaned back on the bed and opened a fresh page.

Dear Diary,

I feel silly. I haven't done this in almost ten years…but let's face it, I am older, wiser and I have a great social life. So… guess it's okay that I haven't written in a while. Anyway, I feel this is the only place I can totally say what I feel without any kind of conviction.

So, Mitchell proposed to me a few weeks ago and I know I have in the past scribbled Mrs. Natasha Jonas and Mrs. Natasha Raymond a million times before. But every girl has that dream or fantasy of marrying one of the Jonas brothers or Usher Raymond at some point right? But people tend to think that Mitchell is my own Usher Raymond, Nick Jonas and everything nice plus a bag of chips rolled up into one great thing. But I'm scared. What if he changes? I mean right now he is the coolest, sweetest person. I mean the man rented out the Griffith Observatory just for me…and that was our first date!!! He listens. I am sure he is a great guy but people change. I mean mama did, Pop did too when he started beating on Nan. I am so scared but I might push him away.

Rita tells me that so far, he has not given me a reason to doubt him and she is right. Maybe I should just say fuck it and give it a chance. I hope I am right on this one. But I must be, right? Even Nan likes him and Nan never likes anyone. That's a sign right?

Sometimes, I wish you would talk back. Maybe then I wouldn't feel like the complete idiot I am right now…talking to a stupid journal. At least I know that I'm not alone. Maybe at this moment, statistically speaking, there are a million people writing weird things in their journals.

"Hey, princess," she heard her father Eric's voice from the doorway. She looked up and slammed the book shut as he walked towards the bed.

"Hey daddy," she said smiling up at him.

"Your Nan told me you were around," he said before kissing her forehead. "You have been coming over a lot lately, not that I'm complaining," he said. "Anything the matter?" he asked sitting down on the bed.

She looked at him and shook her head. "Just escaping the busy life that has become Natasha Black's latest script," she said smiling at him. Eric looked at her and smiled.

"You know when you were a little girl, you'd run up here and grab that diary any time you were upset," Eric said. "And old habits die hard," he added as Natasha's gaze fell to her knees. Eric used his index finger to lift her face up. "Does this have anything to do a little proposal I heard about?" he asked. Natasha's eyes grew wide.

"You knew?" she asked looking at her father in surprise.

"That Mitchell Schmidt is a very upright young man. Very traditional," he said. Natasha looked at her in surprise.

"What do you even mean by that?" she asked looking at him, a questioning look on her face.

"He called me up last month. Surprised me too. I didn't even know he had my number," Eric said as Natasha looked on. "So, he took me out for a great dinner and asked me for your hand," he finally said smiling.

"He did?" she asked feeling a wave of emotion come over her.

"You know honey," Eric said, a serious expression suddenly coming over his face. "Mitchell is a good man and he is not your grandfather," he said taking her small hands in his. "And you are certainly not your mother," he added with a smile.

"Thanks dad," she said looking at Eric. "I really needed to hear that," she said with a smile. "And I think I am ready to give Mitch my answer," she said still smiling.

"So, what are you still doing here? You had better skedaddle," Eric said patting her knee.

Natasha looked at him and smiled even more. Her father was right. Mitchell was not just some guy she had bumped into at the flea market. He was the real thing,. The ideal man. The greatest thing that could ever happen to her. She could not let him slip away.

"You are right, daddy," she said planting a kiss on his forehead. "I got to go," she said practically running out. She stopped in her tracks and ran back to quickly grab the diary from the bed. "Not today, Eric Black," she said before running out.

"You were a child," he called out as he heard her run down the stairs.

"And I'm still your child!" he heard call out from downstairs. He smiled as he heard the door slam shut. He was about to get a son-in-law.

Chapter 7

When Mitchell heard the front door slam shut, his first instinct was to reach for his gun. He reached for his piece cleverly concealed underneath one of his cushions. He suddenly aimed it at the door, his index finger almost squeezing the trigger.

"Bring it buster," he thought. "Breaking and entering can be an excusable reason for getting shot," he said as he kept his eyes fixated on the hallway.

"It's me, Mitchell," he heard. Natasha's small voice coming through the hallway. He took a deep breath as he put the safety back on. "I'm sorry," she said as she walked towards him.

"It's okay," he said looking at her. *"Fuck, she's beautiful,"* he thought as he looked at her. "What are you doing out so late?" he asked as he looked at her.

"I needed to talk to you," she said looking up at him. Mitchell looked at her as he felt his heart pounding a bit faster.

"Oh shit. I'm about to get the it's not you, it's me speech," he thought as he struggled to maintain a brave face.

"Right now?" he asked.

"Yes, Mitchell, Right fucking now," Natasha said obviously getting pissed off at his question. It was one in the freaking morning. This was either a booty call or a serious talk.

"Damn you Mitchell Schmidt!" He thought as he looked at the floor and then back at Natasha. "What's on your mind? Why

don't you sit down," he said not sure what he wanted her to do first.

"No, I don't want to sit down. I can do this just fine standing," she said tugging at her jacket.

"Okay," he said. She looked up at him and at that moment, he just wanted to take her into his arms and hug her and then give her the most passionate kiss known to man.

"I talked to my dad. He told me you asked him for my hand," she stared as she looked into his eyes. Mitchell felt himself panic.

"Should I not have done it?" he asked confused. She shook her head.

"No, I just….I was impressed. I think I…" her voice trailed off as she looked into his eyes, lost for words. She then took a step forward and kissed him. Mitchell closed his eyes and held her shoulders as he kissed her back.

"Wait," he thought. *"This is not good,"* he thought as he began to slowly push her away.

"No, we are supposed to talk. You cannot just fuck me into submission so I can forget about it," he said in a soft but stern voice.

"That's not what I'm doing," she said looking into his eyes.

"Yes you are," he said looking at hr. "You have been coming to 'talk' for the longest time but we just end up having crazy sex. Not that I'm complaining," he said looking at her. "You cannot avoid the situation forever, baby," he told her.

"I am not avoiding the situation Mitchell," she said as she took another step towards him. "I just want to have an intimate moment with my fiancé," she added looking into his eyes. Mitchell looked at her in surprise. This was exactly what he wanted but he had definitely not expected for her to come around this soon.

"Really?" he asked as he looked into her brown eyes. She smiled and nodded.

"I have been so stupid Mitchell," she said looking up at him. "I just don't know…I love you and I don't want to lose you," she said as a tear rolled down her cheek. Mitchell rubbed the tear off her cheek and held her face in his hands.

"I love you too," he said. "But is the fear of losing me the reason why you want to be my wife?" he asked looking closely into her brown eyes. She closed her eyes and shook her head.

"No, never," she said as another tear rolled down her other cheek. "It's just that I didn't realize just how much you meant to me until I almost lost you and…" she felt a tightness in her throat as she choked back a tear. "I am just…I want to spend the rest of my life with you, I have always seen a future with you," she said looking into his deep brown eyes. He felt overjoyed as he held her in his arms, something that he had not done in a long time. She lost all control and began sobbing into his shirt. He kissed the top of her head and gently squeezed her in his arms.

"I'm just happy you are here," he said before kissing her again. She pulled away and looked up at his smiling face. His perfect facial features looking down on her. Those beautiful dark eyes, that thick wavy hair. She was still looking up at him dreamily when he lowered his head and kissed her lips. She closed her eyes as she felt his lips on hers, slowly interchanging as the warm tongue threatened to get inside her mouth. She slowly wrapped her arms around his neck as he retaliated by wrapping his own arm around her dainty waist. He slowly pushed her coat off and pulled away to marvel at her perfect figure in the long top and skinny jeans she wore. He felt his excitement grow a little more when he saw her long heels, maybe because his mind went back to that day she surprised him with a whole lot of BDSM, much to his delight.

"What?" she asked. Without realizing it, he had been staring at her. He smiled and pulled her closer to him.

"Nothing, I just missed you," he said in a whisper. "Come here you sexy woman," he said as he lowered his head again, meeting her lips in a smooth sensual kiss. She slowly let a moan escape her lips as he kissed her long and hard, unwilling to let her go. His hands went down to her waist and began to slowly lift her shirt up. She pulled away and raised her arms over her head as he pulled her top off.

"Gorgeous," she heard him say when he laid eyes on her breasts secured inside her burgundy bra. He suddenly pulled away as if he had remembered something.

"What? What's wrong?" she asked looking into his eyes, a worried look in her eyes.

"I don't wan to have sex tonight, baby," he told her looking into her eyes. Natasha felt a sadness befall her. She wanted him so much right now, but maybe it was for the best. After all they did have a lot to work through. She smiled at him and grabbed her shirt from the couch. "What are you doing?" Mitchell asked looking at her.

"Getting dressed," she said looking at him confused.

"Why?" he asked looking at her.

"You don't want to have sex," she said looking up at him especially hard when he grabbed her hand.

"True," he said yanking the shirt from her hands. "I want to make love," he said kissing her again. Natasha felt herself get wet. This kind of random, arbitrary behavior made him even more hot than he already was. She shrieked as Mitchell suddenly lifted her up with one swift sweep. He walked them to the bedroom and slowly lowered her onto the bed. She watched him as he slowly took his pants off. She gasped when she saw that his penis was already erect, the angry veins threatening to burst its boundaries. He then slowly undid the zipper of her pants before slowly pulling them off.

The way he slowly undressed her, looking into her eyes with a certain intensity but without a word, made her loins crave him. He then slowly lowered his body and began to slowly plant small kisses on her navel, so close to tearing off her panties with his teeth. She closed her eyes as he felt his lips slowly going down her thigh that was now cold thanks to his ever efficient cooling system. She involuntarily spread her legs when she felt him running his tongue along the smooth skin of her inside thigh. Her soft moans had been replaced by hard labored breaths that showed her eagerness to have him inside her, to have him take her and ravage her.

"Oh my…God," she moaned when she felt him take the soft skin in between his teeth, slowly nibbling at her, making her wetter than she already was.

"You like that, don't you," Mitchell said softly, almost in a whisper. "What about this?" he said as he ran his tongue up her thigh, to her navel and finally to her upper breast. She felt herself tingle as his soft lips began planting small kisses on her perfect mounds.

"That too," she said as she held his head against her breast.

"And this?" he asked as he quickly unclasped the bra at the front. For a moment, Natasha was impressed at how fast he had managed to figure out the clasp. She sighed and shivered as he slowly licked the tip of one hardening nipple.

"Yeah, yes baby….like that…" she struggled to answer as he took one nipple inside his mouth. He sucked on it long and hard before he began to softly nibble on it, making her squirm with pleasure. He placed a hand on her other breast giving it equal pleasure from his flicking fingertips. "Ah,…babe… baby…" she moaned softly as he nibbles on the soft skin of her nipple. He resumed sucking on her hard nipples, tugging and pulling on it, making her squirm and moan and scream at some point.

He suddenly pulled away from her and looked at her lying there, eyes closed, tits rising and falling in rhythm with her quick breaths. He lightly touched his cock and could almost swear he could feel his pulse through the raging flesh. *"It's not yet time,"* he thought as he put his hands on either knee and slightly spread them before straightening them on the large bed He went back to kissing her legs and finally, what she longed for happened. He grabbed the top seam of her panties and slowly pulled them down. She felt a shiver as he let his warm finger slightly touch her wet slit.

Mitchell kept his gaze fixated on her face as he began his exploration of her hot, wet pussy. First he ran his finger up and down her slit, slowly moving along it, careful not to go too fast. He wanted this feeling she had presently to last longer if not all night long. He then lowered his mouth and began to kiss her lower lips almost as if he was kissing her face. She moaned as he expertly interchanged his lips, taking each lip in between his warm lips as if her labium was kissing her back. By this time, she was moaning loudly as she rubbed her nipples to try and keep some kind of sanity in her body because he was clearly bent on killing her tonight with pleasure.

Mitchell settled between her thighs, a little bemused by the outlook of what she wanted him to do to her, what he had already began doing to her. He looked up to see her head raised, looking down on him buried inside her.

She suddenly threw her head back and began moaning loudly as he pushed his mouth and nose into her warmth, his tongue niggling out between his lips to land on her distended clit that was calling out for him. He let one hand roughly grab her ass and squeeze it as he tasted her salty juices. He inhaled her familiar whiff with a breath loud enough for her to know just how much he loved it. Her hands slowly dropped from her breasts and held on to his head, involuntarily pulling him in as she slid down on the mattress.

His tongue suddenly plunged into her depths making her squirm and moan loudly as the hot surge of ecstasy raged through her loins. "Mitch…oh shit…Mitch that is so good, right now," she moaned as Mitchell used his tongue to furiously fuck her. The more he rammed his tongue against her, the harder he felt himself getting. By now his cock was simply pulsating, ready to go inside something, anything. With the way he was moving, it was not long before she felt herself shuddering against him, feverishly humping her sex on his face.

Mitchell retracted his tongue from her insides and began to slowly suck on her pussy, taking in all her saltiness, all her sexy nature. He wanted it all. She was still shuddering when he brought himself up to kiss her. She moaned as she tasted herself in his mouth, his magic mouth that had just sent her over the edge. He then looked down on her and pushed his pulsating cock inside her. He gasped when he felt his girth engulfed by her tight pussy, almost like a vise. He was finally inside her. He looked down on her as she wrapped her arms around his broad back and started to slowly move in and out of her, careful not to go so fast that he would finish off soon. His pace was slowly increasing as he drove himself in and out of the woman he loved, the woman he wanted to call his wife.

"I love you, Tasha," he said as he fucked her a bit faster now.

"I love you too baby," she said as she received his thrusts happily. She raised her legs and wrapped them around his waist. She gasped for air the first few times he slammed into her after she did so. It was so deep this way, almost touching the very wall of her cervix. Mitchell withdrew a few inches of his girth when he felt her writhe and resumed fucking her. She grabbed onto the bedding as she felt him driving her hard, almost as hard as a fucking porn star. By this time, her soft moans were loud and erotic, making him drive himself faster into her. He felt her nibble at his ear before burying her face in his neck.

"Baby, I'm cumming again," she said in a whisper. "You are going to make me cum again Mitchell," she said as Mitchell felt himself grow harder, longer inside her.

"Cum for me baby," he whispered as he fucked her faster and harder, feeling her hard clitoris every time he rammed into her. She moaned loudly as her thighs clamped together, her pussy squeezing his manhood with her vise-like cunt. He had held back enough. There was just no going back this time. He thrust into her one last time as he felt his seed flowing out of him, bringing with it a certain surge of hot release.

They lay in a tight embrace, shivering from the wild orgasm that had just ripped through their bodies, panting and heaving.

"You really meant it when you said you wanted to make love, huh," she said.

"Definitely," he said as he felt his cock slip out of her making their cum drip on the bedding. He then stretched out and opened the drawer on the bedside table. "Natasha Black," he said when he pulled the velvet case that had the ring inside. "Will you marry me?" he asked as he opened the case. Natasha smiled and held out her hand.

"When?" she said before kissing him.

"No that's not how it works," he said frowning.

"Okay, Mitchell Schmidt," she said with a smile. "I will marry you," she said as he slipped the ring on her finger. Natasha kissed him again before Mitchell cradled her in a spooning position. "Is that a pickle or are you seriously getting hard again?" she asked.

"I guess things change when you know you are going to have your soul mate by your side for life," he said as she felt him slip into her. She whimpered when she felt him pushing his length inside her depths, her still wet and slippery depth. She was still overly sensitive from her last two orgasms and Mitchell knew it. He began to quickly pummel himself inside her, her hot wetness pulling her in. She moaned as she pressed her mouth against the bed, muffling her sounds. He held on to her hip and used the grip to pound himself into her, every thrust harder and deeper than the first. With his other hand, he slowly began pressing her down, almost forcing her into a vertical doggy position. Natasha began bucking her hips against him, meeting his every thrust until she finally felt him pouring into her once again.

"Tasha I want the world with you," he said as he breathed into her hair. She breathed heavily as he held her close, recovering from the burst of energy that had just left his body twice. She held her hand up and looked at the ring.

"Is it just me or does this rock look bigger to you?" she asked as she looked at the ring. Mitchell smiled and planted a kiss on the top of her head. He was not about to admit to her that he thought the reason she had said no was the size of the diamond.

"It looks exactly the same to me," he said. She shook her head and turned around to face him.

"I was shocked when you first asked me Mitchell but I spent quite a long minute staring at the ring," she said looking at him. "Is there something you want to tell me?" she asked looking into his eyes.

"Trust me, there is nothing different about that ring. Maybe it looks bigger because of your small hands," he told her. She frowned at him.

"Besides, things are always bigger with Mitchell Schmidt," he said before draping an arm around his perfect woman. She smiled and kissed him deeply.

"Corny," she said. "Very corny," she added as she closed her eyes and drifted off to sleep in his arms. There was no other place she would rather be.

Book 3.

Wedding Planning With Mr White

Chapter 1

As she walked down the aisle, Natasha Black, soon to be Natasha Black-Schmidt, could feel the butterflies in her tummy. This was definitely the happiest day of her life. Everything she ever wanted was in this one very nice man who any woman would be lucky to call her own. She felt herself shake a little as she slowly made her way down the walkway scattered with rose petals. Her breasts looked full in her strapless Vera Wang embroidered gown. Her curly hair was pulled back in a bun giving way to the lovely tiara that adorned her forehead. In her hands she had a full bouquet of white roses. She looked like a princess, Mitchell Schmidt's princess.

Her heart was pounding faster as she made her way towards the man of her dreams. She could see her father and Nan smiling at her, so proud of their baby. Rita, who was her maid of honor, was also looking on, smiling at her best friend. Natasha smiled back as the distance between her and her future husband got shorter.

She suddenly felt the color drain from her face when she saw Jay smiling at her. Unlike all the other guests in the chapel, Jay was seated rather than on his feet. On his lap, he had a brown haired bimbo who wore a seriously short white dress.

"Who wears white to a wedding?" Natasha wondered. But the dress was the least of her problems. What she saw next made her sick to the stomach. The bimbo and Jay were in a tight lip lock, not caring for the fact that they were in the house of God. She felt sick as Jay's hand slowly ran up and down the girl's thigh and then under her dress. What the hell was this? He was not even invited. This was not happening. She suddenly realized that she was rooted to the ground. She was no longer walking. Her legs actually could not move. How could this

happen? How had it gone from being the happiest day of her life to the worst and how could Jay do this? He was a douche, granted, but not this much. She felt her heart rate rising. She could see people talking to her, asking her what the matter was but her voice seemed to fail her. She suddenly noticed that the petals of her bouquet were slowly withering; the chapel was no longer bright and beautiful. There was darkness around her, in the chapel....

Natasha woke up with a start and sat upright in her seat. *"Thank God none of that was real,"* she thought as she took a sip from her half finished bottle of water. She then took a deep breath, crossed her legs, and began typing away on her computer. From the corner of her eye she could see the time: 11:49 p.m. She sighed. This was so not how she intended to spend her evening. She had her Wednesday evening all figured out by lunch hour. She was going to leave work early since it was supposed to be her day off anyway, head to the salon for a manicure, and then maybe, just maybe, do some shopping for her upcoming wedding.

She smiled as the thought crossed her mind. Her wedding. It seemed so unreal. She was actually going to get married to one of the best, most charming, most good looking...no, drop dead gorgeous men she knew. She took a deep breath and closed her eyes. Of course, she hoped that it would be better than her dream. Though she had not told Mitchell about it, Natasha had been having some pretty nasty dreams as far as her wedding was concerned. Her best friend and family had convinced her that it was just wedding jitters, something that happened to every bride.

"You're just nervous and want everything to be perfect," her father had said reassuringly. "Every woman I know has them, it's nothing to worry about." Rita, on the other hand, was convinced that it was more than just jitters.

"You are exhausted. All you need is some sleep, a good massage and a wedding planner," Rita had said on a separate occasion. For Natasha, planning her own wedding had been her dream and even though she wanted a small intimate ceremony, she wanted to be the one to oversee everything. But somehow, this seemed to take a toll on her. She was tired all the time, she dozed off in meetings and she was barely getting her beauty sleep. She looked at the wedding planner's card on her desk and sighed. *"Maybe it would not hurt to have someone take the load off my shoulders,"* she thought, her eyes still on the card. God knows she needed it, badly.

"Pull yourself together Tasha," she thought as she shrugged her shoulders. Suddenly, the serene environment of her office was interrupted by the shrill ringing and loud vibration of her phone. She looked at the screen and smiled.

"Hey, baby," she cooed despite the fact that she was exhausted.

"Hey beautiful. What you up to?" Mitchell asked. She took a long deep breath before leaning back in her chair.

"Nothing much. Just finishing the reports for tomorrow," she said looking at the figures on her laptop screen. The numbers just did not make sense anymore, and who would blame her? She had been sitting in the same spot working on the same thing for almost six hours.

"Are you for real?" Mitchell asked. Natasha could hear the surprise in his voice. "Girl, I own the damn company but even I don't stay that late," he said.

"Well, my name is not on the door so…."

"…so what?" Mitchell asked, cutting her short.

"This is a major deal for the company. You said so yourself," she said in her defense.

"Yes but not as important as my fiancée," Mitchell said. Natasha smiled.

"That sounds good," she said. She knew that Mitchell knew she was blushing. She did not know how he did it, but somehow, he always knew.

"What? Fiancée?" he asked.

"Yeah," Natasha said in a voice almost as sexy as she wanted it to be. "Say it again," she cooed.

"Fiancée," Mitchell said softly. "If you like that how about wifey, Mrs. Natasha Black Schmidt?" Natasha laughed.

"Nah, there is something about the French and the Britons," she said. "Somehow, wifey does not at all match up to fiancée," she added.

"Fine," Mitchell said. "So, what did you have for dinner? Take out?" Just then Natasha felt the hunger pains sting her belly. She had not eaten yet!

"Oh my God, Mitchell. I did not even remember," she said. She knew how stupid it sounded but somehow Mitchell understood her.

"Seriously?" Mitchell asked in a shocked voice. "I am coming over right now," he said. She could hear a distortion of the signal, letting her know that he was getting up from wherever he was.

"No, honey…you really don't have to," she said. "I have half a sandwich from lunch and…."

"…the new Chinese place that serves that kung pow chicken you love so much is open 24 hours," he said obviously paying no attention to her pleas. "I'll be there in twenty." She heard the familiar click that signified the end of their conversation.

"Did he just hang up on me?" she wondered looking at the phone. **Mitchell Schmidt: Call Ended.** *"Yup, he just did,"* she thought as she put the phone down. For some people, that would have been a major factor to fuel an argument, but for Natasha…she knew she was in the wrong. Mitchell hated it when she overworked and neglected her own health. She pushed her chair back and stood up to stretch. She suddenly looked up when she felt the door creak before it was flung open. Her heart almost skipped a beat. She did not expect anyone to come barging in her office, at least not for another nineteen or so minutes.

"Oh Miss Black. I not know you here," Juan, the late night janitor said apologetically. Natasha took another deep breath.

"It's okay, Juan," she said with a smile.

"Too much work today?" Juan asked smiling back at her. She loved the way his warm brown eyes seemed to dance in the light.

"A lot," she answered.

"Okay, I will wait for you to finish, then I come clean," he said before leaving.

"Thanks Juan," she called out as he closed the door. She looked around her office and then slowly walked to the window. She kicked her shoes off as she looked at the beautifully lit city below. She had always thought that major cities looked their best in the evening, each skyscraper competing with the next in lighting, height and art.

She was still looking outside her window when Mitchell walked in carrying two take out bags.

"Kung pow chicken, my love?" Mitchell said with a smile. Natasha turned around with a smile.

"Kung pow chicken my love to you too," she said walking towards him.

"Barefoot," he said walking to her office couch. "Foot rub?" he asked as she sat down.

"Oh, would you?" she asked looking up at him. He nodded as he put the bags on the table.

"Anything for my baby," he said as he kissed her forehead. He then took her leg in his hands as she helped herself to the food.

"Hope you don't mind," she said as she opened up the boxes.

"No, you do your thing up there and I'll do my thing down here," he said as he began rubbing her sore feet. Natasha gave him a questioning look.

"You do realize how bad that sounded, right?" she asked as she looked at him. He nodded nervously. She could notice that he was avoiding her gaze. She smiled as she took a large bite and closed her eyes.

"Oh, food," she said her eyes still closed. Mitchell smiled.

"I know," he said. "So, how was your day?" he asked as Natasha took another bite.

"My God the McLane thing tomorrow…"

"…I don't want to talk about work right now," he said taking her hand. "Tell me about you. How was your day?" he asked looking into her eyes. She smiled at him.

"I have had better," she said. "But I'm still alive, aren't I?" she added. Mitchell looked at her and smiled back.

"Yes you are," he said before taking a long sip of his juice. "So, tell me, what is this I hear about you not getting a wedding planner?" he asked, his voice suddenly turning serious.

"Not you too," Natasha said as she leaned back on the couch.

"You are overworking yourself," he said. "And you have too much on your hands right now," he added. Natasha looked at him sternly.

"We are not talking about this, Mitchell," she said before taking a large bite of her rice.

"You do realize that a wedding planner would mean less time in the office, more time to relax," Mitchell said. He smiled at her and put a warm hand on her thigh. "More time for us," he added leaning close for a kiss. Natasha put her finger up just in time and gently pushed Mitchell away.

"Nah uh, no sugar for you," she said sternly.

"I don't know what you are so worried about. This woman has planned every major wedding I know," Mitchell said. "She is really good," he added with a smile. Natasha looked at him.

"Oh really? Like who?" she asked crossing her arms over her chest.

"Well, Phil from the New York office had an 800 guest wedding planned by her. Felicia Kane..."

"...the Malibu goddess?" Natasha interrupted quickly. Felicia was one of the company's top clients and even though she was a great asset, she could drive you crazy. But that was what growing up a spoiled brat could do to a person.

Mitchell nodded. "Yes, the Malibu goddess" he said. "Angelina Jolie, Kim Kardashian..." Natasha suddenly put her hands up.

"Hold up," she said. "You mean to tell me this planner is responsible for Brangelina's hush-hush wedding?" she asked in surprise.

"You know I only get the best for you," he said smiling at her. His smile slowly faded away when he noticed Natasha's frown. "What?" he asked.

"Kim Kardashian," she said. "What if this planner is a bad omen? What if she makes us also have a three month long marriage?" she asked in a panic. At this moment, she was surprising even herself.

"Wow, these jitters are really bad," he said looking at her. ""Just calm down. I am not Kris Humphries and you are not Kim. So you are stuck with me." He pulled her close. This time, Natasha offered no resistance. He lifted her chin with his index finger and slowly gave her a short but sensual kiss. "Forever," he said in a whisper. Natasha smiled and wrapped her arms around him.

"Yes I am and I love it," she said kissing him again.

"So does that mean that you will call her?" he asked looking at her. She sighed and relaxed in his arms. It was getting increasingly difficult to think with his hands slowly running up and down her back.

"Maybe," she said smiling at him. "We'll see how it goes," she said before pulling him close for another kiss.

*****

After a mere four hours of sleep, Friday morning was a bit tough for Natasha. She quickly walked down the hallway to her office, carefully avoiding eye contact.

"Good morning Natasha," her assistant Stacy called from her desk. Natasha flashed her a smile before proceeding to her office. When she opened the door, the familiar, delicious aroma of fresh coffee drifted up her nostrils. She stopped in her tracks and turned around. Stacy was already on her feet, following her, ready to give her the day's schedule. When Stacy saw her boss smiling at her she knew exactly what was going through Natasha's mind. "Triple espresso and warm bagels," Stacy said as she took Natasha's bag from her hands. "Juan told me that you were working late and I knew exactly how to get you fired up for your nine o'clock with McLane-Kane," she added as the two of them walked in together. "Which you almost missed by the way," she added politely.

Natasha frowned. "Please don't remind me that I have to face that Malibu goddess today," she said as she sat down. "God knows why McLane even partnered with her," she said as she took a long sip of the coffee.

"Because she made 70 million dollars in the last six months alone," Stacy answered.

"Yeah, there's that," Natasha said before taking another sip. "What else?" she asked.

"A representative from the Fiddler Group will be here at two for an update on their ad campaign and then you are done," Stacy said as she stuck a post-it note on a file that was on Natasha's desk.

"So, I am free from midday to two?" she asked. Stacy looked at her iPad and nodded.

"Pretty much," Stacy said.

"Would you call the Fiddler Group office and ask if they are willing to reschedule to midday?" Natasha said, looking up at Stacy.

"Sure," Stacy said before glancing at her watch. "But now, you have to take the rest of your espresso in the board room because McLane and Felicia are almost here."

"Bagel?" Natasha asked in a small voice. Stacy smiled as she handed her a bagel in a napkin. No one ever understood the two of them. Most people in the company had assistants for one reason and one reason only: humiliating them to feel better. The assistants had to get coffee, pick up their kids from school, attend parent teacher conferences, do grocery shopping...just simply annoying stuff. But Natasha and Stacy had maintained a healthy professional relationship that had slowly bloomed into a strong friendship.

"The projector is already set up. Just go on and I'll bring your stuff in," Stacy said as Natasha walked towards the board room. When she walked in, she was surprised that Felicia and McLane were right on her tail. Talk about being punctual.

"Miss Kane, Mr. McLane," she said smiling at them. "Very nice to see you again," she said stretching her hand to shake their hands. She noticed McLane giving her breasts a long lingering look and Felicia sizing her up.

"It is so on," she thought as they sat down. "So I have been looking at Miss Kane's returns for the last year and I can tell you Mr. McLane, you are on the best roll right now," she said politely.

"I know. I signed on, didn't I?" he said more matter-of-factly than was possible.

"Well, we have already begun the ad campaign in the Americas and Europe," Natasha began as she waited for Stacy.

"Actually, we were thinking of a European market," Felicia Kane said, taking Natasha by surprise.

"A European market?" Natasha asked looking at Felicia. "We spent four months planning for the North and South American market, African market too, not European, Miss Kane."

"Well, I had a talk with my good friend here and changed my mind," Felicia Kane said lightly. "I am allowed to do that right? After all I am pumping 15 million dollars into this," she added.

"Could you excuse me?" Natasha said as she got up. She didn't care whether they permitted her or not. She needed to get out.

"The reports and.....Natasha are you okay?" Stacy asked as

Natasha walked past her.

"Fine," she said without looking back. She needed air. She needed to do something. She needed to do Mitchell…yeah. She quickly walked towards his office, straight past his secretary and slammed the door behind her. Mitchell looked up in surprise.

"Tasha, you okay?" he asked looking at his heavily breathing fiancée.

Chapter 2

"Honey, are you okay?" Mitchell asked looking at Natasha who was breathing heavily. "You look a bit...flushed," he said after struggling to find the right words, worried that he might be saying the wrong thing at the wrong time. Natasha leaned against the door and took several deep breaths. She could feel a cold sweat breaking on her forehead.

Without a word, she walked to his mini bar and poured herself a shot of bourbon. Mitchell watched as she downed a glass, then another and then another.

"Okay, that's enough," Mitchell said standing up. As he walked to the mini bar, he was interrupted by a brief knock on the door. He turned his attention to the door where his assistant Sheryl had poked her head in. There was a concerned look on her face. "Oh good Lord, what now?" he asked looking at Sheryl.

"I didn't want to disturb you Mr. Schmidt but McLane and Felicia Kane are in the board room," she said. Mitchell looked at her, not sure what to say.

"Yeah, Natasha was doing the meeting...and she is here," he said almost getting the reason why Natasha was in his office.

"Yes, I just wanted Miss. Black to know..."

"...I know the Malibu goddess is in the freaking board room because I left the bitch there!" Natasha said in a stern but hushed whisper. Mitchell could literally feel the color draining from his face as he and Sheryl stared at Natasha.

"Sheryl, we are going to need a moment," Mitchell said. Sheryl nodded and shut the door. He turned his attention back to

Natasha. "Why don't you sit down," he said taking her hand. He could feel her shaking as he led her to one of the guest seats at his desk. She pulled her hand from him and walked around the desk before she finally sat in his chair.

"Okay," he said looking at her in surprise.

"Your guest seats are shit," she said as she leaned back.

"Really?" he asked looking surprised. "I got them from Furniture Palace," he said. She looked at him and leaned forward to rest her elbows on the desk.

"I got mine from the same place," she said. "And they are 100 times better on a bad day than yours," she added.

"That can't be right. They were a thank you after an ad campaign…" his voice trailed off as he suddenly realized what was happening. "Oh shit, I got played," he said sitting down in one if the guest seats.

"Yup," Natasha said rolling her eyes.

"Wow, this really is uncomfortable." He shifted his weight left and right. "This is ridiculous," he said, standing up and sitting on the desk. He pressed the intercom button. "Sheryl, call Furniture Palace and get them to bring in two new guest seats tomorrow. Preferably the same ones as Miss Black's," he added. Natasha smiled. He only needed to hear some things on some of her honest days to get him to do stuff. "So, what is wrong with my beautiful wife to be?" he asked looking at Natasha.

"That damn Malibu bitch," she suddenly snapped. Mitchell looked at her. He could tell she was highly agitated. He had never seen her like this.

"What happened?" he asked calmly. She took a deep breath and stood up. "I'd rather just not talk about it right now," she said beckoning for him to come closer to her.

"What do you want to do?' he asked walking towards her. "How can I help you? I'm really worried about you, sweetness," he said as he held her by the waist.

"Don't talk. I just need a release," she said in a whisper. She looked into his eyes as he looked back at her, in a defining moment that would determine the fate of the next few minutes. She closed her eyes as she pulled his neck down for a long, lingering kiss. He kissed her back and slipped an arm around her waist as their lips met in a unified, sensual kiss. Before long, he was kissing her roughly as he struggled to get his hand under her shirt, cupping her soft full mounds as he kissed her. The randomness of this whole thing was getting him more excited than a fat kid in a pastry shop. He pulled away and began to kiss her chin, trailing his lips all the way to her neck.

"The door," she whispered in his ear. He pulled away and smiled at her.

"No one's coming in," he said looking into her eyes before resuming his kisses. She placed a hand on his chest and turned her head away. He looked at her and sighed before walking to the door. She smiled as he quickly bolted it and walked back to her.

"Happy?" he asked as he approached her. She smiled and pulled her blouse off just as he stood in front of her. He then lifted her and placed her on the desk as he continued kissing her neck, slowly coming down to her breasts. She let out a small whimper when he pulled one bra cup down, exposing a fully engorged nipple. She felt herself blush as Mitchell pulled the other cup down and stared at her perfect tits. She ran her fingers through his thick hair as he took one nipple inside his mouth, sucking and nibbling. She stifled a scream when she felt him gently squeeze one nipple in between his index finger and thumb. She wanted so much to let him have her right there. It was something the two of them had never done before but it somehow seemed the right thing to do at this particular moment. Her mind was so fixed on the way he sucked hard on her breasts that she failed to notice him unbuckling his belt and freeing himself from the constraints of his tight fitting boxers.

When he finally pulled away from her now highly sensitized nipples, she was shaking and breathing heavily. He looked at her beautiful face as he reached under her skirt. He slowly ran his hands along her thighs before finally pulling down her panties. She looked at him as he spread her legs. She whimpered again when she felt his finger playing around with her clit and her moist sex. She saw him smile when she rested her hands on the desk behind her, looking for more support. He was still looking into her eyes when he slowly pushed one finger inside her. By now she was starting to get wetter. He pulled his finger out and pushed it in again. He leaned forward and looked at her eyes which remained closed.

"Open your eyes," he said in almost a whisper. "Look at me baby," he said. She opened her eyes and looked at him as he retracted his finger from her now wet cunt. She moaned her disapproval as he smiled. He then reintroduced his finger inside her and began fingering her hard and fast. Her face winced in pleasure as she struggled to keep her pleasure sounds to herself. She soon began bucking her hips forward, meeting his over eager finger as he continued finger fucking her. He suddenly pulled his finger out and positioned his cock head at the entrance of her pussy. He slowly pushed in the head of his cock while looking into his lover's eyes. She gasped as Mitchell took advantage of her wetness and pushed in his whole length.

Natasha wrapped her arms around Mitchell and kissed him, obviously to drown the scream that would soon escape her lips. She had never known him to be this rough but she loved this side of him. She held on for dear life as he pumped into her, hard and fast, never showing any intention to slow down. She wrapped her legs around his waist as he continued thrusting into her hard. She bit her lip in an effort not to scream or cry out. She could have sworn that every time she did something to help her keep her moans in, it only made him thrust into her harder. She suddenly let out a gasp when she felt him pull his cock out of her without any kind of warning. In a split second, he had pulled her off the desk and turned her around. He bent her over the desk in a doggy style position and entered her from behind. She huffed when Mitchell stuffed his full cock into her again, filling her every fold.

Natasha grabbed the edge of the desk and held on as Mitchell began to slam himself into her. Each thrust was harder than the last, each thrust was driving her wild and the fact that she could not vocally show him how he made her feel was killing her. She felt her breasts pressed against the smooth glossy finish of Mitchell's desk as his balls slammed into her round ass. She suddenly let a slight moan escape her throat as she felt Mitchell's driving force gain momentum. She turned her head to look at him but he had his eyes closed, lost in his own erotic world. At that moment, she felt a hard orgasm rip through her insides, tearing down every twitch that was held up in her vagina. Her pulsating cunt must have triggered Mitchell's own violent orgasm, because not long afterwards, Mitchell plunged into her hard as he deposited his seed into her. She held on to the edge of the desk as long as she could with Mitchell working himself in and out of her for as long as he possibly could.

When his pulsating cock relaxed, Natasha felt relieved as it slipped out of her. She felt a sudden warmth on her inside thigh as a mixture of their cum dripped out of her pussy. She grabbed a tissue from the desk and cleaned herself up before turning to look at an exhausted Mitchell who was slumped back in his seat. She smiled and planted a kiss on his forehead before walking to his bathroom to freshen up.

When she finally emerged from the bathroom, Mitchell was still in his seat, breathing heavily and looking ever so drowsy.

"Hey, mister," she said snapping her fingers loudly in front of his face. "It's only nine. You have a long day ahead," she said smiling. She walked back to the bathroom and came back with two damp towels. She placed one on Mitchell's forehead and began cleaning his cock up with the other one.

"Oh that feels so good," he said as he closed his eyes. Natasha smiled as she wiped his cock and thighs before going back to the bathroom and rinsing it off again.

"Just so you know, I deserve an office with a complete bathroom too," she said as she walked back in. "I mean, really, when do you ever find time to shower in your office, anyway?" she asked as Mitchell pulled his pants up.

"You'd be surprised," he said taking the damp towel from her.

"Really? Do random women come in and screw you to your desk every so often?" she asked in a mocking voice.

"Well, just the one. Crazy woman," he said as he pulled Natasha down. She smiled as she sat on his lap. "She is so crazy, I want her craziness every single day for the rest of my life," he said looking into her eyes.

"If you love crazy so much, how about you get the Malibu

goddess instead?" Natasha said smiling. Mitchell laughed.

"By the way, about that," he said placing a hand on her thigh. "What exactly happened? You ready to talk about it now?" he asked. She nodded before taking a deep breath.

"Well, we all thought Felicia Kane partnering up with Evan McLane was the best deal we could ever ask for, right?" she began. Mitchell nodded.

"Yeah, that account added a few extra zeroes in my pay check last quarter," he said smiling.

"Well, it is good. Especially their new liquor line that was aimed at an African and North and South American market," she said.

"What do you mean was meant to? Didn't I sign a requisition for four million in funding?" Mitchell asked looking at her, more confused than surprised.

"Yes but now, it turns out that Felicia and McLane want it aimed towards a European market," she said. "We have already spent $2.7 million of the company's fund in marketing. We cannot simply begin a new campaign," she said. Mitchell looked at her and nodded. "Not forgetting the fact that we are literally weeks away from the official launch," she added.

"So where are McLane and Felicia now?" he asked. Natasha looked at him guiltily.

"In the board room," she said in a small voice. "I did not know what to say or how to handle myself without slapping the bitch across the face," she said quickly. Mitchell gave her a half smile.

"I get it," he said. "You know, the only way to handle Felicia is to show her that you are the one in control, not her. McLane is a sissy. All he will do is hide behind the stronger person, in this case Felicia," he said matter-of-factly. "Just go in there and show her who's boss," he said looking into her eyes.

"I was hoping you would do that for me," she said pouting. "Pretty please," she said. Mitchell shook his head and cupped the side of her face.

"You know why I hired you?" he asked looking into her eyes.

"My great ass?" she said jokingly.

"Well, yeah plus you are a strong, spirited woman. The kind that gets shit done. The kind that does not let anyone walk all over her," he said. "And I know you can do this because the woman I love is just out of this world." He stroked the side of her face with his index finger. She smiled down at him and stood up.

"Thanks, Mitch. I needed that," she said before walking towards the door. "By the way, baby," she said as she placed a hand on the door handle.

"Yeah," he said.

"Quit looking at my ass as I walk away," she said before closing the door behind her. She smiled as she approached Sheryl's desk. "Just one of those days, sorry for the outburst," she said before walking out of the office. As she headed down the hallway, she felt better than she did when she was walking down the same hallway a few minutes earlier. She walked to Stacy's desk and smiled at her. "Get me the financials to the McLane and Kane merger right away. Bring them to the board room," she said without giving Stacy a moment to respond.

"I am sorry about the wait," she said as she walked into the board room. She cold tell that Felicia was highly agitated.

"I hope it was worth waiting for forty-five minutes," Felicia said sternly. Natasha looked up at her and smiled.

"Oh it was, Miss Kane. In more ways than one," she said as her eyes glimmered. At that moment Stacy walked in and handed Natasha a flash drive and a paper file. "Thanks, Stacy," Natasha said as she stood up and walked to the projector. "Well, as you know we began the official ad campaign for your product three months ago," she started as she inserted the flash drive into the USB slot of her laptop. "We are talking models, photo shoots, traveling and of course, boarding and lodging. And Miss Kane, you opted to go for Mila Asimbi and Maria de Mayo, both top notch models," she added as the monitor came alive with the financial records.

"Yes. We wanted the best for our products," McLane said. "These two are very well known in Africa and the Americas," he added.

"Get to the point. This is really boring," Felicia said. Natasha shot her a look before turning to a page that gave the break down of their expenditure.

"Being top range models in Africa and the Americas, we incurred a $10,000 fee per hour per shoot," Natasha said. "We had eight photo shoots in five different locations," she said.

"So…"

"…Be patient, Miss. Kane. I am getting to the point," Natasha said interrupting Felicia. "We also had a crew of about 30 people who were all being paid by the company not forgetting their basic need costs. So all in all, we spent $2.7 million of the four million dollar fund allocated to us on marketing for an African and North and South American market. Should you choose to change this, as the contract states, you have to pay back the funding in full plus you will be completely ruined. The success of any new product rides high on the success of the product we have been pushing for the last two months," she said as she sat down. "And I must say that we would not work on anything else apart from the agreed on African and America's market. We would hate to have our name tainted."

"So you will not work with us. Is that what you are saying?" Felicia asked. Natasha shook her head.

"Not if you make a snap judgment like this because believe me, it doesn't matter whether or not you have been successful in the past. A bad decision like this can and will end you," Natasha said calmly.

"Felicia maybe she…"

"..Oh please Evan. What does she know? After all she is just the CEO's whore," Felicia said interrupting McLane.

"Miss Kane. I am a professional and my personal life has nothing to do with you or this," Natasha said angrily. "I have already forwarded this to Mr. Schmidt. If you do decide to pursue this, then all the best," she said as she gathered her files together. "But if you want to make money, then call my assistant and let us go ahead with what was already in place." She stood up.

"Miss Black, I am sure we can come to some sort of understanding," McLane said standing up. Felicia was still giving her a cold stare.

"I am sure we can. Just as soon as you come to an

understanding with Miss Kane," Natasha said before walking out, leaving a bewildered McLane and an angry but shocked Felicia. For once, it felt good having the final word instead of the freaking Malibu goddess.

Chapter 3

Rita almost choked on her iced tea as she laughed. She had not laughed this hard in a long time. Natasha had invited her and Stacy for lunch and had just finished telling them how the Malibu goddess almost ruined her day.

"I am sure working with you is not something to look forward to any time soon," Rita said.

"You should have seen Felicia walk into the building last week," Stacy said, biting into her crispy chicken. "She actually walked straight to Mr. Schmidt's office without even causing a scene like she normally would," she added laughing.

"Serves her right," Rita said. "Someone needed to humble the bitch," she added a bit too sternly. Stacy and Natasha looked at her.

"Whoa, hold your horses there. We admire your loyalty but the Malibu goddess has never done anything to you," Natasha said. Rita almost dropped her fork when Natasha said this.

"I must have forgotten to tell you," Rita said looking at Natasha.

"Tell me what?" Natasha asked, a questioning look on her face.

"Felicia Kane came to my gallery some time back. She came there all 'Mitchell Schmidt told me this was a fabulous establishment,'" she said her voice slightly high pitched to emulate Felicia's. Natasha and Stacy laughed. "Well, so anyway, me and Celine…"

"…wait. Who is Celine?" Stacy asked cutting her short.

"Her assistant," Natasha said quickly hoping to get back into the juicy details of the story.

"So anyway, after about half an hour of going through the gallery, she said that some of the work reminded her of an untalented Van Gogh," Rita said.

"What?" Natasha asked, both surprised and appalled. "Why the hell would she say that?"

"It comes naturally with being a bitch," Rita said quickly. Natasha smiled.

"Wow, you must have really wanted to get that out of your system, huh?" Natasha asked.

"Like you wouldn't believe," Rita said rolling her eyes.

"Her and everyone else, me included," Stacy said as she cut her meat into tiny bits. Rita and Natasha looked at her.

"Now, why would you have issues with her?" Natasha asked. Stacy looked at her in surprise.

"Hello? I have been at NSCS for three years and for a whole year before you joined us, I had to deal with the bitch first hand," Stacy said. "And daily because at the time I was at the front office," she added, shaking her head. "Sad days those were," she said in a small voice.

"Sad days indeed," Rita said. "So anyway, she ended up taking two pieces, paid cash and I know this is the worst thing to say as a struggling artist but if I ever see that bitch again it will be too soon," she added before taking yet another bite of her chicken. Natasha smiled and leaned back in her seat.

"Tell me about it, you are preaching to the choir sister," Stacy said.

"But on to better things. How are things on the wedding front?" Rita asked looking at Natasha.

"I got overwhelmed and got a planner," Natasha started.

"What got over you?" Rita asked. "I can't believe a control freak like you would actually let another person plan the biggest day of her life," she added. Natasha shot her a dirty look.

"Hey," Natasha said defensively.

"What? Tasha I've known you since we were kids and you have always wanted things to go in a certain way or not at all," Rita said.

"You *can* be a wee bit controlling, boss lady," Stacy said without looking up. Natasha looked at her and then shifted her gaze to Rita.

"Well, Mitchell talked me into it…"

"…of course he did," Rita said cutting her short. "This is definitely not something you would have thought of on your own."

"I got this lady who apparently planned Brad and Angelina's wedding," Natasha said totally ignoring Rita's comment.

"Lucky you," Stacy said looking up. "Brangelina's wedding was a blast," she added excitedly.

"Oh my God," Rita said as she looked past Natasha.

"What?" Natasha asked looking at Rita.

"Don't look now because you do not want to know who just walked in," Rita said putting her hand on Natasha's.

"Why? I am sure it can't be that bad," Natasha said turning her head. "Oh holy fuck," she said as she saw Jay walking towards their table. "This guy is like a fucking stalker," she said turning back to look at Rita.

"Oh, the ex? He's kind of hot," Stacy said smiling.

"Don't even go there, sister," Rita said sternly.

"If it isn't the lovely Natasha Black," Jay said smiling. "And her council of ladies," he added looking at Stacy and Rita.

"What the hell do you want Jay? Why aren't you somewhere getting your head blown off or something?" Rita asked as Jay walked towards them.

"Always nice to see you, Rita. And you," he said turning to Stacy. "I have never seen anyone rock red locks the way you do," he said with a smile. Stacy smiled and almost blushed. Natasha looked at her in surprise as Rita kicked her under the table.

"Ow!" Stacy yelled as she rubbed her leg under the table.

""Why don't you girls head on over to the bar and order me a drink," Jay said.

"They have waitresses, you punk ass," Rita said angrily.

"Oh, pardon me," he said. "I was just trying to get some alone time with my woman, politely." He pulled up a seat.

"I am not your woman, Jay. That ship sailed at the same time dinosaurs became extinct," Natasha said sternly as she felt her anger rise.

"Well, can I please talk to you?" Jay asked in a low voice trying not to draw attention to himself. "Alone," he stressed looking at Rita. Natasha looked at Rita and nodded.

"It's okay Rita. Just give us five," Natasha said as Rita took Stacy's hand.

"We'll be just here if you need us," Rita said as she and Stacy took a seat two tables from Natasha.

"Okay, they're gone," Natasha said. "What do you want?" She crossed her arms over her chest. She noticed Jay's eyes lingered a bit over her breasts that she had involuntarily pushed up by crossing her arms. She uncrossed her arms and tried to pull the two sides of her blouse together. Jay smiled.

"You always were very feminine," he said. Natasha took a deep breath and looked into his eyes.

"You need to say what you came here to say, Jay," she said angrily. "I don't have all day."

"Since you got this big job you are a different person, Tasha, aren't you?" he said. "But somewhere inside there is the woman I fell in love with."

"Well, you cheated on that woman and she moved on," she said. He looked into her eyes and reached for her hand. She quickly yanked it away just in time. "Me and you are done, Jay. Please try and move on like I did," she said in a low voice.

"I still love you. I still care about you," he said. "It hurts me that you would let me find out this way," he said as he pushed a copy of the local daily towards her. Natasha looked down and noticed the paper was the same one where she and Mitch had advertised their 'save the date' article.

"What good would it have done if I told you Jay?" she asked leaning forward. "I wouldn't want to see you at the wedding, ever."

"Really? You would not want to have me see you on the one day you are the most beautiful woman in white even after Labor Day?" he asked. Natasha shook her head.

"Look at the way you keep on harassing me. Do you think I would want you there?" she asked. Jay's gaze dropped to the table and then rose to look at her.

"Do you really want to do this?" he asked looking at her. "Do you really love Mitchell so much that you want to see him every day for the rest of your life?" he asked. She smiled and looked at her ring before she slowly lifted her hand.

"This is something you never even thought of, Jay," she said. "Maybe if you were man enough to allow yourself to be held down to one woman, you would have me," she added as she took her purse. Jay reached across the table and took her hand. She looked into his eyes and almost felt sorry for him, or was it some remedial feelings?

"Don't marry him, Tasha," he said. She pulled her hand away and looked at him.

"Bye, Jay," she said before walking away with Rita and Stacy not far behind. She felt her heart rate rise as they walked towards the exit. She could still feel Jay's staring at her.

"You okay?" Rita asked holding her hand.

"Just get me out of here," Natasha said thinking of how Mitchell would take this news. He wouldn't like it one bit, but he had to know. That was the kind of relationship they had, an honest one.

*****

When she pulled her car into her driveway and switched off the engine, she lay her head back on the head rest and sighed. It had been a long day, maybe too long. Why was it exes could never really remain as ex-factors? Why did they have to make a comeback every so often if just to do some mockery? This was too much for her to handle. She knew exactly what she was going to do to get herself relaxed. She reached inside her bag and pulled out her phone. She scrolled briefly before seeing the number for Wu Ling Hot Pot.

"Hi, Mr. Ling. It's Tasha," she said when Mr. Ling picked up the phone. She had ordered so much from the same restaurant that her calls were almost regular.

"Miss Black, the usual?" Mr. Ling asked in a heavy Chinese accent.

"No, today I want to do some sweet and sour chicken and rice," Natasha said.

"Plain, fried or spiced?" Mr. Ling asked.

"Fried of course," Natasha answered, smiling almost as if Mr. Ling could see her.

"It will be there in an hour," Mr. Ling said before hanging up.

"Dinner, check. Now for a bath" she thought as she got out of the car. She could not help but need to stretch out to ease her tired muscles. As she walked into her apartment, she took a deep breath and kicked her shoes off. She had just put her bag down when she heard her phone beep. She took her bag and took the phone out. She looked at the screen and smiled. It was an email from Mitchell.

TO: **Natasha Black**

FROM: **Mitchell Schmidt**

SUBJECT: UPDATE

Hey sweetness. I miss you so much. This damn place has shitty reception, I've been trying to reach you for hours. Hope you are okay though. Tell me when you get home.

She smiled and sat down as she typed.

TO: **Mitchell Schmidt**

FROM: **Natasha Black**

SUBJECT: Re-UPDATE

Hey honey. I missed you too. My day was good. No Malibu goddess drama lol!! We can always email if we can't call. I just got home. I want to relax in a nice warm bath.

Natasha stood up and walked to her bathroom. She switched on the water heater and turned on the taps. By the time the tub was full, she would have already had her dinner. She poured in a few drops of her favorite oils and then headed off to the bedroom where she changed into a bathrobe. She then pinned her hair up and headed back to the living room.

"Some music would be good," she thought as she set her favorite playlist on the iPod. *"That's the stuff,"* she thought smiling as the smooth tunes of Sade filled the apartment. She then walked back to the couch where her phone was vibrating. She picked it up and saw that it was yet another email from Mitchell.

TO: Natasha Black

FROM: Mitchell Schmidt

SUBJECT: Re-UPDATE

Ha ha, very funny. I wish I was there with you. I love taking baths with you. You always look so much sexier when your body is covered in that beautifully scented oil and the soap slowly sliding off your body...the thought of it might just make me come back early.

Natasha smiled.

TO: Mitchell Schmidt

FROM: Natasha Black

SUBJECT: Re-UPDATE

Oh I would like you to just throw in the towel. It has been a while since I felt your hardness in my mouth, I miss the way you twitch inside my mouth as my tongue twirls on your pulsating head. I can't wait to have you in my mouth again...

Her erotic thoughts were interrupted by the loud ringing of her door bell. She quickly hit send before she put the phone down and walked to the door.

"Evening, Miss Black," the delivery boy Terry said with a smile.

"Hey there, Terry," she said as she gratefully took the sweet smelling food. "Busy night?" she asked as he handed him a few bills.

"Not really. I'm actually headed home. You were my last delivery," he said.

Is that right?" Natasha said. "I guess then it's a good thing I want to say keep the change," she said with a smile. Terry looked at her and smiled back.

"God bless you, ma'am," he said as he walked away. She smiled as she locked the door and walked back to the couch. She picked her cell phone up but then put it back down, took her laptop from the table and headed to the dining room table. After quickly setting the computer up she opened the bag and took her food out. She took a long deep breath, inhaling the rich aroma of her sweet and sour chicken. She checked her inbox and smiled. Mitchell had already replied.

TO: Natasha Black

FROM: Mitchell Schmidt

SUBJECT: Re-UPDATE

Woman are you trying to get me to come home sooner than I am supposed to? I have to wait for this seminar to be over you know. That's the only way I have even a remote chance of landing this account.

Natasha smiled as she clicked reply. She was wrong. This was far much rewarding than a bath.

TO: Mitchell Schmidt

FROM: Natasha Black

SUBJECT: Re-UPDATE

I do want you back home, I want to give you the best time of your life in more ways than one, baby.

She stood up, quickly walked to the bathroom and turned the taps off. As she slowly made her way back to the dining room, she thought of calling Rita so that she would not have to spend the night alone. But if she did she would not be able to do what her emails got her in the mood for. She walked to the couch and picked her phone up before rushing back to the bathroom.

Once in the bathroom, she undid the long straps that held her bathrobe together and felt a shiver as the cool evening air blew on her skin. She felt her nipples harden as she stepped into the bath. She sat down carefully, trying not to get her phone wet. She looked at the phone and clicked on the new email.

TO: Natasha Black

FROM: Mitchell Schmidt

SUBJECT: Re-UPDATE

Two days, just two days. 48 hours and then I come and lick you dry. After getting you as wet as I possibly can I am going to push myself inside you and listen to you moan and scream because I will make you have the biggest orgasm you ever had and that's a promise. I will work you so hard it will be a surprise if you have any

energy for our honeymoon.

Natasha felt more horny than ever. Mitchell's words although somewhat psychotic made her want to get on him, ride him till she had no more energy. She dreamed of the day he came home. She would probably have to call in sick or something because she did not dream of leaving the house that day.

Just the thought of Mitchell's return made her even wetter. Even though she was in the tub, she knew she was getting wet just from thinking of what she would do to him once he came back. She turned on the showerhead and held it under the water against her pussy. She began moaning as the water's growing pressure splashed hard on her clit. She leaned back as her clitoris became more and more stimulated under the water pressure. She heard herself scream out as she continued to hold the shower head tight. The growing sensitivity in her clitoris made her moan. She wanted to let go of the shower head but at the same time she needed to hold on to it.

"Oh my God…." She thought as she felt her insides burst with intense pressure. She let go of the shower head and closed her eyes and relaxed her body. *"That ought to hold for 48 hours,"* she thought as she picked up her phone again.

TO: Mitchell Schmidt

FROM: Natasha Black

SUBJECT: Re-UPDATE

Shower head fun….Nothing compares to you. I miss you.

She placed the phone on the bathroom counter before holding on to the sides of the tub. The day had been eventful, with some parts of the day being something she wished had not happened but she was happy at the way it ended. Her phone vibrated. She picked it up and scrolled down. It was Mitchell again.

TO: Natasha Black

FROM: Mitchell Schmidt

SUBJECT: Re-UPDATE

Change of plans. Annette Lee from the Las Vegas NSCS office is replacing me in the seminar. I have some 'business' I have to take care of. See you tomorrow evening. I love you.

She smiled and closed her eyes. "*24 hours and counting,*" she thought.

Chapter 4

Natasha looked at the wedding planner in surprise. She could not believe all the weird suggestions the woman was giving her. After she finally agreed to have a wedding planner, she and Rita set up a meeting with the infamous Pam, the woman who was supposed to be magical as far as weddings were concerned. However, the meeting was not going as well as either of them thought. Natasha was getting increasingly irritated at some of the suggestions the woman was making. Apparently theme weddings were the "in thing" and for some reason this woman seemed to think she would fancy a "Christmas" wedding.

"I think that a Schmidt wedding is definitely one you want to couple with the magic of Christmas," Pam Sanders said with a smile. Natasha stared at her in surprise.

"I'm sorry. Pam," Natasha said. "But Christmas is magical on its own," she added matter-of-factly.

"Yes, but the magic of Christmas and the magic of a Schmidt wedding…"

"…okay, I've got to stop you right there," Natasha said holding up her hands at the hyper brunette. "This wedding is my wedding too," she said looking at her. Rita put her hand on Natasha's.

"I think we need to take a little break here," Rita said. "Pam, um, I think Natasha is getting a little worked up because you are treating this as a media oriented thing while it's the biggest day of her life," she said calmly. "I'm sure you understand," she added. Pam took her glasses off and looked at Rita and then Natasha.

"I am sorry if I did anything that would make you feel that way, Miss Black, but I'm sure you understand that Mitchell Schmidt is a kind of a quote unquote "big deal" as far as the entertainment industry is concerned," Pam said. Natasha looked at her in surprise.

"Why? Has Mitchell featured in some Justin Timberlake video I don't know about or something?" she asked, looking at Rita who had raised an eyebrow.

"Well, of course not," Pam answered. "But like Paris Hilton, you come from money and you are instantly a celebrity." Natasha looked at Rita and shrugged.

"I'm sorry Pam. I really thought this would work out," Natasha said putting some bills on the table. "But this was clearly a mistake." She stood up.

"Tasha, don't you think we should maybe sit through the entire meeting?" Rita asked, surprised that for once Natasha was the one eager to end things.

"Rita, I only intend to get married once and this is someone who plans weddings for people who get married a bazillion times," Natasha said angrily. "I'm sorry Pam, but you clearly don't get me," she said more calmly.

"But what about TMZ?" Pam asked looking at Natasha.

"TMZ?" Natasha and Rita asked in unison.

"Being an heir and all, this is a wedding every tabloid wants as a front page story," Pam said. "It is part of my job to ensure you get the highest bidder," she added as Natasha sat back down.

"I'm sorry, did you say bidder?" Rita asked. Pam nodded.

"Are you trying to tell me people will pay to cover my wedding?" Natasha asked in surprise.

"Yes, apart from TMZ, US Weekly and Hollywood Spotter also seem promising," Pam said turning her laptop to face the two women. "US Weekly and Hollywood Spotter both offered five hundred thousand for the ceremony and an extra three hundred for exclusive honeymoon photos. TMZ on the other hand are offering $1.2 million for the same," she said as Natasha and Rita looked at the laptop screen in disbelief. "The others were thinking of raising their bids," she added with a smile.

"Okay. I have heard of ridiculous, but this is it," Rita said, smiling. "Absolutely unbelievable."

"I know. It's actually quite a haggle," Pam said still smiling.

"I can't believe this," Natasha said shaking her head. "I want a simple wedding. A small intimate ceremony," she said looking at Pam. "Maybe I didn't get that across well enough?" she asked, convinced that maybe she had indeed sent the wrong message to the wedding planner.

"Oh honey, you did," Pam said. "But maybe we just need to re-navigate?" she asked looking at Natasha.

"Yes, let's do that," Natasha said standing up again. "Call me when you come up with a new plan," she added walking out.

"Really nice to meet you," Rita said standing up. "Oh, I would go with TMZ, Hollywood Spotter are kind of all propaganda no truth," she added as she quickly followed

Natasha out. "Are you okay, honey?" she asked when she found Natasha leaning on her car. She looked at her best friend who was all worked up.

"TMZ?" Natasha asked looking at Rita. "I am just a public relations officer who happens to work for NSCS," she added. "Where the heck do tabloids play into this equation?" she asked looking at Rita.

"I don't know. But Mitchell is a big deal. You have to admit that," Rita said.

"Not that big a deal," Natasha said frowning.

"Actually, I am surprised he is able to take a poop without the world knowing all about it," Rita said. Natasha smiled at her.

"What am I going to do? I cannot have people who think that Christmas needs any more magic planning my big day," Natasha said, opening her car door.

"We will figure this out," Rita said. "We still have time," she added as she joined her friend in the car.

*****

When Natasha got home that evening, she felt tired and worked up, not just from the meeting with the wedding planner but also having to deal with very unyielding clients. She was expecting to spend some time with Mitchell that evening but he had just called her to cancel, something about a late client meeting that he had to take in Miami that afternoon. She looked at her watch and sighed. It was only seven-thirty. He would probably be on his way back.

She walked to the kitchen and took a bottle of water from the refrigerator before switching the TV on. Her favorite show was on. There was always something about people trying to compete in the kitchen that made her happy. She dropped herself on the couch and held the remote in her hands. After a few minutes, she realized she was not even concentrating on the show. All she wanted was just to be in bed, but she didn't want to sleep without talking to Mitchell.

"Maybe I should email him," she thought as she turned her laptop on.

Hey baby. I hope your meeting went well. My day on the other hand, horrible. Pam Sanders who is supposed to be Wonder Woman is a sham. She was talking about a Christmas wedding because apparently Christmas needs more magic than the birth of our Lord. And did you know about tabloids bidding to cover the wedding? I mean, what's up with that?

She looked at her screen and sighed before she took a few gulps of water from her bottle. She heard a beep from her computer just as a balloon popped up at the top left corner of her screen.

To: Natasha Black

From: Mitchell Schmidt

SUBJECT: Re-UPDATE

Hi honey. My meeting did go well, very well actually. The company has a new client, some business mogul from South Africa. I am sorry your day went so badly. I really thought you and Pam would hit it off. And yeah, I had heard some buzz about the bids but I didn't think anything of it. I thought it was a rumor but LOL.

Natasha looked at the message and smiled. Mitchell would never type in LOL…unless of course he was under the influence of…well he never did. She looked at the screen and begun typing again.

To: Mitchell Schmidt

From: Natasha Black

SUBJECT: Re-UPDATE

Did you just type in LOL? How long was your day? Anyway, about the tabloids, did this happen with your first wedding? I hate to ask this but I really feel that our wedding should be a small intimate affair, something that we have control over and not for the entire world to moon over. It makes me feel like the world expects so much of me. And by the way, me and Pam never came to an understanding. All her suggestions were just….I was not feeling them.

She hit send and leaned back in her chair. Somehow, today nothing seemed to cheer her up. Not even the clumsy chefs on Hell's Kitchen. She looked at her watch again and sighed. This was definitely one of those days she wished Mitchell was around. Her laptop beeped again and she noticed the message icon. She clicked on it and smiled again.

To: Natasha Black

From: Mitchell Schmidt

SUBJECT: Re-UPDATE

I am sorry about Pam. I really thought the two of you would click. Maybe you didn't tell her exactly what you wanted. She only probably dealt with things the way she did with all her other high end clients. I won't get back until late, so I might not see you tonight. I miss you so much though, baby.

She smiled as she typed her final message for the night before finally stretching out on the couch. Just then, she heard her doorbell.

"That's odd," she thought as she got up. *"I am not expecting anyone tonight."* She walked to the front door and looked through the peep hole. She smiled when she saw Rita standing outside with a bottle of wine.

"What are you doing here?" she asked after opening the door.

"Well, I'm your best friend and I feel you shouldn't be alone after that meeting from hell," Rita said walking in. "And I have liquid therapy," she added, raising the bottle of wine. Natasha smiled as she closed the door. Just then she noticed that Rita was wearing in a satin evening dress and a pair of red peep toe heels to match the coat she was wearing. If she didn't know any better she would have thought that Rita was on a date just before she got here.

"Honey, did you and Dave have plans tonight?" Natasha asked, looking at Rita who was now making her way to the living room.

"Actually yes," Rita answered as she sat down. "But he had a business meeting today that ran late. We missed our reservation," she added. Natasha walked to the kitchen and came back with two glasses and a corkscrew.

"I don't know whether to be happy or sad that I was your second choice," Natasha said as she sat down. Rita smiled and took the corkscrew from her hands.

"I brought wine. Just be happy am here," Rita said as she worked the corkscrew. Natasha laughed. "So, that's the sad story of why am alone tonight. What's your excuse? Where's Mitchell?" she asked as she poured two glasses of wine.

"I'm afraid we are birds of a feather," Natasha said taking a glass. "He had a meeting with a prospective client out of town. Some high end guy from South Africa. Apparently the meeting went well," she added before taking a long sip from her glass.

"Really? Did the guy book them a room later?" Rita asked smiling.

"Guess so. That's the only explanation why his flight got late," Natasha said laughing. Rita laughed and took a sip from her own glass before turning her attention to the TV.

"Hell's Kitchen," Rita said. "Do you still watch this shit?" she asked making Natasha look at the TV herself.

"Yeah, I do," Natasha said shrugging her shoulders. "But for some reason I just can't seem to enjoy it tonight," she added.

"Okay sweetie. You need to get this wedding planning situation out of your head before it drives you mad," Rita said. Natasha put her glass on the table and buried her face in her hands.

"What am I supposed to do?" she asked looking at Rita. "I am too busy to plan my own wedding. I cannot find a planner whose thoughts sync with mine," she added looking at Rita. Suddenly her eyes lit up as if she had a brilliant idea.

"What? Why are you looking at me like that?" Rita asked. She knew that look. She had seen it on her best friend's face so many times before, always just before she had great news, or shocking news. She felt her face flush as she looked at Natasha, who was now smiling broadly. "Tasha, you are freaking me out," she said. *The wine couldn't be that strong. It's only aged five years,"* she thought still looking at Natasha.

"I just had the best idea ever!" Natasha squealed, her eyes beaming with delight.

"I'm afraid to ask what the news is," Rita said.

"You planned almost all events I know. High school homecoming, prom, fire and ice ball…" Her voice trailed off as she bounced up and down on the couch excitedly. Rita shook her head.

"Oh no, I am not doing it," she said still shaking her head.

"Come on, Rita. Why not?" Natasha asked taking her friend's hands in hers. "You have planned every successful event I know," she added.

"That was high school, Tasha," Rita said still not believing that Natasha would ask her to do this. "If your wedding turns out to be disastrous, you would never forgive me," she said looking into Natasha's eyes.

"But you get me," Natasha said. "You know exactly what I like, and what I don't. Who's a better person to do this than you?"

Rita looked at her and shook her head again.

"Honey, this is YOUR wedding," Rita said. "The biggest day in your life. What if I mess this up? And who is going to be on maid of honor duty anyway?"

"Think of it as a wedding gift," Natasha said. "And you still get to be the maid of honor. Only a more awesome one," she added rubbing her hands together anxiously. "Please," she said making a sad face. Rita looked at her and took a deep breath.

"Okay, I'll make you a deal," Rita said after taking another long deep breath. Natasha looked at her eagerly and nodded excitedly. "I will be a liaison between you and Pam," she said looking into Natasha's eyes. Rita quickly held her hand up when Natasha opened her mouth to protest. "As you said, I get you but I cannot in good faith take on a task this great knowing full well that I have never planned a wedding. I do not want my best friend's big day to be my practice test," she said. "So, I will take the role of being your voice to Pam Sanders so you can have the wedding you deserve," she added with a smile as she gave Natasha's hands a firm squeeze.

"You would do that for me?" Natasha said in a small voice. Rita smiled.

"Who else would I do it for if not for you?" Rita asked as she looked into Natasha's eyes.

"I really don't know what to say," Natasha said as she felt tears well up in her eyes. Rita looked into her eyes and wrapped her arms around her.

"When the time comes and maybe me and Dave get to where you and Mitchell are, I intend on calling in a few favors," she said smiling. Natasha smiled as she pulled away.

"So we are planning on a wedding soon, huh?"" she asked as she looked at Rita.

"Hey, you are in way over your head," Rita said reaching for her glass.

"Come on," Natasha said. "You just admitted that you intend on walking down the aisle with him some day," she added.

"No, I most certainly did not," Rita protested.

"Rita and Dave, sitting in a tree," Natasha said playfully clapping her hands. Rita looked at her in mock anger.

"Tasha stop it, how old are you?" she said. "And this is only your first glass? Girl you have terrible tolerance," she added taking a sip of her wine. Natasha wrapped her arms around Rita, surprising her.

"I am just so happy for you," she squealed. "You finally have someone who you genuinely like and he is with you out of his own free will," she added. Rita looked at her in surprise.

"What is that supposed to mean?" Rita asked. Natasha smiled and placed a reassuring hand on her shoulder.

"Honey, you are beautiful and hot and everything but you and Leila Ali have one thing in common," Natasha said. "You would kick anyone's ass if they even tried to threaten you in any way. Physically, spiritually, intellectually…."

"..Shut up," Rita cut her short, laughing. "I don't think I'm that bad," she added putting her glass on the table.

"Sweetie, I am sure you will be the Madea Simmons of our generation once we turn 70," Natasha said as Rita's phone buzzed on the couch. She looked at it and frowned.

"I have a meeting with some art collectors tomorrow morning," Rita said. "I should be in bed." She stood up. She staggered a little bit before Natasha held her steady. "I should not be driving tonight," Rita said. Natasha looked at her and nodded in agreement.

"Sleep over!" Natasha squealed again. Rita looked at her and shook her head.

"Seriously, your alcohol tolerance is terrible," she said.

"I don't care about that. My best friend is sleeping over!" Natasha said switching off the TV. "Come on," she said taking Rita's hand. Rita pulled her hand away and looked at her in surprise.

"What are you doing?" she asked.

"Taking you to my room," Natasha answered looking at her in surprise. Rita shook her head.

"Nah ah, I am taking the guest room," she said walking towards the guest room.

"Why? Don't you love me anymore?" Natasha asked in a mock child's voice.

"I am not sleeping in the same place where you and Mitchell have done the nasty," Rita called out before closing the door after her. Natasha smiled.

"I wonder if I should tell her that we have also done it in the

guest room," she wondered as she walked to her bedroom.

Chapter 5

Natasha was not sure what she heard, whether or not it was part of her dream. She smiled as she felt a warm sensation trailing her shoulder blade and then up her neck. It was such a great feeling, she was loving every moment of it even though she had no idea what was going on. For some reason, it seemed as if she was being licked by a dog, her dog....wait, she didn't own a dog. She jolted up, her heart threatening to jump out of her chest and saw Mitchell holding his palm over her mouth. She was not sure whether to scream or not...all she knew was that at that particular moment, she was confused.

"I am going to take my hand away from your mouth, but you have to promise to stay still," he said in a whisper. Natasha nodded as Mitchell pulled his hand away, slowly. "Hey there," he said smiling down at her. She looked at him and smiled back, not caring what he was doing sneaking in like a cat burglar.

"What time is it?" she whispered.

"I don't know, three, four," Mitchell whispered back.

"What are you doing here so late?" she asked as Mitchell kicked off his shoes and snuggled in next to her.

"Are you complaining?" he asked kissing her forehead. She smiled and closed her eyes as he planted a soft, warm kiss on her forehead.

"No, not at all," she said turning to look at him.

"I had to see you, that's all," he said. "It's been what, four days?" he asked, still in a whisper. She nodded.

"Yeah. Sometimes I wonder whether we really are in the same office," she said looking at him. Natasha smiled.

"I know. It kills me sometimes," he said. "By the way, why are we whispering?" he asked. Natasha laughed.

"Rita's asleep in the guest room," she answered.

"But your walls are sound proofed," he said. Natasha looked up at him. She could barely see him in the moonlight.

"How would you know that?" she asked.

"Because I knew the tenants of this place before it became a residential area," Mitchell said smiling. "It was a recording studio," he added.

"The whole building? All nineteen floors?" she asked in surprise.

"No of course not," Mitchell said laughing. "Just the floor you are on," he added.

"Oh that's so cool," she said silently. "Wait, why am I still whispering?" she asked in a normal voice. Mitchell laughed.

"Search me," he said. "So what exactly happened with Pam? I thought you guys would hit it off," he said.

"Seriously Mitchell, that woman thinks she is planning the royal wedding or something," she said looking up at him. "What the hell is a Christmas wedding?" she asked leaning on Mitchell's outstretched arm.

"Christmas weddings are quite nice. You get little trees and gifts…"

"…the only gifts I want under any tree during Christmas are my Christmas gifts," Natasha said, cutting him short. "What happened to our little intimate event?" she asked. Even in the dim light, Mitchell could tell that she was frowning.

"We are going to have whatever you want," he said kissing her forehead. Natasha looked up at him.

"You don't mind?" she asked. Mitchell shook his head. "Even if I plan an outrageous rainbow colored wedding?" she asked. Mitchell smiled but still shook his head.

"It's your day, you do whatever makes you happy," he said. "And so long as you don't pick out an outrageous outfit," he added smiling.

"Then you won't mind that I have appointed Rita as my official wedding coordinator?" she said.

Mitchell reached for the bedside lamp and switched it on. Natasha squinted as her eyes got accustomed to the sudden bright light. *"Now he wants to see me,"* she thought shielding her eyes from the glare of the bedside lamp.

"What does that even mean?" he asked, looking at her.

"Pam Sanders thinks I am the next Angelina Jolie or J-Lo," she stated. "I need her to understand my preference and I need her to give me the wedding that I have always wanted. Not some reused royal wedding she did." Mitchell could hear contempt in her voice.

"That meeting went really bad, huh?" he said looking at her. She rolled her eyes and sat up.

"You have no idea," she said leaning against the headboard.

"And the fact that I had seen Jay yesterday with all his you-really-wanna-marry-Mitchell gimmicks…" Mitchell put his hand up cutting her short mid-sentence.

"You talked to Jay?" he asked looking at her. Natasha felt her heart beat faster. She had totally and completely forgotten that she had yet to tell Mitchell of the talk she had with Jay.

"Yeah, we were having lunch…"

"…you had lunch with him?" he asked cutting her short again.

"No, Mitchell," she said. "Jeez, relax. Me, Rita and Stacy were having lunch and he found us there," she added. She was a bit happy that he was jealous.

"What did he want this time?" he asked passively. Natasha took a long deep breath.

"He asked me if I was sure about marrying you," she said. "And that he was still available should I change my mind or anything," she added silently. She looked over at Mitchell who was breathing heavily. She knew that a lot of things pissed him off and Jay, well, he just happened to top the list. "Baby," she said placing a hand on his clenched fist. "You okay?" she asked in a quiet voice. There was sadness in her voice as well as concern. She hated that this was happening, especially now. Especially since she had not seen Mitchell for so long.

"I hate it that he gets to me so much," Mitchell said taking Natasha's hand in his.

"I know, but don't let him get to you," she said. "I'm here. That's all that matters," she added resting her head on his shoulder. She gasped when he pulled her away from his shoulder. It was all so sudden; some strands of her hair had actually gotten caught up in his zipper. She looked into his eyes as he held the back of her head.

"You are mine," he said in a hushed voice, almost a whisper.

"And you are mine," she said looking into his eyes. She gasped again when he suddenly pulled her down and got on top of her in one swift move. She looked up at him, in fear but somewhat turned on as he looked down at her. He kissed her briefly before he moved his attention to her neck and chin. She smiled up at him.

"I missed that," she said. "Do that again," she said to him. Mitchell smiled.

"What this?" he asked as he kissed her neck. Natasha moaned as she felt his warm lips on her neck. "And this?" he asked again as he continued trailing kisses down her neck. His hand went down her torso, feeling her hardening nipples press against his palm.

"Yeah, like that," she said as she felt him teasing her already hard nipples.

"What about this?" he asked as he slowly ran a hand up her bare thigh. She closed her eyes and arched her back as she felt his hand getting dangerously close to her core.

"Yeah, baby," she moaned. "Yes, just like…" Her words were cut short by Mitchell claiming her lips in a long sensual kiss. She kissed him back long and hard, never intending to let him go. Mitchell brought his body on top of hers as he kissed her. His cold belt pressed on her tummy against the sheer fabric of her lacy night dress. Mitchell pulled away from her, breaking their kiss. She looked up at him, her eyes full of longing. He cupped her face and brought his face down again only this time he did not kiss her lips. Instead he kissed her neck, her chin and continued to pull the sides of her nightdress off her shoulders, exposing her full breasts. She felt a shudder go through her body as he kissed her breast, proceeding down to take her full nipples inside his hot mouth. She put a hand over her mouth to keep in the screams that threatened to escape her lips as Mitchell circled her nipples with his increasingly hot and wet tongue.

Mitchell continued sucking on her nipple as he gave her other nipple equal attention from his flicking fingertips. She tried reaching for his crotch but he held her hand down as he continued sucking on her nipple. He pulled away from her and she opened her eyes, thankful that his erotic torture was over. Her relief was short lived as he took in her other nipple, only to suck as hard if not harder than he had sucked on her at first. She gave in to her pleasure and began moaning. She was still moaning when she felt Mitchell's lips pulling away from her again.

"You are clearly over the top and I have only just began," he said smiling. She opened her mouth to respond but he was quick enough to silence her with a long kiss. She wrapped her warms around him but again he managed to free himself from her grip, moving lower on her body. He touched her thigh through the soft lacy material and smiled when he heard her breathing heavily. He slowly raised the fabric over her legs. She shivered slightly when the cool evening air blew across her naked skin. She raised her head to look at Mitchell who was now slowly kissing her leg, working his way to her soft and sensitive inner thigh. She wanted to hold his head against her so much at that moment. She let her head drop back to the pillow as he slowly caressed her slit with his finger. He was right. She was already wet and judging by the way he was taking things slow and the fact that he was still fully dressed, he had only just began.

Mitchell smiled as he pulled her panties to one side exposing her bare pussy. He could tell that she had been to the salon just a few days before. Her pussy looked invitingly smooth. Her soft lips were slightly bathed by the juices that seemed to flow endlessly from between her legs. He looked at her and smiled before he slowly lowered his head and kissed her warm lips. She heard him whimper as he planted soft kisses on her wet lips and then back to her thighs. He knew she was burning already. Burning with desire for him. Burning with a passion that yearned to be quenched, a fire that longed to have its flames stilled as soon as he possibly could. He kissed his way from one thigh to the other while intentionally avoiding her warm inviting pussy. When he finally used his fingers to peel her panties away from her, he could hear her breathing a sigh of relief. He spread her knees and looked at her now drenched pussy. He looked at her blushing face and smiled.

"Tell me what you want," he said in a low voice. She looked up at him, shaking from desire.

"I want you," she said her voice shaking. He smiled and buried herself in between her legs, attacking her distended clit with his tongue. He sucked on her very core, making her squirm on the bed. With one hand on her tummy, he held her down as he continued sucking on her clit. Just when she thought she had it all, she gasped when she felt his tongue buried deep inside her. She grabbed the sheets in a bid not to scream out as he used his tongue to expertly drive her wild, pushing it in and out of her as if he were a machine.

"Baby…no more…please," she pleaded as Mitchell slowed down. His tongue was still inside her even as she pleaded as if Mitchell held her life in his hands. He slowly brought himself up and kissed her.

"That's how delicious you are," he said after pulling away. He kissed her again as he kept a hand steadily over one of her breasts. "Is that what you wanted?" he asked looking at her. She shook her head and kissed him again.

"That and much more," she said in almost a whisper.

"What will you do for me?" he asked looking down at her. She smiled and rolled over, resting on top of him.

"I want to take your shirt off," she said, slowly undoing the zipper of his jacket. He looked up at her in silence as she slowly undid the buttons on his shirt, exposing his well built chest. She held his hands and pulled him up before pushing the shirt and jacket off his shoulder.

"What now?" he asked looking into her eyes. She gently pushed him back down and brought her head down to plant small kisses on his pecs. She trailed her kisses down his torso and then back up to his chin. She could already feel his cock pressing against her crotch with great urgency. She smiled as she continued kissing his neck and chin. She worked her way up to his ear and gently kissed his ear lobe. She knew that always drove him wild and that was exactly what she wanted to do. He was exactly where she wanted him to be. She smiled as she gently kissed his ear lobe and then slowly ran her tongue over his ear. She smiled when she heard his first pleasurable moan and pulled back. She looked down at him and gave him a quick kiss before moving on down his tummy. She undid his belt and fly and then pulled his pants off. His cock was definitely in need of some service, the same service she had wanted to give him the whole time he was away. She pulled his boxers off, revealing his pulsating cock. She smiled as she gently rolled the boxer shorts off his legs.

"Not fair," he said. "you are still dressed," he added pointing at Natasha's lacy nightie even though it was at her waist. She smiled and pulled the nightie over her head and threw it down. She looked at him and smiled.

"Happy?' she asked as he raised his hands up to touch her breasts. She shook her head and pinned his arms to his sides. "My turn," she whispered as she brought her head down and continued kissing his tummy. His breathing got heavier and heavier as he felt her lips getting dangerously close to his cock. "Tell me what *you* want," she said looking at him. He looked at her in both surprise and a bit of anger. *"So this is how it feels when your own tables are turned,"* he thought looking up at her, wondering why she would use his own words against him, especially so soon.

"I want you," he said. She smiled and lowered her head. He moaned as he felt her run her wet tongue over his cock head. He bucked his hips indicating that he would like a bit more than what she was offering at that moment. She held him down and looked at him again.

"Like that?" she asked smiling. *"What a cock tease,"* he thought as he looked at her.

"More," he said. She smiled and took him inside her mouth again. this time, sucking him in long strokes, letting her tongue swirl over his head as he sucked hard on him. He moaned and whimpered as she went on, showing no signs of stopping any time soon. Mitchell was worried. If she didn't stop soon, he was going to explode. "Baby…" he moaned.

As if she read his mind, she withdrew him from his mouth and straddled him. They both moaned as she lowered herself onto his waiting length. She looked into his eyes, panting. He held her around her waist and kissed her. "You are a cock tease," he said in a whisper.

"You started it," she said as she felt him begin to move in and out of her. He did not even go slow like he normally would to give her pussy time to stretch. All he knew was what he wanted and what he wanted was to be buried deep inside her. And that was exactly what he was doing. She tried holding in her moans as much as she could but she couldn't. She held her hand tightly over her mouth as Mitchell began dropping her onto his waiting cock. She whimpered in silence as she buried her face in his neck. He suddenly stopped, making her want to scream out in agony.

"I want to hear you," he said as he caressed her back. "Moan for me baby," he said as he began dropping her onto his cock again. She suddenly let loose and began moaning loudly as he went on, fucking her with great intent. He suddenly grabbed her legs and straightened them before laying her on her back. She looked up at him as he held her under her knees. She immediately knew what this meant. She suddenly felt a powerful thrust that literally knocked air out of her mouth. She looked up at him but what or who she saw was something else. Mitchell was kneeling in front of her thrusting into her like she was some kind of fuck doll. She could no longer hold in her moans. She cried out and held on to the sheets as Mitchell drove himself inside her. His thrusts did not last much longer before she felt her walls giving in, quaking as her orgasm ripped through her. She cried out as Mitchell struggled to keep his cock inside her through her violent orgasm. She tried holding still as she felt another force, a foreign strength going through her repeatedly and she knew Mitchell had just met his release. She opened her eyes to look at him as he poured himself into her, load after load before finally collapsing on her.

"You are going to kill me one day," he said panting. Natasha smiled and stroked his neck.

"Death by pussy," she said. "I think that's an honorable way to go," she added as she felt him slipping out of her.

Chapter 6

Five months down the line, Natasha knew that making Rita her liaison between herself and Pam Sanders was the best choice ever. In just four months, Rita had put together the wedding of a lifetime. She had dealt with all the stresses that came with the seamstresses, wedding gown, bridesmaids' dresses, venues…in short, she had done what most planners would have called impossible. She smiled as she looked at what Rita called the "Wedding Manifest." The manifest had every little fact laid out in extreme detail. There were photos of the hotel, reception area, seating arrangements, visual testimonials of the wedding decorating committee, caterer's numbers….it was all there. She looked up at Rita, more impressed than amused. She had decided to meet up with her, Mitchell and Leo for the last time as the wedding was just days away.

"This is…simply amazing," Natasha said, smiling at Rita who was busy biting into a cookie. Rita looked at her and Mitchell and smiled.

"All in a few months work," she said. "So, all you have to do today is just relax. I am taking her off your hands, pamper her and shit and you do the same," she added looking at Mitchell.

"Don't worry about that," Leo said. "Me and Dave have got plans for this gentleman right here," he added playfully slapping Mitchell's shoulder. Natasha looked at the two of them suspiciously.

"What?" Mitchell asked looking at her.

"Are there going to be strippers?" she asked looking into Mitchell's eyes. Mitchell raised his hands in defense.

"Hey, I'm the groom. Whatever Leo has planned is beyond my control," Mitchell said.

"Tasha Black, I never figured you to be the jealous type," Leo said smiling. Even though it had only been a couple of months since he met Natasha, he felt like he knew her already. Like Mitchell said, she was so easy to get along with. To Leo, Natasha was like a little sister since she and his younger sister Bess had so much in common. Natasha smiled at Leo and then looked at Mitchell.

"I am not," she said leaning close to her fiancé. "But she had better give you value for your money because the wedding night might last a whole lot longer than the actual honeymoon," she added in a sexy voice not giving a damn about the fact that there were other people at the table. Rita and Leo exchanged glances and laughed.

"Did I get this wrong or did your wife to be just give you a go ahead to have a stripper at your stag night?" Leo asked. Mitchell smiled and slid an arm around Natasha's small waist.

"That's exactly what happened," Mitchell said before giving Natasha a kiss on her forehead.

Leo looked at Mitchell with an ounce of jealousy and then looked at Natasha.

"Tasha, baby, I am not as rich as Mitchell here but trust me I can rock your world so much more than he ever did on his best day," he said winking at her. Rita smiled at Mitchell.

"Whoa dude. Looks like you are about to be single again," she said to Mitchell in what was meant to be a whisper.

"I highly doubt it, but what's your point?" Natasha asked

smiling.

"You don't want to marry Mitchell. There are too many Schmidts in the world as it is. Marry me," Leo said in mock seriousness. "I could do with a girl who lets me have strippers," he added. Natasha looked at him and then at Mitchell.

"Watch it Hayes, I might just take you up in your offer," Natasha said smiling at Leo. "But let's just see how this one works out first," she added giving Mitchell a slight nudge with her elbow. Leo frowned but then his face lit up again as he looked at Rita.

"Birds of a feather?" he asked looking at Rita just as Dave walked in. Rita gave Leo a smile before giving Dave a huge bear hug. The two then exchanged a brief kiss before finally sitting down.

"And we are the ones being accused of PDA," Mitchell whispered to Natasha. He was loud enough for even Leo to hear him. The three exchanged glances and smiled.

"Alas, I might have made my proposal a bit late," Leo said in an old English accent. Everyone except for Dave laughed.

"I have the distinct feeling that I'm missing something," Dave said looking at Rita.

"Oh baby, you are not missing anything at all," she said smiling up at him. His boyish looks appealed even to Natasha who sat snuggled in the comfort of Mitchell's arms. "Anyway, Dave, you already know Tasha and Mitch. This is Leo, Mitchell's best friend and the best man," Rita said as Leo and Dave shook hands.

"Pleasure my man," Leo said. "You came in just in time," he added with a smile.

"Just in time for what?" Dave asked looking at him and then at Rita.

"Let's just say you would have been the fifth wheel here," Natasha said smiling at Dave.

"Well, then I guess it's a good thing I'm already here," Dave said.

"Looks like you will be having company soon enough, though," Mitchell said smiling. Leo looked at him questioningly and then at Natasha who was pointing at the entrance. Leo gasped when he saw a beautiful curvaceous woman talking to the maître d'.

"Please tell me you guys know her," Leo said under his breath.

"Actually, we do," Rita said. "That's the other bridesmaid, your escort," she added with a smile. Leo was still looking at the woman who was wearing a royal blue wrap around sleeveless dress and a pair of black silver studded sandals. Her long black straightened hair was pulled back in a loose bun and she wore a pair of huge sunglasses. As she walked towards them, everyone at the table could tell that Leo was getting increasingly excited.

"He probably has a bead of sweat on his forehead by now," Mitchell whispered to Natasha as the curvaceous woman walked towards them.

"Whatever you do to stay looking so damn young, I need to get that for when I am in my forties," Rita said stepping down from her stool to give the woman a hug.

"Girl. I already told you what it is," the woman said smiling as she pulled away from Rita. "You must be Dave, " she said shaking Dave's hand. "Why so formal? You are already family," she said pulling Dave closer for a hug. A shocked Dave looked at her as he nervously wrapped his arms around Natasha's cousin.

"Bride and groom," she said looking at Natasha and Mitchell who were now on their feet. Natasha smiled and gave her cousin a tight squeeze like she would never let go.

"Hey Mona," Natasha said as Mitchell took his turn in hugging Mona. "Guess we'll have to wait for another wedding in the family so that I can see you again," she added with an evil grin. Mona pulled away from Mitchell and placed a reassuring hand on Natasha's shoulder.

"You know I would see you more if I could but that place…" she paused and took a deep breath. "And there's Dash and his school," Mona added. "But I'm thinking of moving closer to home if you know what I mean," she added winking at Natasha.

"Where is Dashiell anyway? It's been a minute," Natasha said as she sat down.

"Somewhere around this damned hotel. Nana Estelle is with him," Mona answered. "The woman can't get enough of that boy but I ain't complaining," she said as she turned her attention to Leo, who had remained quiet all this time obviously taken aback by her strong presence. Mitchell cleared his throat, perhaps to get Leo's attention.

"Leo Hayes, this is Mona Simone Daniel, Natasha's cousin," he said. "Mona, Leo, my best friend," he added as Leo shook Mona's hand.

"So you did find me a good looking escort, Tasha," Mona said taking her glasses off just in time for Leo to feast his eyes on her warm piercing brown eyes. "Very nice to meet you," she said as she smiled at Leo.

"Believe me, the pleasure is all mine," Leo said still looking into Mona's intense eyes.

"So, what's on the menu today?" Mona asked taking a seat next to Leo. "Because trust me child I have three days away from that damned law firm and I can't wait to burn this baby up," she said with a clap of her hands.

"Well, today is the last day the boys have with us," Natasha said.

"Yeah, sadly," Leo said looking at Mona. "Apparently you ladies have to do some spa thing or something," he added with a smile.

"Oooh, that's of major importance. We got to look good for ya'll," Mona said with a smile.

"I don't think you have a problem there," Leo said looking at her. The other two couples quickly exchanged glances.

"He works fast," Dave whispered to Rita, Mitchell and Natasha.

"Tell me about it," Mitchell said shaking his head.. He rubbed his hands and stood up. "The sooner we get started, the better. Otherwise, we might be the ones getting mani-pedis," he said as he pulled Leo to his feet. Leo gave him a look of disapproval.

"Am in 704, maybe we could catch up for a night cap," Leo

said looking at Mona.

"Looking forward to it," Mona said as the three boys walked away. Rita looked at Mona in surprise.

"Man, you are really on a major rebound, aren't you?" she asked as Mona moved closer to Natasha. Mona looked at Rita and smiled.

"The rebound period is already over sister. I just need a man to oil up the old machines," Mona said. Rita and Natasha looked at each other and laughed.

"Same old Mona," Rita said. "How is Dash dealing with the whole divorce thing?" she asked.

"Thank God it happened when he was old enough to understand everything," Mona said. "He knows me and Pete love him but we just can't stay under the same roof. So he gets to spend two weekends with me and the other two with Pete. We alternate the weekdays," she added.

"Smart kid," Rita said as Stacy walked towards them. Mona smiled as Stacy took a seat next to Natasha.

"Everything is set, Tasha. Felicia Kane's advertising is underway and the two new projects are already being looked at by legal. Everything should be set by the time you come back from your honeymoon," she said looking at her iPad. Natasha looked at Rita and smiled.

"Well, hello little elf," Mona said smiling. Stacy looked up from her iPad and her face flushed a bright red.

"I'm sorry, I didn't see you there," she said in a shaky voice.

"Aren't you a sweetie," Mona said beaming, still looking at a red faced Stacy. Natasha took the iPad from Stacy's hand and put it in her bag.

"Stacy, as your boss I command that you let loose and have fun," she said. "This is Mona Daniel, she's my cousin. Mona, this is Stacy, my friend and also my assistant," she added as Mona smiled at Stacy.

"You are quite the busy bee," Mona said. Stacy nodded.

"I don't like leaving any stone unturned," Stacy said.

"Well, your boss has officially given you the weekend off," Rita said smiling at her. "Just for three days, act like Natasha and Mitchell are not your bosses," she added. Stacy frowned.

"I don't really know if I can do that," Stacy said. "They do command quite a strong presence you know," she added. Mona laughed.

"Ignore them, girl," Mona said as she looked at Stacy's full chest. "Are those real?" she asked pointing at Stacy's breasts that were fully visible in the sleeveless dress she wore. Stacy's face reddened again.

"Mona!" Rita and Natasha said in unison. Mona looked at them innocently.

"What? I have never seen a white woman with knockers like those," Mona said as if what she had just asked was the most normal thing in the world. "Can I touch them?" she asked still looking at Stacy who was looking back at her with her mouth slightly gaped.

MONA!" Rita and Natasha said again.

"Seriously guys, no homo. I just want to know what real ones feel like," Mona said. Rita and Natasha looked at her in disbelief.

"*We* all have real ones," Rita said staring at Mona, still shocked.

"Yeah, but we are black women. She's white with great knockers…God-given," Mona said trying to justify her point.

"Never mind her," Natasha said to Stacy, her arm still draped firmly around her shoulders.

"Oh holy hell," Stacy finally spoke up.

"Okay, it's not that bad. I am straight," Mona said leaning back in her chair.

"It's not you," Stacy said looking at the entrance. "It's *that*," she said pointing towards the doorway. The three looked up to see a slender blonde haired woman walking towards them.

"Now those I can tell are implants," Mona said to Natasha who was too busy trying to recall where she had seen the blonde to actually notice Mona's highly inappropriate comment.

"And so we meet," the blonde said when she finally got to their table. "Stacy, still sucking up to the mistresses I see," she added looking at Stacy. Natasha looked at Stacy and then at Rita.

"I'm sorry but I do not appreciate people being rude to my friends," Natasha said firmly.

"You got one that stands up for you," the woman said smiling.

"Who the fuck is this?" Mona asked looking up at he blonde.

"Lisa Maslow," Stacy said.

"Formerly Lisa Maslow Schmidt," the blonde said stretching out her hand to shake Natasha's hand.

"Mitchell's ex?" Rita asked, more of exclaimed actually.

"Can I have a few minutes with the bride, ladies?" Lisa said looking at Stacy, Rita and Mona.

"Please bitch, whatever you have to say…" Mona started saying before Natasha touched her hand.

"I got this," Natasha said calmly.

"Nah ah, we ain't leaving you with this psycho bitch," Rita said standing up. "How did you even know which hotel we were at?" she asked angrily.

"Please. It's Mitchell Schmidt getting married," Lisa said. "There are lot of people on this side of the Hamptons that are willing to give you information for a couple of hundred bucks," Lisa added with a smile.

"Seriously guys, I got this," Natasha said. Rita looked at her, unsure.

"That's the same thing you said when Jay…"

"…I am getting married in a couple of days. No blonde airhead is going to ruin that," Natasha said cutting her short, loud enough for Lisa to hear. Rita, Mona and Stacy slowly walked away as Stacy mumbled something like, "every time I am around there is a weird case of the ex."

Page 245

"So, Lisa, something I can help you with?" Natasha asked sitting down. She crossed her legs and leaned back in her chair. She was wearing a strapless maxi that not only showed off her great curves, but also gave people an excellent view of her generous cleavage, her *real* God given cleavage.

"Actually, it's what I can do for you," Lisa said smiling. "Do you mind if I sit down?" she asked.

"Suit yourself," Natasha said giving her a cold hard stare.

"I know this is a bit intrusive, but has Mitch asked you to sign a pre-nup yet?" Lisa asked. Natasha smiled.

"You're right, that is none of your business," Natasha said. Lisa smiled and tucked a strand of hair behind her ear.

"I'm really sorry about this, but you know we women that Mitchell hopes to wrong in his lifetime ought to stick together," Lisa said leaning forward. Natasha could hardly believe her ears.

"I hate to break this to you, Lisa," Natasha stated. "But you ceased being Mitchell's woman the day your divorce was finalized," she added, giving her the same cold smile she had earlier given her.

"I know this is a bit offensive to you but I just want to make sure you will be taken care of in case this whole thing goes to the dogs," Lisa said. Natasha looked at her in disbelief. This woman had some nerve.

"What makes you think it will go to the dogs?" she asked.

"Well, look at me Natasha. I am every man's dream," Lisa said standing up and turning around. *'Yeah, every man except for*

Mitchell," she thought as she looked at Lisa. "And he could not hold *all this* down," Lisa added. Natasha laughed cynically as she took her bag and zipped it up.

"Lisa, the only reason you and Mitch didn't work out is because you couldn't hold those damn long legs together," she said. "Yeah, he told me all about that and so much more like you going psycho on him and shit," she added when Lisa's eyes grew wide. "But let me tell you one thing. You can come to the wedding but so help me God if you try anything, I will shove my foot so far up your ass that even if you ever get children, they won't be able to sit down till they're at least ten. You hear me?" she said standing up. She surprised herself that she maintained her cool even though her words were highly violent in nature. By this time, her cousin, Stacy and Rita were already making their way back to the table.

"Is everything okay here?" Mona asked staring daggers at a dumbfounded Lisa.

"Everything's just fine," Natasha said. "We have an appointment at the spa, ladies. Lisa," she said as she began walking out.

"You better watch yourself bitch. I'm from The Bronx," Mona said in a threatening tone. The four walked away leaving a scared, tongue-tied Lisa at the table.

"Mona, you are not from The Bronx," Natasha said giggling.

"It feels good telling people that. It commands some respect," Mona said smiling.

"You are preaching to the choir, sister," Rita said giving Mona a high five. Stacy giggled.

"I don't think I have ever seen her that quiet or white in my life," Stacy said. Mona put an arm around Stacy's shoulder and smiled at her.

"Hang out with us more, we'll teach you how to instill the fear of God in people," she said. "So seriously, can I touch them? Just a light squeeze?" Mona said again. Stacy looked up at her shocked all over again. Natasha and Rita jerked their heads to look at Mona, still not believing she had not dropped the topic.

"MONA!" The two yelled in unison.

Chapter 7

On the eve of their wedding, Mitch and Natasha had the entire bridal party fooled that they would not see each other. But for some reason, like two sex crazed teenagers, they just had to sneak out of their rooms. Natasha peeped out of her room, thanking God that Rita was downstairs in Dave's room doing God knows what. She tiptoed quietly past Leo's room and knew exactly what was happening. There were uhs and ohs being uttered and that could only mean one thing, Mona had taken Leo up on his night cap offer. She found herself breathing a sigh of relief that her Nan was around which meant that Dash was probably staying over with her.

She smiled when she heard Leo's familiar voice commanding Mona to say his name.

"Harder!" she heard Mona's voice plead.

"Like that?" That was Leo's voice.

"Yeah, don't stop!" Mona screamed. "Oh my God! Just like that …oh baby please don't stop!" Natasha quickly walked past the door. She would hate for someone to associate her with the two "perverts" in the room. She thought of taking the elevator but then she thought that chances of bumping into someone she knew there were too high. Maybe even her dad. *"Oh my God, I would die,"* she thought as she imagined how her father would look at her should he bump into her in the elevator. She smiled when she thought of the lecture he would give her.

"Couldn't you just wait a few more hours, honey?" he would ask looking concerned. In his eyes would also be a slight hint of embarrassment caused by engaging his daughter in a topic so sensitive. When she got to the floor above hers, she looked at the doors and sighed. *"Was it 804 or 805?"* she wondered looking at the two doors in front of her. She tried to remember what room the guy at the reception had said but she was too drunk when the room keys were being handed out. *"804...I hope I'm not wrong,"* she thought as she put her hand on the door knob and twisted it. She breathed a sigh of relief when she found that it was unlocked. It was definitely Mitchell's room, it had to be Mitchell's room. Why else would someone leave their room unlocked? She twisted the doorknob and froze in her tracks when she saw Stacy in the arms of Tyrone, Mona's brother. She quickly closed the door silently before going into the next room.

Mitchell jerked his head around when he heard his room being opened. He smiled when he saw Natasha. She looked a bit white faced like she was shocked or something. Oh God, was she having second thoughts? Was she rethinking the whole marriage? He felt his heart beating faster as he looked at his fiancé's pale face.

"Tasha, is everything okay?" he asked standing up. He slowly walked towards her. She looked up at him.

"Sweet innocent, bubble-eyed Stacy is being fucked raw in the next room by Tyrone," she said in a quiet voice. Mitchell breathed a sigh of relief.

"Tyrone, your cousin Tyrone?" he asked as she looked up at him. She nodded. Mitchell smiled. She looked immensely disturbed by the fact. "They grow up so fast," he said holding her by the waist. "So, can't get enough of me? You couldn't wait till tomorrow?" H asked as Natasha put her arms around his neck. She nodded.

"Something like that," she said. He looked into her eyes and saw it, no matter how much she tried to hide it. She just couldn't hide the truth from him.

"What?" he asked looking at her.

"Nothing," she said smiling up at him.

"It's so cute when you think you can hide stuff from me," Mitchell said. "What is it? Tell me," he pressed. Natasha looked into his eyes and knew at that moment that she could not hide the truth from him any longer. She was actually scared of how he would take it.

"I think….I think I have wedding jitters," she said in practically a whisper. Mitchell smiled when her gaze fell. He pulled her close to him and inhaled the familiar scent of her tropical island shampoo. He planted a kiss on top of her head and then held her at arm's length.

"When I look at you I feel scared, happy, afraid, confused…." His voice trailed off as he looked into her warm brown eyes. "What I feel for you scares me. I have never felt like this for any other woman," he said.

"Yeah right," she snapped. Mitchell looked at her in surprise.

"Why would you say that?" he asked. She pulled away from his grip and walked towards the dresser. She then turned around and leaned on it as she looked at Mitchell who was still rooted to the spot she had left him in.

"You were married before. How do I know that you didn't say the same words to Lisa?" she asked looking at him. He smiled.

"Do I smell jealousy?" he asked as he walked towards her. She shrugged her shoulders but she still held her gaze at him. "You know the thing about wedding jitters?" he asked as he continued walking towards her.

"One person is always wondering whether they are making the right choice, more of doubt really. The other one is usually worried that the other one might realize what kind of loser she is marrying and leave him hanging at the altar," he said finally standing in front of her. "That would be me and I will be honest with you baby, I never got that feeling with Lisa," he added.

"Not ever?" she asked, her eyes beaming like a child who had just discovered the secret cookie stash her parents had hidden away. He nodded.

"The jitters I got while marrying Lisa were more like, dude run away," he said dramatically. She laughed as once again he put his hands around her waist. "One of us is scared that he might lose the best thing that has ever happened to him, especially when she realizes that he is not as awesome as she thinks," he said looking at her. She took a long deep breath.

"I just don't know what to expect. This is all so new to me," she said, her eyes closed.

"Tasha, open your eyes. Look at me," Mitchell said softly in a commanding voice. She looked up at him. "I am not going anywhere. I am yours until you say otherwise." She smiled up at him.

"I'm never saying otherwise," she said smiling. "Especially since it is quite obvious that your ice queen ex-wife is still in love with you," she added. Mitchell looked at her ,confused.

"What?" he asked.

"Oh I forgot to tell you. Lisa is here," Natasha said matter-of-factly. "She wanted to try to talk me out of...or about a pre-nup or something," she shrugged. "I don't really remember," she said. Mitchell looked at her in disbelief.

"What do you mean *here*?" he asked.

"Here, in The Hamptons," she said looking at him.

"What?!" he asked in surprise. Natasha kissed him.

"It's kind of sweet actually. Made me think of hooking her up with Jay," she said with a smile. Mitchell laughed.

"We do have some pretty crazy exes, don't we?" he said looking down at her.

"I'm not worried. Mona gave her the whole 'I'm from The Bronx' thing and I also gave her a piece of my mind plus, you just told me that you're here to stay," she said. Mitchell looked at her.

"I am and tomorrow I tell that to the world in front of God and all our friends and family," he said. She looked up at him, a bit tongue-tied. She wanted to go back to her room but somehow she could not break away. "You do know we cannot spend the night together, right?" he said, feeling himself getting hard, to his dismay. She nodded.

"I know," she said quietly as she pulled away from him.

"But," he said pulling her back into his arms. "I can give you a quick taste of tomorrow night," he added as he turned her around. Natasha smiled as she looked at his reflection. His face was burning with desire as he looked at them in the mirror. He undid the bath robe at the front and let it fall to the floor. "You naughty girl," he said when he saw that she wore nothing underneath.. She smiled as she undid his own robe.

"You are not wearing anything either," she said as she felt him pressing against her bare bottom.

"Yeah but I am in my room, unlike you," he said as he palmed one of her breasts. She gasped a little as her nipple instantly became hard in response to his soft touch. "Want me to stop?" he asked looking at her reaction in the mirror. She shook her head and held on to the dresser. He smiled and let his hand drop down to her core. He gently parted her legs and looked at her closing her eyes as he gently touched her sensitive clit. "Open your eyes," Mitchell said when she attempted to close her eyes to hide her pleasure from his stare. She looked at him as he suddenly bent her over the dresser and pushed his hard cock inside her moist cunt. "You are mine," he said as he sunk inside her. He pulled out and sunk back deep inside her, feeling her and filling her every fold. She moaned a little when she felt him inside her. He palmed her breasts again, this time both of them before he thrust into her again. She raised her head to look at his reflection in the mirror. His eyes were shut tight as he pushed himself inside her over and over again.

"Say it again," she pleaded in almost a whisper as he worked himself in and out of her.

"What?" he asked as he opened his eyes to look at her.

"You know what," she said as she steadied herself when his thrusts became more insistent, more resilient. He pulled himself out of her completely, making her gasp. He then played head of his cock around her opening before he pushed himself inside her again.

"You. Are. Mine." He said as he thrust into her deeply, insisting on each word as he buried himself inside her.

"Yeah I am," she said as he fucked her hard. "And you are mine," she said looking into his eyes. She felt him slow down as he looked into her eyes in the mirror.

"Yes, Tasha. I belong to you and no one else," he said in a soft voice before he begun moving himself in and out of her again, this time a bit more gently than when he first began. She grabbed on to the edges of the dresser tightly as she felt herself about to give in to the pleasure. "Come on baby. Give it to me," he said looking at her. He knew. It was written all over her face. She tried holding back as much as she could. He suddenly increased his pace, encouraging her to let go. "Come on, baby," he said again as he thrust into her hard. Natasha moaned loudly as she felt herself releasing all over his length. Soon enough, he was pumping his own life into her as their gazes interlocked. He stood behind her panting as he regained his strength. She pulled away causing him to slip out of her. A messy mixture of their orgasm dripped down their legs and finally to the floor.

"I can't wait to call you my wife," he said turning her around. She reached for her bathrobe and kissed him while fastening it.

"I can't wait to call you my husband," she said before walking towards the door. Mitchell turned around and looked at her.

"You are just going to leave like that. We won't even have a quick shower?" he asked. Natasha turned around and smiled.

"This is us, Mitchell. We never have quote unquote quick showers," she said smiling. "And if I stay the night, we will definitely be late for our own wedding," she added. She blew him a kiss and shut the door softly behind her. She could still hear Tyrone and Stacy moaning loudly as she walked past their door. Clearly, no one was going to sleep without a fix tonight.

*****

Natasha looked at her reflection in the mirror. She could hardly believe that it was her. She loved the gown Rita had picked out for her. It was a strapless Vera Wang dress with a single purple strip for a belt and a tousled finish. It was simple but just right for her. As per her Nan's advice, she had decided to have her natural curls rather than have her hair straightened. The curls were pulled up in a simple bun piling up on her head. There were a few loose curls on either side of her face giving a perfect view of the pearl earrings she wore. She looked at her reflection as her Nan hooked the matching pearl necklace around her neck.

"I don't believe I have ever seen anyone look so effortlessly beautiful," Estelle said standing behind her granddaughter. Natasha smiled back at her and put a hand on her Nan's.

"Thanks for being here," Natasha said. "This is traditionally a mother's role…" her voice trailed off as tears welled up in her eyes. Mona quickly walked up to her and raised a warning finger.

"You better not mess up that make up," Mona said wagging her index finger at Natasha who was now fanning her face frantically and trying to blink back the tears that threatened to fall. "That's better," Mona said smiling.

"Yea, because if you cry then we will all start crying," Stacy said as she held a finger under her eye. She was officially in charge of the flower girl and page boys. Natasha looked at Rita, Stacy and Mona and smiled. This was the most lovely bridal party she had ever laid eyes on. Rather than do the traditional ugly dresses for the bridesmaids so as to flatter herself, she had chosen to go with short sleeveless v-necked satin dresses, all purple. They wore silver strapped heels while the flower girl had on a white dress to match the bride, decorated with purple flowers.

"You guys look so good," Natasha said just as Pam entered the room.

"Miss Black, I have to say, your wedding must be among the top ten loveliest weddings I have ever had the pleasure of planning," she said beaming. "I must say that these small intimate ceremonies are simply charming," she added.

"I hate to say I told you so," Rita said smiling at Natasha. "But I told you so," she said in unison with Natasha.

"Yes, less is more," Pam said as Estelle walked towards the door. Natasha turned around.

"Nan, why do you have to leave so soon?" she asked looking at Estelle.

"I have been with you for 26 years love," Estelle said with a smile. "But I have to go and take care of my other baby."

Natasha smiled back at her. As much it had been almost a year and a half since she moved out to her own place, she knew that her father was still super attached to her, being an only child and all.

"It's okay, Nan," she said looking at Estelle. "See you inside," she added as Estelle walked out.

"So, everything is just the way we talked about. We have exactly two hundred guests," Pam said as she walked over to where Rita was standing. "Unless there is something you'd like to change I think everything is fair play," she added.

"There are forty guests leaving tonight," Rita said looking at Pam. "Are their flights in order?" she asked. Pam nodded.

"Everything is in place," Pam answered as she handed Rita a document to sign. Natasha figured that it was probably the last payment she would have to sign for that evening.

"All right. I will leave you guys to finish up but the procession is in ten minutes," she said before walking out. Mona walked towards Natasha, holding the tiara.

"You ready?" Mona asked. Natasha took a deep breath and looked at her reflection. She nodded and Mona began to put the tiara in place. The tiara was custom made to match the pearl wedding set she had on. "Beautiful," Mona said in a whisper after putting the tiara in place.

"Now for the finale," Rita said as she fixed the veil on and finally brought it over Natasha's face. "If that isn't a work of art, I don't know what is," she said as Stacy walked up to them. Natasha felt her eyes well up again. "Tasha, so help me God, if you mess up your make up I will kill you," Rita scolded. Natasha smiled and looked at her beautiful bridesmaids in the mirror.

"I love you guys," she said before turning around and giving them all a group hug.

"Okay, now we have got to go," Rita said as she handed Natasha a bouquet of red roses. Natasha smiled at them as they left the room. Her heart was pounding faster by the minute.

"I thought your mother looked beautiful on our wedding day but I think you are the prettiest bride I have ever seen," Natasha heard her father's voice coming from the door. She turned around and slowly walked towards him.

"Thanks daddy," she said as Eric planted a kiss on her

forehead through her veil.

"Ready?" he asked smiling. She took a deep breath and nodded. Eric took her arm and led her to the chapel. For Natasha this moment, being with her father ready to give her away to the man of her dreams, this was the best moment of her life.

Book 4.

My Honeymoon With Mr White

Chapter 1

"Dearly beloved, we are gathered here to join this man and this woman in holy matrimony," the priest began. Natasha looked at Mitchell through her veil and smiled. She could tell that he could not wait to have her alone once again, to have her in his arms, to have her as his wife.

"If there is anyone here who has any reason why these two should not be joined together in holy matrimony, please say so now or forever hold your peace," the priest said and paused, obviously to give people a chance to come forward. Mitchell looked at Natasha again. This was definitely the most tense moment in a wedding but he had nothing to worry about…or did he? Natasha shifted her gaze from Mitchell and then to the crowd and finally back to the priest. She looked over at Rita who was now smiling at her. At that moment she saw Rita mouth the words "all good." She smiled again.

Suddenly, a gasp fell over the crowd. She turned around. There was a commotion among the guests, but she was yet to know what it was about.

"Oh hell no," she heard Mona's unmistakable voice. She looked around to give her the evil eye but Mona was looking at something else, at someone else in the crowd. She followed Mona's cold look and felt as if she had just been stabbed in the spine. Right in the middle of the crowd, wearing a white strapless dress…wait…white? *"Who wears white to a wedding?"* she thought as she squinted to get a better view. Her heart almost skipped a beat when her brain registered the familiar female form.

"Mitchell, get that bitch out of here," Mona said as she approached Natasha. "Get her out, NOW!" she commanded.

She was clearly getting agitated. Natasha knew exactly what she was thinking. If only they had given her the few minutes alone she had asked for with this woman, this wouldn't be happening. "It's okay honey, we are not going to let some woman ruin this for you," Natasha heard Mona whisper in her ear. She wanted to talk but for some reason, she could not find her voice. She was tongue tied, for the first time in a long time, she was literally tongue tied. She looked at Mitchell as she felt a stream of tears rolling down her cheeks.

"What the hell are you doing here, Lisa?" Leo asked. Natasha looked at Mitchell, confused by what was happening. He took a step forward and placed a reassuring hand on her shoulder.

"You can't get married, Mitchell," Lisa said as she began walking towards the front. "You and I still got something going on and you know it," she said. Natasha could see the uncomfortable look on Mitchell's face as she walked towards them.

"Is this some media thing? Is this being staged?" the priest asked in a hushed whisper as he looked at Rita and Mona.

"Does this look staged to you?" Rita asked angrily.

"Mitch, baby…why would you do this when you know what we have isn't over?" she asked.

"Shut up, Lisa!" Mitch said angrily. "Leo, you've got to help me, man," he said as he nervously looked at Natasha. "Everything's going to be all right, sweetie," he said. "I'll take care of this." He walked away, towards the crowd.

Normally, she would have so much faith in Mitchell, but not today. There was something off about this day. Why would his ex-wife show up at their wedding? Why would she make a scene? Why....just why? She needed answers. She needed to know why the best day in her life would suddenly become her worst nightmare.

"Lisa, you need to leave," Leo said walking towards Lisa who had now walked up to the front. Everyone was looking at them in shock. Cameras were clicking away like crazy. This was not what Natasha had in mind when she decided on a small intimate wedding. All she wanted was one day she could be proud of, the day she deserved.

"No! Not until I get what brought me here!" Lisa said as she ran towards Mitchell. At that moment, Natasha noticed that she had something in her hand. She had a gun! She needed to get Mitchell out of there. She needed to make sure he would live through this. Again she tried to open her mouth to speak...but still nothing.

"Get out, bitch!" Leo said as he grabbed Lisa by the waist.

"Gun!" Natasha yelled as she found her voice. "Leo, gun!" she said again before a loud bang paralyzed the entire place. People ran around in panic. Women were screaming as the men tried desperately to shield their wives and girlfriends from the gunfire. She watched in a panic as her guests hurried towards the door, trying to escape the nightmare that was meant to be the best day of her life. Her breathing got increasingly labored as she struggled to catch a breath.

She suddenly felt weak in the knees. It was as if her legs suddenly couldn't hold her weight. The voices around her became distant as her legs gave in...

*****

To say that Natasha Black was over the moon would be a bit

of an understatement. This was the woman who was destined to be the newest Schmidt in town, the newest addition to the Schmidt legacy. She and Mitchell were actually expected to be the new power couple. Screw Barack and Michelle; these two would definitely be the new force to reckoned with…at least that would be what the tabloids would be publishing.

As she walked down the aisle, she not only felt like the most beautiful woman in the room, but also the luckiest. She smiled at the guests as she walked holding on to her father's arm.

"You ready?" Eric asked as they approached the priest. Natasha took a long deep breath and nodded.

"I guess so," she whispered to her father with a smile. She looked over at Mitchell and felt herself melt. He was wearing the classic three piece black suit with a white shirt, a purple bow tie…perfectly in line with the color theme of the day.

"Who gives this woman to this union, today?" the priest asked calmly. There was a warmth about him. Apart from the robes he wore, you would have never suspected he was a man of the cloth had you met him in a bar or club.

"We do," Estelle and Eric said in unison. Natasha smiled as her Nan stepped forward and gave her a long hug.

"No one has ever looked more beautiful," Estelle said as she gave her a kiss through her veil before walking to her seat.

"I have seen many brides, but you….you make me wonder why I married so damn early," Eric said. Natasha laughed.

"I don't know whether to be happy or grossed out," she said in a whisper. Eric laughed and planted a kiss on her forehead. He stretched out his hand and took Mitchell's hand.

"I can already tell that you will make a great husband. Take care of her, she is my most important gem," he said to Mitchell as he shook his hand.

"I plan to do nothing less, sir," he said with a smile. He gave Natasha a little wink before turning his attention to the priest. He gave the man of the cloth a light nod as a go ahead.

"Dearly beloved, we are gathered together here in the sight of God to join together this Man and this Woman in holy Matrimony; which is an honorable estate, instituted of God in Paradise, and into which holy estate these two persons present come now to be joined," he began. There was a hush over the crowd as he spoke. It could have been for the respect, the joy or simply just people eager to hear each word coming from the two most important people of the day. Natasha gave Mitchell another smile as the priest went on.

"You are both obligated to present forward any reasons as to why there could be a hindrance to the two of you being joined together in matrimony as it is an obligation on judgment day when all the secrets shall be disclosed. So if you, Natasha Black, and you. Mitchell Schmidt, have any impediment as to why you cannot be joined on this day, please say so now," the priest said.

"I have none," Mitchell and Natasha said in unison. Though everything was going as planned, Natasha was having a hard time keeping her focus. She was sure that the chapel was well ventilated but for her, it was as if the air was being sucked right out of her. She began breathing heavily as the priest went on. She felt someone, maybe Rita, touch her hand.

"You okay?" she heard someone ask. She could not make out who whispered to her. All she could do was nod. But she was not fine. The next thing she knew, it was all dark around her and she had no idea where she was or who she was with. All she saw was darkness, but somewhere in the darkness was the soothing voice of a woman. A familiar voice. She had no idea where she had heard the voice but she was sure that she knew the voice from somewhere.

Suddenly, she saw a woman who had a striking resemblance to her except for the fact that she was a bit lighter in complexion …or was she white? She felt her heart beat faster as the woman seemed to float towards her.

"Who are you? What do you want?" she asked, her voice shaking.

"Tasha, baby. It's me, mommy," the woman said with a smile. Natasha shrugged. There was suddenly a light around her. She noticed that she was in some kind of meadow. She still had her gown on but she had no veil.

"What the hell? Don't call me your baby," she said as she struggled to get up. The light was still too much for her eyes. She squinted as she pulled herself to her feet.

"You've always been my baby," the woman said.

"Then why did you leave? Why would you go away and leave your child and you husband?" she asked as tears welled up in her eyes. "Didn't you love us?" By this time, the woman was already in front of her. Natasha was now able to see that she had the most beautiful blue-green eyes she had ever seen. Her long blonde hair was secured in a braid that hung over her shoulder. She was in a floral strapless maxi dress, soft pink in color; it was definitely something she would have considered wearing. They had the same taste in clothes? No…she could not possibly have the same taste as a woman who had left her. "Why'd you leave, mommy?" she asked again as a tear rolled down her cheek.

"Baby, I would never leave you just like that," the woman said as she took Natasha's hands. "No one in their right mind would ever walk away from such a perfect baby."

Natasha knew that this was unreal. She had not seen her mother in years. No one ever talked about her. She did not know where she disappeared to or what ever became of her. She suddenly looked around as reality set in. What was she doing here? Why wasn't she at her wedding? Why did she feel as if she was losing her mind?

"I need to go. It's my wedding day and I need to be there!" she yelled as she frantically looked around for a way out. She had no idea how she got here but she knew that one way or another, she would have to get out of there.

"Tasha," the woman said calmly as she took her hand. "Look at me and stay calm," she said. Her voice was surprisingly soothing. "Take deep breaths and relax…you will be back where you belong," she added. Natasha looked at her.

"Why can't you come with me?" she asked, still unsure whether she was seeing her own vision. The woman laughed and planted a kiss on Natasha's forehead.

"I no longer belong to that world. I did my part," she said. Natasha felt a fresh flow of tears threatening to roll down her cheeks. "You are the most beautiful bride I have ever seen," she said before Natasha once again felt a weakness taking over.

When she opened her eyes, she saw the familiar faces of her father, Rita and Mitchell staring down at her, worried. "What happened?" she asked trying to sit up.

"No, no, no. you have to lie down," Rita said.

"What happened?" she asked again.

"You passed out. Dave says that it could be stress or your iron levels being too low," Rita said. Natasha's eyes grew big.

"Did you say passed out?" she asked looking up at Rita who nodded. "In front of all my guests?" she asked again. Rita looked at Mitchell and nodded again. Natasha buried her face in her hands.

"Worst wedding ever!" she said. Eric walked towards her with a glass of orange juice and a pill in his hand.

"Here, this will boost your glucose and iron levels," Eric said as Rita helped her up. "Dave said..."

"...since when do we take medical advice from Dave, anyway?" Natasha asked as she sat up. She noticed Mitchell and Rita exchange glances.

"Apparently, Dave is a doctor," Mitchell said as the door opened and Leo, Stacy and Mona walked in. Dave followed soon after. Natasha stared daggers at him.

"How is it you have been dating my best friend for almost a year and I am only finding out now that you are a doctor?" Natasha asked almost angrily before taking the pill and some juice. "Are you an intern or something?" she asked before taking another long sip of the juice. Dave shook his head as Leo and Mitchell suppressed their laughter.

"I'm doing my second year of residency," he said coolly. Mona rolled her eyes.

"Seems I'm the only one who wouldn't bag a moneybags boyfriend," she said just before Leo pulled her close.

"I beg to differ," he said. His head began to lower as if he was getting ready to kiss Mona. Eric loudly cleared his throat to return the room to normalcy.

"We still have a wedding to attend," Eric said. "Unless of course...." His voice trailed off as he looked at Natasha.

"There is no unless. We are going through with this!" Natasha said giving her father a look that screamed "I will cut you."

"All right then. Leo, tell the priest to get ready to continue," Eric said as the bridal party headed out.

"You okay, baby?" Mitchell asked looking at Natasha. She smiled up at him and nodded. "For a moment there I thought you might not want to go through with it," he said. She smiled.

"In your dreams," she said as she noticed Eric leaving the room. "Daddy," she called out. "Mitch, give us a sec," she said. Mitchell nodded and walked out, leaving the two of them in the room.

"Anything the matter, sweetie?" Eric asked, taking a seat next to Natasha. She shook her head and took another sip of her juice.

"I saw mom, when I was passed out," she said looking at Eric. "Do you know what really happened to her?" Immediately she asked that, she noticed her father's face get gloomy. He obviously knew something but didn't want to tell her. "Daddy, please. It's important," she said again.

"I never wanted you to find out," he started as a tear rolled down his cheek. "Your mother had wanted for a long time to work in war torn areas and I told her that after you were born, she would have to choose her work or us." He paused and took a handkerchief from his pocket then dabbed his eye with it. "She was a photojournalist. All I knew was she went to the Middle East and never came back," he said.

"Her workmates never said anything? No one knows where she went?" Natasha asked. Eric shook his head.

"No, but two years after she went there a friend in the Peace Corps told me she went on assignment to some dangerous area without any escort…chasing some story and never came back. They did find some of her stuff, her camera, her scarf… but not her," he said sadly. "No one knows this, not even your Nan," he added looking up at Natasha. "It was a painful subject for me, so we never talked about it," he said holding his daughter's hand.

"Why didn't you tell me?" she asked. Eric shook his head.

"I don't know," he said. "I probably wanted you to hang on to the hope that she would maybe come back some day…I don't know," he said again as Natasha leaned on his shoulder. He draped an arm around her shoulder.

"I think she meant to come back," she said sadly. "Somehow I know it," she added as she pulled away from her dad. He smiled at her.

"We can talk about this later. I am sorry I hid the truth from you for so long," he said apologetically. She smiled.

"You had your reasons," she said standing up. "But right now, I need to go get married." She took her father's hand. He smiled up at her and nodded.

"That you do," he said walking her towards the door.

"Random question, daddy. Was there a gunfight in the chapel?" she asked. Eric looked at her surprised.

"Gunfight? In the chapel? No, why?" he asked still surprised. Natasha smiled and shrugged. She must have been out for a while.

"No reason," she said as her father once again walked her to the chapel.

Chapter 2

Mitchell looked at his lovely bride walking towards him and smiled. Natasha could tell that he was not only happy but proud. The hardest part of the day was over...as well as the most scary part. The rest of the ceremony was a smooth sail. There were no people passing out. There were no gun fights and there was definitely no hallucinations. It was officially time for the first dance. Natasha smiled as Mitchell held her close. For their fist dance, Rita and Mona had decided to stick with the classics and chose Elvis Presley's "Can't Help Falling In Love." Natasha had to admit, it was a nice touch.

Though she had initially been a bit reserved with Pam, the wedding planner, she had to admit that with Rita calling the shots, she had gotten the wedding she always wanted. 150 guests, buffet reception under the moonlight, open bar... everything was simply perfect, not forgetting the fact that Rita and Mona had almost threatened to crush the TMZ cameras if they didn't hand over the memory cards that had photos of Natasha passing out. She smiled as she leaned her head against Mitchell's shoulder. She could not remember a day when she had been happier.

"Penny for your thoughts?" Mitchell asked as they danced. Natasha's smile broadened as he spun her round.

"You would have to give me an entire bank for my thoughts," she said when she was back in his arms again. Mitchell smiled and pulled away from her again.

"The Schmidts don't really own a bank but I could make it happen," he said. Natasha almost stopped dancing. He was serious!

"Mitchell, I'm kidding!" she said resting her head on her shoulder again. He laughed.

"I know, but maybe I was too," he said. Natasha rolled her yes, thankful that he could not see her. *"Maybe being the keyword here,"* she thought.

"I need to have a dance with the bride now," they heard Eric's voice. They turned around to find Eric and Estelle standing next to them, all smiles.

"And I'll have the groom," Estelle said as Mitchell took her hand and gave her a slight bow. "What a gentleman, Where were you some 40 years ago?" she asked as they danced. Eric smiled and took his daughter's hand.

"Is it just me or is my grandmother flirting with my husband?" Natasha asked as she began dancing with her father. Eric laughed.

"I think I saw it too," he said laughing. Natasha smiled up at her father and shook her head. "You okay?" he asked looking into her eyes. She looked at him and nodded.

"Of course. Why do you ask?" she asked.

"Tasha, you just found out that your mother may be dead not less than six hours ago," he said. "Anyone would be excused if they felt a bit unsettled," he added as a cameraman approached them and began clicking away. She gave a small laugh. Eric was not sure whether the laugh was genuine or if it was for the cameraman's benefit.

"I cannot think about that today," she said. "Today, I need to make sure I live this day exactly as I had always planned it," she added with a smile. The smile suddenly faded away as she recalled her mild mishap earlier. "Well not exactly, but close," she said quickly.

"Yeah," Eric said laughing lightly. "But seriously, I hope you understand that I had to do what I thought was right to protect you. You were too young," he said looking into her eyes. She nodded.

"I have never doubted anything you did for me, daddy," she said in almost a whisper.

"Okay, everyone. It's time for the bouquet toss," they heard Rita's cheerful voice breaking the intensity of the moment. Natasha smiled at her father and took the bouquet from Stacy who had walked up with the flowers in her hand. Excited females gathered behind Natasha as she readied herself to throw the flowers over her head.

"Ready?" she asked before she threw the flowers backward. She quickly turned around to see her bridesmaids scurrying around. She closed her eyes, tossed the flowers over her head and quickly turned around to watch who would catch them. She laughed when she saw Mona reaching for the bouquet with ease. After all, she towered over the rest of the women there at six feet two. Natasha gave her a smile and a wink before she turned around. She noticed Leo walking towards her with a beaming smile.

"It's sad that you wouldn't consider me," he said jokingly.

"Leo Hayes, if only I had met you a couple of years earlier," she said hugging him. They laughed and pulled apart.

"You guys are about to leave and I must say that I think you have finally made an honest man out of my man Mitchell," he said with a smile. "You take care of him. His family can be, well…bitchy," he said after a long pause. Natasha playfully punched his arm.

"Watch it," she said laughing even though she knew it was true.

"What? It's true. I'm sure his aunts are calling you the newest gold digger," he said in a whisper. She laughed and leaned close to him.

"Well, if I am a gold digger then I already hit the jackpot," she said before they both laughed. Their light moment was interrupted by Rita and Mona who were both at the PA system announcing that it was time for the couple to leave. Natasha couldn't believe that time had flown that much. It was already eight in the evening. They would leave and their guests would be left partying till God knows what time. She gave Leo a quick hug and smiled at Mitchell who was walking towards her.

"Time to go, Mrs. Schmidt," he said cheerfully as he took her hand.

"So, do I get to know where we are going for the honeymoon or do you still insist it's a surprise?" she asked as they made their way to the limo. The limo had been tastefully decorated and as fate would have it, there was a big 'Just Married' sign on the rear bumper and about a dozen cans tied on to it. *"Definitely Mona,"* she thought as she looked at the décor. No one else would have even remembered to do that what, with all the drama the day had.

Mitchell smiled as they approached the vehicle. The driver, fully clad in a black tuxedo, stood there holding the door open for them.

"That's for me to know and you to find out," he said as he

waved to the crowd. Natasha smiled and blew her family and friends a kiss as they drove away.

"What can I do so that you can tell me?" she asked. "I do have a number of things I can do for you, you know," she added matter of factly. Mitchell smiled and gave the driver a go ahead.

"I know you do. But I am not about to ruin a surprise that took me six months to put together," he said holding her hand. He leaned back on the seat and turned his head to look at her. "Don't worry. I went the extra mile to make sure it is something that tickles your fancy," he added with a wink.

"I am sure it does; after all, I am traveling in a private jet to go to my honeymoon," she said with a giggle. Mitchell laughed.

"I would have thought you would be used to the life by now," he said. She looked at him, surprised.

"When you grow up middle class and for your wedding your father in law just happens to give you a mansion as a wedding gift, you don't really get used to it," she said matter of factly. He smiled back at her and took a long deep breath as his phone buzzed wildly in his pocket. "Why is your phone still on?" she asked, almost angry that even today of all days, he would not have afforded her the courtesy of staying away from all matters business. He smiled and showed her the phone screen.

"Because I was expecting *this* call," he said. Natasha squinted when she saw her father's name on the screen. "He has just found out about the gift we gave him and your Nan," he explained. Natasha smiled. She and Eric had gone fifty-fifty on a summer home in Princeton. Initially, Mitchell had wanted to foot the entire bill, but Natasha, being the "hard-head" she was (as Mitchell would say) would not settle for anything less than splitting the cost. The house...no, mansion, was a tastefully decorated three bedroom, complete with an outdoor pool and Jacuzzi. "Hey Eric," he said casually as he picked up the phone. He put the phone on speaker so Natasha could be part of the conversation.

"Hey daddy," Natasha said beaming. Eric was gasping and sighing obviously trying to get the right words to express just what he felt.

"Mitchell....this is too much..."

"Oh please daddy, you and Nan deserve it," Natasha said casually, cutting him off mid-sentence.

"But why?" Eric asked. He seemed to be more confused at the gift than happy. Natasha laughed.

"Because, you are the best there is," she said. Even though Eric was quiet when she said that, she knew that he was fighting tears. Tears of pride, happiness perhaps.

"I can never thank you two enough," Eric said.

"And remember you can do with it as you please. It is not a rental or anything. It is in your name," Mitchell said excitedly. For the first time, Natasha thought she heard a hint of pride in his voice.

"Thanks guys, I love you. Safe journey," Eric said.

"We love you too, daddy," Natasha said before Mitchell hung up. She looked up at Mitchell and smiled.

"What?" he asked.

"You still need to tell me where you're taking me," she said as she moved closer to him. Mitchell closed his eyes and shook his head.

"I already told you. I am not giving it up," he said avoiding eye contact. There was a look she would give him that made him melt. "Stop that," he said when she tried turning his face so that she could look into his eyes.

"What, Mitchell, I just want to look at you," she said in a mock baby voice.

"Seriously, Tasha. Stop it," he said again. This time, she was not only making the face, she had her hands inside his pants. The fact that they had not been seriously intimate for a long time except for the few minutes on the eve of the wedding had made the idea of the honeymoon more desirable than it already was. Her hands inside his pants just aroused him more. He had actually managed to keep his alcohol consumption to two glasses of champagne because he tended to get horny any time he was under the influence. "Tasha please..." he said as she began stroking him. She smiled and looked at him getting tortured.

"Tell me what I want and I'll stop," she said, leaning dangerously close to him. She was so close to his neck, he could feel her hot breath on his skin. He wanted to cry out. She was tormenting him and she loved every minute of it. "Just a hint, that's all I need," she said as she began planting small kisses along his neck. He was literally between a rock and a hard place. He needed her to stop but at the same time, he could not tell her what he had taken so long to plan. It was just not like him to give in so easily. On the other hand, giving her this vital information would mean that she would stop doing what she was doing altogether and he didn't want that either. He leaned forward and locked the partition before leaning back on the seat.

"Let's see what you got, first," he said looking into her eyes. She smiled and straddled him. It was especially hard with her still in her gown. He looked up at her and gently wrapped his arms around her supple waist. "Come here, wifey," he said pulling her close. He smiled as their lips met. For the first time that day, he could kiss her for however long he wanted, without the awkward feeling of people watching them or being on the clock. She pulled away slightly and looked down at him.

"What?" he asked, wondering why she would stop now.

"Maybe we should..." she began saying, but her words were soon cut off by a long kiss that claimed her lips. Obviously, what she had to say was not of any major importance, at least right now. She smiled and let herself loose, their lips crushing against each other. "The wedding night, Mitch," she said in a whisper when she finally pulled away from his lips.

"We have a whole eight hours before I get to the wedding night. I don't think this," he paused and softly thrust his hips upwards. "...would wait for eight hours," he said before kissing her again. "Right now, this is what I want," he said softly as he zipped down the her gown. She looked at him and smiled as he exposed her breasts in the sheer white bra she wore. "God you're beautiful," he said in a low voice, almost a whisper as he looked at her breasts. She felt herself blush a little especially when he began sliding the bra off. She looked at him as he looked back at her, slowly undoing the clasp behind her. She moaned as she felt the tightness around her chest disappear when he finally took her bra off. "You are mine," he said in a whisper before kissing her again. Natasha smiled. She had known Mitchell to be possessive but never like this. He then pulled away and began sucking on her nipples ruthlessly. Her soft moans soon graduated to be gasps of breath as his tongue flicked over her tender nipples, testing her very edge of sensitivity She held on to his head as he sucked hard and nibbled as he went on. She wanted so much to scream. She had never known him to be this vigorous.

"Mitch…baby…slow down," she pleaded as she gasped for breath. But her pleas fell on deaf ears as all he did was suck harder. It seemed the more she pleaded, all he did was suck more. She put a hand over her mouth to keep from screaming when he switched to give her other breast equal torture. "You're going to kill me," she said as he sucked on one breast and let his hand rub the other one. Before she knew it, one of his hands was struggling to get his pants off as he held on to her back using his other hand. "I'll do it," she said raising herself to get his pants off. He quickly wiggled out of his pants as he pulled her panties to the side "Oh my…God!" she suddenly cried out when he filled her up. She looked down at him panting for breath. His pupils were dilated from the lust that had taken over. She felt him secure his arms around her before he began pushing himself inside her, slowly. She looked into his eyes as he pushed himself into her until every inch of his cock was buried deep inside her. Without knowing it, she had begun digging her nails into the rich leather of the seats as she felt him pull out and then push back in. She closed her eyes and eased herself on and off his cock, letting her cunt coat him with her juices.

She was his and he was hers. They both knew it and they had confessed that in front of all their friends and families. Something about that thought simply drove her over the edge. Subconsciously, she had taken over and was now almost drop fucking herself onto his rigid cock. She had not even noticed that he no longer held her. All she knew was that the feeling of Mitchell's cock buried deep inside of her was all she needed right now. "Mitch…I want to…" she began saying but her voice trailed off as her body erupted in a rhythm of violent orgasms.

She buried her head in his shoulder as she felt her muscles giving out. Mitchell was not left behind either. The wonderful feeling of her pussy convulsing against his hardness was enough to send him over the edge. He cried out as he held her close, waiting for his orgasmic state to pass.

As they lay in each other's arms, panting, tired, spent, they never felt the limo come to a slow stop.

"We need to dress up," Mitchell said in a whisper. She nodded as she climbed off him. She looked around for her bra and noticed it dangling on the door handle. She giggled as she put it on and looked over at Mitchell who was tucking in his shirt.

"I need to change," she said. "And something to drink," she added as she turned around so Mitch could zip her up.

"You can do that on the jet," he said zipping her gown up.

"So I still have to wait and find out what it is you have planned?" she asked as the driver opened the door for them. Mitchell leaned over and kissed Natasha softly.

"I love when you blackmail me with sex and trust me, I'm not complaining," he said. "But this time, Natasha Black-Schmidt, it won't work," he added and planted another kiss on her forehead. She suddenly felt her cheeks flush.

"Let's go, my blushing bride. A beautiful time awaits," he said in a mock old English voice.

"Why yes, my Lord," she said with a smile as she took his hand and followed him out. She would just have to trust him.

Chapter 3

Mitchell had been right to deny all details pertaining to their honeymoon to Natasha because there were no words that could describe their honeymoon destination. It could be because there was no way his very financial talk would ever measure up to magical island of Antigua.

Everything about the island was perfect, including the fact that it was a Caribbean island. Once they landed, she could immediately tell that her honeymoon was not only going to be amazing but also one everyone would be envious of. Mitchell had her blindfolded in the car until they got to the hotel suite. At some point, Natasha had scolded him about the fact that people would look at them strangely.

"So, let them," was his reply. Once in the suite, Mitchell removed the blindfold and stepped back as his wife took in the lovely scene.

"Oh my God," she said in a low voice. "This is so...." Her voice trailed off as she struggled to get the right words to finish her sentence.

"Perfect, right?" he asked. All she could do was nod. The suite was up on the thirtieth floor overlooking the beach and community pool below. Outside on the balcony was a beautiful Jacuzzi that Natasha silently made plans to get to know a little better, or maybe a lot better. The king size bed looked luscious and inviting with a white spread and red rose petals scattered all over it. Right in the middle of the bed was a bowl of strawberries and melted chocolate for dipping them. There was a bottle of champagne on ice, two glasses and a plate of chicken wings on the bedside table. She turned around and looked at Mitchell.

"You planned all this?" she asked looking at him. He smiled and nodded.

"But the wings are mine. The chocolate is obviously for the lady," he said as he closed the door. He walked towards her and took her in his arms. "I told you the quickie in the limo wouldn't ruin our wedding night," he said. Natasha smiled up at him and wrapped her arms around his neck.

"Technically it's the morning after the wedding night," she said. "We've been flying for eight hours remember?" she asked smiling.

"Of course," he said. "So, what do you want to do first?" he asked.

"I don't know. This is my first honeymoon. What did you do on your first honeymoon?" she asked looking up at him. Mitchell frowned.

"That's way below the belt," he said. "You have to pay for that you know," he said.

"That' is exactly what I want," Natasha said kicking off her shoes. "I have been a very naughty girl and maybe I need a spanking," she said in a mock child voice. He smiled as she let go of his neck and moved towards the bed. "But first," she said as she picked up the bowl of strawberries. Mitchell smiled and dramatically rubbed his hands together.

"I have never been one to shy away from a steamy situation," he said. Natasha smiled and put the bowl down.

"Maybe we can soap each other up while we talk about our plans for the future. You know, the normal boring stuff that married people do," she added as she walked towards the bathroom. "Oh and Mitchell," she said stopping in her tracks. She looked over her shoulder and gave him a sexy beckoning smile. "Now that we are in the Caribbean, maybe you should bring your A-game," she said before practically running to the bathroom.

"Woman, when have I ever not brought my A-game?" he asked as he walked after her. He quickly got out of his clothes and dumped them on the floor. "I'm about to show you what my B-game can do," he said. Natasha frowned as she started the shower. "If you survive that, I will bring my A-game," he said with a smile. She laughed as she wriggled out of her dress.

"Sometimes I wonder how I never managed to see that humongous ego you have," she said as she stepped under the shower. He joined her under the running water and looked into her eyes.

"I wanted to make sure I marry you before I showed that ugly side," he said smiling. She smiled up at him as he put his hands on her waist. She saw him give her now wet breasts a long lingering look. If she didn't know any better she could have sworn he was staring.

"Ahem, Mitch. They are still the same ones you have been looking at for the past two years," she said. He laughed and turned her around.

"I know. It's just that you seem to be more beautiful every time I see you. I can't believe you...all this..." He ran a hand up her upper thigh to her torso, "...is all mine," he said finally before planting a kiss on her shoulder. She smiled and put her own hands on his.

"What do you intend on doing about having all this goodness

in your hands right now?" she asked. He pulled her backward toward him so that she could lean against him. She could already feel his semi-erection pressing against her ass. Even after eight hours of flying, he still had the vigor of a teenage boy in heat. He brought his head down again and kissed her other shoulder before trailing his tongue along her shoulder blade. She closed her eyes as he reached for a loofah and some bathing gel on one of the shelves. She let out a low gasp when she felt the cold bathing gel being squeezed onto her back before he began to slowly and gently scrub her back using the loofah. He turned her around and did the same to her breasts but instead of using the loofah, he worked the lather up using his hands, obviously enjoying the sensation of her hard nipples pressing against his palms. She put her hand out and as if in a telepathic mood, he immediately knew what she was asking for. He reached for the bathing gel and squeezed a generous amount onto her palm and then put it back. She looked into his eyes as she began to slowly rub the gel on his chest, his abs and finally his now rigid cock. She heard a low moan escape his lips and smiled.

Natasha began to slowly rub the gel up and down his shaft, totally disregarding the rest of his torso.

"The rest of my body needs cleaning too," Mitchell said in a low voice. She smiled.

"I am not interested in the rest of your body right now," she said. "I was hoping you would appreciate it," she added as a frown took over her smile. He leaned against the cool tiled wall and smiled down at her.

"I'm sorry I ever complained," he said as she went on rubbing her hands up and down. She looked at him and smiled, an evil if not erotic smile.

"That's what I want to hear," she said as her other hand made its way around his neck. She pulled him down for a long kiss. It was a sensual kiss with their lips hard pressed against each other, their tongues meeting in glorious eroticism. She pulled away from his lips as her hand also pulled away from his cock. He looked down at her in disapproval but all she did was smile and pull him under the running water. They kissed as the water flowed down their bodies. He suddenly pulled away and turned her around once again. She gasped when she felt two of his fingers finding their way to her already wet insides. She leaned against him and writhed as he began working his fingers in and out of her, slowly at first but rapidly as they went on. She began uttering small moans, especially when his other hand cupped a breast, holding her roughly against his own fiery body.

"Mitchell, I want more," she moaned. He needed no second bidding. He turned the water off and walked her out of the bathroom to the bed. He quickly took the bowl of strawberries and chocolate and placed it on the floor before gently pushing her down on the bed. Their bodies were still soapy, evidence of how unproductive their shower session had been. He brought his body on top of hers and looked into her eyes. "I want you so much, baby," she said again. Her pupils were dilated from the lust she had for him from the way she wanted him to ravage her. Mitchell looked into her eyes as he slid himself inside her. She closed her eyes as she felt him filling her every fold, feeling her depths. She raised her knees and wrapped her legs around his waist, allowing for an even deeper penetration. Mitchell gave a small thrust of his hips to show his appreciation.

"Open your eyes," he said looking down at her perfect face. "I want you to look at me as I make love to you," he said. She looked into his eyes as he began a slow but sure movement inside her, slowly ensuring that each stroke spoke what his words could not. He sank deep inside her and brought himself up. She was having an increasingly hard time keeping her focus on his face, in his eyes. She wanted to bury her face in his shoulder and scream, wincing her face in ecstasy but he didn't want to break the gaze. She looked into his eyes as he sank inside her again and again and again…bringing her dangerously close to her relief. He knew she was about to get to that point of no return. He knew she wanted to cry out, going by the way she moaned and the way her face would flinch every time he thrust deep inside her. "I want to hear you moan for me , baby," he said. Natasha looked at him and let out a squeak when he once again thrust into her. His long soft strokes had now been replaced by long hard ones. His hips were now slamming into her more intensely as he went on. She once again let another loud moan escape her lips when he thrust into her. The intense look he gave her must have contributed to her fast orgasm as she soon began feeling her insides almost crying for help and he, the wonderfully attractive tormenting devil he was, slowed down.

"Why would he slow down now?" she wondered as she raised her hips to encourage him. He smiled down at her and pulled his cock out of her. "No….don 't…please…" she begged. He smiled as he once again reintroduced himself to her wet pussy. She screamed out as one of his powerful thrusts made her own walls explode in the tune of millions. She squeezed her eyes shut and wrapped her arms around his back as he went on thrusting, struggling to stay inside her despite the raging force threatening to push his cock out of her. His perseverance paid off as he soon felt himself erupt inside her, pouring load after load of his own cum into her.

"I love you so much Natasha," he said as he panted for breath. She relaxed her legs on the bed and her arms dropped to her side. At that moment, Mitchell's limp cock slipped out of her preceding a gooey mess on the bed.

"I love you too, Mitchell," she said in a whisper as Mitchell rolled off her tired body. He took her hand in his and the two of them drifted off to sleep.

*****

On the fourth day of their honeymoon in the magical islands, Natasha decided to try out the pool. She had been procrastinating on everything…a walk on the beach, the pool, shopping…all because she and Mitchell were like sex crazed bunnies. On this day, she woke up excited to see what Antigua had to offer. Instead of the usual room service breakfast, the two of them had headed down the poolside café.

"But I want to stay in bed all day," Mitchell had said in the morning.

"Mitchell Schmidt, if you continue screwing the brains out of me, I will not have a vagina by the time we get back to the States," she had told him. "Besides, I need some air. All I can smell in here is sex," she had said before they headed out. Mitchell may not have wanted to make love all day, but as he told her, there was something beautiful about not having to wake up early, not having your phone ringing off the hook or emails popping up every second. It was the life he had always wanted.

"You do realize you would be worth maybe ten, fifteen dollars if you had this life, right?" she asked as they rode down the elevator.

"Hey, I said I wanted to wake up late, not wake up late and carry a sign saying 'will work for food.' I love being rich. I just need a break sometimes," he said as the elevator doors opened.

"And his true colors finally show," Natasha said as they walked out. The sun kissed pool was a sight to behold. The hotel had gone the extra mile to construct a pool that gave the "I am right in the middle of the ocean" impression. It was in the middle of a tropical setting…low hanging branches, rock waterfalls…basically, if you simply focused on the pool, you'd have the feeling of being lost at sea and swimming to a tropical island.

"Good morning, Mr. Schmidt, Mrs. Schmidt," a brown skinned waiter said with a smile. Natasha and Mitchell smiled back at him.

"Good morning, Zeneal," Mitchell said. "Do you think we could have our breakfast in the poolside café?" he asked.

"Well, the café is part of the hotel so I'm sure they won't mind," Zeneal replied.

"Oh good, because there is this beautiful omelet you have been serving that is simply divine. I don't know what I'd do if I couldn't have it," Natasha said in mock drama. The three of them laughed.

"We will make sure you have your usual bacon omelet, Mrs. Schmidt," Zeneal said. "Anything for you sir?" he asked looking at Mitchell.

"Just the usual, but extra butter in the pan for the pancakes. I want the edges nice and crispy," he said as he and Natasha walked towards the pool.

"Just so you know, when we are back home, you will be on brown rice and kale for a week," Natasha said as the two of them walked towards one of the empty tables. Mitchell looked at her questioningly.

"Why would you even say that?" he asked as he pulled out a seat for her.

"You have been having extra buttered pancakes every day since we got here! Heart attack alert," she said sitting down. She thanked God her eyes were well concealed behind the big sunglasses she had on because she would have bust out laughing when he called her bluff, which was going to be any time now....Her thoughts were suddenly interrupted by a cold sensation on her back. She looked at Mitchell who said nothing. He just stood there his mouth gaping open as if he had just seen the most shocking thing ever.

"Oh my God....I am so sorry," she heard a female voice say. She looked around to see a curvy brunette standing next to a dark skinned man....maybe African American? The woman was holding a glass half full of orange juice. Is that what was all over her back? "I didn't see...I mean I did...it's just..."

"...it's okay, it's a bathing suit. It will wash off," Natasha said standing up.

"I'll walk you to the changing rooms," the woman said as she helped Natasha pick up her towel. Natasha smiled at her casually though she really wanted to punch her inn the face.

"Thanks," she said as she quickly walked towards the changing rooms. She rushed to one of the shower cubicles and turned on the water at full force then stood underneath the flowing streams as the orange juice washed off her back. She stood there for a few minutes before she decided to just take the swimsuit off...which she did.

"Is everything okay in there?" Natasha rolled her eyes. Why wouldn't this woman just leave?

"Everything's fine. It washed off like I said," Natasha replied as she put the suit back on. "The laundry people will just have to use extra bleach," she added as she got out of the cubicle. Some strands of her hair were wet sticking on to her neck and the sides of her face.

"Melinda. Melinda Osbourne," the brunette said handing her one of the towels that were on the towel rack outside.

"Natasha Black…actually Natasha Black-Schmidt.," she said as she wiped herself down. "Still getting used to the new name," she said smiling.

"Newly wed?" Melinda asked. She nodded.

"Four days and maybe 19 hours to be exact," Natasha said with a smile. Melinda blushed.

"Guess I will be the bitch that ruined your honeymoon when you tell this story, huh?" Melinda asked with a frown. Natasha laughed and nodded.

"Yeah, most probably," she said. "But really, it's okay. No evidence of anything that ever happened," she added feeling a pang of guilt when she realized that the brunette was genuinely distraught over the incident. "Come on, I'm sure the boys are in a staring contest right now and they need to be saved," Natasha said as she slipped on a bathrobe. Melinda smiled.

Strike two for me is you covering up that beautiful bathing suit because I made the waist wrap wet," Melinda said as they walked out. Natasha laughed.

"Why thank you," she said looking at Melinda. "But it's chiffon. Give it a few minutes and it will be dry as sand in the Sahara," she added as the two headed out.

Chapter 4

"That makes absolutely no sense. It is not even a word!" Natasha yelled as she looked at the word Mitchell had just come up with on the Scrabble board.

"It is too!" Mitchell said faking a frown. The two were getting more acquainted with the couple that they had so unfortunately bumped into when they decided to visit the café for the first time since they got to Antigua and what Natasha had come to know was Melinda was a sweetie. She was a television producer for a travel show who was in Antigua on holiday. She had met her boyfriend Kyle on her second trip to the islands and as Natasha put it, the two were just made for each other Kyle was a brown skinned man, almost as well built as Mitchell, Natasha thought. He did not talk much but somehow Mitchell seemed to enjoy his company extensively. After the four of them laughed off the juice incident, they had decided to break the tension by having breakfast together. This later turned into lunch and dinner and now, it seemed like the two couples could not spend a day without seeing each other.

On this particular day, Mitchell had decided to have a game that called for everyone's participation. He had suggested chess at first but Natasha wouldn't have it.

"All the bishops and kings get me all mixed up," Natasha had said.

"Well, it's an intelligent game," Kyle had said. Melinda and Natasha stared daggers at him.

"Are you trying to say that we are not intelligent?" Melinda asked. Kyle put his hands up in defense.

"No, nothing like that," he said laughing. "I just meant…" his voice trailed off as he looked over at Mitchell for assistance.

"That we men have a different way of playing chess, that's all," Mitchell said.

"Mitchell Schmidt to the rescue," Natasha said looking at her husband. Kyle looked at him and mouthed a quick thank you to him. "So, what exactly are we going to do? It is too damn hot to be outside," she asked leaning against the couch.

"Well, we could go to the pool later," Melinda said. Natasha rolled her eyes and began fanning herself using her hand.

"Yeah later. But what do we do *now*," she asked again. Melinda's face suddenly lit up.

"Scrabble," she said looking at the three of them.

"Scrabble?" Mitchell asked looking at Melinda closely.

"Yes, Scrabble. Easy. Fun. Mental challenge. Everything we need right about now," she said holding up three fingers she had used to show the advantages.

"She is right. And we all know the rules," Natasha said looking at Mitchell and Kyle who looked unsure. She noticed Mitchell had a look that told her he was about to cancel on her any minute now." Plus, it has no kings, queens, bishops and all those Renaissance fools looking to go to war," she added quickly. Mitchell smiled at Kyle.

"She really doesn't know any of the rules as far as chess is concerned, does she?" Kyle asked. Mitchell shook his head.

"Not even one," he said. Natasha playfully elbowed him.

"What? You don't know the rules!" Mitchell said as Natasha stood up.

"Come on Melinda. Let's go make something to drink as the two geniuses figure out how to set up the Scrabble board," she said taking Melinda's hand. Mitchell looked at her and smiled.

"I still love you, wifey," Mitchell called after her.

"Yeah, yeah. I love you too," Natasha said.

"Ouch," Mitchell said loud enough for her to hear. Natasha looked over her shoulder and winked at him as they disappeared around the corner.

"Women, huh," Kyle said leaning back.

"Tell me about it," Mitchell said in agreement as he stood up. "But this one woman, she just lights up my world," he added as he walked towards their room. He disappeared briefly before he finally emerged with a Scrabble board.

"You guys have been together for how long?" Kyle asked.

"Married one week. Together for three years," Mitchell answered excitedly.

"Wow. The longest relationship I ever had was a year and it was like the relationship from hell," Kyle said. Mitchell smiled and sat down.

"Again, tell me about it," Mitchell said as he spread the scrabble pieces on the table.

"Please dude. What do you know? You have the perfect wife,"

Kyle said. "Beautiful, sexy, intelligent....what more could you possibly ask for in a woman?" he asked.

"Well, Kyle my friend, believe me when I tell you that it was not always so good," Mitchell said looking at Kyle. "There were days I preferred to spend the night talking to a bartender and booking a room at a hotel than go back to my wife," he added. Kyle looked at him confused.

"But you have been married for a week," Kyle said still confused. Mitchell shook his head and looked at him in shock.

"Oh God, you thought I was talking about Tasha?"" he asked laughing. "She is amazing. Perfect even," he said looking at him. "I think if you looked up perfect in the dictionary or googled the word, you'd probably find her picture," he added in a whisper as he leaned forward.

"Okay, now I am officially confused," Kyle said as he leaned forward and picked up one of the scrabble pieces.

"This is not my first marriage, you know," Mitchell finally said.

"Now that makes so much more sense," Kyle said pointing at Mitchell who was now laughing quietly. "What happened with the first one? Not as pretty?" he asked.

"Oh she was a looker, don't get me wrong," Mitchell said. "But she was...not in it for the right reasons," he added. Kyle looked at him closely.

"You lost me again," he said. Mitchell took a deep breath.

"Well, let's just say that she is the kind of woman who, if I was president and she was a lesbian, she'd keep it secret for the sake of being first lady," Mitchell explained.

"So you are the president's son or something?" Kyle said in an effort to try and understand Mitchell's explanation. Mitchell looked at him questionably.

"Why would you even ask that?" he asked looking at Kyle.

"President...first lady. Your words not mine," "Kyle said shrugging.

"Okay, simply put, the whole presidential thing is to do with family fortune. I can't believe you thought I was part of the first family...or at least the extended first family," Mitchell said as Melinda and Natasha walked back.

"Oh...you should have just said that. Talk in parables much?" Kyle asked as the girls sat down. "Hey, what happened to the drinks?" he asked as he laid eyes on the chips and dip the girls had just walked in carrying.

"Here they are," Melinda said pouring cold soda in the four glasses she had.

"You know what I mean," Mitchell said with a frown.

"Well, we decided since it is only, what, two in the afternoon? Maybe we should save the good stuff for later on when you show us all the hot spots around this beautiful island," Natasha said as she sat down next to Mitchell.

"Guess you're right," Kyle said as he took a bite of one chip covered in dip. "And worth it," he said as he closed his eyes. Mitchell followed suit, as did the girls.

"Oh my God, this is no regular dip," Mitchell said.

"I know, right?" Melinda said beaming. "I was in love with the dip when I first came here too. Apparently, the secret is in the garlic," she added taking another chip. Mitchell looked at Kyle and then at Natasha.

"Do you mean to tell me that you make your own dips?" he asked looking at Kyle.

"We like to think that the dip is the reason why Americans keep on coming back here," Kyle said smiling. Natasha laughed.

"We do love our dip," she said. "So, what were you boys talking about when the womenfolk were busy making the delicious treats?" she asked as Melinda handed out the glasses of soda.

"Mitchell was going on about being in the first family and stuff," Kyle said without looking up.

"First family? Like the president's family?" Melinda asked surprised. Natasha elbowed Mitchell again.

"That's the man I married. Always making little figurative phrases," Natasha said. Melinda's eyes suddenly grew wild.

"Wait a minute," she said looking at Mitchell. "Figurative talk… your last name is Schmidt, right?" she asked excitedly. Natasha looked at her surprised.

"Yes. Nice to meet you for the second time," she said. "What's the point of this little trip down memory lane?" she asked.

"Like Schmidt, Nolan Schmidt the big tycoon?" Melinda asked.

"Seems I can never really hide from anyone nowadays," Mitchell said. "But guilty," he said as he put an arm around

Natasha's shoulders.

"Am sorry but I am not so sure I understand what is going on here," Kyle said as his gaze shift from Melinda to Mitchell.

"Okay, I don't want you to think I'm a stalker or some shit like that," Melinda started.

"Okay, that's a little freaky that you chose those particular words to start your speech," Mitchell said. Melinda laughed as she shook her head.

"I'm sorry. It's just that before I started working for the travel diaries I was supposed to cover your wedding. Media houses were calling it the American Royal Wedding," Melinda said laughing. "But when TMZ got the deal...well, you know, the wedding would have been my big break," she added.

"TMZ did get the scoop," Natasha said.

"Wait, big break? Honey, I thought you loved doing the travel show," Kyle said looking surprised.

"I do, God knows I do. It's just that at some point I was into broadcast...maybe something behind the anchor desk," Melinda said. "It was to be..." her voice trailed off as she took a long sip of her drink. "But I not only produce the show, I own it. So it was a win-win," she added with a smile.

"I'm sure you do," Natasha said, a sympathetic look on her face.

"No for real. I came up with the idea and everything. The network wanted it so much they decided to retain me and pay me a lump sum plus royalties," Melinda said raising her glass. Kyle planted a kiss on her forehead and smiled at her.

"Yeah, thank God. If it were not for that show the two of us would have never met," Kyle said with a smile. Natasha and Mitchell smiled at each other.

"That's enough, love birds. What are we doing? Boys versus girls or which couple sucks more?" Mitchell asked. Natasha and Melinda exchanged a "oh no he didn't" look.

"Remember when they thought chess was too quote unquote, intelligent for us?" Natasha asked. Melinda nodded.

"All too well," Melinda answered.

"Well, I guess that answers your question, Mitchell Schmidt. It's boys versus girls and which pair is going to whoop your ass," Natasha said as she switched seats with Melinda. Mitchell looked at them and smiled.

"Fine. We'll go first," he said as he carefully spelled out the word "aint" on the board. Natasha looked at the board and then at Mitchell.

"What language are we playing in? Vietnamese?" she asked laughing.

"English. Aint is a perfectly legit word," Mitchell argued. Melinda suddenly burst out laughing.

"Honey, as an African American I have to tell you that my community has worked so hard to terrorize the English language," Natasha said looking at Mitchell apologetically. "That is an example of how good we are at language terrorism," she added pointing at the board.

"This couple is going to kick your ass," Melinda said giving Natasha a high five.

"Ain't that the truth," Kyle said looking at Mitchell who was smiling back at him. "So anyway, you know how the two of us met. How did you two meet?" he asked as he looked up at Natasha.

"It's not as magical as your tourist meets local boy story," Mitchell said. "Well, it's the usual," he added. Melinda looked at Natasha.

"What's the usual? Coffee shop?" Melinda asked.

"Oh no. Mitchell just seems to lose the romance so soon into the marriage," Natasha said. "I was going for an interview at NSCS," she said as a big smile played on her face.

"The government navy intelligence thing? Cool, I've seen that show. I didn't think it was real, though," Kyle said as he took a handful of chips. The three looked at him surprised.

"Not NCIS honey. NSCS," Melinda said in a whisper even though the other three people in the room were quiet. Natasha smiled at Mitchell.

"Don't worry. My dad also thought I was about to join Jack Bauer in the fight against international crime," Natasha said giving a sympathetic look to Kyle.

"Good to know I'm not alone there," Kyle said. "So what's NSCS?" he asked.

"Nolan Schmidt Communications Solutions. The company I work for," Natasha said. Kyle's eyes grew wide.

"This is one of those boss and naughty secretary situations, isn't it?" he asked. Natasha looked at him surprised and offended at the same time. Was this how people perceived her? The little whore who slept with her boss and finally hit the jackpot? Kyle suddenly noticed Melinda's look, the same look that she would give him on nights that he was sure he wasn't getting lucky. It was at that moment that he realized he had overstepped his boundaries. "I'm sorry. I didn't mean to offend anyone. Sometimes I talk faster than my brain processing capability," Kyle said looking at Natasha ruefully.

"I guess you should feel better knowing that you are not the first person to think that," she said.

"So what happened at the interview?" Melinda asked trying to change the topic. Kyle's comment had brought about an uncomfortable situation at the table that she longed to get away from.

"So, I drove to the interview but when I got out of the car, I don't know what happened. I passed out," Natasha said smiling. "I think I was just nervous," she added. Mitchell raised an eyebrow.

"Just nervous? Woman you were a wreck. Thank goodness I was there to save the day," Mitchell said leaning back.

"So you were the Prince Charming to Natasha's Cinderella story? Is that what you are trying to say?" Melinda asked as she circled the rim of her glass using her index finger. Kyle looked at Melinda and then at Mitchell.

"This speaking in parables thing…is it an American thing?" Kyle asked.

"Oh honey….are you always direct in Antigua?" Melinda asked looking at Kyle who was now nodding.

"Yeah…most of the time….when you are not talking to elders

at least," he said before laughing.

"So anyway, there I was passed out and the next thing I know I am looking up at a stranger," Natasha continued. "The most embarrassing part was when I found out that the guy who probably saw my underwear would be one of the people interviewing me," she added rolling her eyes. Mitchell held up his hands in defense.

"Hold on. I never saw your underwear," he said. Natasha smiled.

"Well, I don't know that, at least I didn't, then," she said. "I can't really tell what position I fell in," she added laughing.

"Trust me, no underwear," Mitchell said again. Natasha took a long sip of her drink and gave Mitchell a dreamy look.

"From there it was a roller coaster and lo and behold, three years down the lane, here we are," she said with a smile.

"Aaww, that is the sweetest story ever," Melinda cooed. Mitchell looked at her and laughed.

"Believe me when I tell you it wasn't all smooth sailing. She really meant it when she said a roller coaster," he said matter-of-factly.

"Oh come on. You guys have the perfect story. Don't tell me she ditched you at the altar before you guys decided to elope," Melinda said as she busied herself coating a potato chip in dip. She suddenly noticed the silence that had taken over the room. She looked up at Natasha and Mitchell in surprise. "She left you at the altar? What is this, *Pretty Woman*?" she asked before taking a bite of the potato chip.

"No one left anyone at any altar," Natasha said.

"She just took her time saying yes after I popped the question," Mitchell said. "But she was worth the wait," he added giving Natasha a wink.

"You guys could literally make a romantic movie, screw *Pretty Woman*," Melinda said.

"I am not a romantic but I have seen quite a few chick flicks and if I didn't know any better I could have sworn you have just spent the last half hour giving us an entire plot theme," Kyle said. Melinda nodded in agreement as she bit into yet another potato chip.

"Well, believe me when I tell you that it is all original," Natasha said as she fumbled around with the scrabble board. "And even if 'aint' was a word, it would be worth a mere four points and I have just made 'terror" and whooped both your asses on the first round," she added as Melinda leaned over to look at the board. The two girls gave each other a celebratory fist bump before they looked at the dumbfounded guys.

"I have a better idea," Mitchell said as he intentionally tipped the board over.

"Hey!" Natasha cried in protest as Mitchell stood up.

"I think it's time Kyle gave us an official club tour," Mitchell said taking Natasha's hand.

"Why do I have a feeling that the only reason we are going out is because we were going to win?" Melinda asked as she stood up.

"And we shall never talk about this again," Kyle said as he

draped Melinda's scarf on her shoulders.

"We could always have another go at chess," Mitchell said looking at Natasha hopefully. Melinda and Natasha exchanged glances.

"He really needs to shut up if there is any hope of getting laid tonight," Melinda whispered to Natasha.

"I know," Natasha said looking at Mitchell.

Chapter 5

"You have to tell me what you think and you have to be honest," Natasha said to Mitchell, tugging on her bathrobe. She had just gone shopping for new lingerie and swimsuits. Since meeting Melinda and Kyle, the newlyweds rarely ever spent time alone together. It was almost as if they were on a couples retreat rather than a honeymoon, not that either of them was complaining.

"Have I ever lied to you?" he asked leaning back on the bed.

"Well, there is the time you said exactly what I wanted to hear just so that we could have sex," Natasha said. Mitchell shrugged.

"It was pretty awesome sex," Mitchell said looking at Natasha who nodded.

"Guess it was. But this time I just want to know what you think, okay?" she asked looking at him sternly.

"Oh well, I guess I could do that," he said. "So, what's first?" he asked rubbing his hands together. She smiled at him and slowly undid the front of the robe, parting the two sides carefully. Mitchell took a long deep breath as he caught a glimpse of the one piece purple bathing suit she had on. It was a perfect fit: low cut at the back showing her perfect back, and the front had a high cut but it was still enough to show off her cleavage. The right side of the suit was cut out giving her that sexy Toni Braxton look that's seemed to turn him on so much. "Please tell me you will not be wearing that here," he said looking at Natasha surprised.

"Why? Don't you like it?" she asked looking at her reflection in the mirror.

"No, don't get me wrong, I love it. And so will the hundreds of other male guests in this hotel and the pervs at the beach," he said as he slowly stood up and walked towards her. "But right here, you can keep it on for as long as you want," he said as he stood behind her and slowly placed two gentle hands on her hips. "Matter of fact, never take it off," he added in a whisper as he kissed her shoulder. Natasha smiled.

"If I don't take it off, how will you get to the good stuff?" she asked as she felt one of his hands slide down to her well rounded ass. He looked up at her reflection and smiled.

"I have a very, very creative mind," he said. "Plus, I know for a fact that they can make these things crotchless," he added before again kissing her shoulder. She smiled and held her his head against her shoulder as she felt his tongue slowly teasing her.

"That's good, that's really good," Natasha said as Mitchell's other hand slowly rose to cup one of her breasts. Natasha turned around and wrapped her arms around his neck. She pulled him down for a kiss when he suddenly went rigid in her arms. "What?" she asked looking into his eyes.

"That kind of hurts," he said. She slowly pulled away and looked at him.

"Why didn't you use the sun block?" she asked looking at him angrily.

"I did," Mitchell said. "But somehow I keep on getting sunburns," he added looking at the pink blotches on his arm.

"Oh honey," she said as she took his hand. "Come with me,"

she said as she walked him to the bed. He watched as she walked up to her makeup bag and pulled out a tube of lotion.

"You are not going to put makeup on me, are you?" he asked looking mildly terrified. "Because the last time I had makeup on, I looked like a tranny – a really attractive one though," he added with a smile. Natasha looked at him questioningly.

"I don't even want to know why you had makeup on," she said. Mitchell held his hands up.

"Whoa, it was a TV interview," he said.

"And attractive tranny? According to whom?" she asked as she sat down next to him. Mitchell smiled.

"Really? You've got to ask?" he said. Natasha could not help but get a whiff of bragging in his voice.

"Anyway, this isn't makeup. Just some aloe vera. It's really good for sunburns," she said as she squeezed a generous amount onto her palm. She then rubbed her palms together and began to slowly rub the lotion on his arms.

"How does it help exactly?" he asked as he looked at her gently rubbing the lotion in him. "Though it feels really good," he added.

"I know. It actually just soothes the damaged skin and makes it peel off," she said. Mitchell grimaced in horror. "The peeling off happens eventually. This just helps speed up the process," she added as she rubbed the lotion on his other arm. The serenity of the moment was suddenly interrupted by the loud ringing of a Skype call.

"Seriously? Skype? On our honeymoon?" he asked as she

quickly wiped her hands on a towel.

"What? You didn't hear me complain when you were on phone with the Patricia Lowndes," she said looking at him sternly.

"You knew…you heard that?" he asked as she grabbed her laptop.

"The whole 13 minutes of it," she answered as she sat down. "Besides, it's Rita. It's been a while," she added as she finally connected the call. "Hey girl," she said as she looked at Rita.

"Hey you. How's married life?" Rita asked as she looked at Natasha.

"Awesome, couldn't be better," Natasha answered with a smile. "We even made new friends. Melinda and Kyle," she added.

"Why do I feel like I have been replaced?" Rita asked.

"Oh honey. You cannot be replaced, ever," Natasha said with a smile. Rita smiled back.

"That's sweet," Rita said. Natasha rolled her eyes at her.

"I'm not sure I meant that as a compliment, sweetie," Natasha said. This time, it was Rita's turn to roll her eyes.

"Tell me, how is the Caribbean? Is it as awesome as I always thought and for God's sake, where's Mitchell?" Rita asked as she tried looking around the room. Natasha picked her laptop up and pointed it to where Mitchell was seated.

"Hey Rita," he called as he gave a slight wave,

"There's the man of the hour. And what the…are those sunburns?" Rita asked squinting. "Didn't you use sun block? I mean jeez, Mitchell, you are in fucking Antigua," she scolded.

"I used the freaking sun block!" Mitchell said almost angry. "It's just…."

"…your skin is softer than veal?" Rita asked cutting him short. Mitchell gave him a cold look.

"I fail to understand how two totally opposite people can be friends," he said as he stood up. "I still need some more lotion on my veal like body. Bye Rita," he said walking to the living room. Rita laughed.

"You can be really mean sometimes, you know," Natasha said. Rita laughed again.

"Mitchell and I have a love-hate relationship. He knows I got nothing but love for him," Rita said.

"So, what are you up to? Any mischief with Dave?' Natasha asked excitedly. Rita smiled. "What? What's going on?" she asked. Rita suddenly shifted her weight and let Natasha have a look outside. The surrounding was terribly familiar, almost as if she was looking outside her own hotel window. "Are you… here?" she asked looking confused. Rita shook her head excitedly.

"No, Cabo," she said smiling broadly.

"Cabo," Natasha repeated.

"Yes, Cabo," Rita said again. "Dave had a really good month at work and he took a couple of weeks off just to unwind and what better time to travel than when my best friend is away on her honeymoon?" she added.

"Good for you," Natasha said. "I love how happy Dave makes you. You deserve to be happy," she added with a smile. Rita beamed.

"I am happy, Tasha and that scares the shit out of me," Rita said in a whisper.

"Is Dave there with you?" Natasha asked trying to get as much of the room in eye view as she could.

"He's in the bathroom," Rita said, still whispering. "What do I do? I haven't felt like this since Simon in the tenth grade," she added. Natasha smiled.

"Sweetie, don't over think it. Just live in the moment. You are always the one telling me to do that," Natasha said looking into her eyes. "He loves you. He is a good guy. Don't mess this up," she added.

"I love him too and I don't want to mess it up," Rita said. "But..." she was suddenly lost for words as she noticed Natasha's big eyed stare. "What?" she asked.

"I don't think I've ever heard you say you love him," Natasha said excitedly. "Awww, we're in love," she added with a smile. Rita looked over her shoulder and looked back into the camera in a panic.

"He's out of the bathroom. Talk to you later," Rita said quickly.

"Okay. Say hi. Love you," Natasha said before the chat window closed down. She placed the laptop on the bed and walked to the living room area of the suite. "How's my veal like husband?" she asked as she approached Mitchell who was

Page 311

seated on the couch.

"Don't call me that," he said. She walked round the couch and looked at him.

"Okay, I'm sorry, baby," she said as she leaned forward to kiss his forehead. She pulled away and looked at him. "That didn't hurt, did it?" she asked looking at him. He shook his head.

"I should punish you for laughing at me," he said looking into her eyes. She smiled and kissed his forehead again.

"Are you going to pull me over your knee and spank me like a naughty little girl?" she asked looking at him. "Because I have been a very bad girl," she said in a mock child voice. He looked up at her and smiled before taking her hand. She gasped when he suddenly pulled her down on his lap making her lie face down across his thighs. She felt a thrill go through her body. He was actually going to do it. She smiled as she seductively wiggled her ass. She felt Mitchell slowly rubbing her ass, softly, gently, as if he was afraid she would break. He suddenly surprised her by bringing his hand down forcefully making her gasp. She felt a sting where his hand had just landed, but there was still eroticism all through her body. She looked over her shoulder and looked at Mitchell as he readied himself to land another hard spank on her. She gasped again as she felt his hand come down hard on her yet again.

"You like that, don't you?' he asked in a soft whisper that made her all warm inside.

"Yeah…I love it. Give it to me," she said in a harsh whisper. She grabbed the edges of the couch as he spanked her again, and again and again. His repeated punishment made sure that she was no longer gasping every time he spanked her but moans and groans escaped her very perfect lips. He spanked her one last time as he felt his erection pressing against her underbelly. He finally rested his hand on her ass which was hot from his recent punishment. She stood up and straddled him.

"Finally ready to thank me for your punishment?" he asked looking into her eyes. She smiled and nodded before bringing her head down to kiss him. He wrapped his arms around her waist and kissed her slowly but deeply. She closed her eyes as she slowly ground her hips down on his crotch, feeling the soft material of her bathing suit getting wet from her own horniness. She pulled away and stood up. He looked at her as she slowly wriggled out of the bathing suit. He smiled and looked at her perfect body. "God, you are beautiful," he said as she bent down to pull his shorts off. She smiled at him and straddled him once again before pulling his shirt over his head.

"You are not so bad looking yourself, Mitchell Schmidt," she said as she ran a finger down his chest. He gently grabbed her by the hair and pulled her down to kiss her lips. "I love a man who takes what is his," she said when he finally pulled away. He nodded.

"I will never let you go," he said as he softly kissed her neck. "Not now..." he planted another soft kiss on her neck. "Not ever," he added in a whisper as he kissed the other side of her neck. She closed her eyes as she felt him trailing his kisses down her neck and along her shoulder blade.

"Baby...I will never let you go either," she said in an erotic whisper. He finally let go of her hair and continued trailing kisses down her chest. She gasped as he trapped one of her nipples in between his teeth and gently nibbled. She moaned, but she was unsure whether she moaned out of fear or ecstasy. Her breathing soon tuned into short quick gasps as he began sucking on her nipple, making it become fully distended. She held onto his head as he sucked on, occasionally teasing her with the expert flicking of his tongue. She moaned her disapproval when he released her nipple. She moaned even louder when he trailed his tongue across her chest and softly kissed the top of her other breast before he took in her other nipple. "Oh God, Mitchell," she moaned as he once again began his oral attack on her nipple She moaned and writhed on his groin, threatening to swallow his cock inside her.

"Tell me what you want," he said when he pulled away from her nipple. "Tell me what you want and I'll do it," he added in a whisper as he looked into her eyes.

"Make love to me Mitchell," she said in a pleading voice. He held her ass and stood up before carefully placing her down on the carpet. He knelt in between her legs and very slowly ran his fingertips along her thighs. He then bent down and took one of her legs in his hands and lifted it up to his lips. She looked at him as he kissed her foot, slowly working his way up her thigh. She felt an excitement go through her body as the thought of his lips on her lower lips crossed her mind. She wanted him to suck her clit, to bury his tongue deep inside her, to make her climax by the way he would expertly use his mouth on her. As his lips got closer to her center, she spread her legs wider,, inviting him in but instead of going down on her, he put her leg down only to pick the other one and service it in the same way.

He lowered his body and aligned himself with her sex. He looked into her eyes as he pushed his cock gently into her pussy, making her gasp. She spread her legs as wide as she could and arched her back to ease his penetration. She wrapped her arms around his back as he buried himself deep inside her. He slowly eased himself in and out of her as he kissed her.

It was not long before his slow and smooth strokes became long and hard ones. He was having an increasingly hard time keeping up especially since his sunburned back was still 'untreated'. He slowed down before coming to a complete stop. He pulled away from her and buried himself in her neck.

"The burns?" she asked. He nodded and pulled himself up. "I'll take care of this," she said with a smile as he pulled out of her and rolled over. She got on top of him and straddled him once again.

"Oh yeah...." He moaned as she eased herself down his girth. She looked down at him as she pulled herself to a squatting position. This way, she would ensure that she kept her weight off him and that he had maximum penetration. "Baby...yeah," he moaned. "Just like that," he said as she bounced on and off his cock, not showing any signs of stopping soon.

"Oh fuck, Mitch. I'm cumming," she moaned as she went on riding him. Mitchell looked up at her and held her full breasts in his hands as he gave in to her hard strokes. He felt himself pulsating as he exploded inside her. She struggled to keep herself at bay but to no avail. She suddenly felt herself pulsating in rhythm with his own orgasm. "Baby I love you," she said in a whisper as she collapsed on top of him. He wrapped his arms around her as they lay on the carpet, spent and exhausted.

"Remember when I told you that you are going to kill me one day?' he asked. She nodded and kissed his cheek. "Well, woman, one day you are going to kill me," he said again.

"It would be the kind of death that most men would choose, though," she said panting. He laughed.

"So," he started as she felt his cock getting hard again. "Any plans for today?" he asked pressing his crotch against hers. Natasha pulled away and looked at Mitchell.

"Depends," she said smiling. "Are you going to use that right now or are we saving it for later?" she asked. Mitchell smiled and answered by pushing himself inside her once again.

"We both know that is not a pickle I have in my pocket because my pocket is on the floor next to me," he said as he pulled her down for a kiss.

"You know sunburns and carpet burns don't usually go well together," Natasha said after pulling away.

"Don't ruin the moment," Mitchell said as he pulled her down again for another kiss.

Chapter 6

Being in Antigua had taught Mitchell two very valuable life lessons: first, he didn't tan very well and two, his wife looked ridiculously hot in swimsuits, not that he didn't know it. The friendship the two of them had forged with Melinda and Kyle made their honeymoon an even better experience.

Today, Melinda, having frequented the island more, had offered to take Natasha for some shopping before joining the guys later on that evening for dinner. Being the man he was, Mitchell was not about to be left alone in this. He took the opportunity and asked Kyle to take him to some of the island's hot spots, a special place. Maybe somewhere he could even manage to get a keepsake.

"So, where exactly are we going?" Natasha asked as she put on a pair of white linen pants. She thought they would go perfectly with the yellow halter top she had on. The humidity in the Caribbean had made her hair frizz up, showing off her beautiful black curls. Melinda, who was waiting for her in their suite, smiled.

"Oh there is so much to see here and the massages are just superb," Melinda said as Natasha walked towards her.

"Spa! Awesome," Natasha said excitedly as she walked into the living room part of the suite. She frowned when she saw Melinda's hair still looking beautifully straight except for the curls at the end. "I fail to understand how your hairstyle survives in this weather," she said.

"I got some frizz free serum for my niece sometime back. Just rub a little in every time I wash it and voila," she said as she stood up.

"I hate you," Natasha said as the two of them walked towards the door.

"Come on. Your curls are great and natural," Melinda said. "You'd be crazy not to love them," she added. Natasha looked at her.

"Don't get me wrong I do. I just wish the straight thing would last longer sometimes," she said. "But I am a woman of color and this is the burden I have to bear," she added as they got into a cab. She noticed Melinda look at something in her purse and then frown before looking up.

"Take us to the Zelani Complex please," Melinda said and then turned to Natasha. "They say it's the true Antiguan experience here. Everything you would need under one roof," she added with a wink. Once again, Melinda reached into her purse and pulled out her phone, looked at it briefly before putting it back inside her purse.

"Everything okay there Mel?" Natasha asked. "You look a little bit shaken up." Melinda gave her a weak smile as her phone vibrated yet again. She took the phone and typed something in really fast before switching it off.

"Perfect," she said looking at Natasha who had a worried look on her face by now. "Trust me when I tell you that you will love the complex," she added in what Natasha guessed was an attempt to change the topic.

"I can't wait," Natasha said as she leaned back on the seat. She looked outside as he mind went wild thinking about what Melinda could be hiding. A secret past, maybe, or a hidden identity. She turned her head and looked at Melinda who was busy looking out the window. A hit man...hit woman maybe? She chuckled at the thought that this sweet Melinda could ever carry out a hit on anyone.

"What?" Melinda asked when she noticed Natasha's big smile. Natasha shook her head.

"Nothing. Just thought of something ridiculous," she answered. Melinda smiled at back at her and gave a few bills to the driver.

"Well, we're here," she said as she opened the door. "You want to feel pampered, this is the place to do it," she said as they walked into the complex. As they walked into the complex, Natasha felt a weird sense of déjà vu. The complex was like a mall picked right out of the States and dropped in the Caribbean. She almost felt as if she was home in the blink of an eye. "Awesome right? I come here any time I feel homesick, which is a lot," Melinda said as they walked through the aisles. Natasha looked at her. Did she just say feel homesick? Just how much time did she spend in the Caribbean? She held Melinda's hand and gave her a smile.

"Come on. No need to feel homesick and not exfoliate," she said as they walked towards the spa salon nearby.

"Melinda, looking beautiful as usual," a man, one that seemingly enjoyed the other side of the buffet table, said as the two walked in.

"You are clearly a favorite here," Natasha whispered to her as the man hugged her.

"Who is your gorgeous friend here?" the man asked. Melinda smiled.

"Alfonso, this is Natasha. She is a new friend I made here," Melinda said with a smile. "Tasha, this is Alfonso Navarro," she added looking at Natasha.

"It is true what they say about black women, huh?" Alfonso said with a smile. If she was not so sure he was gay, Natasha could have sworn that he was checking her out. "Black genes make blue jeans tight," Alfonso added. Natasha gave him a confused look.

"The first genes is actually genetics and the second one is the fabric," Melinda said laughing.

"Oh genes and jeans," Natasha said with a smile.

"So ladies, what are we having today?" Alfonso asked as he led them to the reception area.

"Well we were thinking of something more in the lines of deep tissue massages," Melinda said with a smile. Alfonso frowned.

"Crazy ex-husband back?" he asked. Natasha looked at Alfonso and then at Melinda.

"What crazy ex-husband?" she asked still looking at Melinda who was busy giving Alfonso signs to shut up. "Mel, what is he talking about?" she asked again.

"Girl please, what kind of friends are you?" Alfonso asked as she sat down between them. Melinda put her hand up and shook her head trying to get Alfonso to stop talking but he was either not seeing her or doing a very good job of ignoring her. "This girl right here was married to this billionaire back in Florida. Fairy tale wedding, princess tale marriage and everything but the guy," he paused and took a deep breath, a bit too dramatically. "The guy was actually into some illicit business, human trafficking," he said in a whisper.

"Alfonso," Melinda said feeling uncomfortable.

"Girl please. Friends need to know these things," Alfonso said. "He got crazy when she found out about it. He beat on her, threatened her at some point, even came at her with a weapon..." "Alfonso!" Melinda said sternly, making them both turn around. "That was supposed to be between us," she said as she took her purse. Natasha watched in surprise as Melinda stood up and walked out of the salon.

"What just happened?" Alfonso asked.

"I think I'd better go after her," Natasha said standing up. Alfonso nodded.

"I'll keep the slot opened in case you change your mind," he called after her. Natasha stopped briefly and gave him a slight wave before she continued running out. She found Melinda standing at the mall parking lot. At some point Natasha thought she saw Melinda brush off a tear.

"Hey, you okay?" Natasha asked when she got to the parking lot where Melinda was standing. "You pretty much bolted out of there," she added as she looked at Melinda.

"I just hate it when reality hits too hard," Melinda said.

"Come on, let's get some junk in you. Ice cream maybe," Natasha said as she took Melinda's arm.

"Tasha, you don't need to..."

"...hush now. I definitely have to do this. Besides you need to talk," Natasha interrupted as they walked to the food court.

"Thanks," Melinda said. "And Phil's Gelato has the best ice

cream this side of the Caribbean," she added with a smile.

"So, spill," Natasha said when they got to Phil's Gelato. "What is this about the crazy ex?" she asked looking at Melinda.

"What else is there to say? Alfonso said it all," Melinda said as she took a large scoop of her double fudge sundae.

"I want your version of the story," Natasha said sympathetically. Melinda took another scoop and began playing around with her spoon. "Well?" Natasha pressed.

"Okay. I met Earl on a trip I had taken to London. I was covering a G8 conference," Melinda started as a faraway look came over her face. "He was nice. Great actually. He was sweet, a gentleman and he had a height I loved. His body looked like it was cut out of some male underwear catalogue," she said with a smile. "He was just great. And he wasn't just all about looks either. He was just the kind of guy I had been looking for in a man." She paused and put a spoonful of ice cream in her mouth.

"So what happened?" Natasha asked.

"Well, ten months later he asked me to marry him and I was ecstatic. Then a few months into the marriage, he began taking more trips. I hardly ever saw him," she paused again. "But I was always comfortable. I drove high end vehicles, wore designer perfume, all my clothes were couture." Natasha knew exactly where this was going, or so she thought. She maybe found out her husband's secret and moved to the Caribbean.

"Earl was an investment banker, at least that was what I thought. Imagine my shock when I found a letter of dismissal in his office when I was cleaning. The letter was maybe a year old but the bank statements told another story. I actually thought that he had been promoted some few months earlier because our cash flow had actually improved. So I did the one thing I thought I should do," she said and took another spoonful in her mouth. At the rate she was going, Natasha was surprised she was not getting a brain freeze by now.

"You asked him?" Natasha asked. Melinda nodded.

"Yeah, I asked him. And he gave me some cock and bull story about a new account he landed just after he got dismissed but that he was too scared to tell me," Melinda said.

"Why would he be scared to tell you? You are his wife," Natasha said surprised.

"I asked the same thing too. He told me that the account he had landed was not done in very legal ways. I thought he had bribed people for the job or something," Melinda said sadly.

"So how did you find out?" Natasha asked.

"Some months after that, I happened to eavesdrop on a conversation he was having with someone on the phone. In my defense I had no idea that he was on the phone." Natasha smiled at her attempt to prove her innocence. "He was talking about the next shipment from El Salvador and some club house. It was weird plus he had become really secretive. I actually thought he was cheating on me, so I followed him," she continued.

"And?" Natasha asked when she thought Melinda's pause was too long.

"It was not another woman," Melinda said with a smile. "At least not one woman. There were two trucks laden with women right in the middle of the road heading out of town. I don't know why but I drove right up and got out of the car and honestly, I don't know who was more surprised between the two of us," she added as she looked at her melting gelato. "I asked for an explanation and all he could tell me was that I need not ask any questions because after all I have never lacked anything," she said.

"Was that when he threatened you?" Natasha asked. She nodded.

"That evening, he told me if I breathed a word to anyone, it would be that last thing I ever do," Melinda said. "I wanted to call his bluff and call the cops but he got violent. I had to get out of there," she added.

"The phone calls," Natasha said. Melinda nodded again.

"He must have got a private investigator or something because he called me two days ago and he told me that he knows exactly where I am," Melinda said. "I am not sure if he is telling the truth or…" her voice trailed off as she brushed off another tear. "I just don't know what to do and I am so scared," she said.

"Mel, does Kyle know?" Natasha asked concerned. Melinda looked up and shook her head. "Does he even know there is an ex?" she asked.

"He knows about Earl but he doesn't know the whole story," Melinda said.

"You lost me," Natasha said.

"Earl never signed the divorce papers. So in the eyes of the law, we are just separated," Melinda said.

"And Kyle doesn't know?" Natasha asked as Melinda once again shook her head. "Oh, sweetie. You need to tell him. Otherwise he is just a booty call, long way from home," she said. "Or is he?" she asked when she noticed Melinda's long silence.

"It started off as a hook up. I didn't expect to fall for him," Melinda said. "Now, I'm scared that if he find out all the ugly stuff in my life that he will up and leave," she added.

"Okay, we need to fix this," Natasha said as she reached into her bag and pulled out some bills. "You need to talk to Kyle because if you love him, he needs to know the truth. I'll talk to Mitchell and see how we can help," She added as they stood up.

"Why would you do that for me? You hardly know me," Melinda said as the two walked out of the complex.

"Because you are much like someone I know," Natasha said.

"Oh yeah? Who?" Melinda asked with a smile.

"Me," Natasha said with a smile.

*****

"You're back," Mitchell said when Natasha walked into the suite. "I missed my wife. How was the massage?" he asked as Natasha walked towards him. She took a long deep breath and sat on Mitchell's lap.

"We didn't have one," she said before kissing him lightly on the lips.

"Oh? Then where did you go for four hours?" he asked as he

looked at her. "Is there someone else already?" he asked, a mock frown on his face. Natasha laughed.

"Keep asking questions like that and there will be," she said as she kissed Mitchell's nose.

"You know that makes me feel like a cat," he said.

"I know. That's why I do it," she said as she grabbed Mitchell's soda from the table. "Anyway, we had an hour's drive to some mall and then Mel had some kind of breakdown so we had gelato," she said before taking a long sip from the can.

"What do you mean breakdown?" he asked. Natasha shook her head.

"Not a bad one. Mild-ish," she said as she took another sip.

"I'm sorry, honey but I have never heard of a mild-ish breakdown. What exactly happened?" he asked worried.

"Let's just say that the past has a way of catching up with you," Natasha said. "And babe, she needs help," she added as she looked into Mitchell's eyes.

"What kind of help?" he asked. Natasha took a long deep breath and began telling Mitchell about Melinda's situation.

"Remember that suit guy we met at last Christmas party? You said he was in law enforcement?" she asked.

"Yeah, FBI actually" he said nodding. "What does he have to do with anything?" he asked.

"I think Melinda may need to get into witness protection," Natasha said looking at him.

"Is it that bad?" Mitchell asked. Natasha looked at him in disbelief and slapped his arm. "Oww!" he yelled as Natasha climbed off him.

"Did you not hear the words human trafficking, Mitchell?" she asked. "Women are being sold as sex slaves!" she said angrily. Mitchell took her hand in his.

"Relax. I was just trying to lighten the mood," he said.

"Well, I don't need my mood lightened. I need to know my friend is going to be okay," she said. He pulled her close and wrapped his arms around her.

"She is going to be just fine. I'll make the call today," he said. "And I love how much helping people makes you happy," he added. She looked up at him and smiled.

"At least now you are not making any more corny jokes," she said. "Thanks," she said in a whisper as she looked into his eyes. He smiled and brought his head down and kissed her. "Hey, we're having dinner with Kyle and Mel. Don't get me started," she said as she pulled away.

"I'm sure they'll understand," he said. "After all we are on our honeymoon and we need some honey on this moon," he added as he pulled her close.

"Really?" she asked. "That's all you could come up with?" she asked with a smile. He stood up and began undoing his pants.

"There is a lot more I could come up with," he said as his pants fell to the ground. "If you know what I mean," he added with a wink. She looked at him and stood up.

"Too bad," she said as she took her top off. "I had special

lingerie I wanted to surprise you with," she said. She looked at him and took the pins out of her hair, letting her curls loose.

"We still have a couple of days more in the Caribbean," he said as he pulled her close. "Besides, that lingerie is probably going to end up on the floor anyway," he added as he undid her bra. She smiled and returned the favor by unbuttoning her shirt. Dinner with Kyle and Melinda would have to wait.

Chapter 7

Melinda looked at Mitchell and frowned. "Are you sure you used suntan lotion, Mitchell?" she asked. Mitchell rolled his eyes at Natasha.

"Why does everyone ask me that? I used the damn lotion and that's the last time I am saying those words," he said. "Because of this darned sunburn we have to have dinner here," he said.

"I'm sorry bro but I do love the room service," Kyle said as he bit into a blueberry. The four of them were having dinner at Mitchell and Natasha's suite. This would actually be the last time they would be seeing each other since it was the last night of their honeymoon.

"Mitchell, I must admit that you have grown on me so I have to tell you the truth," Melinda said. "I have been to places that seem to have more than one sun and I can tell you that I have never seen burns like these," Melinda added.

"My baby just has sensitive skin, that's all," Natasha said as she put a hand on Mitchell's shoulder.

"Okay, let's not talk about my skin anymore," Mitchell said. Natasha looked at him and smiled.

"I love you with or without sunburns, baby," she said.

"Hey, aloe vera works great with sunburns," Melinda said matter of factly.

"I know. This one has been rubbing aloe lotion on me every single day since these damn burns appeared," Mitchell said.

"Not that I'm complaining," he added in a whisper looking at Natasha.

"Wine anyone?" Kyle interjected in an attempt to change the topic. "I brought some of the best wine from the island. Grape never tasted better," he said as he poured the wine.

"You are right. This is divine," Natasha said after taking a long sip. "I know just what would be perfect with this wine. Mel, would you care to help me?" she said standing up.

"Sure," Melinda said as the two of them walked to the mini-bar.

"So, did you tell Kyle? You know about the separation?" Natasha asked in a whisper. Melinda smiled.

"Yeah, he was very supportive. A bit angry about the whole deception at first but supportive all the same," Melinda whispered back.

"Mitchell has a friend in the FBI. He is going to put in a good word for you so you can go into witness protection," Natasha said. Melinda looked at her and then threw her arms around her.

"How can I ever thank you?" Melinda asked.

"Just be safe," Natasha said as she pulled away from her. "Come on. We'd better get back before the boys come looking," she said as she led Melinda back to the living room area.

"I thought you were supposed to bring something that would go perfectly with the wine," Kyle said. Natasha looked at Melinda and then at Kyle with a smile.

"Come to think of it, the wine is just good as it is," Natasha said as she sat down. Mitchell and Kyle looked at each other and smiled.

"Oh please, let the women folk gossip on, Schmidt. We need to talk business," Kyle said with a smile. Natasha looked at the two men and took a sip of her wine.

"Business? What is this new venture?" Natasha asked.

"Well, I got some run down property a few blocks away and I needed to make something of it," Kyle said. "An inn, spa maybe," he added.

"That is really good," Natasha said.

"I need to make sure I can still earn and visit my lady," he said winking at Melinda.

"Hello, adventure!" Natasha said with a smile.

"By the way, we've been here for five weeks and I still haven't gotten around to asking something Kyle," Natasha said.

"And what's that?" Kyle asked looking at Natasha.

"How is it you have such great English. No accents or anything?" Natasha asked. "All the people in the Caribbean have something...a lisp...I can't quite put my finger on it," she added.

"That's thanks to twelve years of foreign schooling," Melinda said.

"Yeah. I went to school in Tokyo and then Boston," Kyle said. "My dad has been to almost every international station as far as his job is concerned," he added as he took a bite of his steak.

"I feel you there," Mitchell said in between bites. "If it were not for my grandmother putting her foot down, I would be somewhere in the Middle East," he added.

"Why?" Natasha asked.

"My dad had to try out business in Arab countries and he planned on taking his family with him. That's why," Mitchell said. Natasha looked at him and frowned.

"Then I would have never met you," Natasha said.

"Yeah, you would have never met all this, huh?" Mitchell said. He suddenly tensed up when he felt Natasha's hand on his cock. He looked at her in surprise, trying hard not to show his arousal to their guests.

"No, I wouldn't have," she said, a broad smile playing on her face.

"Well, I hate to break this up but we have to call it a night," Melinda said touching Kyle's hand.

"It was so good of you to come over," Natasha said with a smile.

"We had to see you on your last night here," Melinda said. "Plus we couldn't go down to the restaurants because of the sunburn situation. You should really use sun block" Melinda added with a smile.

"I swear if anyone mentions the sun thing again…" Mitchell said giving a stern look at Melinda.

"Come on Mitch, I'm sure she was kidding," Natasha said. "So, anyway, here is my number. Office, home, cell. All there," she said as she handed her card over to Melinda. "Don't be a stranger," she said as she hugged the redhead.

"Why would I? You've done so much," Melinda said as she moved on to give Mitchell a hug. "And you, you need sun…"

"…if you finish that sentence Melinda, so God help me, I will kill you," Mitchell said cutting her short.

"You're too sweet," Melinda said as she turned around to look at Kyle and Natasha who were still hugging.

"You guys have to be the best thing to come out of an accidental juice spill," Natasha said brushing off a tear.

"Don't do that. Now you're going to make me cry," Melinda said using her hands to fan her face. Kyle walked towards Melinda and took her hand before walking her to the door.

"If I don't get you out now, we will never leave," Kyle said. Melinda smiled at him and squeezed his hand. "So, what time is your flight?" he asked.

"Midday. But don't worry, we'll take a cab," Mitchell said. Kyle shook his head.

"We would never let good friends take a cab. We'll drive you," Kyle said. "Right babe?" he asked looking at a nodding Melinda.

"Sure. It's the least we can do," Melinda said as Mitchell handed his own business card to Kyle.

"Make sure you use that card. I want it to have a permanent

place in your card holder," Mitchell said with a smile.

"It will," Kyle said as he opened the door. "Have a good night," he said as the two of them left.

"You too!" Natasha called after them before closing the door. Mitchell pinned her on the door and gave her a long hard stare. She looked spectacular in the green wraparound dress she wore. "What?" she asked looking at him.

"You are such a naughty girl," he said looking at her. She smiled.

"I was just giving you a taste of better things to come," she said as she walked towards the bedroom. "So, that was fun," she said as she took her earrings off.

"It was," Mitchell said walking towards her. "I know something that could be more fun," he said as he put his hands on her waist. "By the way, that dress was killing me all the way through dinner," he said as he pulled her close.

"Really?" she asked. "What part of you died a little every time you saw me?" she asked looking into his eyes.

"This, right here," he said as he pressed his pelvis into her. "And I wanted to do this," he said as he kissed her neck. "And this," he added as he kissed her chin again. "All night long." Natasha looked at him and kissed his lips, long and slow.

"Let's do something a little different tonight," she said. Mitchell raised an eyebrow.

"Like what?" he asked, his hands still on her waist.

"Tell me what you want to do to me," she said as she took his hand and led him to the bedroom.

"What if words won't be enough to describe it?" he asked as they walked to the bedroom.

"Then you'll just have to show me," she said as she climbed onto the bed. He smiled and took a seat next to her.

"Okay, I will first get you out of that dress and kiss your neck," he started. "And then I will kiss your neck, work my way down to your nipples and suck them, hard. I will then use my tongue on your navel and then down to your perfect little wet pussy and peel your panties off with my teeth," he said as he leaned in close to her. She smiled at him and slipped one strap of the dress off her shoulder.

"Go on," she said in a whisper. He smiled and placed a hand on her leg and slowly let his fingers brush the soft skin of her leg.

"I will make sure you are comfortable on your back and spread these beautiful perfect legs and let my tongue flicker over that soft clitoris of yours. I will get it inside my mouth and let my tongue rub on it as the heat of my mouth engulfs your sensitive core," he said. Unknowingly, he put his other hand on his crotch and began to slowly rub himself. "I shove my tongue deep inside your pussy making you arch your back. That always turns me on. I feel you struggling with your decision to cry out loud, to scream out your pleasure, almost begging me to stop but I'm just getting started," he said as Natasha took her dress off.

"So do I let you stop or do you defy me?" she asked as she leaned in and began undoing the buttons on Mitchell's linen shirt. He smiled.

"I hardly ever listen when any part of me is inside you," he said smiling. "But now I have to show you what I really meant. Because a picture is worth a thousand words and I want to paint the perfect one," he said smiling.

"Well come on up here, baby," she said as she pushed his shirt off his shoulders.

He smiled and pulled her down on the bed making her squeal a little. He smiled at her as he looked at her body. Natasha loved how he looked at her like he was seeing her for the very first time every time they made love.

"My wife," he said in a whisper. "My beautiful, sexy wife." He leaned down and kissed her. She wrapped her arms around his shoulders as the two of them mashed lips, their tongues crushing against each other. She closed her eyes and let one hand run down one side of his back, feeling the moistness on his skin. Mitchell pulled away from her and pinned her arms above her head. She looked up at him surprised but so turned on.

"Make me yours Mitchell Schmidt," she said in a whisper. He looked down at her and smiled. He brought his head down and kissed her lips.

"You are already mine," he said. "You will always be mine," he said again before kissing her neck. She gasped when he quickly undid her bra as he kept her arms still pinned down on the mattress above her head. She closed her eyes and arched her back a little just as he had said she would when he took one of her hardened nipples in his mouth. She moaned when he sucked on it hard, harder when she tried to break free.

"Mitchell," she moaned as he released one nipple only to take in the other one. His crotch was pressed hard against her wetness and she longed so badly to have him inside her. He released her hands and pulled her panties off. Just like he had said he would, he spread her legs and again looked at her. "Mitch, please," she begged looking up at him. He slowly went down and lay with his head in between her legs. She screamed out loud as she felt his tongue deep inside her. At that moment, she felt her pussy pulsate and she struggled to keep her scream inside her throat. She grabbed the bedding and shut her eyes tightly as he began moving his tongue in and out of her, slowly at first but faster as he went on. The pleasure made her want to squeeze his head in between her legs. He suddenly pulled his tongue out and used it to flick her already swollen clitoris. She moaned loudly when he went on sucking on her clit, getting her dangerously close to her orgasm only to pull away. "Mitch...please don't stop!" she screamed out.

He pulled away and took off his pants. Natasha looked at his cock, bulging with veins with a longing to be inside her. He laid himself on her and with one strong shove, got his cock inside her. She gasped and let go of the bedding she held in her hands.

"Open your eyes. I want you to look at me," he said. She opened her eyes and looked into his. She could see his pupils dilated, from the lust he felt, from the longing he had. "Yeah, baby. Just look at me," he said again as he began moving in and out of her slowly. Her pussy felt so tight around his cock, almost as if it had been years since the two of them made love. He looked at her face which slightly winced every time he pushed himself inside her. She closed her eyes again as he buried his head in her shoulder and fucked her long and hard. His thrusts, long and searching, filled her up every time he pushed himself inside her.

She gasped loudly when she felt him pulling his cock out of

her without any warning. She looked at him as he flipped her over on the bed and looked at her lying there bottom up. He reached for her waist and slowly pulled her up on all fours. She turned around and looked at him.

"Not yet," she said before bending her head to take him inside her mouth. This time it was his turn to close his eyes. He held her head as she sucked him, taking every inch of him inside her mouth. He restrained himself from thrusting deep inside her throat. He maintained his composure as she withdrew him from her mouth and slowly ran her tongue around the tip of his swollen head. He suddenly felt an urge to explode inside her but he could not let himself finish yet. He held her head in his hands and pulled his rigid cock out of her mouth.

"I need to be inside you," he said softly as he turned her around and once again positioned her on all fours. He knelt in between her knees and spread them further, making her moan. He ran his fingers along the smooth surface of her waist and her well rounded ass. She turned around and looked at him as he positioned himself at the opening of her wet pussy. She wanted to so much push herself back and take him in but he seemed to have his own well thought out plan. She turned around and held on to the bed rails as he entered her again. He felt deeper than he was when he was on top of her. She involuntarily bucked her hips backward, meeting his every thrust.

"Baby, I'm about to cum," she screamed out loud.

"Don't hold back baby," he said as he continued thrusting. "Just do it. Cum for me, baby," he said as his palm landed hard on her ass, making her scream. "Cum for me," he said again as he spanked her. Natasha held on to the rails as she felt her insides pulsating, almost forcing his cock out of her wet pussy.

"Yeah, that's it," he said as he went on thrusting. Natasha suddenly felt Mitchell's thrusts get harder, longer and more intense as he began pouring himself into her. "Oh shit, baby!" he cried out loud as he drained himself into her. "I love you so much," he said panting as he pulled out of her.

"I love you too," she said as she collapsed in a heap on the bed. He held her close and planted a kiss on her forehead. "So, we go back home tomorrow," she said.

"Yeah, back to reality," he said closing his eyes.

"It's been great though, hasn't it?" she said. He smiled and gave her a tired nod.

"It's been too great," he said as he ran his hand along her arm.

"Mitchell Schmidt, are you complaining?" she asked looking up at him. "Because I could stay here," she added with a smile.

"I would never complain," he said. "Let's just enjoy our last night here," he said as he snuggled in closer to her.

"Mitch, is that a hard-on?" she asked smiling. He smiled down at her and nodded. "Round two?" she asked.

"Oh yeah, round two indeed," he said as he rolled over so that she could be on top. She smiled and put her arm around his back as she lost herself in his kiss. She planned to savor each moment of this night because she wanted to remember every detail of their honeymoon for the rest of their life together.

Book 5.

Making Babies With Mr White

Chapter 1

The weather was beautifully warm when the Schmidts finally got back home. The trip from the airport was seemingly short especially since the two had decided to nap all the way home. It seemed the jet lag was a bit too hard on them.

"Ahem," the driver said loudly when they got home. He looked at the couple in the rear view mirror and was not surprised to see that they were still asleep. "Ahem," he said again, a bit louder this time.

"Oh, sorry. We're just a bit exhausted from the flight, that's all," Mitchell said as he gently shook Natasha's shoulder.

"It's all right, Mr. Schmidt. I understand," the driver said and got out.

"Tasha, we're home. Wake up," Mitchell said as Natasha's eyelids fluttered open.

"Already?" she asked as she stretched. Mitchell smiled and opened the door on his side.

"I know. We can continue this little nap inside," he said as they got out of the cab. The driver was walking towards the door carrying the last bag.

Mitchell reached into his pocket and pulled out a hundred dollar bill when he walked back to the car.

"Keep the change," he said as he handed the driver the money. The driver beamed.

"Thank you, sir. Very generous of you," the driver said as he got back in the vehicle. They turned and slowly walked towards the door, both tired and exhausted from the flight.

"Wait," Mitchell said as they approached the door. "I have to do this right," he said. Natasha looked at him in wonder.

"Mitch, what the…whoa," she said when he took her up in his arms. She looked up at him and smiled. "Oh, so this is what you meant," she said as he carried her into the house.

"Men have been doing this since way before time began. So, welcome home, my wife," he said before bringing his head down and kissing her. She pulled away and smiled, then looked around the house. She suddenly felt as if this was a different house. Things were not the way she remembered them. She could have sworn that walls had been moved and repainted, and the furniture she remembered was no longer there. In its place were new seats, black in color. There were multicolored throw pillows all over the living room…the same way she would have redecorated.

"Mitch…what happened to your house?" she asked as he placed her down. She walked towards the living room and noticed that his frat house table that had beer and tea stains was out and in its place was a black marble top dining table. The new paint and the low hanging chandelier gave the entire room a colonial feel.

"That was *my* house. I needed to turn this into *our* house," Mitchell said as he walked over to her. He put his arms around her waist and kissed her neck. "I made sure everything was made exactly how you would like it," he added. She turned around and kissed him. "Wait, you haven't seen anything yet," he said, pulling away.

"Haven't I seen enough?" she asked. He smiled and shook his

head.

"Come on," he said as he took his hand. "You have to see the bedrooms," he said, leading her through the hallway.

"Bedrooms? How many do we have?" Natasha asked with a smile.

"Three," he said. "The other two don't really matter. The master is what you must see. After all, you'll be spending a lot of time in here," he said as he opened the door to their bedroom.

"What the…" her voice trailed off as she looked around. The bed she had come to know for so long as his had been replaced by a beautiful king size bed. The light brown carpeting was a perfect match to the drapes and wallpaper. She turned around and looked at him. "How did you orchestrate all these without my knowledge?" she asked smiling.

"I do have a few tricks up my sleeve. I made all the plans before we left and left the project in the able hands of your good friend Rita," he said. Natasha giggled at the thought of remodeling the house being called a project. She walked to the bed and sat down. He watched her run her hand over the smooth bedding. "She's pretty talented if you ask me. Maybe she has more than just art in that hot headed mind of hers," he said as he walked towards the bed.

"Your house was beautiful as it was," she said looking at him. He shook his head.

"I needed it to be our house plus I knew how uncomfortable you were with the fact that I had fraternized with other women in this very house," he said putting an arm around her shoulders. "I needed to make sure that you would feel at home and not like a guest," he added as he planted a kiss on her forehead. She smiled.

"This has to be the grandest gesture you have ever shown me," she said. He laughed.

"Grandest? What are we now, old English?" he asked with a smile. She shrugged.

"Certain gestures call for certain measures of kindness, kind sir," she said as she let her hair loose and began unbuttoning her blouse.

"What are you doing?" he asked, looking at her. "I thought we were tired," he said. She smiled and stood up to take her pants off. He looked at her standing before him in just her underwear.

"We are tired. But before we get into bed, we have to test the shower," she said as she unhooked her bra. He looked up at her and smiled.

"You do know that the head that is tired will not be accountable for the head that demands…entry?" he asked looking at her. She smiled.

"If you are going to, quote unquote, demand entry, then I would rather have a shower alone," she said as she walked towards the bathroom. He took his clothes off in a rush and followed her. He caught her just before he she opened the door.

"There are golf clubs in the closet downstairs. If I ever turn down the opportunity to see you naked as water streams down that sexy body, do me a favor and use one of them to beat me to death," he said as he opened the door for her.

He smiled when she gasped at the sight of the new bathroom. There was a beautiful steam shower cubicle and a huge cream colored tub a few steps away from the shower.

"I am never leaving this room," she said as she stepped into the shower.

"We don't ever have to," he said as he closed the door behind them.

*****

"I just love what you have done with the place," Stacy said as she took a sip of her wine. "I mean, I just saw it once before but even I can tell that there's been a drastic change," she said leaning back.

"I know. And people have to pay for this shit. Can you imagine," Mona asked as she bit into a piece of cheese.

"Um, honey, I got paid for this," Rita said matter of factly.

"What? But you're family," Mona said with a smile. "I wouldn't have paid you if you were me," she said as Natasha walked into the living room carrying a bowl of fruit. The girls had decided to drop by when they heard of the couple's return.

"Don't get me wrong, Mona. I was willing to do it for free but he seems to really love ripping those leaves off his checkbook," Rita said.

"True that. Mitchell had me send her another check after she declined the first one," Stacy said. Mona took another piece of cheese.

"Why wasn't I in on this damned party when you got together with Prince Charming in the first place?" Mona asked looking at Natasha.

"Don't look at me, cuz. I invited you over for the longest time. You were always doing something," Natasha said as she sat down.

"Or someone," Rita added without looking up. The girls looked at each other and laughed. "So anyway, this made me realize that I may be looking at a great career in interior décor," she said with a smile.

"What about your art?" Mona asked. Rita smiled and took a long sip of her wine.

"That's still in the keeps. I am not dropping it," Rita said. "But interior design looks like something I would want to pursue," she added. Natasha giggled making Rita give her a stern look. "What?" she asked.

"Do you know how many things you have thought of doing?" Natasha asked as she took a seat on the floor.

"How many? It's not like I jump on every good idea or anything," Rita said looking at Mona. "Right?" she asked. Mona shook her head.

"I love you too much not to tell you the truth," she said. "But every time you do something and it turns out well, you always talk of dropping everything and doing the latest thing," Mona added.

"That's not true," Rita said looking at Natasha and then at Stacy. "Is it?" she asked.

"Honey, I hate to be the bearer of bad news, but, isn't that how you landed on art in the first place?" Natasha said as she placed a reassuring hand on Rita's knee.

"I think you just have to accept that you are multitalented," Stacy said without looking up.

"Guess you are right," Rita said. Natasha smiled at her.

"At this rate we'll have a Rita events company, Rita arts gallery and Rita interior décor," Natasha said.

"Whitey is right. Just admit you are a woman of many talents," Mona said. Natasha rolled her eyes.

"Stacy, Mona. Her name's Stacy," Natasha said sternly. Mona smiled.

"You know I don't mean anything by it, don't you?" Mona said with a smile. Stacy nodded.

"Otherwise I would question the relationship between you and Leo," Stacy said as she took a sip of her wine. Natasha and Rita smiled at each other. "Even Whitey here noticed," Stacy joked.

"Yeah, how is that going?" Natasha asked with a smile. "It's been what, a month?" she asked looking at Rita who was now nodding. Mona shrugged.

"Nothing serious yet, I hope," Mona said as she leaned back in her seat. Natasha leaned forward. Her cousin had a look that she knew only too well, a look that only came about when Mona was smitten. Natasha had only ever seen that look twice, once when they were kids and the other time when Mona met her son's father, right before he screwed her over.

"Oh my God," Rita and Natasha said in unison. Stacy looked at them, confused.

"What? What happened?" she asked looking at Rita and Natasha, who were still staring at Mona. "Guys, what?" she pressed.

"You see it too, don't you?" Rita asked. Natasha nodded and took a sip of her wine, still looking at Mona.

"Okay this is getting really annoying," Stacy said. "Is this some kind of inside joke I don't get?" Natasha shook her head.

"No, sweetie. What we have here is a case of Mona falling in love," Natasha said. Mona stared daggers at her.

"I most certainly am not!" Mona said.

"Watch it, Pinocchio, your nose is getting a bit long there," Rita said. Mona felt her whole face flush.

"Wow, I thought it was a friend with benefits kind of thing," Stacy said as she turned around to look at Mona.

"Trust me, us too," Rita said. "So, Mo, when did this happen?" she asked. Mona shrugged.

"First off, you all need to chill with the stare contest. Man, if looks could kill," Mona said tugging at the sides of her sweater as if the room had suddenly become cold.

"If looks could kill, you'd be the skeleton in my closet," Rita said, making Natasha and Stacy laugh.

"Not funny," Mona said wagging a warning finger at them. "Anyway, I don't want to count my chickens or anything but there could be something real with Leo," she added, blushing.

"Awww, our hard hearted Mona is finally falling in love," Natasha cooed. Mona threw a cushion at her.

"We're happy for you," Rita said with a smile. "I haven't known Leo for long but from the little I have come to know him I can say that he is a pretty decent man," she said as she stretched her arms out. Natasha smiled and looked at her phone vibrating on the table. She giggled and typed frantically before putting it back down. "Really? You guys just spent an entire month together," Rita said.

"How do you know it's Mitch I'm talking to?" Natasha asked.

"Tasha, no one else can make you giggle the way he does," Stacy said. Mona and Rita nodded as Mona gave Stacy a fist bump.

"Word," Mona said. Natasha rolled her eyes.

"Well, we're still newlyweds, so screw you!" she said.

"Is the bathroom still in the same place or is that one of the rooms he knocked out to make room for your fuck pad?" Rita asked standing up. Natasha laughed.

"Down the hall to the right," she said as Rita walked off. "So, Mona, are you in town for long?" Mona shook her head.

"Just for the week. I just had to take care of a few legal formalities for Leo. Comes with the new job and all," Mona said.

"Oh yeah, how's that working out for you?" Stacy asked with a smile.

"Couldn't be better! This is the first job I have had that has a good medical plan. It even covers Dash!" Mona said excitedly, making Natasha laugh. "Beats working at a drive-thru any day," she added.

"Really happy for you, honey," Natasha said with a smile. She was glad that things were working out so well for Mona. She was the one person who had gone through hell and could still stand up holding her head high. Natasha had always looked up to her for as long as she could remember for being so strong willed. Mona had stayed strong through a messy divorce, when her ex cleaned her out and when he bailed out on child support despite the fact that Mona had spent all of her savings to get him started on his business. Natasha always thought that if she had been in Mona's shoes, she would have probably taken her own life by now or something else equally ridiculous. She looked up to see Rita walking back. There was a really concerned look on her face.

"Tasha, is there something you want to tell me?" Rita asked as she sat down. Natasha looked at her in surprise.

"Like what?" Natasha asked still looking at Rita.

"OK, this family has way too many secrets," Stacy said under her breath as she looked up at the newly unfolding drama.

"Should you even be having that?" Rita asked, pointing at the glass of wine in Natasha's hand. Natasha looked down at the drink and shrugged.

"The wine?" Natasha asked, looking confused. "Why shouldn't I be having wine? It's not like I'm pregnant or anything," she said before putting the glass on the floor beside her. Rita walked up to her and looked into her eyes.

"Are you sure?" Rita asked. Mona and Stacy's gazes were now shifting from Rita to Natasha questioningly.

"I think I would know if I was pregnant," Natasha said.

"So the nursery is just for show?" Rita asked, looking at her. Natasha raised her eyebrow at her friend.

"Say what? What nursery? What the heck are you talking about?" she asked looking confused.

"The one down the hall to the right? Guess you are yet to get used to your new house too," Rita said as she held out her hand. "Come on," she said taking Natasha's hand. Stacy and Mona followed soon after even though they were not really part of the mini invite. As Natasha walked towards the said nursery, she felt a tightness in her throat. "Right here," Rita said as she opened the door. Natasha gasped as she laid eyes on a full on nursery. She should have taken the damn tour last night when they got home. She looked around at the beautiful room, unsure of what she should feel. Happy, sad, or confused?

"You didn't know about this?" Stacy asked as she walked towards the crib. Natasha shook her head.

"I was yet to take the tour of the whole house. We just got home last night," Natasha said.

"But this is good, right? You always wanted a little one of your own," Mona said as she draped an arm around Natasha's shoulders.

"Yeah, this is what you always said you wanted. To be the mother your mother never was," Rita said as she looked around.

"Why are you even shocked? Wasn't this your job?" Mona asked. Rita shook her head.

"No, this was the one room I was not allowed to touch. I actually never went in. He must have wanted to be sure I wouldn't blabber anything out to you," Rita said.

"Well, I am surprised. That's for sure," Natasha said. Stacy walked up to her and gave her a hug.

"This is good. I'm so happy for you," Stacy said with a smile.

"Hey, I'm not pregnant yet. Don't pop the champagne," Natasha said, laughing. Though she was smiling, she was still trying hard to wrap her head around the whole idea of being a mom. Not that she didn't want to become a mom. She just always thought she would have more time after being married. But maybe this was a good thing.

"Well, been there done that and I can tell you, there is no greater feeling than knowing you are going to bring something beautiful to this world," Mona said. Natasha smiled.

"I have a feeling I will love the experience," she said as they headed out of the room.

"I have a feeling you will be a great mom," Rita said with a smile. Natasha smiled and nodded. Somewhere inside of her, she knew Rita was right.

Chapter 2

When Mitchell got home later that evening, he was not sure whether Natasha was in or not. There was a deafening silence in the house and except for the lights in the porch, the house was completely dark. Mitchell thought that was a bit odd. Natasha would have called if she was heading out. He looked at his wrist watch. It was a quarter to ten. He steadied the pizza box in his hands and unlocked the door.

"Tasha, honey! Are you here?" he called from the door. Immediately after he said this, he felt a bit stupid. Of course she wasn't home. There were telltale signs of her not being in the house, after all. This thought was maybe the reason he almost jumped out of his skin when he heard her voice call out from the living room.

"In here," Tasha said. Mitchell flicked on the lights in the foyer before making his way to the living room. He walked towards the couch and placed the pizza box on the table before he sat down next to Natasha. He knew her well enough to tell that something was wrong. There was a warm fire crackling in the fireplace.

"Are you okay?" he asked, placing a hand on her knee. She nodded without looking at him. "Then why in God's name are you sitting here in the dark?" he asked as he tucked a strand of her curly hair behind her ear. "Did I already do something wrong, so soon after our honeymoon?" he asked jokingly. Natasha turned around and the look on her face wiped the smile right off his own.

"Why didn't you tell me about the nursery, Mitch?" she asked looking at him. "Why did you have to wait for me to find that out?" she asked again. He looked at her, defeated and disappointed.

"I was going to tell you. I was going to show you last night but we were tired and jetlagged," he paused and looked into her eyes. "And if I remember correctly, at some point you couldn't keep your hands off me," he added with a smile. Natasha pulled away from him angrily.

"Oh, so now it's my fault?" she asked, looking at him. He shook his head and took her hands in his.

"No, never," he said looking at her. He did not understand why she was getting so worked up. "Tasha, I want kids and I want them with you," he said. She looked at him and shrugged.

"I want kids too, but don't you think it's a bit too soon?" she asked. Mitchell pulled her close.

"Baby, I never said I want them tomorrow," he said smiling. He wrapped his arms around her and planted a kiss on the top of her head. "I am just saying that I am ready any time you are," he added as he slowly ran a hand up and down her upper arm. She closed her eyes as she leaned on his chest. Mitchell had come from what he liked to call a loveless family. His parents were always too concerned with their careers to pay any attention to him. To make it worse, they shipped him off to boarding school in Europe to avoid feeling so guilty about missing so much of their son's life. Life for Natasha had been a little different. Even though her mother walked out on them, she had all the love she ever needed from her dad and grandmother. Mitchell was never so lucky; after all, that's what happens when your surname carries a billion bucks.

"Do you think we're ready?" she asked. "Because people with kids say that being a parent is the most fulfilling sensation you could ever have. Even those who were not ready to have kids," she added. He smiled and nodded.

"I'm sure it is," he said.

"But Mitchell…" her words were quickly cut short as he brought his head down and claimed her lips in one long kiss. She looked up at him when he pulled away and smiled.

"I had the house remodeled for us, for our family. I told you once that I want to be the father to your kids," he said. "What better way to start our lives together than like this?" he asked. She looked at him, speechless. She knew that he was right but she had no idea how she was supposed to react. She had always thought that this would be her choice, hers alone. But maybe he was right. Maybe it was about time she accepted that she was no longer in this world alone. That she could no longer make life changing decisions on her own. She looked at him and sighed.

"You could have told me this any time in the Caribbean," she said sadly. Mitchell looked into her eyes and could have sworn there were tears threatening to flow down those flawless cheeks. He ran a finger along the side of her face.

"I wanted to," he said softly. "But if this feels rushed then we can wait. I will wait for as long as you want me to," Mitchell said with a smile. She leaned on his chest again and sighed.

"But what about work? What happens to my career?" she asked. Mitchell frowned.

"What do kids have to do with your career?" he asked.

"I always said that I don't want to be one of those parents who leave their kids with nannies. That's how my mother…that woman who bore me did. And that's why she never had any second thoughts leaving me alone in the house with no one…" Mitchell gently squeezed her shoulders, cutting her off.

"You are not your mother," he said in a whisper. "You will *never* be your mother," he said again.

"I want to be a stay at home mom," she suddenly said. Mitchell pulled away from her and looked down at her, surprised.

"Are you sure? Because I know that more than anything you love your career," he said looking at her. She nodded.

"Some things are more important than work. My babies for instance…"

"…*Our* babies," he interjected. She smiled at him.

"Our babies are more important than my career," she said with a smile. "But I have to take you up on your offer, now," she added, as a more serious look played on her face. Mitchell's eyes lit up.

"Are you sure?" Mitchell asked with a smile. She smiled back at him and nodded. One year after working at Nolan Schmidt Communications Solutions, Mitchell had proposed that he would like to grant her a 20 percent share of the company. Natasha had brought in more business in twelve months than more people do in ten years. Her performance appraisal was glowing, especially since she was the only one who had managed to bring in $14 million in revenue in the first year alone. The NSCS board valued Natasha as an employee more than she thought she was worth. She turned the offer down the first time because she thought it would give the wrong impression of her involvement with the boss.

"What changed your mind about being a shareholder?"

Mitchell asked smiling.

"Well, now I am married to the boss and not just fucking him," she stated.

"Ouch," Mitchell said.

"Now that I am not just fucking the boss, I guess being a shareholder is acceptable," she said, totally ignoring his earlier comment.

"But you know you're irreplaceable, right?" he asked. She looked at him and nodded. "Who is going to take your place?" he asked. She took a long deep breath and looked into his eyes.

"Stacy Reynolds," she said without batting an eyelid. Mitchell's eyes grew wide.

"Stacy? Your assistant, Stacy or another Stacy that I am yet to know?" Mitchell asked.

"Yeah, my assistant, Stacy," Natasha repeated. He looked a bit surprised. "Mitch, Stacy has three degrees. Public relations, advertising and finance. She is more than capable of taking over, plus, I have absolute faith in her abilities," she added. Mitchell leaned back on the couch.

"Three degrees? How did I not know that?" he asked as Natasha opened the pizza box.

"Chicken, bacon, barbecue! My favorite," she said excitedly as she helped herself to one large slice.

'Why did she keep this a secret?" he asked as Natasha chewed enthusiastically on her slice.

"Because certain people only see her as an assistant," Natasha said cynically. Mitchell smiled at her and helped himself to another slice.

"Again, ouch," he said before taking a bite of his pizza.

"Extra cheese…mmm," Natasha said again, ignoring his words. "But like you said, it's not like I am quitting tomorrow. I'll ease her into the news. I'm sure she will be more than happy to take the position," she said as she took the last bite of her slice. He looked at her and smiled.

"Maybe you do have a point," he said looking at her.

"Correction, I just made *the* point," she said as she reached for another slice. He reached over and took the pizza from her hands. "Hey, I haven't eaten all day save for the wine and cheese I had this afternoon. Give it back!" she said sternly. He shook his head.

"I need you to be at your best because I think we need to begin working on the baby right now," he said in a low voice, almost a whisper. She put a hand on his chest and gently pushed him away.

"Wait right here," she said before walking towards the bedroom. Mitchell looked at her and shook his head.

"Should I follow you?" he called after her.

"No! I'll be right back," she called back. He leaned against the backrest and closed his eyes. A smile played on his face as he thought of how happy they would be with two or three kids around the house. The smile soon turned to be a frown as he pictured all three beautiful kids screaming around the house and Natasha exhausted. Maybe he would have to change her mind about the nanny. There was no way she could manage being a full time caregiver to their children. He knew that she would once in a while dive into work to get away from the impending boredom. "I'm back," he heard in a voice that made him open his eyes. He gasped when he saw Natasha standing at the fireplace dressed in just a silk nightie. He could see that she had a packet of pills in her hand.

"What do you have there?" he asked. She smiled and held one hand out.

"My pills," she said. "My birth control pills." He looked at her as she tossed the packet in the fireplace. "Now we can get started on baby making," she said with a smile. Mitchell smiled and slowly walked towards her. He took her hands in his and pulled her close for a kiss.

"Are you sure about this?" he asked when he pulled away. She nodded and kissed him again.

"I have never been so sure of anything in my life," she said. He smiled and brought his hands to her shoulders. She let out a gentle sigh when he slipped the nightie off her shoulders. He stepped back and looked at her before walking around her body, like an artist looking at a fine piece of art. He slipped his hands under her armpits and gently grabbed her full breasts in his hands. She let out another sigh and closed her eyes, resting her head on his shoulder. He kissed her neck as he slowly kneaded her breasts, making her gentle sighs quickly turn to loud moans in no time. He released one hand and let it go down her stomach and then to her pussy where he gently caressed her smooth runway. She let out a moan when his fingers made their way down to her clit and softly brushed it. She felt a shiver go through her body as he began brushing his finger rapidly over her clit. She felt her legs getting weaker by the minute as her pussy got wet, drenching his fingers.

"Mitch…oh baby," she moaned when he tested her wetness using one long finger. She could hear his breathing getting more labored as he moved his finger in and out of her swiftly. The soft kisses on her neck had turned to become rough and wanting. She could feel his cock pressed hard against her bare skin as he involuntarily thrust against her even though he was still fully clothed. She reached behind her and quickly unbuckled his belt before pulling his zipper down. Mitchell was actually kind of amused at how efficiently she got him out of the clothes without actually looking at what she was doing. She slipped her fingers inside the front of his boxers and slowly pushed them off. They proved to be a bit more challenging than the loose fitting pants but that was not what mattered. She gasped when she felt him push in another finger, spreading her out.

He withdrew his fingers and walked around her to look into her eyes. She smiled as she put her arms around his neck and kissed him deeply. He pulled away and got on the floor before gently tugging on her hand to join him. As soon as she was on the floor, he took her legs and raised them high to rest them on his shoulders. She knew exactly what she was in for. He slowly lowered himself to settle in between her thighs. She was already so wet, but he seemed to think that it was not enough. He suddenly put his mouth on her pussy and began taking each lip as if he was still kissing her mouth. She moaned and squirmed, especially when she felt his tongue deep inside her.

Soon, her moans had become loud gasps as Mitchell worked his tongue in and out of her, all the while keeping his hands on her breasts, feeling her hard nipples pressing against his palms. When he finally pulled out, Natasha did not want to give him any time to breathe. She lowered her legs and wrapped them around his waist before flipping around so that he could be under her. Mitchell looked up at her in surprise.

"My turn," she said in a whisper. She lowered her head and began to slowly undo his buttons as she kissed his neck, in the same way that he had done her. He moaned as she ran her tongue along the contours of his neck. When she undid the last button, she trailed her kisses down his chest and finally to his navel but instead of running his kisses down to his crotch, she ran her lips back to his arms. He moaned softly when she began taking his fingers inside his mouth. She could still taste herself on his fingers. He was about to beg her to stop when he felt a warmth engulf his cock. He raised his head to see her head bobbing on his crotch as he sucked on him. She played her tongue on the head of his cock as she kept her mouth on his hardness, making him moan loudly.

"Oh God Tasha," he said when he felt her cup his balls and gently squeeze them as she went on sucking on his cock. She was sucking so hard, he thought she was going to drain him right then and there. "Slow down baby," he begged as she continued working her lips on him.

She suddenly pulled away from his cock and sat on him. He moaned when he felt his cock slip effortlessly into her wet pussy. She looked down at him and smiled as she began to slowly move herself up and down his cock. She moaned louder and louder as she bounced on and off his cock. He put his hands on her waist and began helping her on and off, dropping her hard onto his waiting girth. She put her hands on his shoulders and held on as he went into her hard, slamming against her each time.

He suddenly pulled his length out of her and turned her around. She held onto the table as he got behind her and mounted her once more. She always loved how it felt having him inside her from behind. He always seemed to get a little deeper from that position. She held onto the table as he rammed into her over and over again. She screamed out as she felt him grab her tits roughly. She moaned when he squeezed them gently and brought his lips down to kiss her shoulders.

"Mitch…slow down…you are going to make me cum," she begged as he fucked her hard.

"I can't…I'm too close…" he struggled to say as he thrust into her hard. She suddenly felt herself lose all feeling in her legs as an orgasm tore through her insides. She struggled to hold on to the table as his thrusts got more persistent, a sure sign of his own orgasm. He cried out loud when he felt himself pouring into her waiting pussy. "God…I love you so much," he said panting.

"I love you too, baby," she said as he slowly slipped out of her. They both collapsed on the floor and held on to each other.

"You are a great wife and you will make an even greater mother," he said as he planted a kiss on her forehead. She smiled.

"I think with you by my side, there is no way I would suck at parenthood," she said.

"Natasha Black, are you sucking up to me right now?" Mitchell asked with a smile. Natasha laughed.

"Depends," she said as she gently pressed her ass against his crotch. "Is it working?" she asked. Mitchell tightened his grip around her.

"It most definitely is," he said softly.

Chapter 3

It had been a couple of months since Mitchell and Natasha had the baby talk. Natasha was still active at work though there were instances when she wished she would have stayed home. She could have sworn that her breasts were a bit bigger. She had actually had to get new bras, a size bigger than she was used to. She wanted to tell Mitchell about it but she didn't think it was important. For all she cared it could have just been a hormone imbalance as a result of getting off the pill.

On this particular day, she was on her way to the office in a black wraparound dress and a pair of royal blue heels. She matched this with a blue blazer and a silver necklace. Her hair was straightened and flowing over her shoulders as she walked into the living room where Mitchell sat watching Anderson Cooper.

"This is one of those days I just know I am leaving you at home," she said with a smile.

"I do have a meeting on the other side of town, so yeah. You are flying solo," Mitchell said as he flipped channels. Natasha smiled and walked to the kitchen. She frowned when she opened the fridge. It had been a while since she did the grocery shopping. All that was in there was half a carton of milk, some pizza, a few boxes of Chinese and a half eaten banana cream puff pie.

"Hey honey, we are not having take out again till I say so," Natasha said walking back to the living room. "How about today I do some shopping and cook us a nice dinner?" she asked, hugging him from behind. He smiled and put a hand on the other side of her cheek then planted a soft kiss on her.

"Sure," he said. "All set up for the Japanese meeting?" Natasha nodded as she walked around the couch to sit down.

"Yeah. But I'm thinking I'm going to let Stacy head this meeting. She is much better at smartphones applications than I am anyway," she said. Mitchell frowned.

"You're sure?" he asked looking at her. Natasha nodded.

"Yeah, I'm sure. Apart from the all too obvious chatting app, they have also come up with an app to monitor stocks. Great for all businessmen across the globe but I am not very conversant as far as accounts go. That's where Stacy comes in," she said.

"I always trust your instincts, but I hope this is something you have thought through," Mitchell said. "Well, enough, not that I have any reason to worry," he added with a smile.

"Everything is fine. I have it all under control," she said, sitting down.

"You do know that Nakamura is more annoying than the Malibu princess, right?" Mitchell asked, looking at her. She nodded.

"Give me some credit, Mitchell. I have everything I need right here," she said pointing to her head. "Those Japanese are going to know why we won the war," she added, giggling. She grabbed her bag and kissed her forehead. "I love you," she said as she began walking towards the door.

"I love you too," he called from the couch. He suddenly frowned and looked at her. "We won the war because we hit where it hurt, Tasha," he said just as she opened the door. She turned around and looked at him.

"Actually we won because there were people like me who considered hitting where it hurt," she said before closing the door behind her.

As she drove to the office, she thought of just how her life would change when she became pregnant. She was so used to this routine every single morning that it actually felt like a part of her. The waking up early, going through her closet to decide what to wear, breakfast at home. Maybe it would be for the better. The serenity of the moment was suddenly interrupted by the loud ringing of her phone. She reached for her Bluetooth earpiece next to the gear box and put it on.

"Natasha Schmidt," she said when she answered the call.

"I thought you were not giving up your name. What happened to hyphenating?" Natasha smiled when she immediately recognized Rita's voice.

"Answering the phone saying Natasha Black-Schmidt is a bit too much. How are you?" Natasha asked.

"Not bad. Just missed you," Rita said.

"Missed you too, sweetie, but you're up early," Natasha said looking at the clock. "It's only eight. Dave driving you crazy?" she joked. Rita laughed.

"Nothing like that. I was supposed to be doing inventory. The delivery is late," Rita said in a disappointed tone.

"Like I said, it's only eight. How late could they possibly be?" Natasha asked as she made the final turn to the office building.

"I was expecting some Egyptian sculptures and Greek

paintings yesterday morning. The company said they would be here by the evening but that didn't happen, so they told me that they would do it first thing in the morning," Rita explained. "The bastards cost me my morning sex and you know I love me some morning Dave," she added. Natasha laughed.

"You are having a hard day, aren't you?" she said as she parked her car.

"More like a bad week. There is a collector who has been coming in every week to check on the Greek pieces and I don't even know what to tell him when he comes in today and I still have nothing," Rita said sadly.

"Honey, pop a few buttons and explain the delay," Natasha said as she slammed the door shut. "He will not even know what hit him," she added.

"I don't think Dave would approve," Rita said.

"Fine, but I tried," Natasha said. "Hey, I've got to call you back. I'm going in for a meeting with some guys from Japan, old clients, new product," she said.

"You don't sound very excited," Rita said.

"That's because I am not really looking forward to it. I'd rather be lost in space with the Malibu princess," Natasha said.

"That bad, huh?" Rita asked. "But you got this. You always do," she added. Natasha sighed.

"Guess I do," she said. "Talk later," she said quickly as she hanged up. She was not even sure she had given Rita a chance to say anything. She felt a little guilty as she thought of how rude she had just been. *She would understand,* she thought. After all, she was under immense pressure.

"Good morning, Tasha. Your coffee is on your desk, the Nakamura file is next to it and the board room is prepped," Stacy said excitedly as Natasha walked into the office.

"Thanks Stacy, would you come into my office?" Natasha said with a smile.

"Sure," Stacy said as she followed Natasha into her office. "What's up?" she asked as she sat down.

"Tell me what you know about the Nakamura smartphone app," Natasha said leaning back in her seat. Stacy took a long deep breath.

"Well, they came up with a chat application that works on all operating systems unlike the earlier versions that were only developed for Android phones. They launched a trial version a few months ago in the UK, South Africa and some states right here," Stacy said. "Why do you ask?" she asked looking at Natasha questioningly.

"What do their options look like in trading?" Natasha asked completely ignoring Stacy's question.

"Depends, if they tailor it the same way as the WeVibe application, then they are set for greater things. But if they are only concerned with the Android market then they are set to lose billions with iPhone users and people using Windows Mobile phones. Again, why do you ask?" Stacy asked looking at a smiling Natasha.

"Because you are running point at the Nakamura meeting," Natasha said. Stacy shook her head.

"No, no, no, no," she said. "I know nothing of their product," she added. Natasha smiled.

"You just told me everything I need to know about their product in five minutes," Natasha said. "And you are the one who compiled the file for the meetings, both this one and the one we had six months ago," she added.

"But I was just preparing them. I didn't have any....I don't know if I can do this," Stacy said twiddling her thumbs nervously.

"Stacy, I know about your degrees. I know that being a receptionist was not what you wanted to do all your life," Natasha said. "I think it's time we let you out of the nest, don't you?" she asked. Stacy ran her fingers through her brown hair.

"I'm not even dressed for the presentation," she said looking down at what she had on. Natasha looked at her and laughed. She was in a black pencil skirt and pink sleeveless silk shirt and a pair of black soled pink pumps. She looked beautiful.

"What exactly are you supposed to wear to a presentation? You look lovely," Natasha said. She pointed at her skirt. "Do you know how many times I have closed deals in pencil skirts?" she asked. Stacy smiled.

"Forty-eight," Stacy said. Natasha's eyes widened.

"You kept count?" she asked. Stacy nodded. "Why?"

"You are kind of my mentor," she said.

"Really?" Natasha asked smiling. Stacy nodded.

"You're right. I need to do more with my degrees. I always

hoped I could do more but I'm Stacy Reynolds. No one knows me. My dad is not some senator or rich guy. I didn't know how to progress," Stacy said.

"Hey, my dad isn't rich either, or a senator," Natasha said. Stacy smiled at her. "We make our own name. We shape our future. We make our own legacy," she added smiling. "Three years ago, no one knew who Natasha Black was, but I changed all that," she said again.

"I guess you are right," Stacy said. She looked up at Natasha. "But why now?" she asked. Natasha smiled.

"Remember that day after my honeymoon when we hung out at my place?" Natasha asked. Stacy smiled.

"Those were fun times," Stacy said smiling. "Hey, that's the time we found out about the nursery. Did you ever talk to Mitch about it?" she asked. Natasha smiled and took off her blazer. The wrap around dress was even more flattering on its own. She hung the blazer on her seat and then leaned forward.

"Yes," she said in almost a whisper. Stacy looked even more confused than when she first asked the question.

"And?" Stacy pressed.

"Let's just say that the new Natasha Black is about to be revealed," Natasha said as she slowly flipped through the pages of the Nakamura file.

"What? Already?" Stacy asked. "Congratulations! I thought you looked different but I didn't want to say anything…" her words trailed off when she noticed Natasha looking at her as if all she had said was gibberish.

"I look different? How?" Natasha asked. Stacy shook her head.

"You…um…you know what, you could be glowing because you are happy," Stacy said quickly, avoiding her gaze. Natasha looked at her.

"Stacy Michelle Reynolds, you had better tell me or so help me God…I will kill you with my bare hands!" Natasha said sternly. She looked as the color drained from Stacy's face.

"You know my full names?" Stacy asked surprised.

"Don't change the subject," Natasha snapped. Stacy took a long deep breath.

"Your skin has always been flawless but lately it's been even more glowing, and your breasts…they are not the same size they've always been," Stacy said. "No offense," she added quickly.

"None taken," Natasha said as she leaned back in her seat. "I have noticed my breasts are a bit bigger too. I even had to go shopping because what I had no longer fits," she added. "But I did get off the pill. It could be a reaction," she said in a low voice.

"You got off the pill? You are serious about this!" Stacy said excitedly. Natasha smiled.

"Yeah, and I don't think I want to be one of those women who leave their kids with perfect strangers," Natasha said. Stacy's eyes widened.

"Does that mean what I think it means?" she asked. Natasha nodded.

"Yes," Natasha said with a smile. "But right now, we have to go and show the Nakamuras what you've got," she added.

"I will need a celebratory lunch when I am done with this. Maybe Italian," Stacy said. Natasha frowned as she picked up the file.

"Chinese. Something about Italian makes me sick of late. I don't know why," Natasha said. Stacy looked at her questioningly. "I know what you're thinking and it's not that. I took a test," she said as they walked out of the office.

"You've heard of false negatives right?" Stacy asked matter of factly. Natasha shrugged.

"Yes but…"

"…but nothing. You peed on a stick. Go to hospital and get a proper test done," Stacy said, cutting her short.

"Yes, ma'am," Natasha said with a smile as they walked towards the boardroom.

*****

"You are a natural," Natasha said as they walked out of the boardroom three hours later. "You were born for this," she added as the two walked down the hallway together.

"Learned from the best, I guess," Stacy said with a smile as she took a turn towards Natasha's office. Natasha stopped and held her hand.

"I think this working day is over. We need to celebrate!" Natasha said excitedly. Stacy looked at her surprised.

"It's only midday," Stacy said looking at her wrist watch. Natasha nodded.

"Yes, perfect for our celebratory lunch," Natasha said as one of the office secretaries walked past them. She cringed and held her breath. "What is that smell?" she asked pinching her nose. Stacy looked at her and frowned.

"That's Linda's new perfume. We all got it in the French Volce thank you package," Stacy said. "I got it too, so did you," she added.

"Please don't tell me you wanted to go to the office and dab some of that on you," Natasha said as she felt herself getting nauseated. Stacy shook her head.

"No," she said. Natasha slapped a hand over her mouth.

"I think I'm going to be sick," Natasha said before running to the bathroom. She was still crouched over one toilet bowl when Stacy walked in.

"You okay, sweetie?" Stacy asked, knocking on the door of the cubicle Natasha was in.

"I don't know," Natasha said. "I just puked out last night's dinner and today's coffee and bagel," she added. Stacy placed her hand on the doorknob.

"I'm coming in, Tasha," she said as she opened the door. "Oh my God," she said when she saw Natasha seated on the floor. "Has this happened before?" she asked. Natasha nodded.

"Yeah, twice or thrice," she said. "Last week it was after dinner. Last Tuesday it was just after lunch," Natasha said as she flushed the toilet. Stacy helped her up and walked her out where Natasha began rinsing her mouth out.

"Tasha, you are off your pills, your tits look like a Hooters girl and you are getting sick because of perfume?" Stacy said as Natasha rinsed her mouth. "Don't you think it's time you took a test?" she asked. Natasha looked at her.

"It could be a stomach virus," Natasha said hopefully.

"If it was a stomach virus that has carried on for this long, you'd be dead or dying. Plus Mitchell would also be sick," Stacy said. Natasha looked up at her. Stacy had a point. Natasha had also completely overlooked the fact that she was late. She thought it could also be another effect of coming off the pill but maybe Stacy was right. Maybe she needed to get a test done. She shook her head.

"I'm fine. Let's just do the lunch," Natasha said.

"I'll make you a deal. If we go for lunch we must have Italian and I am going to wear the perfume in my bag," Stacy said. This time, it was her turn to be stern. Natasha cringed again.

"Fine! We'll go to the damn doctor just to get you off my back," Natasha snapped as she looked at her reflection. "Do you have a mint?" she asked looking at Stacy.

"I'll meet you in the parking lot," Stacy said as she walked out of the bathroom. Natasha looked at her reflection and then stood sideways. She looked at her breasts and acknowledged that she did look like a Hooters girl. She grabbed her tits and nodded. They were fuller. She noticed that her ass was also bigger. Just then, the door flung open startling her. She looked at the cleaning lady and felt her cheeks flush.

"Mrs. Schmidt…I'm sorry…I…"

"It's okay. I was just leaving," Natasha interjected with a smile as she walked out feeling embarrassed. She knew that the news about her fondling herself would be leaked in the next few hours. She walked hurriedly to the parking lot. She was surprised to find Stacy already there. "Which path did you take exactly?" she asked. Stacy reached into her purse and handed her a tic tac.

"Let's just go. I called Dr. Mauler when I was at the office. He is expecting us," she said as Natasha walked round to the driver's seat.

"I always thought you were too good to be just an assistant, Stacy," Natasha said as she slipped the key into the ignition. Stacy smiled at her.

"Well…okay, I've got nothing," she said shrugging her shoulders. She fastened her seat belt and put her bag in the back seat.

"Can I have the rest of the tic tacs?" Natasha asked as she began backing out of her parking space. Stacy opened her mouth to talk but then handed Natasha the tiny jar. She must have known that she was about to fight a losing battle. "Thanks! So we're still having Chinese after this?" Natasha asked as they began to drive off. Stacy took a deep breath and nodded. Where to eat was another losing battle.

Chapter 4

Mitchell opened the bedroom door and poked his head through. Natasha was still lying on bed in a fetal position. He felt sadness go through him as he looked at her. She had been like this for two months now. He knew exactly how she felt because he had also been excited to be a father too. He longed to see that beautiful baby Natasha carried…the first, second and third time. He hated going through the same thing over and over again, having to get all excited about the baby and then losing it all over again.

The first time she told him she was late was just a couple of weeks after she decided to toss her pills. To say that he was excited was an understatement. He was glad he had seen the nursery, through. He had even gone shopping, getting onesies and color coordinated outfits. He smiled when he recalled the argument he had had with Natasha about buying unisex colors.

"Three generations in the Schmidt family have always been characterized by a first born male. This one will not be any different," he had said in his defense.

"Well, you could be wrong and I would hate for my baby girl to think she was an accident," Natasha had said with a smile.

"How exactly would she come to that conclusion?" Mitchell probed. Natasha shrugged.

"Remember those photos of you as a baby where you are wearing a pink bunny suit? You know, the one with cuddly bears all over?" she asked. Mitchell frowned.

"We were never to talk of that again," he said. Natasha

laughed.

"I am surprised that bit of your past didn't mess up with your sexuality," she said. "And that is exactly what I am talking about when I say I need to ensure my child is not traumatized seeing herself in blue sailor uniforms," she added. Mitchell smiled and put an arm around her.

"We could make this easier on ourselves and just get a scan," he said. Natasha smiled when she heard a hint of hope in his voice. "They do have special machines for that kind of thing you know," he added. Natasha rolled her eyes.

"I'm sorry Mitch. I know you are a big part of this but I get to puke, I get to hate all the food I love and I get to have a nine pound baby pushed out of my you know what," she said looking at him.

"Don't forget the pooping on the table," Mitchell said matter-of-factly. Natasha gave him a look that screamed 'I would kill you if I didn't love you enough.'

"So, Mitchell Schmidt, all points considered, I call shotgun," she said with a sly smile. Mitchell nodded. He knew when to and when not to engage his wife in a battle, especially when she was already on a winning streak.

All this excitement had been cut short when Natasha woke up one day bleeding. At the time, she was still in her first trimester. This being her first pregnancy, she did not know what to expect. Even the "What To Expect When Expecting" literature proved to be pointless at this time. In the first few seconds, she had all the wrong thoughts going through her mind. It could have been implantation bleeding…but she was way past four weeks which meant only one thing. She was miscarrying. By the time she got to the emergency room, the pain in her abdomen confirmed the painful truth the doctor uttered. She had lost her baby.

As much as she was devastated, she was still willing to try again. So, as soon as she was all healed, she was back on the horse trying everything she could to get pregnant again. And she did but only to be disappointed once more.

After two consecutive miscarriages, she didn't think she could do it anymore. She was even thinking of adoption. After all, a baby was a baby, right? All she needed was some little person to love. It didn't matter who the baby came out of. All that mattered was that the baby would be hers. Mitchell was against adoption at first but Natasha managed to twist his arm eventually. But the adoption process was not as simple as they expected. There were too many logistics. The lady at the adoption agency had even told them that some parents could be on a waiting list for as long as two years. Natasha didn't think she could handle another two years without a baby.

During that time, Mona, Rita and Stacy had almost moved into Mitchell and Natasha's home on Mona's proposition.

"As a mother I can tell you that there is nothing worse than losing your child. We need to be there for her," Mona had said. "She is our family and she'd do the same for us," she added.

After a couple of months, Natasha thought of a third try. Mitchell was unsure. He began doubting his ability to be a father.

"Maybe there is another way. Surrogate maybe," he'd said. Natasha shook her head.

"We're not there yet. We are not that desperate," she said with a smile.

"Tasha, baby, I cannot watch you suffer again. I don't think I can handle it," he said. For the first time since she knew him, Natasha saw Mitchell shed a tear. She looked into his eyes and wrapped her arms around him.

"Third time's the charm, right?" she said before kissing him. He looked into her eyes and smiled.

"We'll be okay, right?" he asked. She nodded.

"We'll be just fine," she said.

Those words were like burning spears now. She shed a tear every time she relived the moment she said them. For the third time, she lost the baby....AGAIN. This was too much for her, and for the first time ever, Mitchell witnessed firsthand, the love of his life shutting down. She never talked, she hardly ate and she was always in bed curled up like a cold kitten. Mitchell sighed and walked into the room carrying the soup he had just made her.

"I brought you soup, babe," he said as he put the bowl on the bedside table. She opened her puffy eyes and gave him a weak smile. "Aren't you going to sit up and eat it? It's shredded chicken, just how you like it," he added.

"I am not hungry," she mumbled. Mitchell took a long deep breath and looked at her.

"You need to eat something, Tasha. You need to keep your strength up," he said. She shrugged and turned away from him. Mitchell felt his rage beginning to rise. He grabbed her and sat her up.

"Let me go!" she yelled as she tried to shake him off.

"You need to eat. Stop acting like a baby and pull yourself together, for God's sake!" he said angrily. Natasha looked at him and shook him off. "I made you the damn soup and you are sure as hell are going to eat it. Now!" Natasha looked at him in surprise.

"What did you just say to me?" she asked in disbelief.

"You heard me. I am not going to repeat myself, you are not a child," Mitchell said. Natasha looked at him, still shocked. She had never known him to be like this.

"You can't make me," she said in a stubborn voice. Mitchell took a scoop of the soup and shoved it into her mouth, spilling a few drops on her pajama pants as he did so. She looked at him as he held her chin, waiting to see her swallow.

"If that is how you want this to work, then this is damn well how we are going to do it," he said. She placed a hand on his and yanked her chin away from his grip. Mitchell looked at her still angry and stood up. "Stop acting like such a spoiled brat, Natasha. Life has to move on," he said as he began walking towards the door. He stopped in his tracks when Natasha tossed a pillow at him, hitting him squarely at the back of the head. He turned around and looked at her. "I don't think I deserved that," he said.

"You think so, you stupid arrogant bastard?" she yelled as tears began streaming down her cheeks. "I lost three babies, Mitchell. Three! Do you even have the faintest idea what that is like?" she asked, her voice quavering.

"As a matter of fact, Natasha, I do. I lost the three babies too, remember?" he asked angrily.

"It is not the same for men," she said before burying her face in her hands. Mitchell's anger slowly subsided as he watched her crying.

"You're right. I have no idea what you are going through, but I was ready for this too," he said as he began walking towards the bed. "We are two peas in a pod. I am hurting too," he added. He took a seat next to her and put an arm around her. "I need my wife. I miss my wife, Tasha," he said as he kissed the top of her head. He pulled away from her and looked at her tear stained face. "For better or worse, remember? You and I are on this ship together. We need each other," he said before bringing his lips down to claim hers.

She closed her eyes as she lost herself in the exhilarating feeling of his lips. It had been so long since she felt his touch, his lips on hers. Without knowing it, her arms were around his neck, involuntarily pulling him down on her. He gently pulled away and looked into her puffy eyes. She wondered what he was up, to especially when he got up from the bed and began undressing. He pulled his polo shirt over his head and then began undoing his pants, letting them fall to the floor. He then pushed his boxer shorts off, revealing his semi-hard cock. She looked at him, more confused than turned on when he stretched his hand out to her. She reluctantly took it as he helped her to her feet. He slowly trailed his index finger on the side of her face and then pulled her own t-shirt over her head. He slowly slid his hands off her shoulders and onto the front of her breasts, her nipples gently pressing into his palms. He then pushed her pajama pants off and slowly led her to the bathroom.

"Mitch, what are you…" Her words were cut off when he kissed her again.

"It's been two months since me and you did anything remotely marital. I need you," he said as he turned on the shower. "I want you," he said, this time in a whisper. He pulled her under the water and held her close as the warm water trickled down their bodies. His hands slowly worked their way from her waist and up to her full breasts. She sighed as she felt him slowly kneading her mounds, attempting to make them perkier than they already were. She leaned against his shoulder as he rubbed her, loving the feeling of her husband making her his once again. One hand released her breast and travelled down her navel to her moist pussy. She gasped when she felt his thumb brush over her over sensitive clitoris, urging her desire on.

"Mitch…I want you," she said in a hushed whisper.

"Not yet," he said as he began working a finger into her, testing her wetness. His cock was already pressing hard into her rear, indicating that he wanted to be inside her, that he longed to be engulfed in her warmth. He suddenly pulled his finger out, liberating her, but her relief was short lived as he pushed in two fingers this time. She winced as she felt herself stretching out, against his fingers. He turned her around and looked into her eyes that were now dilated. Her eyes screamed lust, pain and love. He could not decide what was more important right now except for the fact that she had never looked sexier than she did at that moment, with her wet hair sticking to the sides of her face, her breasts perky and wet as the water flowed down her body. He pulled her towards him and then turned around, pinning her to the cold wall. She gasped as the cold ceramic tiles made contact with her full sexy ass.

She looked into his eyes as he took her in his arms. She looked at him as she felt his cock head pressing into her pussy. She moaned as she felt him pushing inside her, feeling her and filling her every fold. He slowly pulled back and pushed back inside her again, making her gasp and cry out loud as she felt him stretching her out to her limits.

"If this time it does not work…" once again, Mitchell kissed her cutting her words short in midsentence.

"I am not doing this for a baby, Tasha," he said looking at her through the flowing streams of water. "Right now I just want to make love to my wife," he added with a smile.

"All pressure off?" she asked looking at him. He bucked his pelvis into her making her shriek.

"All pressure off," he echoed and began moving in and out of her pussy, his thrusts getting more insistent as he went on. She held on to him as he worked himself into her, feeling her pulsating against his cock. Soon, he was nibbling on her neck as he stroked his cock into her. She could feel his passion rising at an alarming rate, hers too. She almost hated herself for going this long without feeling him deep inside her. She wrapped her legs around his waist, securing herself around him and against the wall. His thrusts by this time had become so forceful that the only sounds she could hear at that time except for the drops of water hitting the floor were of his scrotum slamming against her. With each thrust, a violent shiver went through her making her pussy wetter than ever before.

He pulled away from her and looked at her. She felt another shiver go down her spine as his stare probed through her. His gaze was fierce; his body shook with erotic frustration as he struggled to maintain his thrusts while looking at his wife. She felt herself growing breathless as she looked back at him. She had never seen him look so aggravated, so driven, so….hot. He suddenly bucked his hips into her, making her scream once again. He maintained the look as he thrust into her again, and then again, and then went into full blown piston mode. She held on to his neck as he soon became like a jackhammer, punching into her waiting pussy. She could feel his breathing, labored like an irritated bull readying itself for battle.

She squealed as she felt her body giving in to her pleasures when her orgasm tore through her. She trembled violently as he struggled to keep his rigid cock inside her viciously pulsating cunt. She screamed out as the concluding chapter of her climax finally came to pass. She felt her legs getting weak as Mitchell continued going at her even more strongly this time. She felt a tear roll down her cheek as he fucked her though her post-orgasmic sensitivity before he finally began depositing his seed inside her. He held onto her ass cheeks, squeezing them as he poured himself inside her.

"God, I missed you," he said as he felt his cock slipping out of her. "Whoa," he said when she almost fell over. He turned the water off and took her in his arms. "We can shower later," he said as he carried her to bed.

"I'm sorry," she said as he put an arm around her. He planted a kiss on her forehead and pulled a blanket over them.

"It's okay," he said as the two of them snuggled under the blanket. All that mattered at this moment was that he had his wife back and even though all was not perfect, he had his wife back. "This moment right here, this is the best moment of my life," he whispered as the two drifted off to sleep.

*****

It had been a couple of months since the steamy bathroom sex which then preceded some sort of honeymoon. After that day, Mitchell and Natasha were going at it like sex crazed bunnies. They were literally all over each other, in the living room, on the dining table, in Rita's gallery….everywhere. It was no shock when Natasha missed her period. But this time around, she was in no particular hurry to know whether or not she was expectant. She was not ready to be disappointed again. She was just starting to relive her life in love with Mitchell and she was not about to do anything to ruin it. But when she could not hold any food down, it was time to face the facts.

As she walked into the house after her appointment with the doctor, she was not sure what to think of the whole situation. She looked at Mitchell who was busy watching his Sports Weekly.

"Mitchell, I'm pregnant," she said in a low voice. Mitchell looked up at her and muted the TV. "Three and a half months," she added as a tear rolled down her cheek.

"That's good, right?" Mitchell asked looking at her. She shook her head.

"I don't know. I'm scared," she said as he walked towards her. "I can't lose another one," she said. He wrapped her arms around her and kissed her neck.

"We won't lose another one, Tasha," he said in a whisper. "Not this time," he added. She did not know what it was about his voice that told her everything would be just fine.

Chapter 5

Natasha pulled a t-shirt over her head and sighed. She was well into her second trimester and she could not conceal her baby bump anymore. She could no longer put on the beautiful pencil skirts and mini-dresses she loved so much. Strutting in heels was also a major no-no. Her wardrobe had been reduced to oversized t-shirts, slacks and sandals.

Estelle looked at her as she walked into the living room and smiled. She thought Natasha looked like a cute kid overfed on chocolate cake, especially now that she was showing. Mitchell had to run off to England on an urgent meeting and Rita had clients from Prague coming in every day that week. Getting away for even a second was close to a nightmare and Stacy… well, Natasha's shoes, though dainty, were not easy to fit into. With all her cravings and morning sickness, Estelle had thought it best for her granddaughter to stay with her till her husband came back and it was not an easy fight either. She took the breakfast tray she had prepared earlier and walked to the dining room.

"You know I never let people eat in there," Estelle said to Natasha who was just about to take a seat in the living room. Natasha groaned.

"Why can't I have it in here for once? For the baby?" she asked, looking at Estelle who was now walking towards her. Estelle smiled and took her hand before slowly walking her to the dining room.

"Not even for the baby, honey. Rules are still rules," Estelle said. "Even though I am about to get a great grandbaby!" she added excitedly. Natasha looked at the beaming smile playing across her grandmother's face and smiled. "So, don't you think it's about time we got you some maternity clothes?" Estelle asked looking at the t-shirt.

"Why, Nan? Are you trying to tell me I look fat?" Natasha asked taking a large bite of her pancakes. "God this is like heaven on maple syrup," she said closing her eyes, savoring every bite.

"Well, honey, you know I always tell you the truth, so yes. You cannot wear the clothes you are used to. They make you look....weird," Estelle said looking into her eyes. Natasha shrugged.

"I love my clothes, Nan. I am not about to trade them in to look like a pillow case," Natasha said as she took another bite. Estelle smiled.

"I didn't want to say anything but, have you looked at yourself in the mirror lately?" she asked. Natasha looked down at her clothes.

"What's wrong with what I have on?" she asked. "I know it's a bit big but, hey, it serves the purpose," she added as she poured more maple syrup on her pancakes. Estelle sighed.

"For starters, you have on your father's old and stretched out t-shirt and a pair of gym pants," Estelle said. Natasha took another bite and ran her fingers through her hair.

"Ouch!" she yelled as her fingers got caught up in her tangled strands.

"Plus, you need to brush your hair when you sleep. Avoids all that mess going on right there," Estelle said pointing at Natasha's hair.

"The shampoo smells really gross," Natasha said looking at her grandmother.

"Then buy another scent," Estelle said as she made her way back to the kitchen. She came back a few minutes later carrying a glass of freshly squeezed orange juice. "I can take you shopping later on this afternoon. I don't think I have anything to do then," she said as she handed Natasha the juice. Natasha looked at her and smiled.

"Thanks Nan," she said before taking a sip of her orange juice.

"Any time baby," Estelle said and kissed Natasha's cheek. "Right now, I have to get dinner started," she added as she walked away. Natasha frowned and looked at her wrist watch.

"Dinner? It's only ten," Natasha said. Estelle turned around and smiled at her.

"Well, I'm going shopping later. Didn't you hear?" Estelle asked before walking to the kitchen. Natasha smiled as she looked at her plate. She took the last bite and pushed the plate away. She wanted to go to the kitchen for more pancakes but she was confused between the sudden urge to take a nap and the need to grab a bite. The former won. She gulped down her juice and walked back to the living room where she slouched down on the couch. She grabbed the remote and began flipping through TV channels trying to decide on what to watch. She was still flipping channels when she heard the distinct beep of her computer. She looked around frantically trying to remember where she last saw it, or placed it.

"Fuck!" she thought as she looked around. One of the most annoying things about being pregnant was the way her memory seemed to deteriorate. She would forget the little

things like where she placed her phone or what she went into a room to do. Sometimes she would even go down to the grocery store for some bread but come out empty handed because she had no idea what she was doing at the store in the first place. "Hey, Nan! You seen my laptop?" she called out as she flipped the cushions over.

"On the shelf, under the cable decoder!" Estelle called from the kitchen.

"Finally," she thought as she picked it up. "Thanks Nan!" she yelled as she walked back to the couch. She set the laptop on the coffee table in front of her and flipped the top open. *"Good news, I hope,"* she thought as she clicked on the "new mail" icon popping up at the bottom left corner. She smiled when she saw it was from Mitchell.

TO: Natasha Black

FROM: Mitchell Schmidt

SUBJECT: MISSING MY BEAUTIFUL FAMILY

Hello, my love. I am just back from a meeting with the English dude. He was a bit disappointed you couldn't come, kind of made me a bit jealous. He sends his best though.., but that is not why I am writing. How are you? How is the baby? Are you still waking up in the middle of the day?

She smiled and clicked reply.

TO: Mitchell Schmidt

FROM: Natasha Black

SUBJECT: RE-MISSING MY BEAUTIFUL FAMILY

I miss you too love. I am just fine, getting bigger every day. Sometimes I think whales are smaller and the thought that I will only get bigger freaks me out, big time! And yes, I am still waking up in the middle of the day after all I am carrying your baby. Today I got up a bit early though. I went to bed at five last night, okay, last evening. Long day. And he is not 'that English dude,' he has a name. It's Luke. If you were here you would notice just how much I am rolling my eyes at you right now. Wait, technology *has* made that possible. Why are we e-mailing? Why can't we Skype? By the way, I felt the baby move for the first time today. Such a great feeling. Wish you were here.

She smiled as she clicked "send" and leaned against the back rest. She looked around for the remote and then realized that she had misplaced it, yet again. She sighed as she looked around, wondering if there was a chance it could have slipped in between the cushions. She was still looking when she heard another beep.

TO: Natasha Black

FROM: Mitchell Schmidt

SUBJECT: RE-MISSING MY BEAUTIFUL FAMILY

Okay, it's official. I am jealous. The baby moved and I wasn't there! Man, this is unfair. But I'll be back in a couple of days and I will not let you go till I feel her move. Skype…hmmm, can't work. Something about the hotel's servers. And Luke will always be 'that English dude.' I don't get how women just fall all over themselves just because a man has an English accent. So, 'that English

dude,' Red Alert!

Natasha found herself laughing when she read the last sentence.

TO: Mitchell Schmidt

FROM: Natasha Black

SUBJECT: RE-MISSING MY BEAUTIFUL FAMILY

Correction, dear husband. It is not the English accent that makes women weak in the knees, it's the <u>British</u> accent. And Luke's not even that hot. He would have never have caught my attention if it wasn't for that package of...you know what it doesn't matter. What makes you so sure that it's a girl I'm carrying? You realize that there's a fifty-fifty chance right?

She leaned back and with her free hand, slowly caressed her tummy. She had never thought of knowing the sex of the baby. She wanted to be surprised. There was a thrill in not knowing. But what if Mitchell was right? Or did her husband know something she didn't? She looked at her computer again and noticed the "new mail" icon pop up again.

TO: Natasha Black

FROM: Mitchell Schmidt

SUBJECT: RE-MISSING MY BEAUTIFUL FAMILY

I don't know what it is that makes me so sure it's a girl. Maybe I have been praying for a girl for so long I am hoping that my prayers have finally been answered. We'll see. But whatever happens, you are mine and what you

are carrying, male or female, is ours and I will always love you both.

Natasha smiled and clicked on reply again.

TO: Mitchell Schmidt

FROM: Natasha Black

SUBJECT: RE-MISSING MY BEAUTIFUL FAMILY

Nice save. But we'll see. Patience pays….I'm sure our baby will be the definition of awesome! Feeling sleepy now, I have to take a nap. I have a busy afternoon ahead. Nan is taking me shopping later today.

She smiled as she sent her last email and got comfortable on the couch. *National Geographic* would have to do. She was not about to break a sweat looking for the remote. She heard the beep again and opened the new email.

TO: Natasha Black

FROM: Mitchell Schmidt

SUBJECT: RE-MISSING MY BEAUTIFUL FAMILY

I am a bright man, so nice saves are kind of what I do. Sleep away my beautiful wife. I will call you tonight. Say hi to Estelle. I love you.

She smiled as she slowly stretched out on the couch and reached for the small blanket draped over the couch. She smiled as she pulled the blanket over her body and drifted off to sleep.

She woke up a few hours later to the delicious aroma of fresh bread. She rubbed her eyes and slowly made her way to the kitchen.

"And behold, there she is," Rita said when she walked into the kitchen. She smiled and leaned over the counter.

"Hey, you. I didn't think I would see you this week with all those new European clients and stuff," Natasha said, hugging her. Rita shrugged and smiled.

"Today was one of those days I got to leave early," she said. "What's with you and your dad's clothes?" she asked looking at the oversized t-shirt. Natasha rolled her eyes.

"Not you too," Natasha said as she took a seat.

"Maybe someone in her generation should tell her," Estelle said as she walked towards them carrying a tray of fresh bread and hot soup. "I have taken all I can, you know," she added smiling.

"Nan, I said I would let you take me shopping. Give it a rest, jeez," Natasha said angrily. Rita and Estelle looked at her in surprise.

"You do know she was just kidding right?" Rita asked looking at Natasha in shock. Natasha felt a guilty feeling take over as she looked at the two. She hated what this damn pregnancy was doing to her.

"Yeah, I don't know what came over me," Natasha said. "I'm sorry, Nan. I've been having these short angry episodes, which is weird because I am usually very slow to anger," she added. Estelle smiled and took a seat on the other side of the counter.

"It's okay, the hormones mess with your head and all," Estelle said. "When I was pregnant with your father I could not stand anyone changing the channel even if I wasn't watching it," she said. "Drove my friends nuts," she added with a laugh. Rita smiled.

"See? It's normal. Don't beat yourself up over it, okay?" Rita said as she pushed a bowl of soup towards Natasha. "Your Nan tells me you are only able to stomach a few foods. You better eat that up before it gets cold," she said as she took a spoonful of her own soup. "Mmmm, chicken and mushroom. How is it you manage to pull off great recipes without using a cookbook?" she asked looking at Estelle.

"A true cook comes up with her own and you know I love experimenting," Estelle said. There was a hint of pride in her voice as she talked. "Maybe that's why I'm such a hit at potlucks," she added.

"Talk about blowing your own trumpet," Natasha said as she took a bite of the bread.

"Hey, she blew it first," Estelle said with a smile.

"So how's the morning sickness?" Rita asked. Natasha rolled her eyes.

"It should be called all day sickness," Natasha said irritably. "I don't get why I am still getting sick in my second trimester," she said sadly.

"Well, for some people, the sickness carries to term," Estelle said.

"I miss having pizza and deli meats and Chinese...," Natasha's voice trailed off as she recalled the good days. "But right now I can't even stand the smell. I tried having dinner at Wu's last week but imagine, I wasn't even halfway through the door when I suddenly got the urge to hurl," she said poignantly. Rita put a hand on hers and smiled.

"The good news is it's all worth it in the end," Rita said. "Isn't that right, Estelle?" she asked, looking at Estelle.

"That's so right. Your daddy would get me pissed off on a daily basis kicking me, making me hate chicken. Can you imagine me hating chicken?" Estelle asked. Rita and Natasha laughed.

"Really?" Natasha asked. Estelle nodded and leaned forward.

"I went for nine months without ever having chicken," she said before getting a faraway look in her eyes. "Maybe that's why I got to love chicken that much," she said. Rita nodded.

"Could very well be," Rita said.

"Anyway, you better get ready. Wheels up in fifteen," Estelle said walking to the kitchen. The girls broke into giggles.

"Wheels up? Do you have a private jet now that I don't know about?" Natasha asked. Estelle turned around and smiled at them.

"I watch TV too. I am familiar with the lingo," she said as she walked out of the kitchen. The girls laughed again.

"Your Nan has definitely lost it," Rita said.

"Tell me about it," Natasha said laughing. "All that cable TV is getting to her head," she added.

"Clearly," Rita nodded. "So anyway, how is our girl doing?

Does she love being the communications liaison at NSCS or what?" she asked. Natasha laughed.

"She was a bit freaked out in the first months but she is doing great. I hear she is about to broker a great deal venturing into the African market and everything. I am so proud of her," she said excitedly.

"Who knew that timid little girl had it in her?" Rita said as she helped Natasha off the stool.

"What about you? How is the beautiful world of art?" Natasha asked as the two walked up the stairs.

"Never been better. I met this new guy who takes great photos. I just began featuring his work in my gallery," Rita said with a smile. "Those photos are flying off the shelves," she added

"You better save me one then," Natasha said as they approached her room. Rita nodded.

"You know I got you, right?" Rita said as she opened the door for her. Natasha walked in and was surprised to find an outfit in a laundry bag on her bed. She looked at Rita in surprise.

"What's this?" she asked. "Because I am quite sure that wasn't here when I woke up," she added as she took a seat on the edge of the bed. Rita smiled.

"I know that the only reason you don't want to have maternity dresses is because you think they are unflattering but I got you this to prove you wrong," Rita said as she took a lovely plum colored knee length dress from the bag.

"That's really cute," Natasha said looking at it. "Give me that," she said as she grabbed the dress and headed to the bathroom.

"I hope you've showered already," Rita said jokingly.

"Ha ha, very funny," Natasha said as she closed the bathroom door. She quickly got out of the baggy clothes she had on and pulled the dress over her head. She took a hairbrush from the cabinet, smoothed out the tangles and held her curls in a high pony tail. She looked at her reflection in the mirror and smiled. The sleeveless dress was designed to flatter her feminine features while carefully disguising her baby bump. The V-neck made her breasts look luscious and perky. She walked out of the bathroom and smiled at Rita.

"Girl, you make me want to get pregnant," Rita said when she walked out.

"Really? You are not just pulling my leg?" Natasha asked. Rita crossed her arms over her chest.

"You know I always keep it 100 with you right? I would never lie to you and I swear girl, you look hot!" Rita said.

"Did Nan put you up to this?" Natasha asked as she sat back on the bed. Rita laughed.

"Have you met me? I put Estelle up to this, not the other way around," Rita said. "So, you ready to go shopping?" she asked as she took Natasha's hands in her own. Natasha smiled and nodded. "This time, nothing is going to happen. You are already out of the woods, okay?" Rita asked. Natasha smiled as s tear rolled down her cheek.

"Thanks for that. I needed to hear it," she said.

"What are friends for?" Rita asked as she hugged her friend.

Chapter 6

There was a delicious aroma of chicken, fried bacon and toast when Natasha's eyelids fluttered open on Friday morning. She thought she heard her father's voice downstairs but she was unsure why. She looked at the clock on her bedside table and sighed. It was eleven-thirty. She had been sleeping for long hours…sometimes too long, it was disturbing. But on the flip side, she did actually love how rested she felt…except of course for the occasional puking.

"Wait," she thought as she looked at the clock again. Eleven-thirty? And breakfast was still on? Estelle was the most predictable person as far as consistency was concerned. You could set your watch by her. Breakfast at eleven-thirty was odd. One thing about the Black household was that breakfast was strictly served at seven on weekdays to ensure that no one, absolutely no one, got late for work and on weekends at nine. Granted, sometimes weekend breakfasts would go well over ten but never eleven-thirty. But then again, miracles could happen, especially when Estelle Black was involved.

"Could be a Christmas miracle in November," Natasha thought as she struggled to get out of bed. As she slowly walked to the bathroom, she felt a sharp pain in her side causing her to stop in her tracks. She took long deep breaths and tried to remain calm just as her doctor had advised. The pain, she had been told, was quite a normal occurrence especially in the third trimester. A relief flowed over her as the pain slowly disappeared. She walked towards the bathroom and turned the shower on before walking back to the bed. She smiled to herself when she remembered that in less than two days, Mitchell would be back home. This was the longest that the two had ever stayed apart and quite frankly, she hated it. She quickly made her bed and got undressed before finally

stepping in the shower. Even though she weighed a ton, the best thing about the third trimester was the fact that she did not have to hurl every single moment. Of course, there was the occasional hurl but at that moment, she couldn't even remember the last time she threw up.

As the water streamed down her body, she placed her hands on her huge bump and smiled. It was hard to believe that the little person she had inside her would one day come home introducing a pretty blonde girl as the girlfriend, or some guy who looked like Calvin Klein's cover model as the boyfriend. She felt a shiver at the thought that she was carrying a girl. Well, she didn't really care what the sex was, so long as the child was healthy but she often wondered what being a mother really meant. She stepped out of the bathroom and sat on the bed as she dried herself and thought of how she was going to spend the rest of her day. She needed to be outdoors. It had been three whole days since she got any sun and quite honestly she was beginning to feel a bit jaundiced. She slowly walked to her closet and picked out a blue floral print maxi dress and put it on the bed. She sat down to put on her panties and sighed.

"There are days when this took less than five minutes," she thought as she fastened her bra at the front. *"Aiden had better be a star child,"* she thought as she pulled the dress over her head.

"Oh my god," she said as she felt a kick in her belly. Just then, the door to her room creaked open; a lovely looking Rita was poking her head through.

"What? What's wrong?" Rita asked as she walked in. Natasha smiled and stood up.

"I think I just named my son," Natasha said. Rita looked at her as a smile played on her own face.

"You know the sex?" she asked. Natasha shook her head no.

"No, I was just thinking of everything I am going through and called the baby Aiden," she said. "And he kicked," she added excitedly.

"He?" Rita asked. Natasha nodded.

"I don't know what it is, but I think it's a 'he,'" Natasha said. Rita threw her arms around her friend.

"Somehow, I feel it too," Rita said as she pulled away. She frowned as she looked at Natasha's tangled curls. "What's going on here?" she asked pointing at her hair. Natasha rolled her eyes.

"I was just about to take care of that when you walked in. So…," she walked to her dressing table and picked up a hair brush. "You're on hair duty," she added as she handed Rita the brush.

"Gladly," Rita said as Natasha sat down in front of her dressing mirror.

"So why are you not at work? And why is Nan making breakfast while she should be making sandwiches or something for lunch?" Natasha asked as Rita began working on her hair.

"Work's fine, I finally got a new assistant," Rita said with a smile. Natasha smiled at her friend's reflection.

"That's wonderful," Natasha said. "And does she or he know everything artsy?" she asked. Rita's smiled seemed to be renewed when Natasha asked that.

"That's the best part. She knows her stuff plus she's eye candy," Rita said excitedly. "In her first two days we made over three grand in sales. The men come in, look and buy," she added.

"You sound like a pimp," Natasha said laughing.

"Well, I kind of feel like one too," Rita said as she gathered Natasha's hair in a ponytail. "I have so much more time now to spend with my beautifully pregnant best friend," she added as she fastened the last bobby pin leaving her curls loose at the top of her head. "There," Rita said as Natasha looked at her reflection. She looked classy, if not simply gorgeous. Her breasts, which were a few sizes bigger, looked wonderfully full in her dress and her facial features popped thanks to her new hairstyle.

"I feel so pretty," Natasha squealed. Rita gave her a brief hug and quick kiss on her cheek.

"You are," she said. "Now let's go down and get some food in you," he added.

"Yeah, what's up with that?" Natasha asked as Rita helped her up.

"Estelle had brunch today, remember?" Rita asked looking at Natasha wondering how that slipped her mind. But then again, she had become very forgetful of late. Natasha looked at Rita as a look of familiarity struck her.

"Oh yeah," Natasha said. "Oh well," she added as they made their way down the stairs. Rita suddenly stopped and looked at her. "What? Let's go. I'm hungry," she said looking at Rita.

"Some of Estelle's guests are still here," Rita said. Natasha looked at her confused. She didn't understand why this was a big deal. After all, they had guests over all the time.

"Okay. So?" Natasha asked looking at Rita questionably.

"Sherea is here," Rita said looking at Natasha who rolled her eyes. Sherea was one of the people who never really liked the whole idea of Mitchell Schmidt. To her, Mitchell was the monster who robbed her of the nice girl who was once a promising future daughter in law.

"Oh," Natasha said. "But she should really get over the whole idea. I mean Jay did and he was the one I was in a relationship with, she added. Rita raised an eyebrow.

"Did he, Tasha? Did he really?" she asked looking into Natasha's eyes. Natasha knew exactly what that look meant. Jay had been a thorn in her side ever since she started going out with Mitchell with late night phone calls, showing up at her workplace and even sometimes camping outside her apartment. He had actually gone into full blown stalker mode.

"Well, mummy and son will just have to suck it up," Natasha said as she let go of Rita's hand and continued down the stairs on her own.

"This will not end well," Rita said under her breath as they got to the bottom of the stairs.

"There is my beautiful granddaughter," Estelle said excitedly as Natasha walked towards her.

"Hi Nan," she said as Estelle kissed her cheek.

"Well, I'm sure you remember my friends Marci, Leanne, Moira and of course, Sherea," Estelle said as Natasha shook their hands.

"Yes of course. Nice to see you all again," Natasha said with a smile.

"You were always one of the good ones, Natasha, Leanne said as she gently tugged on Natasha's hand, urging her to sit down. "Coming back home to visit. My Annette never even calls," she added. The ladies laughed.

"I hope you are carrying a boy because they never forget where they came from," Marci said with a smile. "But girls? After bringing home a quote unquote nice boy, you'll be lucky to have them for Thanksgiving every leap year," she added as Natasha joined them on the couch. "So how are you holding up?" Marci asked as Estelle set up some food on two plates for the girls.

"Good. At least the morning sickness is a bit more relaxed now," Natasha said. Rita laughed.

"A whole lot," Rita said matter of factly.

"You poor thing," Leanne said with a smile. "But trust me when I tell you that it is all worth it when you see that little baby's face," she added.

"Speaking of, do we know what we are carrying? Blue or pink flannels?" Marci asked looking at Natasha.

"That Tasha is more old school than me. She said she wants to be surprised," Estelle said as she walked to the table carrying a tray.

"There is a chance that we are talking blue flannels though,"

Rita said with a smile as she stood up to help Estelle.

"Did someone take a little peek at the sonogram?" Marci asked with a smile. Natasha laughed as she took one of the plates from Rita.

"No, nothing like that at all," she said. "It's just that, I think I may have named my baby and he agreed," she added smiling. The ladies looked at each other.

"Did you just say he?" Estelle asked looking at Natasha who was already digging into the food. Natasha nodded. "How would you even know that?" she asked, still looking at her granddaughter.

"It's not fool proof, just that I called the baby Aiden and for the first time, he kicked," she said excitedly.

"First time? How far along are you?" Marci asked.

"Five months," Natasha said as she took a big bite of her turkey bacon. "Damn that's good," she said under her breath.

"Isn't that a bit late?" Leanne asked looking concerned.

"Oh please. I didn't feel her father move till I was in my third trimester," Estelle said with a smile.

"Planning to go back to work after the baby comes?" Leanne asked. Natasha looked up at Rita and then at her Nan and shook her head.

"I don't know. I don't think so," Natasha said. "I don't think I want my child being raised by a stranger," she added.

"Of course you don't. You have all the money to just jet around the world on holidays," Sherea said. Natasha looked at her surprised.

'Do you have something to say to anyone, Sherea?" Rita asked looking at her. Sherea shook her head.

"Not anyone, just Tasha," Sherea said without flinching.

"Okay, what do you have to say to me," Natasha asked looking at Sherea.

"That could have been my grandbaby in you right now," Sherea said. Leanne and Marci rolled their eyes.

"Well, maybe if your son had been half the man Mitchell is, it could have been," Estelle retorted.

"What did you just say about my baby?" Sherea asked looking at Estelle.

"You heard her. You are always cuddling him making him some cry baby," Rita said. Sherea rolled her eyes at Rita.

'Girl, ain't nobody talking to you right now," Sherea said. By this time, what had started as an altercation between Sherea and Natasha had become a brutal exchange between Estelle, Rita and Sherea. For Natasha, she had always known that neither Rita nor Estelle liked Jay, not when they were dating and definitely not now. Sherea had always blamed Natasha for the failed relationship and even though Natasha tried being the bigger person, Sherea always seemed bent on being out to get her. Leanne, Marci and Natasha watched in horror as the three got into it.

"Well, someone is talking to you, Sherea, and this someone is telling you that you had better snap out of that damned box you are in," Rita said angrily. "Tasha and Jay are over. That ship sailed a long time ago and it is not about to make a three-sixty," she added looking at Sherea.

"Rita is right Sherea," Estelle said. "You are my friend and I hate being in this position but you cannot keep on tormenting my granddaughter for the sins of your son," she added. Sherea grabbed her purse and looked at Estelle.

"I don't have to sit here and listen to this," she said looking at Rita and then at Estelle.

"Well, you don't have to," Rita said.

"Rita, be respectful," Estelle said in a warning tone.

"I would be if she deserved it," Rita said still looking at Sherea.

"Rita!" Estelle said again, this time her voice a bit more stern than the first. Natasha put her plate on the table and looked at Sherea.

"Sherea, I respect you and I know you know that," Natasha started. "But you have to understand one thing, Jay is not the good boy you always knew. He is a mess, at least he was when we broke up and I got someone good. Someone who puts my needs first and genuinely cares for me," she continued. "I did not want this, any of this but it happened and it's been two damn years so I think you need to get into that thought," she said.

"Tasha's right Sherea. Jay had his chance and he lost," Marci said sympathetically.

"So did you leave him because he didn't have a net worth of a billion dollars? Is that it?" Sherea asked. Natasha shook her head. She still couldn't believe that Sherea was angry with her for the train wreck of a relationship with her son.

"It was never about the money and you know it," Natasha snapped at Sherea.

"Really? Because you did not end things with my son until you hit the banker's jackpot," Sherea said looking at Natasha. Rita rolled her eyes and stood up.

"I don't know about everyone else but I think it's time for you to leave Sherea," Rita said to the surprise of everyone on the room.

"Excuse you?" Sherea asked looking at Rita.

"You heard me, get the fuck out of Estelle's house. You are just a big bag of bad fucking aura around here right now," Rita said.

"Rita! Language!" Estelle and Natasha said in unison.

"I'm sorry, Estelle but it's going to be a freezing day in hell before I let someone disrespect you or my best friend at their own home," Rita said as she stared daggers at Sherea.

"I know when I am not wanted," Sherea said as she stood up.

"Do you really? Because no one wanted you around half an hour ago but you are still here," Rita said crossing her arms on her chest.

"Of course you would defend her," Sherea said as she walked towards Rita. "Because when one gold digger hit the jackpot she dragged the other gold digger in the mines with her," she added.

"What did you just say?" Rita asked angrily.

"Sherea!" Marci and Leanne exclaimed in shock.

"Seriously Sherea, hold your fucking tongue," Natasha said standing up. This time it was her turn to be vulgar.

"Rita was right. Sherea, it's time you left," Estelle said as he walked towards the door and held it open. "Get out of my house," she said looking at the woman she had once called her friend. Sherea smiled and walked towards the door.

"I had a feeling our friendship had run its course," Sherea said as she approached the door.

"It did and I was just being nice," Estelle said angrily.

"Hey Sherea!" Natasha called out. "I hope you take something from the friendship you had with my Nan," she said.

"And what's that?" Sherea asked.

"Let go of the reins you have on your son and maybe he will not be a total and complete disappointment," Natasha said before sitting down. Sherea rolled her eyes and walked out; Estelle slammed the door behind her.

"Good riddance," Rita said in a low voice but loud enough for everyone to hear.

"Can you believe the nerve of that woman?" Leanne asked.

"I always thought she was such a good woman," Marci said sadly. "Decent even," she added as Estelle sat down.

"I have known her for thirty years. The joke's on me," Estelle said with a sad smile. Rita walked over to Estelle and gave her a hug.

"Enough about her. You okay?" Rita asked looking at Estelle.

"I've never been better. But you have got a mouth on you," Estelle said with a smile. Rita laughed.

"When you deal with snobby art people all day, you learn a few tricks," Rita said looking at Natasha. "You good, Tasha?" she asked.

"Me and Aiden are just fine," Natasha said with a smile. The two older women smiled at each other.

"I hope you have a plan B in case Aiden turns out to be a female," Leanne said smiling. Natasha looked at her Nan and smiled.

"Let's cross that bridge when we get to it," Natasha said with a smile. Marci took Natasha's plate from the table and handed it to Natasha.

"Well, eat up now. You need to keep your strength up," she said.

True, childbirth is no joke," Estelle said. Natasha looked at the older women and then at Rita.

"Let's not talk about that. That shit is weird," Natasha said as she took a bite of her now cold turkey bacon.

"Tasha, language!" Estelle yelled angrily.

Chapter 7

Mitchell looked at the dinner table and smiled. He had managed to pull off a great dinner from scratch – so unlike him. He walked to the kitchen and put on a pair of oven gloves before taking the baked potatoes out of the oven. He walked to the dining table and carefully set the potatoes down. He smiled as he looked at the generous spread. He knew that cooking would definitely not be enough to make up for not being around for two weeks but he hoped that Natasha would see that he was trying to make up for it. He had been called out to Europe on an emergency and it was too much of a short notice for him to get someone to represent him, especially since the company was right in the middle of not one, not two but three major campaigns.

As much as his reasons made perfect sense to him, he knew that his wife saw things a bit differently as Rita had told her.

"You know that you are not neglecting her and I know that you are not but she doesn't," Rita had told her earlier that week. "You need to talk to her," she had said.

"I will, as soon as I get back," he said. "But this time around I had to leave. There were no two ways around it," he added.

"I know, but you need to let her know that. Maybe it's the miscarriages, I don't know, but she feels a bit alone, especially since Stacy and I don't hang out with her as much as we used to," Rita explained.

Mitchell knew what he had to do. The talk with Rita had actually psyched him up to get home, so much that he took an earlier flight. When he got home, Natasha was not there. He took this opportunity to surprise her. It had been a while since he made her dinner, especially her favorite, baked potatoes. He had just finished setting the table when he heard the front door open.

"Hello, Maria is that you?" he heard Natasha calling out.

"It's me, babe," he called from the dining room.

"Mitch, hi. I thought you were not getting home till tomorrow night," she said as she walked up to him. He kissed her and hugged her.

"I couldn't wait to see you," he said as he pulled away.

"Is that right?" she asked. He could hear the sarcasm in her voice. He looked at her blue sleeveless maxi dress and smiled, choosing to ignore her comment.

"You look so sexy," he said a she led her to the table.

"Thank you," she said looking at the table. "You cooked?" she asked. He smiled and nodded.

"I just thought that I needed to do something special for you," Mitchell said. "Making up for lost time," he said as he pulled out a chair for her. She sat down and looked at him.

"You know I love me some baked potatoes but there is a whole lot more you need to make up for. Food, however delicious will not hack it," she said coldly. He looked at her and gave her a defeated smile. If there was anything that he had learned being with Natasha it was how to choose his battles in their relationship.

"We can talk about that later," he said as he began serving her. "Want me to pour some gravy on that?" he asked looking at her. She nodded and poured herself a glass of water. "So, how've you been?" he asked when he finally set the plate in front of her.

"Good. The baby kicked again and you didn't get to feel it," she said without looking up. Mitchell sighed as he leaned back against his chair.

"I know, and I'm sorry," he said looking at her. "But I'm here now. I want to make up for lost time," he added.

"Yeah until the next conference call that begs you to hop on the next flight to Prague," she said sarcastically. Mitchell looked at her and sighed. He didn't know what to tell her. She needed to understand his position. He needed her to understand that his position at the company was not just another job. It was what his family had worked so hard to achieve and it was up to him to make sure that the sacrifices the generations before him had made were not in vain.

"You know that I don't leave because I want to, right?" he asked looking at her. She shrugged and went on eating without looking up. The rest of the dinner was relatively quiet, maybe because he didn't want to say something wrong, or maybe because she didn't want to engage him in an argument. "I'm sorry," he said as he looked at her from across the table. She rolled her eyes and took a last bite of her food. "What?" he asked looking at her.

"Nothing," she said without looking up.

"Tasha, what?" he pressed. She raised her head and looked at him.

"I told you, nothing," Natasha said, getting irritated. She looked into his eyes and saw the familiar look of love, and concern and some anguish. "I'm okay," she said again in an attempt to get the whole argument, or whatever it was over with. Mitchell let out a cynical laugh. He knew exactly what that tone meant. Normally, he would have let it go but this had gone on long enough and even though the therapist told him that the problems in his marriage were a passing wind, he could not wait another month to address this. It had to be now. It had to be today.

Natasha put her fork down and reached for her glass. He watched her as she took a long sip of her water before she finally set the glass down.

"Thanks for dinner," she said plainly as she smiled at Mitchell weakly.

"Anytime," he said with a smile. She was about to stand up when Mitchell stopped her. "I think we need to talk," he said looking at her.

"Okay. Is anything the matter?" she asked as she sat back down. He looked at her and ran his fingers through his thick hair. She felt a warmth go through her when he did that. He still had some effect on her, it seemed.

"A lot actually," Mitchell said looking at her. "I feel like I am still in the dog house," he said looking at her. Natasha gave him another weak smile.

"That's because you are," she said without blinking. Mitchell took a long deep breath.

"I told you what happened and I am sorry. But there was nothing I could do about it," Mitchell said. She could sense the frustration in his voice. "You know what this new account means to me, to the company," he said as he looked at her.

She rolled her eyes and took another sip of her water.

"That's the problem right there. It is all about you and the company," she said angrily. "Call me when you finally realize that you are no longer single but married with a baby on the way1" she added as she tried to stand up. Mitchell got up and quickly walked over to her. "Move, I want to go to bed," she said looking into his eyes. He shook his head and sat on the edge of the table looking down at her.

"We are going to talk about this tonight," he said as he felt his anger begin to rise. "You know very well that Nolan Schmidt Communications is my family's legacy. I have responsibilities there. I cannot just walk out on them," he said.

"And I am not asking you to," she said looking up at him. "It's just that you are away so much and the baby is almost here," she said sadly. Mitchell looked at her and raised an eyebrow.

"I know and I'm sorry. It is not something that is going to take forever," he said as he took her hand in his. "I am sorry but I have to ask, Tasha," he said looking at her. "Could you be acting this way because you are bored?" he asked. Natasha's eyes widened as she yanked her hand from his grip.

"What the fuck is wrong with you?" she asked angrily. "So, just because I have one issue, you think I'm jealous?" she asked looking at him. She pushed her chair away from the table. "I can't deal with this right now," she said as she started walking towards the living room. Mitchell sighed as he followed her.

"Tasha, we have a problem and I need you to understand where I am coming from," he said as he watched Natasha take a seat and switch on the TV. "Babe, talk to me," he said standing behind the seat. She ignored him and cranked up the volume even though he was sure that she was not into whatever was on the TV. He walked round the seat and stood in front of her and grabbed the remote from her grip. "Why don't you understand that whatever I am doing, I am doing it for us?" he asked looking at her.

"How exactly is leaving me for days on end for us?" she asked.

"I told you, I can't just walk away from my responsibilities. There are things I need to do for the company and I am doing them now so that I don't have to leave when the baby comes," he said.

She looked up at him, suddenly feeling guilty that she had been acting like such a brat, like it was always about her.

"Really?" Natasha asked looking at him.

"Yes, really. I do not want to stay away from my family and at the same time, I do not want my business to fail," he said kneeling down in front of her. "I told you once and I'll tell you again, whatever I do, I do for us," he added. A tear rolled down her cheek. "Tell me what is really bothering you, babe. Because I think there is something more," he said as he brushed away the tear.

"I…I…it's just that…" her voice trailed off when Mitchell brushed her lips with hers.

"Out with it, my love," he said in a soothing voice.

"I don't want to be in the delivery room alone. Anything can happen…"

"Nothing will happen," he said cutting her short. "You see this baby you're carrying right here?" he asked placing a hand on her tummy. "This is the healthiest baby in the world and there is nothing, absolutely nothing that could go wrong," he said looking at her. A fresh flow of tears rolled down her cheeks. He got up and sat next to her and draped an arm around her shoulders.

"I don't even know why the hell I am acting like this. This is not me," she said sobbing into his shoulder. He smiled and planted a kiss on her forehead.

"It's okay. I understand. The therapist said that the hormones would be kicking in soon and maybe they're just taking a toll on you," he said with a smile. "Maybe that's just what is happening right now," he added as he trailed a finger down her bare arm. She closed her eyes as she felt his other hand slowly rubbing her thigh. She sighed and placed a hand on his. "What? What's wrong?" he asked,

"I just don't feel...it right now," she said, a guilty look on his face. Mitchell sighed and lifted her chin. He gave her a long sensual kiss, making her breathless when he pulled away. She looked at him panting, almost dizzy. It was obvious that she wanted him too.

"The way you are looking at me, the shortness of breath tells me that you want me just as much as I want you," Mitchell said as he tugged on the cords that held her dress up. She closed her eyes as he began kissing her neck, slowly working his way to her shoulder blade.

"Mitch, the baby..." she started before Mitchell claimed her lips once more, silencing her.

"The baby will be just fine. The doctor told us so," he said as he pulled away. She smiled at him weakly as he got to his feet. He took her hands and pulled her to her feet before pushing her dress off her shoulders. The long blue dress gathered around her feet like a small ocean. The fabric felt cool around her bare ankles as Mitchell began unclasping her bra.

She gasped when she felt his big hands on her bare breasts. It had been a while since the two of them had been intimate. Finding time between her hormone imbalances and his trips was just hard, plus the fact that Natasha did not feel particularly sexy had really taken a toll on their romantic life. He took her hand, helped her step out of the dress around her ankles and pulled her close to kiss her. She gasped when she felt his lips on hers, his tongue searching hers, showing desire and want, pain and anguish. She gasped again when he held one of her nipples in between his thumb and index finger. He gave her nipple a little squeeze and tightened his grip around her waist. She let out a moan when he gently squeezed one of her breasts.

"Not too hard," she said as he began kneading her mounds. He smiled, put his hands on her shoulders and slowly pushed her down on the seat behind her. She looked at him as he took one nipple in his mouth and began sucking. His other hand slowly made its way to her inner thigh, stroking and sending flickering sensations as he did so. She moaned loudly when he suddenly began flicking his stiff tongue over her hardened nipples, making her moan loudly.

After what seemed like forever, he released one nipple and trailed his tongue across her chest to take in her other full nipple. She gasped and moaned loudly when he did and held his head tightly. She squirmed on the seat as he worked on her breasts. Her eyes remained shut as Mitchell worked his magic, causing her a mild shock when he slipped his fingers into the sides of her panties. She opened her eyes to find him pulling down her panties. She felt a bit strange, shy even, sitting there naked when he was still fully dressed. She looked at him as he spread her legs wide. It was a bit difficult to get in that position seeing as she was thirty-five weeks along. She threw her head back as she felt him gently flick his tongue on her clit. A moan escaped her lips when she felt his lips engulf her sensitive clit and begin sucking on her. She held onto the edges of the couch as he sucked hard on her, occasionally plunging his tongue into her.

Mitchell was pleased to find that she was already wet, proving that she felt the same burning desire in her pussy as he did in his own trousers. When he released her clitoris, it was pleasantly distended and her breathing was enough to let him know that she was ready for him. He looked into her eyes as he tested her depths with his index finger.

"Mitch, I want you so bad," she moaned as he fingered her slow and long. He smiled and pulled his finger out. She looked up at him as he stood up and began undressing. She wanted to scream at him at that moment. He was taking his sweet time undressing, obviously enjoying tormenting her. He finally put his hands on her shoulders and motioned for her to lean back. She looked up at him as he brought his face down to kiss her again.

He tried getting on top of her but it proved harder than the last time. After all, the last time he was on top, she was a mere five months pregnant. He smiled down at her and climbed behind her in a spooning position. She gasped when she felt him get inside her in one shove. Mitchell planted little kisses at the back of her neck as he slowly caressed her thigh. She moaned softly when she felt him begin to move in and out of her. She appreciated him starting out slowly, stretching her out, getting her cunt used to his girth. Her moans got louder with each gentle thrust as he fucked her. One of his hands found its way to her tummy as his thrusts got harder and longer. She squeezed her eyes shut and bit down on the couch as she felt him slam against her. It was as if he had totally lost all thought and was just operating under the power of his loins.

Natasha gasped when she felt Mitchell holding one of her legs under the knee allowing him a deeper penetration. She felt herself getting weaker and weaker as she got closer and closer to her orgasm. She hated that she could not turn the tables on him and just fuck him hard. She longed for the day she would once again straddle him or just bend over and let him slam up against her. She suddenly let out a loud scream as she felt her insides pulsating against Mitchell's cock. Her climax must have triggered his own because he suddenly began thrusting harder into her. He released her leg and squeezed one of her breasts as he poured himself into her.

"Fuck, Tasha!" he said when he finally slowed down. "I wish you knew what you do to me, babe," he said as his cock slipped out of her pussy. She smiled and snuggled up against him.

"I think I do," she said as the two drifted off to sleep.

Book 6.

Giving Birth To Mr White's Baby

Chapter 1

Natasha felt a cramp go through her tummy for the umpteenth time. She was not sure if she was going into labor or if it was the damned Braxton Hicks contractions. God knows she'd had enough if those during her pregnancy. She stood up and walked around the living room again. Her OB/GYN had suggested walking it out and taking long deep breaths every time the contractions came around. He had said that Braxton Hicks were a common feature for many women whether they were on their first or tenth pregnancies.

However, today was different. Natasha had been walking up and down for hours and she could have sworn that the contractions were only getting more intense. She had been trying to call someone, anyone, but all she got were voicemails and phones turned off. Mitchell was in some meeting, he'd told her in the morning. Rita's phone was turned off. Mona and her Nan were not picking up; they were probably having some bake off. Her father and Stacy's phones were on voicemails. She was all out of options. But then again, this could just have been the Braxton Hicks.

She clutched her tummy tightly when she felt another nerve wrecking contraction. She grabbed the phone and punched in the first number she thought of, Mona's.

"Hey girl," Mona answered cheerfully. Natasha felt a thrill of relief go through her body when she heard her voice.

"Oh my god, you picked up," Natasha said almost out of breath.

"Honey, you sound like you've been doing laps on the track. You okay?" Mona asked sounding concerned.

"I think I'm in labor, Mona," she said panting. "These damn pains won't go away," she said again leaning against the wall. She was now in the kitchen trying to get a grip on whatever sanity she still had left.

"Okay honey. I want you to relax. Tell me, how frequent are the contractions? Five, ten minutes apart?" Mona asked. She sounded frantic. Natasha guessed that she was looking for her car keys. They never seemed to be where she left them.

"I don't know...maybe twenty, half an hour maybe?" Natasha said. "Oh my God!" she cried out when she felt another contraction. She slowly made her way to the kitchen and yanked the freezer door open. She took some ice cubes and put them in a cup. "I think I need to go to hospital Mona. Get here, now!" she said before stuffing two large cubes in her mouth.

"Okay baby. I will be right there," Mona said and hung up. Natasha sunk to the floor and put one hand on her baby bump. She did not understand how something so beautiful could cause so much anguish. She took long deep breaths as she sucked on the cold ice cube. Apparently, the ice was supposed to help but she was not seeing the effect. She had heard stories of how labor would sometimes get worse than this. She wanted to cry. This could definitely not get any worse. Her whole pregnancy had been about mood swings and a dry spell. She had probably had sex three times during her entire term. She felt another tear rolling down her cheek. She could not tell what was going on, whether she was crying because of the pain or the frustration of the entire situation. She heard her phone ring and rolled her eyes. She had just gotten settled on the floor, no pain, no discomfort, no nothing. This was the first time in hours she had actually felt her body being relieved. She pulled herself to her feet and slowly made her way to the living room. She looked at her phone and almost smiled. It was Mitchell.

"Baby, what's up? I found all these missed calls and I know...."
His voice trailed off when he heard her heavy breathing.
"Tasha, what's wrong? You sound all out of breath," he said.

"I think the baby is coming Mitchell," Natasha said. He
suddenly went silent. Natasha knew that he was freaked out.
He had always planned on being there when the baby came
and it seemed that he could miss it.

"I'm on my way," Mitchell said.

"No, Mona's coming. You could meet us at the hospital,"
Natasha said. She heard Mitchell breathe a sigh of relief.

"I'm on the other side of town. It might take a while," he said.
Natasha could hear the sadness in his voice.

"I'll be okay Mitchell. Women have been giving birth in jungles
for centuries. I'll be fine," she said as calmly as she could as
she felt another cramp in her tummy. If she didn't know any
better she could have sworn that the contractions were getting
more intense.

"You sounded a little off there. Everything okay?" Mitchell
asked sounding helpless.

"Yeah. Just another bad contraction," Natasha answered. She
stood up and began walking around again. She had heard that
walking sped up labor and she was willing to do anything to
hurry this up.

"Okay. I'll see you soon. Okay. I am driving as fast as I
possibly can," Mitchell said. Natasha smiled. She knew that he
was not bluffing.

"Just don't get yourself a ticket. Today is the worst day for that to happen," she said lightly.

"I love you," Mitchell said. Something in his voice let her know that he was smiling as he said that.

"I love you too," she said before hanging up. As if on cue, she felt another contraction that made her lean against the wall. When it finally passed, she sank down to the floor and sat down. Even though walking might have sped the process up, she didn't feel like she was strong enough to keep it up.

By the time Mona arrived, Natasha was sweating it out big time. Her contractions were now a bit closer; this was definitely the real thing. Natasha turned around to look at Mona who was walking fast towards her.

"Oh, honey. How are you feeling?" Mona asked looking at her. She bent down to lift Natasha up. "Let's get you off the floor," she said as she struggled to help the once petite woman to her feet. She held on to Natasha's waist as they walked towards the living room. Mona breathed a sigh of relief when she finally set her on the couch. "Okay, how far apart now?" she asked looking around.

"About fifteen minutes," Natasha said panting. Mona looked at her and then looked around.

"Okay, then we don't have time to wait for the ambulance. That baby could be coming any time now," Mona said. "I need your supplies. I am taking you to the hospital," she said looking into Natasha's tired eyes.

"There's a go bag in the bedroom. It has everything I might need," Natasha said. Mona ran to the bedroom and emerged momentarily holding a brown travel bag.

"Is this it?" Mona asked holding the bag up. Natasha nodded and Mona quickly opened the bag.

"What the hell are you doing?" Natasha asked as Mona rummaged through the contents of the bag.

"Making sure you have everything. Only one of us has been through this, you know. Where is your baby layette? All these are your clothes," Mona said looking up. Natasha looked a little confused for a moment.

"There is a baby bag in my closet. It was supposed to be next to the go bag," Natasha said. Mona did another sprint to the bedroom which Natasha found quite impressive considering she was in six inch heels.

"And this is why I had to go through the bag," Mona said as she ran out. She came back after Natasha figured she had dumped the bags in the car. "Okay, what hospital is your OB/GYN at?" she asked as she helped Natasha up.

"First General," Natasha answered. She appreciated how much Mona was trying to help but she was having a very hard time. Staying on her feet alone was proving difficult. "I am never having sex again, Mona, I swear," she said her voice trembling. Mona laughed as she helped her into the car.

"Even girls who have seven kids say that every time they are in labor. I am sure you will be giving it up to Mitchell really fast once all this is over," Mona said as she typed on her phone frantically. "Okay. I just texted your husband to meet us at the hospital. Now watch as I show you why I should be a driver in the presidential motorcade," Mona said as she started her car engine. Despite the discomfort Natasha was feeling, Mona had managed to put a smile on her face and she was just about to make her heart skip more than a beat. The way she drove…Natasha had seen Formula One drivers driving safer. Even dirt bike racing seemed safer than the stunts Mona was pulling. What was supposed to be a forty minute ride to the hospital quickly became a fifteen minute drive. As soon as she pulled to the ambulance bay area, Natasha sensed trouble especially when two security guards began walking towards them first.

"You can't park here ma'am," one guard said as the two guards swiftly walked towards them.

"Get me a wheelchair and I'll move. This woman is in labor and I think she's crowning," Mona said. Natasha turned to look at Mona. There was a look of fear in her eyes.

"I'm crowning?" she asked worried that her wait could have cost her more than she would have bargained for. Mona smiled and shook her head.

"No, I just need a wheelchair ASAP. You good," Mona said as one guard rushed outside pushing a wheelchair in front of him. "Bingo," she said in a whisper. Natasha was about to smile when another nerve wrecking contraction ripped through her belly.

"Oh fuck! I can't do this…It's too much," Natasha said in a whisper as a tear rolled down her cheek. "I want the drugs. Get them to give me an epidural, Mona. Please….get me the epidural," she said again as Mona and one guard helped her to the wheelchair. A doctor walked towards them and took the chair.

"I got this, thanks guys," the doctor said. Mona looked at the doctor and gave her car keys to one of the guards.

"Here, park it," she said dumping the keys in the shocked

guard's hands.

"I'm not a valet," the guard said as Mona followed the doctor into the hospital building.

"I'll give you one hundred dollars for it!" Mona called out as they walked into the hospital building. "Okay, sweetie. I need you to tell the good doctor..." she trailed off and looked at the doctor.

"Mason," the doctor said as he pushed the wheelchair through the hallways.

"Doctor Mason, would you tell him the name of your doctor?" Mona said practically running after them.

"Georges," Natasha said still panting.

"Do you know a Doctor Georges?" Mona asked looking at Doctor Mason who was now nodding.

"Matter of fact, Mr. Schmidt called and told us that his wife was being brought in by her cousin. I'm assuming that's you. So Doctor Georges sent me to get her. He is finishing off in the ER, he should be with us soon," the doctor explained as they came to a halt in front of one of the rooms. "Here we are," he said pushing the wheelchair through the door. There was a young nurse in the room who quickly rushed to help Natasha out of her clothes and into a hospital gown. Normally, that was the kind of situation that would make her uncomfortable but right about then, she didn't give a crap. The nurse helped her onto the bed just in time for another contraction. She held on to Mona's hand as the pain, which seemed to last forever, tore through her again.

"Okay, you need to get her an epidural," Mona said when

Natasha got her relief. The doctor walked round the bed and put Natasha's feet in stirrups. Natasha felt her cheeks flush as the doctor took a long look under her gown.

"How long ago did your labor begin?" he asked as he checked her dilation.

"Four, five hours ago?" Natasha answered. By this time, strands of her hair were sticking onto the sides of her face. The doctor seemed concerned when she answered. "Why? Is there a problem?" she asked worried. Was this another joke like Mona had done a few minutes earlier?

"Your amniotic fluid is still intact. For someone whose contractions are so close, your water should have broken by now. We'll need to do it manually," he said.

"That should not be a problem. Should it?" Natasha asked looking at the doctor more worried than ever.

"No, but it is a bit too late for an epidural. Either way, we will have to operate," Dr. Mason said just as Natasha's OB/GYN walked in. She looked at him, her eyes hopeful, but Doctor Mason pulled him aside and whispered a few words to him. Dr. Georges then walked to Natasha's bedside as the nurse applied some gel to her tummy. She was so tense; she didn't even notice how cold the gel on her tummy was.

"He says I have to have surgery. Is my baby okay?" Natasha asked her doctor. Dr. Georges gave her a reassuring smile. He always seemed to be able to comfort her every time he smiled. There was honesty in his eyes, integrity in his smile.

"Nothing at all. But given how weak you have been in your pregnancy, a natural birth is not a very good idea. And your little guy is just fine," Dr. Georges said as the nurse moved the scanner on the surface of her tummy. "Look, strong heart beat," he said again as he pointed the screen. Natasha looked at the ultrasound and smiled. Her baby was fine. She was okay. "But we have to go right now," he added as he looked into her eyes.

"What about Mitchell?" Natasha asked. Mona gave her hand a gentle squeeze.

"I'll be here. I'll tell him," she said with a smile. Natasha gave her an appreciative smile before the nurse and Doctor Mason wheeled her off.

"Can I talk to you?" Dr. Georges asked touching Mona's hand. Mona immediately felt her heart go up her throat.

"It is not just about the amniotic fluid, is it?" Mona asked. The doctor shook his head.

"I didn't want to say anything in front of her. I didn't want her to panic but the baby is in distress. The labor has taken its toll on the baby. We need it out of there as soon as possible," he explained. Mona shook her head and then held her hands up.

"What do you mean distress?" she asked looking at the doctor.

"Sometimes during labor, the baby can defecate and at that moment, the fluid around it is no longer safe. The toxicity could kill him and if that doesn't, then struggling to catch a breath could cause the cord to get wrapped around the baby's neck," Dr. Georges said. "But she'll be okay. Don't get too worked up," he said as he quickly rubbed her hand.

"Whatever happens, do not under any circumstances let my cousin die," she said as a tear rolled down her cheek.

"I'm in the business of saving lives. I would never let that happen if I could help it," he said before hurrying away. Mona stood looking at him as he rushed down the hallway to the operating room. Now she was charged with telling her cousin's husband that his baby could be in distress and that his wife knew nothing about it.

"Where is she?" she heard Mitchell's voice. She turned around to see the whole gang: Mitchell, Rita, Eric, Estelle and Stacy.

"Where'd all of you come from? Natasha said she had been calling you," Mona said as she wiped her tears and tried to compose herself.

"I called them. How is she? Where is she?" Mitchell said looking frantic.

"She is fine but they had to take her to surgery," Mona said. She saw the fear in everybody's eyes when she said that.

"What do you mean surgery? Is she okay?" Rita asked pushing her way past Stacy and Mitchell. Mona nodded and then shook her head.

"I don't know....she was almost fully dilated but her water hadn't broken yet and then there was something about the baby being in distress," she said.

"What does that even mean?" Eric asked.

"It's when the baby poops while the mother is in labor," Estelle said. Everyone turned to look at her surprised. "You were in distress," she added looking at Eric.

"The doctor said it is a relatively common surgery. So everything should be okay," Mona said.

"Of course they did. They are doctors. The fuckers," Stacy said. Everyone's attention now turned to Stacy. She never used curse words, at least not in front of them.

"Actually it is a regular surgery. They should be done in two hours tops," Estelle said. "Speaking from experience," she added. Mona and Mitchell sighed. This might have been the best news they'd heard all day. Estelle looked at the small group that had now formed a circle. "God is on her side. My grandbaby and great grandbaby are going to be just fine," Estelle said with a smile. Mitchell took her hand in his and smiled.

"Amen," he said in a quiet voice. Rita walked up to Mitchell and looked at him.

"I've never had a baby but I am told that when you look at that little face, it is all worth it," she said smiling at him.

"It's true. For you, for Tasha, it's all going to be worth it in the end," Mona said. Mitchell choked back a tear. He was trying to be strong for him, for Tasha but everything was proving so hard. He was about to give in to his emotion when he saw Dr. Georges walking towards them. He suddenly felt a lump in his throat as he watched him slowly make his way to the small group.

Chapter 2

With every step the doctor took, Mitchell longed for the ground under him to just open up and swallow him whole. He was not so sure what could be worse: losing the baby or losing Natasha….or both. He took a deep breath and tried to gain composure as the doctor approached them. There was a sudden panic when he finally got to where everyone who mattered to Natasha was standing, eagerly awaiting an update. As soon as he got there, everyone was suddenly talking. Mona and Rita had gone all hood, roughing him up as Estelle and Eric tried to get their own information. Mitchell did not need this.

"Will everyone just shut up," he suddenly yelled making everyone around him go quiet in surprise. Estelle and Stacy looked at him in surprise. They had never known Mitchell to be a loud person. This was definitely a first for him. "I just need everyone quiet. I can barely hear myself think," he said before turning to face the doctor. "Dr. Georges, how is my wife?" he asked looking at the doctor. Whatever answer the doctor was about to give would definitely shape his mood. He braced himself for the worst as the doctor placed a hand on his shoulder.

"Oh shit. This is it. I lost them," he thought as a tear rolled down his cheek.

"There was a slight complication but it was nothing we could not handle. Natasha is doing great and the baby is even better. Seven pounds, eight ounces," Dr. Georges said with a smile. Mitchell breathed a sigh of relief and ran his fingers through his thick hair. Stacy walked up to him and gave him a hug.

"Congratulations daddy," she said as Rita and Mona patted his back

"When can I see my grandson?" Eric asked excitedly. The doctor frowned.

"Granddaughter," he said looking at Eric, Estelle and then at Mitchell.

"What?" Mona and Rita exclaimed in unison. "

"But the scans…the ultrasounds…." Mitchell began saying before his voice trailed off.

"The scans can sometimes be wrong. And she never really did come in for a confirmation in her third trimester. So we had no way of knowing," the doctor said with a smile.

"Though in all fairness the only reason Tasha thought she was carrying a boy was because she called him Aiden one day and he kicked. She thought it must have been some cosmic force confirming the sex of the baby or something," Rita said laughing. Mitchell looked at her and raised an eyebrow.

"You mean she never…"

"No," Rita quickly said cutting his sentence short. Mitchell seemed more confused than ever. He looked at Estelle who was smiling broadly and Eric who was almost shedding a tear.

"What the hell. I'm a father!" he yelled as he took Estelle in his arms and hugged her tightly, lifting her off the ground.

"Mitchell Schmidt, you had better put me down!" Estelle said as she tried to slap his shoulder. Mitchell was either too fit or too excited to feel it.

"So when can we see her?" Eric asked looking at the doctor.

"Well, Natasha is in recovery, so maybe just one person can go in. The rest of you can follow the nurse to the nursery to see the baby," Dr. Georges said.

"I'll go see her," Mitchell said almost immediately.

"I want to see her too," Estelle said crossing her arms.

"Yes, so do I," Eric said still looking at the doctor.

"You better count us in too, mister," Stacy said pointing to herself, Mona and Rita. The doctor looked at them defeated.

"Well, I'll make arrangements for her to be moved back to her room within the hour. But I must warn you she will be a bit off, drowsy even," he said.

"We don't care. We just want to see her," Eric said. The doctor smiled and walked away. Mitchell looked at the group and laughed. Rita, Mona and Stacy joined in soon after. "If there was a time I was glad that I didn't opt to become a medical professional, this would be it. The poor man looked confused," Eric said as he sat down.

"We are all here. It is his own fault for expecting anything less," Estelle said with a smile. Mona looked around and opened her purse.

I don't know about you guys but I suddenly became hungry. I think I'll run down to the canteen," she said looking up. "Anyone else need anything?" she asked.

"Coffee, cream two sugars," Eric said quickly.

"Latte," Estelle said with a smile.

"Potato chips and juice," Stacy said. "And maybe some chocolate. Two bars," she added. Everyone turned to look at her.

"Is there anything you want to tell us, sweetie?" Rita asked looking at Stacy.

"Why?" Stacy asked looking at her.

"You are the one person I know who strictly sticks to her diet and suddenly you want chips and not one, but two chocolate bars?" Rita asked still looking at her. "I don't know about everyone else but that is a cry for help if you ask me," she added with a smile.

"I've had a long day, okay? I'm just hungry and a bit stressed. That's all," Stacy said as she tucked a long strand of hair behind her ear. Mona smiled and reached for her arm and pulled her up.

"Come on. You can tell us all about it as we go down to the canteen," she said looking at Rita.

"Us?" Rita asked looking up at Mona.

"Well, child, it's either she takes you on errands or me or Eric and frankly I don't see myself or my son getting up unless the doctor comes and tells us that we are going to see Tasha," Estelle said. Rita rolled her eyes and stood up.

"These damn heels are killing me," she whined.

"Get some flip flops from the gift shop," Estelle said.

"Come on, Mother. It's a *gift shop.* Flowers and cuddly toys maybe but flip flops? Really Mother?" Eric asked looking at Estelle.

"You'd be surprised at what shops stock nowadays," Estelle said as she leaned back on the chair. Eric shook his head as the girls walked away.

"So, I'm a grandfather. Wow," Eric said with a faraway look in his eyes. Estelle let out a laugh.

"What are you complaining for? Have you met me? I'm a great-grandmother," she said looking at Eric.

"Why are you saying it like it's such a bad thing? I know you like it," Eric said. If whatever he was feeling was anything to go by, then he could bet his life that his mother as over the moon.

"Love it," Estelle said excitedly. Eric took his mother's hand and leaned against the chair.

"What do you know, my little girl has her own little girl now," he said with a smile on his face. "Do you think it's appropriate for me to still call her my little girl?" he asked turning to look at Estelle.

"I still call you my little boy," Estelle said with a smile. Eric frowned.

"What? When?" he asked looking at her.

"When I'm talking about you at Bible study or with friends. And when I'm really angry with you," she said with a smile. Eric laughed.

"I guess once a child always a child, huh?" he said and closed his eyes. He did not hear her reply. He had drifted off to a world of his own where he and a young girl, probably six or seven years of age were having a tea party. The area was strangely familiar, maybe his back yard or Mitch and Natasha's place. He was not very sure where they were. The girl had beautiful heavy black curls just like Natasha's. He looked lovingly at the child who was busy serving him a cup of cinnamon tea and a cupcake. He smiled. Being a grandfather was definitely going to be fun.

All this time, Mitchell was pacing up and down the hallway. He could not get himself to relax, not even for a minute. He would definitely not be okay, not before he saw his wife and daughter.

*****

Mona and Stacy slowly walked out of the canteen laden with goods. Mona was staring daggers at Stacy for buying more than she intended. Apart from her potato chips and chocolate bars, she had gotten a milkshake and a double beef cheeseburger and as if this was not enough, she had Mona holding everything while she munched on her burger. They had decided to wait for Rita who had gone into the gift shop right before they went to the canteen. Rita thought they would save more time that way.

"Hanging out with us black folk has really boosted your appetite," Mona said as she looked at Stacy whose face was almost covered in ketchup. Stacy nodded.

"If you had half the day I had, you'd be eating a whole cow," she said as she took another bite. Mona looked at her and then looked around.

"Okay. I need to sit down," she said as she walked to a nearby waiting area. Stacy followed her and sat down before taking another bite. "So, what happened?" Mona asked looking at her.

"Well, do you want the long version or the short version?" Stacy asked as she took the last bite of her burger. Mona raised an eyebrow.

"Girl, you know I'm a sucker for details right?" she asked looking at Stacy.

"Long version it is," Stacy said as she used a paper towel to clean her mouth and hands. "So as it turns out Mitchell's ex wants NSCS to manage her campaign," she started. Mona let out a scornful laugh.

"Of what? Whores R' Us?" she asked laughing cynically. Stacy rolled her eyes.

"I wish. The bitch has decided that she will be the new name in fashion jewelry and she wants, get this, Beyoncé to be her envoy," Stacy said. Mona almost dropped the bags she was holding.

"Wait up," Mona said as she put the bags down. "Are we talking the one Beyoncé or is there another Beyoncé that I don't know about?" she asked looking at Stacy who was now nodding.

"The one and the same. So, for that to happen, she must be ready to pour millions. I mean, it is Beyoncé but she won't hear of it. She wants Mitchell to personally negotiate the deal," Stacy said angrily.

"What? Why?" Mona asked looking confused. "Isn't she rich

on her own? She did get a generous divorce settlement, right?" she asked.

"That's just the thing. It's not about the money," Stacy said. Mona looked at her and rolled her eyes.

"You lost me," she said looking at a really angry looking Stacy.

"I think she is still trying to get Mitchell back," Stacy said in a whisper.

"Who's trying to get Mitchell back?" Rita asked. The two looked up at her in surprise. None of them had noticed her walking up to them.

"The ex-wife," Mona said as Rita sat down on the chair next to them, her eyes wide.

"Who, Lisa?" Rita asked.

"Uh huh," Stacy said as she pulled her hair back into a pony tail.

"But what proof do you have that she is trying to get back with Mitchell? Because if her demands are the only thing you have to go by, we all know the bitch is crazy," Mona said matter of factly. Stacy nodded.

"I know, but how would you explain her coming to trash the office demanding to see Mitchell? You know she got so crazy, I had to call security," Stacy said. Mona and Rita exchanged glances.

"I don't know about you, cuz, but I am seriously considering a job at NSCS. The drama in that place, whoa," Mona said laughing. Rita gave her a playful nudge.

"Stop it, it's not funny," she said before turning to Stacy. "Does Mitchell know about this?" she asked. Stacy shook her head.

"No, and I am not going to tell him, at least not until after Natasha's feeling better. It's my house now and I will clean up the mess," Stacy said looking a bit distracted. Mona placed a hand on her shoulder.

"You know the hit squad is always here if you need us, right? That stupid white bitch can't take us. We're from The Bronx," she said. Rita rolled her eyes.

"No, we're not," she said looking at Stacy.

"Well, she does not need to know that. The last time I told her that she was literally shaking in her boots…or sandals. Whatever she was wearing. Doesn't really matter to me," Mona said. Stacy laughed and then sighed. "What? There's more?" Mona asked looking at her surprised. Stacy nodded.

"You know me and your brother hooked up on the eve of Natasha's wedding right?" Stacy asked. Rita and Mona smiled.

"I thought it was a rumor!" Mona said excitedly. Rita shook her head.

"Nope. It happened alright," she said as she slowly bent over to rub her feet.

"Damn, he's a heartbreaker that boy, isn't he?" Mona said looking at Stacy whose face spelled out more sadness than anger. "Oh no, please don't tell me you fell in love with him?" she asked as she noticed a tear roll down Stacy's cheek.

"Oh come on. It's Tyrone!" Rita said sitting upright and looking at Stacy. "There is no way you can tell me you had any genuine feelings for him," she added still looking at Stacy who was now using her finger to brush the tears off her cheek.

"I did but I think I was just a one off thing for him. He does not pick up or return my calls. Even my emails have gone unanswered," she said as a fresh flood of tears overcame her. Rita put an arm around her and rolled her eyes. If there was one person in the entire world who loathed Tyrone, it was Rita. To her, he was stupid, self absorbed bastard who could not tell a great thing even if it hit him in the balls. Mona reached over and squeezed Stacy's hand.

"Look, I know he's my brother and all but he is dumb if he cannot realize that he is missing out on what could very well be the greatest woman I have ever met." She looked at Rita and squeezed Stacy's hand again. "You are better than this. You are stronger than this. Just let it go, have some mimosas or something. Get wasted," she said. Stacy pulled herself from Rita's embrace.

"Mona's right you know," Rita said. "Where else is he going to find a white woman with super boobs like yours?" she asked. Stacy laughed and wiped off another tear.

"Don't forget, they are one hundred percent real," Mona said looking at Stacy. She gently stroked her hair and then held her face in her hands. "As far as I'm concerned, consider his butt kicked, okay? And then me, you, Rita and maybe Tasha if she gets a sitter will go out and paint this damn town red," she added. Stacy sniffed and then nodded. Mona smiled. She thought Stacy looked like a living doll. "Come on, it's time I met my niece," she said as she stood up. Rita got up and bent down to help Mona with the coffee as Stacy walked ahead. "Hey, what do you know, they do sell flip flops at a hospital gift shop," Mona said looking at Rita's feet.

"Who knew huh? Maybe this hospital will be the new Oz," Rita said before the three of them broke into bouts of laughter.

When they got back to the waiting area, Estelle was seated silently, Eric looked deep in thought and Mitchell was still pacing restlessly. Stacy took one of the coffee cups and walked up to Mitchell.

"Here," she said handing him the cup. "You need to relax. We already know that they are fine," she said. Mitchell looked into her eyes and for a minute, Stacy thought she saw fear in them.

"Stacy, I am a father now. How do I know I won't mess this up?" he asked in a whisper. Stacy looked over her shoulder at Estelle, Eric, Mona and Rita who were now too busy chattering to hear anything.

"Listen, the fact that you are freaked out is proof that your daddy instincts have already kicked in. You will do just fine," she said in a hushed whisper. A half smile played on Mitchell's lips.

"When did you become so smart?" he asked looking at her.

"I was always smart. You just took longer to notice," she said as Dr. Georges walked towards them. He was holding a bundled up baby in his arms. "Oh my God, Mitch. The baby," Stacy squealed. Mitchell turned around as the doctor approached them. By this time, everyone else had already walked up to them.

"I'm afraid our beautiful mum is out. The sedatives were too much but here is baby Schmidt," Dr. Georges said as they gathered around him. Mitchell took the baby from the doctor and looked down at her. As much as everyone was busy making cooing noises, all Mitchell could see was the most beautiful, most precious thing in the world. She had the most beautiful pink pouty lips and a full head of dark curly hair. He suddenly felt all emotional as he looked at his daughter.

"She is so beautiful," he said in a low voice.

"She gets that from our side of the family," Mona said making everyone laugh.

"So, no name," Estelle said. Mitchell shook his head.

"Unless we call her Aiden," he joked. "But as soon as Tasha is up, we will have a name for my daughter," he said as Eric took the baby from him. Mitchell smiled as his last words echoed in his head.

"My daughter." He smiled. That was one thing he was going to love hearing over and over again.

Chapter 3

When she woke up, Natasha could not tell how long she had been out. The last thing she remembered was Dr. Georges telling her that she had a baby girl. But he could have been mistaken. She was carrying a boy. She knew it, she felt it. She was carrying Aiden Schmidt. Just then she noticed Mitchell standing at the far corner of the room. She noticed the bundle in his arms and knew that he was holding the baby. He was whispering sweet nothings as he rocked the baby. She smiled to herself. He looked so….calm. Who knew Mitchell Schmidt had a soft side.

"Hey there stranger," she said weakly making him turn around. He smiled as he walked up to her bed.

"You're up, finally," he said as he planted a soft kiss on her forehead. Natasha longed to take him in his arms and give him a nice, long hug but she was too tired, not to mention the pain in her abdomen. "Do you want to see her?" he asked with a smile. She looked up at him and nodded.

"So it was not a dream. I did have a girl," she said as Mitchell lowered his arms so that she could see her. She smiled as she looked at the newest addition to her family. If there was one word that she could use to describe her, it was beautiful. She brought her fingers up and gently stroked the side of the sleeping baby's face. She smiled when the baby stirred a little. "She is so beautiful," she said as she suddenly felt tears welling up in her eyes.

"Whoa, no tears on the baby," Mitchell said in a low voice so that not to startle the child. Natasha laughed.

"I'm sorry," she said still laughing.

"Don't be. I shed my fair share when I first saw her. And your dad was there. He must think I am some kind of sissy or something," Mitchell said. Natasha looked at him.

"Speaking of dad. Where is he?" she asked as she tried to get comfortable. "Ow," she said when she felt a discomfort in her abdomen. Mitchell put the baby down in her crib and walked up to the bed.

"You need to take it easy. Let me do that for you," he said as he began adjusting the bed angle while fluffing her pillow so she could lean back comfortably. She looked at him in appreciation as he busied himself in making her comfortable. "So, your dad and Estelle and Mona, Rita, Stacy…everyone was here but they had to stay out. Only one person was allowed in at a time," he said. Natasha smiled.

"Everyone came?" she asked. Mitchell smiled and nodded.

"Seems like you are a pretty popular lady, Tasha Schmidt," he said looking down at her.

"I like to think I am," she said smiling at him. She was trying her best to be conversant but she was in pain. She could barely feel the bottom half of her body and the stitches in her abdomen were nearly driving her wild. It suddenly hit her. The stitches. "I had a C-section," she said looking at Mitchell who was looking back at her questioningly.

"Yes, we all know that," he said looking at her. "Why? Did you think that was a hallucination too?" he asked with a smile. She shook her head.

"No, it's not that. It's just…get me Dr. Georges," she said in a panic. Mitchell held her hand and looked into her eyes.

"Baby, why are you so worked up?" he asked looking at her lovingly.

"Just get me the doctor. Now!" she said. Mitchell took his pager and briefly clicked on it before putting it back in his pocket. "There, I paged him," he said.

"No you need to call him so I know you are not running some kind of scam so some nurse can come and pump some sedatives in me," Natasha said looking at him. Mitchell knew that look. He had seen it so many times before. It was his wife's no nonsense look. The look that said, "if you don't do what I ask there will be hell to pay. "

"Baby, we are in a hospital. It's not like I can just pop my head out and call out his name like some imbecile at a bar," he said as he took her hand in his. "Everything will be fine," he said looking at her. Natasha still looked restless. His words were not convincing enough. Just then, the door opened and Dr. Georges walked in with a smile. He still had his scrubs on. Natasha guessed that he was either headed to surgery, from surgery or just doing rounds. At that moment, she didn't even think to notice that this was the first time she was seeing her doctor in scrubs.

"How are mother and daughter doing?" the doctor asked cheerfully.

"They were fine until the mother started acting weird," Mitchell said. The doctor frowned.

"How weird? Anything out of the ordinary? Natasha?" he asked looking at her.

"I hate to be one of those annoying bitchy women but I have to ask. Did you do a clean job with the cut? I mean I need to know that I can still wear a bikini someday if I feel like it," she said. Mitchell grinned. He could not believe it, that was her big emergency. At some point he even chuckled before Natasha stared daggers at him. "You better laugh when you still can, Mitchell," she retorted angrily before turning her attention back to the doctor. "So, was it a nice clean cut? Should I be worried?" she asked looking at Dr. Georges. The doctor looked at Mitchell and smiled.

"I had a plastic surgeon, the best I have, do the work. You have nothing to worry about," he said. Natasha breathed a sigh of relief.

"I can't believe you had me page the doctor for this," Mitchell said laughing.

"Trust me, Mr. Schmidt, that is a very common concern," the doctor said. His smile slowly disappeared as he looked at Natasha's chart.

"What? Is there anything wrong?" Mitchell asked looking worried. The last thing he needed right now was to be told that something went wrong. The doctor shook his head and looked up at them.

"I know that you would like to be out of here as soon as you possibly can but we need to keep you here for at least a day for observation. Though it was a simple surgery, you lost quite a lot of blood," he explained. "We just need to keep you here for observation, make sure you do not relapse at home. Better here than there," he added with a smile. Natasha looked at Mitchell and then at the doctor and then nodded.

"I understand. But my baby is okay, right?" she asked looking worried.

"Your baby is the healthiest baby I have had the pleasure of delivering in a long time. You should be proud," Dr. Georges said looking at her. She smiled and felt her cheeks flush. She knew she looked a mess but all that did not matter. At least not now. All she needed to know was that her baby was fine.

"Bring her over. I need to hold her," she said looking up at Mitchell. The doctor smiled at them as Mitchell carefully picked up the baby and gently placed her next to her mother. "I guess I need to get more pink stuff, huh?" she said smiling up at her husband who nodded.

"Thank God the nursery was not gender specific, right?" Mitchell said with a smile. The doctor stood up and walked to the door. He was obviously tired of being the third wheel…or fourth wheel in this case. He opened the door and turned to look at the young family.

"I'll let the others know you are awake," Dr. Georges said before he walked out. Natasha looked up at Mitchell and smiled.

"Now that we cannot have a daughter named Aiden, what do you suggest?" she asked. Mitchell looked at her and then at the baby and shook his head.

"I don't know. Taylor?" he asked looking at her. Natasha shook her head.

"Taylor Schmidt? That sounds like a failed version of Taylor Swift," she said. Mitchell laughed.

"You are right. We could call her Madeline," he said. Almost as soon as he had said that, Natasha suddenly thought of a name and said it at the same time.

"Alexis," she said and then laughed. "I like Madeline too," she said looking at him.

"I like Alexis just as much," he said smiling. "There is no reason why she cannot be Alexis Madeline Schmidt," he said suggestively. Natasha looked down at the sleeping child.

"Alexis Madeline Schmidt. Why not?" she said in a whisper just as the door opened and everyone came into her room. She lifted her finger to her lips. "She's asleep," she said in a whisper.

"So, how are you guys? Except for the obvious pain and disorientation from the meds,' Rita asked as she walked to Natasha's bed and kissed her cheek. Mona and Stacy followed suit before giving way to Eric and Estelle. Eric planted a kiss on her fore head and smiled down at her.

"You made me a grandfather," he said with a smile. "It's a great feeling," he added still smiling. Natasha smiled and looked at the baby again.

"Thank God one of us feels great. It's like these damn meds are not working," she said frowning. Estelle made her way through and gently draped an arm around Natasha's shoulders.

"They can only give you enough to help you manage the pain, nothing more. You are breast feeding now remember? We would hate for baby…what's-her-name to be an addict this early," she said.

"By the way guys, what's-her-name has a name now," Mitchell said excitedly.

"Really? What is it? Oh I know – it's Mona," Mona said quickly.

Rita looked at her and rolled her eyes.

"I think Rita is a better name." She looked over at Estelle who was giving her a stern look. "What? We've been best friends since we were kids," she said shrugging as she looked away from Estelle to avoid her icy look.

"Okay, if we were to honor each one of you, our daughter would either be Rita, Mona, Stacy, Estelle or Erica. And not forgetting my parents also wanted their names somewhere in there," Mitchell said pointing at the small group. "So, we decided on names that are not connected in any way to the family," he added.

"Where are your parents anyway?" Mona asked looking at Mitchell.

"Somewhere in the Maldives. They are unreachable till they get back home. That's how seriously they take their vacation time," he said smiling.

"Bummer," Mona said under her breath.

"I know," Stacy and Rita whispered in unison.

"So, what is it? Don't keep us waiting," Eric pressed. Mitchell looked at Natasha and smiled.

"Alexis Madeline," Natasha said with a smile. Stacy walked over and looked down at the sleeping baby.

"May I?" she asked. Natasha nodded, giving her the go ahead to pick the child up. Stacy looked at the sweet angel and sighed.

"You better thank God she is so cute. Otherwise, I would have never forgiven you for not naming her Stacy," she said with a smile. The nurse walked in and everyone knew what that meant. They had to say goodbye. Estelle looked at Natasha; her eyes were full of pride.

"The last time I felt this happy was when I looked at you when you were born. Seems like just yesterday," she said as she held Eric's hand. "We will always be here if you ever need us, okay baby?" she added as she kissed Natasha again.

"I know," Natasha said weakly as they left the room.

"By the way, Mitchell, tell your daughter to call me Pa," he said as he held the door. "No one is calling me grandfather," he added as he made his way out of the room.

"Will do," Mitchell said laughing. He looked at Natasha who was being made to lie back down so the nurse could look at her dressing. The nurse looked at Natasha and then at Mitchell nervously. "I'm the husband," he said leaning forward. The nurse smiled as she slowly opened up Natasha's gown.

"You might feel a little sting as I apply some antiseptic," the nurse said in a soothing voice. Mitchell held Natasha's hand as the nurse carefully redressed the wound and gave her another dose of painkillers. "That's it, and we're done," the nurse said as she covered Natasha up with the gown. She smiled at both of them before she left. Mitchell looked down at Natasha and smiled.

"I'll be here when you wake up," he said in a low voice. She shook her head. She had no idea how long she had been out for and at the rate they were dosing her with painkillers, she had no idea how much longer she would be out.

"You need to rest. Go home," she said weakly as the drugs

began to kick in.

"I cannot bear the thought of letting my two favorite girls out of my sight," he said as he kissed her forehead. "Get some rest. I will be right here when you wake up," he said again. Natasha smiled as she felt herself drift off into a deep sleep.

*****

Two days after giving birth, Natasha and Alexis were still in the hospital even though the doctor had only talked about keeping them in the hospital overnight. Needless to say, Natasha was becoming worried. Again she was afraid that something could have gone wrong with the baby and no one had bothered to tell her. She was becoming infuriated. She longed to be back in her own house, sleeping in her own bed, putting Alexis to sleep in her crib. She wanted to be in that nursery, rocking in her chair as Alexis fed. There was just something about the hospital that was sucking the sanity out of her. Just then, Dr. Georges came in looking cheerful as ever.

"Good morning Natasha. How are we feeling today?" he asked as he picked up her chart. Natasha sighed and rolled her eyes. The doctor had seen this before. He could tell that Natasha was agitated.

"I want to go home, Dr. Georges. Why am I still here?" she asked looking at him. "You had told me that we would only be here one night for observation. It's been two nights and three days and I want to take my baby home," she said. Dr. Georges looked at her and sat on the edge of the bed.

"Natasha, you have been my patient for what? Two, three years? And I always want to make sure that you are in perfect health before I let you go home," he said. Natasha shrugged. "I really like you but I hate making house calls unless of course they are about a nice pot roast and wine," he added with a smile. This made Natasha laugh. He always had a way with words.

"But I am in good health, am I not? Or is it Alexis? Is something wrong with my daughter?" she asked suddenly feeling herself panicking. The doctor shook his head and put a consoling hand on her own.

"Your baby is fine. I told you. But as I said before, you lost a lot of blood and we had to ensure we replenish it and nurse you back to health as soon as possible, for your baby's sake. Plus your blood type is not that easy to come by. Don't worry. It won't be long now," he said before getting up. Natasha sighed again as she watched him scribble something on her chart before he headed for the door.

"Could I at least get a timeline?" she asked. The doctor turned around and looked at her. A slow smile played on his lips.

"Not more than twenty-four hours, I promise," he said and then left. Natasha smiled. That gave her so much hope. She looked over at the baby cot where Alexis was sleeping soundly.

"We'll be going home soon, Alexis," she said in a whisper. She smiled to herself as she looked at her baby girl. Looking at that little angel had to be the greatest feeling ever. It was no wonder babies were called bundles of joy. She immediately began thinking of what lay ahead for her, for Mitchell and for their daughter. Alexis' first words, first steps, first date…she shuddered at the thought of her baby girl dating. If it were up to Mitchell, Alexis would never, ever know that she was a girl. Natasha had no idea how he intended on making that happen. She would just have to wait and see.

As she looked at the baby, she suddenly felt herself getting angry at her mother for walking out on her and her father. How could anyone look at something so innocent and just walk away? Without even flinching? She came to the conclusion that her mother must be one cold hearted bitch to just walk away from her one and only daughter. She would never do that to Mitch or Alexis or herself. How could she live knowing that she left the two people she loved most? Natasha stretched out and gently stroked Alexis's cheek for the umpteenth time.

"You are mine, Alexis. Nothing would ever make me turn my back on you. I will never, ever let you go," she said looking at her baby. She smiled when the child stirred a little and almost fluttered her eyelids, still deep in sleep. She let out a small, silent laugh. This moment right here, with nothing else between her and Alexis, this was the best moment of her day. Of her life.

Chapter 4

Three months after having Alexis, Natasha had begun to resent her body. Every time she went to the bathroom was a nightmare. Her tummy was still headed down, literally, and she no longer had that supple waist or a nice, firm butt. All she saw every time she looked at her reflection was a big blob of baby fat. She had declined every invitation Mitchell had given her to go for dinner or one of the company functions. She had always been the one person who stood out without even trying but now everything she wore made her feel like Sponge Bob or a Chucky Cheese employee.

"You okay?" Mitchell asked as he walked into the room. Natasha sighed and nodded as she walked out of the closet. She had been staring at her clothes for…she had no idea for how long. "You are not still mooning over your body now, are you?" he asked as he walked towards her. He slowly slipped an arm around her waist and pulled her close to him. "You do know that you are still the most beautiful person I know, right?" he asked looking into her eyes. Natasha nodded.

"Except for Alexis," she said with a smile. Mitchell laughed and nodded.

"Yes, except for Alexis," he said looking at her. He pulled her close and held her in his arms. "Get that awful thought about your weight out of your mind," he said with a tone that commanded finality. She pulled away from him and looked into his eyes.

"You do know the likes of Beyoncé and Jessica Alba lost their baby weight in a couple of months, right? That really concerns me," she said looking at him.

"God, Tasha. Are you serious?" he asked laughing. She nodded and began walking towards the bed.

"Yes, I fucking am. They are women like me, right? So what's the big difference?" she asked as she sat down.

"The big difference is that they worked out like crazy while they should have been eating healthy while breastfeeding. And I will die before I let you starve yourself just so you can look good," he said with a smile. Natasha smiled back at him.

"At least I have you," she said as Mitchell walked towards her. He sat down and looked into her eyes before gently slipping a hand behind her neck. She smiled as he brought his face down and gently kissed her. Her hand slowly came up and held the side of his face as their lips crushed together. Soon, they were both breathing heavily as desire took over. Natasha could not remember the last time they got intimate, sexually. Her wound was yet to completely heal and there was the little fact about her not feeling sexy. She let out a moan when Mitchell began to slowly kiss her neck. She could feel his tongue slowly running down one side of her neck. She wanted him so bad. One of his hands slowly made its way down her front and gently cupped a breast, making her moan. He was just about to begin taking off her t-shirt when Alexis's familiar wail came through the baby monitor. He pulled away from her and sighed.

"That's a buzz kill," he said burying his head in her neck. She smiled and patted his back.

"I know. It's your turn now," she said as she pushed him away. He groaned and stood up.

"I love that girl to death but I do not understand how something so small can make so much noise," he said as he walked towards the door. Natasha smiled.

"She probably just needs a diaper change or daddy's familiar face," she called out as he walked away. She smiled as she lay down on the bed. She looked at the ceiling and an idea struck her. If she could not have sex, she would have to find another way to pass the time. She rose from the bed and walked to the bedside table. She pulled one of the drawer handles and took out her diary. She smiled as she flipped through the pages. It had been almost three years since she had last made an entry or even gone through some of the entries in there. She made herself comfortable and randomly opened the diary. She looked at the date and almost let out a laugh. It was from 2007. Things were still a bit too weird in her life at the time. She was in her third year of college and was still trying to figure things out. She leaned against the headboard and began reading.

Dear Diary,

Today was the most awful day. I am done with men. DONE. I cannot keep trusting in some guy who will never do me any good. It's almost as if I only ever seem to attract assholes. I am not sure what about me screams, "Desperate and looking for the next bad boy." The last one was a serial liar but I have just found out that Darryl is a serial cheater! I do not think there is one girl on the entire campus he has not hit on or slept with. Bastard. This is what happened.

Last night, Darryl and I had plans to go to dinner. I have been working my ass off for the last week just so I could have last night off. That's what I get for having a double major. But Darryl did not even consider that little fact when he unceremoniously cancelled on me even after I spent half the day shopping for an "appropriate" outfit since everything I own somehow "does not do my body justice." I should have known better. Imagine my surprise, after he texted me saying that he is bedridden with a cold, when I saw him with some dumb ass re head outside my damned dorm building. And apparently this is not the first time. He has been doing this forever. I thought me and him were exclusive. Well, maybe I could simply just go on and start liking girls.

"What are you doing? Is that your old journal?" Mitchell asked as he walked in carrying Alexis. Natasha smiled and nodded.

"I needed to pass the time," she said. Mitchell shrugged.

"There is so much you could do to pass the time. You could watch a movie or just some TV. We do have cable, remember?" he said in a low voice as he sat on the edge of the bed.

"I know. Sometimes I just like to think of myself as Robinson Crusoe and just delve into pen and paper," she said with a smile. Mitchell looked at her and shushed her. "What? Why are we whispering?" she asked putting the journal away.

"She just went down," he said in a whisper.

"Oh, so she was just cranky?" Natasha asked looking down at the sleeping baby girl. Mitchell shook his head.

"No, it was the usual suspects. Hungry, diaper change," he said as he rocked Alexis. "So, who were we reading about today?" he asked looking at her.

"Darryl Jones. Third year of college," she said looking at him.

"The jerk?" Mitchell asked with a smile. Natasha laughed.

"They were all jerks," she said looking into his eyes.

"So," Mitchell said as he slowly laid the baby on the bed. "Is there anything there about me?" he asked looking at her. Natasha smiled and felt her cheeks flush. For some reason, even after so long, Mitchell still managed to have this effect on her. She looked at him and nodded. "Really?" he asked looking more interested. She nodded again and ran her fingers through her thick curls. Her hair was a big frizzy mess; at least, that was how she saw it. She had become so accustomed to weekly salon appointments but lately, she barely had enough time to sleep, let alone get her looks in check. Mitchell touched her chin and turned her face so that he could look at her. "Can I read it?" he asked, his eyebrow raised in hope. Her eyes widened as she shook her head.

"Hell no!" she said so loud that he almost woke the baby up. Mitchell put his finger to his mouth and shushed her. "Why would you want to read that?" she asked in a whisper.

"I would want to know what you first thought of me when we first met," he said with a smile. She gave him a disapproving look.

"I don't know," Natasha said looking at him.

"Come on," Mitchell said, almost in a pleading voice.

"Well, what's in it for me?" she asked looking at him.

"Oh, so we're being businessy," he said with a smile. She looked at him and nodded.

"I married a man who tells me that in every little thing, there is a hidden business transaction. So maybe it's about time I took his advice," she said with a smile. Mitchell took one of her hands in his and looked into her brown eyes.

"That's some wise man. I would like to meet him some day," he said with a smile. "So what do you say, one entry about good old *moi*?" he asked. She looked at him and rolled her eyes and finally gave up.

"Fine. One, just one," she said as she picked up her diary again. "Okay let's see…..oh, here's a good one. This is about the first time we met," she said looking at him. "Okay here goes," she said as she got comfortable.

Dear Diary,

Today was supposed to be the best day of my life. I finally landed the interview of my life: Nolan Schmidt Communication Solutions but the day had to start on an all-time low when I passed out at the parking lot and guess who found me? My future boss, Mitchell Schmidt! As if that was not embarrassing enough, I was blushing, and I know he noticed. I am a black woman who does not have the darkest skin. Damn it! I'll be damned if I even manage to get a second interview.

Working at NSCS has been my dream job and the fact that I have to work under His Royal Hotness! ☺ Okay, maybe that is a bit immature but anyone who has a pulse must have noticed just how hot Mitchell is. He is tall, he is muscular, and he has great hair. He is like a very real Derek Shepherd. Maybe that's what I'll call him. McDreamy, or is it McSteamy? Maybe he is both McDreamy and McSteamy rolled into one.

Natasha looked up and smiled at Mitchell.

"Why did you stop?' he asked looking at her. He could tell that her cheeks were flushed.

"I never promised to read you one full entry," she said as she put the diary back in the drawer.

"Come on, Tasha. Why not?" Mitchell asked looking at her. She shook her head and smiled.

"At this rate I might need to get a safe installed here somewhere," she said looking at him.

"What are you talking about? This house is full of safes," he said laughing. Natasha rolled her eyes.

"I'm sorry but two safes in a three bedroom house is not my definition of, quote unquote, 'full of safes,'" Natasha said with a smile. She climbed of the bed and walked to the bathroom.

"Where are you going?" he asked looking at her.

"To shower," she said as she turned on the water. "I'll be out in a few," she said walking into the bathroom. Mitchell sighed. Since she gave birth, she barely let him see her naked. She would get dressed and undressed in the bathroom, cover up that lovely body in his oversized t-shirts. It was about time he showed her that he still appreciated her. He got up and picked up Alexis slowly and then placed her in her crib. He made sure she was comfortable before he stripped down and walked to the bathroom. He opened the door and looked at Natasha standing under the running water and smiled.

"What are you doing?" Natasha asked when she saw him standing there. Mitchell walked in and slipped an arm around her waist. "Mitch, you know I still can't," she said in a whisper as he pulled her closer to him. He smiled and gently claimed her lips.

"I just want to make love to my wife. We don't need sex for that," he said as he kissed her again. Natasha wrapped her arms around his neck as they kissed. She loved the way her naked body felt against his own muscular one. It had been a long time, too long since she felt this way. She felt his tongue slowly make its way inside her mouth as one hand slowly caressed her back. She let out a moan when she felt his hand on her ass, squeezing and kneading gently. He slowly pulled away from her and looked down at her. She gasped when he suddenly turned her around, letting his already fully engorged cock press against her ass. She closed her eyes as he slowly lifted both of her arms and secured them around his neck. He went on to slowly run his fingertips along the fine skin of her body, expertly avoiding any spot that would suddenly turn her into a fire engine. She moaned as she felt him exploring her, softly, gently, lovingly. She let out a moan as his fingers trailed upwards from her waist and her navel. She gasped loudly when he cupped her breasts. Her nipples were already hardened, pressing hard against his palms. She moaned again when he began to slowly rub his palms on her breasts, making her want him, lust for him.

"Mitch..." she moaned as he continued his torture on her breasts. Just when she thought she could not take any more, he slipped his hand down to her pussy and gently touched her clit. He smiled when she suddenly twitched and pressed harder against him. He got both hands on her thighs and forced them apart. She let out a moan again when he began rubbing his finger against her already distended clit. She leaned against his shoulder and squeezed her eyes shut as he pleasured her. She felt her legs get even more weak when he slipped a finger inside her. He smiled when he found that she was already drenched. He was surprised that there was no pre-cum leaking down the side of her leg but then again, it could have very well have been already washed away. She suddenly cried out and he knew, she was ready.

Mitchell turned her around again and held her against the cold tiled wall of the bathroom. He looked into her eyes and kissed her again. He slowly pulled away so he could admire her face. He thought she looked beautiful, with her hair all wet, sticking to the sides of her face and neck. She watched him as he sunk to his knees and slowly kissed her thighs before he slipped his hand under her knee. She looked down at him as he placed it on his shoulder. He leaned forward and began kissing her pussy. He loved the way she tasted, that beautiful taste of her being so close to an orgasm. He slowly kissed her pussy in the same manner he would have kissed her mouth. He interchanged her labia as he slowly ran his tongue along the inside of her outer lips. She sighed and gasped especially loudly when he engulfed her clit with his mouth. She moaned loudly as he sucked hard on her. She could not hold herself back any longer. She was about to explode and he knew it. He could feel her spasming against his mouth. She screamed out when he suddenly shoved the entire length of his tongue inside her pussy, making her cum hard. He held her close to his mouth as she shook against him before he finally pulled away from her. He released her leg and pulled himself to his feet.

Natasha looked at him as she gasped for breath. This was the first time she had felt like a woman in a long time. She looked into his eyes and smiled. He pulled her from the wall and held her against his body as they stood under the running water. She could still feel his raging cock pressing hard against her ass.

"Thank you," she said in a whisper. "Pity I can't take care of this," she said as she reached behind her and held his cock in his hands. He sighed loudly and held her tighter.

"You are taking care of it just fine," he said as she began stroking his cock. She stroked him long and hard as he began moaning. A few strokes in, she could already feel his cock get harder and twinge in her hand. She obviously needed to get him some servicing and soon. But she had to wait for a couple more weeks before she got back in the saddle. By that time, her stitches would be completely healed. The doctor had recommended six weeks but it was too uncomfortable. Her doctor had told her that the wound would be a hundred percent healed after twelve weeks and she intended to wait. She could remember how great her sex life was before the baby and if she had to wait to feel that again, she was willing to make the sacrifice.

She suddenly felt Mitchell's hot jism all over her hands and smiled. "God, you are still the sexy goddess with all the tricks up your sleeve I married," he said holding her close. She smiled and leaned against his shoulder. "I hope your screams did not wake Alexis," he said in a whisper. She turned around and kissed him deeply.

"You better take the blame if you ever hope to tap this again," she said with a smile.

Chapter 5

Mona's eyes grew wide as she looked at Natasha.

"What do you mean you have not had sex in two freaking months?" she asked in a whisper. Rita looked at the two and rolled her eyes.

"You must be kidding. There is no way the Natasha I know goes for a week let alone two months without getting freaky," she said making goo goo noises at the baby. Natasha had decided to spend the day at her Nan's after Mitchell had to rush out suddenly that morning. This was actually the first time he was away from the house in a long time since he had opted to take some time off work so that he could spend time with Natasha and Alexis. When he left, Natasha took the baby and drove straight to her Nan's house. Halfway down there, she decided to call the girls. She was going to turn this into a girls' day out. God knows she didn't have enough of those lately. Needless to say, the girls jumped at the idea almost immediately except for Stacy who could not get away from work.

"Trust me when I tell you, I am serious," Natasha said. "And given the way I look like a big tub of Jell-O lately, I doubt anyone would be willing to even see me naked," she said. Mona playfully slapped her knee.

"Have you seen your clothes? I don't blame Mitchell if he can't get it up," she said pointing at the oversized t-shirt Natasha was wearing.

"Hey, what's wrong with my t-shirt?" Natasha asked frowning.

"It's not yours, for starters," Rita said without looking at her.

Natasha shot her a dirty look.

"None of my clothes fit right now," she said. Mona snapped her fingers and rolled her eyes.

"You are married to a millionaire. Buy clothes that fit," she said matter of factly.

"Come on, I will never look as good as I used to," Natasha said looking at Rita and then at Mona.

"Have you looked in the mirror lately? You are still the hot mama we know. In an oversized t-shirt," Mona said smiling. Natasha smiled as she looked at Mona.

"And by the way, Mitchell has no problem getting it up, thank you very much," she said giving Mona a wink.

"Wait, you mean that in all this he is the long suffering victim?" Rita asked looking at Natasha who was nodding. "What is wrong with you?" she asked. Natasha shrugged.

"I look like a pumpkin and he is not seeing me naked," she said. "Well he did see me in the shower the other day – well, he did a little more than simply see me," she added looking at Rita.

"Okay, that's it. We are taking some well-deserved girl time at the salon," Rita said. Natasha laughed.

"Have you met me? I have a baby now. I can't just up and leave when I want," she said looking at Rita. Just then Estelle walked in carrying a tray of tea and freshly baked muffins.

"Hey Estelle, we need a favor. Could you watch Alexis for a few hours?" Rita asked looking up.

"Actually for the night. Natasha here and Mitchell need some time alone if you know what I mean," Mona said smiling. Estelle smiled and sat down.

"You don't need the baby around you when you are doing the nasty. Of course I will watch her," she said pouring some tea for them.

"No muffins for me. I am already too chubby to continue stuffing my face," Natasha said.

"It's just one muffin. It's not like it will make a big difference," Estelle said. "The only problem would be if you have more," she said holding a muffin up to Natasha's face. Natasha pushed her hand away and shook her head.

"I know you made some for me to take home. So no way," she said before taking a sip of her tea. "Come on guys, we have work to do," she said as she stood up. She picked Alexis up from Rita's arms and kissed her. "See you later princess. I love you so much," she said as she planted another kiss on the baby's forehead before handing her to Estelle.

"You won't even finish your tea?" Estelle asked looking up at Natasha.

"I'm sorry Nan. There are not enough hours in the day," Natasha said as she pulled Rita to her feet. Mona smiled and picked up two muffins before following the girls out. Natasha was ecstatic as they drove to the salon. She had not been pampered in a while. She could not wait to get to the salon. The first stop was obvious, a manicure and pedicure before she headed off to get waxed. She was a little sore as they headed to the hairdresser.

"Oh my god, Tasha? Girl you are a mess," Ivan, her hairstylist said as soon as they walked in.

"Tell me about it," Natasha said as Ivan hugged her. Ivan was almost like one of the girls. He was masculine but everything about him was ever so feminine. He liked shopping, did hair and gossiped better than a Stepford wife. "Ever since I had the baby, I never get time for myself," she said as Ivan sat her down.

"You could have called me. I make house calls you know. I would hate for any of the competition to know I am your stylist especially now that you look like that," he said pointing at her clothes.

"Oh please, Ivan. Don't we know it. We are going shopping after this," Mona said. "Our girl needs to get laid," she added. Natasha's face flushed.

"Mona!" she yelled as she stared daggers at Mona.

"What? It's true," Mona said as she sat down. Ivan smiled as he led Natasha to a chair.

"When I am done with you, people will be begging to get into your pants. Even you," he said winking at Natasha's reflection. Natasha felt her cheeks flush again.

Ivan was right. He did a fabulous job. He got her highlights and got rid of her split ends before he turned her frizzy mess into a glamorous pile of wavy curls. She looked absolutely gorgeous. She looked at the time and sighed. She had exactly three hours to get something to wear and make dinner. She would never make it in time.

"Oh please. We can totally make it work," Rita said as they walked into a boutique.

"How do you suggest we do that?" Natasha asked looking at Rita and then at Mona. Rita took her phone out and quickly scrolled through her contacts list.

"You don't have to cook. What are you in the mood for?" Rita asked as she looked at Natasha.

"I don't know...."

"...never mind. I know of a great Moroccan place. They make great chicken," Rita said cutting her short. Natasha smiled at her as Mona walked over to a rack of dresses. She pulled out one short dress and held it against her body. Natasha shook her head and frowned.

"That will never fit,' she said.

"It's a stretch. Just go inside there and try it on. If it doesn't fit then we can always get another one," Mona said.

"Chop, chop," Rita said clapping her hands. Natasha laughed as she walked inside a changing room. "Here, try these on too," Rita said handing her a pair of black peep toe heels. Natasha took a deep breath and took off the t-shirt and pulled the dress over her head. She then took off her flip flops and put on the shoes Rita had just handed her and then walked out.

"Oh my God. If you leave that dress, I will kill you," Mona said as Natasha looked at her reflection in the mirror. Mona was right – not only did she look great, she looked sexy too. Who knew all she wanted to do was just get her hair done and wear a fitted dress? She could not wait to see Mitchell later on that night.

When she got home, she quickly set the table and lit some

candles. She then popped the food in the microwave but didn't switch it on. She had no idea when Mitchell would get home. She took some red wine from the kitchen and some glasses and walked to the dining room. She poured two glasses of wine and then walked out of the dining room. She laid the dress on the bed and the quickly got undressed before she walked into the shower. She took a shower cap and then looked at the tub for a few minutes. She suddenly decided she deserved a long luxurious soak in the tub. She held her hair up and put on the cap as she ran the bath water before she stepped into the tub. She closed her eyes and felt the great smelling scents of lavender and vanilla coating her skin.

"God bless Nan and dad," she thought as she closed her eyes. Even though Alexis's loud wails and cries sometimes got to her, she thought the house was a bit too quiet. But all the same, she needed it. She had no idea how long she had been in the tub before she finally got out. She walked to her dresser and quickly moisturized her entire body before she took the dress from her bed. She slowly slipped it on and then walked over to the full length mirror. Again, Mona was right. The form fitted short sleeved below the knee dress was just what she needed. The way the dress was all cropped up in a single line down the center distracted the attention from her baby fat to her more glamorous curves around her hips. She slipped on the new black peep toe shoes she bought earlier that day and let her hair down. She put on some silver dangling earrings and quickly did a touch of her makeup, nothing too much, just enough to accentuate her features. She took some cherry flavored lip gloss and dabbed her lips before standing up to look at herself. Even she thought she looked fabulous. She was still staring at her reflection when she heard the front door open and close.

"Perfect timing," she thought as she walked out of the bedroom and slowly made her way to the living room.

"Honey! I'm ho….whoa," Mitchell said when he saw her. Natasha smiled. She was glad to know that her effort had paid off. The way he was looking at her at that very moment was the same way he had looked at her that night he took her to the Griffith Observatory and then on the night he first proposed to her, and it was the same look he had given her when he said his vows on their wedding day. "You look….whoa," he said again as words failed him. She laughed and walked over to where he was and gave him a nice long kiss. "I'm guessing we are almost out of the woods," he said smiling at her. She shook her head.

"We are not 'almost' out of the woods. We *are* out of the woods," she said looking at him. His eyes widened.

"You mean…,"

"…yeah. It's been twelve weeks already," she said cutting him short. "So I thought we would have dinner and just get crazy," she said before planting another kiss on his lips.

"What about Alexis?" he asked looking around. She smiled.

"She's with my dad and Nan. We have the whole night to ourselves and I already pumped so there is no chance of…" her voice trailed off when she saw him frown. "What? I'm sorry my sexy talk is not what it used to be," she added with a smile. He pulled her close and let his hands run wildly on her back.

"Whoa, hold up tiger. We need to have dinner first. You will need your energy for later," she said as she tried to push him off. He pulled her closer to himself again.

"We could always have a break in between," he said as he carried her to the bedroom. She giggled when he literally threw her on the bed. He threw his jacket on the floor and climbed on the bed. She quickly flipped over as soon as he laid his body on her so that he could be under her. She straddled him and felt his cock pressing hard against her crotch. She looked down at him and giggled again. "You naughty horny little devil. Is that a semi? Already?" she asked seductively. He nodded and held her waist as he looked up at her.

"Three months and two days? A semi is not all you are going to get," he said as he pulled her down for a kiss. She slowly ground herself on him, gently bouncing her ass off his groin, the way he liked it any time they made love with her on top. Natasha pulled away and smiled at him before climbing off the bed. She pulled his pants off almost as quickly as she had conceived the idea and then pulled his shorts off. She looked at him and smiled as she held his already firm member in her small hand. She brought her head down and slowly planted a kiss on his throbbing head making him moan loudly. "Shit Tasha, you are definitely going to kill me," he said lifting his head to look at her. She looked at him and smiled.

"And I have only just began," she said looking at him. Mitchell held his hands out, an invitation to hold her in his arms. She smiled and stood upright and then slowly undid the zipper on the side of her dress. She let the dress slip off her shoulders before kicking her shoes off. She saw him take a long deep breath as he looked at her black matching lace underwear. He was already breathing hard just by looking at her. She slowly slipped two fingers on either side of her waist and wriggled out of her panties. She stood there for a few more minutes letting him see her smooth, cleanly waxed pussy before climbing onto the bed again. She looked at him as she straddled him once more. He looked at her and reached behind her to unclasp her bra. She looked down at him as she slowly lowered herself onto his waiting cock. She moaned slightly as she felt herself slowly being impaled on his cock. The months of waiting had turned her into one tight glove, almost like a virgin. She looked down at him as she slowly moved herself up and down, letting him fill her every fold. She suddenly began riding him hard, sitting up the entire time. She looked down at Mitchell as his face became contorted. She could tell by the way he was thrusting into her that it wouldn't be long before he exploded into her. She suddenly felt her insides shuddering as he gave in to his orgasm.

Natasha laid her full weight on him and kissed him deeply. She smiled when she pulled away and looked into his angelic brown eyes.

"Wow," he said as he held her. She nodded and kissed his neck.

"I know, right?" she said matter of factly. "Three months can do a whole lot, huh?" she asked as she rested her head on his shoulder. He nodded and laughed. Her eyes widened as she felt him hardening inside her again. "Is that what I think it is?" she asked pulling her head up to look at him.

"I told you. You are getting more than just a semi tonight," he said as she flipped her over. His cock almost slipped out of her when he did. He looked down at her and smiled as he brought his head down and took one nipple inside his mouth. She moaned loudly and wrapped her legs around his waist, making his cock go deeper inside her pussy. She moaned and shivered under him as he let his tongue circle her hard nipples. She held his head steady as he sucked her gently while he slowly moved in and out of her. He slowly released her nipple and trailed his tongue across her chest to take in her other nipple. She moaned again as he sucked on her and gave her other breast equal attention from his flicking fingertips. She suddenly cried out loudly when he began thrusting into her hard. He fucked her long and hard as he struggled to keep his lips around her nipple. He gave up sucking on her breast and buried his head in her shoulder. She slipped her hands under his shirt and clawed on his back as he worked to almost drill her to the bed. She was now screaming loudly as he fucked her. Her body had completely given in to her pleasure as she felt her pussy tightening around his cock. She suddenly let out a loud scream when she felt herself cumming wildly. Once again, she felt him releasing. Her own orgasm must have beckoned his. He collapsed on her, panting, as she released her legs around his waist.

"Oh my god," she gasped as his cock slipped out of her pussy. "That was definitely worth waiting for," she said panting.

"Tell me about it," Mitchell said smiling. "Now, what's for dinner? Because I need energy for another round," he said. Natasha looked at him in surprise.

"The long wait has definitely got you in better shape than ever," Natasha said. Mitchell brought his head down and kissed her softly.

"Get some food in me and I will show you just how much better time has made me. I'm better than good wine," he said as he pulled himself out of bed. Natasha smiled and walked over to pick up her bathrobe. For some reason, she could not wait to get done with dinner.

Chapter 6

Natasha had always heard people say that sex made women glow but she thought it did more than that. It was almost as if she'd had an awakening, like she had been reborn. There was something about an orgasm that made her excited about the day ahead. Ever since she "got her groove back," Natasha no longer cursed when morning came. Before this, every single day had been a drag. Getting out of bed, walking to the nursery, feeding Alexis, rocking her to sleep, pumping more milk for later on and don't forget the occasional sore breasts. As if this was not enough, there was the little fact of Mitchell's occasional meetings. Even though they had both agreed that Mitchell would take some time off so that he could spend more time with his new family, he still had to run off every so often when the need arose. That was the life he led, being an heir to a million dollar empire.

Today was no different than every other day had been. When she woke up, Mitchell was already out of bed. She was glad to hear Alexis's soft moans through the baby monitor. She got out of bed and quickly made her way to the nursery. She smiled when she saw her baby lying peacefully in her bed. She was aimlessly kicking around while sucking on both her hands. Natasha thought she looked even more beautiful than ever. With every day that went by, Natasha thought her daughter looked more like Mitchell. Her hair was thicker, and except for the curls that framed her face, the baby's hair was almost a replica of Mitch's. Her big brown eyes looked the same as Mitchell's did every time she looked into his eyes. Natasha reached down and touched the baby's cheek. She smiled and gently rocked the crib as the baby smiled up at her showing off her toothless gums.

"Hey there little princess," Natasha said with a smile. The baby grinned even more when she spoke. Natasha found herself laughing when the baby tried getting her leg all the way to her face. "You are quite the little gymnast, aren't you, darling?" she said as she stroked her cheek. The baby squealed and Natasha laughed again. "Well, mama has to go take a shower and then she'll be right back, okay?" Natasha said as she picked the baby up from her crib. She kissed her cheek and then her other cheek before she held the baby at arm's length to look at her. Alexis was almost six months old now and to say that she was growing up fast was an understatement. Her cheeks and thighs were a chubby affair and her weight had nearly doubled since the last time Natasha checked.

"Now that is what I call a Kodak moment," Mitchell said making Natasha turn around. Natasha smiled as Mitchell walked towards her.

"I smell breakfast. What time did you get up?" she asked before Mitchell gave her a good morning kiss.

"Maybe two hours ago. I didn't want to wake you up. I heard how fussy Alexis was last night and I knew you needed the extra sleep," he said as he took the baby from her. He lifted her up and made funny faces as he brought her down again to kiss her. The baby squealed in excitement as he did it again. Natasha out a hand behind her neck and nodded. Alexis had been a bit restless that night for some reason and no matter what Natasha tried, she just could not get her down for the night. At some point, Natasha was so frustrated that she almost cried with the baby.

"Tell me about it. I do not understand how something so small can make so much noise," she said looking at the baby who now seemed more joyous than ever. "I was just about to go take a shower," she said as she made her way out of the door.

"You do that. I'll wait for you so we can have breakfast together," Mitchell said as Natasha walked back to their bedroom. Once she was back in the bedroom, she walked to the bathroom and turned on the shower before she stripped down to her birthday suit. She then held her hair in a bun before she stepped under the hot shower. She was not sure what happened next. All she knew was that she felt light headed before everything went dark.

When she came to, Mitchell was holding her in his arms looking as worried as ever. She could see his lips moving but she could not hear a word. It was as if everything was happening in slow motion. She felt some movement and it took a while before she finally realized that Mitchell was shaking her a she spoke.

"What the hell happened?" she thought as she looked into Mitchell's eyes. Somehow, she was still a bit groggy. She could not even make out his face. Everything was so blurry. She suddenly remembered the baby. She felt a panic go through her.

"Alexis..." she said as she tried to get up. Mitchell steadied her on the floor and shook his head.

"Alexis is fine. Are you okay?" he asked still looking at her. Those were the first words she heard from him even though she knew that he had been talking for a while. She nodded and looked around.

"Where is she....oww," she said as she felt a prick on her arm. She suddenly noticed that Dr. Georges was in the room and that had just given her a shot of something. *"What the fuck is going on?"* she wondered as she looked around. She felt even more confused as she looked around the room. She could see that she was still in her bedroom, but then again, this could very well be the product of her presently delusional mind.

"Is she okay, Doctor?" Mitchell asked looking worried. Dr. Georges nodded as he packed his bag.

"She is just a little low on iron causing some anemic symptoms. But that is weird because most women experience it while expectant. That's why we give them iron supplements and encourage a specific diet," he said as he turned to look at Mitchell. "Has she been under any kind of pressure lately? Something that might cause her to forgo eating healthy?" he asked. Mitchell shook his head no. He could not imagine, for the life of him, anything that might have caused Natasha's weakness.

"I had no idea she had anemia. What do I do?" Mitchell asked. The doctor sat down beside him and looked at him.

"The thing about anemia is that it is not a disease. It is a condition that can be managed by eating iron rich foods such as green leafy vegetables and liver," he said. Mitchell frowned.

"She hates liver," he said smiling.

"She has no choice. She must eat it," the doctor said with a smile. Mitchell nodded. "I will write up a diet plan. It should be followed to the letter for the first week and since it is mild, you can then do it every so often later on," he said as he stood up. Mitchell nodded and stood up to shake his hand. He felt a sigh of relief when the doctor gave Natasha a clean bill of health, or at least predicted one.

"May I make a suggestion?" he asked.

"Anything," Mitchell said.

"With Natasha's fragile condition, I would like to recommend the services of a nanny," Dr. Georges said. "That way you have your eye on Natasha and the nanny has her eye on the baby. Everybody wins plus I know Natasha will not be a stay at home mom forever. She is far too talented for that," he said. Mitchell knew he was right. He ran his fingers through his thick hair as he walked the doctor to the door. The nurse was walking behind them silently. "Make sure she sticks to the medication and the diet," the doctor said as Mitchell opened the door.

"Um hello?" Rita said when the door opened. The doctor smiled at her as he walked out. Rita looked at Mitchell's worried face and immediately knew that something was wrong. "Where's Tasha?" she asked. "Is everything okay?" she asked as she walked in. Mitchell stepped aside for her to get in and nodded.

"Yeah, for now. Tasha passed out while she was showering. I thought she might have had a concussion or ....worse," he said as a tear rolled down his cheek. Rita was shocked. She had never seen him look so vulnerable. Rita felt her heart go out to him. She took a step forward and threw her arms around him. "I thought I lost her, she was just lying there," he said all the while sobbing on her shoulder. She pulled away from him and closed the door behind her.

"Come on, I'll make you some tea," she said as she led him to the kitchen. She could feel his hand shaking and almost sweating, a sure sign that he was freaked out. She had never seen him like this. He was always the one who managed to hold his shit together, whatever happened. This was an all time low for him. "You sit down right there," she said as she sat him down on one of the kitchen stools. There were two untouched plates of Spanish omelet, sausages and some toast. They had obviously not even had breakfast yet. She put the kettle on and then took one big mug. She put a teaspoon of honey and some chamomile as she waited for the water to come to a boil. When she looked over at the table, Mitchell was still crying, even though he was trying hard not to show it. After a few minutes, she poured some boiling water into the cup and then walked over to the table. "This cures anything," she said as she set the cup down in front of him. "Except for cancer," she added. She noticed Mitchell's half smile when she said that. "That's more like it. Now, drink up, Schmidt, and tell me soberly, what the heck happened," she said as she sat down next to him. Mitchell nodded as he took a sip of his tea.

"Alexis was a bit restless last night. A lot of crying, fussing. Natasha was up till about four so when I woke up this morning, I didn't want to wake her. I figured she needed her sleep. I made breakfast and she woke up later," he paused to take another sip of his tea. "When she woke up, she decided to take a shower before breakfast and I was waiting for her but she never showed. So I went to the bedroom, I thought that she went back to sleep but she was on the bathroom floor and she was not moving and..." his voice trailed off again as a fresh flow of tears rolled down his cheeks. Rita reached for her bag which she had thrown on the table on their way in. she opened it and took out a small bottle of pills. She took one pill out and handed it to Mitchell. "What's this?" he asked looking at the small pill in his hand.

"Valium. You need it," Rita said. Mitchell looked up in surprise.

"Since when do you walk around with Valium in your purse?" he asked looking surprised. Rita smiled.

"You would be surprised at the things I carry in my purse. Now, take that," she said sternly.

"But I have to look for a nanny and..."

"…I'll handle it. Swallow that pill and join your wife in bed. I'll have you a great nanny by the time you wake up," she said. Mitchell shook his head.

"I don't know…" his words trailed off again when she took the pill and stuffed it inside his mouth and then held her hand on his mouth for a few minutes. He looked at her in surprise as he swallowed the small pill.

"Now, off to bed, mister," she said.

"Can I just watch some ESPN first?" he asked looking at her. She nodded and took his tea before she walked him to the living room. She handed him the cup and waited for him to finish it. It was not long before he began dozing off before he finally collapsed on the sofa. She smiled as she tucked him in.

"You have got to admire the power of good old valium," she thought as she walked to the master bedroom. She smiled when she saw Natasha peacefully sleeping in bed. The doctor must have given her a sedative because normally, Natasha was not a very heavy sleeper. Under normal circumstances, the sound of the door opening would have woken her up but not this time. Rita smiled as she then made her way to the nursery. She looked down at Alexis who had fallen asleep with the pacifier in her mouth. She gently stroked her black curly hair before she made her way out of the room and back to the kitchen. She sat down as she took her cell phone and called her assistant at the gallery to inform her that she would not back. She then made a call to Mona.

"Hey girl, what's happening?" Mona said when she picked up.

"Tasha needs a nanny," she said when Mona picked up.

"What? I thought she wanted to be a stay at home mom,"

Mona said surprised.

"Well, she still does but a few things have changed," Rita said as she sat down.

"Oh yeah? Like what?" Mona asked.

"I caught the doctor on his way out. Anemia or something," Rita said.

"I'm forwarding you a list right now," Mona said before hanging up. Rita waited for a few minutes for Mona's message. It didn't take long before Mona's message came through. She sighed when she opened the message. Mona had sent her almost twenty names. She might have well just taken the entire week off. She took a long deep breath as she called the first person. *"The things I do for love,"* she thought as she waited for the person to pick on the other end.

*****

When Natasha woke up, she thought she was dreaming. The clock on the bedside table read that it was four in the afternoon. That could not be right. She tried to get up but the pain in her head was just too much. She pulled herself to a sitting position and grabbed her phone from the night stand and sighed. The clock was right. It was four in the afternoon. She slowly got out of bed and put on her slippers before she began walking to the nursery. This had become routine for her. Every time she woke up, even if it was from a nap, she had to make her way down to the baby's room and check on Alexis. She suddenly stopped in her tracks when she saw an attractive man holding her baby. The man was not old; he was maybe in his mid to late twenties. He seemed to be very free with the baby in the way he rocked her and fed her from the bottle.

"Who the fuck are you and what are you doing with my baby?" she asked looking at him. "Get the hell out before I call 911," she said. She was trying to sound calm but without knowing it, she was yelling. The man looked confused. He placed the bottle on the changing station and then slowly lowered Alexis in her crib.

"I think there's been a misunderstanding here," he said calmly as he looked at Natasha.

"Damn right. Get out!" she yelled. Her sudden yell must have startled the baby because she began crying almost immediately.

"What the hell is going on?" Rita asked running into the room. Natasha looked at her confused.

"I found him holding my baby," Natasha said as she ran towards the crib. She picked up Alexis and stood at the far end of the room. "I don't even know how he got in," she said looking scared. Rita sighed.

"That's my fault. Marcus this is my best friend Natasha. Natasha, meet Marcus, your new nanny, or manny if you like," Rita said looking at Natasha. Natasha looked more confused than ever.

"What the hell are you talking about?" she asked looking at Rita and then at Marcus. Rita smiled at Marcus.

"Give us a minute, Marcus. You can wait in the kitchen," she said. The man smiled at Natasha before walking out.

"Where's Mitch?" Natasha asked still shocked.

"Asleep, on the couch. I gave him a valium," Rita said.

Natasha's eyes grew wide.

"What the fuck, Rita? You bring in a strange man to my house, you drug my husband…."

"You are overwhelmed. When I came this morning, I found the doctor leaving. You are handling too much," Rita said as she slowly walked towards Natasha.

"I've been sleeping all day?" she asked in surprise. Rita smiled and nodded. She then took the baby from Natasha's arms.

"You need to go back to bed. I am not going anywhere," Rita said. She could not even explain the whole nanny interviewing process or why she had decided on a male nanny. This was too much for Natasha to process. Rita thought that she still looked confused and that the drugs were yet to completely wear off.

"Go on. I'll bring you some soup," Rita said as Natasha slowly walked back to the bedroom. Rita smiled. She was still clearly under the influence of the sedative. She did not even ask to check on Mitchell. She would explain all that once she was a hundred percent sober. Right now, she needed to make sure her best friend stayed in bed and that the baby was comfortable and fed. Marcus would handle that, she thought as she walked back to the kitchen.

Chapter 7

Natasha was not sure what she hated more, being treated like an invalid or not being able to move around as she pleased. She was grateful to Rita for getting Marcus though. He had completely taken over the day to day running of the household. Who knew male nannies could be this good? He watched Alexis, took care of the feedings, cleaned up around the house and shopped for groceries. Just like that, Natasha had more time to relax and catch up with all her favorite TV shows. She was still staring out into space when Mitchell came in holding a tray of freshly squeezed orange juice, a banana and her pills.

"Hey there," he said with a smile as he handed her the banana.

"At this rate I will never lose this damned baby weight," she said as she quickly devoured the banana.

"Don't worry. Everything you have been eating is low in calories. I know how much you want to get back into your slim fit dresses," he said as she placed the peel on the tray. He handed her the juice and two tablets. "By the way, congratulations are in order. These are your last three pills," he said as she took big gulps of the juice. She looked at him and smiled.

"Awesome," she said putting the glass back down. "So, what plans do you have for today?" she asked looking at him. He shook his head as he took the tray and placed it on the bedside table.

"I have a meeting in an hour," he started.

"That explains why you are all dressed up," she said looking at him. He was in a pair of blue jeans and a black and grey pinstriped shirt. She thought he looked handsome. Pinstripe was always her weakness.

"This old thing?" he asked jokingly. "But anyway, apart from that, I am pretty much yours all day," he said as he put an arm around her.

"Where's Alexis? I can't hear her," she asked looking at him.

"Marcus took her to the park. He really has a way with her," he said with a smile. Natasha nodded. Marcus seemed to have a magic touch. If Alexis cried, she got quiet almost immediately after he picked her up. She did not throw food at him either, the way she did with Mitchell and Natasha. "Speaking of which, we are alone. That does not happen often nowadays," he said as he began to slowly pull her closer. She looked at him as he brought his head down to kiss her.

"But your meeting," she said as he forced her down on the bed.

"It can wait. I can't," he said as he kissed her again. She could feel him pressing his crotch hard against her own pelvis. She could actually feel his cock hardening against her leg. As Mitchell kissed her, she could feel her own desire raging in her. Getting time alone lately had been next to impossible. Marcus was always around because of the baby and if it was not him, someone else. She closed her eyes as she felt him kiss her lips softly before he trailed kisses down one side of her neck. She could feel herself getting wet already. Maybe it was the fact that Marcus could come back any time that made her feel this way. The mere thought of being busted made her even wetter than she wanted to be. She gasped when Mitchell suddenly pulled open the pajama shirt she was wearing, exposing her full breasts. She looked at him as he breathed heavily. She threw her head back when he suddenly engulfed one of her full nipples with his mouth. He had not done this in a long time. She moaned as he slowly sucked on her breasts while his other hand gave equal attention to her other mound using his flicking fingertips. She moaned loudly when he began pleasuring her hard nipple using his tongue, twirling it around the hardened tip.

He suddenly pulled away and quickly undid his pants. She looked at him as he pushed his jeans off and then finally wriggled out of them. He climbed on top of her and kissed her again. Instead of pulling her panties off, he pulled them aside and in one swift move pushed himself inside her. She yelped as he held her tightly, giving her pussy a chance to get used to the new force that had just been plunged into her. This was definitely different. Usually Mitchell was more of a lovemaker. He would normally do the whole candles and dinner thing but sex, down and dirty, was not his style.

She looked up at him and smiled. Mitchell smiled and kissed her again before he began moving himself in and out of her. She moaned as he fucked her; slowly at first and then he picked up his pace. Soon he was thrusting into her hard, slamming against her with tremendous force. Natasha wrapped her legs around his waist and interlocked them as he moved himself in and out of her. This felt so good, so different, and almost illicit.

She suddenly began crying out loud as she felt her orgasm approaching. Mitchell showed no signs of slowing down. He seemed to fuck her harder with every thrust. She began shaking in his arms as her orgasm took over. She squirmed and writhed under him making it hard for him to stay inside her. He pulled his cock out and waited for a few seconds for her orgasm to run its course. The wait seemed to take forever before he finally pushed his cock into her once more.

She screamed out when she felt him reintroduce his cock to her pussy again. He seemed to have a newfound energy as he began fucking her hard. She held on for dear life as he thrust into her long and hard. She suddenly felt him go rigid in her before he began pulsating hard. She moaned loudly as she felt him emptying inside her, almost tearing her insides.

"Damn," he said breathlessly as his cock slipped out of her.

"The meeting," she said panting. He slowly climbed off her and sighed.

"I have to cancel that. There is no way I can make it now," he said breathing hard.

"Was it important?" she asked as she turned to look at him. He let out a laugh.

"I might have cost the company a couple of millions today," he said with a smile. She slapped him playfully and climbed off the bed.

"Make that call," she said as she walked to the bathroom. She could not believe that he had blown off a meeting for a quickie, but then again, she was that good. She smiled as she turned the water on.

*****

When she woke up the next morning, Natasha was determined to have a personal day. She took a shower, dressed up and headed straight for the salon. She needed to feel relaxed and pampered. After four hours of a manicure, pedicure and full body massage, Natasha felt that she was ready to go home. Mitchell had texted her telling her to stop by the store for some groceries. She thought that was odd because she could have sworn she saw Marcus walk in with grocery bags the day before but she didn't mind going to the store. It had been a while anyway. When she got back, she noticed Mona's, Stacy's and her father's car in the driveway.

"This is a coincidence. How could they all think of visiting on the same day at the same time," she thought as she opened the door.

"Surprise!" she heard everyone yell. She almost dropped the bags she was holding. She looked around at Stacy, Mona, Rita, Estelle and Eric who were all smiling despite the fact that she wanted to kick each of them at that very moment. "What the hell is this?" she asked as she put the bags down.

"We just wanted to show you that we appreciate you," Eric said as he walked towards her. He threw his arms around her and planted a small kiss on her forehead. "And happy birthday sweetie," he added when he pulled away. Natasha looked confused.

"Wait, what?" Natasha asked looking at Eric.

"Oh my God. You forgot your own birthday?" Rita asked looking at her surprised. Natasha was the one person who never forget anyone's birthday, especially her own. She always made a point of issuing threats to anyone who dared forget her birthday. "You just cost me two hundred bucks," she said angrily.

"And you just won us a hundred bucks each," Mona said pointing to Stacy and then herself. Natasha felt more confused than ever.

"We bet that the baby would cloud your head so much that you'd forget your own birthday," Stacy said smiling.

"Seriously guys, today is August fifth?" Natasha asked as she looked at her phone. Eric nodded.

"I never thought I would see the day when you wouldn't make a big deal of August the fifth," Eric said. Estelle emerged from the kitchen carrying a big cake.

"She forgot?" Estelle asked looking at a shocked Natasha still standing at the doorway. Eric looked at her and smiled. "Child, you just cost me fifty bucks!" Natasha shook her head.

"Did everyone take a bet on this?" she asked. She had never felt any more loved than she did at this very moment. Everyone who mattered to her was there. Stacy looked especially sweet holding Alexis, Rita and Mona had their usual glamorous glow, Estelle and Eric would definitely not have missed this and Marcus, the nanny she had come to adore so much was also present. Mitchell was also there holding a somewhat small box considering that it was supposed to be her birthday present. "Thanks you guys," Natasha said as she finally said hello to everyone. She gave people short hugs and kisses on their cheeks before she took Alexis from Stacy.

Estelle put the cake on the table as the group walked back to the living room. "Okay, because we know Mitchell here has something planned, we will make this really quick and then give you a proper birthday dinner when you get back," Stacy said. Natasha looked at Mitchell.

"What does she mean 'when I get back'?" she asked in a whisper. Mitchell held her hand and squeezed it but never said anything.

"Open mine first," Stacy said handing her a medium sized box. Natasha pretended to shake the box, trying to guess what was inside. When she opened it, she gasped as she laid eyes on a pair of nude colored Christian Louboutin peep toed heels. The room was silent for a while as Natasha mouthed a low "Oh my God."

"FYI those are straight from the catwalk in Milan. It was fashion week last week," Stacy said proudly. Natasha looked up at her and gave her a hug.

"Thank you so much," she said when she pulled away from her.

"Yeah, we know of late you have not had enough time to go shopping, so mine's next," Mona said handing her a bigger box. It looked more like a box of roses than anything. When she opened it, she gasped yet again. Mona had given her a short strapless red dress complete with a silver studded lining. "It's not from Milan, but I am sure you will get some use for it soon enough," she added with a smile.

"Okay. Now me," Rita said as she jumped in holding a huge present. Natasha excitedly tore the wrapping paper off to reveal the most beautiful black and white glamour shot of herself.

"When did you even do this?" Natasha asked. She could not even remember posing for it.

"Just before you found out you were expecting Alexis, we went swimming, remember?" Rita said. Natasha nodded as she recalled the day. Rita had insisted on not swimming, something about being under the weather. "Well, I might have had an ulterior motive," Rita said.

"I know the perfect place for that," Mitchell said with a smile. "Now mine," he said as he handed her the small box. Natasha frowned.

"It looks a little small. The girls have really set a standard you know," she said as she quickly tore wrapping revealing a velvet case. She suddenly had an idea of what was inside. She slowly opened the case and gasped when she saw the beautiful pearl necklace inside. "Wow," she said as Mitchell gently picked up the necklace and fastened it around her neck before kissing her.

"Happy birthday baby," he said in a low voice.

"Get away from her. You have the rest of your lives to be all mushy," Estelle said as she pulled Mitchell away from her. "Anyway your father and I got you something too," Estelle said as she gave her an envelope. Natasha smiled as she shook the envelope. "Just open it already," she said as Natasha tore the top of the envelope.

Her eyes got watery as she looked at the contents of the envelope. Her father and grandmother had given her the one thing she had always wanted ever since she was a little girl: a princess trip to the Maldives. There was a hotel there that would literally give you a royal treatment beginning with a horseback ride from the airport, a lavish meal serviced by the "squires" and a royal ball on your final night. She had always said that she would go for the royal treatment but as a child she had no idea how she would ever come up with twenty thousand dollars all for a three day hotel stay however special the experience would have been.

"Nan, this cost a fortune," Natasha said as a tear rolled down her cheek. Estelle shook her head.

"Never mind that," Estelle said looking at her.

"Wait, Alexis…" Natasha suddenly protested.

"….do you know how many of us are dying to spend the next three days with Alexis?" Estelle asked cutting her short. "After all, this little girl will be off to school soon. We need to get her out of your protective shadow," she said looking at Alexis and then back at Natasha.

"Now, blow out this damned candle before it gets the wax all over my perfect chocolate cake," she said pointing at the cake on the table. "Make a wish," Estelle said in a whisper. Natasha looked around and smiled.

"I already have everything I could ever wish for," she said before she blew the candle out. After everyone had their share of cake, Estelle took a few of Alexis's clothes and packed them in a bag. She then went to the kitchen and took out all the milk bottles that were in there before she finally walked back to the living room. "Wait, we are leaving *now?*" Natasha asked looking at Estelle carrying Alexis's bag. Mitchell smiled and nodded.

"You've been through too much lately. You need the time off," he said as he draped an arm around her. She smiled and rested her head on his shoulder.

"This is all so sudden," she said in a whisper as Stacy, Mona and Stacy gave her a group hug.

"You need to get away," Mona said with a smile. "Plus, we will all be here with Alexis and Marcus is helping out," she added. Natasha smiled. Eric was next. He walked towards her and kissed her forehead before giving her a hug.

"Have fun," he said before he finally let go.

"Thanks Daddy. I will," she said. Finally, Estelle walked over holding the baby. Alexis was as jumpy as ever and had not the first clue of what was happening. Natasha took her briefly and held her tightly for a minute. "God, I can't believe I have to spend three whole days away from her. I've never been away that long," she said as she handed her back to Estelle.

"Sometimes I think God made friends and families for such situations," Estelle said making Natasha laugh. She looked up and noticed that Marcus and the girls were already outside and Eric and Mitchell were engaged in a heavy chat, too busy to notice them. "Listen, I know you feel guilty and everything but remember, you are not your mother. You are taking a holiday. If anything, we are forcing it down your throat without giving any regards to whether you have a gag reflex," Estelle said with a smile. "You are your father's daughter. You would never be that woman," she added looking into Natasha's eyes. Natasha sighed with relief. It was as if Estelle had read her mind. Her biggest fear was making mistakes with Alexis, the same mistakes her mother made with her. Being a neglectful mother was something she promised herself she would never become.

"Go have fun and don't feel guilty about it," Estelle said as they walked towards the door.

"Rita and Marcus already packed up the car. See you in a few days," Eric said as he and Estelle walked to the car. Stacy and Mona had already driven off. Mona was at that moment pulling out of the driveway. Mitchell put his arm around her

"So we get to spend a whole three days away. It's just like when we met. Just me and you," he said as they waved goodbye to Eric, Estelle and Mona. "Maybe we should have some quick celebratory sex before we leave," he said as he pulled her in and pinned her against the door. She shook her head and pushed him away.

"Remember what happened yesterday? The meeting? And I want to go to the Maldives. We can have celebratory sex there," she said as she kicked off her shoes. He looked at her and nodded.

"That flight cannot be in the air fast enough, because this guy also wants some royal treatment," he said as he pulled her against him again. She smiled. This holiday could not have come at a better time.

Book 7.

My Future With Mr White

Chapter 1

Natasha ran her hand through her hair as she looked at her computer screen. She had heard that it was best to have a good preschool in mind long before a child reached school age but the prices she was looking at were simply not encouraging. She sighed and leaned back in her chair.

"This is a nightmare," she thought as she looked at the list of schools. She was still looking at her computer screen when Mitchell walked in.

"Hey," he said softly. She looked up and smiled.

"Hey. I officially hate education," she said as she shut down her laptop. Mitchell smiled as he walked in and took a seat in front of her desk.

"Why? What's going on?" he asked. Natasha sighed and looked at him.

"Do you know how much preschools cost these days? I think it's cheaper to pay for college," she said. Mitchell shrugged.

"I have heard quite a few people complain about it," he said. Natasha rolled her eyes.

"That's all you've heard?" she asked. "Do you know there are schools asking for up to fifteen thousand dollars a term? Julie from accounts told me she had to be on a two year waiting list to pay eight thousand a term and that was after a very quote unquote good recommendation from one of the school's major donors," she said. Mitchell looked at her and laughed. She looked at him and shook her head. "What?" she asked.

"Well, I fail to understand why you are so stressed out about Alexis' school, yet she is only seven months old," he said. Natasha shrugged.

"Well, *Parenting Today* reports that eighty percent of troubled teens never had a good education. I want Alexis to be successful," she said softly. He looked at her and shook his head again. He stood up, walked around the desk and took her hands in his.

"Hey, sweetie. You are an amazing wife and an even better mother and the fact that you are this worked up about what school our seven month old daughter will be attending is proof of that. Right now, I just want to take you home, and pass by Estelle's because if we miss that fried chicken she is going to hold our daughter hostage till kingdom come," he said before kissing her forehead. She looked into his eyes and smiled.

"That may work really well for us. We have had the entire house to ourselves for almost three whole days and love being able to relive our glory days," she said with a smile. Mitchell frowned. "I know it's not something mother of the year would say but you like it too and I know it," she said as she packed up her stuff.

"I have no idea what you are talking about," Mitchell said as Natasha zipped up her laptop bag. She looked at him and smiled.

"You know that thing you did last night in the dining room or this morning in the kitchen? Yeah, you can't do that with Alexis in the house," she said as she stood up. Mitchell smiled.

"Guess you are right," he said as they walked out.

"Said the hypocritical father of the year," she said.

"Hey, I already gave in. Not fair," he said.

"I heard you but I have always to call someone a hypocrite and doing it to my husband, well..." she went silent as she tried looking for the right thing to say. "Okay fine, I'm sorry," she said before walking out of the office. Mitchell reached for her hand.

"When Alexis goes to sleep later tonight, I will make you pay for that," he whispered in her ear. She looked at him and smiled.

"I am looking forward to it," she said as they approached Stacy's desk. "Hey Stacy, I've emailed you details about the new energy drink clients. Set up studio time and photo shoots for tomorrow afternoon, okay?" she said. Stacy nodded.

"Sure," she said as she looked at the bottom right corner on her screen. "Wow, it's only four. Is everything okay?" she asked.

"Yeah sure. We are just headed to my Nan's for dinner. You know how she gets with time," she said.

"Yeah. We need to go now or we'll miss the soup," Mitchell said.

"Soup, really?" Stacy asked looking at him.

"I have it on good authority that she is making potato leek soup and I happen to love potato leek soup," he said matter of factly. Stacy shook her head.

"Well, I would hate to get between a man and his love of potato leek soup. See you tomorrow, Stacy," Natasha said as she and Mitchell walked out to the hallway. They decided to stop by the grocery store and got some food and a cake she had pre-ordered earlier that day because she was supposed to bring dessert and that had completely slipped her mind.

"What makes you think Estelle won't know that the cake is store bought?" Mitchell asked as Natasha took the cake out of the box.

"I especially asked the Cake Factory to make pineapple upside down cake, my specialty, and I even paid extra so they would follow my recipe and put it on my own cake stand," she said. "My Nan cannot know that this cake did not come from my kitchen and if she does I swear you will be denied all this for a year," she said, looking at Mitchell.

"Fine," he said as they got out of the car. "I just don't like lying," he said as he walked towards the front door.

"Well, no one is asking you to. Just select your words carefully and don't answer unasked questions," she said in a whisper as she rang the doorbell. Mitchell shrugged as Eric came to the door.

"Hey Daddy," she said when the door opened.

"Hey princess," he said kissing her forehead. "And my favorite son-in-law," he said, turning to look at Mitchell. Natasha walked off towards the dining room where Estelle was just finishing setting the table.

"Hey, Nan," she said smiling.

"Hey baby. You actually remembered the cake. I'm impressed," she said as she kissed Natasha's cheek.

"Of course I did. Why wouldn't I?" Natasha asked as she walked to the kitchen. She placed the cake on the counter and smiled at Estelle who was now serving the soup.

"Well, you work sixty hours a week even after having Alexis and you are still in your work clothes. If I didn't know any better I'd think that cake was store bought," Estelle said smiling. Natasha silently cursed in her head. She had forgotten the most important factor in lying, covering your bases.

"Well, Nan, it isn't. I baked it in the morning and then I had Stacy do the frosting and bring it back to me in the office. I had a meeting in the afternoon, so I couldn't go home," she said quickly.

"Sometimes I wonder if you pay that woman enough," Estelle said smiling.

"Well, she is the best paid assistant in the entire company so yeah, she is well compensated and she is not complaining so neither should you," Natasha said. Estelle smiled at her. "Can I help with anything?" she asked looking at Estelle.

"Actually I am done. You can carry the soup to the table though," she said as she handed Natasha the tray.

"Where is Alexis, by the way?" Natasha asked as she and Estelle walked towards the dining room where her father and Mitchell were.

"She's with Rita upstairs getting changed," Estelle said. Natasha turned and looked at Estelle.

"Rita's here?" she asked.

"Yes, since last night," Estelle said. Natasha put the tray on the dining room table and put bowls of soup in front of her father and husband before she took one.

"I'll take mine upstairs. I need to say hi to Alexis," she said. Estelle gave her a disapproving look.

"You came for dinner," she said.

"I know but I will be back in a few minutes," she said looking at Estelle. "I promise to be here for the main course," she said before walking out. Mitchell looked at Estelle and shrugged.

"Is she okay?" he asked. Estelle nodded and sat down.

"I just told her that Rita was here since yesterday and she just...well, you saw what she did," she said.

"Well, if Rita was here, even I am intrigued," Mitchell said as he took a spoonful of his soup. "Great soup, Estelle," he said before taking another spoonful. Estelle smiled in appreciation and began eating her own soup.

Meanwhile, Natasha made her way up the stairs to her old room. She pushed the door open and saw Rita playing peek-a-boo with Alexis on the bed. It was the perfect picture. She smiled and softly knocked on the door.

"Can a tired old mummy join the party?" she asked.

"Hey. You are here," Rita said smiling.

"Yes I am and so are you," Natasha said as she walked towards the bed. She took a seat on the edge of the bed and gave Rita a hug before picking up Alexis.

"Yeah, I am," Rita said exhaling.

"How's my little girl doing," Natasha said as she rubbed her nose against the baby's nose. The baby hated that, she could tell by the way she frowned every time she did it, but she thought it was cute. So she always did it for her own sake. She put the baby back down on the bed and turned her attention to Rita. "So, do you want to tell me why I had to find out that you spend the night here from my Nan?" she asked. Rita took a long deep breath as Natasha took a spoonful of soup.

"I…it's complicated. I didn't want you to make a big deal out of it," Rita started.

"Make a big deal out of what? What the hell is going on, Rita?" Natasha asked. Rita leaned back and looked at Natasha. "Come on, tell me already. I can't stand the damn suspense," Natasha said again. She could see the exhaustion in Rita's eyes, as if she had not had a good night's sleep in a while. Whatever it was, she did not understand why Rita felt like she could not talk to her. After all, the two had grown up together and seen each other through the hardest times. "Sweetie, please talk to me," Natasha begged as she looked into Rita's eyes.

"It's Mama," she started. Natasha looked at her.

"Okay. What happened? Is she okay?" she asked.

Rita shook her head and brushed a tear. "I don't know. I think she's using again," she said. Natasha reached over and placed a hand on Rita's. Six years ago, Rita's mother had been hooked on prescription painkillers and it had been a hard time in Rita's life especially because the two of them were never really close. The road to her mama's recovery was hard and long but she did manage to get clean eventually even though she fell off the wagon a couple of times.

"Are you sure?" she asked.

"No, I don't know. She is just weird and distant. I never see her and when I do she is always in a hurry to go somewhere and there is this new guy in her life and..." Natasha shook her head and put her hand cutting her short.

"New guy?" she asked. "Since when?" Rita shook her head again.

"I don't know. No one knows. I can't reach her, she is not answering her phone and she is not at home and I am freaked out Tasha," she said. Natasha looked at her sympathetically and smiled.

"Why didn't you come to me earlier?" she asked.

"I wanted to...but there is also work and...." Her words trailed off as Natasha noticed a tear rolling down her cheek. This was not just about Rita's mother. There was something else.

"How are you and Dave doing?" Natasha asked, looking at Rita. Rita brushed away another tear.

"I don't know," she said in a whisper.

"What do you mean, you don't know?" Natasha asked. "When was the last time you talked to him?"

"Last week. I just can't talk to him right now," she said. Natasha raised an eyebrow.

"What do you mean right now? What happened?" she asked. She looked at Rita and she could have sworn she had never seen her so sad.

"Last week, he was supposed to be in Miami on some conference and we even Skyped in his supposed hotel but I saw what I thought to be his car heading into the Four Seasons, so I followed him just to be sure," Rita paused and took another long deep breath.

"So, what did you find out?" Natasha asked.

"I saw him there with some woman and they were a bit friendlier than usual and I.....I really don't know what to do," she said.

"So, why don't you ask him who she was? Why don't you just talk to him?" Natasha asked. Rita looked up at her.

"I don't want to know if everything is true...I can't handle it right now. I need some time before I talk to him," she said. Natasha shook her head.

"That is not like you. You usually tackle a problem head on and this is one of those situations that need you to do exactly that. You just can't bury your head in the sand and assume everything is fine while you know for a fact that it isn't," she said. She gave Rita's hand a little squeeze and smiled. "You need to make that call," she said in a low but reassuring voice. Rita looked at her and nodded. "Now about your mother, maybe she is just out with this new guy. She is finally moving on and you should be happy about that. Don't rain on her parade," she said smiling.

Rita laughed. Her mother always said that any time she embarked on a new endeavor.

"At least I got you to laugh," Natasha said. "And now, we are going downstairs and have that dinner Estelle slaved over and the cake I brought and then you are coming home with me. You need me and you know it," Natasha said as she picked Alexis up. Rita looked at her, surprised.

"When did you get time to bake?" she asked.

"Who said I baked? But Nan cannot know that or I swear to God I will kill you faster than you can say store bought," Natasha warned her as they walked out of the bedroom. She suddenly stopped when she remembered the soup. "Do me a favor. That soup is already cold and I know Nan is going to give me an earful about it. Dump it," she said in a whisper. Rita looked at her surprised.

"I thought you liked potato leek," Rita said looking at her.

"Correction, Mitchell likes potato leek. I endure it," she said as Rita walked to the bathroom and poured it down the toilet. Natasha stood guard at the door

"We are going to hell," Rita said giggling as they walked down the stairs.

"Not if she doesn't find out," Natasha said.

"There you are. Are you okay?" Estelle asked looking at Rita who nodded.

"Everything's fine Estelle. I just needed some time to myself," she said. Estelle smiled at her.

"Good. Take a seat at the table. You guys are just in time for the main course," she said. "You look like you enjoyed the soup. I have never seen a bowl so clean after serving you potato leek soup. Maybe I'll give you some to take home with you," Estelle said looking at Natasha.

"I'm sure Mitchell will love that," she said as she walked into the dining room. Mitchell's eyes lit up when he saw Alexis. He took her from Natasha's arms as she took a seat next to Rita.

"So, baby, how do you like being a working mom?" Eric asked, looking at Natasha. It had only been a couple of months since Natasha went back to work. Initially, she had considered the idea of being a stay at home mom but that did not go so well. She was always in a bad mood because she lived what she termed a life of confinement.

"It's amazing, Daddy. At least I actually look forward to going back home at the end of the day," she said. Mitchell looked at her.

"Was there a time you did not look forward to being home?" he asked.

"Why do you think I insisted on going back to work? I love Alexis but I can't handle her 24 hours a day without any other company around. I need a change of scenery every so often. We all do," Natasha said as Estelle sat down.

"Okay everyone. Dig in," she said. Natasha looked at Mitchell and smiled.

"I have invited Rita to stay with us for a few days," she said in a whisper.

"Okay. Is there anything I need to know?" he asked.

"She is just going through some stuff right now. I'll tell you later," she whispered back. Mitchell smiled at her before turning his attention back to the baby. Natasha smiled in appreciation as she took a bite of her food. Estelle had really outdone herself this time, not that she did not deliver every time she worked in the kitchen. She looked at Rita and sighed. Her best friend had been there for her so many times before and this time, she had to be the one to offer a shoulder to cry on. She took another bite as she thought of the possibility of Rita and Dave breaking up and her mother heading back to rehab again. She would do anything and everything to be there for her friend, even if it meant taking a leave of absence. She turned to Mitchell again. "If worse comes to worst I will need to take some time off work," she said. Mitchell smiled at her and nodded.

Chapter 2

Almost a month after she had asked Rita to move into her place, Natasha noticed that Rita was avoiding any and all instances that could lead to her bumping into Dave. She would open the gallery an hour earlier than usual and leave way before closing time, leaving her assistant to do the closing up for her. If Natasha knew anything about Rita, it was that she loved avoiding uncomfortable situations. But Natasha thought that there was probably more to the whole story than what Rita had told her and she had no way of confirming the whole thing since Rita was not talking.

Natasha hated being in this situation. She hated feeling helpless when her best friend was hurting, and what was even more nerve wrecking was the fact that Rita was not talking about anything. Natasha had half a mind to call Dave and give him a good talking to, or at least try and find out what was going on between the two of them.

It was on a Thursday when Natasha finally decided to break the ice. After taking a shower, she put on a pair of sweat pants and a t-shirt and then headed to the living room.

"Good morning," she said as she walked into the kitchen where Rita was sipping on a glass of orange juice.

"Morning. You look....motherly," Rita said smiling.

"Don't start with me. I am not going anywhere and if I wear something nice, Alexis will probably find a reason to puke all over it," Natasha said as she poured herself a glass of orange juice. "Pancakes?" she asked as she walked over to the fridge.

"Sure," Rita said as she took a seat. She watched Natasha

take the batter from the fridge and then walk over to the stove.

"So, any news on your mama?" Natasha asked as she put a pan on the stove. Rita shook her head.

"I don't know whether to just wait it out and see what happens. That was what I used to do anyway," Rita said as she took another sip of her juice.

"I know, but this is what, ten years later? Rita, something else is up. She has no reason to fall off the wagon. She has been clean for ten years," Natasha said.

"Well, the time has changed but maybe she hasn't," Rita said. "You know what, I won't even bother. She wants to talk to me, she can call me," she said shrugging. Natasha knew she needed not press any more about Rita's mother.

"What about Dave? Have you talked to him yet?" she asked. Rita shrugged again.

"I don't want to talk to him," she said curtly. Natasha smiled as she flipped a pancake.

"Well, honey, you know I love you, but is there a possibility that you might be overreacting?" she asked.

'You do realize we are in a room full of knives, right?" Rita asked. Natasha looked at her and shook her head.

"You know what, sweetie? I think it's time for a little tough love. I have known you for more than twenty years and the one consistent thing about you is running away from stuff you don't want to face, but did you ever consider that maybe just maybe, if you talked to Dave you would solve all this shit? Dave is a great guy, Rita. Talk to him. Find out his side of the story before you take the villagers to his house armed with pitchforks," she said as she looked at her. There was a long silence before Natasha put another pancake on the pan. "I know you don't want to hear all this but it's about time someone told it like it is. Dave loves you and I know you love him too. Swallow your pride and talk to him, or at least pick up his damn calls," she added before removing the pancake from the pan. She switched off the stove and then walked over to one of the cabinets and took two plates. She served two pancakes on each plate and then sat down after setting one plate in front of Rita. She knew there was a lot of awkwardness in the room but someone had to tell her.

After breakfast, Natasha gave Alexis her breakfast and then sat down to watch a movie. Everything was relatively calm but there wasn't a lot of conversation between them. When Mitchell came back home that evening, he noticed that everything was not right.

"What's going on?" he asked Natasha in a whisper. Natasha looked over at Rita who was playing with the baby at that moment.

"I went all tough love on her," she whispered back. Mitchell smiled and then frowned.

"Really? How did she take it?" he asked.

"How do you think?" she asked as she looked over at Rita again.

"Well, I need to talk to you. Now," he said as he took Natasha to the bedroom.

"What's going on?" she asked when she got to the bedroom.

"I had a talk with Dave," he said. She looked at him and then sat down on the bed. This was not something Mitchell would normally do. He was the one who always insisted on letting things be.

"This is...new," she said as she looked at him. "So, what happened? What did he say?" she asked.

"Well the whole thing must have been a misunderstanding," he said. Natasha raised an eyebrow.

"Must have been?" she asked. Mitchell shrugged and sat next to her.

"Fine. It was a misunderstanding," he said. "Dave wants to propose," he said smiling. Natasha's eyes grew wide.

"What?" she asked. "How do you know that? I mean, how can you be sure?" she asked excitedly.

"Well, there was a conference in Miami, true, but Dave didn't go until a day later because this woman, the wife of one of his bosses, works at a jewelry store and was willing to give him a generous discount. So that was the only day he could see her to make sure that the ring was ready by the time he got back from Miami," he said.

"So, the compromising situation Rita was talking about?" she asked.

"Well, I know she is your best friend and everything but Rita can be a bit....you know, exaggerating," he said. "I'm sure whatever she saw was not that bad. Maybe it's the situation with her mama that made her a bit paranoid," he explained. Natasha smiled.

"This is good news," she said and then frowned. "In a way," she added quickly when she remembered that they still had no news about Rita's mother.

"I know. But I guess we have to celebrate every bit of good news," Mitchell said before planting a kiss on her forehead. Natasha smiled and closed her eyes.

"Guess you are right. It is good news about Dave and everything but what about Rita's mama?" she asked.

"I've got my friend at the precinct looking into it. I'm sure she will be okay," he said as he ran his hand up and down her back. Natasha smiled and pulled away from him. "Hey, where are you going?" he asked.

"To the living room. Rita needs to hear this," she said. Mitchell held her hand and shook his head.

"You have all day to tell her that. I have not seen you, any part of you, since last week and I must say I miss you," he said pulling her closer to him.

"Do you miss me or are you just horny?" she asked as she looked into his eyes.

"Wow, excuse your French," he said as he slipped a hand behind her neck and pulled her down to kiss her. As their lips touched, she felt a surge of electric energy go through her body. Mitchell was right. They had not been intimate for a while and yeah, she could talk to Rita any time, especially now that she was crashing at their place. Mitchell slowly pushed her onto the bed and pulled away. She lay there, staring up at him, her eyes burning. He pushed the shirt she wore upwards and breathed on her bra covered breasts. She closed her eyes as he slowly brought his head down again and planted soft kisses on her chest. She opened her eyes when she felt him raise his head from her body. She smiled at him as he brought himself up and kissed her softly as he caressed her thighs. She wrapped her arms around him and arched her back, giving him a chance to slip his hand under her to unclasp her strapless bra. She sighed as she felt the bra slipping away from her body, exposing her bare breasts to him. She shivered when he brought his hand up and cupped one full breast, making her nipple press hard against his palm.

He slowly let his hand run down her torso and pushed her sweat pants off. He then pulled away from her and stood up to get undressed. For some reason, Natasha still got turned on when she saw him undressing. It was as if he was her kryptonite. She smiled up at him as he rejoined her on the bed. She could feel his hardness pressing against her thigh. She slowly spread her legs and looked at him. She knew that he wanted to fill her just as much as she wanted him to feel her. He looked down at her as he settled in between her legs. She wrapped her arms around his shoulders and kissed him deeply as he rubbed his cock against the opening of her pussy. She loved the way the head of his hard cock felt against her wet pussy. She wanted to beg him to get inside but at the same time she did not want to deny herself the pleasure that she was getting from his teasing.

Mitchell pulled away from her lips and looked at her, then smiled. He loved the way she looked at that moment. Her eyes screamed desire and her pussy was wetter than ever but it had been so long. He did not want this to just be some conventional sex.

"Baby....I want you," she moaned. He looked at her and ran his finger down the side of her face.

"Not yet," he said. Natasha wanted to scream out. Why would

he do this to her now? This was torture but she knew a thing or two about torture. She flipped him over so that she was on top and smiled down at him.

"Fine. Then we'll do things my way," she said. Mitchell was intrigued as he watched her crawling up to his waist. She did not waste any time as she simply lowered her mouth onto his throbbing cock and began licking his highly sensitive glans. Holding his cock in her hand, she began sucking on him as she stroked him hard. She then kissed the length of his cock and ran her tongue on either side before she finally lowered her mouth onto his cock, taking most of his length inside her mouth. Mitchell's breathing had been reduced to gasps of air as he struggled hard not to moan out loud. The last thing he wanted was awkwardness at the dinner table later on that evening. She then pulled away, getting his cock almost out of her mouth before taking in the entire length again. This time it was too much for Mitchell. He let out a loud moan and Natasha pulled away from him.

She pulled herself up and kissed him softly. "Keep it down baby, we don't want to draw any attention to ourselves," she said before going back down on him. He closed his eyes as he felt her warm lips engulf his cock once more. He could barely contain his groan as she sucked him, especially when her hand found his sac. Mitchell could have sworn she was on a mission by the way she was sucking him. She had never gone down on him like this. He was always the one with mad oral skills, not that she did not have a number of skills up her sleeve but this, this was unlike any other thing she had ever done to him.

Mitchell put his hand on her head as she bobbed up and down on his crotch. He raised himself up to look at her and that was enough encouragement for her to pick up the pace, slamming her face onto his raging hard-on.

"Tasha....don't....oh shit...baby," he moaned giving her the warning she so much needed. By this time, she was breathing hard through her nose as she held him in her mouth, taking all he had to offer until she felt his orgasm dangerously close. She let his cock out of her mouth and looked at him. He was panting and finally ready for her. She looked at him as she straddled him. She closed her eyes as she slowly worked her pussy onto his wet cock. Mitchell exhaled loudly and held her by the waist. Her mouth was good but her pussy was even better. She began working herself up and down his cock, slowly and teasingly. By this time, Mitchell wanted to cry out and just slam himself into her. He held her tightly and begun thrusting into her with long slow strokes, but given the way she had just worked him, long slow strokes were not going to cut it. He suddenly pulled out of her and in one move turned her over and entered her from behind. He knew Natasha must have been surprised at how he managed to turn the tables on her so quickly. He spread her legs and positioned himself in between her knees. The first stroke was a long deep one, almost as if he was making her pay for the long oral torture he had just endured. He entered her again before finally holding her by the hips and worked her over in long hard strokes.

He was mesmerized by the way her pussy seemed to cling to his cock with each stroke. He spread her cheeks and let his finger flick her now fully engorged clit while nudging his cock into her. He slowed down and released her cheeks and then reached for her breasts. She moaned as she felt him slowly working in and out of her. He knew that by now she was not only exhausted, but also almost at her very end. He grabbed her hips and leaned over her, driving into her, filling her. He could feel her wetness grasping at him as her orgasm approached. She turned her head and looked at him.

"Do it, please," she begged.

Mitchell did not need any further bidding. He slammed his full weight into her, unable to resist the urge any longer. It was not very long before he erupted inside her. Almost immediately, she cried out loud as her own orgasm ripped through her body. She shivered over and over again and the tightening muscles in her pussy forced his now limp cock out of her. The two collapsed on the bed, exhausted and panting.

"God, I had missed that," Natasha said gasping.

"And you thought I was being an ass by saying I had missed you?" he asked. Natasha laughed.

"At least I admit I was horny. You tried to charm that big cock into me," she said. Mitchell looked at her and smiled.

"I don't remember you resisting," he said.

"I had ulterior motives," she said.

Mitchell laughed again. "Of course you did," he said and yawned. Natasha put a tired hand on his damp chest.

"No, you have to help me with dinner. You promised," she said.

"That was before you allowed me to miss you," he said as she rolled over. He draped a hand over her.

"You made your bed, and now you have to lie in it," she said as she pulled away.

"Actually, you made it and right now I would like to just lie in it for thirty minutes," he said as she walked towards the bathroom.

"Five minutes. That's how long I need to take a shower," she said as she stepped into the bathroom. After she had her shower, she thought of waking Mitchell up but she also had to make her peace with Rita. She walked into the living room and looked at Rita. The way she was with the baby made Natasha smile. It was as if her motherly instinct came alive any time she was with Alexis. She slowly made her way to the middle of the room where Rita and Alexis were seated, playing with the baby's toys. "Hey," she said as she joined them on the floor.

"Hey," Rita said as she gave her a smile.

"Friends again?" Natasha asked. Rita smiled again.

"We never stopped being friends," she said as she looked at Natasha.

"So you don't think I overstepped my boundaries?" she asked. Rita shook her head. "Good, because I think my husband might have," she said. Rita frowned.

"What did Mitch do?" she asked.

"Well, he has a friend at the precinct that is looking into your mama's case, and, um, he also talked to Dave," Natasha said. Rita sighed.

"Wow, you guys..." Rita trailed off.

"There is an explanation and I think you need to talk to him. Pick up his call the next time he calls, or just call him – or I swear to God I will bring him right here," Natasha said before she stood up and walked to the kitchen.

"Why? What did he say?" Rita called after her. Natasha smiled. She was not about to give everything away and take her best friend's proposal from her. She knew that Rita loved

Dave and that when she heard his reason, she would be all too happy to get back with him.

"I love playing Dr. Phil," she thought as she took a chicken from the freezer.

Chapter 3

Mitchell smiled as he walked into the living room. Natasha looked up at him and shook her head.

"No, it's not going to happen," she said as she typed away on her laptop.

"What's not going to happen?" he asked.

"Sex. I am not having sex with you," she said without looking up. Mitchell frowned.

"Um, okay. Good to know but that was not even in my head right now. But ouch," he said as he joined her on the couch. She looked at him and smiled. Lately Mitchell had an insatiable appetite for sex. He would get her in the bathroom, while fixing dinner, after putting the baby down...pretty much any time. Natasha thought that Rita being around had a lot to do with it. Maybe it was some kind of voyeuristic kink.

"Well, don't blame me, but seriously, Mitch, you are going to fuck me raw one of these days," she said. She looked at the time displayed on her computer screen and frowned. "It's almost midday. What are you doing home?" she asked.

"I needed a break from the office, plus we need you down there," he said. She put her laptop down on the coffee table and looked at him.

"Why? What do you mean?" she asked.

"We just lost millions of dollars in billable hours," he said. She crossed her arms in front of her chest and looked him in the eye.

"You'd better stop these charades and just tell me what the hell is going on. What do you mean we lost millions of dollars? Who's we?" she asked, trying hard to remain calm.

"The company," Mitchell said as he exhaled loudly. "Remember Fiona Barnes Energy?" he asked. Natasha nodded.

"Yeah. That was one of the accounts I worked on when I first started working at...wait. Please don't tell me that's the account we lost," she said, looking at Mitchell, who was now nodding. "Mitchell, what the hell happened? If anything that was our most solid account. If you asked me, I would have said that the account was guaranteed for at least the next five years," she said.

"Sweetie, if there is anything guaranteed in business, it's that there is never a guarantee," he said as he looked at her. She slammed the laptop shut and then stood up. "Babe, where are you going?" he asked as he held her hand.

"I need to do damage control," she said. Mitchell pulled her back down on the couch and then looked at her.

"Okay, you want to do damage control. What kind of damage control do you have in mind?" he asked. She shook her head and frowned.

"I don't know...just...I don't know. I just need to go to the office," she said. Mitchell smiled at her.

"Whatever you need to do, you can do it right here. And that's why I came home. I knew you would need the help," he said as he took his phone out of his pocket.

"What are you doing?" she asked.

"Checking in with Stacy," he said.

"What for?" she asked.

"I left her in charge of damage control. She's got everything covered," he said as he typed away on his phone. "See?" he asked as he showed her a reply from Stacy assuring him that everything was fine. "You don't need to go in. Plus you have two girls and a man who need you right here," he said, looking at her. She smiled and leaned back on the couch.

"I really need to get back to work. I am beginning to feel like a sad housewife," she said. Mitchell laughed.

"Well, most sad housewives don't look this good," he said as he moved closer to her.

"I said no sex. Seriously, what has gotten into you?" she asked as she pulled away from him.

"I don't know. But it's like Rita being here makes it exciting, like we'll get busted or something...I don't know why. But I just can't seem to relax around you nowadays," he said in a whisper. Natasha looked at him, surprised.

"I honestly hoped for a better explanation," she said, looking at him. "Sometimes I don't think you are the man I married," she added as she leaned back on the couch again. Mitchell laughed.

"Forgive me for bringing the spontaneity back to our marriage," he said. Natasha looked at him and smiled.

"Honey, save that for our fortieth anniversary," she said. She then leaned forward and took her laptop.

"What were you working on?" he asked.

"Reports. Last fiscal year," she said. Mitchell shook his head.

"Why are you doing reports?" he asked.

"I'm not *doing* them, just going over them. Just the reports from my department, though," she said. Mitchell looked at her computer screen and frowned. "What?" she asked.

"Can it wait?" he asked.

"No...."

"It has nothing to do with sex. I promise," Mitchell said, cutting her short.

"Okay. What do you have in mind?" she asked.

"Where's Rita?" he asked.

"She went out to meet Dave. It was a while ago so I guess she should be back any time now," she said.

"She has a spare key to this place, right?" he asked. Natasha nodded.

"Really, what do you have in mind?" she asked.

"Well, I was not entirely honest about why I was home," Mitchell said. Natasha shook her head.

"Okay, so we didn't lose the account?" Natasha asked.

"No, we lost the account, all right. But I got a call from Pete Faulkner," Mitchell said.

"Okay, who is Pete Faulkner?" Natasha asked, looking confused.

"My friend from the Thirteenth Precinct. He said he has a lead on Rita's mother," he said. Natasha smiled.

"Awesome. So where is she?" Natasha asked excitedly.

"It's a lead, sweetie. Not a location. We still don't know where she is," Mitchell said. Natasha frowned. "It's better than nothing. So I was thinking we could go over to the station and meet up with him," he said. Natasha smiled and nodded.

"I'll be ready in ten minutes. You get Alexis' bag," she said as she rushed to the bedroom. She took off the oversized t-shirt and sweat pants she was wearing and changed into a dress. She put on some light makeup and then pinned back her curly hair. To complete her look, she put on a pair of high heeled sandals and then walked back to the living room.

"Wow," Mitchell said as she walked towards him. "Talk about a transformation," he said, looking at her. She smiled.

"Thank you. Thank you very much," she said in a mock Elvis Presley voice.

"Do you have some guy down at the precinct that you are looking to reel in?" he asked as he raised an eyebrow.

"Why, Mitchell Schmidt. I never took you to be the jealous type," she said as she picked up Alexis. "Hi there, beautiful. Mommy and Daddy are going to take you for a ride," she said as she walked out of the living room. She strapped the baby in her car seat in the back and then took a seat next to her where she could keep an eye on her.

All the way as they rode to the station, Natasha felt herself getting tense. She was prepared for anything but she was not so sure that Rita was. Back when Rita's mom was still using, every single day was a struggle for Rita. Natasha could count more days when Rita's mother was found on the street somewhere than days she spent at home. For Rita, microwave dinners while watching her mother wasted on the couch was the life she knew and the life she had become accustomed to.

"What if she is...?" Natasha started to ask when they got to the station. Mitchell looked at her and smiled.

"Let's just take it as it comes," he said as he took her hand. She smiled, picked up the baby, put her in her stroller and followed him in.

"Hi, we are here to see Officer Cameron," he said to the woman seated behind the desk. She pointed to a desk where a brown haired man was seated. Mitchell and Natasha walked up to the desk. "Does the state pay you enough to work this hard?" Mitchell asked. Officer Cameron smiled and stood up.

"It doesn't but that I can live with. It's the idiots who lounge at their desk all day without working that piss me off the most," he said as he shook Mitchell's hand. "Long time no see," he said.

"Yeah, I know it's been a few, but work and my family always come first," Mitchell said. "Speaking of which, Officer Cameron, meet my wife Natasha and daughter, Alexis," he said proudly.

"I have heard a lot about you both," Cameron said as he shook Natasha's hand and then picked the baby up.

"Good things I hope," Natasha said smiling.

"Well, yes, but he did not do you justice," the officer said, lifting the baby up. Alexis squealed excitedly. "Any of you," he added as he looked at Natasha.

"Thanks," she said blushing.

"So, my man, what do you have about my friend's mother?" Mitchell asked. The officer put the baby back in the stroller and then walked back to his seat.

"Okay so, I put out a BOLO for your friend, Lydia Dennis. No one in the vicinity has seen or heard from her but we got a hit in Seattle. There was a charge to her credit card," he began. Natasha frowned.

"Seattle?" she asked surprised.

"Yes. Does she know anyone there? Family maybe?" Cameron asked. Natasha shook her head.

"Rita's family is estranged. They hardly communicate and I don't think they have any family in Seattle," she said.

"Well, the charge was to a motel. We had Seattle PD look in on it but by the time they got there, she was long gone," he said. Natasha took a long deep breath.

"So this could be another dead end?" she asked.

"Yes and no. It could be if the credit card was stolen but it could also be a major lead," the officer said. "I am liaising with the team down in Seattle and they reported something interesting. They put out posters and flyers with Lydia's picture on them and a woman called this morning. She said she saw someone matching Lydia's description at her place of work," he added.

"Where is this exactly?" Mitchell asked.

"A supermarket, Pay Less," the officer said.

"So, what does this mean?" Natasha asked.

"Right now, that's all we know but I think we'll have an update soon," he said. Natasha took Mitchell's hand.

"Thanks, Cam. We will be in touch," he said. Natasha looked at him.

"That's it?" she asked.

"Well, for the moment, that will have to be it. We have absolutely nothing else right now," Cameron said sadly. Mitchell smiled at him.

"That's better than nothing, Cam. Thanks a bunch," he said as he stood up. Natasha gave a smile to Cameron as she stood up.

"I'm sorry if I am not as excited as I should be. It's just that I thought you'd tell us where she is," she said. Cameron smiled at her.

"I understand. This is not the first missing persons case I am handling. But I can tell you from experience that this right here is better than most families hope for. Your friend will be very happy," Cameron said to her.

"Actually, we haven't told her that we contacted the police," Mitchell said.

"May I ask why?" he asked.

"In the past, her mother would just come around eventually so I guess she was hoping that this would be one of those times," Mitchell said.

"Yeah, she made so many reports back when she was in high school, the police didn't want to hear anything about Lydia. To them, she was the girl who cried wolf one too many times," Natasha said sadly.

"That explains a lot," he said.

"What?" Mitchell asked. "What explains a lot?" he asked again. Cameron took a long deep breath and looked at the two of them.

"Sergeant Polson, one of the senior guys here, probably one of the oldest guys in this precinct, found me as I was sending the email to Seattle PD. He said that Lydia was probably lying in some strange man's bed wasted. I didn't know what he meant by it then. I just thought he was being the usual judgmental ass he always is," he said.

"He must have known Rita and Lydia from way back then," Natasha said.

"Yeah, probably," Cameron said. "But don't worry, I got this covered. I will give you a call if anything comes up," he said. Natasha smiled and walked toward the door, pushing the stroller in front of her. Mitchell stayed behind and had a few words with Cameron before he finally followed her out.

"This is the worst thing that could ever happen. But at least she is alive, right? At least I think she is," Natasha thought as she looked down at Alexis. *"What happens if something*

happens? How will I tell Rita?" she wondered as Mitchell walked towards her.

"Hey," he said softly as she strapped Alexis in the car seat once again.

"Hey," she said standing up.

"You okay?" he asked. She nodded and looked into his eyes.

"You know I am lucky to have you, your family, and my family," Nathasha told him. "And this beautiful baby here, but Rita, she has no one. As much as her mom messed up, she was Rita's whole world. She's always been her whole world and I don't even know what..." Her words trailed off yet again. He held her face in her hands and smiled.

"This, right here, is one of the very many reasons I love you," he said.

"Me freaking out?" she asked.

"No, you being caring and concerned. Just the wife and the mother for our baby that I need," he said before giving her a long kiss. "Everything will be fine," he said.

"I hope so," she said.

"Don't hope. It is going to be fine," he said smiling at her. "What do you say I take my two favorite girls somewhere special?" he asked.

"Babe, I love you but any time you take me and the baby somewhere, it is usually a place where curly fries and high chairs are the special offers," Natasha said smiling.

"Well, how about we do something else?" he asked.

"Like what?" Natasha asked.

"The last time we had a picnic was way back before we got married," he said. She smiled and nodded.

"Yeah, it has been a while, hasn't it?" she asked.

"So, what do you say we introduce the girl to our little tradition?" he asked. She smiled and nodded, then frowned. "What now?" he asked.

"Well, I know you mean well but we can't have a picnic without the essentials. Blanket, picnic basket, you know, the usual," she said.

"I'll handle it. I just want to take your mind off things for a few hours," he said. She smiled and got in the car. She could not wait to see what he had planned.

When Mitchell began driving to the unknown location, Natasha once again found herself thinking about Rita and her misfortunes. She could not help but wonder what her life would have been like if she was the one in Rita's shoes. She remembered what her father and Nan had told her about her own mother. How she left Natasha because she didn't think she could give her daughter the life she deserved. And maybe her mother was right to do so, because the life she knew as Natasha Black, that was the best life she had ever known.

"What if my own mother was actually like Lydia or worse?" she wondered. She would have never met Mitchell. She would have never known or even had Alexis because she would have probably turned out as terrible as her mother. She looked over at Alexis and brushed the curls off her face. She smiled

when the baby took her index finger in her own little chubby hand.

"Are you okay back there?" Mitchell asked, looking at Natasha in the rear view mirror. She smiled and nodded.

"I'm fine. We both are" she said with a smile. "I love you, Mitchell," she said, meeting his eyes in the mirror. He smiled as he held her gaze before returning his eyes to the road.

"I don't know what it is about you that makes a shiver go down my spine every time you tell me that," he said.

"I'm sure you say that to all your wives," she said laughing.

"Ouch. That's just cold," Mitchell said. "And no, my ex-wife never had this hold you have on me," he said.

"Normally flattery would get you nowhere but today, we'll see how it goes. There might be a little something, something for you when we get back home," she said with a smile.

"Mrs. Schmidt, you shouldn't say that in front of the baby," Mitchell said with a smile.

"We can say a lot in front of the baby. That is, until she begins to talk," she said with a smile.

"And here I thought you were the world's best mom not too long ago," he said. She smiled.

"I still am," she said. "Being a good mom simply depends on knowing the right timing," she added.

"The right timing? What for?" he asked. She smiled as they pulled into the Pizza Hut.

"I can't let you in on everything. Some mystery is vital in our relationship," she said. "And the Pizza Hut? Really?" she asked.

"Just chill, woman," he said as he got out. She smiled as she watched him disappear into the Pizza Hut. Moments later, he emerged with two pizza boxes and a picnic basket. She smiled. He must have planned this. There was no way he just left the house without having all this planned out. "Is your faith in me reaffirmed yet?" he asked as he climbed back into the driver's seat.

"I always had faith in you. It's believing that all this was spontaneous I'm having a problem with," she said. He smiled and started the car again.

"Well, get ready, girls. I am about to rock your world," he said as he drove away.

Chapter 4

Tension was high as Mitchell and Natasha rode to the precinct. It had been a long afternoon for everyone, especially Rita. While they were on their family picnic, Natasha and Mitchell made a decision to talk to Rita and let her know everything they had done to find her mother. For Natasha, that would be the hardest conversation she would ever have if Rita reacted the way she thought she would.

"So you all decided to keep this from me?" Rita had asked her, looking disappointed.

"Yes. We had to. You had a lot on your plate and we felt it was for the best," Natasha said.

"Okay," Rita had said, making Natasha surprised.

"Okay?" Natasha asked her, still shocked at her reaction. Needless to say, she had expected a lot of fireworks and profanity, which was not happening right now.

"Yeah okay. I can't be mad at my best friend for trying to help me," she said. "Right now, I just want to go and see what kind of mess she has got herself into this time," she said. Natasha nodded and placed a reassuring arm around her shoulders. "Seattle? What the hell was she doing all the way in Seattle?" she asked looking at Natasha.

"Beats me, Rita," Natasha replied. She was dying to ask her what happened with Dave but she just didn't have the heart to ask, at least not now.

When they got to the precinct, Rita was having a hard time getting herself to walk through the front door and Natasha understood. After all, no one could understand what she was going through.

"Hey Cameron. This is our friend Rita," Mitchell said when they walked in. "Rita, this is my friend, Officer Cameron. He's been looking into your mom's case," he said. Rita gave him a smile and then whispered, "Pleasure to meet you."

"Okay, guys. A woman was brought in by a couple from Seattle. One of them is the woman who recognized Lydia from the photos in the posters," Cameron said. Rita nodded.

"Where is she? Where is my mother?" Rita asked. Cameron looked at Mitchell and then at Rita. "What?" Rita asked when she noticed the look. Cameron was just about to answer when Dave came running in.

"I was hoping I would find you here," he said, panting.

"Dave, hi!" Natasha said, surprised. "I didn't expect to see you here," she said, making it almost too obvious that she was fishing for information.

"Yeah, I thought I had an emergency ACL but it turns out that the patient won't be coming in until six in the evening," he said. Natasha frowned. She had no idea what he was talking about and this was neither the place nor the time to get him talking. Dave looked at Rita and then slipped an arm around her waist. "You okay?" he asked, looking at her. Rita nodded. "Have you seen her?" he asked. Rita shook her head.

"Actually, Officer Cameron was just about to tell us about Lydia right about the time you walked in," Natasha said as she gave Mitchell a nudge in the ribs. Mitchell gave her the "grow up" look before he turned his attention to Cameron.

"Yes, I was saying that the woman who was brought in is a bit off," he said. Rita shook her head.

"What do you mean, 'off?'" she asked.

"Well, she did not have any ID on her so we are guessing her wallet must have been stolen because we had tracked one of her credit cards to a motel but it was not Lydia. The woman who was brought in does not know her name or how she got to Seattle," Cameron said.

"What? Then how do you know that it's her?" Rita asked.

"Well, the lady who brought her in says she kept on calling her Rita. It is a long shot but...." Rita put her hand up.

"I want to see her," she said with finality. "I want to see her right now," she said again. Cameron nodded.

"Our medics are checking her out. She will be here in a minute," he said as two people, a Caucasian man and an African American woman walked towards them. "Perfect timing, guys. This is the woman who brought Lydia in. She's Desiree Young and this is her boyfriend, Taylor Ericson," he said.

"Nice to meet you. I hope she didn't stress you out," Rita said. Desiree shook her head.

"She was cool. We wanted to send her here on a bus but she wouldn't hear of it. So we just drove down here," she said.

"Well, thank you," Rita said before giving Desiree a hug. "This is my boyfriend Dave, my best friend Natasha and her husband Mitchell," she said when she pulled away. Mitchell and Natasha smiled at each other when she introduced Dave as her boyfriend.

"Nice to meet you," Natasha said with a smile.

"Yes, we could never thank you enough," Mitchell said warmly.

"So, do you mind if I ask, how exactly was she acting?" Dave asked.

"Apart from the obvious memory loss, there were also some times when she had difficulty in communication and her judgment was also a bit off sometimes," Desiree said.

"Yeah, she also had a hard time focusing and paying attention to the most minor details," Taylor said. Rita shook her head.

"I'm sorry. I don't understand," she said. "What do you mean she could not pay attention to detail?" she asked.

"We stayed with her for four days and she almost burned the house down three times when making us dinner. She would just get started and then forget that she was cooking," Taylor explained. Dave rubbed Rita's back.

"Babe, they just gave all the symptoms of dementia," he said in a low voice.

"But I don't know anyone in our family who has dementia. At least the side of the family I know about," she said.

"Well, it is a possibility that the side of the family you don't know about may have a history of dementia. But don't worry. I'll make sure she gets all the tests needed to confirm everything before we make any conclusions," Dave said with a smile.

"Yeah, Dave's a doctor. I'm sure by now you have realized," Mitchell said with a smile.

"Yeah, we noticed," Desiree said smiling.

"Oh my God, Mama," Rita said in a whisper as a medic holding Lydia's arm walked towards them . "You're okay," she said as she hugged a confused Lydia.

"Rita, who is this woman? What is going on?" Lydia asked, looking at Desiree. Rita pulled away and looked at her.

"Mama, it's me. It's Rita," she said, looking at Lydia.

"Rita?" Lydia asked again, still looking at Desiree.

"It's okay," Desiree said, walking towards Lydia. "See this lady, her name is Rita too, and you are her mother," she said with a smile.

"I had twins and named them the same?" Lydia asked, looking confused.

"No, it's...Ericson, help me," Desiree said. Taylor took a step forward and then took Lydia's hand in his.

"Come on, Lydia. Why don't we go down to the vending machine and see if they have those chips you like," he said as the two of them walked off. Desiree looked at Rita, who was now fighting the tears that were threatening to roll down her cheeks.

"I'm so sorry," she said looking at Rita.

"It's fine. You were there for her when I wasn't," Rita said, smiling sadly. "Do you know what she was doing there? How she got there?" she asked. Desiree nodded.

"Well, her memory comes back in flashes. She said something

about meeting Zack. Does that mean anything to you?" she asked. Rita nodded as a tear rolled down her cheek.

"The name on my birth certificate, my father's name is Zachary Albert. Maybe they reconnected. Maybe she was going to see him or something," she said as she brushed off a tear.

"I'll make a call to the hospital to get everything set up," Dave said as he walked away. Rita walked to a nearby couch and sat down, and Natasha followed.

"I never had a mom. I grew up in foster care and seeing someone's mother like this...it's hard," Desiree said as she and Mitchell looked at Natasha, who was now holding a sobbing Rita in her arms.

"I know. I can't imagine this being easy on anyone," Mitchell said.

"But for us, the glass is half full. I mean, when she was not almost burning down the house, Lydia was quite a delight. Only we called her Meg. We had no idea what her name was or even the first letter of her name," Desiree said. Mitchell laughed.

"You guys are just the best," he said as Dave walked up to them

"I have an MMSE test scheduled for her beginning tomorrow. She has to be admitted today, though," Dave said. Mitchell looked at him and shook his head.

"MMSE?" he asked.

"Sorry. Sometimes I forget I am not at the hospital all the time.

MMSE is a mini mental state exam. The test will determine her concentration span, short and long term memory and ability to understand instructions. It's pretty standard," he explained. "After that, then we'll have the CT and MRI and see how it goes," he added. Mitchell nodded.

"I'm just glad she is back. Rita can breathe again...but she is going to need all the help she can get," Mitchell said.

"Well, she is not alone. She has me and you guys," Dave said. "And a new family," he added as he looked at Desiree.

"So, it's official. You guys are back together?" Mitchell asked. Dave smiled and nodded.

"What? You had let that gorgeous woman go?" Desiree asked.

"It was just a misunderstanding," Dave said quickly. Desiree laughed. "I would never let her go," he added.

"And did you...?" Mitchell asked. Dave shook his head.

"There is too much going on right now. I'll let it rest for a while," he said with a smile as Taylor and Lydia walked back over to them. Natasha and Rita walked towards them and then Cameron followed.

"So, what is going to happen now?" Cameron asked. Dave looked at Rita and smiled.

"I have made arrangements for the necessary tests to be made. We can get her admitted to the hospital tonight," he said. Rita looked at Natasha and then at Desiree and brushed off a tear. She looked at Taylor who was still walking towards them with her mother and then nodded.

"Do it," she said in a whisper before walking away. Dave looked at her and then at the group.

"I better go after her," he said before following her outside. Cameron went out after them, probably to discuss how Lydia would get to the hospital.

"I guess Taylor and I had better get started. It's a long drive back," Desiree said. Natasha shook her head.

"Are you kidding? You leave now, you'll probably get there at two in the morning," she said.

"Well, yeah, but..."

"Stay the night," Natasha said cutting her short as she looked at Mitchell who was nodding. "You can stay at our place if you'd like. We have more than enough room," she said, smiling.

"So, what do you say?" Mitchell asked just as Taylor and Lydia approached them.

"Ericson, it looks like we will be heading back home tomorrow because these two won't take no for an answer," Desiree said with a smile.

"Okay," Taylor said smiling. "I was about to suggest to you we get a motel because I am beat but their offer sounds better," he said.

The six of them, Natasha, Mitchell, Taylor, Lydia, Desiree and Cameron waited until Dave had calmed Rita down. After that, Dave, Cameron and Rita took Lydia to hospital as the two couples drove to Eric's and Estelle's to pick up Alexis. Mitchell advised Taylor to leave his car at the station where he would pick it the next morning, to make the transit to Estelle's and then back to his place easier. Once they were home, Natasha and Mitchell made dinner and when they sat down, they realized that their new friends were two of the best people they had ever met.

"You know the last time we met people, it was on our honeymoon," Natasha said after putting Alexis down to sleep.

"Yeah, the two of us lead a crazy lifestyle. She is lucky she got time off after having Alexis," Mitchell said.

"Time off? I would have swapped places with you if you would have asked me," Natasha said.

"Actually, maternity leave is not really a leave, per se," Desiree said as she looked at Mitchell.

"Of course you would take her side. But Taylor, you are on my side, right?" Mitchell asked. Taylor shook his head.

"I'm sorry, man. I'm with the ladies on this one," he said.

"Oh come on," Mitchell said.

"No seriously, babies are a twenty-four-seven commitment. They are usually crying, puking or pooping or sometimes all three. And not forgetting the fact that they sleep for two seconds before screaming for four hours in the night," Taylor said.

"Man after my own heart," Natasha said, laughing.

"You talk like you've been through this. Do you have any kids?" Mitchell asked. Desiree looked at Taylor and smiled.

"Oh no," Desiree said.

"The answer should be not yet," Taylor said with a smile.

"Oh, that is so sweet. How long have you guys been together?" Natasha asked.

"A year and a half," Desiree said.

"Have you thought of making an honest man out of him yet?" Mitchell asked.

"Mitchell, honey. You are prying," Natasha said.

"No, it's okay. But I would also love to hear the answer to that," Taylor said. Desiree smiled and nodded.

"Yes, I will make an honest man out of him one day. Just not yet," she said with a smile. Taylor took her hand in his and smiled.

"I don't think I would have heard that if it weren't for you," he said. Natasha looked at the time and gasped.

"I had no idea it was this late. We should probably leave you guys alone. Mitch and I have a long day tomorrow," Natasha said.

"Yeah, we probably should," Mitchell said with a smile.

"Thanks again for letting us stay here tonight," Desiree said with a smile.

"Oh, we owe you," Natasha replied. "Well, the guest bedroom is down the hall to your right. You guys can bum here, watch TV or even get something to eat if you're hungry," she added.

She smiled at Desiree and Taylor as Mitchell stood up.

"We'll see you guys in the morning," he said as the two of them walked towards their bedroom.

"That was a long day," he said as Natasha took off her earrings.

"Long but interesting. I am too tired to even shower," she said.

"You and me both," he said as he watched her take off her top. He looked on as she took off her skirt and then tossed her dirty clothes in the laundry basket.

"What?" she asked when she turned around. Mitchell shook his head and smiled.

"Nothing. Nothing at all," he said with a smile. "Just looking at my beautiful wife," he said as he stood up. He walked over to her and held her close before he gave her a long kiss. She smiled as she pulled away from him.

"What was that for?" she asked. He smiled and undid the clasp of her bra.

"Oh, that's what it was for," she said as she looked into his eyes. "I thought you were just as tired as I am," she said.

"There is a bunch of golf clubs in this house. The day I claim to be too tired to make love to you, I want you to beat me to death with all of them," he said as he backed her up towards the bed.

"Oh sweetie, I might just do that," she said.

"I would not blame you," he said as he kissed her. Natasha

suddenly laughed.

"I'm sorry," she said looking at him

"What is it?" he asked looking down at her.

"Normally what you just said would turn someone off but for some reason I am still kissing you," she said.

"That's what makes us so perfect for each other," he said, smiling down at her. Natasha brought her hand up and ran his fingers through his thick hair.

"I guess we are, aren't we?" she said as he brought his head down to kiss her again. She shivered when she felt his hand on one of her breasts. She suddenly grasped the tails of his shirt and pulled them apart, sending his shirt buttons flying all over the floor.

"Thank God I can afford my wardrobe because you are one woman who makes Marks & Spencer very happy," he said before kissing her again. She pushed his shirt off his shoulders and then flipped him over. She undid his belt buckle as she straddled him before climbing off his crotch to pull his pants off. She then took off her own panties before climbing back on him and letting his cock slide inside her. He exhaled loudly and held her waist as she began working herself on him, rocking her hips back and forth in a slow motion. Mitchell pulled her down so that she could rest her head on his shoulder as he began thrusting into her. Mitchell and Natasha made love long into the night, throwing all caution to the wind about getting up early the next day.

As they made love and allowed themselves to get lost in their own world, what the two did not know was that down the hall, their guests were also doing the same.

Chapter 5

"I will not even ask," Natasha said as she walked into Rita's gallery. Rita looked up and smiled when she saw her.

"What are you doing here?" Rita asked, standing up.

"Well, I just went back to work and on my first day I closed a major deal. So, I was so happy about it, I decided to give myself a personal day off," Natasha said as she walked towards Rita. The two hugged briefly before Rita looked over at her assistant.

"Keep an eye on things. I won't be long," she said before leading Rita to a room in the back.

"So, how's Lydia doing? Is the treatment working?" Natasha asked as she sat down. Rita took a long deep breath as she poured two cups of coffee. She had transformed the room into her own little haven where she could get away from everything. She had a coffee maker set up, a table and a couch that sometimes (well, most of the time) doubled up as a bed. Rita sat down on the couch next to Natasha and smiled sadly.

"The first few days are usually the hardest. It will be at least another ten days before they allow me to even see her," she said.

"Well, the important thing is that she is getting the help that she needs," Natasha said with a smile.

"I know. But I just don't get what would have driven her to substance abuse after all these years," Rita said.

"Well, these things happen honey. Maybe she had a major

stressor that pushed her to the edge," Natasha said as she took a sip. Rita nodded.

"Thank God those guys from Seattle got to her in time," she said. She then looked at Natasha and frowned. "I never really understood how they got to her in the first place," she said, shaking her head.

"Well, like you, I believe she was there to meet up with..." her words trailed off when she realized what she was about to say. The subject of Rita's biological father had always been a sensitive topic and Natasha more than anyone knew this. Rita smiled.

"It's okay. You can say it. Don't take my word for it, but I am a hundred percent sure that she was there to meet my dad," she said, smiling sadly.

"Well, yeah, that, and when the Alzheimer's got out of control, she happened to be at the store, probably buying something. Desiree, that's the woman she mistook for you, must have walked up to her at the exact opportune moment," Natasha said. She placed her hand on Rita's and smiled. "She is in the best care facility," she added. Rita shrugged.

"Care facility my ass. She is at a hospital," she said.

"Well, she needs to get treatment and then she will be in the best care facility," Natasha said, smiling. Rita looked at her best friend and smiled at her.

"I know you have absolutely no idea as far as this situation is concerned but I am happy that you're trying," she said.

"Well, what are friends for?" Natasha asked before taking another sip.

"I'll need to go home...to my mama's and pack a bag for her. Will you come with me?" Rita asked. Natasha nodded.

"Sure. When?" she asked. Rita looked at her watch and smiled.

"You know what? Now's as good time as any," she said as she took Natasha's cup from her. Natasha frowned.

"Hey, I wasn't done with that," she whined.

"There's plenty of coffee at my mother's house," Rita said as she put her cup down and pulled Natasha to her feet.

"Okay fine. Easy on the Christian Louboutins," Natasha said as the two practically ran out of the room and back into the gallery.

"Hey guys, I have to step out. Will you be okay in the meantime?" Rita asked.

"Go right ahead," one of her two workers said.

"Yeah, Rita. They have practically been running this place on their own for the last three weeks," Natasha said as they walked out. "It's midday. I have to pick up Alexis from daycare in exactly three hours. So keep that in mind," she said as they got into her car.

"Sure. We are just taking a few clothes, some of her favorite books and DVDs," Rita said as she buckled in. The drive to Lydia's place was short and almost quiet. There was not much to talk about anyway. Natasha could see that Rita was still unsettled about her mother and Rita knew that the last thing Natasha needed was to have to listen to her whine about her mother. For Natasha, the one thing she really wanted to ask was whether Dave had popped the question but the fact that she had not mentioned anything was a clear message to her that Dave had decided to wait it out.

"This place is a dump," Natasha said when Rita opened the door. "No offense though," she said quickly as she looked at Rita.

"None taken. I mean look at this place," Rita said as she walked around the living room. There were dirty dishes on the table, the couch cushions were not as neat as they usually were and the throw pillows looked to have lived up to their name, thrown around the room. "I'm afraid to go to any other room of the house," she said as she picked up one pillow.

"Three hours is more than enough to smooth the place out and pack a bag. You take this room. I'll take the kitchen," Natasha said as she removed her shoes and pinned up her hair up. Rita gave her a thankful smile as she began taking off her own shoes. As she rearranged the pillows, she had half a mind to tell Natasha that the reason she was so quiet was that she was scared she would end up just like Lydia. She had no idea how everything was going to work out. Being sick would mean that she would never have a friend again because she would not be able to recognize her. She would not know the man she loved or even recognize herself. There was also the fact that she did not trust Dave not just because of the "misunderstanding" as he had put it, but there was also the fact that she had walked in on him a dozen times talking on his phone but he had hung up as soon as he noticed her. She was so engrossed in her own thoughts that she did not notice Natasha walking back in the room.

"What have you been doing for the last hour?" she asked, looking at Rita who was holding a cushion in her arms.

"Well..." Rita began talking before Natasha put up her hands. She took the cushion and began straightening up the living room.

'Don't worry. You have a lot going on," Natasha said. "But if I am going to make that pickup at three, we need to pick up our slack," she added as she quickly bustled around the room. Rita smiled and helped her out before she walked to her mother's room. She pulled out a bag out of the closet as Natasha pulled out a few clothes and began folding them.

"What is this?" Rita asked as a piece of paper fell out of one of her mother's favorite books.

"What?" Natasha asked.

"This," Rita said as she bent down to pick up the paper. "From my experience, notes hidden in books are usually the bearers of bad news," she said as she looked at Natasha.

"So, what do you want to do?" Natasha asked even though all she wanted to do was grab the paper from her and read it out loud.

"Screw it," Rita said as she sat down on the edge of the bed. She unfolded the paper and began reading through it.

"What? What does it say?" Natasha asked.

"It's a letter from my mother. It is dated three years ago. I think this is the day she was diagnosed with Alzheimer's," Rita said, looking up. Natasha walked up to her and sat down.

I would tell you if I could but we have had a rough run and I have just recently got my daughter back. I don't want your last memories of me to be sad ones. I still have a few good months left and I want to spend them living my life to the fullest, being a good mother to my daughter.

Natasha took Rita's hand in hers and squeezed it gently.

"She knew and she didn't say anything," Rita said.

"But it was a selfless act," Natasha said as she squeezed her hand again. "She only did that because she loves you. You are her only baby, remember?" she asked, smiling.

"I know. Maybe one day I will understand why she did this," Rita said. Natasha squeezed her hand again. This was the first time she was seeing her friend this vulnerable, this defeated.

"Hey, let's get this stuff to your mama, okay?" Natasha said as she stood up. She folded a few dresses and sweaters before looking at Rita again. She could not hold back anymore. This was an inevitable question. "How are things between you and Dave?" she asked. Rita took a long deep breath and sighed.

"Oh wow, that is a whole other story," she said.

"What? I thought you guys worked everything out," Natasha said.

"He apologized for the quote unquote misunderstanding," Rita said, putting up finger quotes. "But that was the explanation for that day. What about all the other women I have seen them with?" she asked.

"I'm curious. Just what explanation did he give you?" Natasha asked. She had not seen any ring on Rita's finger and Dave had confirmed that he had not had a chance to go down on one knee yet.

"Some story about the woman being an event's organizer and that he was planning something special, an office party or something," she said. Natasha rolled her eyes. Dave was hopeless. That was the best he could come up with?

"Sweetie, there could be so much more to it than just that," Natasha said. Rita shrugged. "Then why did you get back together with him if you did not believe him?" she asked.

"I have a lot going on, Tasha and honestly, I needed the distraction. I know you think I'm terrible but I..." Rita sighed as she thought of what she could say. Anything she could say at this point would not be right.

"I am not judging you, sweetie. I'm just saying you need to give him a chance," Natasha said. She would have hated for Rita to miss out on a great guy because of her insecurities. Rita looked at her and raised an eyebrow.

"Why are you in his court? You are my best friend, not his," she said with a smile.

"I know and I am on your side. One hundred percent but still, you might be surprised," Natasha said. Without knowing it, Natasha had almost blown the entire secret.

"What do you know?" Rita suddenly asked. Natasha felt her face get red.

"Nothing," she said quickly.

"Tasha, I have known you for more than ten years and I can tell when you are lying and right now, you are lying," Rita said.

"No, I most certainly am not," Natasha said sharply.

"Fine, then you are holding back on the truth," Rita said, smiling. Natasha was still looking at Rita, trying to convince her, when her phone suddenly rang loudly, piercing the uncomfortable silence. "I'm sorry, sweetie. I have to take this," she said as she walked out of the bedroom.

"Natasha Schmidt," she said as she walked to the living room.

"Hello, Mrs. Schmidt. My name is Miranda Simms. I am calling from the Lockhart Academic Complex," the woman on the other side said. Natasha's heart almost skipped a beat. Lockhart Academic Complex or LAC as most people called it, was the Oxford of the preschool world.

"Hi...thanks for calling," Natasha said trying hard not to stammer from the excitement.

"Well, it is my honor," the woman said. "I am calling about an application you placed with us for Alexis Schmidt, your daughter, and I had to ask, is there any relation to Nolan Schmidt, the businessman?" the woman asked. Natasha rolled her eyes. Of course the Schmidt name had to come up.

"Yes, I am. I am married to Mitchell Schmidt, Nolan's grandson," Natasha said. She could almost see the dollar signs going ka-ching in the woman's eyes.

"That is just great. Having a member of the Nolan Schmidt family as one of our students here at Lockhart Academic Complex," she said. Natasha smiled.

"So does that mean we are off the waiting list?" Natasha asked excitedly.

"Oh yes. We are happy to have your little girl as part of our family," the woman said. Natasha said goodbye and almost danced around the living room. This was just perfect.

"What are you all randy about?" Rita asked as she walked into the living room carrying a bag.

"Alexis just got accepted into LAC," Natasha said excitedly. Rita frowned.

"LAC?" she asked.

"Lockhart Academic Complex," Natasha said.

"What? That is like the Oxford or Harvard of elementary education," Rita said.

"I know. Isn't it great?" Natasha said excitedly. Rita frowned again.

"I know I have said this before but you do remember that girl is only seven months old, right?" she asked.

"Okay, please don't tell me you have joined the 'Alexis is only a baby' bandwagon. I don't need any more people on that train," Natasha said.

"Well, as your best friend I have to give you both sides of the coin. The first side, you doing this shows how good of a mother you are, but also how you get your head wrapped around something and never let go of a stupid idea, and at the same time, I know Mitchell hates all this. So this is more of a cons than pros situation," Rita explained.

"Well, he hates it now but I am sure he will come around," Natasha said.

"I hope so," Rita said with a smile.

"Is that everything?" Natasha asked pointing at the bag Rita was carrying.

"Well, we cleaned up, packed up her books and clothes...so yeah, this is everything," Rita said looking at the bag in her hands.

"Good. Let's get going," Natasha said as she got out of the living room. As the two rode to the hospital, Natasha could barely hide her excitement.

*****

Mitchell looked around at the strong minds seated at his conference table to the board room. He had just made the pitch of his life and even though he was sure he had done a good job, he was still unsure of himself. He had not done a pitch in a long time. He usually left pitching jobs to the junior associates. What he did was just identify the people he wanted to work with and the associates would do the rest. But not this time. This time he was not just pitching to some random company. It was his grandfather's closest friend, Ralph Peterson. At the time, it was the most profitable business decision he had ever made.

"I must say, Mitchell, you are truly a direct bloodline from Nolan," Simon Cryer, one of the associates at Peterson Parker insurance, said.

"I'm glad you liked it. We are all about our client's product and for a company such as Peterson Parker, we can make a campaign so big that it will blow your mind," Mitchell said imitating his grandfather. The three associates laughed as they recalled Nolan's comical voice.

"You are right. He is his grandfather's grandson," Lawrence

Simms, another associate said.

"So, what do you say? Deal or no deal?" Mitchell asked. Normally he would not use that phrase but he knew he had nailed it. He would have danced naked on the table and they would have still offered him a deal.

"We would be honored to work with you," Cryer said as he stood up to shake Mitchell's hand.

"Good. I'll have the contract drawn up and sent to your attorneys," Mitchell said as he led them out.

"Perfect," Simon said.

"Well, if you are not in a hurry I would like to indulge you in some of the best English tea and some pound cake downstairs," Mitchell said smiling.

"Of course," Simms said, smiling.

"Yes, we have been known for our sweet tooth," Cryer said. Just as they were making their way past his office, his assistant came running up to him.

"Sir, you have a call," she said.

"Take a message, please. Well, Peggy?" he said.

"It is Lockhart Academic Complex and it sounds urgent," she said. Mitchell pointed out the break room to his guests and then walked to his office. He had no idea why a school like LAC would be calling him. Perhaps they needed him to make a speech at one of their events.

"This is Mitchell," he said when he picked up the phone.

"Mr. Schmidt. Hi, my name is Alicia from Lockhart Academic Complex. I am calling to confirm your daughter's social security number," the woman said. Mitchell shook his head.

"I'm sorry but why would you need my daughter's social security number?" he asked.

"For our records," Alicia said.

"What records?" he asked wondering what the hell she was talking about.

"Oh your wife must have not talked to you yet. Your daughter got accepted to Lockhart Academic complex," Alicia said excitedly. Mitchell felt anger shoot through him when she said that.

"I'm sorry, what?" he asked.

"Your daughter Alexis will be going to school here as soon as she is of school going age. Now all I need is her soci..." Mitchell did not have it in him to listen to her anymore. He hung up and ran his fingers through his hair. He had already told Natasha to quit with the whole early admission thing but obviously, she had chosen to defy him. He rose from his seat and walked out of the office. By this time, he had forgotten all about his guests because all he could think of was having a long talk with his wife.

Chapter 6

"Will you at least talk to me?" Natasha asked as Mitchell walked right past her and to the kitchen. He walked to the fridge and took a bottle of water.

"What do you want me to say? I asked you not to do something and you went right ahead and did it," he said before taking a sip.

The Schmidt household had been almost impossible to be in since Mitchell found out that Natasha had met up with Lockhart academic Complex officials. To Mitchell, getting into the school was not such a big deal and if anything, it was going to put unnecessary pressure on Alexis as she grew up. Mitchell had sworn to protect his daughter from the kind of childhood his mother had forced on him, because he had only been too lucky to get away from the disadvantages that came with that lifestyle, but his sister, that was another story altogether.

"Okay, so are we going to be one of those couples?" Natasha asked angrily. "You just want me to be seen not heard. Is that right?" she asked. Mitchell shrugged and took another sip of his water.

"I never said that. Those are your words, not mine," he said.

"But all I did was make sure my daughter..."

"Our daughter," Mitchell interjected looking at her.

"Fine. Our daughter. All I did was make sure she got in the best elementary program there is," she said. Mitchell laughed cynically and shook his head.

"Preschool does not matter, Tasha. If you are this uptight about preschool, I don't know what you will be like when Alexis is going to college," he said. Natasha rolled her eyes.

"I already have that all planned out," she said.

"God damn it! Tasha. That is exactly what I am talking about," Mitchell said. "You cannot force our daughter to live a life that she does not want. Let her grow up to become what she wants to be," he said angrily.

"Really? You can sleep at night knowing that your daughter chose to be a waitress?" Natasha asked.

"Of course not. But I don't want to force her into a career that she does not want and that is exactly where you are headed," he said as he took another sip of his water. Natasha rolled her eyes and crossed her arms on her chest.

"How exactly am I doing that?" she asked.

"Remember how I told you about my mother, how she forced things on us that we did not want? This is how she started," he said.

'But I am not your mother!" Natasha yelled angrily.

"Not yet," he said as he looked at her.

"Okay, just what is that supposed to mean?" she asked.

"Well, in not so many words. Natasha, I love you but you are doing things that remind me why I sometimes hate being related to Nolan Schmidt," he said. "I never wanted to learn piano and my sister never wanted to learn the violin. We never wanted to be the golden children and that is what pushed my sister to substance abuse," he said. There was a long pause before he finally spoke again. "I will not let my daughter hate herself. Not in this lifetime," he said before walking out. Natasha quickly ran after him and touched his arm.

"We are not done yet," she said. He turned around and looked at her.

"What do you want to say now? Because if you are not about to tell me that you will forfeit that position at LAC, I have nothing else to say," he said.

"Why don't you just try and see things from where I stand? Have you tried to walk a mile in my shoes yet?" she asked.

"Let's see if your shoe fits, Tasha. Let's see, would you ever trade the life you had as a child, your childhood, to be in some quote unquote good school?" he asked. Natasha looked at him, unsure of what was expected of her at that moment. The truth was, she did not live a very privileged lifestyle but she still managed to carve out a great life for herself. She knew more than anyone that her life and career were the result of her father's hard work...and hers, and she also wanted to do the same for Alexis.

"No, I wouldn't, but I would have done anything to help my dad out," she said. Natasha looked into his eyes for any sign of Mitchell yielding but there was none.

"And I must say, Eric and Estelle did exceptional work with you but my point is, you did not have to be in an over-glorified school, especially, preschool, to turn out the way you did. This, you being who you are now, had absolutely nothing to do with whether or not you went to a twenty-five thousand dollar a term preschool. It was all in you and in your dad," Mitchell said.

Natasha shook her head and sighed.

"But I...." Mitchell put his hands up, silencing her immediately. He walked to the bedroom and undressed before he stepped into the shower while Natasha paced around the kitchen. She was dreading going to bed. It would be an awkward situation for both of them. She checked up on the baby and then took the monitor with her before finally getting into bed. Mitchell got out of the bathroom and walked straight to the nursery. He walked back to the bedroom and got into bed without a word. "So, you are giving me the silent treatment?" Natasha asked.

"Tasha, not now," he said without turning around.

"This is not the kind of marriage I want," she said in a low voice. Mitchell turned around and looked at her.

"What the hell is that supposed to mean?" he asked.

"This, fighting and you ignoring me, this is not what I want," she said.

"So, what are you saying?" he asked. He was afraid of saying the exact words for fear that she would answer in the affirmative. She shook her head and shrugged. "Natasha! What do you mean?" he asked. She looked into his eyes as a tear threatened to roll down her cheek. He shook his head and got out of bed.

"Where are you going?" she asked.

I am sleeping in the guest room tonight," he said as he walked out of the bedroom. Natasha felt the tear rolling down her cheek. There was no point holding back anymore. For the rest of the night, Natasha cried herself to sleep as she thought of the mess she had created. She would have to fix this but she had no idea how.

*****

When she woke up the next morning, Mitchell was long gone. He had left a note for her on the nightstand.

"He had to have been extremely quiet," she thought because she had not heard him leave. She took the note and sat up as she read it.

Hey. I had to leave the house early. Something came up at work and it could not wait. But we need to finish our talk. I will try and come home as early as I can. We need to work this out, the sooner we do it the better it will be for all of us. We cannot just disagree on stuff anymore. It is no longer just us, we have a daughter and if not for us, then we owe it to her.

She took a deep breath as she read the note over and over. She then glanced at the clock on her nightstand and sighed. She was late for work. It was already eight. She took her phone and called Stacy.

"Hey boss lady," Stacy said in a cheerful voice, like she always did.

"Hey. Do I have any pressing matters today?" Natasha asked.

"No. It's a pretty free day. Why? Aren't you coming in?" she asked. Natasha sighed.

"No, I don't think I can," she said.

"Are you okay, boss lady? You sound sick," Stacy said. Natasha could hear the concern in her voice.

"Yeah, I just need some personal time," Natasha said.

"Okay. I'll hold down the fort for you," Stacy said.

"Thanks a bunch," Natasha said before she hung up. She got out of bed and took a quick shower, then put on a pair of jeans and a top. She would probably go out later that day for some retail therapy so one of Mitchell's shirts would definitely not cut it. She then made her way to the nursery where Alexis lay happily in her crib. "Look at you, not making any noise," Natasha said in a mock baby voice. She picked her up and did a quick diaper change. She put the baby in the playpen and then walked to the kitchen. She found herself thinking of Mitchell as she poured herself some juice. How she longed for him to understand her and where she was coming from. Was that so hard? She took out a can of baby food and heated it up in the microwave as she took small sips of her juice. She had just taken the baby food out of the microwave when she heard the doorbell. She quickly walked to the door and opened it. She gasped in both surprise and happiness when she saw Mona standing at her doorstep.

"Don't just stand there. Give your cousin a hug," Mona said with a smile. Natasha laughed as she threw her arms around Mona. She had not seen Mona in almost a year thanks to Leo's busy travel schedule.

"What are you doing here? When did you even get here?" Natasha asked when she pulled away.

"I haven't been here for long. I literally just got here," Mona said with a smile. Natasha looked at her and smiled. She could not believe just how much Mona had changed. She was no longer the tomboy Natasha had always known. Mona had been transformed to a very ladylike person that Natasha didn't recognize anymore. She had even given up her box braids that had long been her signature look. Instead, her hair had been straightened out and highlighted to perfection.

"If I met you on the street, I honestly wouldn't have recognized you. You look fabulous," Natasha said as she stepped aside for Mona to walk in.

"Well, I needed something new after ditching the old tired me," she said. "So, where is my beautiful baby girl?" she asked as she walked into the living room.

"She has grown so big and so fast," Mona said as she picked Alexis up from the playpen.

"Well, apparently, that's a good thing," Natasha said as she walked to the kitchen. "I hope you haven't had breakfast yet because I am about to make us some," she yelled from the kitchen. She was not very sure Mona had heard her since she was busy making goo-goo noises at the baby. She made some bacon and a spicy omelet before walking back to the living room.

"That was fast," Mona said looking at the tray Natasha carried.

"Well, when you live with a toddler and you are still a working mom, you learn how to multitask," Natasha said as she sat down next to Mona. She took a bib and the baby food from the table and looked at Mona. "Are you going to give her to me or are you going to feed her?" she asked. Mona nodded.

"I'll feed her. Give me the goo," she said as she sat Alexis in her high chair.

"Are you sure?" Natasha asked.

"Why not? Are you forgetting that this is not my first dance?"

Mona asked. Natasha smiled and gave her the bowl before leaning back.

"You can't say goo. When she learns what that means she won't want it," Natasha said.

"But we call it what it is. Don't we, Alexis?" Mona asked in a baby voice. Alexis chuckled.

"She seems to like you. So you are officially on goo duty as I catch up with Alejandro, Miguel and Sonia," Natasha said as she bit into a bacon strip. Mona looked at her and smiled.

"Did you join a drug cartel and didn't tell me?" she asked. Natasha laughed.

"No, those are my favorite characters on *Sacrificio de Salvador,* my favorite soap on Telemundo," Natasha said.

"Since when do you watch Telemundo? I thought you hated soap operas," Mona said as she fastened the bib around Alexis' neck.

"I did. I probably still do. It's just that daytime television is just not as interesting as it used to be," Natasha said. "Trust me, I did not begin watching it by choice," she added with a smile.

"Of course you didn't and I am a virgin," Mona said before she fed Alexis a spoonful of the mashed vegetables. "So, I called the office and Stacy said you were staying home today. She seems to think you are under the weather," Mona said as she went on feeding the baby. She looked at Natasha and shrugged. I don't know about you, but you look perfectly okay to me. So, what is wrong, mama?" she asked as she gave Alexis another spoonful of her food. Natasha leaned back and took a long deep breath.

"That bad, huh?" Mona asked.

"Well, not really," Natasha said.

"Come on. Are you going to tell me or are you going to make me guess?" Mona asked.

"When did we start talking about me? We haven't even gone through how you and Leo are," Natasha said. Mona smiled.

"Leo and I are fine. So, why are you at home and not at work?" Mona asked.

"Just fine?" Natasha said ignoring her question.

"We are more than great. We are perfect," Mona said smiling.

"Good. Have you heard about Rita's mother?" Natasha asked. Mona raised an eyebrow.

"What happened with Lydia?" she asked as she fed the baby another spoonful.

"She has Alzheimer's. We could not find her for weeks and when she was tracked down, it was in Seattle," Natasha said. Mona looked at her, surprised.

"Seattle? What was she doing there?" she asked.

"Rita's biological father lives in Seattle. We think she was going to see him when it all happened," Natasha said. Mona shook her head.

"Wow, I had no idea. I just happened to be around for work and Leo is around for the week..." Her words trailed off and Natasha knew exactly what she was feeling. She was probably giving herself the "I am a horrible person speech." "I am a terrible friend," Mona said.

"Don't beat yourself up. The important thing is you are here now and Lydia is getting the help she needs," Natasha said.

"Where is she?" Mona asked.

"Right now, Dave had her admitted at the hospital where he works but she will be moved to a care facility soon. Maybe in a few weeks," Natasha said.

"I'm around for a few days. I should go check up on Rita. How is she doing?" Mona asked as she put the bowl on the table and wiped Alexis' mouth.

"How do you think? Her own mother does not know who she is," Natasha said biting into another bacon strip. Mona shook her head as she finished cleaning the baby up.

"I can only imagine. Maybe you can come with me later. You are not going anywhere are you?" she asked.

"No, not today," Natasha said.

"Cool, then we could pass by the gallery and see how she is doing," Mona said. She then looked at Natasha. "Did she ever make up with Dave or are they still having issues?" she asked.

"Oh they made up all right. And Dave is planning to propose soon," Natasha said. Mona's eyes grew wide.

"Really?" she asked.

"Oh yeah. He would have done it already but by the time they made up the whole Lydia situation was a full blown saga. It was just not the right time," Natasha said.

"So, about you," Mona said. Natasha smiled. There was no escaping Mona's drilling questions.

"What about me?" Natasha asked.

"Are you going to tell me what's going on with you or are you going to make me work for it?" Mona asked. Natasha closed her eyes and took a long deep breath.

"Mitchell and I had a fight last night," Natasha said.

"What kind of fight? A no sex fight or I can't deal with you right now fight?" Mona asked.

" A sleeping in the guest room fight," Natasha said. Mona gasped.

"You cried yourself to sleep," she said. Natasha scoffed.

"No I did not," she said.

"Yes you did. The whole time I've know you, any time you would have a fight with your boyfriend you would cry yourself to sleep. That's why you took a personal day, isn't it?" Mona said. She looked at Natasha who was taking a sip of her juice. "What happened?" she asked.

"I got Alexis on a waiting list to Lockhart Academic Complex and Mitchell doesn't approve," Natasha said.

"I hate to say this, but I don't either. Why would you do that? Alexis is seven months old," Mona said.

"I just want to make sure Alexis gets the best," Natasha said.

"But she already has the best. You and Mitchell," Mona said, concerned. "What are Mitchell's reasons for being angry?" she asked.

"He says I am turning into his mother," Natasha said. Mona shook her head.

"Alexis is not a personal project, Tasha. He has a say too, and if he sees his mother in some of your deeds than it's time you took a step back and listen to him," Mona said.

"But I..." Mona shook her head.

"I know you want to say that you have listened to him but the truth is that you have been hearing him, not listening to him," Mona said. Natasha sighed. Mona was right. "Talk to him and this time, listen to his side," she added.

Natasha nodded. She would give Mitchell a chance to explain himself and tell his side of the story.

Chapter 7

After the talk with Mona, Natasha felt guilty. Maybe Mona was right. She needed to hear Mitchell out. As she waited for him to come back home that evening, she could feel her heart beating fast and hard, almost threatening to beat out of her chest. She could still hear Rita and Mona's words ringing in her ears and they were right. Mitchell and Natasha were good together and part of this reason was the fact that they did the one thing most couples didn't do...talk. And Natasha felt bad that she had forgotten this important step. How to talk things out. For some reason she had decided to take all matters concerning Alexis into her own hands, completely disregarding his feelings. It was almost like what her mother had done to her when she left her and her father alone. She had to sort this out and she had to sort it out soon.

It had been three hours since Mona left and she had just tucked Alexis in. Putting her down was getting harder by the minute. The older the baby grew, the more she wanted to stay awake longer. Natasha found herself missing the few hours a day Alexis would sleep. Sure, she would wake up every four hours, but at least she was down every four hours. It was almost as if Alexis felt the need to stay up more the older she got. At this rate, Natasha hated to think what her sleep patterns would be like when she turned four.

She looked at the clock and took a long deep breath. It was already eleven. Maybe she had scared Mitchell away. Maybe he was going to spend another night away from their bed, this time at a hotel or something. She sat down and sighed as she began taking her bra off. She pulled the bra down over her arms and then walked into the dining room. She grabbed a piece of paper and sat down. If Mitch was not going to listen to her, he would at least read a note. She took a minute to gather her thoughts. She had no idea what to write or even how to begin. She sighed again as she started to write.

Hey Mitchell,

I really don't know how to begin because all I can think about right now is that I hate fighting with you. You are the best thing that ever happened to me and I do not believe that being the person I am, wanting the best for our child can make us fight this much. All I want is for Alexis to have everything I never did. I hope that is not too much to ask because I have you now but I did not always have you. I want her to be secure and this is the best way I know how....

Natasha suddenly looked up when she heard the door open. She felt her heart skip a beat when she saw Mitchell standing at the doorway. A huge relief swept over her as she looked at him.

"I'm sorry. I got held up. Some new clients and all," he said as he walked into the living room.

"I was just writing you a note," she said as she tore the paper from the notepad and crumpled it in a ball. "We need to talk," she said in a small voice.

"Yeah, we do," he said as he loosened his tie. She stood up and walked over to the couch and then sat down. He caught a glimpse of her bra on the arm rest and smiled. "What's with the bra?" he asked. She smiled and shrugged.

"It was getting too tight. I felt like I had a noose around my rib cage," she said smiling as he sat down. There was a long uncomfortable silence before they both spoke at the same time. Mitchell smiled at her.

"You first," he said. She smiled and nodded.

"I'm sorry," she started. "I didn't mean to hurt you or anything. I just wanted to make sure Alexis got the best education," she said.

"I understand that. But do you understand me?" he asked. Natasha shook her head. This was what Mona was talking about. Getting his side of the story. "I love my mother, Tasha. I really do but it is not the same love I see between you and Eric. The love I have for my mother is, well, obligatory. She forced stuff on me, music, art, science. I was better in business studies and commerce but she had to force what she wanted and when you begin things like getting her in Lockhart Academic Complex when she is barely a year old, I can't help but think that history is repeating itself," he said looking into his eyes.

"Is that the only reason?" she asked. Mitchell nodded.

"I cannot bear to think that my daughter will spend the rest of her life enduring my company rather than enjoying it," he said in a quiet voice, almost a whisper. She looked into his eyes and for the first time, she could see the honesty and the pain in his eyes. It was something he had kept hidden for so long.

"Why didn't you ever tell me about the whole thing with your mom?" she asked. "We are a team. We are in whatever it is, together," she added.

"I was trying to protect you. The whole when you marry a man, it's your family you are really marrying...well, that does not really work with me," he said smiling. "I wanted to make sure our marriage had a chance before my mother got to you like she got to my first wife," he added. Natasha raised an eyebrow.

"Got to her? How?" she asked.

"She wanted a woman who was exactly the same as she was to be my wife and unfortunately, that is exactly who I married. But I will not let you turn into her," he said.

"Again Mitchell, why would you keep all this from me? I am your wife. We need to talk about stuff," she said.

"I know but this is not the time for that talk. It is time for this talk. Alexis is our daughter. Not yours or mine, ours. We need to make all decisions about her life together because when you go ahead and do stuff without talking to me, I feel like you do not trust me enough to share the facts," he said.

Mona was right. All she needed was to hear Mitchell's side of the story. She smiled and put her hand in his.

"I'm sorry, babe," she said looking into his eyes. He draped an arm around her shoulders and pulled her close to hug her.

"I'm sorry too," he said in a low voice before pulling away. He looked into her eyes and sighed. "There's something else. What did you mean when you said this is not the kind of marriage you want?" he asked.

"I don't want to fight. I hate living a life of fighting, that's all," she said looking into his eyes. He exhaled in relief and she shook her head. "Why do you look like you were expecting something else?" she asked.

"I thought ...." His words trailed off as he brought his head down and kissed her.

"What did you think Mitchell?" she asked. He took another long deep breath again.

"I thought you were going to ask for a divorce. I thought you were going to leave me," he said. She looked into his eyes and she could have sworn she had never seen anyone look so vulnerable. She held his face in her hands and kissed him passionately.

"I would never do that. I love you," she said. He smiled and kissed her again. She stood up and took his hand before leading him to the bedroom. As soon as they got to the bedroom, Mitchell kissed her passionately under her chin and then up the sides of her neck, moving shoulder to shoulder as he brushed his lips gently across her chest. She gasped when she felt his lips on each of her breasts. He pushed his face into her breasts, loving the feeling of the weight of her beautiful breasts on his face. Natasha interlaced her fingers behind his head and let out a moan as he kissed her breasts, letting his tongue circle her hardening nipples.

He pulled away from her and looked into her eyes. He smiled as he slowly pulled her top up, untucking it in the process. She looked back at him as he slipped the blouse off her shoulders before letting it fall to the floor. She lifted her arms and put her hands behind her head, flaunting her breasts. Mitchell felt his cock twitch when she did this. She was still the same hot, provocative woman he had fallen in love with. This he knew well and he could see it too. He longed to hold her breasts in his hands, to squeeze and caress, to feel her nipples pressing hard against his palms. He smiled as he once again buried his head in her cleavage, slowly inhaling the rich scent of her perfume as he trailed small soft kisses in her most sensitive areas. By this time, Natasha was slowly arching her back, pressing her crotch against his own. Mitchell let her know how good this was for him by letting out muffled moans and gasps every time he tried coming up for air.

Natasha slowly spread her legs, letting him settle in between them. She looked at him as he slowly trailed kisses down her tummy until he finally got to her waist. He quickly undid the button and zipper on her jeans before he went on to pull her pants off. He looked at her for a long minute, almost as if he was seeing her for the first time before he went on to pull her panties off. She sighed as he placed his hands on either knee and slowly spread them, giving him a perfect view of her pussy that was at that moment almost completely drenched.

Mitchell smiled. He was just getting started and she knew it too. He slowly brought his hand to her center and began to gently caress her slit with the tips of his fingers, all the while being careful to avoid her clit. He was not ready for that yet. There was plenty of time to deliver his torment. He was teasing her and he loved the way she gasped and writhed as he played his fingers close to her pussy. Soon, he had her purring as he went on making her wet. He could tell that she was practically begging for more of his attention. She tried rocking her pelvis to lure his fingers into her pussy but Mitchell was quick enough to pull his hand away. He then brought his head down and kissed her thighs softly. She hated how he would get dangerously close to her pussy and then pull away, making her moan loudly.

"I want you," he heard her whisper urgently. He brought his head up and smiled at her.

'Not yet," he said before going back down to kiss her thighs. She moaned and clutched the bedding tightly when he ran his tongue along her skin. All this was too much for her. He brought his head up and kissed her chin before claiming her lips once more. The way she kissed him, with great urgency, with great passion...she was definitely at the point of no return. She reached down and undid his pants and then used her legs to push them off. She probably thought that if she did not take matters in her own hands, her torture would last much longer. The way she roughly pushed his pants off ensured that not only did she get his pants off but his boxers too. She flipped him over, getting him under her, and then held the two ends of his shirt before pulling them apart sending his shirt buttons flying all over the room. At this point Mitchell thought, *"I am going to need an entire wardrobe."* He looked up at her as she pulled his pants off his legs. She wanted to get his cock inside her so much but she needed to make him feel the same torture he had taken her through.

She kissed his chest and then slowly worked her way down his torso until she got to his waist. She teased him by slowly running her fingers across his stomach and then deliberately brushed the head of his cock. She smiled when she felt his cock twitch again in response to her touch. She looked at him and smiled again as she ran her fingers on the head of his cock again before moving lower down his legs to give her a complete view of his throbbing cock. She used her knees to force his legs apart and then brought her head down to kiss his thigh the same way he had done to her. By this time, Mitchell was moaning his pleasure, dying to have his cock inside her – anywhere inside her really, in her mouth or in her pussy. He just needed to be inside her but she would not let him. It was her turn to make him beg for her attention. He moaned as he felt her running her tongue on his thigh, dangerously near his cock, only to pull away. The height of his troubles came when she slowly ran her tongue on his sac and then sucked his balls. This time, a mere moan would not cut it. He groaned and reached for her head, missing her by inches.

She looked at him and smiled. Maybe it was time to make him moan even louder. She slowly took his cock in her hand and began running her tongue along its length, making him moan again. She ran her tongue on one side of his cock and then on the other side before she let her tongue circle the bulbous head of his cock. She could feel him getting harder in her mouth and she decided to just go all the way and took him inside her mouth. She took him as deep as she could, making her almost gag as she felt his cock pressing at the back of her neck. She bobbed her head on his crotch for a while as she held his balls in her hands, slowly massaging him. By the way she was going, she knew that she was not giving him much of a choice. He would blow any time now unless she slowed down. She pulled his cock out of her mouth and looked at the monster she had helped create before she lay down next to him.

"My turn," she said in a whisper. She knew that Mitchell at that moment was only thinking of getting inside her, but he had to yield too. She had already done it and it was only fair if he would do it too. Mitchell found all the strength he had in him and got in between her legs. She spread her legs and looked up at him as he looked at her pussy. By this time, she was wetter than ever. This time around, he did not have to hold back. Without any warning, he pushed his index finger inside her, making her let out a sharp moan.

"Shhh, you are going to wake up the baby," Mitchell said as he fingered her. She turned her head and bit into the pillow as Mitchell pulled his finger out of her, only to push two long fingers deep inside her. She muffled her moans and screams for as long as she could before she finally felt an orgasm building up inside her.

"No more...I want you now," she begged as she looked into his eyes. Mitchell smiled and pulled his fingers out of her. He settled in between her legs and let himself slide inside her in one swift move. She wrapped her arms around him as he began thrusting into her. He was clearly making up for the torture he had made her endure earlier because this time, all he was doing was just thrusting into her as if his life depended on it. The only sound in the room was of his balls slamming against her pussy and their moans.

When Mitchell finally slowed down, Natasha took this opportunity to take the reins. She once again flipped him over so that she could be on top of him. She looked down at him as she began to slowly grind herself against him, making him moan loudly. She was moving slowly as she looked at him, almost too slow. His moans were more of a complaint than pleasure. For Mitchell she was moving too slow for comfort. He suddenly grabbed her hips and began pulling her down on his cock. She moaned as control was taken from her. Mitchell was drop fucking her onto his cock with immense pressure and even though she knew that he would bust his nuts any time now, she was relieved because her own orgasm was approaching fast. It was not long before Natasha began bucking her hips on him as her orgasm rocked through her. The pressure of her pulsating pussy on his cock was too much for Mitchell as he exploded inside her almost immediately.

"I had really missed that," Natasha said panting as she collapsed on top of Mitchell.

"I missed you," Mitchell said before planting a kiss on her forehead.

She smiled and closed her eyes. This was definitely worth making up for. "I don't ever want to lose you. I can't lose you," he said in a whisper. Natasha lifted her head and kissed him softly.

"Don't worry, because you never will," she said with a smile.

Book 8.

Igniting The Passion With Mr White

Chapter 1

Natasha took a long deep breath when she came home from work. She could not remember the last time the house was that quiet…maybe before she had Alexis. She kicked her shoes off and walked to the kitchen to fix herself a snack. She had at least a couple of hours before Rita called it quits on playing mommy.

"Salty snack or sugary sweetness…salt…sugar…" she wondered as her eyes shifted from the leftover club sandwich to the red velvet cake. She suddenly decided that she could have both. After all, she had a few more years before she could start worrying about setting a bad example for her daughter. She placed the sandwich and cake on the counter and quickly washed her hands. She then leaned against the counter as she waited for her sandwich to heat up in the microwave. *"A glass of wine would be perfect,"* she thought as she noticed the bottle of wine on the counter. Maybe it was a good thing her cleaner Aurelia was on her leave. Natasha would not have noticed the bottle otherwise. She poured herself a glass and then took a bite of the cake. She frowned at the weird combination of tastes before spitting it out. She put the cake back in the fridge and then sat down to enjoy her now warm tasting sandwich.

As she ate she thought of her day at work. Actually, the last couple of weeks had been great…or at least they had the potential to turn out great. What happened was that after the company lost one of its top clients, it was all hands on deck trying to get another one to fill the void. That meant working like crazy in Natasha's department what with all the advertising campaigns that had to be prepared. And because of this, she was out of the house as early as six-thirty and the earliest she would come back was around eight in the evening. By that time, little Alexis was already in bed and she and Mitchell, well, the only thing they wanted to do was go to bed and sleep. Their marriage had been a weird kind of schedule. Wake up, drive to work, drop Alexis in office day care, spend the day in numerous meetings and finally, come home. Basically that had been her life, at least, the life she had come to know for the past few weeks. Matter of fact, the only reason she was home this early was because one of her meetings got cancelled and she had given strict instructions to Stacy not to schedule another meeting. This was the only way she would get to have a few minutes to herself....a few very needed minutes. She had everything planned out. She would get home, have some food....well, in this case, half a club sandwich and a glass of wine and then have a long luxurious soak as she watched the night's episode of America's Got Talent. Well, that never really happened. All she wanted to do was lie in bed and think of how everything had been between her and her husband. The thing was, she wanted to keep the flame alive but there was never enough time. She and Mitchell worked all day and Alexis had so much energy when they got back home that by the time they got to bed, they fell asleep almost immediately.

When she finished her sandwich, Natasha stood up and walked to her room. She still had her glass of wine in her hand and the one prayer she kept on reciting in her head was that Mitchell would not come home in the next hour and a half. She took a sip of wine as she started the bath. As she took off her jewelry, she heard a buzz and a definitive "ding" from her computer that showed she had a message, an email maybe. She sat on the edge of the bed and scrolled her messages.

"Work, who knew?" she thought sarcastically. Her private page suddenly popped up and she smiled. She had resorted to an online diary after getting married since she started losing track of her hard copies. *"Maybe I should have an entry. It*

has been forever and that water is going to take another few minutes," she thought as she got comfortable on the bed. She took a deep breath and began typing.

Dear Diary,

*Wow. It has been forever since my last entry. Maybe I am becoming a lazy writer, maybe it's about time I switched to video diaries...*she paused and smiled. *Yeah that is not going to happen. So, of late I feel like I am not having fun in my marriage. Okay, don't get me wrong. People always tell me that what me and Mitchell have is exactly what they want, and I love my husband to death. He and Alexis are the two most important people in my life and I would never trade them for anything in the world. But that is the upside. There is a downside. Not that I am complaining but I miss the alone time I used to have with Mitchell. For starters, I have not had sex for almost two weeks. That never happened before. Me and Mitchell would get down and dirty anywhere, anytime but...yeah, those were fine days. So now, it's just me and long showers and even those don't help. Yeah I know most women use the shower nozzle but honestly, there is a way Mitchell uses his magic wand that just makes me shiver and yes, I just called his manhood a magic wand. He would kill me if he found out. So, yeah that is what I have been reduced to. But I will make it work.*

She was still typing when she heard the front door open and close.

"You have got to be kidding me," she thought as she slammed her laptop shut. *"Rita is not supposed to drop Alexis over for another hour,"* she thought as she walked to the living room.

"Oh, you *are* home already," Mitchell said as he pushed Alexis' stroller into the house. Natasha forced a smile.

"Yeah, I just got home. I was about to have a bath," she said. "I thought Rita was supposed to drop off Alexis tonight," she added as she looked down at a sleeping Alexis.

"Yeah, she was apparently cranky and she was running a fever..."

"...a fever? What the hell? Why didn't she call me?" Natasha asked in a panic, cutting him short. She touched Alexis' forehead to feel her temperature. Mitchell closed the door and leaned forward to kiss her.

"She's fine and Rita did call you. She said you were not picking up," Mitchell said with a smile.

"Really?" Natasha asked. Mitchell nodded.

"Yeah, I called you too," he said. Natasha walked to where she had dropped her bag earlier and rummaged through the contents of her purse.

"I can't find my phone. I probably left it in the car," she said looking at Mitchell.

"Don't worry about it," he said with a smile.

"I'm really sorry," she said again.

"Hey, I already told you. Don't worry about it," he said. "Our little girl is teething by the way. That's why she was cranky and feverish," Mitchell smiled proudly.

"Aww, she is growing up so fast," Natasha said, squealing.

She walked back to the stroller and picked the baby up. "I'll tuck her in. She must be tired," she said. Mitchell leaned forward and kissed Alexis' small forehead before Natasha carried her to the nursery.

Mitchell walked to the kitchen and, like his wife, made himself a quick snack. He was seated at the counter when Natasha walked back in.

"So how was your day?" he asked. She smiled and took a deep breath.

"Good, but my last meeting got cancelled," she said as she sat down next to him. "I thought I would come home and relax," she added with a smile.

"Good for you. Have you already had your bath yet?" he asked. Natasha smiled and shook her head.

"I was just about to," she said.

"Good. Maybe I should join you," he said smiling. Natasha looked into his eyes and nodded.

"Maybe you should," she said as she got off the stool and slowly walked to their bedroom. She was carefully swaying her hips, making sure he noticed her effort. As she walked she raised her dress, showing her soft inside thigh to him. She could hear Mitchell's soft footsteps behind her. When she got to the bedroom, she took her dress off and let it drop to the floor. She turned around and then undid her bra, letting her full breasts free before finally taking off her panties. She looked at him and smiled before she went into the bathroom.

Mitchell did not waste any time. He quickly took off his own clothes before he joined her in the bathroom. She was pouring her bath oils and gels into the water when he finally came in. Her eyes could not help but drop to his already hard and inviting cock. She looked up at him and smiled. "Are you just going to stand there or are you going to join me in this very inviting water?" she asked as she swirled the water with her hand. Mitchell walked up to her and held her by the waist. He had half a mind to bend her over and push his cock inside her right there and then. But after the way things had been between them, the distance and the estranged sex life, he wanted to savor the moment. He turned her around and kissed her lips softly. He let out a soft moan when she playfully bit his bottom lip. This always made her smile. She pulled away and looked into his eyes.

"What is it about you, woman, that makes me so damn weak?" he asked. She slipped an arm around his neck and smiled.

"I don't know about you sweetie, but I think it's called love," she said before kissing him again. She pulled away and looked into his eyes. She let her gaze drop down to his throbbing cock and smiled. "I'll do you if you promise to do me," she said smiling. Mitchell turned off the water and pulled her out of the bathroom. He sat on the edge of the bed and threw his head back as Natasha knelt in between his legs. He closed his eyes as he felt her lips engulf his girth, making him let out a long low moan under his breath. Natasha put his hand under his scrotal sac as she went on sucking him. She knew how much he loved having his balls squeezed gently while she sucked on his cock. Natasha let her tongue roll around the top of his cock, tasting the salty pre-cum as Mitchell struggled to stay still. Natasha knew that he would not last much longer, not with the way she was working his cock. She sucked on him, long and hard as Mitchell moaned and groaned as he felt himself about to explode inside her mouth.

He raised his head and looked at Natasha who was now

bobbing her head on his crotch. Seeing his cock disappear in her wet mouth was a sight to behold. She did it so well, so naturally…in another life, one that Mitchell would never have known her, she would have done this professionally. He suddenly held her face in her hands and pulled her away from his crotch, making his cock pop out of her mouth.

"I am going to cum," he said in a whisper, perhaps from being so turned on, pushed almost over the edge.

"That's okay. I want you to," Natasha said smiling. Mitchell let go of her face and she went back to sucking him long and hard. And he was right. It was not long before he exploded in her mouth and Natasha, like the star she was, swallowed every drop. When she finally brought her head up, he was still hard but he had made her a promise and she was not about to let him off the hook before he fulfilled it.

She looked at him as she lifted her head to kiss him. He could still taste himself on her lips. "Now, do me. You promised," she said in a whisper as she rolled herself off his body. She lay on her back and spread her legs. Mitchell was already weak from his powerful orgasm just moments earlier but she was right, he had promised her. She closed her eyes and tried to control her breath as she felt his lips on her soft inside thigh. He let his tongue run up and down her thigh as he pushed his index finger inside her pussy which by now was sopping wet. He smiled to himself as he began working his finger in and out of her, slowly at first and then faster as he went on. He could not help but get even more turned on when he looked at his wife who was now panting and moaning as he fingered her.

He slowly lowered his head and inhaled the rich scent of her pussy before he took her clit into his mouth and sucked hard. This was too much for her. He tasted a fresh gush of her pre-cum in his mouth. He took his finger out of her pussy and thrust his tongue deep inside her. Natasha cried out loudly as she felt the double pleasure of Mitchell's sucking and tongue fucking. She held on to the bedding and grabbed a fistful in each hand as her vaginal muscles worked against her. She was getting closer and closer to the point of no return and by the way he was going, Mitchell was not about to slow down.

He suddenly pulled away from her and brought his body up. She looked into his eyes as he lowered his head to meet her lips in one long sensual kiss. She wrapped her arms around him as she allowed herself to get lost in his kiss. They were still in a tight lip lock when Mitchell decided to just go in for the kill. Natasha let out a loud scream as she felt Mitchell bury his cock inside her in one sudden move.

"Oh my god..." she moaned as he began fucking her. He did not start slow like he usually did. He just went right into her, slamming himself against her hard. His long strokes were hard and rapid, knocking the air right out of Natasha's mouth. She suddenly cried out as she felt the pressure building inside her pussy. Mitchell put his hands on her shoulders and began shaking her. She looked into his eyes and suddenly cried out. Mitchell was no longer Mitchell. It was Rita.

Natasha sat up in bed. She had beads of sweat running down her forehead. She looked up at Rita who walked to the bathroom and turned the water off.

"A few more minutes and that bathroom would have been flooded," she said as she walked back into the bedroom. Natasha was still confused. All that was a dream? She never had sex dreams....**ever.**

"Are you okay?" Rita asked. Natasha nodded and climbed off the bed. She splashed some cold water on her face before walking back to the bedroom. She could feel the wetness in her panties.

"Where's the baby?" she asked looking around.

"In her room, fast asleep," Rita said.

"How did you get in?" Natasha asked as she walked back to the bedroom.

"My spare key but that is not the important thing right now. What's up with you?" she asked as Natasha sat down on the edge of the bed.

"Nothing…just tired and a bad dream," she answered. Rita smiled.

"I don't think that dream was as bad as you are letting on," she said. Natasha felt her cheeks flush. "Oh my God, it was a sex dream, wasn't it? Who was it? Was it Mitchell or some other hot fantasy guy?" she asked.

"Of course it was Mitchell but I have never had a sex dream in my life," Natasha said.

"Never?" Rita asked, surprised. Natasha shook her head. "Then what triggered it?" Rita asked.

Natasha shrugged. "Girl, I'm your best friend. We have no secrets and you know you need to tell me. You are going to tell me anyway so just let it rip," Rita said. Natasha shrugged again and then took a long deep breath.

"I have not had sex in two weeks," Natasha said in a low voice.

"What? Have you guys been fighting or something?" Rita

asked, surprised. Natasha and Mitchell were like sex crazed rabbits. Getting them to keep their hands off each other was harder than feeding broccoli to a five-year-old. Natasha shook her head. "Then what is it? Are you guys okay?" Rita asked, concerned.

"Yeah we are but work has been draining us. We barely have time to talk, let alone have sex," Natasha said sadly as she heard the front door open and close. This time she pinched herself to make sure she was not dreaming.

"I think that's him. I better make myself scarce," Rita said as she stood up. Natasha smiled at her.

"Thanks for taking Alexis," she said.

"That little princess is fun. It was my pleasure," Rita said as she walked out. She smiled at Mitchell and gave him a high five as she walked past before whispering "You got a lot of work to do in there, brother," to him.

Mitchell gave Rita a puzzled look before he walked into the bedroom. He sat next to Natasha and shook his head.

"What was that about?" he asked. Natasha blushed. She had no idea how she was going to start explaining the last few minutes.

Chapter 2

Mitchell looked at Natasha and smiled. He snapped his fingers in front of her face.

"Earth to my beautiful wife. What was all that about?" he asked. Natasha smiled as he sat down next to her. "Rita just told me I've got work to do? Is there something I missed?" he asked. Natasha rested her head on his shoulder and sighed.

"Don't worry about it," she said, giving him a weak smile.

"Come on, babe. I can see that there's something on your mind," he said. Natasha took a long deep breath. She looked at him and shrugged. She might as well just tell him. Otherwise, he would bug her all night.

"I had a sex dream, Mitchell," she said looking into his eyes. "With you," she added quickly when she saw the disapproving look in his eyes.

"That's a good thing, right?" he asked. She shook her head.

"Sweetie, I never have sex dreams. Ever," she said as she held his hands in hers. "I need to have sex. Crazy, wild, porn sex," she added. Mitchell smiled.

"How many times have I told you I love you?" he asked as he pulled her close. "Right now I feel so in love with you," he said before bringing his head down to kiss her. She smiled after pulling away from his grip.

"I know you are tired but Alexis is asleep and I just had a sex dream. What do you say you fuck me right here?" she asked as she pushed his jacket off his shoulders.

"Ditto," he said before kissing her again. She hated to admit it, but this kiss was nothing compared to the way Mitchell had kissed her in the dream. He suddenly pulled away and pushed her down onto the bed. He looked down at her as he took off the rest of his clothes. Natasha smiled and took off her dress before lying down on the bed. She looked at him as he got on top of her. He smiled as he brought his head down to kiss her again while his free hand worked to push her panties off. She closed her eyes as she felt him pushing his cock inside her. Again, she hated to admit it, but this time, the sex was just too boring. It was like so unlike them, so routine, like some old boring couple.

"I don't think I can cum and I can't fake it either," she thought as she lay there. She put her hands on his shoulders and pushed him away. He stopped thrusting and looked down on her.

"What's wrong? Did I hurt you?" he asked. She smiled and shook her head.

"This is not us, baby," she said. "Our sex has always been explosive and fun and I don't want to be one of those people who pretend that everything is okay when it's not," she said. Mitchell smiled and kissed her forehead before rolling off her.

"That's what Rita meant, huh?" he said as he lay next to her. She nodded and interlaced her fingers with his.

"We are either at work or sleeping. We forgot what it meant to have fun and I need it, baby," she said in a low voice.

"I agree," Mitchell said. "How about some sun and sand?" he asked. She shrugged and shook her head.

"I was thinking something cooler, in terms of temperature at least. Aspen?" she asked. Mitchell laughed.

"You want to ski?" he asked.

"Who said anything about skiing? I just want to have an excuse to spend long hours in bed, naked," Natasha said.

"Well, we need a sitter for Alexis," he said smiling.

"My dad is always a willing candidate," Natasha said. Mitchell smiled. He had promised himself that he would always put his family first and this time, he was about to do exactly that.

*****

Mitchell and Natasha had everything planned for the next morning. The baby's bag was already packed. They had already talked to Eric and Estelle, who were all too happy when Natasha mentioned she wanted to leave Alexis with them for a few days. After making all the plans that needed to be made, Natasha stepped into the bathroom. She had just stepped out of the shower when a frantic Mitchell walked into the bedroom.

"Whatever happens, you need to know that I love you and that I had no hand in this," Mitchell said. Natasha unwrapped the towel that held her wet hair in place.

"Okay, this sounds serious but before you tell me your big news, who was at the door?" she asked as she sat down in front of her dressing mirror. She took her body lotion and squeezed a generous amount on her hand.

"My news has everything to do with who was at the door," Mitchell said as he rubbed his hands together. Natasha looked at him and raised an eyebrow.

"Honey? What's wrong? You look nervous and agitated," she said.

"My parents are here," Mitchell suddenly blurted out. Natasha shook her head.

"I thought they were in Europe," she said. Mitchell rolled his eyes.

"They are always in Europe. I'm actually surprised they made it to our wedding. But apparently they are in town and they are here, in our house," he said. "Right now," he added.

"Then that's a good thing, right?" she asked as she rubbed the lotion on her legs.

"Well, there is that and there is the little fact that they want to take Alexis," Mitchell said.

"Take her where exactly?" she asked as she stood up. Mitchell looked at her as she began dressing herself,. first her panties and then her bra. When Natasha noticed that he had gone silent and was now staring at her, she looked at him and snapped her fingers. "Keep talking, Schmidt. There is nothing here that you haven't seen before," she said as she pulled on a pair of sky blue skinny jeans.

"I just wanted to have some mental picture so I know where to escape to when my parents begin talking," he said.

"Fine. Where do they want to take the baby?" she asked again as she pulled on her pink chiffon sleeveless top.

"Well, Mother and Father know that we are planning a vacation and they want to take Alexis for a few days," he said. Natasha smiled.

"That's great. We did not even know if Nan and Daddy would be free. This is a load off our shoulders, Mitch," she said smiling.

"Sweetie you don't understand. These are MY parents. They are not the same as Eric or Estelle. They are horrific, button pushing people. I really don't want all that negative energy around my daughter," he said. Natasha rolled her eyes as she sat down in front of her dressing mirror again.

"It's a few days. They cannot do that much damage in just a couple of days," she said as she applied a coat of mascara.

"Clearly you don't know who my parents are," he said as he sat down at the edge of the bed. He took a deep breath and buried his face in his hands as Natasha touched up her face. When she turned around and saw him seated there with his face in his hands, her heart went out to him.

"It's really that bad?" she asked. Mitchell looked at him and nodded. "But they can't be that bad if they raised you," she said as she looked at him smiling.

"I just don't know why we have to keep up appearances except for the mandatory Fourth of July, Christmas and Thanksgiving," he said as he rested his head on her shoulder. Natasha smiled.

"We can handle this just fine," she said. "Come on," she said as she pulled him up to his feet. Mitchell groaned as they walked to the living room where Mitchell's parents were busy making goo-goo noises to the baby and Alexis seemed to love it. She was chuckling loudly as Mitchell's father lifted her up and Mrs. Schmidt was busy playing peek-a-boo.

"Something is wrong," Mitchell said in a whisper. Natasha

looked at him as they stood at the entrance of the living room.

"Why? What makes you say that?" she asked looking concerned.

"These people are too human to be my parents," he whispered. Natasha smiled and punched him playfully on the arm before she walked into the room.

"Mr. and Mrs. Schmidt. So nice to see you," she said with a smile. She gave Mrs. Schmidt a hug and she was given a kiss on the cheek in return before Mitchell's father gave her another kiss on her other cheek. Natasha gave a little wave to Alexis who was at that moment in the arms of Mitchell's dad.

"Natasha, you look better by the day. Having a baby agrees with you. Maybe you should have another one?" Mrs. Schmidt, or Naomi as she liked to be called, said. Natasha laughed.

"Please, I am still recovering from this one," Natasha said laughing.

"Well, for the time being this little girl will do. Yes you will," Mr. Schmidt said as he rubbed his head in Alexis' tummy, making her squeal loudly.

"Mitchell told me that you guys just got here. You should join us for breakfast," Natasha said smiling.

"But we're not insisting. You can leave at your own pleasure," Mitchell said loud enough for his parents to hear.

"Come on Mitchell. Be nice to the people who gave you life," Natasha said as she led Naomi to the kitchen. "I had already prepared some batter. I can make some waffles," she added with a smile.

"Waffles sound lovely darling," Naomi said as she sat down. She held Natasha's hand and whispered, "It is good to see he landed a good one." Natasha laughed.

"I heard that, Mother," Mitchell said as he walked into the kitchen followed by his father who was still making faces at the baby.

"I intended for you to hear that, honey," Naomi said as she looked at Natasha who was pouring some batter onto the waffle iron.

"When did you guys even come back? I thought you were still in Europe," Mitchell said as he sat down.

"We had to come back for Elijah Parsley. His mother-in-law just died," Mr. Schmidt said. He looked at Natasha whose face was as red as a beet from holding back her laughter. "It's okay, sweetie. You can laugh. I did too the first time I heard his name," he said with a smile. Natasha giggled.

"So his name is Parsley? Like the herb?" she asked as she looked at him.

"Yeah," Mitchell said smiling. His smile died down as soon as he remembered that the name had come up with some bad news. "So, what happened?" he asked looking at his father.

"Well, the woman had a long fight with leukemia. I guess it's better this way but Eli is not taking this too well. And since he is the only friend I have since my college years, I have to be there for him," he said.

"And now we have this little princess to light up the mood," Naomi said with a smile.

"Yeah, how did you know about us taking some time off, anyway?" Natasha asked as she served the waffles on individual plates.

"His sister is not as secretive as he is, lucky us," Mr. Schmidt said smiling.

"So, the two workaholics have finally decided to take some time off," Naomi said smiling. "What gives?" she asked as Natasha set the plates in front of them. She walked to the fridge and came back with some orange juice.

"Well, since we got Alexis we have found that we rarely get time to ourselves and the situation only got worse when I went back to work. Mitchell and I just need some time to work on our marriage," she said as she poured everyone some juice. Naomi and her husband exchanged glances.

"Work on the marriage? Is there trouble in paradise already?" she asked looking at her son.

"No, not like that. We…um…need some alone time…away from all the madness at NSCS and it is hard doing something romantic with this bundle of joy," Natasha explained.

"Yeah, the Windsor Resort in England said they don't allow baggage when I mentioned I have a ten month old daughter," Mitchell said. "Baggage," he scoffed under his breath.

"Ah, your story reminds me of the good old days when your mother and I were trying to rekindle our romance. The only reason some of the leading hotels accepted our reservation was because of a generous donation here and there," Mr. Schmidt said smiling.

"You bribed them?" Natasha asked her eyes wide.

"No, I would never do something that heinous. As I said I made a donation to various charities," Mr. Schmidt said quickly. Mitchell looked at him and smiled. "Don't you dare judge me, son," he said before using his free hand to take a sip of his juice.

"It has been thirty years and this is the first time he has admitted to having had a hand in getting us a reservation. I knew that phony story about you having quote unquote friends in high places was a hoax," Naomi said with a smile. "So, where are you two going?" she asked. Mitchell took a long deep breath and shrugged.

"We were thinking of taking some time in Mexico but Tasha wants some time in Aspen. So we got the cabin for the long weekend," he said smiling.

"By the way, when he said 'we' at the beginning of the sentence, he actually meant him. I wanted Aspen right from the get go," Natasha said matter-of-factly.

"God knows you will need the chilly weather," Naomi said. Natasha felt her cheeks flush. She suddenly regretted inviting them over for breakfast.

"So Mother, you have to promise not to do anything drastic with Alexis," Mitchell said quickly. Naomi frowned.

"What makes you say that? And even if I could, it's not like I could get her away from Charles," Naomi said as she glanced at her husband who had gone back to playing with the baby.

"What? You can't blame me. She is adorable," Mr. Schmidt said with a smile.

"Of course she is. She is mine," Mitchell said proudly.

"Hey, those are my genes. Your father's side of the family is all fat and double chins," Naomi said quickly.

"Guess I hit the genetic jackpot," Mitchell said sarcastically.

"No, the one who hit the jackpot is Alexis. With your hair and her mother's great features…" Mr. Schmidt took a long deep breath. "Please tell me you will get all men within a hundred feet screened before they even think of talking to her?" he said looking at Mitchell.

"Please, she will not know what sex she is until she is thirty," he said laughing.

"Good luck with that. I tried that with your sister," Naomi said laughing. "It's a good thing she joined that Christian club thing," she added.

"So anyway, mother. You cannot dress my baby up like the queen of England or Lady Gaga and most importantly, you cannot enter her in toddler pageants," Mitchell said with finality.

Natasha looked at him and then at Naomi. "You do *that*?" she asked, shocked.

"Come on, that's the old me. How could I possibly pull off getting her into a pageant in one weekend? I don't even think there are any pageants this weekend," Naomi said. "Unless I stage one myself," she added in what she thought was a whisper.

"Don't even think about it, Mother," Mitchell said sharply. The last thing he needed was photographs of his daughter on the internet. So far, he had managed to lead a normal life despite the paparazzi that fought tooth and nail to get a snapshot of the latest addition to the Nolan Schmidt family tree.

"Don't worry son. I am not letting this one out of my sight," Mr. Schmidt said with a smile.

"So when are you leaving?" Naomi asked before she took a bite of her waffle.

"In a couple of hours. I just wanted to drop by my dad's and see them before I leave," Natasha said with a smile.

"Yeah that will give us enough time to get to the airport and check in before the rush," Mitchell said. His father looked at him and frowned.

"You are flying commercial?" he asked. Mitchell smiled and nodded. "Since when?" his father asked surprised.

"Well, I loaned the jet to one of our newest clients. He gets back tonight and I didn't want to wait that long," Mitchell said. "If it helps, it is first class," he added. Naomi took the last bite and then took her last sip before standing up.

"We'll get going then. I don't want Eric thinking that we are influencing you negatively," Naomi said.

"He would never think that," Natasha said.

"I am taking his grandbaby away. He is going to be pissed but I need time with my favorite granddaughter," Naomi said as she picked Alexis from her husband's arms.

"Alexis is your only granddaughter, Mother," Mitchell said as he walked to the nursery to get Alexis' bag. When he got back, Natasha was giving Alexis little hugs and kisses. It was always hard for her to say goodbye to the baby, even at the office daycare. He was actually surprised that she was willing to leave her behind for three long days but he was determined to make the trip count. By the time they got back he would have made sure that the only sex dreams in his wife's life would be the ones she witnessed on TV. He was prepared to sex her out…as soon as he called Eric and Estelle to cancel the weekend plans. He knew that talking himself out of this would be hard but three days in Aspen with his wife was worth it.

Chapter 3

After Mitchell's parents left, Mitchell and Natasha did not waste any time. Being the last minuters that they were, they went right to packing their bags for the weekend.

"I don't think you will need all that. I doubt you will need any clothes at all," Mitchell said as he watched Natasha packing. She looked up at him and smiled.

"Well we are going to be seen in the airport and we cannot travel in our birthday suits," she said as she put the final item of clothing, a pair of boxer shorts for Mitchell, inside the suitcase. He looked at her and smiled.

"There is that and there is the little fact that I noticed you packed your laptop too," he said. Natasha looked at him and shook her head.

"No, Mitchell. I need to carry my laptop," she said. He stood up and walked towards her.

"Give me one reason, one good reason, and I'll let you bring it," he said as he looked into her eyes. Natasha shrugged.

"Well, I…I need to, um….," she looked into his eyes and realized that she was fighting a losing battle. "Okay, fine. I don't have a good reason, any reason," she said. Mitchell gave her a smile, that all knowing "I'm right, you're wrong" smile. She looked at him and shrugged again. "Don't you dare gloat," she said.

"I was not about to. I just want to make sure that the only thing keeping you busy is me," Mitchell said as he brought his head down to kiss her. Natasha closed her eyes and let herself respond to his soft kiss.

Their romantic moment was interrupted by the loud ringing of her phone. Mitchell pulled away from her and looked at her. "Yeah, we will have to talk about the phones too," he said. Natasha smiled and walked towards the night stand where she had placed her phone. She looked at the screen and then looked at Mitchell. "What? Who is it?" he asked looking concerned.

"It's Stacy. She knows better than to call me today," Natasha said.

"Had you told her about us taking the weekend off?" Mitchell asked. Natasha nodded. "Don't answer it," he suddenly said.

"It could be important. She would not have called otherwise," she said as she slid her finger on the screen to answer her phone. "Hey Stacy," she said.

"Hi, Tasha. I am sorry to call you today. I know you and Mitchell are probably on your way to the airport but this is important," Stacy said. Natasha looked at Mitchell and then sat down at the edge of the bed.

"Okay. What's up?" she asked.

"I've tried to reach Mitchell too but his phone keeps on going straight to voicemail," Stacy said.

"Hold up, he's right here. I'll put you on speaker," Natasha said looking at Mitchell. "Right, you're on," she said.

"Hey, Stacy. Everything okay?" Mitchell asked as he took a seat next to Natasha on the bed. They heard Stacy take a long deep breath.

"Well, it depends on how you look at it. If I was in your shoes, this would not be very good but it is generally good news for the company," Stacy said matter of factly.

"Stacy, what is going on?" Mitchell asked in an authoritative voice. Stacy knew she was no longer dealing with her laid back boss.

"I had a call this morning about a Naima Nassir, the daughter to Sheikh Fayed Nassir," Stacy began.

"*The* Fayed Nassir? The Arab billionaire?" Mitchell asked.

"Exactly. He has been looking for opportunities to invest in the States and he has decided on what he wants to do," Stacy said.

"Okay, what is it?" Mitchell asked.

"As of ten minutes ago, the Nassir Foundation owns sixty percent of Lovell Telecommunications and Naima made a call to Natasha's office," Stacy continued.

"My office? Why?" Natasha asked. "I don't even know this Naima Nazir," she said.

"Nassir," Mitchell corrected her.

"My point exactly," Natasha said. "Why would she call my office?" she asked.

"Well, your work is known far and wide Tasha. She said the only company she wants handling her campaign is NSCS but only on one condition," Stacy said. "That Natasha personally handles her campaign," she added. Natasha looked at Mitchell in surprise.

"Okay," she said not sure of what she was supposed to say at that point.

"Okay? Baby, the Nassir family is worth billions. Business with them would be a great bump in our financials," Mitchell said excitedly.

"Really?" Natasha asked.

"Um Tasha, the campaign is already priced at thirty million dollars," Stacy said. Mitchell looked at her as his eyes grew wide.

"I'm sorry. Did you just say thirty million dollars?" he asked.

"Yes and that said, you guys have to reschedule your plans because Naima will be here in half an hour," Stacy said. Mitchell and Natasha exchanged glances. "So, yeah. I told you it was kind of good news, bad news situation," she added.

"I see what you mean, Stacy. See you in a few," Natasha said as she hung up. She looked at Mitchell and shrugged.

"So much for flying commercial, right?" he said.

"Guess we will just be taking the jet after all," Natasha said as she walked to her closet. She took off her comfortable pants and top and pulled out a green sleeveless dress. It was just what she needed. Pencil design, knee high and it was the kind of dress that you could wear from the office and straight to happy hour. She pulled out a pair of black peep toe pumps and a red and black checkered coat and then put it on. By the time she walked out of her walk-in closet, Mitchell had loaded their bags in the car. It seemed he had the same thoughts as her. They would do the meeting and then go right to the airport. She waited for him to get changed and then walked out to the car.

"This is it, huh?" she said as she buckled herself in the passenger seat.

"Yeah. Maybe losing a four million dollar account was the pathway to getting a thirty million dollar client," he said as he started the car and pulled out of the driveway.

"So, what do I need to know about this Nassir Foundation?" she asked as she pinned her hair back, letting her rich black curls pile up in a ponytail.

"The Nassir Foundation was set up in the late eighties. It was initially just another charity but soon they began venturing out to more commercial business to fund their charities. They support over four hundred shelters and they also run a school, one of the biggest schools in the Middle East. My grandfather worked with the foundation sometime in the early nineties but that relationship did not last," Mitchell explained.

"How so?" Natasha asked.

"They were out of commercial business for a while. I had heard rumors about them in merger talks with Lovell but I thought they were just that, rumors," he said and then looked at Natasha. "If they asked for you specifically, then baby you are the star I always knew you were," he added.

"Well, I knew I was good but this is the golden feather in my hat," Natasha said as they pulled into the company parking lot.

"You got this, honey," Mitchell said looking into her eyes. She smiled and nodded.

"So, one more thing. On a scale of one to ten, where one is

the Malibu Princess and ten is the royal family, where would you rate the Nassirs?" she asked. Mitchell smiled.

"Like fourteen," he said. "These guys could buy not just England but the entire United Kingdom, the United States and still have enough money left to have at least a hundred thousand dollars in every bank account in the world," he said excitedly. Natasha frowned.

"Really?" she asked.

"Okay, I may have exaggerated a little," Mitchell said smiling.

"A little?" Natasha asked as she got out of the car.

"Okay, a lot but I did not exaggerate about their net worth. These guys are the definition of filthy rich," he said as the two of them walked towards the elevator. As they rode up to the office, Mitchell looked at her. "I'm sorry," he said in a low voice. Natasha shook her head and frowned.

"What for?" she asked.

"Our perfect weekend is ruined," he said. She smiled and shook her head.

"No it's not. It's a meeting. We will strategize and then fly off to Aspen. Then when we come back on Monday we go back to work," she said as she leaned forward to give him a small kiss just as the elevator doors opened. She smiled at him as they walked out of the elevators.

Natasha was not surprised that it was business as usual. That was the kind of place she worked in. Stacy had already set up the board room.

"You look spectacular as usual," Stacy said smiling at Natasha who smiled back at her and mouthed a "thank you." "It's good to see you, Mitchell," she added.

"Hey Stacy," Mitchell said.

"You guys are just in time. Naima should be getting here any time now," Stacy said. "I assume Mitchell has already briefed you on everything you need to know about the Nassir family?" she asked turning to Natasha.

"Bits and pieces," she said. Stacy handed her a tablet.

"That's everything on the family, their foundation and basically anything that could come up," Stacy said. Natasha frowned.

"You do know I am not some crazed paralegal with a photographic memory right? I can't have all these in my head in five minutes,' she said scrolling through what seemed like hundreds of files.

"I should have said for future reference," Stacy said before turning to look outside. "I think she is here," she said as Natasha noticed a tall brown-skinned woman walking towards the board room.

Natasha had to admit, Naima Nassir was not what she expected. She had the whole image of her in a burqa but the woman making her way towards them was tall, maybe five nine, and had a slim figure like a model or something. She had long brown wavy hair cascading onto her shoulders and she wore a short black dress and a matching pair of black platform heels.

"So, I am guessing she is one of those reformed Muslim people?" Stacy asked as they looked at her.

"Actually there is no such thing as a reformed Muslim. According to my knowledge," Mitchell said.

"Hmm, just smile, people. We can talk about this when she leaves," Natasha said as the front office girl opened the door to the boardroom.

"Mr. Schmidt, Mrs. Schmidt, this is Naima Nassir," she said before turning to Naima. She whispered a few words and then walked away, leaving Naima and two other gentlemen with Mitchell and Natasha. Natasha guessed that they must have been her bodyguards.

"Miss Nassir, it is nice to meet you," Natasha said smiling.

"Oh, please call me Naima," Naima said shaking Natasha's hand.

"It is an honor to meet you," Mitchell said. Naima smiled at him.

"The tabloids were not exaggerating. You are ruggedly handsome," Naima said smiling.

"Well, the camera never lies, now does it?" Mitchell said smiling.

"And you have an even better looking wife. I can imagine that little girl that you have kept a well-guarded secret is a killer in her looks as well," Naima said looking at Natasha.

"I do not want to sound like I am patting my own back but she is the most beautiful little girl to me," she said. "But then again, I have to say that. I am her mother," she added laughing. Naima laughed.

"I'm sure she is a looker," Naima said. She turned to Stacy and smiled. "You must be the lovely lady I talked to on the phone," she said.

"Yes, Miss Nassir. I'm Stacy," Stacy said, trying hard to hide her excitement. "But my work here is done. I'll be at my desk if you need me," she said before practically running out. Naima smiled as one of the men pulled out a seat for her as Mitchell did the same for Natasha.

"So, shall we get started?" she asked as she sat down. Mitchell sat down and looked at her.

"I understand that you are now the managing partner at Lovell, congratulations," he said with a smile.

"Actually, my family's foundation is. I am merely a representative for the foundation's interests. I have been a big fan of the work done by NSCS and I found out that most projects were headed by Mrs. Schmidt here. That is why I thought she would be perfect to head this project," Naima said as she took two files from the other man and gave them to Mitchell and Natasha. "As you can see, we have big plans for Lovell," she added.

"Are you not planning to change the name?" Natasha asked as she flipped through the pages. Naima shook her head.

"No. Lovell is a brand everyone is familiar with and that is our biggest bargaining chip because we plan to expand to the Americas. Having a brand that was already known will work in our favor," Naima said.

"The Americas? Just how big of a campaign are you planning on?" Natasha asked.

"Eight weeks, maybe more. We will see how the first phase goes, but I know the project is at least eight weeks," Naima said. "I trust Stacy already gave you our budget. I was hoping your CFO would be here to discuss that," she added.

"I am representing the CFO. He is away on another business meeting in New York but he will be briefed," Mitchell said.

"Okay in that case please mention that the Nassir Foundation would like to have NSCS on retainer," Naima said, looking at Mitchell and then at Natasha, who was struggling not to swallow hard.

"We will be happy to have you on board again. At least this time I get to work closely with you," Mitchell said with a smile. Naima smiled at him.

"Yes, I heard that you worked with my grandfather…or is it that our grandfathers worked together?" she said. "So, Natasha. When can you start working your magic?" she asked.

"We can schedule the first meeting for Monday and then I'll have a full report for you by the end of the week. How does that sound?" Naima looked at her and nodded.

"Perfect. I love what you have done with other brands and I am sure that you will be great with our Lovell acquisition," Naima said. Natasha smiled.

"The pleasure will be all mine," she said.

"Good. Then I guess I will see you all next week," Naima said standing up. Natasha was surprised. After working with the Malibu Princess, she had expected a headache of a client in Naima but she was exactly the opposite. She was actually likeable. Natasha stood up and shook her hand.

"Yes we will," she said. "I'll have our lawyers liaise with yours on the contract before then," she added with a smile.

"By the way, your shoes are to die for. What are they, Christian Louboutins?" Naima asked. Natasha laughed and raised an eyebrow.

"Good eye," she said.

"And here I thought a Middle Eastern woman would be different," Mitchell said as he shook Naima's hand. "Shoes seem to be an international language with women," he said. Naima laughed.

"Shoes are the one language women of all nationalities, color and creed understand," she said smiling. "By the way, I am sorry for interfering with your travel plans. Stacy told me that you were supposed to be leaving for a vacation today," she said.

"Yes, but don't worry. It's no problem," Natasha said.

"Where are you off to?" Naima asked as she picked up her clutch bag.

"Aspen," Natasha said smiling. Naima raised an eyebrow as her glance shifted from Natasha to Mitchell and then back to Natasha.

"Aspen? Is there some romantic skiing trip that I don't know about?" she asked.

"No, why?" Mitchell asked. Naima laughed and opened her purse. She took out a card and looked at them.

"There is only one reason a couple takes some time off and

Aspen is the farthest thing from romance I can think of. Here, my friend owns this place. I'll make a call. You guys should have the best time there," she said as she handed Mitchell the card. "I look forward to our meeting next week," she said before she walked out of the board room. Natasha looked at Mitchell and shrugged.

"What's the name of the place?" she asked. Mitchell shook his head.

"I cannot even pronounce it. Some chateau in France," he said.

"So, no Aspen?" Natasha asked. Mitchell sat down and did a quick search of the chateau. He looked at her and smiled.

"Definitely no Aspen. This place looks amazing!" he said as he showed her the search results. It was just what they needed. A lakefront manor and a never-ending tree cover. It looked so peaceful. She smiled and kissed his cheek.

"I'm game," she said just as Stacy walked in.

"So, how did it go?" she asked. Natasha smiled at her.

"We have a new client," she said proudly. "And that is one of the good reasons I should give you for carrying my laptop on vacation," she added as she looked at Mitchell.

"This is after the fact," Mitchell said.

"It does not matter. The point is we got a new high end client because of me," Natasha said.

"Wow, way to be modest," Stacy said. "So is this a good time to ask for a raise?" she asked, looking at Natasha. Mitchell stood up and took Natasha's hand.

"Yes, this is a very good time to ask for a raise but after we come back," he said as he led her out of the board room. Natasha looked at Stacy and smiled.

"I'm sure we can make something work," she said as she walked past her.

Chapter 4

After a great meeting with Naima, Natasha had to admit her mood was more than set. She was never really worried about herself when it came to company matters, but she did worry about the rest of the employees. She lived a life of luxury but she also never forgot where she came from. She would have hated to make cuts in the budget that would affect the lives of some of the hard working employees of NSCS. She could not help but smile as she walked out of the board room. The day had been a great success even though it was still morning.

"Can we leave already? I'm thinking of a number of ways in which I would like to celebrate," she said to Mitchell in a whisper. Mitchell looked at her and smiled.

"Well, I share the same thoughts but the fact is that since we were flying commercial…" he shook his head. Natasha frowned.

"We missed the flight didn't we?" she asked.

"Well, yes, but the jet should be back in a few hours. We can leave then," he said.

"How many hours is a few?" she asked looking at him.

"A couple," he said, smiling sadly. Natasha looked at him and shook her head. "But I can promise you one thing. We will be in that chateau tonight," he added in a whisper.

"Until then?" she asked. Mitchell shrugged and then looked at Stacy who was back at her desk.

"Girl talk?" he asked. "She needs to talk to someone,

especially after..." his words failed him as he looked for the right way, the politically correct way, to tell his wife that her cousin had broken her assistant's heart.

"What happened?" Natasha asked.

"Well, there have been a number of developments," Mitchell said in a serious voice. Natasha playfully hit his arm.

"Just tell me what you are holding back on, already," she said in a hushed whisper.

"Your cousin and Stacy...it didn't work out," he said. Natasha frowned.

"What? When?" she asked.

"I also just found out...like two days ago. She put on a really brave face," he said. Natasha looked at him and frowned. "So, girl talk," he said again. She smiled and nodded.

"And where will you be?" she asked.

"Let me worry about that. See you in a few," he said before giving her a quick kiss on the cheek and then walking away. Natasha slowly made her way to Stacy's office.

"Hey, I thought you would be long gone by now," Stacy said as Natasha made her way to her desk.

"Well, we planned on taking a commercial flight but the meeting made sure we missed it so Mitchell thinks that it's just better to wait for the jet," she said as she sat down.

"With what they are worth, you would think the Schmidts would have more than one jet," Stacy said as she typed something on her computer.

"They only needed the one. And Mitchell had to go above and beyond the call of duty for some client. So I guess that cost us in one way or the other," Natasha said, frowning. She was not so sure what she had said had made any sense to Stacy. It hardly made any sense to her. Stacy smiled, probably due to confusion. "So, how are you?" she asked looking at Stacy.

"Good. Why are you asking?" she asked.

"Because I just found out that things between you and my cousin hit the rocks. I can't believe you didn't tell me," Natasha said. Stacy looked up and shrugged.

"I didn't think you needed to know…I mean, not in a bad way. Just that, there was a lot happening…and I'm over him anyway," she struggled to say. Natasha frowned.

"You are?"

"Yes. Are you surprised?" Natasha shook her head.

"Depends. How old is this information?" she asked.

"Three months," Stacy said as she gave her a guilty smile.

"Three…three months? Are you serious?" Natasha asked standing up.

"Where are you…." Stacy started asking before Natasha snapped her fingers.

"We are going out. You and I need to have a talk, a long one," she said.

"But what about this, um…file…that, um…"

Natasha rolled her eyes. "For God's sake, Stace, I know there is no work related thing on your screen and I'm your boss. You have the rest of the day off," she said, pulling her from her seat. Stacy smiled and grabbed her bag.

"Awesome. Where are we going?" she asked as she followed her out of the office.

"Right now, the coffee place outside the office building. After that you can go wherever. I only have a couple of hours," Natasha said as they got inside the elevator. As they rode down, Natasha tried thinking of all the things she wanted to ask as she adjusted the laptop bag on her shoulder. She had a billion and one questions. What happened? Did he cheat on her? Did she cheat on him….wait…was that even possible? The innocent Stacy she knew? But she did sleep with…no, fucked her cousin so the innocence was long gone. Once they were out, they casually made their way to the coffee shop.

"May I take your order?" the waiter asked when they sat down.

"Latte, please and…what will you have, Stace?" Natasha asked looking at the menu.

"I'll just have the same," Stacy said. When the waiter walked away, Natasha put the menu down and looked at Stacy.

"So, what happened?" she asked.

"Gee and I were okay at first…." Stacy started before Natasha put her hand up.

"Wait up. Who the fuck is Gee?" she asked.

"Oh, that's how he first introduced himself to me. I kind of liked the name so...yeah. I stuck with it," Stacy said. Natasha shook her head. That was a classic move from her cousin. He had once introduced himself as James Bond to a Russian model. Natasha could not put anything past him.

"So, what happened?" Natasha asked. Stacy paused for a minute as the waiter came back with their coffees.

"Well, Gee was a great guy at first in every way but what was supposed to be a one night stand became so much more than what I expected. I developed feelings for him and it was weird because I normally take a considerable amount of time before I even consider liking someone," Stacy explained. "He was just what I needed at the time, a good friend who I occasionally slept with. I guess I overdid it," she added smiling.

"What do you mean overdid it?" Natasha asked.

"About a month after your wedding, we hooked up again and then he moved back here for a while and we sort of decided to define the relationship. That was the beginning of the end. He was too....what's the word...possessive, clingy, take your pick. I could not answer a call from a male workmate without him throwing a fit," Stacy continued. "It was a living hell. So I broke it off," she said, looking at Natasha.

"That was three months ago?" Natasha asked.

"No. That was four years ago. It was just after your wedding remember?" Stacy asked. Natasha nodded and then took a long sip of her coffee. It was evident that she had not been a very good friend to Stacy for a while.

"So? What happened next?" she asked, eager to know what

had happened in Stacy's life since then.

"Nothing much. We have been on and off for three years but he only seemed to get worse. Suddenly, he wanted to be around me all the time. He was talking about moving in together and, get this, he wanted me to quit my job," Stacy said. Natasha's eyes grew wide. She had known her family to have the crazies but this was a kind of crazy she had never expected.

"He wanted you to do what?" Natasha asked surprised.

"I know, right? I told him that was crazy. And he told me to choose. It was either him or my job and of course I chose my job," Stacy said. "I just liked him. I did not love him nor was I in love with him and unfortunately, I think he was already there with me. I just could not handle it. So I made my choice," Stacy said. Natasha looked at her and shook her head.

"So this was three months ago?" she asked. Stacy nodded. "I can't believe you were in a relationship with my cousin for almost four years and I never knew about it," she added. Stacy laughed.

"Technically, he was the one in the relationship. I just had an enthusiastic fuck buddy," Stacy said, laughing. Natasha laughed and took another sip of her coffee.

"I just feel really bad that I didn't know about this. I consider you one of my closest friends," she said. Stacy smiled at her.

"I know and it is for that reason that I chose to keep the truth from you. You had a lot going on with you and work and the baby and Rita's mother. There is only so much you can handle in your life at a given time, you know. You are not Wonder Woman," Stacy said. She took another sip of her coffee and smiled. "Now that you have given me the day off, I think I will spend it with my new man since he is around this week," she added. Natasha looked at her, surprised again.

"New man?" she asked, looking at Stacy who was now nodding. "The way you have just described your life left me thinking you would not have enough time to meet any new people. When did the new man happen?" she asked.

"Well, somewhere between Gee being an ass and me deciding to have a life," Stacy said smiling. "It has not been so long. I met him a few months ago but it's going so well. He is simply awesome," she added.

"Okay. I need to know more about him. Like his name, where he's from, what he does...that kind of thing," Natasha said, smiling. Stacy laughed.

"Okay, but this feels like me being grilled by my parents the first time I brought my high school boyfriend home," she said. Natasha laughed.

"I'm sorry. I'm just trying to make up for all those years," she said. Stacy shrugged.

"His name is Larry. We met on one of those days I wish I was married to your husband," she said. Natasha frowned.

"Say what?" she asked.

"Hey, don't go all black girl on me. Sometimes there is so much work in that office I wish I could just go MIA for a week and get some much needed spa treatment," Stacy said. "Yeah, so I was working late and there was literally no one to send on a food run. So I thought I would carry the work home. On my way I walked into one of those late night delis to get a sandwich and Larry had the same idea. He was working on a case and he needed some brain food. His words," she explained.

Natasha could not help but notice the dreamy look she had in her eyes as she talked about him. She had never seen her like this with any other guy, not that she knew a lot of the men she had dated before.

"A lawyer," Natasha said smiling. Stacy's cheeks flushed.

"Yeah. He is a family lawyer at Smithson and Associates," she said, smiling.

"Cool. You are never winning any arguments. You know that, right?" Natasha asked. Stacy shrugged and nodded.

"Sadly, I came to terms with that fact a long time ago" she said.

"You said he will be around for this week? Where is he going to be?" Natasha asked.

"He is working on something in New York starting next week and it may be a while. So I am taking all the time I can with him," Stacy said, smiling. Natasha looked at her and smiled.

"You really are happy with him, aren't you?" she asked. Stacy's cheeks flushed again.

"Yeah, I am and I know it is still too early to say this but this is definitely the sort of guy I want to settle down with," she said smiling. Natasha's eyes grew wide. She reached across the table and took Stacy's hands in hers.

"I am so happy for you, sweetie," she said looking into Stacy's

By Saucy Romance Books

beautiful blue eyes.

"Thanks," she said before she pulled a hand out of Natasha's grip. She took one last sip of her latte and looked into Natasha's eyes. Natasha smiled.

"It's okay. You go on ahead," she said. Stacy smiled and picked up her bag.

"Have fun in Aspen," she said smiling.

"France," Natasha corrected. Stacy frowned. "Naima gave us a place there. I think her friend owns it or something," she added.

"Wow, you guys are sure lucky. You hit the jackpot with the Schmidts," Stacy said. Natasha laughed.

"Really?" she asked still laughing. Stacy shrugged and then bent down to whisper in Natasha's ear.

"Wherever you go to do the nasty, have a blast," she whispered before walking off. Natasha smiled. This time it was her turn to blush. She took her bag and pulled out her laptop. She thought that since she had to wait for Mitchell, she might as well journal.

Dear Diary,

It has not been so long since my last entry but except for work, there hasn't been much happening in my life. So let's see....today was an awesome day. We were supposed to leave for Aspen in the morning but we got called into work. I know it sounds silly since we were supposed to be taking time off so that we could take some space from work and we got called back...haha...interesting. So, anyway, turns out that my work is globally acclaimed. This is a good time to give myself a well deserved pat on the back. So....applause...WHOOP WHOOP!!!

Natasha looked up feeling stupid at what she had just typed. She looked around and realized that no one had seen her goofy smile and after all, it was her diary anyway. She did not have to feel stupid for anyone. She looked down and went on typing.

*So this woman from the United Arab Emirates walks into the office building and asks for me personally. That was a great honor. So we drove down to the office and had a great meeting. She is officially our new client on retainer plus she has just given us a thirty million dollar contract. I know!!! Thirty freaking million dollars! This has to be the greatest day of my life...okay, maybe the third greatest since there is my wedding day and the day Alexis was born. But then again, they will never see this so maybe this once I can say that today was greater than both days combined...*she paused and then shook her head. *Okay maybe not but it is a close second. And she also gave us a place to have our perfect weekend in France. I am so excited. I have only been to France once and it was for business plus Mitchell wasn't even there!! But this time around I am a hundred percent sure that I will enjoy my time there. But I am a bit nervous. I want everything to be perfect but I am not so sure I'll be able to. I am kind of out of practice...that sounded ridiculous in my head but it's true. Me and Mitchell have actually become strangers in the bedroom. We only use our bed to sleep nowadays. It's like work has taken all the magic out of our sex life. Sad face galore. But maybe I should just be relaxed and let everything come at its own pace. Kind of roll with the punches...we'll see how it goes.*

She looked at the bottom right corner and saw the time. Mitchell should have been back by now. She paid the bill and shut down her computer. She needed to get back before Mitchell did because she had every intention of taking her computer with her. As she walked back to the office, she could not help but feel like she was on top of the world. This was what she had dreamed of when she was in college, getting so good in her career that people come from all corners of the world just to work with her. And it was happening. When she got to the parking lot, she opened the trunk and put her computer under some of her clothes.

"Thank God for private jets," she thought as she pictured Mitchell's disappointed look at customs. She then walked back to her office and sat down at her desk. She thought back to the first day she walked into the doors of NSCS. She remembered the awkward feeling she got when she saw that one of the men who would be interviewing her would be the same hunk who had helped her out after she passed out in the parking lot earlier. The same guy who had made her get wet just by smiling at her. The guy who she never thought she would end up marrying. She smiled to herself. Things had a weird way of working themselves out. It had been one of those blessed embarrassing moments, if anything like that existed. She smiled to herself again. Stacy was right, she had hit the jackpot and it had nothing to do with the Schmidts' net worth. It was to do with the fact that she had it all, the best of both worlds. Most people had either one or the other, a happy marriage or a great career, but not her. She was happy, she had a great career and she had a great family. What more could a girl ask for? This was so much more than most people ever got in their lifetime.

Chapter 5

After having coffee with Stacy, Natasha made a call to Rita. She was right to take a vacation but the truth was, she had no idea what to do for two whole days. Of course, the whole idea was to rekindle the romance but she had become so much of a workaholic that she didn't know how to just live a life of fun anymore, not just with her husband, but in every aspect of her life.

"Hey girl. I thought you'd be in some posh resort in Aspen by now," Rita said when she picked up. Natasha smiled.

"Well, there was a last minute change of plans. Something came up at work," she said.

"What? I thought the whole point of taking time off was to get work out of your system," Rita said surprised.

"I know, but this one was a major one. There was no one to take the meeting and the lady asked for me in person," Natasha explained.

"Really? What made her so special?" Rita asked.

"Well, I can think of thirty million reasons and that's just off the top of my head plus she looks like a great art collector too. This may be a win-win," Natasha said. She heard Rita take a long deep breath.

"Forget I said anything," Rita said. Natasha laughed. That was so predictable of her. "So, I am in kind of some deep shit. I think I may have lost my touch in bedroom matters," she said. She heard Rita laugh.

"That is not possible. You are like Spartacus and the arena," she said. Natasha shrugged as if Rita could see her.

"Well, I don't feel that way," she said. Rita laughed again.

"Look, the more you stress about it, the more terrible you will be at it. If you have such a hard time getting in the mood, let him lead. You'd be surprised at how much potential playing the humble servant can unlock," she said. Natasha laughed at her choice of words.

"There is no hope for you, girlfriend," she said in a mock Madea voice before she hang up.

As they rode to the airport later that evening, she could still feel Rita's words ringing in her ears. Maybe she was right. Maybe letting Mitchell lead would work in her favor.

And it did. As soon as they were airborne, she caught Mitchell giving her a look, that all-knowing "I want to rip your clothes off" look. She smiled at him and shook her head.

"What? You have a look that tells me that this is not one of my ordinary flights," she said. Mitchell shook his head.

"I am not looking at you any different than I have for the last four years," he said.

"Really? Because that bulge in your pants can hardly wait to get to the chateau so that it can be freed," she said. Mitchell laughed. "And there is the guilty laugh that tells me I am right," she added as she ripped open a bag of peanuts. Mitchell reached for the bag and placed it next to his seat making Natasha give him a confused look.

"You know one of the perks of not flying commercial is the

privacy," he said, pulling her close to him. She smiled.

"Mitchell Schmidt, what do you have in mind?" she asked.

"Roll with it honey, roll with it," Mitchell said as he pulled her down to kiss her. She closed her eyes as their lips met in one passionate kiss that almost left her breathless. She felt a tingle run down her spine as he kissed her. She had to admit, he had not kissed her like that since…back when they were dating. She was almost out of breath when he finally pulled away from her. She opened her eyes and looked at him.

"Babe, the pilot is still here in this plane, you know," she said in a whisper.

"That makes it even hotter," he said smiling. Natasha shook her head. It was like making out with a teenage boy behind the bleachers. She hated the fact that thinking about it that way made her feel even more aroused than she was supposed to be. She smiled and allowed herself to get lost in his kiss. He pulled her down and Natasha got the point. She sat down on his lap and wrapped her arm around his neck. She loved every moment of his kiss. The way he was caressing her back was sending shock waves through her body. She began cursing herself for not wearing pants. She would have straddled him right there but then again, a dress gave him the perfect leeway to get his hand up under the thin fabric and feel the smooth skin of her legs. She let out a soft moan as she felt his hand slowly running up and down her thigh. She pulled away from him and then looked into his eyes as she ran her fingers through his thick hair. He smiled as he let one of his hands go up her back and slowly pull the zipper down. She breathed slowly as he let the dress slip down her shoulders.

He looked at her breasts concealed behind her royal blue lace bra. He could have sworn her breasts looked bigger but that was just probably because he had not seen her undressed in a long time. She looked into his eyes and began to loosen his tie.

"I must say that you in a suit, looking all official, makes me all hot," she said as she let the tie drop on the floor. She smiled and pushed his coat off his shoulders before she began undoing his shirt buttons.

"Well, I'm officially turned on by all these right here," he said as he put his hands on her breasts. She gasped when she felt her nipples respond almost immediately to his touch. He smiled as she ran her fingers down his chest. She could feel his body tingling as he brought his fingers closer to his crotch. The excitement was not only being dished out to her. He took the reins and began running his lips along her neck. She snaked an arm around him as she felt him kissing her neck, slowly at first and then more intensely as he went on. She was still getting used to his lips being on her neck when he suddenly began running his tongue up and down her neck slowly. She was not sure whether it was the fact that this had not happened in a long time or that it was his expert moves, but she was sure of one thing, whatever he was doing was good…too good.

When their lips met, it was like a soft dance as their tongues slowly brushed against each other. He put his hand on the side of her face and tilted it to give her an even deeper kiss before he let his hand slowly drop onto her breasts. He wrapped his arms around her as she gave in to her body's desires and began grinding on his leg.

He pulled away for a few seconds and looked at her. He smiled and then went on to kiss her as he worked on undoing the clasp of her bra. She let out a soft moan when she felt her bra loosen around her ribs. He pulled the bra away from her and feasted his eyes on the taut nipples that had been well hidden by the fabric of her bra. He kissed her again as he began to tease her nipples by running his flicking fingertips on then. Her breathing became labored as she struggled to keep her cool in the heat of the moment.

But what happened next really threw her over the edge. Mitchell pulled away from her lips and held her hand motioning for her to stand up. As if by telepathic communication, she stood up and he followed before pulling her dress down to reveal her long legs. She could have sworn she saw a half smile form on his lips as he looked at her now dressed in only a pair of panties and her shoes. Mitchell quickly took off his shirt and let it fall on the floor. She looked at him with half a mind to get his pants off but it was clear that she was not in the driver's seat.

Mitchell sat back down and tugged her hand. She straddled him and wrapped her arms around his neck. She wanted to kiss him again but again, Mitchell had other plans. He took one nipple in his mouth and sucked hard, making her moan loudly, so loud that Mitchell thought the pilot would be distracted. Her moans only made him want to suck her harder. He put a hand behind her and held her tightly as he let his tongue circle her breasts, knowing fully well that this was driving her crazy. When he finally pulled away, she gave him one of her sexy "fuck me" looks through partially closed eyes.

Natasha was as hungry for him as he was for her. As they struggled to fit in the small seat, their lips continued to explore each other. Mitchell felt her suddenly tug at her belt before undoing his buckle. She unzipped his fly and let her hand seek out his now hard member. He moaned as he felt her small fingers slowly caressing his cock. She pulled away from him and stepped off the seat. She hated that he was still dressed, well mostly, while she was in nothing but the dress around her waist. She looked at him as she pushed the dress down off her waist, letting it gather around her ankles before she stepped out of it. She kicked off her shoes and then slowly got on her knees and helped him out of his pants. She did not have the patience to take them off all the way so she just let them hang around his ankles as she got closer to him. She could almost see the throbbing in his cock as he looked down at her, eager for her to begin whatever had caused her to get on the floor.

Mitchell closed his eyes when she finally put her hand on his cock, slowly and softly caressing his length. She did that again before finally lowering her mouth to lick the head of his cock, He was not sure whether it was the fact that it had been a long time since this happened or if it was how good she was with her tongue. The fact was that he loved it, everything about what she was doing and how she was doing it. She again ran her tongue on the tip of his cock making his hardness ooze some pre-cum. He stifled a moan as she did it over and over again, teasing him and making him want to grab her head and just face fuck her right there.

"Oh baby, please don't stop," he moaned when she suddenly took his entire length inside her mouth and sucked softly. She smiled as she took him out of her mouth and ran her tongue along the length of his cock before taking him inside her mouth again. She sucked him long and hard, making him moan loudly and hold on tightly to the sides of the seat.

This was definitely one of the benefits of not flying commercial. There was no way they would have been able to kill the two birds with one stone. It was either giving in to their bodies' desires or taking the flight. But here, in the Schmidt Airborne (as Nolan Schmidt had named it), they could do whatever they wanted to do, be whomever they wanted to be.

She sucked him hard like there was no tomorrow, making him writhe as she went on. Natasha gave herself a mental pat on the back. He never writhed even when she thought she had outdone herself. She pulled him out of his mouth and looked at him, waiting. They were both holding their breath: Mitchell waiting to see what her next move would be and Natasha waiting to see how he would react when she pulled her next move. She ran her hand up and down his leg, making her way to his inside thigh, getting dangerously close to his cock. She suddenly ran her hand all the way down to his ankles and pulled his pants all the way off.

"What…" Mitchell began asking before Natasha spread his knees. She looked at him and smiled as she moved closer and closer to him until she positioned his cock right in between her breasts.

Mitchell was now certain that he had unleashed a madwoman. He closed his eyes as she held a breast in each hand and carefully began rubbing his cock. She had never done this before and he had always wondered what a boob job felt like, and now he knew. He was in heaven. Every minute she spent rubbing her soft mounds against his cock was a minute he wanted to explode. The sensation was, in a word, intense and by the way she was going, he was sure he would not last very long.

He held her face in his hands and looked into her eyes. "Come up here," he said in a whisper. She stood up and he wasted no time. He pushed her panties off and let them fall to the floor. "Mitchell, we are naked…" she whispered.

"We will not be landing for at least two more hours," he said smiling as he stood up and pushed her back in her seat. She smiled at him as she sat down. This time, it was evident that he was in control and there was no fighting him as he went right ahead and spread her knees. He got on the floor and knelt in between her legs.

She knew exactly what he was up to and there was no stopping him. She closed her eyes and threw her head back as he began kissing her pussy, softly sucking on her clit. Natasha was having a hard time trying to keep her moans to herself. He was driving her to the point of no return and she was sure that she could not control her senses for much longer. Mitchell sucked and thrust his tongue deep into her hot depths, making her gasp and whimper as she approached orgasm.

She suddenly jerked in her seat and Mitchell knew this was it. He raised a hand and cupped her breast as she writhed in the seat. She shivered and shook as she felt a surge of hot energy go through her as her climax took over. Mitchell pulled away and looked at her, smiling. He always loved looking at her when she was in this state, the state he had labored to get her in. When she finally stopped shaking, Mitchell took her in his arms and sat back in his seat, carefully positioning her legs on either side of his thighs. She held on to his neck as he guided his cock inside her.

"Oh my….God…" she moaned in a whisper as she felt his cock getting deep inside her. She buried her head in his shoulder as he lifted her on and off his cock slowly. It was not only the sex that gave her this exhilarating feeling but also the fact that they were fucking with two people less than ten feet away. His strokes were getting harder and faster and soon he was slamming against her crotch like his life depended on it. She slapped a hand over her mouth and stifled a scream as she felt her second orgasm taking over. She breathed deep and hard as she felt herself releasing, her pussy pulsating around his cock. It did not take long before Mitchell got his own orgasm. He held her tightly and thrust into her harder than ever, in time with every gush of his cum.

"Wow," Mitchell said as he felt his cock slipping out of her.

"Yeah wow," she echoed as she got off his thighs. She wobbled onto her own seat before getting dressing. She was surprised the flight attendant had not come to check up on them. Maybe it was just their luck but she was not taking any chances.

"You are dressing already?" he asked as he looked at her. She gave him a tired smile.

"Right now, I want nothing more than to lie down and just sleep but we are almost there and Alanis might walk in," she said as she pulled her dress up. She noticed a smile playing on Mitchell's lips. "What?" she asked.

"You forgot your bra," he said smiling. Natasha looked at her bra lying next to his feet and frowned.

"Crap," she said under her breath. She took the dress off again as she reached for her bra using her foot. Mitchell smiled and picked up his pants. She could tell by the way he moved that he felt the same way as she did. As they lazily got dressed, she could not help but think about what the rest of the weekend was going to be like. Their perfect romantic getaway had been delayed, yes, but it had started out so well, better than she would have even hoped.

"Mr. and Mrs. Schmidt, please fasten your seat belts. We are about to touch down," they heard Alanis' smooth voice on the intercom. Mitchell looked at Natasha and smiled. He picked up his glass and raised it.

"To us," he said. Natasha smiled.

"The glass is empty," she said.

"The gesture isn't," Mitchell said looking at her. Natasha took a glass and raised it before clinking it gently with his.

"To us," she said as the plane touched down. This was going to be one of those weekends you could not write home about but you sure had a desire to do so.

Chapter 6

When Mitchell and Natasha got to the chateau, they realized that Naima was right. This was in no way any comparison to Aspen. The area was beautiful, serene…just what they needed to get away from everything. The chateau was a lakefront property and the room they got had a perfect view of the lake. There was a fully equipped gym downstairs and a heated pool. When they got to their room, Natasha gasped. This was better than the presidential suite at the Four Seasons and with better scenery. She turned around and looked at Mitchell as he tipped the concierge.

"This is the best delayed romantic getaway I have ever been on," Natasha said with a smile. Mitchell closed the door and walked towards her, smiling.

"I know, right? How about we make the best of it?" he asked as he wrapped his arms around her waist. She smiled and gave him a quick kiss before pulling away from him. "Hey? I thought we were going to make the best of it," he said as he pouted the same way Alexis would when she did not get her way. Natasha laughed.

"First, I need to check up on our daughter," she said as she walked over to the bed and opened her suitcase. Mitchell frowned when he noticed she had managed to sneak in her laptop.

"I thought we said no computers," he said as he walked over to the bed.

"We did, but this is not for work. I just want to Skype your parents and mine. See how everything is," she said as she entered her password. Mitchell sat down and looked into her eyes.

"Fine. Just this time, I will let you get away with it," he said, wagging his index finger at her. She smiled as she waited for Mitchell's mother to pick up.

"Natasha, darling. How are you doing?" Mitchell's mother said in a cheerful voice.

"I'm good. How are you doing? How is the little lady treating you?" she asked.

"She has been great, a bit jumpy but who's complaining? It's good to have the pitter patter of little feet around the house again," she said. Natasha smiled. "Mitchell's father is the one not coping so well," she added. Natasha frowned.

"Why? What happened?" she asked, concerned.

"It's nothing to be concerned about. He was like that with Mitchell and his sister too." Natasha shook her head.

"Like what?" she asked. Mrs. Schmidt smiled and shook her head.

"Over exerting himself, playing with the kids only to tire himself out. Never mind about him. He is just taking his fourth nap of the day. He should be fine," she said, smiling. Natasha laughed and then breathed a sigh of relief. "Where is my boy anyway? Are you not with him or did he leave you again to go to some meeting?" Mrs. Schmidt asked. Natasha giggled. That was so Mitchell.

"I'm right here, Mother, and I am no longer your 'boy,'" Mitchell said as he leaned forward to make his face visible to his mother. "I am a married man and the father of your granddaughter. Remember her? Alexis? Oh yeah, you have her in your house right now," Mitchell said in a cynical voice. "Boy," he said under his breath.

"Honey, you are a father now and you'll see. Even when Alexis is in her forties, she'll still be your little girl," Mrs. Schmidt said, smiling. "So, how is Aspen?" she asked. Mitchell looked at Natasha and smiled.

"Actually, we are not in Aspen," Natasha said. Mrs. Schmidt frowned.

"Really? What happened? Where are you?" she asked confused.

"France," Mitchell said proudly.

"France?" his mother asked again.

"Yes, Mother. France," he confirmed. He looked at his mother as she tried to figure out the change of plans. "We had a last minute meeting this morning and long story short, we have a new client and this chateau in France was a favor from her," he added. His mother smiled.

"Enjoy the perks of the seat of power," she said. Natasha giggled.

"The seat of power?" she asked, looking at her mother-in-law who nodded.

"Yeah. That was what my mother called it once. Anyway, you kids have fun. I need to check on the little lady. I love you darling and you too, my dear boy," she said smiling. Mitchell frowned.

"I love you too, Mother," he said.

"Yeah, bye Mrs. Schmidt," Natasha said before she signed out. She looked at Mitchell and smiled.

"Don't you dare," he said in a warning tone. She smiled and shrugged as she dialed her father's number.

"I was not going to say anything," she said as she waited for her dad to pick up.

"You better not because when you hang up I will show you just what this boy can do to you," he said as he gently touched her thigh. She smiled at him just as her father picked up.

"Hey there, stranger," she said with a smile. "I have missed you," she added.

"Hi sweetie. How is Aspen?" Eric asked. Natasha looked at Mitchell and smiled.

"Actually Eric, we had a change of plans. We are in France," Mitchell said. Eric smiled.

"Do I really need to ask?" Eric asked. Natasha rolled her eyes and smiled.

"It's a long story, Daddy. But how are you? How is Nan?" she asked.

"Yeah, Eric. Where is Estelle?" Mitchell asked.

"Who knows? Grocery shopping or bible study…one of the two places. I was at work when she left," Eric said. "And how is Alexis dealing with the other grandparents?" he asked. Natasha laughed.

"Apparently my dad is not as energetic as you are," Mitchell said.

"Really? Why? What makes you say that?" Eric asked. "I mean, I know I am the younger one and the one who is more physically fit," he added quickly. Natasha looked at Mitchell and shook her head. It was just like her father to have an unnaturally high self esteem.

"He has to keep on taking power naps to keep up with Alexis," Mitchell said, laughing. Eric laughed.

"Yeah. It takes a special kind of tolerance to keep up with her," he said. "So, how is France so far?" he asked. Natasha smiled.

"Wait. I want to show you something," she said as she picked up her laptop and walked to the window. She pointed the camera outside so Eric could see the lake.

"Okay, I know I am not supposed to be jealous of my daughter but I officially am," Eric said. Natasha heard him take a long deep breath. "It is breathtaking," he said in a whisper.

"I know. I should bring you over," Natasha said as she turned the laptop to face her. "Anyway, I was just checking up on you guys. Say hi to Nan when she gets back. I'll see you guys next week," she said.

"Sure. We can do dinner when you two get back," Eric said. Natasha looked at Mitchell and then smiled.

"Sounds great, Dad," she said.

"Yeah Eric. Can't wait," Mitchell said. "But Estelle has to make her awesome Peking pie. I can never have enough of it," he added. Eric laughed and nodded.

"Will do. Stay safe," he said. Natasha nodded.

"You too. I love you," she said.

"Love you too," Eric said before hanging up. Natasha shut down her laptop and looked at Mitchell.

"I need a shower," she said.

"I'll come with you," Mitchell said excitedly. Natasha looked at him and shook her head. "Why?" he asked as he looked at her.

"Because a shower with you means sex and I have a few things in mind before I fuck the living daylights out of you," she said with a smile.

"Really? Any spoilers?" he asked. She smiled and shook her head.

"Let's just say that one of your old girls will be making a comeback," she said. Mitchell closed his eyes and smiled.

"Which one? Shower cop? My Dandelion?" he guessed. Natasha walked towards him and placed the laptop on the nightstand before giving him a long kiss, one that made him hard all over again.

"You are not that far off but you are not right either," she said before disappearing into the bathroom.

Mitchell smiled to himself. Sometimes when people told him how lucky he was, he just thought they were being nice but at times like right now, he knew that there was no way he could have ever found anyone who would be better than Natasha. She was the complete package. She was a beautiful African American woman who had both brains and a hot body. She had given him everything he could ever want: a happy and perfect marriage, a beautiful baby girl and she was rocking the corporate world. Who could ever have all that in just one package? You had to be extremely lucky, or God himself.

He sat on the edge of the bed and kicked off his shoes. He could not help but smile to himself when he recalled their airborne sex. They should have been busted. They actually came very close to being busted but it did not matter. It was worth it. He would not even have cared if they were busted because after all, Natasha was his trophy wife.

When Natasha finally emerged from the bathroom, she quickly got dressed in a pair of blue capri pants and a hot pink flowered halter top. She put on a pair of flip flops and took her sunglasses before she kissed a now sleeping Mitchell on the forehead and walked out.

Rita had mentioned to her that she had to dig deep in order to give Mitchell the awesome weekend she had in mind all along. But for her, getting to know just what to do was a struggle. Given the long period of time since the two of them had been intimate, she was surprise she had been able to pull off the plane sex. But in her mind, she thought that the only reason it happened was because Mitchell was leading. She needed to get her own groove back. She had no idea where she was supposed to go but she was sure that she would find something hot and sexy that would knock her husband's socks off. When she got to the front desk, she smiled at the man seated behind the rich mahogany desk.

"Hi. I was wondering if I could get a map of the area," she said with a smile. The man nodded.

"Of course, *madame,*" he said in a heavy French accent. He turned around and gave her one of the pamphlets behind him.

"Thank you so much," she said before walking out.

"Have a good day, *madame,*" he replied. She turned around and smiled at him before going out. She got into a cab and told the driver to take her downtown as she did a quick web search on where to buy sexy lingerie in the area. As she was scrolling through the results, one store called out to her.

"Le Monde Pleasures, for all your BDSM needs," she read. She opened the page and held her breath as she looked at the various products. They had everything from butt plugs to cat-o-nine tails. She looked at the address and then asked the driver to take her to that specific place. She could not wait to go there. She had not delved into her bondage side since before she got married. When they got to the shop, she paid the driver and walked into the store.

She could feel a thrill going down her spine as she made her way through the door She noticed that each product had a brief description underneath it. The store owner walked towards her as she walked around looking at the various products.

"Good day, *madame,*" the woman said to her with a smile. Natasha was surprised that she did not have an accent like the man back at the chateau or the cab driver. Natasha had also expected the store attendant to be a woman dressed in spandex and probably carrying a whip but she was simply clad in a black sleeveless pencil dress and a pair of nude colored heels. Her long black silky hair cascaded over her shoulders complimenting her smoky blue green eyes.

"Good day to you too," Natasha said with a smile.

"My name is Leah. How can I help you today?" the woman asked. Natasha shrugged.

"I have no idea. I just know I want almost everything in here," she said excitedly. Leah looked at her and smiled.

"That is normal. Just take your time," Leah said. "I'll just be at the counter of you have any questions," she said before walking away. Natasha smiled at her and then continued walking around. She literally wanted everything in that shop. Some silver balls caught her eye and she walked towards the stand and read the description below the balls.

If you are into the Fifty Shades kind of anal play then these balls are just what you need and so much more! They come with a special vibration feature that gives you and your partner more pleasure than you could ever hope for. And all these for only €30.

Natasha smiled to herself and picked the balls. They would not be her cup of tea on a normal day but this was a special occasion and she was willing to go above and beyond the call of duty. She had tried a butt plug before so maybe this would be almost the same if not better. She walked over to the next shelf where there was a nipple suction. She had always wanted to try it out. The last time she played the bondage card, she was the one in charge but this time she intended on letting Mitchell do all the driving. She was sure she would not mind playing second fiddle, especially since she suddenly had a desire to be a submissive. She picked the nipple suction and then walked over to the more familiar shelves. She frowned at the cat-o-nines. She knew she had a high tolerance for pain but cat-o-nines were simply not for her. Her threshold was not that high. She picked a spanking paddle and some lube before walking over to the counter. Leah looked at her and smiled.

"First time?" she asked. Natasha felt her cheeks go red.

"Actually, second time. Is it that obvious?" she asked. Leah shrugged and nodded.

"Unfortunately," she said. Natasha smiled.

"Well, it happens to the best of us," she said as Leah rang up her bill.

"So, forgive me for prying but by your accent I can tell that you are American. So are we here on a honeymoon or something?" Leah asked. Natasha smiled and shook her head.

"Actually, I got married four years ago. We just needed some time to ourselves for a few days," she said.

"In that case, may I suggest something?" Leah said. Natasha shrugged.

"Anything," she said with a smile. Leah smiled and walked over to the costumes section. She came back holding a naughty Cinderella costume. Natasha had to admit. It was the most beautiful costume she had ever seen. It was a blue and white bustier and short skirt, open at the bust with only a sheer fabric covering it. The fabric could be removed to expose the breasts for either sadistic play or simply to arouse you. It also had an open crotch, a pair of high heeled open toe sandals and a tiara to complete the look. Natasha smiled and looked at Leah.

"I'm sure your husband will love this," Leah said.

"I'm sure he will," Natasha said as she took the costume from her. "Ring it up," she said excitedly.

Leah smiled, rang up her bill and then handed her a bag with all her purchases. Natasha smiled and thanked her before getting out of the store. She walked to a lingerie store and picked out a black sheer negligee with a matching thong. That was right out of Mitchell's hot book. She knew she would make him happier than he had been in ages.

As she rode back to the chateau, she could not help but smile. She had half a mind to call Rita and tell her what she had just been out shopping for but she had to keep a few things about her marriage sacred even though Rita knew for a fact that she was the epitome of "lady in the streets and a freak in the bed." When she got back to the chateau, she asked for room service with extra chocolate covered strawberries before she walked back to her suite. Mitchell was still asleep but he had a bathrobe on.

"Maybe he showered and then went back to sleep. That's good, because he will need his strength," she thought as she waited for room service to get there. She did not want to anything to ruin her perfect lovemaking session.

It was not long before the concierge came to their room pushing the food trolley. She tipped him generously and then closed the door behind him before going to the bathroom and changing into the black negligee. She took a pair of black heels from her suitcase before walking to the bed. She planted a soft kiss on Mitchell's forehead. Mitchell's eyelids fluttered open.

"I hope you are naked under that robe," she said in a sexy voice. Mitchell smiled and nodded. "Good, because I have something for you to see," she said as she stood up. Mitchell smiled and breathed a long low "wow" when he saw her. Just like she thought.

"You look beautiful. I just want to…" he took a deep breath, unsure of what to say. Natasha smiled. "I just want you," he finally managed to say. Natasha felt proud of herself but if this lingerie got him this breathless, what would he do when he saw her in the naughty Cinderella costume? She could not wait to see his reaction then. But now, it was all about what he wanted to do to her.

Chapter 7

Whoever sang the song 'Easy Like Sunday Morning' must have been on vacation in France, exactly where Mitchell and Natasha were or its equivalent. When the two woke up on Sunday morning, Natasha could not help but take a long deep breath. The area had pine trees and the scent was at its strongest in the mornings.

"Smells like Christmas," Natasha said as she woke up. Mitchell laughed.

"Really? Seasons have smells now?" he asked.

"What? Pine trees are Christmas trees and their sweet scent makes me think of Christmas," she said in her defense.

"Uh huh. Just don't start singing 'tis the season' all up in here," he said as he draped an arm around her. Natasha smiled and looked at him.

"'Tis the season to be jolly, fa la la la la la la la la," she began singing. He laughed and silenced her with one long kiss. She looked into his eyes when she pulled away from him. "You were great last night. At some point I thought we would wake up the entire chateau," she said in a low voice.

"Well, I can't take all the credit. That black lingerie you had on had a lot to do with it," he said. "A lot," he added, nodding. She smiled and shrugged.

"Well, wait till you see what I have planned for you later," she said. Mitchell's eyes lit up. He almost looked like a kid who had just been told that he was being given a free trip to Disneyland.

"You do remember that we have to be getting back today, right?" he said. Natasha frowned.

"Don't remind me. I don't ever want to leave," she said. Mitchell smiled.

"I know," he said as he used his index finger to softly caress her cheek.

"Does that make me sound like a terrible mother? Am I becoming one of those women who neglect their children just because they need time to themselves?" she asked, still frowning. Mitchell smiled and shook his head.

"You will never be one of those women. You are one in a million and there is no way I could have ever done better," he said before kissing her forehead. She smiled and looked into his eyes.

"Sometimes I think I am the one who could have never done better. Most of the times I consider myself the lucky one," she said. He shook his head.

"That is not possible," he said in a whisper before he kissed her softly. "So, where do we go today?" he asked.

"I don't know. Let's just get out of bed first and then we'll see from there," she said, smiling. Mitchell smiled and let her go. He watched her as she walked to the bathroom where she turned on the shower.

The better part of the next hour was spent with them arguing about the bathroom situation. Mitchell wanted them to shower together to "save time" but Natasha thought that saving time meant some shower quickie and she was not up to that, at least not before breakfast. The way Mitchell had handled her the night before ensured that she was famished. After showering, Mitchell put on a pair of jeans and a fitted t-shirt that flattered his physique and Natasha put on a long blue strapless dress and a pair of sandals. She took Mitchell's advice to let her hair down and "flaunt her curls" as he had put it and together they went downstairs for breakfast.

When Natasha made her order, she surprised even the waiter. She asked for waffles, a pancake, toast, a Spanish omelet, bacon and coffee.

"Woman, is there something I need to know?" Mitchell asked smiling. Natasha rolled her eyes.

"I'm just hungry, Mitchell and there is so much to do today. I need my energy," she said. The waiter smiled and looked at Mitchell.

"And what will you have monsieur?" he asked.

"I'll have what she is having save for the waffles, toast and pancake," Mitchell said with a smile.

"Oui," the waiter said before walking off. She smiled at him as he looked at her.

"I am tempted to ask why you need all that energy. What do you have planned for me?" he asked. She shook her head and interlaced her fingers.

"That's for me to know and you to find out," she said. For the entirety of their breakfast, Mitchell tried as much as he could to get her to spill the beans about what she had planned but she would not budge. After breakfast they did a little sightseeing for almost three hours before they went back to their room. Natasha looked at Mitchell sadly and frowned. "I am about to ask for a very selfish favor," she said. Mitchell looked at her and shrugged.

"If I can get it, you will have it," he said.

"Well, it is not something that you can get, per se…it's really something that you can do for me," she said. Mitchell looked at her and shook his head.

"Then out with it, baby. Tell me what's on your mind," he said.

"Well, is it possible for us to spend one more night here? I mean, I miss Alexis and everything and I know we have to have a sit down with Naima but with the new account and everything, I have no idea when we will have another chance to just be us," she said. Mitchell smiled.

"I was thinking the same thing," he said as he walked towards her. She smiled back at him.

"Good. Will you do the honors of calling your parents and let them know we'll be twenty-four hours late?" she asked.

"Why do I have to do it? Mother likes you better," Mitchell said frowning.

"I have to call Naima and then I will make it up to you in more ways than one," she said as she took her phone out of her bag.

After making her call to Naima, she walked to the bathroom and changed out of her dress and into the naughty Cinderella costume and then pinned her hair up to make room to flaunt the tiara. When she was done, she got the clear slippers and then retouched her makeup before she finally walked out of the bathroom with her bag of "tricks" in her hand. Mitchell was still on the phone…she was not surprised. Mrs. Schmidt had a talent to talk your ear off. From the corner of his eye, Mitchell caught a glimpse of his wife in the sexy outfit. He never needed a better reason to ignore his mother like he did at that moment.

"Mother I have to go," he said before hanging up. He looked at Natasha from head to toe as he felt his cock getting harder in his pants. If there was ever a time his wife looked attractive, it was that moment, right there. He seemed to be tongue tied and rooted to the ground at the same time as Natasha made her way towards him. She dropped the bag at his feet and smiled.

"Tonight I want you to make me your slave, my Lord," she said in a low sexy voice. Mitchell could have sworn his cock twitched when he heard her say that.

"I'm sorry, what?" he asked, just to be sure he had heard the right thing.

"You heard me. I want you to spank me and fill me up like the naughty cock hungry girl I am," she said again.

Mitchell wanted to pinch himself. He looked at the bag at his feet and smiled. He could put two and two together. A horny, submissive Natasha dressed in a naughty costume and a bag at his feet, he knew exactly what was inside the bag. Mitchell suddenly felt nervous. The last time this had happened, Natasha had totally taken control of the situation. Right now, he had no idea what he was supposed to do.

"Babe, I …" Natasha kissed him and silenced him.

"I know you know what to do," she said when she pulled away. He smiled and kissed her again. Natasha could tell from the look in his eyes that her words had given him new encouragement. She suddenly felt a thrill go down her spine. She was not sure whether it was her desire or fear of the unknown that made her feel like a leaf caught in very bad weather. He held her by the waist and bent her over the bed. He used her hands to caress her softly as he raised the small skirt of the costume.

He swallowed hard when he laid his eyes on his wife's naked pussy thanks to the crotchless design of the costume. He spread her legs further and then lifted one of her legs. Natasha knew he wanted her to kneel on the bed. He had no idea how uncomfortable he made her. She was wet, so wet and there was cool air flowing freely in between her legs...not that it was making anything any better.

For some reason, Natasha was looking forward to what Lord Mitchell had in store for her. It was not that she was looking forward to being belted or whatever it was that he had in mind. All she knew was that the intensity of the moment excited her...everything about the moment. The hungry look on his face, her bare pussy before him, the enraged cock in his pants. She just knew that she wanted him, all of him, all he had to offer. She hankered for him, for his touch. She did not even give a damn whether his touch would be harsh or soft. She just wanted him.

She felt his hands leave her body and then felt a movement at her feet. She knew he was looking for the best toy to play with. It was not long before she felt his hands on her once again. She heard him take a long deep breath.

"You are the most beautiful woman I have ever seen and you are all mine," he said in a low voice. For some reason, the way he said it turned her on so much. "I am going to spank you with my hand as I love doing and then I will use something from your wonderful bag of tricks," he said before bringing his face down to kiss her bare waist. She smiled to herself as she waited anxiously for him to begin his punishment or whatever he wanted to call it. "Promise me you will use our safe word if I get too far," he said as his hand gently caressed her.

"Yes my Lord," she said. Mitchell smiled. He could get used to this. Natasha was still waiting for him to begin but she did not have to wait much longer. She felt a sting on her bare skin as he brought his hand down to spank her. She was not sure whether she heard the sound first or felt the sting first. She struggled hard not to scream as he brought his hand down again to spank her still stinging ass.

Mitchell raised his other hand and brought it down to spank her other cheek. By this time, Natasha knew that her ass was a bright crimson but it did not matter. She loved what he was doing to her. The way he was handling her, owning her. He went on probably for another full minute before he finally caressed her gently. Natasha knew that the first part of the punishment was over. She waited patiently as Mitchell picked up the spanking paddle from the bag. Now this was going to be true punishment.

SMACK!

She buried her face in the mattress to muffle her screams. She would hate to walk through the front doors of the chateau with her head hanging low. The blows were hard…hard enough to sting but not too bad to leave scars. All in all, Natasha knew that she would have a hard time sitting down later that evening. She was happy Mitchell had agreed to spend another night at the Chateau and this was the price she had to pay.

SMACK!

Another blow.

SMACK!

Another hard blow…

SMACK!

By this time, she wanted to scream. She wanted to say the safe word.

SMACK!

She needed to say the safe word…

SMACK!

"Umbrella!" she finally yelled. Mitchell felt terrible. He had hurt her. He wanted to apologize but he did not want to ruin the mood. He caressed her softly and then bent down and planted a kiss on each cheek. He like how hot her ass was against his cool lips.

Mitchell looked in the bag again and saw a bag that contained three silver balls and a remote. He could tell that the balls were definitely for anal play and he wanted to play. He undid the clasp that held the costume together in between her legs, revealing her bare pussy and ass to him. He took a bottle of lube he had seen in the bag and squeezed a generous amount onto his palm. He then went on to lube her ass so that the balls could go in smoothly. He then took one of the balls and gently pushed it inside her ass. He heard her gasp and felt her body tense up. He slowly slipped a hand underneath her and began rubbing her clit. She moaned as her muscles relaxed, allowing him to push another ball inside her.

"Think you can take another one?" he asked, concerned for her comfort and safety. She nodded.

"Yes, Master," she said obediently. Mitchell smiled. He was still having a hard time believing that this was the same woman who could bring the greatest men down in the board room. He grinned as he pushed the third ball inside her, making her moan her pleasure…or was it discomfort? He was not sure. He then took a step back and looked at her.

"Climb down off the bed," he said in a commanding tone. She climbed off the bed and stood in front of him. She was having a hard time maintaining her posture because standing there, it felt like the balls would fall out of the constraints of her ass. "Walk to the window and back," Mitchell said as he began undressing. He was quick to get out of his clothes revealing an angry cock that he had managed to keep behind the restraining fabric of his jeans. She slowly walked towards the window and then walked back towards him. Mitchell pressed a button on the remote and Natasha moaned and froze. Right then, he knew that he could not wait to be inside her pussy. He had to feel what she was feeling. He smiled at her and beckoned for her to walk faster. When she got to where he was, he smiled at her and she knew by the way he looked at her exactly what he wanted her to do. She got on her knees and began running her tongue along his cock head.

Mitchell threw his head back and moaned loudly as he felt her hot wet tongue circling the tip of his cock. Clearly, he had married a woman of many talents. He suddenly let out a gasp when she took his entire length inside her mouth. He looked down at her as she worked his cock in and out of her mouth with tremendous speed. If she kept this up, he was sure he was going to explode inside her mouth. He held her face in her hands and pulled himself out of her mouth. He then took her hands in his and helped her up. He gently pushed her on the bed making sure that the balls stayed inside her.

Mitchell positioned himself in between her legs and guided his cock inside her pussy. As he felt himself slide in, the pressure in her pussy and ass made her almost cry out and Mitchell knew this. He could see it written all over her face. He kissed her to muffle her scream as he began moving himself in and out of her, his momentum building. He reached for the remote that he had earlier thrown somewhere on the bed and pressed another button. He pulled away from her and cried out as he felt a vibrating sensation inside her ass. He pressed the button again and this time, he moaned in unison with Natasha as they both felt the overwhelming sensation take over their bodies. For Natasha the anal play alone made her want to give in to her body's desires and she knew that would mean the balls had to come out.

"Master, I need to cum," she said in a whisper.

"Fine do it," he said as he went on thrusting into her, making it harder for Natasha to maintain control.

"But the balls," she said. Mitchell stopped thrusting into her and looked into her eyes.

"Get them out. Push them out," he said as he looked at her. He looked at her as she closed her eyes and squeezed her vaginal muscles, forcing the balls out and tightening the grip around his cock at the same time. Mitchell moaned loudly as he felt the movement inside her ass and pussy and this was indeed time for his release.

"Babe..." Natasha moaned. Mitchell smiled. The sensation had taken over so much that she had forgotten that she was still a submissive. He suddenly felt her pussy tighten around him again before a gush of hot liquid overwhelmed him. It did not take long before he also exploded inside her. He collapsed on top of her as he panted.

"God, that was amazing," he said amid short breaths. She smiled and wrapped her legs around his waist. She could not even talk. All she wanted to do was just sleep. She kissed his cheek before giving in to the deep sleep that beckoned.

Book 9.

Healing Mr White

Chapter 1

Natasha let her gym bag drop to the floor as soon as she got home, then rushed to the kitchen and opened the refrigerator door. She grabbed a bottle of water and downed it in big gulps before she looked at the contents of the fridge again. There was a leftover slice of cake and half a blueberry pie that called out to her. There were also two slices of pizza that seemed to beckon with every lingering look but she knew they were all not a good idea. She had finally managed to shed her baby weight and stuffing herself was the one thing that would guarantee her looking like Mrs. Porky. She groaned as she grabbed a slice of watermelon, an orange and some strawberries. At least she could make her own shakes...tasty ones, nothing like that nasty stuff sold in stores branded "protein shake." To Natasha, they could have very well taken tar and gravel and called it a healthy shake. It tasted like such anyway.

She combined all the fruits in the blender and in minutes, she had a nice glass of tropical smoothie without the milk. She looked at the time as she drank it and sighed. She had exactly forty minutes before Rita walked in with Alexis and that would be the end of her personal quality time. She quickly walked to the living room and picked up her gym bag before she rushed to her room. She took a quick shower and then put on her night shirt and a pair of sweat pants. She then picked up her laptop and switched it on. She had every intention of working but she found herself looking at a blank page of her diary.

"I may as well just do this," she thought as she took a deep breath.

Dear Diary,

Whoever said that women can do anything and everything that men can had obviously never had a child. Don't get me wrong, I am not complaining, but sometimes I find myself picturing an island where I am all alone... sometimes being fanned by a scantily dressed Hawaiian man. Okay, maybe sometimes I picture Alexis and Mitchell there with me, but hey...that only happens every so often. But on a lighter note, I love being who I am...a wife, a mother and a career woman. The fact that I can juggle the three makes it all worthwhile.

She stopped typing and carried her laptop to the living room where she sat down and reclaimed her smoothie. She took a long sip before she went on typing.

The most important thing that keeps me going is that I have to be the kind of mother to Alexis I always dreamed of having, rather than having to be MIA in her life for whatever reason. It is just that simple. I love my family, and I would do anything for them and there is no way I would ever be a messy mother to my daughter. I learned from the best. I...

She paused as she took another sip. As she sipped on the drink, she could not help but notice just how quiet the house was. With Alexis out of the house and Mitchell away on one of his business trips, the house was like a ghost town. She was still thinking about that when she heard the doorbell. She walked to the door and opened it, smiling at Rita who had a sleeping Alexis in her arms. Natasha relieved her of the heavy two year old as Rita walked to the living room.

"She might be out till tomorrow. She was excited to be at the zoo," Rita said when Natasha came back. "I now understand what people mean when they talk of 'hands on parenting,'" she added. Natasha laughed as she walked to the kitchen.

"Smoothie?" she called out to Rita.

"What kind?" Rita asked.

"Homemade tropical," Natasha said.

"Cool," Rita said. Natasha poured her a glass and then walked back to the living room. "I must say, this new diet thing is a really strange thing for me to get used to," she said as Natasha sat down.

"Well, those love handles were not going to disappear on their own, now, were they? And the only way I make sure that they don't come back is by controlling my eating habits," Natasha said before she took a long sip.

"Yeah, I know that but you have always been petite," Rita said.

"Yeah, until I had a baby. Now I have to make sure that I work hard to bring the sexy back; otherwise I will be a Liza Minnelli till I die," Natasha said smiling.

"So anyway, how is the new job going?" Rita asked. Natasha smiled at her and shook her head as she tried getting the right words to describe whatever emotion she was feeling at the moment.

"Amazing. I don't think I have ever worked on anything so big," she said excitedly.

"Yeah, I can see it in your eyes. Hey, it even got you to the gym so it must be good," Rita said as she took the last sip of her smoothie. "Damn, what was in this? This is awesome," she said as she put the glass down.

"Watermelon, orange and strawberry," Natasha said as she put her own glass down. She looked at Rita and shook her head. "What do you mean, it got me to the gym?" she asked.

"Well, you were not an active gym member before the account came through and now you are spending ten hours a week at the gym. Need I say anymore?" Rita asked rhetorically. "Plus, you have a gym in the house. Why do you have to use a commercial one anyway?" she asked.

"I need to see people who are actually bigger than me so that I can feel encouraged. Plus I needed the trainer," Natasha said. Rita shook her head.

"You can get a personal trainer to come here," she said matter of factly. Natasha nodded.

"True but every time I come through those doors, I just want to sleep because I have to keep up with Alexis, catch up with my husband, sometimes work a little and at times also fix dinner. Trust me, there was no way I was going to work a trainer into that schedule," she said. "Plus, after all that, focusing would be hard especially when I know that my bed is just in the other room," she added. Rita laughed.

"Come on. You could make it work. It's just a matter of self-discipline," she said. "Kind of like you are doing now with the whole healthy eating thing," she added. Natasha frowned at her.

"Hey, you are my friend. You are supposed to be on my side," she said. Rita laughed and leaned back.

"How is Mitchell anyway? I haven't seen him in a while," she said. Natasha shrugged and smiled.

"He is okay. He's in England on business," she said.

"Sometimes I feel like the two of you have a virtual marriage," Rita said smiling. "It's like he is never around. Wasn't he in France last weekend?" she asked. Natasha smiled and nodded.

"Well, thanks to Skype, we talk everyday without fail but you are right. He has been a bit of a tourist lately," she said. Since the Nassir contract got signed, Natasha had been crazy busy at work and coincidentally, Mitchell had to work on another contract, a new client from Europe. Their tight schedules made it almost impossible for them to spend more than two days together before one of them had to be called to work. "But I like to think that it's a guarantee to early retirement,"

Natasha added. Rita smiled at her and nodded.

"I know what you mean, girl," she said. She then leaned in and looked at Natasha closely. "Lupe's gone, right?" she asked in a whisper. Natasha was intrigued. Why would Rita want to know whether the housekeeper was in or not?

"Yeah, she's gone. Why?" Natasha said. Rita moved closer.

"Awesome. Remember Tameka Sohn?" she asked, looking into Natasha's eyes. Natasha frowned and shook her head.

"Well, the name is familiar," she said still frowning.

"Come on, Tameka Sohn? We had her for tenth grade math," Rita said. Natasha smiled.

"Ms. Sohn? Why are you calling her by her first name? Are you guys that close?" she asked. Rita shook her head.

"No, that is how juicy the gossip is," she said. "So rumor has it that she is a cougar and that she is Jay's new play toy," she added excitedly. Natasha's eyes grew big.

"Jay? My ex Jay?" she asked surprised. Rita laughed.

"Yeah, that very one," she said. Natasha suddenly burst out laughing. "Guess you really ruined that one," she said. Natasha wiped a tear and leaned back.

"Well, his loss. But it's a good thing he messed up because I wouldn't have had Mitchell if he hadn't and I wouldn't trade Mitch for anything," she said. "But seriously though, Ms. Sohn? Did he run out of women whose lives he could ruin? How desperate must he have been?" she asked laughing. Rita nodded.

"I know, right? But like I said, you ruined him for other women," she said. Natasha pretended to fan her face.

"What can I say, it's genetic," she said smiling.

"I wonder how his mother is taking it," Rita said.

"Oh my god, does she even know about it? That drama queen may as well have had a heart attack," Natasha said. "Do you remember how agitated she was when we broke up?" she asked.

"When you dumped him." Rita corrected.

"Poh-tay-toh potato," Natasha said. "Bottom line, the relationship was over. But serves her right. She does have a holier than thou attitude. It's about time reality hit her hard across the face," she added. Rita raised an eyebrow and smiled.

"That's a whole new side of you I had never seen," she said. "What have you been keeping all bottled up inside for this long?" she asked. Natasha shrugged.

"A whole lot of stuff. Let's start with the fact that Jay was an ass and anything trickling down from that can be seen as valid collateral information," she said.

"Listen to you getting all legal up in here," she said in a mock ghetto voice. "Anyway, I'm hungry. Got any food?" she asked as she stood up.

"I have every kind of food, depending on what you are hungry for," Natasha said as she followed her to the kitchen. "Leftover pizza, casserole…oh, I made a lasagna yesterday," she said as she watched Rita look at the contents of her fridge. She pulled out the two slices of pizza and walked to the microwave. "None for me, thanks," she said. Rita looked at her and smiled.

"Sweetie, I was not intending to give you any. You are on a diet, remember?" she asked.

"Whoa, thanks for caring," Natasha said.

"What? I'm being supportive," Rita said. "Besides, I'm starved. I was doing inventory today and the only food I had all day was a bagel and cup of coffee," she added. Natasha smiled. Rita reached for some green goo in the fridge and handed it to Natasha. "But in the spirit of being supportive, here," she said. Natasha looked at her and raised an eyebrow.

"What am I supposed to do with this?" she asked.

"You are all about smoothies and nasty tasting fluid and this qualifies for both of those descriptions. So drink it, or eat it... whatever you are supposed to do," Rita said. Natasha shook her head.

"This is Alexis'. It's her vegetables," she said putting it back.

"Now you are making the baby eat the goo too?" Rita asked frowning.

"She has always had the vegetables," Natasha said as she leaned against the counter.

"If they are her vegetables, where is the label?" Rita asked.

"Why do I feel like am being interrogated? You think I would force my child to have some shitty tasting goo?" she paused a little and then snapped her fingers. "Wait, there was that time she had a bad case of diarrhea. Then, I had to make her drink some weird rehydration salts. Tasted like warm pee," she added. Rita frowned as she took one slice of pizza from the microwave before putting the other one in.

"How do you even know how warm pee tastes like? Why would you have an idea of pee...you know what, never mind," she said. Natasha laughed.

"Everyone knows what pee tastes like because somehow, everyone has tasted their pee at some point in their lives," she said as she cut a small piece of Rita's warm pizza. "Oh God, that's heavenly," she said when she bit into it. Rita laughed.

"Come on, have one slice. That won't mess up your diet plan that much, will it?" she asked. Natasha shrugged

"I will be back at the gym for two hours tomorrow. So what the hell," she said as she took another bite. "Oh my God, I have missed the taste of melted cheese," she said dramatically. Rita laughed as she took her own slice out of the microwave. She walked over to the fridge and took out two cans of soda. "Oh no, one slice of pizza is enough. I am not about to have carbonated drinks," Natasha said as she walked to the fridge and pulled out a bottle of water.

"You are really taking this diet thing seriously, huh?" Rita asked as they made their way back to the living room. Natasha smiled and nodded.

"I had love handles, Rita. Love handles. I was one slice of chocolate cake away from getting the entire Mabel Simmons look," she said as she sat down.

"Who's Mabel Simmons?" Rita asked looking at her. Natasha looked at her surprised.

"No self-respecting black woman can ask that question with a straight face," she said.

"Why? Should I know her?" Rita asked. Natasha raised an eyebrow.

"Oh my God, you really don't know her. I thought you are a Tyler Perry fan," Natasha said. Rita shrugged.

"I am, what does that got to do with…" her words trailed off when she suddenly realized what Natasha had been driving at. "Mabel Simmons is Madea, isn't she?" she asked.

"Ding! Ding! Ding! We have a winner," Natasha said dramatically. Rita laughed and shook her head.

"I will never understand why you didn't go for a career in show business," she said.

"Oh no, I don't have the stomach for it," Natasha said. Rita squinted.

Are you sure?" she asked. Natasha nodded.

"One hundred percent," she said. Just then they heard Alexis' shrill cry pierce the serenity of the room. "Duty calls," Natasha said as she stood up. She walked to the nursery and found Alexis standing in her crib. "Hey sweetie," she said as she picked her up in her arms. "I thought you'd be out until tomorrow. Why are you up?" she asked as she made faces at Alexis, making her smile even though her cheeks had tear streaks. "You want to go say hi to Auntie Rita?" she said as she walked to the living room.

"There is our girl," Rita said as Natasha sat down next to her. The baby reached for Rita's pizza. "Whoa, hungry already?"

Rita asked as she cut a small piece and fed it to her.

"Yeah, she will have that for the next hour," Natasha said smiling.

"They are so cute when they are this young. Why can't some scientist come up with an antidote that makes them remain this way?" Rita asked as they watched her struggle with the small piece of pizza.

"I know, right? I am not looking forward to her teenage years," Natasha said.

"Why do you have to be like so uncool mom? I hate you. Urgh!" Rita said in a mock teenage voice. Natasha shook her head.

"We really need to get that scientist before we get to that age," she said just as her phone rang. She smiled. "I think this is your daddy, Alexis," she said before she picked up. "Hey Mitchell," she said.

"Actually Natasha, it's Patrick Keller." Natasha frowned and looked at Rita.

"Oh hi, Patrick. Is Mitchell there with you?" she asked.

"Well actually yes, but there's been some sort of accident," Patrick said.

"What do you mean, some sort of accident? Where's Mitchell? I want to talk to my husband," Natasha said as she stood up and walked to the kitchen. Rita looked at her and picked Alexis up. She had no idea what was happening but she needed to know. She put Alexis in the playpen and then walked to the kitchen where Natasha was talking in hushed tones.

"Tasha, what's going on?" she asked as she looked at Natasha who was still talking on the phone. "Natasha!" she called again when she saw Natasha hanging up. Something was definitely the matter and she was either too scared or too shocked to speak. Rita walked over to her and draped an arm around her shoulders before she walked her back to the living room. "Tasha, I need you to tell me what the hell is going on," she said as she looked into her eyes.

"Mitch…he…" Natasha started.

"Yeah, what did Mitch do? Is he okay?" Rita asked looking at her. "Sweetie, I need to know what is going through your head. What happened? Where is Mitch? Is he okay?" she asked, not sure which question she wanted answered first.

"That was Patrick Keller, Mitchell's business associate in England," Natasha said. She seemed to be staring into space.

"Okay. What did he say?" Rita asked.

"That there was an accident and that Mitchell was hurt," Natasha said as a tear rolled down her cheek.

"Was it serious? Is he badly hurt?" Rita asked but Natasha never answered. She just stared into oblivion with a tear rolling down her other cheek.

Chapter 2

Natasha was shaking as she held the phone tightly. Rita was getting more and more worried. She had never seen her best friend like this.

"Tasha, talk to me. What's going on?" she asked again but Natasha was quiet. Tears were rolling down her cheeks and as much as Rita wanted to help, she couldn't do anything, not without knowing what was making Natasha so upset. She slowly took the phone from her hands and put it on the table before she put her hands on Natasha's shoulders. She looked into her eyes even though she knew that Natasha's blank look was looking way past her. "Let it out," she said in a low voice.

Natasha became hysterical. She cried on Rita's shoulder for a long minute before she finally pulled away.

"Can you talk now?" Rita asked and Natasha nodded. "Okay, who was that on the phone and what did they say to get you this upset?" Rita asked again.

"Remember when I told you Mitchell is in England on business? Well, that was one of his associates, Patrick Keller. He said that Mitch had an accident," Natasha said as she choked back her tears.

"What kind of accident?" Rita asked. Natasha shook her head.

"I…I don't know," she said.

"Okay, you go lie down…" Rita said.

"But Alexis…." Natasha started to say before Rita shook her head.

"I spend most of my time with that baby. I will feed her, bathe her and get her to bed. You just lie down," she said.

"Rita, I can't...I can't just sleep. Not when Mitch is..." Rita shook her head again, shutting her up.

"Mitchell is all the way in England and you are here. There is nothing you can do. Not right now anyway. Come on, I'll give you a Valium," Rita said as she walked her back to the living room.

"Why do you have Valium?" Natasha asked.

"Sweetie, every time I visit my mother at the hospice, I need a Valium and every time some weirdo art collector comes into the gallery, I need another one. Story of my life," Rita said.

Natasha smiled. "At least I got you to smile," Rita said as she got a bottle of pills from her purse. She gave a pill to Natasha and then walked to the kitchen to get her some water. When she came back, she handed her the glass and watched as she took the pill. "Good, now go lie down. I'll give the baby some of the green goo I saw in the fridge," Rita said as she watched Natasha walk towards the hallway. She felt sorry for her friend but she also needed to know what was going on if she was going to help. She looked at Alexis who was busy nibbling on her teething toy in the playpen before she went to the kitchen to heat her food. A few minutes later, she had Alexis in her high chair. She looked at the big eyed toddler and smiled.

"Now, we've been on this rodeo before, Alexis, and I need you to cooperate with me if we are going to make this work," she said. Alexis chuckled and Rita rolled her eyes. "Of course, you would laugh at me. You do that every time I talk to you," she said and then sighed. She was talking to babies now...

After a long hour, Alexis was fed and bathed and Rita could finally breathe easy. She looked at her clothes and sighed. Her top was covered in the baby's vegetables, and her pants, well, they also shared in the same fate. After she put the baby to bed, she walked to the guest room where she had left a few of her clothes the last time she stayed over at Mitchell and Natasha's place. She changed into a pair of pants and a sleeveless top before checking in on Natasha, who was now sound asleep. She then walked back to the living room with the baby monitor in her hand and then pulled her phone out of her bag. She sat down as she dialed Stacy's number.

"Hi Rita," Stacy said excitedly. Rita never understood why Stacy always seemed so happy.

"Hi girl. How's your day?" Rita asked.

"Good. Can't complain. How's yours?" she asked.

"Not so good. I need a favor," Rita said.

"Sure anything." Rita smiled. She could always count on Stacy.

"Would you happen to know a Patrick Keller?" she asked.

"Sure. That's Mitchell's associate from England. As a matter of fact, that's where Mitchell is right now. Why do you ask?" Stacy asked.

"Keller just called Natasha about some accident Mitchell was in," Rita said.

"What? When?" Stacy asked. She sounded frantic.

"Sometime today. Natasha got the call maybe an hour, an

hour and a half ago but we don't know the whole story. I need you to call Keller and find out everything for me, for Tasha's sake," Rita explained.

"Oh man, how is Tasha?" Stacy asked. Rita took a long deep breath.

"Not so good. I gave her a pill so that she could rest up. So will you make that call for me, like right now?" Rita asked.

"Sure. I'll call you back when I find out anything," Stacy said before hanging up.

Rita made herself busy and cleared the table and then did the dishes. She liked being busy when nervous to get her mind off things. After she was done, she looked at the time and sighed. It had almost been forty minutes since she asked Stacy to make the call.

"What could be taking that long? It's just a call," she thought. *"What if it's something serious? What if Stacy couldn't get any information because…"* Her random traumatic thoughts were interrupted when she heard her phone ringing. "Hey, what did you find out?" she asked when she picked up.

"It was a minor accident, nothing to worry about," Stacy said. Rita could tell that even she was relieved.

"Oh, thank God. What happened exactly?" Rita asked.

"The clients decided to have a game of soccer and one of them had a not so clean game. So, Mitchell ended up getting injured. He will be jetting in later this evening. So, let Tasha know, will you?" Stacy said. Rita breathed a sigh of relief. "It will be at around eleven," she added.

"Thanks Stace. I will let her know," Rita said before she hang up. She looked at the time and sighed. She had a couple of hours until Mitchell came back and she was a hundred percent sure that the effects of the Valium would not have worn off. She took her phone and called Dave. He would know exactly what to do.

"Hey babe," he said when he picked up.

"Hey," Rita said.

"What's wrong? You sound exhausted," he said.

"Well, I had to take care of Alexis and Natasha. So yeah, I'm trying hard to hold myself together," she said.

"Why? Is Tasha not okay?" Dave asked, sounding concerned.

"Well, she went frantic when she found out that her husband was in an accident," Rita said.

"What? When? Is Mitchell okay?" Dave asked.

"Yeah, he is okay. It was a petty accident. Nothing major but I do need your help," she said. "Are you on call tonight?" she asked.

"I was actually about to get off when you called," he said. "Why do you ask?"

"Well, Mitchell is coming in at eleven and I gave Natasha a Valium," she started.

"Why the hell would you do that?" Dave asked.

"Did you not hear me say that she was frantic? I could hardly calm her down and I needed her out of my hair so that I could think of my next move," she said in her defense.

"So you gave her a Valium?" Dave asked. Rita could hear the criticism in his voice.

"Well, I had to do something. Anyway, you are a doctor, so I will need you at the airport when Mitchell touches down and because I can't leave Alexis and Natasha on their own, I need you to do it and then bring him back here when you are done with your preliminary doctor check-ups," she said. Dave laughed. "I'm serious," she said.

"I know you are. It's just like you sound like my boss when you order me around like that," he said.

"I'm sorry. I'm just trying to get control of the situation and it is not working very well," she said.

"You don't have to defend yourself, I get it. I'll see you in a few, okay?" he asked.

"Thanks Dave," she said before hanging up. She sat down and took a long deep breath. Everything was sorted. All she had to do was just wait for Dave to get home…

*****

When Natasha woke up, her head felt heavy. She could hear voices coming from the living room. When she raised her head, she noticed that she was on top of the covers and wondered why. Her heart suddenly started beating faster when she realized what had happened just before she came to bed. She'd gotten a call from Patrick Keller about Mitchell. There had been some sort of accident. Her head suddenly felt heavy and even though she wanted to get out of bed, she found herself struggling. She remembered Rita giving her a pill…Valium. Could this have been why she felt so weak? She then felt her head getting heavier and heavier….

She was not sure how long she had been out but when she woke up, she felt stronger than she did when she woke up the first time. She could still hear the voices from the living room. She got up from the bed and walked to the bathroom. She quickly brushed her teeth and then splashed some cold water on her face before she walked to the living room. It was a full house. Rita, Dave, Mona, Leo, Mitchell's mother and sister, and even her own family, Estelle and Eric, were there but Mitchell's mother and Eric were seated in the kitchen…not that Natasha really cared. The person she was really worried about, Mitchell, was seated in the reclining chair with his foot elevated. He had a brace on but she did not care. He was fine. She did not even care to say anything to the rest of the people in the room. She walked straight up to Mitchell and kissed him hard right on the lips.

"Whoa, great to see you too, Tasha," Mitchell said when she finally pulled away.

"Don't you ever scare me like that again or so help me God I will kill you myself," she said in a whisper.

"Oh, you are stuck with me, babe," Mitchell said before Natasha kissed him again.

"We are also fine, babe, thanks for asking," Mona said loud enough for everyone to hear. Natasha laughed as she pulled away from Mitchell. Estelle stood up and walked towards them. Natasha smiled at her and hugged her.

"Hi baby," she said as she held Natasha closely. "At first I was upset you didn't call me but then I found out that Rita drugged you," she added, loudly enough for Rita to hear.

"I did not drug my best friend," Rita said frowning.

"Honey, you gave her a Valium without a prescription. Do you have any idea how strong diazepam is?" Dave asked.

"I take it all the time and I'm fine," Rita said in her defense.

"That can't be good. Right Dave?" Mona asked. Dave shook his head. "Take care. You could be a junkie in the making," she added, laughing. Rita threw one of the throw pillows at her.

"The pill was especially strong because of Natasha's new diet, which by the way I do not support," Dave said. Estelle looked at Natasha and frowned.

"Are you starving yourself in the name of a diet?" Estelle asked.

"I need to shed this baby weight, Nan, and it's not starving. I am just on a strict diet for the duration of my program," she said.

"What program?" Mona asked.

"She signed up for a crazy ten hours a week workout program that is also dependent on what she eats," Rita said.

"But honey, I saw you rock a bandage dress just last week," Mona said.

"And do you know what I had under that dress? Yards and yards of spandex," Natasha said. Estelle shook her head.

"I will never understand you children," Estelle said. Natasha smiled and looked at Mitchell.

"What happened?" she asked.

"Patrick got me to play soccer and let's just say that I am not that good at tackling," he said. Natasha rolled her eyes.

"Not that good? Your leg is in a brace," she said, surprised that he could be so relaxed.

"Chill, babe. It's just a minor injury. I believe they called it a stress fracture," he said. "Relax honey, it's just a fracture," Mitchell said again. Natasha shook her head.

"Just a fracture? That's like telling airport security to relax because it's just a bomb," she said. Leo laughed.

"Yeah buddy. I think Tasha is right. You are taking this a little too lightly," he said.

"Yeah, and I thought stress fractures just occurred because of pressure, not impact," Natasha said. Leo and Mitchell looked at her and raised an eyebrow. "Oh, did I forget to mention that I happen to have an entire army of soccer crazed male cousins?" she said.

"Clearly," Leo said.

"Actually, his x-rays show that he had a pre-existing stress fracture but the impact is why his leg is in a brace. It was literally the straw that broke the camel's back," Dave explained. Natasha looked at Mitchell.

"I think he just referred to you as a camel," she said, smiling.

"Well, he is the proverbial camel in this conversation isn't he?" Rita asked.

"Yeah and the proverbial camel is still in the room. He can't exactly leave at will," Mitchell said. Natasha smiled again.

"So, how long are we going to have the brace on?" she asked looking at Dave.

"Well, he should be back on his feet soon enough plus with the help of the crutches..." Dave started.

"...he has crutches?" Natasha asked, cutting Dave short.

"Did I forget to mention that?" Mitchell asked. Natasha turned and looked at him angrily.

"I literally just woke up. When would you have had the time to mention it?" she asked.

"Dave, would you tell her to calm down? It's not like I am in a wheelchair or anything," Mitchell said. Natasha shook her head.

"It is a big deal, Mitchell, and it's time you realized that," she said. Mitchell held her hand and smiled at her.

"We are going to be okay. We always work things through," he said. Natasha frowned and looked at Dave.

"What should we do? How are we supposed to handle this?" she asked.

"Well, as long as you keep the leg elevated and use the crutches every time you walk, you should be fine," Dave said to Mitchell. Natasha frowned.

"See, we'll be fine," Mitchell said.

"Let me go say hi to my dad and your mom," Natasha said as she walked into the kitchen. She knew she still had a frown on her face but she could not help it. It had been a long day.

"There she is," Eric said as she walked in.

"Hi Daddy," she said as she hugged him.

"Natasha dear, you should turn that frown upside down. After all, Mitchell is fine," Mrs. Schmidt said as she wrapped her own arms around Natasha. "How is my favorite daughter in law?" she asked.

"Mrs. Schmidt, I am still your only daughter in law," Natasha said.

"And that's why you are my favorite," Mrs. Schmidt said with a smile.

"How are you? You were out for quite a while," Eric said.

"Really? How long was I out? What's the time?" Natasha asked.

"It is ten in the morning," Eric said. Natasha's eyes grew wide. "And that's why we don't take sleeping pills without a prescription," he added.

"I didn't just take one, Dad. Rita gave it to me," she said.

"Well, you took it," Eric said.

"Come on, Eric. Leave the poor girl alone," Mrs. Schmidt said. Natasha gave her an appreciative look.

"Guess we all know who my favorite parent is right now," Natasha said as she looked at her dad. The two laughed as Natasha grabbed a bottle of water from the fridge.

"Hey, you should eat something, not just have water," Mrs. Schmidt said.

"Yeah, you should eat," Eric said.

"I'm not hungry," she said.

"That's because of that diet you are on," Mrs. Schmidt said as she climbed off the stool she was seated on. She walked to the fridge and took two eggs out. "I'll make you a proper breakfast," she said as she beat the eggs in a cup.

"You also know about the diet?" Natasha asked.

"We had to find out why you were out for more than twelve hours, so Rita fessed up," Eric said.

"Well, you should know that it is not really a diet but actually a..." she sighed when she realized that even she could not believe whatever she was about to say. "Spice the eggs, Mrs. Schmidt. That should give my brain the jumpstart it needs," she said as she buried her face in her hands. Eric looked at her and tucked a strand of her hair behind her ear.

"For a person who just woke up, you look beat," he said.

"This whole thing is too new for me and I just don't know how to handle it," she said, looking at Eric.

"Oh please, all Schmidt men get a leg injury at some point in their lives. It is kind of like a rite of passage," Mrs. Schmidt said as she seasoned the omelet that was now on the stove.

"His father still has a scar from the fourth year of our marriage, fell down the stairs. His grandfather slipped on ice and his great-grandfather coincidentally had a soccer injury. Relax, he'll be fine," she said as she served the omelet on a plate.

"See, it's not a big deal," Eric said.

"Eat up and relax. My son may have had a few accidents in his past, but the one thing he did well was getting you to make an honest man out of him. And you are the most loving, caring woman ever. So I know he will be okay," she said, smiling.

Natasha smiled and took a bite of her omelet. Everyone was right. She married Mitchell for better or worse and this was one of those lows in their marriage that she would power through.

Chapter 3

Two weeks after the accident, Mitchell and Natasha were at the doctor's office. Natasha had tried to find the perfect balance between work, being a wife and being a mother. She had to; otherwise it was a sure thing that she would crack under the pressure. To say that she was no longer worried would be a big joke because the truth was she was more scared than ever. The accident, even though it was a minor one, was an awakening for her. She realized that any accident, however minor, was a big impact to her family. She began thinking of how life would be without Mitchell, without the father of her child, and it was something that she could not live with.

She took a long deep breath when she saw the doctor walking into the office holding the x-rays he had taken earlier of Mitchell's fracture.. This was the moment of truth. The doctor had said that he would have a better idea of what they were dealing with after the fourth round of physiotherapy and today was the day of reckoning. At first Natasha did not understand why a prognosis would take this long to deliver, but it was something about finding out how quickly a patient responded to treatment, both medicinal and therapeutic.

"Dr. Michelson, hello," she said as the brown haired man took a seat. Mitchell shook the doctor's hand before he sat down.

"Natasha, Mitchell. Good to see you too, and I have some good news," he said smiling at them. Natasha looked at Mitchell and smiled.

"Okay, what's the good news?" Mitchell asked.

"We all know that the injury was not that bad since it was just a stress fracture. And the latest x-rays show that you should be fine after eight weeks of physio," the doctor said. Mitchell raised an eyebrow and shook his head.

"Did you just say eight weeks?" he asked. The doctor smiled and nodded.

"Normally people would go for even six months but I don't see the need of all that. Physiotherapy and keeping the weight off the leg should do it," he said. Mitchell sighed.

"Keeping the weight off means keeping it elevated which means that I should also be immobilized, right?" he asked. Natasha frowned.

"Well, yes. You have to take it easy for a while," Dr. Michelson said. "Try keeping moving around to the absolute minimum," he added.

"That means no office for a while. Your clients will understand," Natasha said. Mitchell ran his fingers through his hair and groaned.

"Do you have any idea how important this week is?" he asked. Natasha put her hand on his.

"We'll talk about this later. Let us just sort this out first," she said in a low voice, even though Dr. Michelson's office was quiet enough to ensure that her whispering was no good.

"You will continue with your physiotherapy, so far so good, but you must make sure that it is not less than three times a week or more than five rounds in the same week. Overworking will only make your already sore muscles worse," the doctor said as he scribbled on his prescription pad. "That's a prescription for a refill of your pain meds," he added as he handed Mitchell the prescription.

"So I can pick this up on the way out?" Mitchell asked. The doctor nodded and smiled.

'I'm sure the pharmacy has everything you need," he said.

"Okay, then I guess we are done here," Natasha said as she took the x-rays from Michelson.

She had a long task ahead and she was not even sure she had it in her to handle everything. She had thought of getting a live-in nanny to help out with Alexis and menial tasks around the house but Estelle wouldn't hear of it. According to her that would have been a waste of money and she would gladly spend time with her great-grandchild for free, in her words.

"Thanks for everything," Natasha said to the doctor as she slowly followed Mitchell out.

"Sure. See you next week," Dr. Michelson said as they walked out.

The longer than usual walk to the car was quiet as Mitchell thought of how he would survive not working while Natasha tried planning how the next couple of weeks were going to be.

"We were signing a new deal with the guys from Wales this week, " Mitchell said when Natasha got in the driver's seat.

"So? You can still do that without having to be at the office," she said as she started the car engine.

"Well, I was supposed to fly out to Wales the day after tomorrow. What is going to happen now?" he asked. Natasha knew that he was just sulking because he was practically bedridden for the next few weeks.

"I don't know what age you are in Mitch, but back in my time they had a little something called Skype. You can call them and explain why you cannot go out and if worse comes to worst I can drive to the office and you can have a conference call there," she said as she drove.

"Yes but…it's just not the same," he said. Natasha smiled.

"Admit it, you just hate being in the house," she said.

"It's literally killing me," he said. "I've already spent two weeks out of work. I don't think I can survive another two months," he added as he leaned back on the head rest.

"Hold on, the doctor did not say anything about you not being able to go back to work for another two months. Your luck may change, you never know," she said smiling.

"Well, Lady Luck has not exactly been kissing my ass lately," he said. Natasha shook her head.

"What do you mean? We've had some of the best business in the last few months," she said.

"Well, that's been all you. This was going to be something that I brought to the table," he said. Natasha looked at him and smiled.

"Mitchell Schmidt, are you jealous that I brought in one of the best clients you have ever had and you haven't?" she asked. He looked at her and smiled.

"Jealousy is a strong word," he said.

"Oh baby, come on. We'll make it work," she said as she maneuvered the last corner before they got home. "We always do," she added. Mitchell smiled and shrugged.

"I know," he said as they pulled into their driveway. Natasha got out and helped him out of his seat even though he was adamant that he could handle everything on his own. She hated that he would not let her get him a wheelchair. She thought that would make everything so much easier but it was his call…this time. When they finally got inside the house, she helped him sit down before she collapsed next to him. Mitchell looked at her and smiled. "Tired?" he asked.

"Not at all," she said shaking her head.

"Tasha, it's okay to admit you are tired. I can see the perspiration on your forehead," he said laughing. Natasha rolled her eyes.

"Then why did you ask?" she asked smiling at him.

"Because I love you and I care about you," he said holding her hand in his. She smiled and lifted his hand up to her lips to give it a little kiss.

"You know what this reminds me of?" she asked looking into his eyes. Mitchell shook his head. "When I was pregnant with Alexis," she said smiling. Mitchell pretended to choke. "What?" she asked as she looked at him.

"Am I moody and hungry for everything?" Mitchell asked.

"I was not moody and hungry for every single thing. I just had a particular palate," she said. Mitchell laughed.

"Oh, you were. We almost tripled our food intake in your second and third trimesters. And the moods, babe, you were getting upset over anything and everything plus you also cried when watching SpongeBob," he said looking at her.

"One, It was Finding Nemo…that is some sad shit, and two, SpongeBob? Really?" she asked.

"I have the home movies to prove it but that might take a while given my current condition and everything," he said smiling. Natasha shook her head.

"Yeah in that same light, you've heard of the no body no crime policy right? Because I watch enough CSI. I know how to get rid of a body," she said.

"And what would you tell Alexis?" Mitchell asked.

"Daddy went on a trip to a place without phones," she said as she squinted. Mitchell shook his head.

"With all the TV you watch, is that all you can come up with?" he asked.

"Well, I will have time to think about that one. Alexis is only two right now," Natasha said as she picked up her phone and dialed Stacy.

"What are you doing?" he asked.

"We are going to prep Stacy together and send her to England for your super awesome meeting where she is going to close the deal for you and consequently, reclaim my respect for you," she said casually as she put her phone to her ear.

Mitchell smiled. He loved how much effort she put into this but again, she didn't have a choice. This was it. He looked at her as she talked on the phone and once again he smiled. He had married her for better and worse and maybe this was not half as bad as nine months of mood swings but still, he knew and understood that it was a difficult time yet she was being a real trooper. Natasha was doing anything and everything that she could in order to make his life easier during this time and she was doing a pretty darn good job at it.

When Natasha finished talking to Stacy, she hung up and turned to look at him excitedly. "Okay, she will be here in half an hour. I'll get you your laptop," she said as she walked to the bedroom.

When she got back to the living room, she found Mitchell trying to walk to the kitchen. She was immediately annoyed and scared at the same time. "What the hell do you think you are doing?" she asked as she put the laptop down on the couch.

"I wanted to go make a sandwich," he said looking at her.

"Why didn't you wait for me? And why are you not using crutches?" she asked as she picked up the crutches and walked over to him.

"Well, you can't blame me for trying," he said as he balanced himself on the crutches.

"Well, bad idea because keeping the weight off that leg is exactly what you need to get better, not the other way round. Damn it, Mitchell," Natasha said as she suddenly took one crutch away. "Actually, sit. I will make you your sandwich; I know how you like it," she said as she helped him back in his chair.

She sighed as she walked to the kitchen and then opened the fridge. She took out the ham and made him the sandwich. She was about to walk back to the living room when she heard the doorbell. She walked to the door and opened it to find Stacy standing at the doorstep. "I thought you were not supposed to be here for another twenty minutes," she said as she stepped aside for Stacy to get in.

"Yeah, something about an impromptu trip to the UK can make you drive like a crazy person," Stacy said. "Don't worry, I didn't get any speeding tickets," she added quickly when she noticed Natasha's look.

"Go on, Mitchell is in the living room. I'll be right there," Natasha said as she walked back to the kitchen. She made an extra sandwich for Stacy and then grabbed a few bottles of water from the fridge before she carried everything out to the two of them. She placed the tray on the table and handed them their sandwiches.

"So, you're kind of like bedridden?" Stacy asked. Natasha smiled. Stacy said the most weirdly (and sometimes inappropriate) things when nervous.

"Not really but I guess you could say that. I should be back to full function in a few weeks," Mitchell said smiling.

"Good to hear that," Stacy said as she bit into the sandwich. "So, were you guys serious about England or were you screwing with me?" she asked. "Forgive my language sir," she added quickly. Again Natasha smiled to herself. This Stacy seated in front of her was the same one she had first started working with, full of potential and yet she did not even know it.

"It is for real and you are here now because you leave tomorrow morning," Mitchell said. Stacy took a long deep breath and nodded.

"Yeah, but don't sweat it. You don't have to make any pitches or anything, Mitch already did that," Natasha started.

"Everything you need to know is that the company is all about online retail marketing. They are really big in the UK and they are making their entrance to the American market and that's where we come in," Mitchell said.

"So, they are like kind of the next eBay?" Stacy asked. Mitchell shook his head.

"Actually no. eBay is a consumer to consumer corporation. What these guys do is basically help you get your everyday product from their site. It's just online shopping dressed in a fancy outfit," he explained.

"Oh okay," Stacy said.

"So you get it?" Mitchell asked.

"Yeah, you need to be very sure about it before you go in," Natasha said.

"I do, totally. Plus I plan to spend the better part of the night going through the file," Stacy said smiling.

"Can't you do that on the plane and sleep instead?" Natasha asked.

"I'm going to be on a private jet. There is no way I am working on board," Stacy said. Natasha and Mitchell exchanged glances and they were not too subtle about it. "What? Am I not going on the jet?" Stacy asked.

"Well, no," Natasha said.

"Bummer," Stacy said under her breath.

"But we'll get you business class tickets. There is no way my representative is going to fly coach," Mitchell added quickly.

"Yeah, we'll definitely do that," Natasha said smiling.

"Well, I will still not work on board," Stacy said.

"Whatever works for you," Mitchell said. "One thing though, how good are you at tennis?" he asked.

"Why?" Stacy asked looking at him.

"Because this client has a thing for outdoor sport. And given the time you will be leaving here, you will most likely get there just as he is about to do his hour long tennis workout," he said. Natasha looked at him and frowned. "Trust me, it's a thing," he said, looking at Natasha.

"Well, I am pretty good. I have all the trophies at my mom's to prove it," Stacy said, smiling.

"Good. Make sure you pack something to wear to the tennis court and make me proud," Mitchell said smiling.

"Don't worry, I will come back with a signed contract," she said as she took a bite of her sandwich. "By the way, Tasha, you will be having a conference call later today. Just a follow up on the new business," she added before taking another bite. Natasha frowned. Between taking care of Mitchell and work, she had completely forgotten that she was handling both of their workloads, and it was taking its toll on her.

"What time?" she asked as she looked at Stacy.

"Two-thirty. But it should be short since it's just a follow up. You know how it goes," Stacy said.

Natasha suddenly had an idea. To her Stacy was more than just her executive assistant. She was basically the next Natasha Schmidt. She had great potential and ever since Natasha realized this, she had been grooming her to take over for her one day.

"If it's no big deal, then why don't you do it?" Natasha asked, smiling.

"Okay, Tasha, are you sure about this?" Stacy asked.

"Yeah, Tasha, are you sure?" Mitchell asked. He was having a hard time believing that Natasha would be okay with charging all this responsibility to Stacy all at once.

"Think about it, Mitchell. Over the past two years, Stacy has been the hands on person on almost all our campaigns. I make the decisions but she pulls the strings. She knows this stuff and she is ready for it. I am sure," Natasha said. "Plus we did send out that memo about your accident. No one expects us to be working for another few weeks," she added.

"You believe in me that much?" Stacy asked, smiling.

"Well you were always too good to be just an assistant," Natasha said. "And I don't want you to be an assistant forever. You are a born leader," she said. Stacy smiled and took the last bite of her sandwich before she stood up. "Where are you going?" Natasha asked.

"I have a long night ahead going over the contract but before that I am going shopping for something executive for that conference call," Stacy said excitedly.

"Sweetie, it's a call. They only see half your body," Natasha said.

"And I will make sure the half they see screams executive," Stacy said, smiling. "Get well soon, boss," she said before she walked out of the living room and out of the house.

"Now that's passion you don't see every day in a worker," Natasha said smiling. Mitchell looked at her and smiled.

"Come here," he said. She stood up from the couch and walked towards him. He took her hand in his and pulled her down to meet her lips in a soft kiss. "The kind of passion I want is right here," he said when he pulled away. She smiled and held the back of his neck before she leaned forward to kiss him again, all the while thinking of how the sex would work now that Mitchell was mildly immobilized.

Chapter 4

Natasha looked around the lingerie shop that Rita had recommended and sighed. Rita had forgotten to mention that the store had so much variety. She was literally spoiled for choice. There were beautiful...no...*hot* corsets, bustiers and every single thing that would drive a man and some gay women nuts. She was still looking at the array of intimate wear when the attendant walked up to her.

"You look like you need some help," the female attendant said. Natasha looked at her and smiled.

"Yes and no...I want everything," she said. The attendant smiled.

"Okay, we have everything for whatever personality you are looking for," the attendant said as she held up a pink pleated baby doll nightie. "This is exactly what you need if you are going for the good old girl next door thing," she said. Natasha nodded and smiled.

"Well, I am looking for something a bit more...um... provocative," she said. The attendant put the nightie back and nodded.

"Well, how about this? Lace trim, low cut bust and with those babies, I don't need to tell you that this will totally work in your favor," she said. Natasha smiled.

"Well, that works. Let's just put a pin on that...no, I'll take it," Natasha said as she put the lingerie over her shoulder. "What else do you have?" she asked excitedly.

"Well, there is this simple, sexy satin and lace slip. We have it in red, blue and pink," the attendant told her. Natasha smiled.

"It has a hint of suburban vibe but I can rock it just as well," she said as she picked up the red one. A green satin bustier caught her eye and she walked towards it. "How about this?" she asked.

"Well, I see you have impeccable taste," the attendant said as she handed her the satin bustier with the lace over lace. Natasha looked at it and smiled. She could definitely see herself in it and she could see Mitchell's face when he saw her. It was complete with garter straps and sheer center cutouts. It would show off every single curve of her body and she just could not wait to see herself in it. "Should I add it on?" the attendant asked.

"Oh yeah," Natasha said smiling.

"So, I have to ask," the attendant said as Natasha handed her a credit card. "Your last name is Schmidt and you look really familiar so...is there any chance you are related to that heartthrob Mitchell Schmidt? The heir to the Nolan Schmidt empire?" she asked. Natasha smiled. No one had ever called Nolan Schmidt's business an empire even though that was exactly what it was.

"Well, that heartthrob Mitchell Schmidt is my husband," she said. The attendant's eyes lit up. It was like a young boy who had just been given a treasure map where X marked the location of the world's best chocolate factory.

"Oh my God, really?" she asked. Natasha nodded.

"Yeah, really," she said.

"I can't believe that I am talking to Natasha Schmidt...*the* Natasha Schmidt," the attendant said excitedly. Natasha laughed.

"Well, as much as this is exciting, I really have to go," she said as she looked at the attendant.

"Yeah, of course. I'm sorry but this is awesome. You look so different from the photos on US Weekly. They must be outdated because you have lost all that baby weight," the attendant said.

"And that is why I don't read the tabloids anymore," Natasha thought as she looked at her. "Thanks, I guess," she said. *"Wait, did she say baby weight? How old are the pictures the tabloids are running anyway?"* she wondered as the attendant rang up the receipt.

"Okay, cool. Just sign here," the attendant said as she handed Natasha the receipt. Natasha signed it as her purchases got packed up. "It was nice to meet you. Come back soon," the attendant said excitedly as she handed Natasha the bag.

"I definitely will," Natasha said as she walked out.

As she drove back home, she felt a bit guilty that she had left Mitch alone. But it had only been a couple of hours and he had just taken his pills so he would definitely still be down at that time, or so she thought. She had taken the time to pass by her dad's place and spend some time with Alexis. After that she had gone to the office and made sure everything was all fine before she went shopping. She was actually happy and proud of herself that she had managed to do all that in under two hours.

Sure enough, when she got home, Mitchell was still asleep. This was perfect. She had all the time to get ready for everything she had planned. She walked into the house and went to the kitchen. She took some strawberries and whipped cream from the fridge and set them on the counter. She then took some milk chocolate and poured it onto a bowl. She put all these on a tray before she headed to the guest room where she took a quick shower so as not to wake up Mitchell. She changed into the green bustier and let her hair down. She put on some light makeup and then walked back to the kitchen. She then took the tray and slowly made her way to their bedroom. She could not help but feel a bit nervous as she approached the door. This would be the first time they had sex when Mitchell was physically…well, challenged, for lack of better words. She slowly cracked open the door and poked her head inside.

"Hey there sleepy head," she said as she stood at the doorway. Mitchell raised his head and smiled.

"Hey, you are back already? How long have I been out?" he said as his eyelids fluttered open. "And what are you wearing?" he asked when he saw her. He slowly adjusted his weight on his elbows, getting himself in a position to get a better view of her.

"Relax," she said as she slowly made her way towards him. "I got this," she added. Mitchell smiled and looked at her from head to toe. She heard him breathe a long low "wow" as he looked at her. She was the epitome of beauty, especially now that she had on that bustier. He wished he could go and take her in his arms at that very moment.

"Baby, you know that I can't…" Mitchell started to say before she put the tray down on the bed.

"Your leg is injured but your penis is just fine," she said. "I will so ride you," she added in a soft but urgent voice. She got on the bed and straddled him. He looked up at her and smiled as wild thoughts crossed his mind. It was all he could do not to tear that sexy bustier off right there and then.

"That would be awesome," he said in a whisper as she lowered her head to kiss him. He held her head and kissed her softly. He loved the way her lips felt so soft and sweet on his own. She pulled away from him and reached for a strawberry. He watched her as she dipped it in some chocolate before spraying some of the whipped cream on it. It looked heavenly. She slowly licked some of the cream off before letting him take a bite. He smiled at her as he bit into the fruit. The varied tastes were like an orgasm of flavor inside his mouth but that was not what made his cock twitch. She then took the other half of the fruit in her mouth and closed her eyes as she chewed. "Damn it," Mitchell moaned when she slowly ground her hips on his crotch.

"I'm just getting started," she said in a whisper as she took another strawberry and bit it first before she offered it to him. She smiled down at him as he purposely took the strawberry and her fingers in his mouth. She felt a tingle go down her spine when he gently sucked on her fingers. She pulled them out of his mouth and brought her head down to kiss his neck.

He closed his eyes and moaned softly as she slipped a hand under his shirt and began pushing it upwards. She helped him take it off and tossed it on the floor before she lowered her head and began trailing small kisses down from his neck to his shoulder. She let her hand slowly go down his chest and then slowly caressed his abs. It was the perfect feeling, him under her, helpless and horny, just the way he wanted him. She let her hand go even lower and slowly cupped his balls, making him moan. She pulled her head up and looked down at him as he moaned every time she let her fingers brush his penis. She gently let her lips brush his as she pulled her hand away from his penis.

She climbed off him and dipped her index finger in the chocolate. She knew he was watching, so when she put her finger in her mouth, she did it so slowly and so sensually that he wanted to scream. She looked at him as she slowly began undoing the straps on her bustier. She could tell that he was aching for her to remove it but she was not about to give him the satisfaction. "You like this?" she asked as she walked over to the dressing table.

"I love this," he said as he watched her putting on some music. She turned around and began swaying her body to the smooth, intoxicating tunes, turning to let him see her well rounded ass as she danced. She liked being in a position of power, making him want her from a distance. She then walked back to the bed and dipped her finger in the chocolate again before she got on top of him and ground her hips on him in rhythm with the music.

"Oh yeah, just like that," he moaned as he put his hands on her hips. She was not sure whether it was just the sexy outfit or the combination of the outfit and the moves she was pulling on him, but whatever it was, he was harder than a rock, pressing hard into her bottom. She took another chocolate covered strawberry and fed it to him. "I want you. I want you right now," he whispered urgently. She smiled down at him and shook her head.

"But honey, I am just getting started," she said as she shifted her weight and got back on the bed. She looked at him as she slowly pulled his pants down. She carefully maneuvered his injured leg out of his pants before she slipped them off his other leg. She looked at him and smiled as she lowered her head to kiss his thighs. The skin under her lips was warm and inviting, so she just went on trailing kisses up his thigh, getting a bit too close to his scrotal sac. She heard him let out a long low moan when she let her fingers brush his rigid cock. "You like that?" she cooed as she went back to kissing his thigh.

"Oh yeah....don't stop," he moaned as she started kissing the sensitive skin of his inside thigh. She wrapped her slender fingers around his cock as her lips pressed hard against his scrotal sac and worked their way to his shaft. She heard him gasp when she began kissing his shaft, slowly working her way up to his highly sensitive glans. He put his hand on her head as she began kissing the bulbous head of his cock, gently circling her tongue on him.

"Yeah, just like that," he moaned as she took him inside his mouth. She let him go so deep inside her that he thought she would gag, but it seemed that over their years together, she had developed amazing gag reflex control. She lowered her mouth on him, letting him go deep in her throat. He moaned so loudly, she was actually glad that Alexis was not in the house. She sucked him long and hard, making him shudder. She could feel his cock pulsating inside her mouth and she knew that if she went on much longer, this would be a short ride.

She pulled away and looked at the monster she had helped create. She then brought herself up and straddled him once again. He looked up at her and once again put his hands on her hips. "Don't you need to get this off?" he asked as he looked up at her in the green bustier. She smiled and brought her head down to kiss him.

"Crotchless undies," she said in a whisper as she held his cock and guided it to her pussy. She rubbed his cock head on her wet opening until he let out a frustrated moan. She then released him, letting him slip inside her in one slick stroke. She closed her eyes and felt him filling her up, feeling her insides. It felt so good having him inside her. She opened her eyes and looked down at him as she began rocking her hips forward, working his cock in and out of her with every movement she made. Mitchell raised his hands and cupped her breasts.

She could tell that he was getting frustrated not being able to touch her, caress her like he wanted. She unclasped the garters and then undid the side zipper on the bustier. She stopped her rocking movements and looked at him before she pulled the beautiful satin bustier away. She looked at him and smiled as he looked at her breasts that were already threatening to burst out of the restraining bra. He reached around her back and quickly unclasped her bra. She let out a gasp when he put his hand on one of her bare breasts, gently caressing her, making her nipple press hard against his palm. The sheer feeling of his hand on her made her even hotter, as she started rocking her hips on him again. She made him get deep inside her and then pulled away almost to the point of withdrawing his cock.

She loved teasing him, lowering herself on him, almost swallowing him, taking him deep inside her, before pulling away, threatening to pop him out of her pussy. All the while, Mitchell was caressing her breasts, rubbing, squeezing and tweaking her nipples. She saw a look in his eyes that made her want to kiss him. As she slowly made her way down, he held her tightly and raised his head. She let out a loud moan when she felt his lips around her nipple. She could feel herself shivering as he sucked and nibbled on her nipples. She felt him tugging at her nipple and the sensation he was giving her was making her rocking movements almost an impossibility.

Natasha breathed her relief when he finally pulled away from her but it was short lived because he took her other nipple inside his mouth. She moaned loudly as he gave the same treatment to this nipple as he had the other one. She was at this point moaning loudly as she tried rocking her hips. She found herself wondering how strong he possibly was, keeping his head up this long. When he released her nipple, she pulled her hips away, making his cock burst out of her pussy. He looked up at her as she squatted on his crotch.

"What….oh my…God…baby…" he moaned as she once again lowered herself on him, taking him inside her in one stroke. He looked up at her and tried holding her but she began slamming herself on him, literally sending him into a state of confusion. The way she had positioned herself on him made her look like she was doing some kind of frog jumps and he did not mind. Having her slamming herself on him made sure that he felt every single fold of her pussy. Soon enough, she had him moaning so loud that she was forced to put her hand over his mouth. She was working herself to an orgasm and she wanted to scream. She could feel her pussy pulsating as her orgasm approached fast. Her pussy tensing up on him sent him to the point of no return. He held her tightly as they both climaxed, their passion entwined. It was a long minute before she collapsed on him panting.

"Wow," he breathed out slowly.

"I know," she said as she breathed hard.

"If I had known that you would be this rigorous I would have hurt my leg a long time ago," he said as he caressed her back. She raised her head and looked at him.

"Shut the fuck up," she said before resting her head back on his shoulder.

"But seriously, that was the best sex ever," he said as his cock slipped out of her pussy. "And this," he said as he tugged at her bustier that was now gathered around her waist.

"A little shopping really, nothing major," she said.

"Well, I want to go again," he said in a whisper.

"Sure, I'll just wait a few minutes and then I will rock your world," she said in a low voice.

"No, right now," Mitchell said. At that moment, Natasha became aware of his cock, hard and pressing onto her ass. She raised her head and looked down at him, smiling.

"You opened a Pandora's box, babe," he said, smiling back at her. She raised her hips and lowered her body on him, taking him inside her once again. If there was ever a time she was glad they were not going to work tomorrow, it was at that moment because by the look of things, she would be riding him long into the night.

Chapter 5

Mitchell was still asleep when Natasha woke up. She looked at his peaceful face and smiled. She thought that she must have worked him out really well for him to be sleeping so late. She got up from the bed and walked to the bathroom. She turned on the water and stripped off the bustier that Mitchell had left around her waist, along with the stockings, before she stepped into the shower and stood under the hot jets of water. She closed her eyes and enjoyed the feeling of the warm water trickling down her back. She could not help but think of the way Mitchell would take her in the bathroom and press her body against the wall as he claimed her over and over. She longed for him to do that again but unfortunately, that was not going to happen, not for a few more weeks anyway.

Without knowing it, she was lowering one hand to her pussy while the other one cupped her breast and began rubbing gently. She thought of the way her husband would squeeze her gently as he worked himself inside her, slowly but surely, making sure that he would have her moaning with every long stroke. She gently stroked her curls as her index finger pressed hard against her budding clitoris. She was wet, so wet that she surprised herself but in all fairness it could have been as a result of all the hot sex she had the previous night or the thought of what the four walls of her bathroom had seen. She just could not make up her mind as to what turned her on more. All she knew was that she needed Mitchell to fuck her again, or the other way round.

She pulled her hand from her pussy and turned the water off. She walked out of the bathroom and back to the bed where Mitchell was still sleeping. She thought of waking him up but a better idea suddenly came to her. She slowly reached for the covers and gently pulled them off. She smiled when she saw that Mitchell had a semi-erection. Good, he was already halfway there. She brought her head down and took his cock in her mouth. She sucked slowly, letting her tongue circling his bulbous head inside her mouth. Needless to say, Mitchell was up, in more ways than one.

"What the…oh my God…" he moaned when he saw her head bobbing on his cock. This was definitely the best way to wake up. He looked at her and smiled. She was sucking him like this was the very last time she was ever going to. This was all too much for him. He began moaning softly, almost in tune with her strokes. He raised his head to look at her and that was when he noticed her wet body. "Were you showering just now?" he asked. Natasha pulled him out of her mouth and raised her head.

"No, talking," she said before she went back to the great oral treatment she was giving him. Mitchell struggled hard to keep himself in check, to keep himself from exploding. All he could do was just moan and put his hand on her head. She was working him a bit too well. She knew just what to lick, just how hard to suck. She was just perfect. Everything about her.

"Baby…slow down," Mitchell moaned softly. Natasha wanted to pull away from him but she did to want to give him the satisfaction. She went back to sucking him harder and harder as she went on. Soon enough, she had him moaning and groaning almost as loudly as he had the previous night. She let her hand cup his scrotal sac and gently squeezed his balls as she worked her mouth on his cock until it came to a point when even she knew that he was well over his threshold. She pulled away from him, looked at his hard cock and smiled.

"Come up here, baby," she heard Mitchell say. She slowly brought herself up and kissed him as she climbed on top of him. She pulled away and looked into his eyes. She could see that his pupils were dilated, probably as a result of his arousal.

"Please Tasha…just fuck me," he said in a whisper. She smiled as she started lowering herself, impaling herself on his big cock. He breathed out loudly and put his hands on her hips. As soon as he did, she placed her own hands on his and pulled them off as she began raising and lowering herself onto his waiting cock. He looked up at her and smiled. She was loving this whole being in charge thing and he was not complaining. He watched her forehead that had formed some vertical lines, showing her arousal as she went on. He loved looking at her face all grimaced, all because of him. He loved this woman; he could not imagine a life without her and now that she was working herself, and him, to a point where they both wanted to cry out only made him feel so much more in love with her. He tried to gently move his hips upwards to meet her downward strokes and it was great. She was moaning loudly and increasing her pace. She was fucking him with harder, more urgent strokes and he was loving the way her tits bounced up and down in motion with her movements. She released his hands and raised her arms up before running her fingers through her wet hair. He had to admit, she looked just perfect, like a hot porn star that was every man's dream. Her skin was still damp from the shower and the way the sunlight hit her made it glow. He held her tightly as she suddenly upped her speed, smacking herself against him harder and harder each time she brought herself down. "Yeah, baby. That's it…that's just it," he moaned as he felt her slamming against him harder and more persistently until they both climaxed in unison. It was heavenly, the way their passion entwined together and brought them to a sheer state of ecstasy.

Natasha screamed out loud before she collapsed on him, panting hard.

"You keep working me like that, I won't need therapy," Mitchell said. She laughed and planted a kiss on his shoulder.

"Well, that's one of the things I'm here for," she said, still panting.

"So, what do you have lined up for today?" he asked.

"To be honest, I think I'll know as time goes on because I literally feel like I am cracking under the pressure," she said as she raised her head to look at him.

"You don't have to do all this, you know," he said, looking at her.

"I know but I am no longer just Natasha Black. I am Natasha Schmidt. The family business is also important to me," she said smiling. He held her tightly and she rested her head on his shoulder.

"Thanks for this, for everything. It means the world to me," he said.

"Just doing my due diligence," she said smiling. "I would like to swing by Nan's and see Alexis," she added.

"I would like to see her too. Can I come with?" he asked. Natasha frowned. She did not like the idea of having him moving around. "I promise I will use the crutches," he said quickly, almost as if he had read her mind.

"Fine. Let me have a shower first," she said.

"Do I get a shower too?" he asked as he looked at her.

"Yes, but not alone," she said as she pulled herself away from him, forcing his cock out of her.

"Oh yeah," Mitchell said in a tone that let her know that this was more than just about the shower.

"No, Mitchell. You can't handle that," she said as she got off the bed. "Keep the weight off, remember?" she asked as she helped him get off the bed. She held him steady and helped him walk towards the bathroom where she restarted the shower. She then slowly helped him get under the water where she helped bathe him before she guided him out of the bathroom. She got his clothes and laid them out on the bed before she went back to the bathroom and finished her own shower.

When she came back out, Mitchell was still getting dressed. She hated that he had to struggle this much. Even though he was trying to show her that he was okay with everything, she knew that at the back of his mind, he was not okay with the whole situation. All in all, she loved the man he was.

*****

Estelle had prepared what was Natasha's favorite breakfast: waffles with syrup, well done eggs and bacon. That always made Natasha's mouth water. When Mitchell and Natasha got there, Estelle had just put out the generous spread.

"If I didn't know any better I would have thought that you are trying to keep us here forever," Mitchell said as he made his way to the table. Estelle smiled.

"Well, I would not mind that at all," Estelle said as she pulled out his chair. Mitchell took a seat as Natasha went on upstairs to check on the baby. Mitchell looked at Eric who was now walking towards them and smiled.

"Guess I am not the only one taking some time off work today, huh?" he said. Eric laughed.

"I would like a few more days actually but I'll just have to do with the one," he said as he shook Mitchell's hand. "How are you doing anyway? Natasha told me that you have a few more weeks before you can fully be back on your feet, literally," he said.

"Yeah, I just have to stick to therapy and see how everything goes," Mitchell said.

"So, this was a soccer injury?" Eric asked.

"Well, in England they call it football, but yeah," Mitchell said.

"I never thought that such a fun sport could do this much damage," Eric said.

"Well, you should have heard some of the horror stories I was being told about soccer. Apparently some guy had a fall so bad that he can never walk again. That is definitely not something you want to hear while you wait for a doctor's prognosis," Mitchell said.

"You hear about these things but you never really think that it might happen to someone you know," Eric said. "And how is Natasha handling all this?" he asked. Mitchell smiled.

"She is great, really great. She has taken it upon herself to handle my workload and hers all the while making sure that I don't miss a single appointment," he said. "Your daughter is hands down the best thing that has ever happened to me. I wouldn't have been able to get through this if she was not there for me," he added. Eric smiled proudly.

"That's my girl. That is definitely the daughter I raised," he said.

"I know. She makes me proud to be the man I am, a husband and a father," Mitchell said. Eric smiled at him.

"You know how people say that a parent always knows when her daughter makes the right choice? Well, I felt it with you and I see why," Eric said. He could remember the sick feeling he got in the pit of his stomach every time he saw Jay but he never got that, not with Mitchell.

"I have to say that I am honored, sir," Mitchell said. Eric laughed.

"How is it that you are worth a billion dollars but you are still humble enough to call common folk like myself sir?" Eric asked.

"Well, sir, that is just how my father raised me," Mitchell said as Estelle joined them at the table.

"What is all these chit chat about? Eat up before it gets cold," she said as she took a bite of her bacon. "And where is Tasha?" she asked, looking at Mitchell.

"Probably with Alexis," he said. "That is definitely where I'd be," he added in a low voice. Estelle smiled at him.

"I know you miss her but trust me, Natasha is not doing herself any favors by being up there. That girl woke us up at the crack of dawn and she just went back to sleep," she said.

"Hopefully for another two hours," Eric said.

"Oh, is she being a handful to you guys?" Mitchell asked. "Because we can get the nanny, no problem," he added. Eric laughed.

"Oh no, it's good to have the pitter patter of little feet again. She keeps me on my toes," Eric said. "Actually, she is the reason I have been taking so many days off work since every day is not bring your granddaughter to work day," he added. Mitchell laughed as Natasha came down the stairs. Mitchell looked at her sad face and smiled.

"She is asleep, isn't she?" he asked.

"You knew? Why didn't you tell me?" Natasha asked as she took a seat next to Mitchell.

"Actually I just found out myself," Mitchell said.

"I have really missed her smile," Natasha said, frowning.

"You guys are here all day, right? You can still see her," Eric said. Natasha took a bite of her waffle and shrugged.

"I have to take Mitchell back home for his physiotherapy at four," she said.

"That's plenty of time. She will be awake by then," Eric said.

"So how is work going?" Estelle asked. Natasha smiled.

"Great. We have had some pretty serious deals this past year and greater ones that almost broke my husband's leg. So I guess business is booming," she said. Estelle looked at Mitchell and frowned.

"I am really sorry about this whole thing, dearie," she said.

"Don't worry about me, Estelle. I am a trooper," Mitchell said smiling. "Plus Tasha is doing a really good job of making sure the company does not crash and burn," he added as he looked at Natasha.

"Really? She is working?" Eric said. "You used to beg to stay home when I had the flu," he said.

"Well, in my defense, Daddy, that was school and I am not working anymore. At least not from the office," Natasha said before taking a bite of her food.

"So who is handling business?" Estelle asked.

"There isn't any pressing business really. We sent Stacy to handle the last bit of urgent business we had," Mitchell said.

"Your assistant?" Eric asked raising an eyebrow.

"That girl is a bit too intelligent to be an assistant," Natasha said proudly. "I might just pick her to replace me when I finally decide to retire," she added.

"Wow, she s that good, huh?" Eric asked.

"You should have seen the fight she put up when one of the guys on the board tried taking Stacy for a few days. Natasha almost threw him off the fortieth floor," Mitchell said laughing.

"You are exaggerating," Natasha said.

"Seriously? You should have seen yourself that day. I had never seen you that pissed off and this was just your assistant. I'd hate to see how you react when someone tries to pull anything on Alexis," Mitchell said, laughing.

"I am not even looking forward to her teenage years," Natasha said shaking her head. "That's when all the weird boys in her life start showing up," she added.

"Oh, I remember those days," Eric said shaking his head.

"Why are you shaking your head, Daddy? I was a star daughter," Natasha said, looking at her father. Eric looked at Estelle and laughed.

"They grow up so fast and forget even faster," Estelle said, smiling. Mitchell's gaze shifted from Eric, to Estelle and back to Natasha.

"Am I missing something?" he asked.

"Yeah, some of my daughter's terrible boyfriend choices," Eric said.

"They were not that bad," Natasha said. Eric and Estelle looked at each other and laughed.

"Let's see, Adam, Zachary, Jay…and that's just the top three," Estelle said. "I don't know the other two but if Jay is in the top three then I agree Natasha you struck gold with me," Mitchell said.

"Don't blow your own trumpet, babe," Natasha said smiling.

"No, he is right. For a moment there I thought that all hope was lost for you," Eric said. "But you bounced back and we are happy and I'm proud to be called grandpa," he added.

"Well, give it another year. Alexis is still at 'opa'," Estelle said. They all laughed.

"I am loving this by the way," Mitchell said smiling.

"Of course you are. That's because they are not bashing you," Natasha said. "You wait until the day I have breakfast with your mom. I'm sure bashing you will be fun," she added.

Mitchell leaned in and kissed her cheek before he whispered in her ear. "I was a golden child," he said. Natasha smiled.

"So was I and behold," she said, holding her hand out to her father and grandmother. She smiled and took another bite before looking at her father and Nan. They were right. Her love life had been a train wreck and it would have probably still have been terrible if Mitchell had not been in her life. She loved each and every minute of having Mitchell in her life, and Alexis and her dad and her Nan as well. She leaned in and nudged Mitchell. "You know I love you, right?" she said in a whisper. Mitchell smiled at her and nodded.

"I know and I love you right back," he said in a whisper.

"Is there something you two want to share with the rest of the class?" Estelle asked. Natasha and Mitchell looked up and laughed.

Chapter 6

"How is it that your Nan made you waffles and you never thought of calling me?" Rita asked as she burst through the doors at Natasha and Mitchell's place. Natasha had just finished cleaning up in the living room when Rita came in. She looked up at her and smiled.

"Nice to see you, Rita. Why don't you come on in?" she said sarcastically.

"I'm sorry, but I just passed by to say hi to Alexis and imagine my shock when Estelle told me to bring this over because you left it there when you had brunch the other day," Rita said as she lifted her hand that held Natasha's blue cashmere scarf. Natasha walked over to Rita, wrapped her arms around her, and hugged her.

"It was kind of a rushed thing. We didn't plan it or anything," she said as she pulled away. Rita looked at her, frowned, and shrugged.

"Well, I just felt left out," she said. Natasha laughed.

"Are you sure you're not just sorry you missed Nan's waffles?" she asked.

"Well, there is that," Rita said laughing.

"But I did invite you here for today's little party, right? That should count for something," Natasha said as she walked to the kitchen, with Rita close behind.

"Yeah, about that. I didn't know what to bring so I just brought two bottles of this," Rita said as she put the bag in her hand on the kitchen counter. Natasha looked in the bag and smiled. "I figured 1960 was a good year for whatever the celebration," Rita added as Natasha put the two bottles of white wine in the fridge.

"This is perfect," she said.

"What are we celebrating, anyway?" Rita asked as she helped herself to one of the sandwiches on the counter. She figured that the trays set out in the kitchen were for whatever Natasha had invited her for.

"Stacy's graduation from mere assistant to full blown exec," Natasha said. Rita raised an eyebrow.

"Huh?" she asked. Natasha shook her head.

"Okay, here's the deal. Mitchell was on the verge of closing a major deal and since he could not travel, we had to send Stacy in to close the deal," Natasha explained.

"I don't get it. Why didn't you go?" Rita asked.

"And leave my invalid husband all alone?" Natasha asked, frowning. Rita shrugged.

"Of course. What was I thinking?" she said. "So, how did she do?" she asked before she took another bite of her sandwich.

"Awesome. She closed the deal for ten million more than what Mitchell thought it would cost. I always said she was too good to be an assistant," Natasha said proudly as she placed an assortment of fruit on one tray. "She went in a girl, she came back a woman with a great ass and big fat boobs," Natasha added as she smiled. Rita laughed.

"You make boobs sound disgusting," Rita said laughing. "So,

what's the plan?" she asked as she looked at Natasha.

"Well, Mona and Leo are in town so they will be picking her up from the airport. Dave and Mitchell are downstairs, and they will join us later," Natasha said. Rita shook her head.

"Wait, Dave is here?" she asked. Natasha nodded. "That makes so much sense. He texted me that he is catching up on some love from a brother. It was a very disturbing thought," she added, making Natasha laugh.

"Yeah, he is giving Mitchell moral support in physio...that's what they are doing downstairs by the way. Not any weird man on man romance kind of stuff," Natasha said, smiling. Rita nodded.

"Good, because I don't think I would have had the heart to look at him again," she said before taking the last bite of her sandwich. "Okay, now that I have some food in me, what can I help with?" she asked. Natasha looked around and frowned.

"Well, I'm pretty much done except..." she walked over to the fridge and came back with a bowl of chopped up mangoes and strawberries. "You could make the smoothie. We have a number of teetotalers today and this will be their drink of choice. Okay, this and some fresh passion fruit juice I made in the morning," she said smiling.

"Wow, you've been busy," Rita said.

"Well, Lupe helped with the sandwiches," Natasha said.

"Yeah, but still," Rita said as she looked at the generous spread on the counter.

"Well, there is nothing more to do. I mean, Mitch feels bad

when I go to work and leave him here. Okay, maybe not mad, just really down. So, I try to work when he is asleep but that rarely happens. I think he is over-rested and yeah, Alexis is not here. So, you get the drift," she said. Rita nodded.

"Which brings me to my next question. How are you guys… you know…bedroom affairs?" she asked. Natasha looked up at her in surprise.

"Really? You want me to discuss my sex life with my husband?" she asked.

'Well, discuss is a very big word. Just an overview, really, is what I am looking for," Rita said. Natasha rolled her eyes.

"Okay. I won't give you the details but to be honest this is the best sex I have ever had," she said before she giggled. Rita's eyes grew wide. She did not think she had heard her best friend giggling since high school. Could it really be that good?

"Oh please, you're exaggerating," she said as she looked at Natasha.

"No, for real. I get to do everything, I am in total control and I love it. I have made control my bitch," she said, smiling. Rita shrugged.

"You were right the first time. This is so not my business," she said as she poured the chopped up fruit in a blender. Natasha smiled.

"What can I say? I love what I love and this is one of the things I actually love," she said.

"Good for you," Rita said as she switched on the blender. "So, that's it? I counted seven when you told me who was coming," she said, a bit louder to be heard over the sound of the blender.

"Well, it's just a small thing, really. Wine, sandwiches, juice. Kind of a brunch but in the evening rather than in the morning or mid-morning," Natasha said. Rita smiled. "And I have to go change, because Mona is almost here," she said as she walked out of the kitchen.

"I'll just finish up here," Rita called out. Natasha rushed to her bedroom where she had a quick shower. She had already picked out what she was wearing, a short blue sleeveless dress and a pair of red heels. She had told everyone to look glam in the invite she sent out. Now that she and Mitchell were not getting a lot of time to go out, this would suffice as their first date night in weeks and she was determined to make it memorable. She straightened out her hair and used her curling iron on it before she styled it into a simple but elegant side sweep. She did some light makeup but went bold red on her lips. After putting on a pair of matching earrings, she walked back to the living room where Rita had just finished putting the glasses on the table. "Wow, are you bent on making me feel underdressed?" she asked when she saw Natasha.

"Oh please. Have you seen yourself?" Natasha asked as she looked at Rita's black and white bandage dress and pink peep toe heels. Rita shrugged.

"Well, I tried," she said. "By the way, I forgot to give you the 411," she added as Natasha took a seat. She looked at Rita and raised an eyebrow.

"What 411? What the hell happened?" Natasha asked.

"Well, I have good news and really shitty news. So what goes first?" Rita asked.

"Shitty news, of course," Natasha said.

"So, Jay came over to my place last week," Rita started.

"Last week? Why didn't you tell me?" Natasha asked.

"I'm telling you now, aren't I? Anyway, he came down to my place and he was weird. I think he had been drinking and he was asking me to give him the address to your house because he's tried calling you and you never pick up his calls," Rita said. "He also said that he tried to come to NSCS but he couldn't get past the gate. Something about the guards being given a direct order?" she asked as she looked at her friend. Natasha sighed.

"Well, yeah. I had to. That guy was turning stalker real fast," she said. "So what did he want?" she asked.

"Well, he told me to tell you that he misses you and that he would like to have a sit down with you," Rita said. Natasha rolled her yes.

"What for? What could he possibly have to tell me that I haven't heard from his lying ass already?" she asked.

"I don't know but his words were that he wants his friend back, and that he misses you. He also said that he would want to be in Alexis' life," Rita said. Natasha scoffed.

"Why in God's name would I let that freak anywhere near my little girl?" she asked.

"Yeah, that's what I thought. He said that and I was like, what?" Rita said as she leaned back.

"Actually what he didn't tell you was that I have been down this road before. I have tried to let him in and everything but that train crashed before it even left the station," Natasha said. Rita raised an eyebrow.

"Why do you say that? How did that train crash?" she asked.

"A few months after I got married, he called me up with some sob story how he missed being friends because we started out as friends first and like a fool, I fell for it. But almost as soon he was back in my life he went all psycho telling me that he would do whatever it took to get me back. That was too weird," Natasha said. "And it only got worse when I got pregnant. He would come up to my work place and tell me that Mitchell didn't have to be in the picture. I had to get a restraining order. He was getting weird and fast," she added.

"So that's why he had to come to me," Rita said in a low voice. "I thought it was some kind of best friend bond," she added frowning.

"You got played, sister," Natasha said as she brushed a curl off her face.

"I feel so used," Rita said. Natasha laughed.

"Enough of that lowlife. What is the good news?" she asked as she took Rita's hand in hers. Rita smiled.

"Well, turns out that you got more business and it had a butterfly effect trickling all the way down to me. I got this great kid from college who does some gorgeous expressionist pieces, and your latest client, the Arab..." she explained.

"Naima?" Natasha asked.

"Yeah that one. She saw something at your offices she liked so someone told her where you got it from and she came down to the gallery. She took a keen interest in the expressionist art and she ended up getting fourteen pieces," Rita said excitedly.

"Oh my God, that is awesome!" Natasha said smiling.

"I know, and she made an order for six more. Apparently she wanted to make sure every member of her family got one," Rita continued.

"Seven, that's a big family," Natasha said. Rita shook her head.

"Actually the seven are for her house. She must have a freakishly huge house. The fourteen are for the family," she said. Natasha's eyes grew wide. "I did some digging. Her dad has the whole four wives thing, hence the many children," Rita added.

"Wow, all that and she is my client. I seriously had no idea," Natasha said.

"Well I like making sure I get to know every little thing about my clients, especially the ones that get fourteen pieces at a go," Rita said, winking.

"True that," Natasha said. "I'm happy for you. This gallery thing is the one thing you've stuck to and with good reason," she added.

"I know. I was not sure when I started out myself but well, everything worked out so I guess I can say that everything worked out for the best," Rita said just as the doorbell rang. Natasha got up.

"That's probably Stacy and Mona. I'll get it," she said as she walked to the door. "There's my star player," she said as she looked at Stacy.

"Oh, thanks but I think we can all agree that Stacy here is the real star player," Mona said as she hugged Natasha. Natasha and Stacy exchanged glances that said, "you can be so full of yourself."

"I was talking to Stacy," Natasha said pulling away. She looked at Stacy and waited for Mona to get in before she pulled her close in a long bear hug. "I am so proud of you," she said in a low voice as she held Stacy close.

"I just did what anybody else would have done," Stacy said.

"Anybody else would not have upped the deal for an extra ten million," Natasha said as she pulled away.

"Oh, I did that one for me. I need a generous commission for that," Stacy said smiling.

"That is definitely a done deal," Natasha said as Leo walked up to the door. "Ah, the prodigal son returns," she said as Leo kissed her cheek and hugged her. "You have become another Santa," she said. Leo looked at her confused.

"And I didn't get you anything," he said. Natasha laughed.

"No silly. It's just that I feel like I only get to see you once a year," she said. Leo laughed.

"I'm sorry about that but don't you worry. All that is about to change," he said. She raised an eyebrow. "I'm setting up office in the States, matter of fact in this very town," he said.

"Yay! When will this be?" she asked as the two made their way to the living room.

"We are still trying to work out the logistics but it should happen soon. Not more than four months if I should give a timeline," he said as they walked into the living room.

"There he is, the prodigal son," Rita said when she saw Leo. Leo turned and looked at Natasha.

"Really? Is this a thing now? It's only been a few months," he said before Rita got up to say hi. Natasha and Mona walked to the kitchen and came back with some of the trays. As soon as Leo sat down, Rita got up to help them. She came back carrying two pitchers containing the juice while Natasha carried the wine into the room.

"Wow, you guys, this is too much," Stacy said looking at the trays the girls were laying on the table.

"Well, if you were working for me I would buy you a car after the deal you just closed," Leo said.

"Watch it, I might just take you up on your offer," Stacy said.

"And I will kill you if you ever take the best employee I ever had," Natasha said as she looked at Leo. At that moment, Dave and Mitchell's voices could be heard as they slowly made their way to the living room.

"Hey! No cast? I came with a pen and everything," Leo said, frowning, as he looked at Mitchell's brace.

"If I had not oversold the concept, you would not have been here," Mitchell said as he sat down.

"It's good to see you, man," Leo said as the two shook hands. Dave and Rita shared a quick kiss before everyone sat down.

"So everyone is here. We might as well get started," Natasha said as Mona poured the wine into the glasses. She handed out a glass to everyone as Natasha gave a glass of juice to Mitchell.

"Bro, no wine for you?" Leo asked.

"I am on medication. So no, not for another few weeks,' he said. Leo smirked and Natasha shot him a dirty look.

"Really? Smirking?" she asked. Leo mouthed an "I'm sorry" before Natasha cleared her throat. "Okay, I think we should all hear something from the special lady tonight," she said. Stacy's cheeks flushed. That always happened any time she was put on the spot.

"Go on, Stace. Tell us what this feels like," Mona said as Stacy stood up. She tucked a strand of hair behind her ear and looked around.

"Wow, I really don't know what I am supposed to say. Like I told Tasha, I just did what any other assistant in my shoes would have done," she started.

"All other assistants make coffee and get dry cleaning. You make me millions," Mitchell said smiling.

"The offer to work for me still stands," Leo said. Stacy smiled at him and nodded.

"You know a few years ago if you had told me that, I would have probably jumped at the idea but working for NSCS and for Natasha in particular has been a great experience. I have never had a boss that believed in me the way Natasha did. I never even thought I would get a chance to work for and be a friend to such a cool boss. So Leo, I guess I would say no because I would want to see what challenge Natasha has for me after this," she said. Natasha walked towards her and hugged her.

"I don't know about you but that's the best speech I ever heard," Mona whispered to Rita. Rita smiled and nodded at her.

"I know, right?" she said. Natasha pulled away and raised her glass.

"This is to the best assistant I could ever ask for and the best employee I will ever see. Here is to Stacy," she said.

"To Stacy," everyone echoed as they clinked their glasses together and drank. Mona walked up to the home theatre and turned up the music. Now the party was complete.

Chapter 7

It had almost been three hours since Leo and Dave picked Mitchell up for some quality guy time...even though the guy time involved having Leo and Dave have a few beers while Mitchell went on with the therapy. Natasha took her phone and called her dad.

"Hey Daddy, how's everything?" she asked.

"Great. How're you?" Eric asked when he picked up.

"Good, I can't complain. How's my little princess?" she asked as she leaned back on the couch.

"Being very good to us. I have never seen a baby with this much appetite," Eric said. Natasha smiled. She had always loved the way Alexis made feeding so easy even after so many people swore by the fact that feeding a child is right up there next to singing to a rock.

"Well, Nan told me that she is just like I was," she said.

"Oh, she was just trying to make you not feel bad about yourself," Eric said. Natasha scoffed.

"Oh please. I was a good baby and I know it," she said.

"Well, you had your days," he said. "Do you think you guys could come over tomorrow for brunch again? Or better still, dinner?" he asked. Natasha ran her fingers through her hair and sighed.

"We have done so much over the past week. Brunch with you the other day, Stacy's party. I don't want Mitch to over exert himself. Maybe next week?" she asked. She heard her father breathe out loudly.

"Of course, baby," he said. She smiled. She loved how her father was always so understanding. "His health comes first," he said.

"Yeah it does, Daddy, but we will be back to our usual traditions soon enough. I promise," she said.

"Yeah, I miss our Sunday dinners," Eric said. She could tell he was smiling as he said it.

"Me too," she said. She then went quiet for a while as she tried to bring up something that had been on her mind for a while. "Daddy, I hate to do this over the phone but I need to know something," she said.

"What is it?" he asked.

"Do you…do you ever hear from my mother?" she asked. She heard her father go quiet before he took a long deep breath. "Hello, Daddy, are you still there?" she asked when Eric got too quiet.

"Honey…." He started to talk before Natasha cut him off.

"I really need to know, Dad," she said. Her voice was full of hope.

"She did, once," he said. "When you were about eight, but she has never done it again," he added.

A sad smile played on Natasha's lips. She thought of a mother's smile, the one she always got when she saw Alexis crawling, when she first saw her daughter sit up all on her own or the time she heard Alexis' first word. How could a parent be okay with missing all that? Missing every little part of your child's life and not even feel a pinch?

"You still there sweetie?" Eric asked when Natasha got too quiet.

"Yeah, I'm here," she said as she shrugged her shoulders. "It's just a lot to take in at once," she said.

"And that is why I never want to talk about it. She wanted out of your life and that's just it," Eric said.

"And that's okay. We don't need her," Natasha said echoing the words she had heard her father say to her as she grew up.

"That's right. We do pretty damn good on our own," he said. Natasha laughed as a tear rolled down her cheek. She brushed it off but another one just rolled down in its place. "But remember, you are a better woman, a better mother than she ever dreamed of being. What you are doing for your husband and Alexis, nothing could ever measure up to it," he said.

"Thanks, daddy. I needed to hear that," she said. And she meant it, too. Having her father and Nan take care of her daughter was hard for her. She felt like this was just like what her mother had done. And even though she tried as much as she could to pass by their house and spend a couple of hours with her, it did not feel the same.

"Don't be sad. You are here almost every day. I'm sure she rarely misses you," he said.

"Ouch," she said laughing.

"You know what I mean," Eric said. She ran her fingers through her hair again.

"I do," she said. At that moment she heard a car pull up in the driveway. She guessed that Leo and Dave must have dropped Mitchell off. "I have to go, Dad. Mitchell's back," he said.

"Try not to think about it, okay love?" Eric said.

"I'll try. I love you, Daddy," she said.

"Love you too, princess," Eric said before Natasha hung up. She wiped away her tears and then walked up to the door. She could see Dave and Leo driving off as Mitchell made his way up the steps. She was proud of him. He was now walking up and down stairs with the crutches with great ease and seeing how far he had come, she was more than proud.

"Hey," Mitchell said as he approached the door.

"Hey," she said before she threw her arms around him and began sobbing.

"Whoa there. Are you okay?" he asked as he held her with one arm. She nodded, her head still buried in his shoulder. "Want to talk about it?" he asked. She shook her head again.

"I...I...just talked to my dad," she said when she pulled away. She looked up at him as he slowly brushed her cheeks with his fingers. He had not seen her this sad for a long time.

"Is it Alexis? Is she okay?" he asked as panic took over. She shook her head.

"Our daughter is fine, Mitch," she said as she pulled away from him. "Come on in," she said as she stepped aside. She looked at him as he made his way to the couch.

"Okay, what's going on?" he asked when he finally sat down.

She walked up to where he was and sat down next to him.

"I asked him about my mother," she said as another tear rolled down her cheek. Mitchell put an arm around her and pulled her closer to him. "I asked if she had ever tried to come and see me or at least ask about me," she said.

"What did he say?" he asked.

"She did, once. When I was eight," she said in a low voice. "And she has never done it again. It's as if I was a piece of garbage that she never wanted around her. She left me like I was nothing!" she said as yet another tear rolled down her cheek.

Mitchell planted a kiss on top of her head. She looked up into his eyes and shook her head. "I know she knows about me and you but she did not even come to my wedding or even try to make contact with me when I had Alexis. She can't say she didn't know because the tabloids were buzzing with the news, Mitch," she said. He pulled away from her and looked into her brown, tear-filled eyes.

"You know what you are, Tasha? Amazing. An amazing woman who captured my heart because of how pure and awesome she is. And because of that, I know for a fact that the woman who gave birth to you does not deserve a tear from you," he said. He held her face in his hands and gently kissed her lips. "You are who you are because of what you went through and guess what, Alexis knows it too," he added when he pulled away.

She looked into his eyes and smiled. He always had a way of making her feel better. She leaned in and kissed him gently before she pulled away. "It's late and I can see you are already in a robe," he said gently. She smiled and nodded. "Let's go to bed," he said before he pulled himself to his feet. She got up and slowly followed him to the bedroom and then sat on the edge of the bed as he got ready for bed. When he came back out, he walked to the bed as she took off her robe. He almost gasped when he saw what she had underneath: a blue stretch lace chemise and matching thong. Natasha looked down at what she had on and sighed. The talk about her mother had completely messed up her plans.

"I'm so sorry, Mitchell. It all slipped my mind and…"

Her words trailed off as he made his way towards her. She looked into his eyes when he stood in front of her before he took her in his arms and kissed her deeply. When he pulled away, her eyes were closed and at that moment, they both became aware of the scent in the room. Natasha had lit some candles earlier but she had waited on Mitchell for so long that the small candles had all burnt out, leaving only their sweet scent in their wake.

His lips closed in on her neck as he leaned into her. Her beautiful dark skin was getting closer to his lips, making his pulse increase as his cock began getting rigid. When she felt his lips brushing against her skin, his name escaped her lips in a whisper as her body tensed up against him. He kissed her neck again and she sighed, the very same seductive sigh that made him want to mount her. At that moment, he wished he could take her, claim her and just make wild passionate love to her way into the night, but because of his injury, all he could do was wait – wait to see what she had in mind. He let his hands explore the softness of her body, slowly kneading her flesh as he kissed her neck. With his lips focused on her neck, he could feel her letting go in his arms. He wanted to take her over more than anything but she was still in charge…she would be in charge until he got a clean bill of health and that was not going to happen, not yet anyway.

Mitchell trailed his kisses along her neck, slowly bringing his lips up to her warm cheeks. With one arm around her, he slowly made her turn around until she had her back to him. He balanced himself on his one crutch as his other hand began undoing the ribbon that held the chemise together. He kissed her neck as he tugged on the ribbon, slowly and carefully until he had loosened the entire garment. With one more tug, the chemise was loose enough and he took this chance to push it down her torso. He felt her nipples brush against his hand as he pushed the piece of clothing down.

He looked down and gasped when he saw that she had on a matching thong. She had gone all out and it was working wonders for him and in his body. She reached behind her and gently brushed his cock with her fingers. Even against the thick fabric of his sweats he could feel her gentle touch and needless to say, he wanted more of her. He held her tighter and exhaled on her nec,k sending a tingling sensation down her spine. She could feel the tiny hairs at the nape of her neck standing rigid as he kissed her again.

She turned around and looked at him before helping him out of his t-shirt. She then took his one crutch and tossed it on the floor before she helped him onto the bed. He looked at her as he laid his back on the bed with her standing so close to him he wanted to grab her and make her join him in that very same bed. She was so close to him, he wanted to raise his head and take one of her nipples in his mouth and suck so hard that he would have her moaning out so loud that she would not be able to show her face the next day.

She pulled away from him and helped him out of his sweats. She loved how hard he was already and could not wait to have him all to herself in just a few minutes. She slowly ran her finger along his chest, making him moan softly. She brought her head down and kissed his neck. He closed his eyes and sighed. Now it was her turn to make him feel hot.

She trailed her kisses down from his neck to his chest before she took one of his hardened pecs inside her mouth. She heard him moan when she began circling his nipple with her tongue. She could feel him getting against on her ass, getting more and more rigid. She pulled away and looked at him. She stared so long that he had to open his eyes.

"How are you feeling?" she asked in a whisper.

"Good, why?" he asked. She smiled at him and shook her head. She had no idea how to tell him that she planned to work him intensely that night. She lowered her head again and kissed him deeply, feeling his tongue exploring her mouth. She slightly parted her lips and let her own tongue dance with his. She pulled away from him and then slowly lowered herself on his body, trailing small soft kisses as she went along. She heard him moan again when she slowly fondled his sac. She watched him get harder, as if that was even possible. All she was thinking was how much she wanted to taste him, how much she wanted him inside her mouth.

She leaned forward and kissed the tip of his cock. This time he let out a low groan, especially when she ran her tongue around his bulbous head and along the slit. This was almost too much for him. He twitched and tried to writhe but her small body held him down so hard, he could hardly move. He never really understood how strong she got when aroused but it was a turn on for him. She went on to run her tongue along the sensitive underside of his cockhead before running it down the shaft to his balls. He moaned out loud as she worked her tongue up and down his shaft, slowly but surely. She pulled away from his cock and then slowly lifted her head to grin at him. She looked into his eyes for a long minute before she took his cock back inside her mouth and sucked hard on him.

Mitchell let out a long growl as she sucked him. He could feel a tingle run down his spine as she worked herself on him. His hand slowly made its way down and took a handful of her hair. He held her head as she bobbed her head up and down, bringing him dangerously close to his climax. But as much as she loved sucking him, she wanted more. There was something she loved a little more than having him in his mouth. She needed to have him inside her – she longed to have him deep inside her.

She pulled her mouth away from him, making him pop out of her mouth. He gasped and moaned his disapproval when he felt the warmth of her mouth leaving his cock. She slowly took off her thong before she got on top of him, straddled him, and took his cock in her hands. She guided his cock to the entrance of her pussy and then let out a loud moan as she felt his hard cock filling her up, filling her every fold. She looked down at him and smiled as she started to slowly move herself on and off his cock. Mitchell held her waist as she moved on him slowly, every stroke terribly punishing. He longed to buck his hips and slam himself into her but the way she was fucking him, so slow, it was almost as if she wanted to kill him.

"Baby please," he begged as he held her tightly. She smiled and began picking up the pace, slowly getting him deeper and deeper into her. She suddenly gasped when she felt his hands on her ass, groping hard, and then pulling her down on him. Every time he did, she landed on him, slamming herself onto him, making her scream out every time he pulled her down. Her moans slowly became groans and then small gasps as her breath got knocked out of her mouth every time she swallowed his cock using her pussy. Soon enough, she was screaming and she was having a hard time understanding how it was that she was on top of him but it seemed like he was the one who was thrusting into her. She let herself collapse on him and he loved the way her breasts felt against his chest, all squeezed up against him. It was the most perfect feeling. She held on to his shoulders as she went on slamming her pelvis onto his own, each thrust making her scream even louder. It was not long before her body shivered in his arms for a long minute before he followed suit and began trembling inside her, sending his seed spurting deep inside her. By the time his orgasm died down, they were both exhausted, spent... all they wanted to do was just sleep it off. She raised her head and looked down at him.

"That was great," she said looking into his eyes.

"I should be the one saying that," he said smiling. She laughed and kissed him as she felt him getting hard again. She was surprised. He usually took a few minutes before he was ready to go again. She looked at him and kissed him again.

"Give it to me, baby," she said as she slowly began moving her hips up and down.

They happily climaxed together a second time. Afterward, as they lay entangled and drifted off to sleep, Natasha forgot that her heart had been wounded, and Mitchell forgot that his leg had been injured. Together they were one. Together they were whole.

The end.

Get Free Romance eBooks!

Hi there. As a special thank you for buying this book, for a limited time I want to send you some great ebooks completely **free of charge** directly to your email! You can get it by going to this page:

www.saucyromancebooks.com/physical

You can see a the cover of these books on the next page:

ONE LONE COWBOY, ONE WOMAN ON A MISSION...

THE LONE
COWBOY

EMILY J

ROCHELLE

IRE MET HIS MATCH?

UCH
LASS

LDING

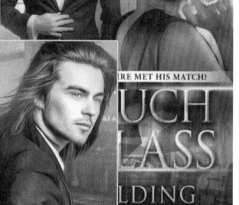

IF IT'S MEANT TO BE...

Him

KIMBERLY GREENFORD

ONE VAMPIRE. ONE COP. ONE LOVE.

VAMPIRES OF
CLEARVIEW

J A FIELDING

PLAYER GONNA PLAY?

SHE'S THE ONE HE WANTS
BUT CAN SHE TRUST HIM?

These ebooks are so exclusive you can't even buy them.
When you download them I'll also send you updates when
new books like this are available.

Again, that link is:

www.saucyromancebooks.com/physical

Now, if you enjoyed the book you just read, please leave a
positive review of it where you bought it (e.g. Amazon). It'll
help get it out there a lot more and mean I can continue writing
these books for you. So thank you. :)

More Books By J A Fielding And Others

If you enjoyed that, you'll love The Next Level by my friend Stacey Pond (search 'The Next Leve Stacey Pond' on Amazon to get it now). Here's what it's about and a sample:

Description:

A one off story with no cliff hanger.

Through their work at an attorney firm, Chelsea and Matt have known each other for a while, and have been dating for the last 6 months.

Now Chelsea is ready to take things to the next level.

Marriage and kids are things they both want, and she's ready to make that commitment to her man.

But by Matt showing his commitment to her, is Chelsea letting herself in for more than she bargained for?

Soon discovering there's more to Matt than meets the eye, it seems committing herself to him will bring up complications that could actually threaten their future together.

Can they overcome obstetrical and surprises, both good and bad, to create the family they both so badly want?

Find out in this Saucy new romance story by Stacey Pond of BWWM Club (search us) and Saucy Romance Books.

Suitable for over 18s only due to smoking hot sex scenes between a billionaire male and sexy, sassy female.

Sample:

Chelsea pulled up to the restaurant just as the time flashed 7:00 on her dash. She pulled down the mirror. Her hair was pinned up for the night, an elegant necklace draped around her neck and a gold and diamond bracelet on her wrist. They were gifts from Matthew, along with the dress. She was in love with it. It was short, pearl colored pink and looked soft and delicate against her skin. The shoes were a gift too, a matching pair of pearl pink heels. Matthew had planned every single detail. On her bed there had been a note: Get dressed, look amazing (as always) meet me at La Blue.

She reapplied a layer of lipstick, smacked her lips together then took a deep breath. There was no way she could be totally sure, but she had that nervous feeling she sometimes got in her gut. She and Matthew had been dating for six months now. What had started as an office rivalry had quickly turned into a passionate romance. Sangi swore this was the night he was going to propose. Excitement tore through her, quickly followed by the nervous knot in her stomach. She forced herself to step out of the car and onto the pavement.

Her tall heels clicked against the concrete loudly. She gripped her small, white clutch a little harder and took her time walking into the restaurant. La Blue was one of Chelsea's favorites. It was a small french restaurant with excellent cuisine and a relaxed atmosphere. It was a Saturday night however and the place was packed. She walked up to the small brown podium and spoke to a man wearing a white shirt under a dark blue vest.

"Rawlins, Matthew?" She asked as if she'd suddenly forgotten who he was.

"Ah yes, follow me."

Chelsea made her way through a group of standing people waiting on a table and through the restaurant. Matthew was sitting at a small table in the middle of the restaurant. His black suit and red tie all the more appealing as he stood when she approached. She knew what was under that suit. A hard body, all muscle and tanned skin she loved to lay against. She smiled wider at the thought.

He pulled out her chair and she sat down. There was a bottle of champagne in an ice bucket. Three little candles floated in a wide, glass bowl giving the table a little more illumination. The dark blue tablecloth brushed against her legs. Matthew looked stunning, his deep blue eyes captivating hers. He flashed a smile at her and she felt her knees go weak. Thank God she was already sitting.

"You look beautiful, babe," he said with his eyes still glued on her.

Chelsea couldn't help but to feel heat rising up through her body. "Thank you. You look really good too."

When the food arrived, Chelsea barely tasted it. She knew the food was good, but she was too nervous to enjoy it. The nervous energy must have been coming off of her in waves, because halfway through dinner Matthew gripped her hand and didn't let go. Just as they were finishing dinner, she began to think she'd been wrong. He wasn't going to propose. That made her both disappointed and slightly relieved. There was some small part of her that was so nervous about the possibility of getting married. That's when it happened.

Matthew stood up and she thought he was leaving the restaurant. When she stood up however, he dropped down to one knee. It was swift, effortless. His hand reached into his pocket and came back out with a baby blue box. He popped the lid open and Chelsea covered her mouth in shock.

"I knew you'd been waiting for it all night. So, I kind of had to make you wait a little longer. I wanted it to be a surprise," he said with a grin.

Chelsea felt tears forming in her eyes, her vision was getting a little blurry. "You jerk."

"Chelsea Ayers, I have fallen in love with you in a way I didn't even think was possible. I want to spend the rest of my life with you. Will you marry me?"

Her voice wouldn't work. The words caught in her throat as tears ran down her face. She nodded, hard. He stood up quickly. Holding her hand he slipped the ring onto her finger. The restaurant burst out into applause and sounds of congratulations as he hugged and then kissed her.

"So, was that a yes?"

"Yes, definitely yes."

*****

Six months later.

Chelsea rolled over in the sheets and groaned. Her fingers reached out for Matthew, but came up short. She raised herself up on one elbow and peered around the room through narrowed eyes. He was gone. She sighed and buried herself back into the sheets. She procrastinated for another five minutes before she slipped out of bed and headed for the bathroom. Sunlight streamed through the curtains, the floor was warm against her feet. She turned on the shower watching the clouds of hot steam rise. Turning slightly, she saw a note halfway tucked beneath the yellow soap dish. She pulled it out gently.

Good morning, babe. I had to leave early to work on the Donovan case. You take care of yourself and have fun planning the wedding. I love you.

It was signed with a little smiley face and Matt scribbled hurriedly on the bottom. Chelsea grinned. As much as she loved the fact that she was getting married, she also couldn't be more stressed out. The cake, caterers, wedding hall, dresses, everything was on her now. On top of that there was still the fact that she still hadn't met Matthew's mother. The woman was on a safari in Africa and wouldn't be back until the next month or two. It was concerning, but also a relief for Chelsea that she didn't have to meet the woman just yet.

She shed the white button up she was wearing, reached out a hand to test the water and slipped inside. The water hit her smooth, brown skin making her moan slightly. It was going to be a long day. Just for that moment, she wanted to enjoy the feel of the water sliding against her skin. She took her time washing her body, thinking about the wedding, relaxing. When the water decided it'd had more than enough and turned chilly, she stepped out and wrapped herself in a thick, green towel.

It was hard to believe just the year before, Chelsea had hated Matthew. He'd come in with his blond hair, blue eyes, gray suit and list of demands. She couldn't stand him. The surprising part was he couldn't stand her either. They'd fought every time they were in the same room together, until the night they were working late into the evening on the same case. The tension had hit a bursting point. Before Chelsea knew what was happening, he was bending her over the conference room table and they were taking their frustrations out on each other. The thought brought a little grin to her face. She still couldn't sit at that conference table without shooting Matthew a little knowing grin and him doing the same.

Water dripped off of her body as she walked into the kitchen. The lingering smell of burnt toast and a burnt pan were the only evidence that Matthew had attempted to cook breakfast for himself. She laughed softly, lifted the pan then let it slide back into the murky water. Matthew was a horrible cook. He was a great boyfriend, now fiance, great attorney, wonderful person, but he was awful in the kitchen.

She left the mess for the maid, Maritza, to deal with. There was no time for her to be cleaning this morning. Chelsea picked up the big, black binder that had become her best friend. Ever since Matthew had proposed six months ago, it had been her constant companion. She flipped through the pages, attached a pink sticky note then shut the book again. Glancing over at the microwave the red numbers flashed at her. 8:30. She sighed.

Stepping into her room she reached into the closet and pulled out her outfit for the day. She and Matthew worked at the same firm. He was mostly interested in attaining property for his father's company, while she just wanted to make partner. She was so close, she could feel it, but she wasn't there yet. She slipped into a black pencil skirt, a white blouse that buttoned up the front and black stockings. As she slipped into her heels her phone lit up and buzzed three times before it went dark again.

Chelsea swiped her finger across the screen and saw a text from her boss. Short, sweet to the point. *I need you here, now.* Of course he did, she was his best attorney. Her fingers ran through wavy black hair before she stood up and grabbed her briefcase. Her heels tapped along the wood floor as she entered the kitchen and slipped the binder into the briefcase.

The weather was just turning warm, she was happy for that. She walked up to her little black jeep and tossed her bag in before she slid in after it. Her routine of the day was about to start. That might have bothered some people, falling into routine, but Chelsea loved it. It was always simple, straight forward; Get up, get coffee and maybe breakfast, go to the office, punch out at 5 or 6, go home.

When she arrived at the office, the familiar sounds made her smile. Jeff was off flirting with one of the women in the office, she could hear his chuckle. The sound of fingers hitting keys on keyboards. Phones being answered in polite voices. It was like music to Chelsea's ears. She made her way to her office. As her fingers gripped the metal handle a voice came up behind her.

"Good to see you've joined us Ms. Ayers. There's a meeting in the conference room in five," the voice said.
Chelsea turned around and was face to face with Mr. Whitehill.

Her boss was on the better side of fifty, graying hair at his temples and streaks of gray in his hair. He was pudgy from years of good eating and long hours in the office. As she watched he ran a thick hand over his blue suit to smooth it.

"Of course, Mr. Whitehill. What's the meeting about?" She asked.

"Some lake front property just became available and that fiance of yours wants to snatch it up. It shouldn't take too long."

Chelsea nodded, watched her boss walk away before she slipped into her office. Sighing, she sat her briefcase down on her desk It was going to be a long day. Add on top of that the planning of the wedding and it would quickly grow longer. She readjusted the files before she stood up, smoothed her skirt and walked to the conference room.

Seated around the dark table there was Mr. Whitehill, a few faces that she knew, but couldn't put names to right away and her fiance, Matthew. He stood in front of the wide, black screen on the wall, his gray suit fitting him in all of the right places. His hair was golden blond, short and lay against his forehead slightly. He would declare it was time to get a haircut soon. Shame. Baby blue eyes locked in on hers and the briefest of smiles touched his thin lips. Chelsea felt her heart flip in her chest. Was it any wonder she'd fallen for him?

She quickly regained control of herself before settling into a seat next to Mr. Whitehill. As Matthew clicked through his file she was both intrigued and distracted. The property was beautiful, a large almost mini-mansion. The land itself would be valuable. Still, in the back of her mind all she could think about was the wedding. It was only six months away and she still hadn't even met his family.

As Matthew wrapped up his presentation, the room quickly cleared out. Matthew gave her a warm smile before he walked over to her. He planted his hands on the table. Seeing him anywhere near the table sent ripples down her spine, but she kept her composure.

"So, I have some news," he said.

"Oh yeah? And what news has you smiling so hard?"

"My mother's back in town. Dad will be getting back soon too. I told them about the engagement and they want to meet you. This weekend."

Chelsea kept her smile on her face, but inside she was nervous. What if they didn't like her? What if they didn't want her to be a part of their family? Matthew's smile dissolved.

"Okay, what's wrong?" He asked.

"Nothing, I'm fine really. Don't give me that look. I have to go over a few of these cases, that's all. Lunch?"

He nodded. "Lunch sounds great."

Chelsea left the conference room quickly and headed back for her office. When she closed the door she gave a deep sigh. She wasn't ready. There was no way she was ready to meet his family. From what little she knew of them, they were pretty well off. Matthew's father ran a construction company that was only getting more popular as the years went by. His mother was a retired attorney herself. Chelsea had come from humble roots. Her father was in the military and her mother was a nurse at the local hospital. She didn't know how she'd fit in with them.

She sat behind her desk. Instead of pulling out one of her work files, she delved back into her wedding planning bible. Picking up her cellphone, she called around to see if they could find a decent caterer. Matthew had told her to plan big and to spend whatever she wanted. That made her briefly wonder just how much money his family had, but she didn't pry. That was something to figure out later.

Before she knew it the time on her phone blinked one. She gathered up her briefcase, tossed the binder back inside and headed out of her office. She rode the elevator down, trying to dodge the many questions her co-worker's had about the wedding, almost wishing she'd taken the stairs. Not in the heels she was wearing.

She stepped off of the elevator and waved to the group of lunch goers. Matthew was waiting, his jacket over his arm. He raised an eyebrow as she rolled her eyes. It always felt like people were watching them as they walked through the building now, the eyes following them to see if they'd kiss, if they'd fight. Once they hit the outside, the sun made Chelsea wince. The cons of life in an office, lit by constant fluorescents and in front of laptop screens.

"Let me guess. They were talking your ear off?" Matthew asked with a grin.

"Ugh, you have no idea! It's like a million questions and you know most of them don't really care. They just want something to gossip about. I wish I could tell them to fuck off," she said with a sigh.

"Please, don't do that. I like working with my future wife."

"Not for too long. Eventually daddy Warbucks will want you to take the throne and I'll be by myself again fighting with these jackals."

"Or," he said grabbing her hand as they walked, "you make partner and then you get to boss the jackals around."

The thought made her smile. His hand slipped into hers even more so. She glanced down at his hand, his skin pale against her brown. It wasn't the first time she'd dated a man of another race, but she definitely hoped it was the last time. Matthew was everything she'd dreamed of in a man; ambitious, trustworthy, funny, intelligent and sexy just to name a few. Sure, he could have a bit of a temper, but he was working on it. No longer letting the stress of the job get to him was one of the things that helped.

They walked into an Italian restaurant that was more high end than where their collages would visit for lunch. Matthew pulled out her chair and Chelsea thanked him. The tinkling of classical music filled the small building. The table cloths were white, heavy linen, not the plastic ones she'd become accustomed to when she was younger. She knew the silverware was all real, the plates and tea cups fine china, the wine vintage and the people rich. She gazed around the restaurant easily picking them out. There was a man with diamond cufflinks, who could afford that anymore? A woman with blond curls was wearing a black Versace dress, her impeccable red nails drumming against the tablecloth. Everywhere Chelsea looked, she could see signs of wealth. She wondered vaguely if Matthew's parents would be the same, oozing wealth and status.

Matthew must have seen the look of concern on her face. He reached over, laid his hand on top of hers and gave it a firm squeeze. That at least made the frown fall from her features. A woman walked up to the table, white button down shirt, black bow tie and black slacks. Her breasts looked like they were about to burst out of her top. Chelsea looked over at Matthew who was looking anywhere, but at the waitress.

They ordered quickly. When the woman was gone Chelsea kept grinning at Matthew, but he made himself busy laying his napkin in his lap. He must have adjusted it ten times before he finally looked up meeting her gaze.

"I didn't look," he said.

"I didn't say you did."

He paused for a minute. "They were like out to here," he said indicating how big her breasts were with his hands.

Several of the other patrons shook their heads or turned up their noses. He didn't care. Matthew had no censor sometimes and it was mostly hilarious, sometimes embarrassing. She laughed behind her hand and swatted at him.

"Stop that! Stop it!"

Matthew grinned as he drank some water and shot daggers at the people around them. She loved that out of the both of them, he was the one who could lighten up. He cared deeply about his job, loved the thought of going into his father's business, but he didn't seem to care for the people. He'd told Chelsea more than once that rich people were like toddlers only with diamonds and cash instead of toys to fight over.

"How's the wedding planning going? Ready to call it quits and hire someone yet?" He asked once their food arrived.

She pointed her fork at him. "No! I told you, I can do this myself. It's been my dream to plan my wedding since I was a girl."

"Yes and now you're a busy woman trying to make partner. I don't want our wedding stomping all over your dreams," he said.

Chelsea smiled. His consideration of her both in their relationship and at her job was what made her love him so much. "It's not. It's just, I really want to do this myself. Besides, Sangi's helping."

"Oh Sangi's helping, well now I'm relieved."

"Stop it," Chelsea gave him a look. "What's wrong with Sangi?"

"Well, let's see. She told you to put laxatives in my coffee when we first met. On several occasions she's asked me if I was gay, oh and tried to set me up with her cousin. Then there's the time we asked her to watch the apartment. She let all the plants die, ate all of the food and didn't even realize we got robbed."

"Okay, lower your voice. I know. She can be a bit...odd, but she's also my best friend. I wouldn't be where I am today if it wasn't for her," Chelsea said.

Matthew sighed, but seemed to let the conversation dissipate for the moment. Chelsea knew Sangi could be a flake sometimes, but she had been there for her through every stage of her life. Both of their moms even worked at the same hospital, although Sangi's mom was an ER doctor. She could trust Sangi, sometimes. It was just keeping her on task that was the hard part.

Matthew wiped his mouth with his napkin. "So, my parents house this weekend..." he began.

"Yay," Chelsea chimed in.

"Look, I know you're nervous. Hell, my mother still has the ability to make me feel like a little kid-"

"Yeah, not comforting."

"*However,* I also know she'll like you. I mean, you two are pretty alike," he said before returning to his plate.

"Does she know you're dating...you know, a black woman?"

Matthew almost choked on his chicken parmesan. He held up a finger to her as he drank down his glass of water. She stared back at him knowing the answer even before he came up for air. No, he hadn't told her, not a thing.

"Matthew-"

"It's no big deal. My parents aren't racists, babe. Besides, race isn't important anymore," he said straightening his tie.

"Then why are you nervous? You only do that when you're nervous. And it may not be important to us, but it is to some people. I mean, how do I know I'm not just setting myself up for an evening of failure?" Chelsea asked.

"First of all, they're going to love you. Trust me. Second, I didn't say evening. I said weekend. They invited us for the whole weekend so you could meet the family and a few close family friends."

Chelsea dropped her fork onto her plate with a clink. She rested both of her elbows on the table and pressed her fingers against the bridge of her nose. As much as she loved Matthew, he sure had a habit of leaving out important details.

It irritated her. When she opened her eyes, his hand was across the table, palm up, waiting for her hand. She looked at it before she turned away.

"Okay, I should have told you earlier, babe. I'm so sorry. I promise you, we will have a great weekend, my parents will love you and if things don't go well, we'll leave. Agreed?" He said.

She looked into his eyes. Those baby blues always seemed to win her over in the end. She sighed heavily. The nervous twisting in her stomach hadn't left, but she couldn't resist that sad look on his face for long. Chelsea rolled her eyes.

"Fine, but you will tell them before we go! And the first minute I don't feel comfortable you will wrangle up some bullshit excuse and get me the hell out of there."

Chelsea slipped her hand into his as he nodded. His fingers curled around her hand. The smile was back on his face making the nervousness in the pit of her stomach lift slightly. She still couldn't shake the slight feeling however that things weren't going to go well.

They finished their lunch and headed back to the office together arm in arm. They'd do that until they were in sight of the building and disconnect as if they were merely friends. They didn't want people in their business, but in the office it was almost impossible to have a secret. Chelsea knew Jeff was a hopeless womanizer, Amy was getting a divorce and Roger had recently attended a sex addicts anonymous group. She wasn't sure how anonymous it was if the whole office now knew.

Matthew opted for the stairs. She followed him into the narrow, dusty white corridor. Looking around to make sure no one was around,, Matthew laid a hand on her cheek. She felt heat sweep her body at his touch. Leaning in, he kissed her softly. It was sweet and innocent but quickly became something more. His tongue slipped into her mouth, wet and warm against her own. She felt wetness collect between her thighs. Her hands gripped his jacket. She wanted to push him up against the wall, slip a hand into his pants, grip his cock and stroke him into a frenzy. Even though they tried to keep a low profile, there was something hot about rubbing up against each other where they worked. They heard footsteps approaching and quickly broke apart.

"I'll see you upstairs," he whispered, a noticeable bulge in the front of his slacks.

Chelsea giggled as if she were back in high school as the stairwell door opened. She slipped past the man going up and headed for the elevators. If they didn't have such an important case coming up, she would have invited him back to her office for a little play time, but she knew better. Mr. Whitehill had already warned her about slacking on her work. Not that she had, he just wanted a reason to lecture. Or maybe a reason to stare at her stocking legs. It was hard to tell.

She disappeared into her office ignoring the stares, whispers and giggles. Let them talk. She was marrying the man of her dreams and so close to making partner she could taste it. After she closed the door behind her, she could feel her cellphone buzzing away. Reaching a manicured hand down into her bag, she pulled out her phone. Sangi's picture popped up. Just in time.

"Tell me you got the flowers squared away."

*

Enjoy that and want to read more? The search 'The Next Level Stacey Pond' on Amazon now.

If you've already read that, you should definitely pick up 6 BWWM romance stories in 1 bundle here (authored by myself and others - search 'BWWM Club' on amazon to get it);

Here's what it's about:

Like black woman white man romance stories? Well you're in luck. In this book you get 6 classic BWWM stories in 1 - that's 828 pages of interracial goodness!

All of the books in this bundle can be enjoyed as stand alone stories. That said, all have further parts in the series, so if you like one more than the rest you can pick up more books with the same characters when you're ready.

Books in this collection are:

1. My Russian Dream:

When she woke that morning, the last thing Sophie expected was to not only meet the man of her dreams, but to enter into a fast moving whirlwind romance with a mysterious Russian billionaire. Will it all be too much for Sophie? Or will this be her dream playing out like she's always felt she deserved?

2. Passion Abroad:

Have you ever felt like you just need to get away from it all? Well that's exactly how Erica feels, and she's going to do something about it!

The tale of a holiday romance which turns into a round the world trip with a passionate and loving new partner.

3. Home Is Where The Heart Is:

When a handsome English billionaire is looking for homes to add to his portfolio, Julie is assigned the job of helping him out. But will this billionaire have another reason for his interest in her?

4. Find Me Online:

After filtering through a ton of pervs on a popular interracial dating site, Cherelle finally finds someone who catches her eye. But is there more to her catch Michael than she originally realizes? And will he be the man she is looking for?

5. Is Mr White Mr Right:

One of the original BWWM books, and largely held as a classic in the genre.

Natasha Black is a strong African American woman, who has always been career focused and level headed. Nothing has ever been able to knock her off her game... until now! Enter 'McDreamy', the hunk of a boss at her new dream job. Will she be able to stay career focused while getting advances from possibly the man of her dreams?

6. My Billionaire Cowboy:

What does a fashion stylist and a fashionably challenged cowboy have in common?! You're about to find out...

Kate is the proud owner of her own fashion boutique. Bruce is a successful business man who now spends his time on his passion: working his ranch.

When fate brings these two opposites together, there's no denying there's something there. But is Kate at a point in her life where she is willing to throw caution to the wind and allow herself to be swept off of her feet by an unexpected love?

Authors of these books: J A Fielding, Esther Banks and Cher Etan; all authors from Saucy Romance Books.

To see more great stories by us, simply search BWWM Club on Amazon Kindle.

Suitable for over 18s only due to all stories having scenes of a sexual nature.

You won't ever get a better collection of BWWM romance stories again, be sure to pick up your copy today.

My Russian Dream Preview

Here's a preview of My Russian Dream, the first book in the series:

The wave seemed to be thirty feet high; she watched it from the shore, rooted to the spot. It was coming for her and there was nothing she could do about it. Her whole body was frozen. She opened her mouth to scream, but her vocal cords were not working either. The huge black wave came closer and closer; but just before it engulfed her in silently screaming agony, she woke up.

Sophie Devereaux had this dream a lot, especially when she was stressed. Ever since Hurricane Katrina had forced her ejection from her home and the loss of her family. She shrugged inwardly trying to shake the dream. Her grandfather Elijah was still with her – that was something at least. But her little brother Joseph was in the wind and her grandmother had been too weak to run. They had tried to save her, but the waves had engulfed the house before they could get the wheelchair out. Sophie and her grandfather had moved to Boston after searching in vain for her brother. There was no news of him that they could find – not in the refugee camps, the message boards, nowhere. Grandpa Elijah had gone back to work as a watchmaker. He had been well known in New Orleans as a master craftsman; here in Boston, he worked in anonymity in the back room of a jeweler's while Sophie interned at an accounting firm. She was trying to earn her qualifications as an accountant. It might not be a happy life, but it was theirs at least.

Sophie got out of bed and wrapped a robe around her full figure. She padded down the hall to her grandfather's room to check that he was still breathing. It was a habit she couldn't quite kick. The smell of coffee wafting down the hall from the kitchen told her that he was not only breathing, he was up and making breakfast. She changed direction to the bathroom to take a shower. Unlike her grandfather who still had until 10am to get to work, she had the office keys so she was supposed to be in by at least 7am.

"Good morning my dear." Her grandfather smiled at her as she walked into the kitchen fully dressed, twenty minutes later.

"Mornin' G. How's tricks?" she asked in turn. Her grandfather glared at her from behind the plate of pancakes he was making. He hated 'young people slang' as he called the funky abbreviations of her generation and so Sophie had taken to calling him 'G-Money' when she was feeling playful. He pretended to hate it, but she saw the way he bit back a smile every time she said it. Anything that made her grandfather smile was just about alright with Sophie.

"Is that how you greet your boss at work? You won't last long at those white people firms if you do," her grandfather said.

"Nah, I save that just for you G-Money. Speaking of, are you good for lunch or do you need me to..." Sophie began before he cut her off.

"I'm fine Sophie", he said very gently, "now eat up quick so you're not late for work."

Sophie smiled at her grandfather and finished her breakfast.

*****

It was a cold day in Boston and Anton "Tony" Romanov was pensive as he strolled slowly down the street. Seven o'clock in the morning and downtown was already bustling with hurrying commuters. Tony's mind wasn't on the traffic though; he was deep in thought about what to do with his current accountant; he was pretty sure the man was stealing from him.

'I should get an audit done.' He thought as he watched his feet move in the shiny black shoes he'd treated himself to on his birthday. He didn't think he'd ever get used to paying $1000 for a pair of shoes no matter how well he was doing. That thought reminded him of his father and he smiled grimly imagining him in this situation. Roman Petrov was not a man to tolerate thieves. But this was America and times and situations were different here.

The sound of a startled squeak caused him to lift his head, just in time to see a rotund young woman almost fall on the slippery sidewalk. He hurried forward to see if he could help her, but she had righted herself and hurried away before he could. He stopped for a minute to contemplate a backside so lush and luscious that it rendered her waist tiny in comparison. Her hips swayed from side to side as she walked up to a door and let herself in a building. Without even thinking about it, Anton followed her.

*****

Sophie checked her watch as she came up to the offices of Rodham, Clarence and Haggerty; Certified Public Accountants. She was five minutes late and Rodham was already at the door, tapping his foot impatiently.

"Good morning, sir," she said as she put the key in the lock and opened up the office.

"You're late," he replied with a frown.

Sophie opened her mouth to apologize, then closed it again. 'What the hell' she thought, 'it's not like he ever really sees me anyway. An apology probably wouldn't even register.' She swept into the office in his wake, unbuttoning her coat even as she turned to close the door. The man standing in the doorway gave her a turn and she made a startled sound, hand to her heart.

"Oh! Err, can I help you?" she asked a bit breathlessly. His eyes were very blue she thought, especially with that blonde hair. Piercing too; and he was staring at her in a way that was a shade under polite.

"Yes, I am looking for an accountant," he was saying, "Have I come to the right place?"

Sophie's eyes slid to the prominently displayed sign on the door, but refrained from saying anything untoward. Clearly he was a client.

"Well, yes, you have. Come in," she said instead.

"Thank you. And your name is…?" he asked, still staring at her with those piercing ice blue eyes. 'Could you possibly look elsewhere?' she thought at him, hoping it would somehow register.

"Sophie. Why don't you come into the waiting room while I see if Mr. Rodham is available?" she said, ushering him in and hoping that would avert his attention. No such luck, he continued to stare at her like he had found the mother lode in a gold mine and he was afraid to take his eyes off it lest it disappear.

"Err; can I get you a coffee or tea, maybe?" Sophie asked.

"No thank you," he said, sitting down.

Sophie hurried away before anything else strange could happen. If she didn't know better, she would think that guy was checking her out. But she'd taken a look at his shoes as soon as he walked in; that brand did not come cheap – he was definitely out of her league. Perhaps he had never seen a black woman working in an accountant's office before? Sophie shrugged inwardly and went to announce him to Mr. Rodham. It was only as she stepped into her boss' office that she realized she did not know the client's name.

She hesitated, wanting to go back out and find out the name before she got another blot on her name before ten o'clock in the morning on a Monday in February but Rodham had already looked up.

"Yes Sophie?" he said.

Sophie frowned, wondering if he'd ever used her name before – just her luck he would choose today to remember it.

"There's…a man in the waiting room wanting to see an accountant," she said.

Mr. Rodham contemplated her for a moment eyebrow raised.

"Send him in," was all he said at last.

Sophie breathed again and went to tell the man with the piercing blue eyes that the boss would see him now.

The office was quickly filling up and Sophie put the strange happenings of the morning behind her in favor of getting to work. Mr. Rodham and the client were in his office a long time and Sophie wondered if he had come for help declaring bankruptcy, or maybe it was a mortgage gone badly. So many people came with money management issues these days. 'Mr.

Blue Eyes could start by buying cheaper shoes' she thought.

*****

"My accountant is stealing from me," Tony began bluntly, "and I need an independent audit."

"Is that so?" Rodham leaned back in his chair contemplating the client. His suit said expensive, but bourgeoisie with it. His shoes were clearly very new. Not Old Money then; and Russian to boot. Mafia, perhaps? But he doubted the Russian Mafia asked for audits.

"Yes. Can you help me or not?" Tony asked.

"Of course. I'll get someone who is skilled in this area to get right on it," Rodham said, picking up the phone and summoning one of the associates.

"This is Curtis Jackson; he is one of our brightest associates with a talent for spotting fraud. He is at your disposal," Rodham said as Jackson came in.

Tony nodded at Jackson, who smiled at him and ushered him into the conference room so as to get the details of his case.

*****

Sophie was typing up some financial reports for clients while simultaneously studying for her CPA exam when a shadow fell over her desk. She looked up to see Jackson grinning down at her.

"Hey Sophie," he said.

"Hi. Can I help you with something?" she asked, narrowing her eyes suspiciously. Jackson smiling never boded well for anyone.

"Au contraire, it's what I have done for you," he said confirming all her worst suspicions.

"And what is that Jackson? Will I need to kill you now or later?" she asked fist curling involuntarily.

"Definitely later. I got you a date," he said grin widening.

"You…what?" she asked, almost choking in her disbelief.

"That Ruski dude that was here this morning? Remember him? Took quite a shine to you," Jackson said, propping himself on the edge of her desk.

Sophie's hand reached out and she grabbed the calendar staring at it, "Nope. It's not April 1st; so what the hell are you trying to do to me?" she was whispering, but the menace in her voice was unmistakable.

"C'mon Sophie, you have no life. You come to work; you go home to your grand pops. You're a beautiful woman. The man likes you. Give him a chance," Jackson wheedled.

"Are you pimping me out to your clients Jackson?" Sophie asked him pseudo-politely.

"No!" Jackson said and sighed, "Look, just hear him out okay? If you don't like him, say no."

There was a small silence.

"Besides, he's way out of my league," Sophie said, and then could have bitten her tongue. Giving Jackson a reason he could argue away was as good as acquiescing to his demands.

*****

"G-Money! You home?" Sophie called as she got in that night. Her feet were killing her! She flung her heels off her feet with more violence than strictly necessary. Being a size sixteen meant that there was quite a bit of weight pressing on her toes. She would have preferred wearing flats, but the office had an unspoken policy on how its female employees should present themselves. Heels were part of the uniform. She walked to her room still calling out for her grandfather, but there was no reply. Then she remembered that Monday nights was poker night for him and his workmates at the jeweler's. He wouldn't be home until later. Changing into a comfortable pair of black sweats she went to contemplate the contents of the fridge. There was some leftover gumbo which she warmed up and ate at the table while Jay Z blasted from her beats headphones, telling her about his 99 problems. This was followed by her guilty pleasure, Justin Bieber, singing about Beauty and a Beat.

Did Mr. Blue Eyes really want to date her? Did she want to date him? She'd never been with a white guy before. They usually weren't into the bigger girls like her; not that she minded. Her voluptuous figure was quite popular enough, thank you; she had no complaints. But Jackson was right. What with money so tight and everything that had happened, she had to admit she was living the life of a recluse. Hell, even her grandfather had more of a social life than her! Maybe if he asked her, she might say yes…just to see what dating was like these days.

Sophie snorted, "Someone would think you're like some middle aged hag instead of a twenty five year old babe the way you talk," she said to herself. She leaned forward, glancing at her blemish free heart shaped features in the mirror. Her short curly hair framed her face in a way that flattered her prominent cheek bones and round brown eyes. Her rosebud shaped mouth smiled a little smugly. She lifted her index finger and touched her full lips with it and then touched the mirror.

"Sssmmokin," she whispered.

Then she went off to bed.

*****

"Good morning," a deep voice said to her as a shadow fell on her desk. She knew it was him before she looked up. She wouldn't be forgetting that voice in a hurry. Her head lifted slowly, as she felt her face glow.

"Down girl," she whispered to her rapidly increasing pulse, "no need to get excited or nothin'"

She pinned a smile to her face and looked up, "Hi," she said breathlessly.

"I'm Tony Romanov," he said.

"Hi Tony," she replied, feeling dizzy. Her smile felt extremely artificial on her face, but she couldn't seem to shift it.

"Um, would you like to have coffee with me?" he suggested, piercing her with those ice blue eyes and leaving her helplessly pinned to her seat. Or at least that's how it felt.

"Sure," she managed to whisper.

"Great. Shall I pick you up after work?" he offered, smiling down at her and literally taking her breath away. She nodded her acquiescence. His smile widened and he nodded back at her before Curtis came to whisk him off to his office.

Sophie stood up and bolted to the ladies room, "What. The hell. Is the matter with you girl?" she scolded herself sternly in the mirror, "Settle down before you make even more of a damned fool of yourself!"

She breathed in and out with her eyes closed, all the while wondering at this reaction. Yesterday she hadn't reacted at all this way to his presence. Maybe she was just nervous about the date. She nodded to herself, deciding that this was the reason and then went back to work.

The day passed without event, Sophie threw herself into her work and studying for her exam, so much so that she was startled when the shadow was back at her desk, promptly at 6pm.

"Hi Sophie," Blue Eyes said...Tony. His name was Tony.

"Hi...Tony," she replied, smiling woodenly up at him. She wanted to slap herself out of this fugue state he seemed to put her in but he was watching her.

"Shall we go?" he asked, holding out his hand. Sophie stood up and smiled at him. She was a tall girl, but he towered over her.

"I'll just go freshen up. Real quick, I promise," she said, hurrying away from him.

Tony watched her go, "I hate to see you go, but I love to watch you leave," he murmured to himself.

"Whoa, down boy," an amused voice said from behind him. He turned around to find Curtis smiling at him.

"Oh, hello Curtis. I was just..." Tony began, embarrassed at being caught out.

"Oh, I know what you were just..." Curtis replied grinning, "Keep it in your pants though. Sophie ain't that kinda girl."

"I was not..." Tony began to protest, but then caught himself. He didn't need to explain himself to anyone. Not anymore.

Curtis saw his discomfiture and changed the subject, "I have something for you by the way, if you want to stop by my office tomorrow."

Tony stared at him in surprise, "Already?"

"Yeah. What can I say? I'm the best," Curtis replied with a pseudo-self-deprecating shrug and a smirk.

Tony nodded and agreed to come and then turned his attention back to Sophie who was just swaying her way over from the ladies' room. She had slicked down her hair with some kind of gel, leaving all the bones of her face exposed and her eyes looking three times as big. Her lips were painted with a brown lipstick and the overall effect was just...electric. Tony wondered if she would let him kiss her after their date. He'd just met her yesterday, but he felt like he'd been waiting for her for millennia. His hands itched to place themselves on those luscious hips; the mere thought caused his penis to twitch.

"Down boy," he whispered to himself, "no need to get excited. All in good time." He smiled as she came up to him.

"You're beautiful," he told her looking her straight in the eye.

He was trying to confuse her with those eyes she thought with resignation. How was she supposed to walk when her knees were so weak?

*

Want to read the rest? Search 'BWWM Club' on amazon to get it;

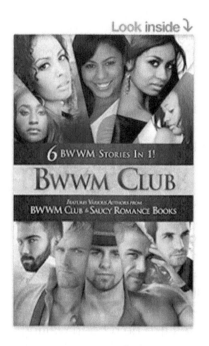

You can see more romance books from myself and other top authors by going to www.bwwmclub.com.

About J A Fielding

Hey my lovelies, J A Fielding here! You want to know more about my writing? Ok, here goes:

I specialize in stories with strong black women (although we're all human and need support at times) and sexy white men. I enjoy this genre so much I've teamed up with other writers to start the website SaucyRomanceBooks.com. Here you can see a selection of books in the BWWM genre, all with different view points and authors.

I'm always open to writing on new related subjects, so if you want to suggest any story ideas for me, leave a review on one of my current books and mention your story idea. If it's something I feel I'll enjoy writing, I may give it a go. I will of course leave you a credit in the book for inspiring the idea. ;)

I hope you've enjoyed this story and go on to check the others out. If you do leave a review, thank you in advance.

J A Fielding.

CPSIA information can be obtained at www.ICGtesting.com
Printed in the USA
LVOW01s1342020915

452388LV00042B/1785/P